W9-CAY-964

The Death and Life of Miguel de Cervantes is not merely a novel; it is an extravaganza – bursting with heroic deeds, tireless action, espionage, extraordinary women, historical and fictional truth (not quite the same), metaphysical bombshells and humour – delicious, unsparing humour.

In the cast, led by Don Miguel de Cervantes – yes *that* Cervantes – appear kings and barbers, terrible Turks, trance dancers, grasping lawyers, a Faustian eunuch astrologer who is growing back his vital bits, William Shakespeare and Christopher Marlowe as secret agents, a lot of gypsies and the real Don Juan.

The narrative careers through Spain, Italy and sea battle to a prison in Algiers, and is propelled by a spy network named 'The Nameless' into Amsterdam and England where Miguel's favourite agent is incognito as Lady Waynescote of Loose Chippings. There is romance – now hopelessly smouldering, now brightly blazing. There are mixed parental blessings, undercurrents of incest and irksome vows of chastity. There are hints of how to remember the future, walk through walls and write the first and greatest of novels.

Stephen Marlowe is a cracking conductor of the pyrotechnics and an engaging and witty companion along picaresque paths as errant as Don Quixote's own. Like Miguel de Cervantes (both fictional and historical), Marlowe is a supremo among storytellers.

BY THE SAME AUTHOR
THE SHINING
THE SEARCH FOR BRUNO HEIDLER
COME OVER RED ROVER
THE SUMMIT
COLOSSUS
THE MAN WITH NO SHADOW
THE CAWTHORN JOURNALS
TRANSLATION
THE VALKYRIE ENCOUNTER
1956
THE MEMOIRS OF CHRISTOPHER COLUMBUS

The Death and Life of Miguel de Cervantes

A novel by Stephen Marlowe

BLOOMSBURY

First published 1991

Copyright © 1991 by Stephen Marlowe
Translations from the Italian and Spanish by Ann H. Marlowe and the author

The moral right of the author has been asserted

Bloomsbury Publishing Ltd, 2 Soho Square, London W1V 5DE

A CIP catalogue record for this book is available from the British Library

ISBN 0 7475 1024 5

Typeset by Hewer Text Composition Services, Edinburgh
Printed in Great Britain by Clays Ltd, St Ives plc

WITH ANN
AND
FOR MARLOWE AND ADAM ZACHARY

CONTENTS

vii

CONTENTS

The delusions of history and the illusions of art both require a suspension of disbelief.

Arthur Koestler

Art gives life to what history killed.

Carlos Fuentes

Prologue

The midday sun casts a foreshortened shadow of the gallows erected for my hanging.

Perhaps, I think, the public executioner has already begun his funereal march down Souk Street, but if so, the dirgeful music of pipe and drum cannot be heard over the roaring of my name, 'Zher*ban*tay! Zher*ban*tay! Zher*ban*tay!' – so angry a sound that at first I believe the crowd would be pleased to do the executioner's work for him. But then I see the anxious knots of turbaned Turks and club-bearing janissaries among the cowled Moors, and I see the Dey of Algiers's own pikemen uneasily surrounding the stage where I stand with my hands roped behind my back and a janissary on either side, looking not at me but where the pikemen are looking, which is at the crowd – for am I not a sign and an omen, a wonder, at whose death the already stricken city will die? And if so, mustn't the crowd's anger be directed not at me but at those who would kill me?

'Got any money?' asks the janissary to my left.

I shake my head no.

'Pity,' he says. 'For a few *zianies* I could help.'

'How?'

'Pulling,' he says. 'See, when a person's dangling from a rope, he strangles slow. Takes half an hour or more. But if somebody who don't like to see his fellow man suffer was to pull on his legs, this would break his neck and put him out of his misery. You sure you don't have any loose change?'

Again I shake my head, the one that will soon be supported by a rope.

I find myself thinking for the first time in years of my grandfather Juan the Patriarch, and how he died so abruptly, the first death in my life, the recollection of which I brush irritably from my mind. Standing under the crossbeam of the gallows, is death all I can think of?

I decide to think of Zoilos instead.

Zoilos was the first literary critic in recorded history, spiteful but shrewd and capable of the killing witticism. He lived in the fourth century BC and was called Homer's Scourge because he made his living tearing apart the

1

Iliad and the *Odyssey* almost line by line, and blind Homer dead four hundred years by then so who was there to defend him?

Still, I'd rather have a Zoilos than nobody at all. In my short life, what have I written to merit the critics working me over? I won't have even a Zoilos.

I brood about this until it makes me wonder: What would I write if I didn't die? I'll never know.

This leads me to some seemingly unrelated speculation. If the universe consists of numberless atoms floating around randomly in infinite space and endless time – as the Laughing Philosopher (what's to laugh?) and others believe – then is this world in which we live (and die) the only world? Why shouldn't there be another world somewhere . . .

(I hear music faintly, then louder, the skirl of pipes and bang of drums rising over the roar of the crowd.)

. . . almost exactly the same, but where a few billion atoms have come together differently so that there are minor changes . . .

(An unremarkable-looking man in a green turban mounts the stage and gives the hempen noose a professional tug.)

. . . one of which is that I don't die today, which happens to be 23 April 1580?

(The unremarkable-looking man in the green turban shoves a crate directly under the dangling noose. 'It's time,' he says.)

I listen to the crowd roaring my name, and this gives me the strength to climb on to the crate. My cheek bumps the noose and sets it swinging. I recoil, as some people recoil from snakes and slugs. The unremarkable-looking man slips the noose over my head.

Though the sky is cloudless, bleached a brassy white by the implacable sun, thunder peals and a twin-pronged streak of lightning forks the harbour – the only implausible element in an otherwise straightforward account of my death – making the crowd of superstitious, miracle-hungry Moors prostrate themselves just as two burly members of the public executioner's entourage kick the crate out from under me so that I am left dangling eighteen inches above the stage.

And then? Why, then, an extraordinary thing happens.

Or is it so extraordinary, all things considered?

Part the First

THE DEATH
OF
MIGUEL DE CERVANTES

I

Being an Exploration of the Columbus Connection
And Other Family Matters of Consequence

My great-grandfather knew Christopher Columbus before he discovered the New World. Ruy Díaz de Cervantes was proud of his acquaintance with the legendary explorer, but his son and my grandfather, the attorney Juan de Cervantes Saavedra, denied to his dying day that his father and Columbus had ever met. There's a story in this, but it's not my story. Not quite, anyway. There's a story in most things, if only you know how to find it.

My great-grandfather Ruy Díaz de Cervantes lived in Córdoba, where he belonged to a drinking club that met at the apothecary shop of two Genoese brothers to weigh such grave matters as physics, astrology, Aristotle's *Poetics* and the then-contestable – to some, detestable – roundness of the earth. One day in 1486 the Genoese apothecaries admitted to their club a disarmingly monomaniacal navigator who himself had been raised in Genoa by probably Spanish, possibly New Christian, parents. This, to give him the name he used on arrival in Córdoba, was Cristoforo Colombo.

Some in the drinking club sailed with Columbus on his first great voyage of discovery and left their bleached bones in the Indies, but most, like the men of my grandmother Leonor de Torreblanca's family, merely drank and argued with Columbus before sinking back into respected obscurity. The people of Andalucía deplore overachieving, except by themselves.

My mother, another Leonor, Doña Leonor Cortinas from the village of Barajas near Madrid, would tell me and my sister Andrea, 'Oh, they did have one thing in common, that lot – there wasn't a Rusty Old Christian among them.' This was an overstatement. Doña Leonor lived in a world of overstatement, doubtless to compensate for the underachievement of her husband, the barber-surgeon Rodrigo de Cervantes.

'Your grandfather the Patriarch' – she always called him that – 'married a Torreblanca, which is to say a New Christian, which is to say a *converso*, which is to say a person of Jewish ancestry, so his purity of blood, if any, did not pass to you children.'

Doña Leonor's Old Testamentally relentless scorn of her father-in-law was so reciprocated that when my father Rodrigo plunged the family into poverty, as he regularly did, Juan the Patriarch never opened his purse to let even a handful of *maravedis* trickle in our direction.

An early memory, which Andrea, who is almost three years older, confirms:

'Well, we're moving! On the old road again,' shouted my father in a simulacrum of cheer.

'Who did you kill this time?' asked my mother.

'Nobody. I didn't kill nobody.'

The double negative, I ought to say, is no indication of a deficient education – my father was speaking Spanish, after all. 'Lazarillo de Tormes had nothing on us!' he shouted, referring to the protagonist of the picaresque novel then a bestseller in Spain. 'No, señora! We travel, we see the world and learn how psychology breeds geography, or is it the other way around?'

'After Lazarillo de Tormes saw the world,' said Doña Leonor, 'he settled down in Valencia or somewhere as town crier – a good steady job that you if anyone could handle.'

My father's deafness got worse every year. It was why he shouted.

'Toledo. Lazarillo was town crier of Toledo,' he shouted.

After this minor literary correction – my father was an expert on the more impractical aspects of book lore, like poetry and picaresque novels – Doña Leonor fell silent, but it was an eloquent silence. Where she scorned her father-in-law the Patriarch, she merely disdained her husband, a subtle distinction, but one Doña Leonor knew how to draw.

Rodrigo de Cervantes was so thin and angular that, although he was a man of barely middle height, at a casual glance he appeared tall. Stamped on his sallow, sparsely bearded face was the wistful expression of someone who wished he had been born in some other place or time.

Andrea asked, 'Why must we move again, Papá?'

'You're too young to understand.'

'Try *me*,' suggested Doña Leonor ominously.

My father sighed. Then he shouted, 'I simply failed to reduce a dislocated shoulder. It's not so easy, you know. A door, you usually use a door and a stout rope. You need shoulders of your own like the bellringer at Sevilla Cathedral.' My father did not have such shoulders. 'Well, what happened, instead of reducing the dislocated left shoulder, I somehow managed to dislocate the right.'

'Who did the shoulders belong to?' demanded Doña Leonor.

'A count. A no-account count,' my father shouted. 'Practically threadbare. Hardly a grandee of Spain, my dear. Still, it would be politic to leave right away.'

It was frequently politic and never a problem. We had few possessions and Doña Leonor always hid enough money somewhere to hire, in the inevitable extremis, one of those long, covered mule carts called galleys. Andrea and my next-oldest sister Luisa and I were all the right age for the roads and inns of Spain to seem limitlessly seductive; my younger brother Rodrigo was just a toddler, and my third sister Magdalena hadn't been born yet, nor the youngest of us, little Juan the Obscure.

Our removal did not deter the count with the two dislocated shoulders from bringing the predictable lawsuit. Litigiousness proliferated in Spain in its Century of Gold no less than in Elizabethan England and other contemporary centres of culture, an unfortunate by-product of Renaissance humanism, which one shouldn't be too hard on. As Cide Hamete – arguably the world's most profound philosopher – would tell me many years later, 'Avoid all isms – except the one good one.' Ah! But which was that? The sage Arab never said.

Another early memory, again confirmed by my sister Andrea:

To go to prison, Doña Leonor dressed me in my best – actually, my only – grey serge suit. Mother's and daughters' homespun gowns parted in inverted 'V's to reveal their kirtles. This modest finery had escaped the depredations of the bailiff who, two days after my father's arrest for debt, came to the small house outside Valladolid where my father's pragmatic travels had deposited us, and distrained before a distraught Doña Leonor my father's guitar and sword, my mother's empty jewel case, a table and three broken chairs, blankets as much moth holes as merino wool, straw-deficient mattresses, and a chipped Christ-child in a lidless wooden box. Only my father's pathetic library of half a dozen books (of which more later) was spared.

'If,' said Doña Leonor disdainfully, 'you could prove you were gentry, you'd be free in five minutes. It's against the law to imprison an *hidalgo* for debt.'

To be married to an *hidalgo* – *hijo de algo*, son-of-something, a man of consequence – you could see the longing in Doña Leonor's eyes.

'I could prove it,' said Rodrigo de Cervantes, 'if they let me out of here.'

'They won't let you out until you do prove it.'

'That's called a paradox, I think,' chirped my sister Andrea brightly.

At eight, insatiably curious Andrea was fascinated by everything in Valladolid prison. 'They put ladies in prison too,' she marvelled.

'Those are not ladies,' Doña Leonor said.

My sister Luisa's head was bowed. Her lips moved in silent prayer.

My father hugged Andrea to his chest, possibly to keep her from seeing too much.

'Well, son of a something,' Doña Leonor taunted him, 'if you're an *hidalgo*, now's the time to prove it.'

Proving *limpieza de sangre*, purity of blood, was out of the question, but a patent of nobility, even a coat-of-arms, these were possible. Yet in all the years of his marriage Rodrigo de Cervantes had never managed to get them.

'What are that man and lady doing?' Andrea asked my mother.

'She's no lady. Don't look. And stop pointing.'

But in the dim light of the visitors' room my sister Andrea looked and looked, her pale blue eyes enormous.

'What *are* they doing?' I asked her.

'Why did I ever bring them here?' Doña Leonor wailed.

'Beg the warden to release me for thirty days. In thirty days I'll prove I'm a gent.'

The warden refused, but sent Doña Leonor to a lawyer, a young Basque named Iñaki Satrústegui Zumalacárregui.

Doña Leonor practised those thirteen tongue-tormenting syllables, but to no avail. Basque does not resemble Castilian. Or any other language.

'Call me Picapleitos,' the young lawyer suggested. 'My fellow students at Salamanca always did.'

Picapleitos was a small intense man in a black baize doublet and tight black hose. He sat with his skinny legs crossed, swinging a brass-buckled shoe. His undersized head rested on a huge starched cambric ruff, like an apple on a stack of platters, and he had an inordinately long nose, the tip of which God had pinched to a point.

'A veritable patent of nobility,' he said, 'would of course cost a fortune. But gentility can also be acquired in much the same manner as its divine equivalent, the state of grace. My ecclesiastical colleagues speak of indulgence. A Janus-faced term. Here in the shop we frankly prefer the word bribery.' Picapleitos stroked the length of his long nose, bridge to tip, his clean hand somehow managing to leave an ink smear. 'Now then. How much are you prepared to spend?'

'Well,' Doña Leonor parried.

Picapleitos stroked his nose in reverse, tip to bridge. The ink smear vanished. 'Contingency,' he complained. 'I should have known. My dear señora, gentility-by-repute or -aspect does not come cheap. What does your man do in life?'

'He's a barber-surgeon.'

'No fixed income.' Picapleitos sighed. The tip of his now unsmeared nose quivered. 'Would a moneylender be helpful at this point in time? It so happens that my cousin – '

'No. No, we want no part of any moneylenders.'

'Then shall we say ten per cent of his gross income for one year commencing on the day I deliver the document?'

'Shall we say five per cent commencing the day he's discharged from prison?'

It took Picapleitos six weeks. Meanwhile, we starved.

I don't mean to the point of death. There was something to eat most days, usually a few overripe fish heads in a pan of *migas*, crumbs fried with garlic in rancid olive oil. But this diet did little more than fight a rearguard action against hunger.

'Enough to keep body and soul together, if God wills,' my pious, pudding-faced sister Luisa put it.

Except for plump Luisa, we were a family of lean people with no fat to live off in an emergency. Luisa was the odd one out in other ways too. Her hair was dark, her complexion olive, while the rest of us had fair complexions and hair ranging from my own bright chestnut to Andrea's glorious wheaten mane. My baby brother Rodrigo even sported some freckles, like a dusting of cinnamon.

In a bare kitchen, we dreamed of food.

Pudding-faced Luisa: 'Fried milk all slathered with honey, please God.'

I: '*Benengeli con queso.*' Eggplant baked with cheese; my favourite.

Andrea: 'Not *benengeli* – it's *berengena*. Try it.'

But ever since I was two, I always mispronounced eggplant as *benengeli*. It was almost the first word I spoke. (It would almost be the last.)

'Be- be-' I tried. '*Benengeli!*'

'Oh, never mind,' sighed Andrea. Then, with spirit, 'Anyway, don't waste your wishes, Miguelito. Meat! A big pot of stewed rabbit, under a golden crust to hold in the saffron steam! Or lambs' tongues braised in sweet Málaga wine. Or a plump pleasant, I mean peasant, I mean *pheasant* – simmered in milk with ginger and almonds!' She banged her small fists in frustration on the empty larder shelves and twitched her hips in an odd new way so that, many years later when I was a prisoner in Algiers, the first time

I saw the groaning table set for the exotic dancer Zoraida, I remembered my sister Andrea.

Doña Leonor also, in her way, prepared me for Algiers. For even when the family had enough to eat, even when the fish heads were attached to fish bodies and the oil was not rancid, *migas* were still crumbs, the crumbs of poverty. But, 'Eat your *migas*,' my mother would warn me, 'or the Barbary pirates will come in the night and get you.'

It was the commonest maternal threat on the seacoasts of Andalucía, where Barbary pirates prowled and where *migas*, like some culinary plague, were endemic. Most of my early youth was spent there in Andalucía as Rodrigo de Cervantes sought haven from ineptitude and litigation in the less unforgiving south.

'Eat your *migas* or the Barbary pirates will come in the night and get you.'

I ate my *migas* – and the pirates bided their time.

One day my father appeared with a paper attesting to his gentility and we, naturally, moved. Rodrigo de Cervantes plied his trade in a dozen towns and villages in the south, and he grew deafer with every season, and we rarely had enough to eat, but Andrea flourished, eight, nine, ten years old, more a beauty each year, and my pudding-faced sister Luisa thought her pure thoughts of God, and my brother Rodrigo was the perfect little soldier with those cinnamon freckles and gaps between his milk teeth. My parents argued (so that in time I thought all parents did, all the time), my father spent more time in debtors' prison despite Picapleitos's document, my sister Magdalena was born with a thatch of red hair. We never stayed put long enough to go to school, not until we settled for a time in Córdoba, but my father taught us all, even my sisters, to read. Doña Leonor didn't mind, even though literacy was a strong indication of a *converso* hiding in the family tree. Nor did she mind that our nomadic existence made youthful friendships impossible: the children in the towns where Rodrigo de Cervantes found fleeting work were, of course, never good enough for us.

Friendless, lonely, I read. I read everything I could get my hands on. I read the books essential to my father's trade, Lobrera's *The Four Diseases*, Vigo's *The Practice of Surgery*, and a serviceable Latin grammar by one Nebrija. I read my father's dog-eared and *migas*-stained copy of *Lazarillo de Tormes*, received in payment for curing one of those four diseases. I read about Orlando, *furioso* and otherwise, in a volume acquired by splinting a broken leg. I read the poetry of Petrarch, that father of humanism – perhaps the one good ism? – presented for the timely application of some leeches. (Knowing no other incomparable girls, I pictured as Petrarch's incomparable Laura my sister Andrea.) I even read summonses for my father's arrest.

But reading, like *migas*, only fought a rearguard action. I would walk along the dusty, unpaved street of our latest port-of-call and watch boys my age chasing each other or taunting girls or wrestling. Loneliness was a hunger as bad as an empty belly.

Andrea, lonely too, studied herself. I mean this in no Delphic or Socratic sense; but her body, with its unmistakable signs of puberty, fascinated her. That made two of us. Secretly I would watch her run her fingers over the curve of a hip, or with her two hands explore the sleek length of a bare leg, or impatiently cup the not-quite-flatness of her breasts. Spanish girls mature early, especially in the south.

Sometimes Andrea took little Rodrigo on her lap and crooned a gypsy melody to him. I felt left out. But invariably Rodrigo would squirm free to play with a mutilated toy soldier, lacking one hand, which he had found somewhere.

Our grandmother, the other Doña Leonor, Leonor de Torreblanca, came to live with us when her husband Juan the Patriarch decided to spend his declining years in their native Córdoba, taking their eighteen-year-old housekeeper with him. The two Leonors spent hours alternately scorning the Patriarch and disdaining Rodrigo de Cervantes.

The word from Córdoba was that the Patriarch, ensconced there as a magistrate, was squandering the family fortune on his housekeeper and in the gambling den of a Frenchman.

This word came from the Patriarch's twenty-year-old black slave – actually he was only a little darker than a gypsy – called Luis, who, bearing a letter, came one day to the nameless village where we were living near the (to us) great city of Cabra midway between Córdoba and Granada.

'The things that go on in that house,' Luis said with a possibly envious shake of his head. 'The money that man pisses away at Pierre Papin's.'

Juan the Patriarch had addressed the letter to Rodrigo de Cervantes, so although both Leonors were literate, they waited for my father's return. He came shortly before sunset, bringing in a blast of cold mountain air, his face and fingers blue except for the bloodstains.

'Hello, Luis, what are you doing here?'

'Letter from your old man.' Luis, in the years since the Patriarch had won him from the gambler Pierre Papin, never señor-ed or señora-ed any of them. He claimed he'd been born the son of a mighty prince on some island or other in the Indics.

Rodrigo de Cervantes broke the seal and read. And this poor, well-meaning failure of a husband and father seemed to swell to twice his usual self.

'I have an offer of steady work,' he said.

Everybody crowded around.

'Surgeon to the Córdoba tribunal of the Supreme and General Council of the Inquisition,' my father shouted.

There followed one of those ear-shattering silences.

'The Suprema,' said Leonor Cortinas finally, 'prosecutes *conversos*.'

'And persecutes those it's too busy to prosecute,' said Leonor de Torreblanca. 'One way or another, everyone in this house figures to be a target.'

'Except me,' said Luis smugly.

'Anyway, you can't work for the Suprema unless you have *limpieza de sangre*,' Leonor Cortinas told her husband.

'Which you don't, as I of all people should know,' Leonor de Torreblanca told her son. 'Purity of blood is a matter of three generations. Nobody in this family can claim that.'

Not true. My mother, from an illiterate and inbred peasant family in La Mancha, could claim it.

'Only those with pure blood,' shouted my father, 'can work for the Suprema. Since they've hired me, it follows that I have it. And if I do, then you all do.'

I remember turning my wrist towards the light of the oil lamp and trying to see if the tracery of veins and arteries looked any different. I saw Andrea engrossed in the study of her own slender wrist.

'Bring water, someone,' my father shouted.

And he washed his bloodstained hands. He washed them again. He washed them a third time.

At dawn my mother produced her hidden galley-money and by nine o'clock we were creaking, swaying and jouncing along the Córdoba road into the teeth of a cold wind.

12

II

In Which My Grandfather Loses an Argument
And My Sister and I Share a Dream

Until then the Rusty Old Christians around us had mostly exempted my father from the intolerance with which they favoured your average *converso*, whose rumoured wealth and power they resented. Rodrigo de Cervantes, after all, was clearly even poorer and less powerful than themselves. He had not married into the nobility to taint the blood of their race, as other New Christians did. Nor, in the (to us) great cities like Cabra where he had plied his insecure trade, could they accuse him of spreading the Lutheran heresy – which converted Jews allegedly did, just as surely as converted Muslims (called *moriscos*) spied for the Barbary pirates who ravaged the sea coasts of Andalucía and came in the night for little boys who wouldn't eat their *migas*. They couldn't accuse him because in the (to us) great cities like Cabra they had never heard of the Lutheran heresy.

Things were different in Córdoba.

'What am I doing wrong?' Doña Leonor asked my grandmother, who had returned eagerly to the city of her birth but now barely ventured outdoors except to walk in awe once or twice a week – a pilgrimage almost – past the apothecary shop where her Torreblanca uncles had shared wine with Christopher Columbus seventy years ago. 'What am I doing wrong? For the first time in my married life, coins jingle in my purse, but the neighbours shun me and I'm lucky if the fishmonger will sell me even the dregs of the catch when I can afford salt cod already soaked. And now I can't find a midwife for when my time comes.'

My father vowed, 'I'll get you the best midwife money can buy or she and all her family will wear the *sambenito* to the Burning Place.'

My formerly gaunt father in a few months had gained so much weight that his excess chins rendered a ruff superfluous. But his eyes had a haunted look. As a surgeon employed by the Inquisition his job was to patch up the victims of torture so they could undergo more of the same.

'I heal them,' he would plead. 'That's the opposite of hurting them, isn't it? I make them better, not worse.'

13

No one would answer, and my father would sit heavily and stuff his face with the rich foods he himself bought on his way home from the Inquisition dungeons.

A terrified midwife delivered Juan the Obscure in September 1555, or was it October? Very little is known about my youngest sibling.

'I'm going to name him Juan, for the Patriarch,' said my mother, surprising everybody. 'Why? Because for once I can afford the gesture. For once the old reprobate won't think I'm angling for anything, that's why.' Hardly pausing to give Juan the Obscure her breast, she told me, 'You're eight years old, Miguel – high time you went to school.'

I gasped. Andrea squeezed my hand sympathetically.

'I know you're not getting along with the kids in the *barrio*,' my mother said, 'but a Jesuit school just opened and you won't be known there.'

The Jesuits were almost as new as the Lutheran heresy. Some say they arose to counter it.

'Amadis of Gaul,' I said in an apparent *non sequitur*, 'was educated by the King of Scotland.'

My father had bought – actually paid cash money for – a copy of the chivalric romance *Amadís de Gaula* for my birthday. Ideas of chivalry, valour, fidelity and purity soon filled my heart, but I had no one to be chivalrous, valorous, faithful or pure to. Or with.

'The Jesuit Academy is as far as we can send you.'

'At birth,' I informed my mother, 'Amadis was abandoned and his cradle set adrift in the sea.'

'If you want to be abandoned, there's still time.' Juan the Obscure's birth had changed Doña Leonor. Or perhaps the coins jingling in her purse had. She showed signs of a humour as dry as the plains of her native La Mancha. 'Otherwise, you're going to school.'

'I'll have nobody to play with,' protested Andrea – which seemed odd, because until then we so rarely had played together.

I looked at Rodrigo on the floor, anxiously marching his one-handed toy soldier back and forth. I looked at Juan the Obscure, nursing. Glumly I told myself I would never have a brother like Amadis's brother Galaor. Galaor would have thought of something.

It's been said that the legend of Amadis of Gaul, already known by the early fourteenth century and written down in 1508 probably by one Rodríguez Montalvo, gave to Spain a vital part of its unique soul which, not quite a hundred years later, I killed. I plead not guilty, or at least extenuating circumstances including the long reign of a king in love with death. But all that comes later.

Now, I'd better say something about the Spanish art of the *piropo*. An ambulatory pastime, allied to the *paseo* or ritual stroll, the *piropo* is a flirtatious compliment which may be aimed with impunity at any woman on any street in the realm. A novice *piropeador* might murmur as the object of his admiration parades by, 'Ah, how lovelier than the full moon' (or springtime, or a garden, or whatever strikes his feeble fancy). In theory *piropos* are always in good taste, but a gifted *piropeador* can skirt the outrageous, and even do it in verse, viz.:

> If the Inquisition learned
> How truly I worship you
> And the false coin you've returned
> They'd burn you for a Jew.

A *piropo* can be suggestive but never sexually explicit. The *piropeador* who oversteps the bounds must be dealt with by the girl's brother(s), and dealt with severely — as I learned on my way home from my first day at the Jesuit Academy.

A girl came skipping towards me.

'What are you doing here?' I asked when I recognized Andrea. She was dressed fetchingly in an arched hood and shoulder cape.

'I missed you.'

We began walking the long way home past the Roman bridge and the honey-coloured stone buildings that hid the great mosque which, at the time, was spawning in its interior a cathedral. As we passed two loitering boys a year or so older than Andrea, a wind swirled in off the river to lift her cape and plaster her bodice and skirts against her.

'If Aeolus the wind-god were no pagan, I'd light a candle tonight to thank him,' the taller boy commendably improvised, and doffed his beret. Andrea's pale blue eyes twinkled as she swept past.

The second boy said something just as the wind gusted again. Andrea froze. With an anguished look the taller boy groaned, 'Tomás, no! Man! How often must I tell you? A *piropo* is not a blunt instrument.'

'My sword,' said the boy named Tomás. 'I said my sword. That ain't a blunt instrument, is it?'

'A taste of his sword?' Andrea said. 'Me? What's he got against me?'

'Nothing,' said the boy Tomás. 'But I wish I did.'

The taller boy groaned again.

'Besides,' mused Andrea, 'he isn't carrying a sword. Or any weapon that I can see. So why say he wanted to give me a taste of . . .' Her voice stopped. Her eyes narrowed.

15

'I assure you, señorita,' said the taller boy with a sigh, 'Tomás's bark is worse than his bite.'

'But I'd gladly bite her too,' said Tomás indefatigably.

Andrea's eyes suddenly flew wide open. 'Sword,' she cried, then, louder, '*Sword!*' Pale, her lips trembling, she told me, 'Hit him, Miguel.'

He was four or five years my senior and outweighed me by half.

'Me?' I temporized. 'Hit him where?'

'You could hit him,' Andrea suggested, 'in his precious "sword".'

I wasn't sure of her precise meaning, but knowing Andrea expected me to defend her honour, I lowered my head and reluctantly charged.

I think he let me butt him in the stomach because he felt contrite. At any rate, he fell backwards. I think he would have apologized to Andrea, but my head had knocked the breath from him. Trying to regain my balance, I inadvertently stuck my knee in his face. His nose began to bleed.

'Ooh,' said Andrea, not displeased.

I might have done more, for I was warming to my obligation, but the taller boy lifted me and deposited me to one side. 'Enough,' he laughed. 'Who wants it written on his tombstone that a seven-year-old beat him to death?'

'Eight,' I bristled.

The stocky boy snuffled blood. He got up.

'This lout who meant no harm,' the tall boy said, 'is Tomás Gutiérrez, and I am Juan Rufo. You're a spunky kid,' he told me, and turned a radiant smile on Andrea. 'You must be extremely proud of your little cousin, Doña . . .'

'Andrea de Cervantes Saavedra y Cortinas,' she said. 'And this is my younger brother Miguel, who just started school at the Jesuit Academy today, which is why I happen to be out on the street. Seeing him home. I mean, there's no telling what riff-raff a child might run into.'

Andrea had packed a lot into those words: that she was mature enough to be given responsibility for my safety despite the reverse having happened; that as a student at the Jesuit Academy I came from an acceptable family; and that she hadn't yet forgiven Tomás Gutiérrez his woeful Piropo but, by introducing us, hinted that she might.

'School?' said Tomás Gutiérrez, horrified. 'Still, it don't seem to have hurt Juan here none.' He shook my hand with a grip like a blacksmith's tongs. 'Someday,' he said wistfully, squeezing, 'someday I'll learn to keep my big mouth shut instead of shoving my boot in it.' He gave my hand a final crush.

Juan Rufo said, 'Man, don't worry about it. The best of friendships often begin with a little altercation to clear the air. Romances, too. Isn't that so, Doña Andrea?'

Our two new friends walked with us until we neared our dilapidated house. Then, as the wind was blowing from the direction of the nearby tanneries, they doffed their berets and swiftly departed.

Doña Leonor told Andrea, 'Absolutely not.'

'But Miguel needs friends.'

'In the first place, they're boys. Nice girls do not have boys for friends.'

'Miguel, Mamá. I only asked if *Miguel* could sometimes play with Juan and Tomás, and I'd look after him. Because they're bigger.'

'What happened to your hand, Miguel?'

'My what? Nothing. Happened to it.'

'In the second place, this Tomás Gutiérrez,' Doña Leonor continued the next day, 'I have discovered, is the son of a hosier. And this Juan Rufo's father is a dyer, an equally suspicious line of work.'

'You mean those are Jew jobs?' Andrea asked.

'Don't say Jew jobs.'

'Then they aren't?'

'You should say occupations appropriate for *conversos*.'

On the subject of New Christians my mother was often ambivalent.

'But, Mamá, aren't we *conversos*?'

'The probability,' said Doña Leonor, 'is not low. On your *father*'s side. But that doesn't matter. They're just not good enough for you children. Miguel will find suitable friends at school.'

But I found no friends at the Jesuit Academy. At first I thought the other boys avoided me because of the tannery stink that clung to my clothes and hair. But then I overheard them talking.

'And after they've tortured their poor victims to the point of death, his father patches them up so they can be tortured some more.'

'I hear he's his father's apprentice.'

On my way home I sometimes met Tomás Gutiérrez and Juan Rufo.

'Where's your sister, man?'

'Home. She's home. You'd be amazed how much she has to do.'

To be friendless without the possibility of friends is bad enough. But to see the possibility and have it denied is worse. Andrea moped around the house. She read desultorily. She no longer took Rodrigo on her lap, and she had nothing to do with Magdalena who, belying the red of her hair, was an almost icily self-possessed child. 'No, thank you, I would rather not,' was her most frequent response to anything. Like all of us Cervantes children, except plump, pudding-faced, devout Luisa, Magdalena was verbally precocious, but she kept her own counsel.

As Andrea's melancholy grew, so did her beauty. My sister Andrea's hair was the colour of a wheatfield, her pale blue eyes luminous. Though her long-legged figure was too slender for the common taste, she moved with numinous grace. Her beauty was like the caress of the sun on a windless winter day in high Castilla, or the silver track of a full moon on the sea bearing the enigmatic silhouette of an exotically rigged boat, or a pool of clear water in all that man-killing expanse of blazing sand and rock between Algiers and Spanish Oran at the exact moment the escaped prisoner realizes it is no mirage.

One day early in 1556 when the oranges hung ripe on the trees, Doña Leonor said, 'Children, you've been invited to visit your grandfather the Patriarch.'

All I knew about my grandfather was what I'd heard from the two Leonors. My hands began to tremble. I saw Gog and Magog, fourteen feet tall and looming colossally over landscapes and things.

'I'll wear my satin-trimmed kirtle,' said Andrea.

'You'll wear plain Cuenca cloth, the oldest you have.'

Juan the Patriarch summoned us for that hour usually reserved for the siesta, so we would expect no hospitality. To reach the front door of his house across the river from the cathedral-spawning mosque, we had to walk single-file along a narrow path through rushes that reached over our heads. Inside, the black slave Luis led us along a chiaroscuro corridor lit by occasional random holes in the wall to a vast, bare and gelid room. Unseen water dripped. Great sea-green patches of mould covered the walls and a terrarium of life teemed in the ancient rush mats underfoot. We sat stiffly side by side on a rickety bench, Doña Leonor with Juan the Obscure in her arms, then Andrea, Luisa nervously fingering her rosary, me, Rodrigo with his mutilated soldier clutched in one hand, and red-haired Magdalena. Luis brought us each a small, a very small, cup of water, icy cold and faintly brackish. 'No, thank you, I would rather not,' Magdalena piped up, just as our grandfather came striding in past our rickety bench, eyes straight ahead, with a gait so impressively martial that Rodrigo held his mutilated soldier up to see. Seating himself on a backless chair facing our bench, Juan the Patriarch waved Luis away. A juicy young woman who had to be the housekeeper María appeared in his place, wearing an opulent gown with deep décolletage and a domed skirt supported by a farthingale (as Andrea explained to me later). 'Blubber and whalebone,' muttered my mother out of loyalty to the other, absent Leonor. 'She's all blubber and whalebone.' The juicy young woman curtseyed in our direction, mumbling the ritual my-house-your-house to which Doña Leonor responded with several sibilant puffs of visible breath, dragonlike, and a muttered, 'Who says it's hers?' The housekeeper María then followed Luis out, perhaps by prior arrangement.

My grandfather Juan was no colossal Gog or Magog. He stood, and sat, below the average height, a stiffly straight old man of martial appearance despite an understarched ruff that looked like a wilted chrysanthemum. From his wizened monkey face he stared out of deep sockets with the terrible eyes of the mythical cockatrice.

'So this is the younger generation.' His stentorian voice, of which his son's deafness-induced shout was so pale a copy, sent the teeming life scurrying from the rush mats underfoot. I could feel the small water cup vibrate in my hand. 'Why have you been hiding them from me?'

'You never cared to see them before,' Doña Leonor reminded him.

The old man brooded, then spoke. 'As magistrate of Córdoba,' he said, 'I have accumulated certain . . . favours.' He rubbed his hands together; they looked and sounded like old parchment. 'A licentiate named Iñaki Satrústegui Zumalacárregui' – my grandfather was the only one I ever knew who could pronounce that name – 'will shortly be taking testimony from various sources to confirm the purity of my family's blood back to the year fourteen eighty-six, when it has been alleged that certain people, many of tainted origin, gathered once or twice in the back room of an apothecary shop. My father Ruy Díaz de Cervantes, it hardly need be said, never met any of these people.'

'Gathered once or twice!' repeated Doña Leonor in visible puffs of disbelief. 'Never met them!'

'Never. Not my father, nor any member of the Torreblanca family, so esteemed for the purity of its blood. As you must convince that foolish woman my wife Leonor de Torreblanca de Cervantes.'

'But the world knows otherwise. The Torreblancas were early supporters of Christopher Columbus. Their drinking club met every week for years at the shop of those Genoese apothecaries who, like Columbus and the rest, were probably *conversos. And*' – puff, puff – 'your discarded wife Leonor de Torreblanca de Cervantes is proud of that association.'

'I am prepared to give that foolish old woman, freehold, the deed to the slave Luis, who as you know is the offspring of a mighty prince of a strategic island across the Ocean Sea, if she affirms under oath to my lawyer Satrústegui Zumalacárregui the facts as I have stated them.'

'She'd never. That crumbling old apothecary shop is a shrine to her.'

'Make her, Doña Leonor – for the good of your own children sitting here on this rickety bench, especially my namesake Juan who, I assume, is that obscure little bundle in your arms.'

19

'So that's it.'

'As you say, that is it. Although we are speaking of a largely hypothetical occurrence twenty or thirty years down the road, I intend leaving everything – in your trust, Doña Leonor, in the unlikely event that he has not reached his majority – to my namesake Juan. Everything including an untainted name. Now do you see?'

'I see you're an old fool to think you can – '

'Married to that son of mine and you call *me* a fool? I carved a career for myself in the law, a career any man would be proud of, while that non-compos son of mine cannot even – '

' – husband, not shameless like some I could name, and he tries his best to pro – '

' – omach for his post, the post *I* ob – '

' – family. He'd die before he hurt a hair of any – '

' – imply that I – '

' – stoop to innuendo. The truth – '

' – can mean nothing, no more than honour can, to an illiterate peas – '

' – always hurts a hypocri – '

' – when my son could have married – '

' – n't accept – '

' – woman who might have hel – '

' – his own heritage.'

On they went, first his stentorian voice overriding her visible dragonlike puffs, then the other way around, in shorter and shorter takes, so that we children could hardly follow the argument that, in some perverse way, even though their faces were turning the colour of arterial blood, I sensed they were both enjoying.

' – overbearing – '

' – inbred – '

' – parsimonious – '

' – I shit – '

' – profligate – '

' – in the – '

' – adulterous – '

' – milk – '

' – excuse for a – '

' – of your – '

' – patriarch.'

' – mother.'

Silence.

For there, finally, it was: the ultimate insult in a land where veneration of the Virgin made a cult of motherhood.

'What . . . did . . . you . . . say?' Doña Leonor demanded in four icy puffs that momentarily enveloped her father-in-law.

'I believe,' said the Patriarch in a conciliatory tone, 'I believe I may have spoken of milk.'

'You spoke of my mother,' puffed Doña Leonor. 'A sainted woman you never even met.'

'I may perhaps have referred to *a* mother,' allowed the Patriarch.

Luisa frantically counted her beads. Rodrigo desperately solaced his mutilated soldier.

My grandfather might have talked his way out, but I was young and naïve and, unlike my father, had acute hearing.

'Grandfather,' I said, 'you said, "I spit in the milk of your mother." ' Naïve or not, I edited the verb.

'My lady mother,' said Doña Leonor, oddly triumphant I thought.

'No, no. I did not mean her,' essayed my grandfather the Patriarch. 'My words, if in fact I spoke some such words, were meant more impersonally, even metaphysically. A sort of universal milk, a milkness. Milk with a capital M, if you will. Platonic. If I indeed said, "I . . . spit in the milk of . . . whomever", it should not be construed as personal. You see?'

My grandfather the Patriarch, his face the colour of one of my father's blood-gorged leeches, pushed himself up from his backless chair and approached me.

'Dear boy, when I said I would leave everything to that obscure little bundle in your mother's arms, I of course meant to him and to all his deserving siblings – yourself included. Now will you please explain to your good mother that what you seem to have heard did not mean what she seems to have thought?'

'With my dying breath,' vowed Doña Leonor, 'I will urge Leonor de Torreblanca to tell the truth about that apothecary shop. Now, leave the boy alone.'

He turned on her. 'Ways! I have ways! Tomorrow in this time there'll be no apothecary shop, not even a gutted shell. At the altar of what ridiculous shrine will that foolish woman then sacrifice the future of her children, and her children's children – not to mention generations of my bloodstock as yet unborn?'

He swung that cockatrice stare away from me just in time, for my knees had turned to water. Or milk. His cruor-coloured face atop the wilted-chrysanthemum ruff thrust itself at Doña Leonor and he opened his mouth to speak again, but he spoke no more. He clutched his shoulder, his left shoulder, bringing to mind the many dislocations his son my father had treated with varying degrees of success, and he staggered back, back towards his backless chair, and half there he gave me one final gibbous glare of those cockatrice eyes, and then he fell, and when he struck the floor it was not gently.

I reached him first, Luis the black slave and the housekeeper María right behind. They knelt. He did something with the Patriarch's eyes. She held a mirror before the Patriarch's lips. My mother meanwhile was herding my brothers and sisters from the room. I heard her call my name. In reply I said something that sounded like 'd-d-d-d', about which more in a moment. I heard the housekeeper María say, 'He's not breathing.' I heard Luis the black slave with his habitual sang-froid say, 'He is not breathing because he is dead.'

And he was. Oh, he was dead. He had not expected to die, he had not wanted to die, but he was dead anyway. It seemed incredible, monstrous, to me. It always would. Staring down then, nine years old, and seeing death, human death, for the first time, I asked myself, did I like my grandfather? Did I hate him? Did it matter? Had their argument killed him? Had I? Or would he have died right then, no matter what? Had the thread of his life been spun, measured, cut – all as ineluctable as the tides? But the tides ebb, then flow back. And the dead? The dead don't flow back. No, but they go elsewhere. But what if it's the wrong elsewhere? Or what, I asked myself, what if there *is* no elsewhere? My grandfather's cockatrice eyes stared and stared and saw nothing. Oh, he was dead, as everyone who ever lived would one day be dead, not wanting to die, yet knowing all their lives, as I now knew, that they must. More than twenty years later in Algiers when I stood on the scaffold, hearing the dirgeful valedictory of pipe and drum as the executioner mounted behind me, I would try to solace myself with the knowledge that we each had a time and this was mine, but as I felt the thick hempen rope surprisingly cool against my throat, my mind still clamoured: in another instant you will be dead as monstrously as your grandfather was that afternoon in the large icy room across the river from the cathedral-spawning mosque. It was absurd.

And was life any less absurd? We had to keep my grandfather on ice for days because the authorities, the very authorities he had been one of, refused to certify his undeniable defunctness until his papers could be found, and his papers could not be found because Picapleitos had misplaced them while trying to prove that in my grandfather's veins flowed untainted blood, a proof so desired that it had led to his death and non-burial.

On the day we were finally permitted to bury him, my father resigned his position with the Supreme and General Council of the Inquisition. Faith, not deeds, motivated his employers, and while he had all the faith in the world, his deeds were mangling his soul. (Is this not the Lutheran heresy? But my father was a good Catholic Christian all his life.) That same day my grandmother Leonor de Torreblanca entered the house in tears to tell us the crumbling apothecary shop had been demolished to make way for a smithy, and after that she went into a decline.

Picapleitos, smearing and then unsmearing his nose, read my grandfather's will to the family and to Luis the black slave and María the housekeeper. Also present was a dapper man wearing the ostrich plume in his velvet hat on the right side, French style, not over the heart as befitted a Spanish gentleman. This was the gambler Pierre Papin. My grandfather left no estate. Zero. In fact, less than zero. He was in debt to dapper Pierre Papin, but it all worked out because my grandfather had bequeathed Luis the black slave to his discarded wife, and she sold Luis back to Pierre Papin for exactly the amount of the debt. Luis had a way with cards. What happened to the housekeeper María I have no idea.

When we moved to a new nameless village near the (to us) no longer great city of Cabra, Andrea had to confront the mysteries of puberty in the face of Doña Leonor's Manchego prudery while I had to confront my affliction.

'Do you think they ever do it?' Andrea asked me.

'Who? D-d-do wh-what?'

'Mamá and Papá. You know.'

I shrugged. Shrugging was simpler than talking.

'I don't. Think they do. Because we'd hear them.'

I thought a moment, and tilted my head towards Rodrigo, playing with his mutilated soldier in one corner of the kitchen, and towards Magdalena, who seemed to be pulling the wings off a large horsefly, in another. Then I made a cradle-rocking motion to signify Juan the Obscure.

'They all happened a long time ago.' Andrea touched my hand. 'You mustn't be afraid to talk, Miguel. It's just a small stutter, really.'

But I shrugged. Not that the family weren't patient with me – my father most of all, who had his own affliction.

'Try again, Miguel. Sometimes when I don't hear too well, you help me, isn't that so?' My father had become his familiar slender self, and he looked at the world with perplexed rather than haunted eyes.

'I said I d-d-don't th-th-' My face turned red. Cruor-coloured, in fact. You will understand.

For, ever since my grandfather died right before my eyes, I stuttered. It wasn't always the sort of stutter that makes spittle fly when you utter plosives such as – well, plosive. But it was more than enough (like the missing hand of Rodrigo's toy soldier, had he been real) to set me apart. Why, even the ancient Greeks, who should have known better, used the selfsame word, barbarians, to denote both stutterers and foreigners.

I tried again. 'I don't think Mamá should treat Andrea like a prisoner just because she – '

My mother interrupted me, as if to say yes, yes, we know what you are trying to say and the answer is, 'You're too young to understand such things, so mind your own business.' Then she apologized for interrupting.

In those few words I'd spoken, most plosives were repeated, some more than once. P-p-prisoner, for instance. But I won't clutter these pages with examples of my lamentable inability to communicate, except for an occasional reminder.

'Because if they don't do it,' Andrea asked another time, 'how can she understand the things I'm feeling?'

Andrea brooded, and retreated inside her changing body.

Drought followed the death of our grandfather the Patriarch, and famine, and hard on the heels of drought and famine came the plague. Soon the villages near the no longer great city of Cabra filled with refugees from Córdoba, and many more hands than necessary were available to harvest the crop from the Duke of Sessa's olive trees, green and silver on the russet hills for miles in all directions. But the drought was so severe that even the hardy olives suffered.

The next year it rained, and the harvest was bountiful.

'Can I, Mamá?' Andrea asked.

Doña Leonor's no was flat and final, but Andrea persisted.

'Everybody harvests the olives of the Duke of Sessa.'

'There's still plague about.'

That was true – just.

'But practically every man, woman and child in all the nameless little villages for miles around – '

'How many times must I tell you no?'

Every Sunday after the priest came from Cabra to celebrate mass, the villagers would take their slow turns around the dusty plaza in front of the church. You hardly needed hawk eyes, which Doña Leonor had, to see how, as Andrea passed and circled and passed again, every man in the nameless little village lost interest in anything but my sister's numinous walk and the lovely face half hidden by her shawl.

Every weekday at dawn the villagers would go into the olive groves and beat the branches with sticks, and the ripe fruit would rain on to the cloths and nets spread beneath. All day the mules would trudge and the great presses would turn and the golden oil would spill into huge earthenware jars. And half the night at the presses and in the groves wine would flow and goat meat sizzle over wood fires, and guitars would strum, and with a pensive, faraway, almost a bored look in the firelight a man would lift his head in the abrupt opening wail of *cante jondo*, deep song, that unique and yet universal expression of pain and, finally, contempt for all the things in the world that eventually must beat a man down.

It was at such a moment, the music but dimly heard in our house in the nameless village, that Andrea disappeared.

Doña Leonor quickly wrapped her shawl around her square, mannish shoulders and we went out into the moonlit night – my mother, Rodrigo and I – to find her. My father had somehow managed to twist his own knee while trying to reduce a dislocated hip, so he stayed at home with Luisa, who was counting her beads, and Magdalena and Juan the Obscure.

As we approached the big oil presses of the Duke of Sessa we heard over the guitar music much shouting and rhythmic clapping, and then in the moonlight we saw Andrea. It would have been difficult not to see her because she alone was dancing, under the spill of golden oil at the end of the sluice – hair plastered to her thrown-back head and shining with golden oil, bodice drenched in oil to reveal the tips of her breasts, and beneath her caught-up skirts those long legs streaming oil as her feet stamped to the music. Her golden-oil-anointed face wore a look that would haunt me, so compounded was it of childlike joy and newly, overwhelmingly discovered sexuality.

'Beat her,' Doña Leonor told my father when she had dragged Andrea home. But Rodrigo de Cervantes declined, pleading the state of his knee. So Doña Leonor herself beat Andrea, with a length of leather she was using to replace the worn hinges of our ancient door.

If my sister was treated like a prisoner before, it is easy to imagine the sequel. For months my mother did not permit her to step outdoors, except to use the privy and to attend mass. Even when we buried my grandmother, Andrea stayed at home with Juan the Obscure.

'I was only dancing,' Andrea would say. 'What's so terrible about what I did?'

'Whose idea was the oil?' I asked.

25

'Well, if you promise not to tell. Juan Rufo and Tomás Gutiérrez came up from Córdoba for the harvest. It was Juan.' Then, a husky whisper, 'Also, he kissed me on the mouth.'

I did not, could not, speak. I felt an inexplicable urge to strike my sister Andrea – and at the same time an even more inexplicable one to kiss her on the mouth myself.

Once, I came into the kitchen as Andrea was sweeping. Bent over her short-handled besom, she backed towards me. I could have stepped out of her way. I didn't. Colliding with me, she straightened and half turned to look over her shoulder. That year we were the same height. She made no sound, but those luminous pale blue eyes laughed.

I looked for other ways to touch my sister Andrea and make it seem accidental. Complacently or complaisantly, she permitted this. Soon I was eating little and sleeping less.

'The boy looks peaked,' my father shouted one day.

'He ought to go to school again,' said Doña Leonor.

My heart jumped. The nameless village had no school. School meant Cabra. Cabra meant I wouldn't return home at night. And that meant I wouldn't see Andrea.

'I don't know,' shouted my father. 'He has his books. I can get more. Probably even from the Duke's library.'

'Not the same as school.'

'I need him on my rounds,' shouted my father, 'to act as my ears. It helps if a surgeon can hear his patients' complaints.'

They argued, and settled nothing. I glanced at Andrea. She averted those pale blue eyes. She looked, for Andrea, almost demure.

The sleeping arrangements in our small, dilapidated rented house in the nameless village near the no longer great city of Cabra were these: Our parents' straw pallet just fitted in a shedlike extension on the north side of the kitchen along with Juan the Obscure's cradle. A curtain closed this cell off at night. The rest of us children slept in the kitchen.

That night I watched Andrea in her worn nightdress silhouetted against the candle before she pursed her lips and blew it out. Then I heard the rustle of her pallet. Staring into darkness, I saw Andrea dancing, her pale blue eyes laughing over her shoulder at me, and then instead of me those pale blue eyes were laughing at Juan Rufo, and then I saw her blowing out the candle again, and that dissolved into her kissing Juan Rufo, and I cried out and heard from across the dark room the sudden intake of breath, and I tasted salt on my lips and felt the tears on my face, and I slept.

And, sleeping, dreamed that I had gone that night with Andrea to the oil press and that Andrea, dancing with her head thrown back, turned to kiss not Juan Rufo but me on the mouth, and I awoke to a softness against my cheek and a fragrance in the breath I took, and the awareness that Andrea lay with me on my pallet and was holding me in her arms. The softness was her breast, and in a hardly willed movement I reached out in the darkness to touch it. I could not have been asleep long, for Andrea lightly stroked with her fingertips the tears still wet on my face, and then she was kissing them from my cheeks, and then from my lips while something strange and stirring began to happen to me. My sister Andrea laughed softly, hardly a laugh at all, and with a single, delicate, burning touch explored the thing that was happening. Then she pulled away and, in the moonlight which now stood outside the window, stretched as if she had just awakened, and in a drowsy voice said she had been concerned that I was crying so. I said I was all right, and she told me she'd had a dream about that night of the harvest, but it was a wicked dream and she didn't know whether she ought to tell me. I insisted. In her dream she had been dancing at the mill, she said, but it was not Juan Rufo who had kissed her on the mouth, it was I. I wanted to tell her I had dreamed the same dream, but my stuttering tongue was suddenly paralysed as over Andrea's shoulder I saw in the moonlight the cockatrice eyes of my grandfather. Then I realized it was only our sister Magdalena watching us.

III

In Which the Crown Prince Falls Downstairs

Which of us has never pondered the difference between historical time and fictional time?

Early in 1562, historical time, three gilded youths came to study at the University of Alcalá de Henares, twenty miles from Madrid and even closer to Barajas where my mother Doña Leonor was born. The trio should have been Fortune's favourites. One was the seventeen-year-old prince Don Carlos, heir to the throne of Spain. Another was Don Carlos's half-uncle, the illegitimate prince Don Juan of Austria, then fifteen (exactly my age), who within a decade would become the number-one hero of the Christian world. The third, seventeen like Don Carlos, was his Italian cousin Alessandro Farnese, later Duke of Parma, who would die full of glory in his mid-forties while taking the waters at Spa.

By surviving into his forties, Alessandro Farnese proved himself luckier than the others. The handsome hero Don Juan would meet his end, also in the Low Countries, a dozen years sooner. As for the ill-fated Don Carlos, twisted in mind and body, hunchbacked – or was he? the enigmatic English spy and part-time playwright Marlowe would tell me of a similar black legend that grew around England's Richard III – he was to die under ambiguous circumstances at twenty-three.

History tells us this:

By the age of seventeen His Highness Don Carlos had deflowered 228 virgins, according to the count of his bodyguard-procurer Pedro de Isunza, a compulsive keeper of records. The 229th on the night of 19 April 1562 (a date universally endorsed by historians) had been brought to the Crown Prince's rooms on the third floor of a minor mansion conveniently near the College of San Ildefonso, where the Crown Prince was a special student.

Whether she stayed the night would depend on how zestfully she yielded her virginity. Provided, of course, Don Carlos himself managed to perform. If not, there would be a princely rage, with blame falling on Pedro de Isunza for the poor quality of his merchandise.

Tonight Isunza had little to worry about; he knew the Crown Prince's tastes. Of partly Austrian blood, perhaps homesick for that eastern land he would never see, Don Carlos fancied lithe, long-limbed, blue-eyed blondes who might have leaped straight from the pages of Tacitus's *Germania*.

Tonight's virgin was perfection itself.

Pedro de Isunza had found the girl at the gambling den near the Santiago Gate run by the Frenchman Pierre Papin. She had been losing recklessly at backgammon, her stake supplied by an obviously infatuated student. Isunza had moved in, squaring the student's account with Pierre Papin, although from the go-to-hell look in the girl's pale blue eyes he was half willing to bet she was no virgin.

But when he asked, the girl said, 'Of course I am.'

'Well, we'll learn soon enough.'

'We,' said the girl, 'may find that we learn nothing of the sort.'

'My principal,' said Pedro de Isunza, 'is most particular on the point.'

'Holy Virgin! You're a pimp?'

The insult did not bother Isunza. But the girl disengaged her arm and turned away.

'Shall we say one hundred gold ducats for the night if you . . . prove out?'

One hundred gold ducats was more than a year's income for a skilled labourer.

The girl turned back to him, her mane of wheaten hair swinging in the lamplight. 'Let's have a look at this Croesus of yours,' she said thoughtfully.

Isunza found her so attractive that he wished she would admit, on the way to the Crown Prince's rooms, that she had misplaced her virginity. Then he would have her for himself in a sort of *droit-du-seigneur*'s-bodyguard.

But she didn't, so Pedro de Isunza was now waiting in the antechamber.

Inside, the girl was saying, 'No, no I don't think so.'

'Why not, for heaven's sake?' whined the Crown Prince.

'I'm just not in the mood.'

'You have, I assume, guessed who I am.'

'Well, your chin.'

The arrogant, prow-like Habsburg jaw was, alone, almost a dead giveaway. And everyone here in Alcalá knew the Crown Prince was at the university. She had even dreamed of meeting him.

The man of flesh and blood was a nightmare.

That he'd taken her for granted was not unexpected. But did he have to guzzle his wine with those unhousetrained little slurping sounds? Or smell so of garlic and stale clothing? Or bray so when he laughed?

'I,' he said, 'shall some day rule an empire vaster than the Roman empire at its height, or the Islamic. The first empire on which the sun never sets.'

'So?'

He fed her geography as if it were an aphrodisiac. 'Spain, New Spain including South America, Central America, part of North America, the Indies and so forth; most of Italy including Tuscany, Parma, Savoy, the Kingdom of Naples, Sicily, Sardinia; islands off the coast of Asia that may soon bear my name; parts of Africa; the Low Countries and more of France than you would imagine; and, oh yes, I almost forgot, the Duchy of Milan. All these will belong to me eventually. I want you to belong to me tonight.'

She drained her fourth – or was it her fifth? – cup of wine. 'I'm not a peninsula, I'm a person.'

'And a beauty, a Lorelei. You can't refuse me. One day I'll command an army of fifty thousand men.'

'Then why don't you choose one,' she said sweetly, stifling a tipsy giggle, 'and bugger him?'

His Habsburg jaw dropped. He slapped her.

Reflexively, she slapped him, harder.

A bodice-ripper by nature, he reached for hers. She evaded his grasp and ran for the door.

A knife thudded into oak inches from her face. She yanked the door open and plunged through.

Pedro de Isunza just missed beating her to the other door across the antechamber. She got it open, hesitated only an instant on the landing, and hurtled downstairs.

Isunza and the Crown Prince pounded after her.

What happened in the dark stairwell is not known. Possibly Don Carlos in his fury tried to push past Isunza. Possibly Isunza accidentally tripped the Crown Prince. Whatever, both lost their balance and went tumbling down to strike their heads on a door standing ajar at the bottom.

The girl disappeared into the night.

Note that history does not, *for reasons that remain to be seen*, name the instrument of Don Carlos's downfall; she is just 'the girl', a bit player in the annals of the Habsburg dynasty, forever anonymous.

And note again the date – 19 April 1562.

Yet it was not until October of 1564 that I accompanied my father, then deaf almost as the proverbial post, to Alcalá, where I had been born and where my sisters Luisa and Andrea were to take the veil.

So in historical time Andrea could not have been in Alcalá when Don Carlos fell downstairs. But in fictional time she *was* there. I know this for a fact because I was there too. I was the one she came to afterwards, the one who along with Juan Rufo hid her and . . .

How to explain this chronological conundrum?

When I asked Cide Hamete long afterwards, the sage Arab – arguably the world's severest critic of Aristotle – would answer obliquely. 'Without Aristotle, your Dark Ages couldn't have been so dark, could they? Once his ideas spread, it would be generations until people saw unbelief, not belief, as the beginning of wisdom. Still, that philosophical fraud got one thing right: poetry – in which he included drama and fiction – is truer than history.'

'But,' I began to object, 'but history is the – '

'Truth?' Cide Hamete supplied. 'Because it's documented? But why should the ledger be truer than the legend? The merely measurable truer than the truly memorable?'

'But history is what really – '

'Happened?' Cide Hamete's smile was indulgent. 'Is it? Doesn't the historian, no less than the poet, have to make choices? If he didn't, he would be swept away by the river of time. But the historian dips into that river, rescues a fact here and lets one drown there, leaves a third to be saved by some other historian – a triage, in short. From the flood of facts, the historian must *select*. Selecting, he endows his chosen facts with a kind of meaning often confused with truth. Doesn't the poet do the same? So tell me, whose is the truer truth?'

When I did not answer, Cide Hamete, to whom past and present and future are one, said this:

'All time, whether poetic or historical, is elusive, elastic, protean – and like Proteus it is almost impossible to capture. But if you capture it, you can win foreknowledge, as Proteus's captors did.'

'All I'm asking,' I said, 'is that you help me get a grip on the present.'

'Yet the illustration I would choose lies in the future. I speak of the curious coincidence of your death occurring on the same date as Shakespeare's.'

At the time I had never heard of Marlowe, let alone Shakespeare. I said the name sounded contrived.

'He'll be as famous as you,' Cide Hamete said.

'I'll be f-famous?'

Cide Hamete sighed. 'Could you try to stick to the subject? I was saying that you and Shakespeare will die on the same date, the twenty-third of April of – oh my, what am I doing?' A pained look crossed Cide Hamete's face. His godlike omniscience was still new to him and he was feeling his way like a toddler. Or was he? Perhaps he only wanted me to think so; perhaps he had a purpose in telling me the date of my death. Whatever, from that time on, most April 23rds I would do something reckless, something I knew desperately needed doing before I died, and the Devil – or Cide Hamete – take the hindmost.

'At least,' the sage Arab went on in self-exculpation, 'I haven't told you the year.' I hardly knew if that was better or worse. 'Now, about the nature of time. It will be the same date, as I said – but a different day.'

'That's ridiculous,' I said.

'I assure you, my friend, I do not deal in the ridiculous. Quite soon Pope Gregory will reform the calendar, and Spain will rightly adopt the change immediately. But stodgy England will characteristically cling to the old Julian confusion for more than a century, during which the two calendars will be separated by a gap of at first ten, then eleven days. So are you and Shakespeare really dying at the same time? According to the diverging

31

calendars – those temporal frames upon which historians drape facts like wet laundry – you are. But logic says you are not. After all, then, is history any more trustworthy than fiction?'

He was leading me, of course, but I went willingly. For, when history and fiction conflict, has a storyteller any choice?

So – the year was either 1562 or 1564, the month was either April or October, and my father and I had just arrived at the house of my sister Luisa's godfather, a devout lawyer named Cristóbal Bermúdez, where my sisters had been staying for some months before taking the veil.

'She's gone!' cried the lawyer. 'A few nights ago there came faintly to the house the sound of guitars and *cante jondo*, and she just disappeared.'

Standing before my father, I relayed Bermúdez's news in a private sign language, our solution to my stutter and his deafness. For in this manner I had been Rodrigo de Cervantes's interpreter since a few days after Andrea and I dreamed the same dream in the nameless village outside the no longer great city of Cabra. Horse and cattle fairs, saints' days, wedding feasts – these attracted us to the numerous other nameless villages in that part of Andalucía, for such events always meant too much drinking, which meant broken bones, dislocated joints, black eyes, split knuckles, and gunshot wounds to treat. About such wounds people believed boiling oil would counteract the poison, but my father was too softhearted to aggravate the pain, so instead applied a simple salve, heavy on the beeswax, and his gunshot victims seemed to fare better than most.

My father would mumble his ritual prayers to SS Cosmas and Damian, and roll up his sleeves to do good. But he was a clumsy man who would have made an equally inept mason or carpenter, and before long he yielded to me the more dextrous procedures. My father was also absentminded. I often had to point out, as he readied his lancet to bleed the fever from a patient, 'Papá, you are probably looking for the vein, the *vein*, Papá, that runs close by that artery there.' To do this, I had either to gesticulate urgently or to shout, neither option instilling confidence in the patient, until I learned with a light touch to guide my father's distracted fingers. In this manner we kept moving, and the inns of Andalucía were home to me, and the open road my neighbourhood, and books borrowed from the library of the Duke of Sessa my school. And if some nights, bedded down in a cattle stall, I dreamed ardent dreams of Andrea – why, surely it was only teenage fantasy combined with a longing for home.

I tried to prepare myself for our homecomings, each time vowing things would be different. But they never were. Andrea's presence, or absence, was so preoccupying that I hardly noticed how my brother Rodrigo now wore his maimed toy soldier on a string around his neck, or how my sister Luisa had developed a beatific smile and my sister Magdalena a self-absorbed one, or how my brother Juan the Obscure had taken to hiding in dark corners.

Doña Leonor too was preoccupied by Andrea. '. . . no time for anything else while you're away,' she complained, 'if I always have to watch her like a hawk.'

'. . . nest . . .' answered my father. His periodic efforts not to shout inevitably turned into a mumble, with only an occasional word distinct.

Once, Andrea had begun to give me what might at first have passed for an impulsive sisterly hug just as our parents walked into the room.

'Now that,' Doña Leonor beamed, 'is the healthy kind of affection the girl needs.'

'. . . but . . .' said my father, looking at us closely. My father's mumblings sometimes masked an insight.

Even if I wanted to break the web Andrea wove around the two of us, how could I? What could I tell her – me, the kid brother with the bad stammer, especially when nervous? If I mentioned the unmentionable, she would say it was just a game she played. Did it help to know that denial, like desire, is strengthened by guilt?

She would give me a sidelong look as she said, 'Juan Rufo's always finding excuses to visit the village. Last week he came with Tomás Gutiérrez, and you know what? The Duke of Sessa's going to pay his way through the University of Alcalá.'

'Gutiérrez?' I asked.

'Of course not. Does Tomás look like scholar material? He'll go along as Juan's servant. He's handsome. He's got a twin-pointed beard. Dark brown.'

'Tomás?'

'Juan! He lets me stroke it. It's all silky.'

I had no retort. My beard still lay in the future.

Our mother, who hardly let Andrea out of her sight, considered her safe with me. We found places where we could be alone – a cow byre at the edge of the village, a shed behind the cemetery, the ruin of a burnt-out house.

One evening, sitting on a fallen beam, we watched the moon rise over the blackened walls of the ruin, flooding it with light. On the floor were the remains of a cookfire.

'Gypsies,' I said.

'Gypsies,' Andrea echoed, her wheaten hair brushing my cheek as she turned to me. 'I dream about them sometimes. Far off I can hear a guitar so distant it sounds like a dream inside a dream, and a man singing deep song, and I get out of bed and you're waiting, Miguel, and I take your hand' – she took my hand now in the ruin of the burnt-out house – 'and we just run away with the gypsies. Just go with them, the two of us, and you set their broken bones and I sew for them, for the whole clan, beautiful clothes, and . . . and nobody has to know whether our blood is pure or . . . or anything else about us. And we lie under the stars together every night, free. Can't you see it?'

I tried not to. I tried not to feel the scalding line Andrea's fingernail traced along my wrist.

'G-g-gypsies are strange people,' I said, desperate to fill the charged silence. 'They came from Egypt, did you know that? "Gypsy" means "Egyptian". I read all about them in a book of the Duke of Sessa's. Egyptians, I mean. They're strange p-people too. Ph-pharaohs,' I blurted. 'They had kings in Egypt called pharaohs, and they built gigantic tombs for when they died called pyramids, and the people believed the pharaohs weren't just kings, they were gods, and because nobody else was good enough for them, the pharaohs kept their blood pure for generation after generation.' I went on, tripping over my tongue, spouting half-forgotten lore from the Duke of Sessa's book to get my mind off what Andrea was doing and what I wanted to do. 'When they were alive, I mean. They kept their blood pure by marrying their sisters.'

Struck dumb by my own words I gazed at Andrea, her lips moist as ripe pomegranate, and if there were ever to be a time it was now, for I found myself holding her face between my two hands and bringing it close so I could touch those lips, now softly saying Miguel Miguel Miguel, with my own lips.

Afterwards I would remember how little warning there was – a faint creak overhead, movement sensed rather than seen, a shadow in the moonlight where no shadow should have been – and as the charred rafter gave way with a splintering crash I hurled myself at Andrea, falling with her in my arms away from the gypsy cookfire as the heavy roofbeam thudded to the bare earth floor.

We held each other, not moving or breathing, until the dust settled. Then in silence we made our way home, side by side, careful not to touch.

And we never talked about what almost happened there.

And we never went back.

The next time my father and I returned from the road, Doña Leonor said, 'Cristóbal Bermúdez was in Córdoba and he took Luisa back with him to Alcalá to prepare for her novitiate.'

'I thought the novitiate *was* the preparation,' said my father.

'He took Andrea too,' Doña Leonor explained.

So now here we were in Alcalá, my father and I, and my father was shouting, 'We'll find her.' But his voice lacked conviction, and for once he was practical. 'While we're about it,' he suggested to his friend Cristóbal Bermúdez, 'maybe you'd better ask the Carmelite sisters what provisions exist for the return of a girl's dowry if the betrothal should unavoidably be called off.'

My father had borrowed 400 gold ducats – roughly four years' income – for his daughters' dowry, and this staggering sum had already been paid over.

While the devout lawyer learned whether such provisions existed (they did not), and while my father prowled the town to learn where Andrea was (he did not), I went to the university and found Juan Rufo's lodgings.

A tall man with a silky, twin-pointed beard opened to my knock, his hopeful smile vanishing when he saw me.

Behind him a voice was saying, '. . . no time for the likes of you, now that she's been royally rogered.'

'But we don't *know*,' pleaded the man at the door, 'that this fellow Isunza – '

'Face reality,' came the voice, louder, and a short, powerfully built man joined us. 'Who the hell are you?' he demanded.

'Miguel de Cervantes,' I said. 'We met in Córdoba.'

'Sure, the brother. You're not armed?'

'Armed?'

The tall man, who of course was Juan Rufo, sighed.

'You got no sword? Dagger? Dirk? Poniard? Stiletto? Misericorde?' Tomás Gutiérrez pursued.

'What for?'

'Man! The point of honour! A girl gets deflowered, never mind if it's the King or whoever, and her family's reputation is shot – unless some blood gets spilled. And I don't mean the blood on the bed sheets.'

'Tomás,' said Juan Rufo, 'must you? I'm still hopeful that the lovely Andrea, whose beauty is like the caress of the sun on a windless winter day in high Castilla, will make this talk of honour and vengeance unnecessary.'

'Not a prayer in purgatory,' Gutiérrez said, with that bluntness that would always plague his social aspirations, and turned to me. 'The code of honour don't bend, friend. The seducer's got to die. Ordinarily. But if he's a royal?' Tomás continued. 'You can't kill a royal. So guess who that leaves.'

I understood, and refused to understand. My sister and royalty? Honour and vengeance? Dagger, dirk, poniard, stiletto, misericorde? My whole being rejected the abomination demanded of me by ancient tradition.

'Miguel!' cried a breathless voice.

I whirled. My knees turned to *cuajada*.

'I knew you'd come – oh, I knew you would!'

We clung. Her face was flushed, her wheaten hair dishevelled. Her heart pounded against mine.

'Did you – ' I asked.

'Of course not.'

'Thank God,' said Juan Rufo.

'Why didn't you?' asked Tomás Gutiérrez suspiciously.

By this time we were all inside, and all ears.

'I couldn't stand him, he was such a boor. I ran away.'

'They let you?' asked Gutiérrez sceptically.

'I don't see how they could have stopped me – not once they fell downstairs.'

Simultaneously, Juan Rufo said, 'Do they know where to find you?' and Gutiérrez said, 'Get her out of here, Cervantes,' and I said, 'We've got to hide you until – '

Until what?

Gutiérrez was unrelenting. 'We want no part of her here. Get her out, friend. Now.'

Juan Rufo gave him a withering glance that still managed to convey anguish. This is as hard as it sounds.

'The porter's lodge at San Ilde,' he told me. 'She'll be safe there until dawn.'

Swiftly, Juan Rufo and I made our plans. Then Gutiérrez opened the door reluctantly and peered to left and right in the moonlight, and I hurried out.

My father stood flanked by two men in the *cercle privé* of Pierre Papin's gambling den.

Luis the black slave wore a turban in the Turkish manner and a huge gleaming scimitar. His smile revealed two wicked gold teeth. He looked prosperous and menacing.

'Find her?' he asked.

I settled provisionally for a noncommittal grunt.

Pierre Papin had a Frenchman's way with words. 'Her beauty,' he extemporized, 'is like the silver track of a full moon on the sea bearing the enigmatic silhouette of an exotically rigged boat.'

I wondered if any man in Alcala, aside from Tomás Gutiérrez, hadn't fallen under my sister's spell. Luis, maybe.

'She make it with Prince Charming?' the black slave asked with his habitual sang-froid.

'The Crown Prince seems to have met with an accident.'

'What?' my father shouted.

'With that girl, it was to be expected,' said Luis, and removed his turban thoughtfully. His pate was shaven. He mused, 'Her beauty is like a pool of clear water in all that man-killing expanse of blazing sand and rock between Algiers and Spanish Oran at the exact moment the escaped prisoner realizes it is no mirage.'

So much for Luis's sang-froid, I thought; so much for his imperviousness to my sister's charms.

But replacing his turban, he said, 'They'll be looking for her, you know. And they torture people. If they come here asking, I owe you Cervanteses nothing. Your grandmother could have given me my freedom. Instead she sold me.'

'So what? You're practically my partner,' said Pierre Papin. 'You're a slave in name only.'

'I feel it, man,' said Luis. 'I feel it. I was born the son of a mighty prince of a great island in the Spanish Main with more gold reserves than Mexico and Peru put together. Now I'm a slave. Expect no help from me.'

'. . . buy . . .' said my father.

'We'd like to buy Luis back from you,' I elaborated for Pierre Papin's benefit.

'. . . debt . . .' continued my father.

'How much,' I asked Pierre Papin, 'did my late grandfather owe you?'

'Four hundred and fifty gold ducats.'

'We'll buy Luis back from you for twice that.'

'I,' said Luis, 'don't care who owns me. I wasn't born to be owned. I have no desire to be owned.'

'Profit,' said Pierre Papin, 'holds little interest for me. But a wager . . . are you a gambling man?' he asked my father. 'I propose a single roll of the dice. If you win, you get Luis and pay me one thousand gold ducats, for I prefer round numbers. If you lose, the deal's off.'

'I,' repeated Luis, 'don't care who owns me.' He said this almost crankily.

Pierre Papin produced the ivories. Luis held out his hand, weighed them, then squinted at one. 'Now really, Pierre,' he chided.

Pierre Papin produced a second pair of dice, which passed his slave's scrutiny.

My father rolled an anaemic two and three. Pierre Papin smirked professionally, spat on the dice, rattled them in his hands, spat again, rolled. A two and a one.

'Give me one thousand gold ducats,' he said with a gambler's fatalism, 'and Luis is yours.'

My father wrote the IOU.

'You're a free man,' I told Luis.

Luis lifted an eyebrow.

'How would you like to be my partner?' Pierre Papin asked him.

Luis lifted the other eyebrow. 'How much up front?'

He was not proposing to buy in. Pierre Papin would do the paying, for Luis knew his value. A gambler depended on his relations with the *hampa*, the underworld of gypsies and other picaresque elements then spreading from Sevilla throughout Spain to drive Frenchmen and even Italians from the *métier* they had long dominated. Luis knew his way around the *hampa* better than Pierre Papin.

The Frenchman said, 'One thousand gold ducats,' and handed Luis my father's IOU.

'Quarterly payments of one hundred ducats, plus forty per cent interest per annum,' Luis warned us. 'And don't even dream of welching. Because if you do, guess who's going to learn the identity of a certain beautiful lady.'

I found Andrea safe at the porter's lodge of San Ildefonso College and in the morning saw her off for the no longer great city of Cabra with a group of superannuated Dominican brothers bound for Córdoba and its near-miracle of a cathedral-spawning mosque. After the betrothal of my sister Luisa to Christ, my father and I returned speedily to Cabra, where we hired the usual galley and left with the family at midnight (rent on the small house in the nameless little village was several months in arrears) for Sevilla, gateway to the New World.

At about the time we were buying Luis and giving him his freedom, Crown Prince Don Carlos regained consciousness in the arms of his retainers. Later that morning, when his bodyguard-procurer Pedro de Isunza came to, he was found to be suffering from amnesia, the hours immediately preceding his fall downstairs blotted from his memory, so that he could not recall procuring Don Carlos's 229th putative virgin, let alone where. He was dismissed in disgrace and for some years lived in obscurity.

Don Carlos seemed to recover. Then one day, without warning, he collapsed. A team of nine royal physicians diagnosed pressure on the brain but disagreed on a course of treatment. They might have settled on benign neglect, but for the presence in nearby Madrid of the greatest physician of the day, Andreas Vesalius of the Low Countries (later condemned by the Inquisition for dissecting cadavers, but not executed). Vesalius, finding the Crown Prince in deep coma, promptly bored a hole into his skull with a thong drill to relieve the pressure on his brain and – possibly – saved his life.

Alternative therapy arrived that night in the form of the late Fray Diego, a Franciscan brother dead almost exactly one hundred years but undecayed. Bearing this grisly cure (for the corpse was said to have amazing restorative powers) were several living Franciscans and a retinue of true-believing peasants. Fray Diego's remains shared the patient's bed while the living Franciscans led the true believers in loud prayer.

When Don Carlos survived, his death-loving father Felipe II credited not Dr Vesalius but Fray Diego's remains with the cure, and badgered four successive popes to sanctify the dead friar. In 1588, the year the Invincible Armada sailed to conquer England, Pope Sixtus V finally consented to the canonization. Later, settlers in California named a small mission in honour of the new saint.

As for the erstwhile bodyguard-procurer Pedro de Isunza, after some years in obscurity he obtained a position with the Investment Branch of the Supreme and General Council of the Inquisition. By then he was waking regularly in a cold sweat of terror from nightmares that featured a fantastically pulchritudinous virgin who whipped him mercilessly with her long mane of wheaten hair.

IV

In Which the Beautiful

Two-Thousand-Two-Hundred-Gold-Ducat Baby

Spurns the New World

Every evening the family would walk south along the Guadalquivir from Triana Bridge to the Tower of Gold to dream the dream in which the port of Sevilla played so great a part.

My father would join us late, if at all. After his full day's work in the poor *barrio* of La Macarena, where we had rented a tumbledown house in the shadow of the ancient Moorish wall, he queued for hours at the Exchange. Every evening, just as he neared the head of the line, the wicket slammed shut. But he persevered, as did thousands of other job applicants besieging the Exchange for a chance at the New World and its irresistible promise – a new life.

'Why would they need a deaf barber-surgeon in New Spain?' Doña Leonor would ask dubiously.

'You'll see,' Rodrigo de Cervantes would shout with evasive optimism.

We promenaded past wharves piled high with iron tools, hogsheads of wine, barrels of salted Baltic herring, bolts of Italian brocade, English kersey, Dutch wool, as hopeful as any in the multitudes thronging Sevilla.

'The thing is, a fellow doesn't have to *be* somebody over there in the New World, he only has to *do* something,' everybody said.

'*Do* something,' Doña Leonor would tell me. She would look meaningly at Andrea.

So would grandmotherly women with benign, toothless smiles. 'It will be a beautiful child,' they would say.

'At least find out who he is,' my mother would implore.

But Andrea had become withdrawn and aloof even from me.

'How can she go with us to New Spain,' Doña Leonor would wail, 'under such a cloud of dishonour?'

'In New Spain,' Magdalena would observe coolly, 'there are twenty men for every woman. She'll make out.'

'We'll fight heathen savages in Mexico,' my brother Rodrigo would promise the maimed toy soldier he still wore on a string around his neck. Rodrigo spent more and more time in Sevilla's labyrinth of Moorish streets deploying his company of youthful soldiers, recruited from families bound for the New World, in elaborate and endless war games.

Juan the Obscure would disappear under some wharf or other until we made our way back to our tumbledown house in the shadow of the ancient Moorish wall.

Daily my mother would take me aside and urge, 'You're closest to her. Find out who he is.'

But how could I even ask her – let alone bear to imagine my sister Andrea in a stranger's arms, her wheaten mane spread on his pillow, her lips parted in ecstasy?

The baby was expected in July. So, according to the calendar, Crown Prince Don Carlos could have been the father. But I believed my sister had spoken the truth about her non-seduction in Alcalá, and anyway, we had moved to Sevilla so soon afterwards that the father could have been someone right here. For a time I half assumed it was Juan Rufo, for he had followed us to Sevilla with Tomás Gutiérrez, and we frequently met during our waterfront *paseos*.

'Looks like a clear case of twins to me,' Gutiérrez would hoot (for Andrea's *embarazo* – literally embarrassment, or pregnancy – was indeed extravagant), while Juan Rufo stood by in awkward silence.

But then he managed to take me aside and, after some hemming and hawing, said, 'Tell her I'll marry her if she'll have me. The child needs a name.'

I told her.

'Tell him I'm grateful, but I can't marry someone I don't love.' And those luminous pale blue eyes met mine, then looked swiftly away.

A week or so later, Andrea asked me, 'How do I find a good lawyer?'

'The only lawyer I know is a fellow called Picapleitos who I've seen around here once or twice.'

Andrea and I were then walking past market stalls in the direction of Sevilla's new royal prison.

'The one that got Papá out of jail in Valladolid?'

'Well, he got him papers of gentility-by-repute,' I said. 'Which didn't always keep him out of debtors' prison. Like that time in . . .'

My sister's arm was tugging at mine. I turned, and realized she hadn't heard a word.

'Andrea?' I said, alarmed.

41

She stood motionless, staring at a coffle of prisoners coming slowly along Sierpes Street under armed guard, heavy chains clanking. Her eyes, enormous and yet strangely depthless, like eyes painted on an Egyptian frieze, followed the chained convicts through the jeering crowds and into the prison. Iron-banded gates thudded shut. Andrea remained petroglyphically rigid. I grasped her arms and shook her. Her eyes rolled back, blankly white. I called her name again, more urgently. She shuddered, and I could see once more the pale blue of her irises. 'Miguel? Miguel?' Her voice was like the echo of a remote wind blowing at us from a tomorrow bereft of all hope. 'Dear God . . . Miguel . . . so many prison cells . . .'

Could my sister that day somehow have been vouchsafed second sight? Could she have glimpsed the future – my future? I cannot say; I only set this down as it happened.

Her fingers dug painfully into my arm, and in almost her normal voice she said, 'Get me an appointment with that lawyer. You've got to leave Spain.'

'Me? Don't you mean all of us?'

'I don't know what I mean. Please, Miguel. Just do it.'

It was the one night a week the employment section of the Exchange stayed open until midnight, and I had just left home to take my father's place in the long queue.

'Cervantes?'

As I turned, strong arms grabbed me and a blanket was thrown over my head. I felt myself deposited ungently on a hard surface that began to sway and jounce: a wagon. Half an hour later the suffocating blanket was removed, and in the moonlight I saw a narrow street and the blind windowless walls of houses turned inward on themselves, secretive houses. Close by I heard a minor-key flamenco wail. I could smell the river. We were in Triana, the gypsy quarter.

My two captors hustled me through an interior patio, along a dark passage, across an open space redolent of urine and littered with the detritus of brutal lives brutally lived, to a hut on the edge of the river. One of the gypsies kicked its sagging door open. I looked down at a small boy on a verminous pile of straw.

'Have you come to rescue me, Miguel?' he asked.

A closer look revealed him to be my youngest brother, Juan the Obscure.

'How long have you been here?'

'Three days, I think,' he said.

The family hadn't noticed he was missing, though I could hardly say so.

'Four. It's been four days,' corrected the first gypsy, who was noticeably *bizco* – cross-eyed.

As they began to shut the door on him, Juan the Obscure called out with laudable restraint, 'You *are* going to rescue me, aren't you?'

In the stinking, littered space between the hut and the blind back wall of the house, the second gypsy fingered his dark, drooping *bigotes* – moustaches – and said, 'He wants to know has he come to rescue him.'

'Four days we've kept the kid here, we can keep him forty more,' Bizco told me. 'Or until you give a certain person what you owe him. Which is two quarterly payments on a debt of one thousand gold ducats.'

'Plus interest,' Bigotes said, and made an impatient twisting motion with his hands.

'Or,' said Bizco, picking up the cue, 'a kid's neck breaks easy.'

'*Plus* interest,' repeated Bigotes. 'And on the rapid side of soon.' He flailed his arms to mime drowning.

'Or,' said Bizco, 'the river is deep.'

I hit him.

This was only my second attempt to inflict bodily harm on anyone, the first having been the Tomás Gutiérrez *piropo* incident. I was by nature non-violent, but what choice had I in the face of their histrionic threats on the life of my brother?

When I say I hit him, I mean that I swung my right fist awkwardly but with all my strength and somehow managed to strike the point of his jaw. This sent an atrocious stab of pain up my arm to the shoulder. The cross-eyed gypsy, much to my surprise, fell where he stood. Reaching down, I plucked the poniard (or was it a misericorde?) from his sash and whirled to face his mustachioed companion.

On the littered ground Bizco wiped a dribble of blood from his chin and said, 'Cut off the baby brother's ear.'

'Which one?' asked Bigotes, and at that instant I kicked his own misericorde (or was it a stiletto?) out of his hand.

I thought of Juan the Obscure, captive four days on a verminous pile of straw. I wanted to kick their faces in.

Instead I kicked the door of the hut open. 'Out you come, Juanito.'

Which he did, hero-worshipful.

Bizco by then had climbed to hands and knees. I kicked all four out from under him. Remembering how he'd told Bigotes to cut off Juan the Obscure's ear, I wanted to hold both their heads under water until bubbles stopped rising.

It's slow to ignite but, my gentle nature notwithstanding, I have this temper.

'Into the hut, both of you,' I said, switching Bizco's stiletto (or was it a dirk?) from my numb, swollen right hand to my left.

I shut the sagging door of the hut behind them. Juan the Obscure found a flat rock and I wedged it at the bottom. It would give us a few seconds.

'. . . if you'd have just told me which one . . .' I heard Bigotes complaining inside.

Then we ran, Juan the Obscure clutching my painful right hand, in what I hoped was the direction of Triana Bridge. At that hour the riverbank was deserted except for the occasional scavenger poking through broken spars, rusty barrel hoops, worm-eaten sea-chests. 'Faster!' – for I could hear pursuing footfalls. I could also see, directly ahead, the welcome sight of the bridge. Just when I began to think we might actually make it, Juan the Obscure tripped, fell, howled. As I scooped him up, I saw Bizco and Bigotes pounding along the shingle not fifty yards behind. I ran on with Juan the Obscure in my arms, the dirk or dagger in my clenched teeth. As we neared the bridge, my heart sank. A veritable army was crossing towards us, their weaponry making an odd clattering sound. At a signal from their leader, they broke into an impressively co-ordinated run, whooping and hollering as they came. I set Juan the Obscure on his feet and crouched in front of him, blade at the ready, determined to sell myself dearly. Then I noticed a strange thing. Even crouched in a knifer's stance, I was as tall as the clamorous soldiers swiftly bearing down on us and parting like white water on a rock in perfectly timed response to a motion of the long wooden lance their leader used as a guidon. Herding Juan the Obscure on to the bridge and between the twin columns of child-sized soldiers, I looked back once to see that strange army clustered at the Triana end, wooden weapons clattering. The gypsies were nowhere in sight. We slowed to a jog, Juan the Obscure squeezing my swollen hand all the way home to our tumbledown house in the shadow of the ancient Moorish wall, where the whole family except my brother Rodrigo was waiting with all lights blazing.

My father shouted, 'Well, on the old road again!' in a paroxysm of pure joy, and even cut a caper or two, while my mother asked, 'What happened to your hand, Miguel?'

'My what? Nothing. Happened to it.'

'He rescued me,' Juan the Obscure explained.

'Where were you all afternoon?' Magdalena asked him.

Then they all talked at once, outshouted by my father. 'On the old road again, only this road's a ship! *María de la Esperanza* she's called, a caravel of two hundred thirty tuns, and we sail for New Spain next October.'

'Some nincompoop of an employment officer hired your father as a barber-surgeon to the Indians in a no-place called Veracruz,' said Doña Leonor, but she was glowing.

Just then Rodrigo came in wearing the motley soldier-suit he'd sewn for himself out of scraps of fabric scrounged from Andrea. Standing his long wooden lance in a corner, he sat down near Magdalena.

'Out playing soldiers again?' she demanded.

'They're not good enough for you, those "troops" of yours,' sniffed Doña Leonor.

Meanwhile my exuberant father lifted Juan the Obscure off his feet, both of them laughing, and raised him to the ceiling. Then my father scowled. 'You smell as though you've been lying for four days on a verminous pile of straw.'

'Miguel rescued me,' Juan the Obscure explained.

When my father sang out for the tenth time, 'On the old road again, road again, road again!' I got a chance to crouch for a moment next to my brother Rodrigo.

'What happened?'

'They couldn't swim.'

A few days later Andrea asked me, 'How does he do it? That trick with the ink smears on his nose.'

After I admitted it bewildered me too, she told me about her first meeting with Picapleitos.

He sat with his skinny legs crossed, swinging a silver-buckled shoe. His undersized head rested on a huge starched cambric ruff, like an apple on a stack of platters, and the tip of his inordinately long nose, which God or the Devil had pinched to a point, was fiery red from a cold.

Stifling a sneeze, Picapleitos stroked the length of his nose, his clean hand somehow managing to leave an ink smear. 'Señorita Cervantes, of course! I got your father released from prison in Valladolid.'

'Actually, you got him a patent of gentility-by-repute,' said Andrea.

'Now I remember. Very little in it for me.' Picapleitos stroked his nose the other way, tip to bridge. The ink smear vanished. 'Well. The family prospers, I hope?'

'We're sailing for New Spain in October.'

'Ah, so you have prospects!' He stroked the smear on to his nose again.

'My father has a pressing debt in the amount of one thousand two hundred gold ducats.'

Off came the smear. 'Then fleeing to New Spain is indeed the wisest course. But why do you require my services?' His eyes wandered to Andrea's embarrassment. 'You wouldn't need a midwife? My cousin – '

'I've already engaged one.' Andrea leaned forward awkwardly. 'I want to sue someone for breach of promise in the amount of one thousand two hundred gold ducats.'

'Aha! The precise amount of your father's debt. But my dear girl!'

'It's too much?'

'It's too little. Were you betrothed?'

'No. I only met him once.'

The red tip of Picapleitos's nose quivered. 'Well, what *did* the fellow promise?'

Her luminous pale blue eyes downcast, Andrea said, 'You know. The usual. I suppose.'

'Embarrassment, by which I mean shyness, has no place in this office. We'll say he promised to take care of you and the child until its twentieth birthday.'

'But – but one thousand two hundred gold ducats, even though it's a fortune, would support a mother and child for no more than ten years.'

'Precisely, my dear girl. Which is why we shall sue the fellow for *two* thousand two hundred gold ducats. My fee will be half of whatever I am skilful enough to collect.'

'But then, even if you get all of it, I only get one thousand *one* hundred gold ducats.'

'Which, I'm sure, shows you how much worse your predicament would have been had you sued for the amount you suggested. Who is the father?'

Andrea told him.

'The nephew,' Picapleitos gloated, 'of a prominent, a very prominent person. Leave everything to me.'

Of their second meeting Andrea had this to say:

'Picapleitos was elated. The court ruled far sooner than he'd dared hope, and they awarded me the whole two thousand two hundred gold ducats. The father must tell the court under oath, next month, how he intends to pay.'

Of their third meeting, shortly before Pentecost, Andrea had this to say:

'Picapleitos was even more elated. It seems the uncle died suddenly.'

Picapleitos, stroking his nose with a clean hand from bridge to pointy tip and leaving the usual smear, had exulted, 'Remember, I told you your seducer was the nephew of a prominent, a very prominent person. He was also, I find, the sole heir of this uncle, who happens to have been Vicar-General of Sevilla, and so, dear girl, monstrously wealthy. We have only to wait until the will is probated and the money shall be ours — that is to say, yours.'

Andrea asked me, 'Isn't that wonderful?' and started to cry.

'I know,' I said. 'I know. You don't have to tell me how awful it must have been.' I wanted to put my arms around her swollen body and pull her close, but she turned away. 'Thinking he cared about you and then finding — '

'But it wasn't like that at all, Miguel. You think I loved him? It had nothing to do with love, or . . . or even lust.' She was facing me again, tears bright on her cheeks. 'I just thought there was no other way to get the money. He was rich, and so I let him . . . let him believe he was seducing me when really all the time it was the other way around and I was thinking how it was going to cost him . . . cost him one thousand two hundred in gold . . .'

Then I did pull her close, and she wept, and I kissed the salty tears on her cheeks as once, long ago on the night when we shared a dream, she had kissed mine.

'. . . because I knew something terrible would happen unless Papá could pay his debt to Luis the black slave. And how could Papá ever get that kind of money? Oh God, if only I'd known he'd be accepted for service in New Spain, then I wouldn't have had to . . .'

I kissed more salty tears. Her wheaten mane snuggled against my throat, tickling. Then her head jerked up, making me bite my tongue. 'Don't you see, I'm no good! I never will be. Because while he . . . while I lay there and he . . .'

'You don't have to t-tell me. I know how you must have hated it.'

And I stroked that glorious wheaten mane, and for a while she was quiet in my arms. But then, so softly I almost didn't hear, she said, 'Hated it? I wouldn't have minded hating it, that was what I expected, to hate it. Or maybe even to enjoy it. If I enjoyed it — does this shock you? — I still could have told myself I was normal.'

She laughed, an unpleasant little sound. 'All those years of fending off men right up to the Crown Prince because I didn't want any . . . anybody I could have. I might as well have gone into the nunnery with Luisa. At least then I'd never have learned how low I could sink. Because I didn't hate it and I didn't enjoy it either. I just lay there in his bed with his weight on me . . .'

'Stop. Stop it, Andrea.'

'. . . doing what every common streetwalker does, and I couldn't feel anything, not even guilt. I could only think how *easy* it all was.'

After that anguished admission, every time I saw my sister Andrea's embarrassment I imagined her in unthinkable positions with her faceless, nameless lover. And I told myself, I'm going to hate the little bastard.

July came and went, but Andrea did not have her baby. At first the family was too busy to notice.

My father was busy buying (on credit extended to those bound for New Spain) various indispensable items including five stout pairs of walking shoes. His eyes sparkled, his stride was jaunty. He even seemed to hear better.

My mother was busy keeping a hawk eye on Magdalena, precociously pubescent at eleven. This did not stop Tomás Gutiérrez from propositioning her. But, 'No, thank you, I would rather not,' said Magdalena.

My brother Rodrigo was busy diagramming the Battle of Las Salinas, where Francisco Pizarro had killed his former colleague Diego de Almagro in 1538. 'Only to be killed in turn three years later by Almagro partisans,' said Rodrigo, trying to interest Juan the Obscure – in vain, since Juan, as usual, was busy disappearing.

Early in August, Picapleitos sent for my sister Andrea. 'I've got bad news.' A smear was already in place on his long, pointy nose. He backstroked it off. 'The will of the Vicar-General of Sevilla has been probated.'

'But that sounds like good news.'

'It is not, I fear. The estate has been besieged by multitudes of trumped-up creditors. It could take months or even years before the residue is passed to the nephew.'

'So we may not get the money for a long time?'

'Worse. Your seducer claimed he could not pay what the court awarded you, and immediately declared bankruptcy.'

An old midwife named Zárate visited Andrea periodically. 'A postmature baby is so much rarer than a premature one. How many weeks has it been, Andrea dear?'

'Forty-five.'

'That's a record, at least here in Sevilla.'

'But what makes a baby postmature?' Andrea asked.

'Nothing, if the mother has miscounted.'

Andrea reddened. 'That just isn't possible. You see, I only . . . met him . . . the one time.'

'Tell me,' said old Zárate, 'has this tumbledown house in the shadow of the ancient Moorish wall been the family home for long? Because if so, I can see why the wee thing might not be eager to – '

'No. We move rather a lot. Actually, I would say, a great deal. In fact, we move more than we don't move.'

'Indeed,' said old Zárate. 'You see, towards the end of her normal thirty-nine-week term in the womb, the child is in her own way aware. And if what she's aware of is – '

'She?'

'I always call unborn children "she". As I was saying, it's natural for the wee thing to fear the unknown. Most *grown-ups* fear the unknown. And with a family like yours – always on the move, as you say – she could fear it even more. She is in no hurry to be born.'

She wasn't. And the fleet sailing for New Spain would hardly wait for the birth of the illegitimate grandchild of an indebted barber-surgeon. Through August and into September that fleet swelled until it numbered fully a hundred caravels and carracks and naos, each at least 130 tuns as the law required. Every day the apparent chaos on the river increased as merchantmen came with supplies from Hamburg and Rotterdam, Ragusa and Venice. Soon so many foreign seamen clogged the labyrinthine streets that it was difficult to find a Spaniard, any Spaniard, in Sevilla.

We knew where to find old Zárate, only a few streets from our tumbledown house. Rodrigo and Juan the Obscure ran to get her when Andrea's labour began one early September morning after my father and I had left for the port to pick up some business. My father spent the entire day ministering to the navigator of *María de la Esperanza*, who had got into an altercation with two Icelanders over a half-Indian whore named, rather inappropriately I thought, Constanza. As my father laboured over his apparently dying patient, the half-Indian whore Constanza never left the navigator's side. 'He paid, I owe, understand?' she said. 'Fix him, doctor.' My father understood with his newly improved hearing, but he was no doctor. No doctor, after examining the navigator, would have taken the responsibility of trying to resurrect him. But my father worked on, and towards sunset the navigator opened his eyes and the whore Constanza whispered the things she would do to him when he was strong enough for her medicine – such promises of earthly delight that the dying navigator had no choice but to stay alive in order to experience them. 'Keep talking,' said my father, and she did, her fecund imagination and wonderful powers of description so engrossing that it was some time before I realized my brother Rodrigo was shaking my shoulder while my brother Juan the Obscure was jabbing my father with his little fists.

Candles burned around the family's one serviceable bed, where my sister

Andrea, propped on the two serviceable pillows with a beautiful little head of tight golden ringlets hiding her left breast, was smiling a classic madonna smile. Looking at the infant, I found myself thinking, so she's got beautiful golden ringlets, so what, I'm going to hate the postmature little bastard.

'Forty-six weeks,' said old Zárate. 'I'd never have believed it, Andrea dear, but you must know.'

'Look at her fingernails,' said my sister Magdalena.

I looked. The baby's fingernails – with one tiny hand she was trying to grip Andrea's breast – were perfectly formed and long, improbably long for a newborn infant. They were also, improbably, green.

'Temporary stains from fluids in the womb,' explained Zárate.

'They look as if they've been painted the colour of emeralds,' marvelled Magdalena.

'Long green toenails too,' said Zárate. 'Indeed, if you happen to like green nails, the outward aspects of postmaturity are not unpleasant.'

'Let's call her Esmeralda,' said Magdalena, 'for the emerald fingernails.'

Doña Leonor said, 'We'll call her Esperanza, after the caravel that will take us to New Spain.'

The infant stopped feeding and lifted her head.

'What better name than "hope",' my mother went on, 'for a child about to embark for the New World?'

The infant began to wail. Her tiny hand with its green fingernails struck puny blows at my sister Andrea's breast.

'Constanza,' said my father suddenly.

My mother rounded on him. 'Constanza? What kind of name is that? We don't even *know* anyone called Constanza.'

'It's a fine name,' my father said. Not shouting, but more assertive than I'd ever heard him. 'A virtuous name. A name with the power of life in it.'

'It's a preposterous name,' sniffed Doña Leonor. 'I won't hear of it.'

I smiled at the irony of my father, the indefatigable optimist, siding against Hope while my long-suffering mother rejected Steadfastness.

Andrea smiled too. She said, 'I rather like the name Constanza myself.'

This, with Andrea's help, was the last argument my father would ever win with anyone.

While it was in progress, old Zárate spoke, but no one paid particular attention. 'No, the outward aspects of postmaturity are not unpleasant,' she said. 'But the seizures will be something else again.'

It was Magdalena who noticed the first stage. 'Baby Constanza is chewing,' she reported.

Andrea, who was dozing, woke and tried to feed her daughter but, chewing instead of sucking, Constanza could get no milk. She began to howl.

Old Zárate was sent for. She said, 'Let her chew on a twist of cloth dipped in sugar water. Wait until she's drowsy before you give her the breast.'

A few days later Magdalena, by then morbidly curious, noticed the second stage. The baby's left leg began to jerk. When both arms began to jerk too, Magdalena called frantically for Andrea.

'She's jumping around so, I can't hold her!'

As Andrea reached for her, Magdalena almost dropped the poor tarantistic infant.

Her right leg now jerking, Constanza began to chew.

Again old Zárate was consulted. 'Weeks,' she said. 'Even months. Who can say, with such a postmature baby?'

The next morning I woke to my sister Andrea's voice. '. . . if you'll take her while I go, please.'

And my sister Magdalena's voice – stuttering, just like me. 'N-no, th-thank you, I would rather n-not.'

'Just for two minutes.' Andrea held out the baby.

Magdalena retreated. 'No! The child's possessed by the Devil!'

'What the devil do *you* know about the Devil?' I asked.

'What everybody knows – fits and spasms and such are signs the Devil's in a person.' Magdalena crossed herself.

'I'll take her,' I said.

While Andrea was out, I tried to still the little bastard's jittery limbs, but her features squinched together, her face reddened, and she screamed at me.

'The Devil Himself,' insisted Magdalena from the other side of the room.

Soon the neighbours began to talk.

'Seizures – the child's a bundle of unholy seizures.'

'She's possessed.'

'It's the powers of darkness moving in her.'

Baby Constanza next began to look everywhere at once. (Being postmature, she already used her eyes a lot.) While her left eye, which was brown, stared at me, her right eye, which was blue, wandered towards Doña Leonor across the room. Then she looked at the ceiling with one eye and the floor with the other. But at least she stopped twitching.

Then she stopped breathing.

Fortunately my father, finding no business at the port that day, had come home to be near his stricken grandchild. He immediately picked her up, pinched her little nostrils shut, forced open her little mouth, and blew his own breath into it. Constanza's face, which had begun to turn blue, regained its normal pale pink. She sighed tremulously and her tiny chest resumed moving up and down.

This was my father's most successful foray into medicine, and it cost us our new life in the New World.

'The fleet sails in three days,' he told us.

Once again old Zárate was sent for.

'If you mean an ocean voyage,' she said, 'it would surely end all your worries. Because little Constanza would never survive it.'

At these words, my brothers and even Magdalena gathered around the bed where, for the moment, Constanza slept quietly, nestled in the crook of her mother's arm.

'In the New World,' said Doña Leonor, 'we might have been anything. Names, pedigrees, none of that matters there. Why, for all anyone knew, Andrea might have been the widow of a courtier who died serv – '

'Or a soldier,' suggested my brother Rodrigo.

' – ing the King.'

'And no questions asked,' said Magdalena.

'Your father might have been a physician with a degree from some minor Italian university.'

'What?' shouted my father. For the first time in months he hadn't heard. He looked smaller. Monkey wrinkles like Juan the Patriarch's seamed his face. It was from that moment that it can be said my father began to *dwindle*, and he would go on dwindling until he was declared dead in a fraudulent attempt to – but all that in its place.

'Go without me!' begged Andrea.

Everyone – Magdalena last – said that was unthinkable.

On sailing day we all went down to the port, standing in the multitudes near the Tower of Gold, to see the great fleet weigh anchor and move downriver with the current, long sweeps dancing on the water, sails tautening with a sound like gunfire. We watched *Esperanza*, third in the line nearest to shore, catch the wind. I wondered if the navigator whose life had been saved (it was inconceivable to think otherwise) by the whore Constanza was aboard. I wondered if *Esperanza* would have a good crossing. I wondered if my father would have regained his hearing a second time, if my brother Rodrigo would have fought red Indians, if my brother Juan the Obscure would have found whatever he sought in dark corners or my sister Magdalena whatever she expected from New Spain's demographics.

I wondered if in a new, possibly a better life, my parents would have drawn closer. I wondered if, sailing in the wake of Cortés, I would have become an explorer, blazing a trail south through the gloomy impenetrable jungles to the fabled headwaters of the Orinoco, or marching north across the desert to find the Seven Cities of Cibola and become richer than Croesus.

At my side stood my sister Andrea cradling the twitching little Constanza protectively in her arms.

'Possessed,' I heard someone say. 'Possessed by the Devil, she is.' And the crowd stirred and gave the Cervantes family a wide berth.

Ostracism and the Old World – instead of optimism and the New. How I hated the postmature little bastard!

When we returned to the tumbledown house in the shadow of the ancient Moorish wall, a big crowd milled outside.

'Out with the spawn of the Devil!' they shouted.

Heavy boards had been nailed across the front and back doors. The window hole was boarded over.

We didn't even try to get our belongings, we had so few and felt so down.

But oh, how I hated the little bastard who chose that moment, not two hours after the fleet had sailed and our hope with it, to cure herself forever of all postmature jerks, twitches, spasms, chewing motions, eye deviations, and breathing difficulties. She gurgled and cooed and suckled hungrily while my father and I rented the usual galley. 'On the old road again,' my father tried, but it sounded like a lamentation. We were *en route* before midnight with a full moon to show the way.

I sat for the first leg of the journey next to Andrea, and in the early morning hours I reached out once to touch her glorious wheaten mane to let her know I loved her with a healthy, brotherly sort of love (as I reminded myself each time the jouncing of the galley brought our bodies together). But just as I reached for my sister's hair, the baby, with a graceful motion of her tiny hand, not at all a twitch, grasped my finger. What happened next, I now suppose, was one of those infant gas bubbles that make a baby's face squinch up, but in the light of the full moon, while she clung and clung to my finger, it looked like a smile of love and trust which, don't ask me why, made my eyes sting as I smiled back at the gassy little grimace or loving smile or whatever it was, and knew I would never again deceive myself into thinking I hated the postmature little bastard.

53

V

In Which I Visit the Palace with High Hopes
And Leave with a Price on My Head

My father often cut his customers' hair and trimmed their beards in the open doorway of his barber-shop just inside the Gate of the Moors, affording them that splendid view – partially obscured by hastily erected new wooden houses – of the steep hill crowned by Spain's first-ever permanent Royal Palace, here in Madrid, Spain's first-ever permanent capital city, proclaimed so at the beginning of the decade by King Felipe II the Death-Loving.

But the barber-shop door would be shut this September day, for a hot hard wind brought dust swirling across the city, dust from the surrounding hills newly denuded of their poplar and walnut trees, pines and oaks, to build those rickety houses that spoiled the view but sheltered Madrid's mushrooming population – 15,000 when we arrived four years ago and now, in 1569, 60,000 people in a city with the aspect of a frontier town placed paradoxically in the centre of the age-old country.

My father was carefully sculpting the moustaches of an Italian named Lomellino or Lomelín, a friend of the *hombre de negocios* Rizio Rizione who had so changed my family's life. It was this businessman Rizione who had set up my father in the barber-shop, and though he'd been back in Italy two years, Rizio Rizione still owned the shop and the rent was still nominal. And it was Rizione who owned the tall stone house near the Gate of the Sun where Andrea and my niece Constanza now lived rent-free. And it was Rizione who had paid off my father's debt to Luis the black slave. All this Rizio Rizione had done for love of my sister Andrea. So I resented him, even long after his return to Genoa. I hoped the wife he had gone back to was a harridan.

A few Italians sat waiting their turn and talking about the latest calamities to befall the Spanish empire – revolt in the Low Countries, revolt right here in Spain among the *moriscos* in the mountains south of Granada. My monkey-faced father looked up, causing a ruby of blood to appear on Signor Lomellino or Lomelín's upper lip.

54

'Trim your beard? Haircut? Won't be an hour – ah, Miguel.'

I was only an occasional visitor. It disturbed me to see my father toady to the rich Italian businessmen and pretend to hang on their every word when he was deafer than ever and couldn't fathom their Spanish-Italian *dialetto* anyway. His barber shop had become, thanks to Rizione, the de facto club for Madrid's colony of Italian, mostly Genoese, businessmen – history in a way replicating the apothecary shop near Córdoba's Iron Gate where my great-grandfather Ruy Díaz de Cervantes had known Christopher Columbus before he discovered the New World.

'So how's the boy?' said Signor Lomellino or Lomelín while my father dabbed at the blood on his lip.

Looking at 'the boy' – the club members always called me that, as Rizione had – what would they have seen? Well, for one thing, not a boy but a man of twenty-two. Broad-shouldered but slender and giving a tall impression though only of average height. Wide forehead over a long, almost gaunt face with a belligerent nose. Chestnut moustaches still boy-silky and a neatly trimmed (by myself) beard. Eyes that had seen no far places but yearned to, aspiring eyes of a mostly hazel colour.

Juan Rufo came in, looking every inch the young courtier with a rapier slung within easy reach of his right hand and a rose tucked behind his left ear. Juan Rufo, man about town, I thought, would never understand why I hated their calling me 'boy'. Four years ago the future had offered me a New World and then taken it back, and every day since, I felt the hope of shaping my own life slipping away. Juan Rufo never lost hope, at least not with my sister. He proposed to her annually on the anniversary of their first meeting. And Juan Rufo was carving his chosen career as a courtier in the very city where I felt like a displaced person.

After trimming my beard and Juan Rufo's twin-pointed one, my father surprised me by presenting for my inspection a rapier of the finest Toledo steel. 'Like it?'

It was a beauty, and I said so, and without further ado my father belted it at my side.

'Very apt. Every courtier must be quick to avenge an offence to his honour,' Juan Rufo said, then added, 'but slow to see one. Come on, we're late.'

I thanked my father. In fact, I kissed him, first time in I don't remember how long, and he blew his nose hard, and we left.

On our way to the palace I asked Juan Rufo, 'What does a courtier do, actually?'

The question gave him pause. 'Why, uh, he courts. Which is to say seeks.

That's it, he seeks. Friends, connections, influence – the ingredients, in short, of power.'

'Power? I don't want power.'

'Everyone wants power.'

'If I had any, I wouldn't know what to do with it.'

All I could think of was paying off the family's debt. But Rizio Rizione had done that. Or buying the barber-shop so my father wouldn't have to pay even nominal rent. Or owning the tall stone house near the Gate of the Sun so my sister Andrea would be beholden no longer to Rizio Rizione.

Was money, I couldn't help wondering, power?

'Listen, my young friend. I've had advantages. The Duke of Sessa for a patron, the university. But you' – here the polished courtier dissolved with a self-deprecating smile into the Juan Rufo hopelessly in love with my sister Andrea – 'have only me for a patron. And I don't altogether understand this courtier business myself yet.'

'Then why are you sponsoring me?'

Again Juan Rufo paused. 'It's quite simple, really – '

'Andrea?'

'She suspects you're not wild about spending the rest of your life as a schoolmaster.'

I wasn't. But I wasn't convinced, either, that my way out was Liars' Walk. As we climbed through the palace gardens, I asked, 'Why is it called Liars' Walk anyway?'

'Because everyone gathers there for talk, talk, talk – half of it false and all of it calculated. Court conversation is an art. Respecting the taboos, for example.'

'Like what? Besides not criticizing the King?'

'That alone can cover a lot.' Juan Rufo grinned. 'Pick a topic, something that sounds safe.'

'The weather,' I said promptly.

'Good. Or not so good if, like every other Madrileño, you moan about nine-months-of-winter-and-three-months-of-hell. The King himself chose this place for his capital.'

'It wasn't the climate the King chose, it was the location. Madrid's dead centre if you look at a map, so it's equally hard to invade from all directions.'

'But that is precisely what one doesn't say. If the King harbours morbid fears of an invasion by the Turks or the French or even the English, that topic is *verboten*. So, I should tell you, is any mention of the King's late unlamented heir.'

'Don Carlos? B-but nobody knows it was Andrea who – '

'I mean *any* mention of that twisted excuse for a Crown Prince. For all you'll hear here, he never loathed his father and never plotted to defect to the Low Countries – a plot uncovered by his bastard uncle Don Juan of Austria who, naturally, is never called bastard. Nor did the Crown Prince, when locked up by the King, starve himself to death, nor, alternatively, did the King have him strangled. Don Carlos died a natural death. And while he may have deflowered two hundred and twenty-eight certifiable virgins before he fell on his head, he left no acknowledged issue. So the Crown has no male heir. Which topic – '

'Don't tell me. Is taboo.'

'Touchy, let's say. A king marries to get sons. After three wives, our lord Felipe has none. So his queens are best not discussed – especially Mary Tudor. That seemed a splendid strategy: marry the Queen of England, give her a Catholic son and reclaim her realm for the Church. But our poor King spent months and months on that soggy island, covering the royal frump like a Spanish stallion, and instead of quickening, Mary-Mary-quite-contrary sickened and died. And now Elizabeth Tudor sits on the English throne hatching her Protestant plots against Felipe. Which we don't talk about.'

'And our own last queen, Elisabeth of Valois? What did she do that we can't talk about her?'

Juan Rufo shrugged. 'She died. All the wives of our death-loving King (a *most* unmentionable trait) seem to die out from under him. Poor lovely Elisabeth, dead only a few months after Don Carlos – for whom, in fact, she was intended until King Felipe claimed permanent *droit du seigneur*. But even *you*, Miguel, wouldn't mention that – at least, you didn't in your contributions to poor Elisabeth's book of obsequies.'

Through the influence of the headmaster at the school where I taught rhetoric and poetry, I had been commissioned to write a sonnet and the dedication. They were, respectively, wretched and pompous. God apparently had not put me on this planet to be a poet – which was to say, the only worthwhile kind of literary luminary, for the whole world knew that playwrights and fiction writers were, like cobblers and cabinetmakers, simple craftsmen.

'But then what's left,' I asked, 'to talk about?'

'You'll see. It's not called Liars' Walk for nothing. But remember,' Juan Rufo had time to advise me before I entered into my brief, almost terminal, career at court, 'a skilled courtier knows that a judicious blending of the false and the true produces something infinitely more effective than a straightforward lie – a newer, higher kind of truth than mere factual truth.'

Before I could digest that, we reached Liars' Walk.

Enclosing what once had been the bailey of the Arab fortress of Majerit and now was the palace courtyard, the tile-roofed arcade was protected alike from sun and wind-driven dust. The gardened interior and deep shadow gave it a monastic air, accentuated by the presence of numerous clerics. But the roar of conversation in that enclosed space, the dashing about of drably dressed commoners seeking the right sub-minister's purse into which to drop their life savings to stave off the Inquisition or the Crown, the more languid movements of the brilliantly bedizened courtiers who clustered about one luminary or another like planets revolving in the Copernican heresy about the sun – all dispelled any notion of monasticism. Anyway, half the courtiers in skirts were not clerics but women.

Threading a path through the crowds, Juan Rufo paused now and again to eavesdrop.

One group's luminary, a military fellow in an impressive uniform, contended that the Duke of Alba still stood numero uno, even though (or perhaps because) the Duke was currently absent, coping with the revolt in the Low Countries. But few listened. They were noisily speculating that the King's real favourite was Ruy Gómez – and since Ruy Gómez was under the thumb of his young wife, the indecently beautiful Princess Eboli, the real question was whose thumb (and not just thumb) the Princess was under nowadays.

Another group's luminary, a maritime fellow in an impressive uniform, insisted the bastard Don Juan of Austria had been sent south not because the *morisco* revolt was really worrisome, but simply because the bastard cut too dashing a figure next to the King. But few listened. They were noisily speculating whether the King was building his new palace in the mountains north of Madrid to house a new bride as broodmare (and if so, whom) or just to be his mausoleum.

As we moved on, I couldn't help observing, 'I thought there were certain things you couldn't talk about here.'

'That depends,' Juan Rufo explained, 'on who does the talking, and how. Now here's a true mistress of the art.'

Juan Rufo steered us towards a group clustered about the most beautiful woman I had ever seen except for my sister Andrea. Even without her looks she would have been unforgettable, as over her left eye she wore a bold black silk eye-patch. This was the Princess Eboli.

Me *sotto voce* to Juan Rufo: 'What happened to her eye?'

Juan Rufo *sotto voce* to me: 'No one knows.'

Nor to my knowledge did anyone ever find out. Doubtless the Princess Eboli wanted it that way. Perhaps the eye was completely intact, as some speculated.

Like her face, the Princess Eboli's voice was indecently beautiful – and beautifully indecent.

'. . . looks fucking fantastic in the saddle, but he isn't worth horseshit in the hay,' I heard.

'. . . and these gentlemen,' Juan Rufo was concluding, 'are Don Antonio Sigura and Don Nicolás de Ovando.'

Sigura, a huge fellow of about thirty, glanced at his companion. Ovando asked, 'Miguel de Cervantes, you said?' When I smiled and bowed, Ovando bobbed his head perfunctorily and turned aside.

I looked at Juan Rufo in puzzlement, but his attention was being claimed by the Princess Eboli. Her forearm on his shoulder, she fingered his twin-pointed beard with reflex flirtatiousness and said, '*Sweetie*, how deliciously your beard curls. I swear it's as perfect as my pubes.'

Her one eye offered more allure than most women could project with two; her lips seemed moister than most lips.

'But the Princess's, er, nether hair owes its perfection to nature,' said Nicolás de Ovando in carrying tones, 'while friend Rufo's beard reflects credit on his barber.'

Juan Rufo's barber hardly seemed conversational material for Liars' Walk, no matter what the blend of false and true, but Antonio Sigura pursued it.

'That would be, I believe, this young *caballero*'s father, who runs a little barber-shop catering to Italians near the Gate of the Moors. Isn't that right, Cervantes?'

I barely had time to nod before the huge Sigura went on. 'It's only natural that Cervantes barbers mostly Italians. The Genoese businessman Rizio Rizione owns his shop.'

And Ovando went on, 'Owns his house too, doesn't he?'

And Sigura went on, 'No, the Cervantes home, I am told, is a mean hovel behind the Virgin of the Granary. It is Cervantes's oldest daughter who lives in Rizione's tall stone house near the Gate of the Sun.'

At this point a magistrate on the edge of the group chimed in. 'This barber Cervantes, unless I am mistaken, is a bona fide *hidalgo* by repute. I processed the papers myself some years ago in Valladolid.'

The courtiers tittered. How droll, a barber acquiring bona fide *hidalguía* by repute! But much of the laughter was uneasy. Half the *hidalgos* in Spain were 'bona fide' only through the legal fiction of repute or aspect.

Nicolás de Ovando: 'They say his son, this barber Cervantes's second son, I forget the name – '

Sigura put in: 'Rodrigo, same as the father.'

Ovando: 'His son Rodrigo tried to enlist in the army mustered for Granada by Don Juan of Austria after the *morisco* revolt last Christmas. Cheeky, beardless, freckled little whoreson – as he didn't look anywhere near twenty, the recruiters told him to come back in three or four years.'

My brother Rodrigo, taking his maimed-soldier talisman with him, *had* tried to enlist in Don Juan's army early in the spring. But how did these men know so much about my family? And why were they airing it on Liars' Walk?

I felt Juan Rufo's hand on my elbow. It gave a small but not insignificant tug.

Ovando: 'You said, friend Antonio, that Rizione owns both the barber-shop and the daughter's tall stone house?'

For the first time I took a good look at this Ovando. He was a handsome, ruddy-faced fellow with the typical arrogant bearing of the aristocrat.

Sigura: 'Indeed he does, friend Nicolás.'

Ovando: 'But why would the daughter want such a tall house? Three floors, isn't it?'

Sigura: 'Four. And you know, in this housing shortage, the government can requisition all but the ground floor to billet civil servants and such.'

Ovando: 'But civil servants have not been billeted?'

Sigura: 'Upon the daughter of Cervantes the barber? No.'

Ovando: 'But how has the daughter managed this?'

Sigura (chuckling lewdly): 'Live-in apprentices. She claims to run a seamstress shop. Is reputed to run a seamstress shop.'

Sigura: 'But repute and reality are not always the same, are they. Seamstresses!'

Later, when it no longer mattered, I would learn that Antonio Sigura was a mason's son and by repute a brawler.

Ovando (disingenuously ingenuous): 'You're suggesting . . .'

'I'm suggesting,' said Antonio Sigura in tones that carried around Liars' Walk and the palace gardens, 'that just as anyone with an ordinary pair of eyes can recognize a genuine *hidalgo* or a genuine twenty-year-old – '

Juan Rufo's hand on my elbow became more insistent.

' – so anyone with an ordinary pair of eyes can recognize a genuine whore.'

Several things happened more or less simultaneously.

The Princess Eboli's one eye narrowed in anger – possibly at Sigura's tactless reference to eyes coming in pairs.

Courtiers and commoners converged on the sound of Sigura's voice and the laden silence that followed it.

To be sure, my lips were moving as I tried frantically to say something in defence of my sister Andrea. But all I could manage was 'B-b-b-b' and then 'th-th-th'.

Not that I think, as I review the events of that afternoon, mere words would have done any good, however eloquent. Spanish pride if tormented will seek some violent outlet, and mine had been Augeanly abused.

With a wordless cry – my one vocal sound – I pulled my brand-new rapier from its sheath.

Juan Rufo shouted something in a despairing voice.

At least one woman screamed.

Nicolás de Ovando smiled and stepped back, leaving the field to Antonio Sigura, twice his size and twice mine.

Had we used broadswords, the outcome would never have been in doubt, so much stronger was Sigura. A few strokes would have put an end to my story right there, or, rather, made it disappear into the maw of un-history, along with the vast majority of human lives.

As it was, rapiers left the outcome in some small doubt. The dextrous hand, not the strong arm, can win the day with those supple, finely tempered, lightweight blades. But I knew nothing of rapier fighting and, it soon became obvious, Antonio Sigura did.

'He'll kill the boy!'

'The boy's as good as dead!'

Did I see a priest off to the left unstoppering a flagon of holy oil?

Steel struck steel as I fought awkwardly for my life. Did some dim awareness of all I had yet to accomplish vouchsafe me a kind of preternatural cunning with a weapon I had never used before? Cide Hamete, who ought to know, believes such things are possible.

'The boy's forestrokes are improving,' observed someone.

'The boy's two-handed blows are oddly effective,' conceded another.

The boy – calling me that, condemning me to the impotent anonymity of youth even as my death hovered close! This indignity lent seismic strength to my arm as I struck with a determined combination of backstrokes, forestrokes and cuts, all narrowly missing. I also maladroitly stumbled to one knee, and Antonio Sigura cut my head off – or would have done, had I not dropped flat – with a prodigious swipe of his rapier that swung him clear around before he resumed his attack.

'The boy is faltering.'

'The point of the boy's rapier is dropping.'

Did I see the Princess Eboli behind Sigura, her transcendentally moist lips parted as if cheering him on, but her one eye still narrowed at his ill-chosen words?

History does not credit the indecently beautiful Princess with an angry one-eyed view of the swordfight that so changed my life. At a certain point in time (it is always a point in time for historians, never a moment in space; we shall return to this strange prejudice), the afternoon of 15 September 1569 to be exact, historians do agree that Sigura and I fought: there is documentation. But about the Princess Eboli they are mute. Was the Princess there? Of course she was. I saw her. A warrant for my arrest confirms that one 'Antonio de Sigura' was my antagonist 'in a clash of arms' and attests to his grievous injuries. Rapiers are not mentioned. Apparently, to historians, arms are arms (broadsword, rapier, cutlass – you've used one, you've used them all), when in reality the characteristic lightness of our rapiers saved my life. The warrant further said the fugitive Cervantes when apprehended would forfeit his right hand to the public executioner's axe and be exiled for ten years from the King's globe-spanning realms. This for wounding the man who called my sister a whore!

Hardly had I caught sight of the one angry eye of the Princess Eboli than I noticed she was hatless, apparently having removed the black velvet beret held in place by a long jewelled hatpin. And hardly had I noticed her hat- and hatpin-less state than Antonio Sigura bounded awkwardly at me as if propelled by some unseen force. This had two results. (1) The point of Sigura's rapier caught in the filigreed handguard of my own. (2) I felt (a) an agony of pain in my temporarily dislocated wrist and (b) a momentary shock of resistance to my weapon followed by (c) its penetration of the right side of Sigura's chest, causing (d) the rapier to jump from my nerveless fingers and Sigura, spitting a froth of blood, to fall at my feet, upon which I stood unmoving just long enough to hear Nicolás de Ovando shout, 'Murderer!'

Yielding to the imperative of self-preservation, I ran through the gaping crowd, along a tile-roofed walkway, through a garden (boxwood maze with its tomcat smell) and a dimly lit passage which made a sharp turn to the left (where a palace guard was pissing copiously in the angle) before opening on the outdoors, where I mounted stone steps to a crenellated wall along which I dashed to more steps, these descending to a patio of orange trees (where a beatifically smiling Franciscan friar was picking off birds with a slingshot) and another wall which, under normal circumstances, I could

not have climbed, but which under these exigent ones I cleared at a single
bound, and so away.

It was nearly dark when, not far from the family hovel beyond the Virgin
of the Granary, Rodrigo intercepted me.

'King's bailiffs,' he said, wasting no words, and showed me his heels,
which I followed towards my sister Andrea's tall stone house near the
Gate of the Sun. Every step jolted my right hand with an extraordinary
pain, and when we paused for breath I observed that it was swollen and
turning blue. Two streets short of our goal one of Andrea's apprentice
seamstresses intercepted us.

'King's bailiffs,' she said, wasting no words, and showed us her heels,
which we followed to the bank of the Manzanares, where in the dusky
light I saw my brother Juan the Obscure. Rodrigo and the girl left us. Juan
the Obscure was, unsurprisingly, completely at home in the darkness, and
led me surefootedly through *barrios* already old when Madrid had been
no more than an Arabic fortress, before King Alfonso VI captured it late
in the eleventh century – as Juan the Obscure explained to pass the time
while we holed up in an abandoned rookery whitewashed with the guano
of long-dead birds. Then:

'Pssst! Boy!'

Juan the Obscure had vanished. In his place was a liveried footman who
led me to a coach drawn by four matched geldings, which presently deposited
me before a plateresque portal in the style of Bustamante or Herrera framing
studded-oak doors, which opened at my approach to reveal a brick-walled
corridor with a splendid marquetry ceiling and a hand-painted tile floor
in, mostly, deepest azure, which led to a flambeaux-lit gallery with a blind
arcade of marble at one end and my family at the other, from whose midst
came Signor Lomellino or Lomelín to welcome me to his excessively eclectic
mansion with these words:

'I promised Rizione I would always help any member of Andrea's family
in need, and that includes you, boy.'

They all gathered around, Andrea releasing sleepy little Constanza's hand
and flinging herself into my arms, more or less sisterly, however it might
have seemed to an objective observer.

'Sigura could have killed you!' she cried against my throat.

'What makes him hate us so?'

'Sigura? But he just does whatever Nicolás de Ovando wants. And
Ovando wants revenge. He irrationally blames my breach-of-promise suit
for blocking his inheritance from his uncle the Vicar-General.'

So, finally, I knew. It was Ovando, Nicolás de Ovando, who had lain a single time with my fecund sister Andrea, Nicolás de Ovando who refused to acknowledge sleepy little Constanza as his daughter, Nicolás de Ovando who —

Doña Leonor cut into my brooding. 'What happened to your hand, Miguel?'

'My what? Nothing. Happened to it.'

'In times of trouble,' offered my father in a tentative shout, 'the medieval physician and diplomat Hisdai ibn Shaprut would — '

'You're no physician and no diplomat,' my mother contemned, and before my eyes I saw my father dwindle some more. Had Doña Leonor always been so much the taller?

'Why don't you enlist in the army?' suggested Rodrigo, and Magdalena either agreed or dissented, with, 'Soldiers aren't the big spenders a girl is led to believe.'

'A rapier,' Doña Leonor reproached her dwindling husband. 'You had to buy a gentle boy like Miguel a rapier.'

'Please, my friends,' said Signor Lomellino or Lomelín. 'This is no time for recriminations. A fast horse will take you to Barcelona, boy, where — '

Baby Constanza, clutching me with that hero worship so common to four-year-old nieces and so misplaced in me, interrupted. 'Is Barcelona at the end of the world?'

I stroked her hair, which was like spun gold.

'Almost,' said Doña Leonor, still glaring at my father as she gently pried the weeping child from my knees.

Signor Lomellino or Lomelín continued. 'From Barcelona you'll sail for Italy, and by the time you arrive, our friend Rizione will have made further arrangements.'

Here, amidst tearful embraces, some parting lines:

My sister Magdalena, her green eyes glittering: 'When you come back, bring me something smashingly Italian.'

My brother Rodrigo, removing the string around his neck that held the toy soldier with the missing left hand and placing it around my neck: 'This will bring you luck, until we're together again.' (A two-part statement, you will notice, and prophetic in both.)

My brother Juan (obscurely): 'There are ways for fugitives to drop from sight as if they never existed.'

Doña Leonor: 'Never forget that your great-grandfather knew Christopher Columbus.'

My father: 'On the old . . . on the old road . . .' But, sobbing, he covered his face and could not go on.

Andrea accompanied me to the stables, where a groom led out a great white stallion. 'Fast but mettlesome,' he informed me unnecessarily as the stallion ramped.

When I had mounted, I understood suddenly, with a hollowness in my soul, that it might be months before I saw my sister Andrea again, or even years. I leaned down from the saddle to touch that glorious mane of wheaten hair shimmering golden in the torchlight. She smiled bravely, but molten silver tears ran down her cheeks. Quickly she thrust into my hand a heavy purse and, when I protested, explained that the money came from Signor Lomellino or Lomelín (which meant, I knew with familiar resentment, from Rizione).

The hollowness in my soul expanded. Months or years – how one consoles oneself with the finite! It was far from unlikely that Andrea and I would never meet again. Never, I despaired, never, never . . . and the great white stallion leaped the paddock gate and broke into a furious gallop as I clung desperately to his mane with my uninjured left hand.

VI

The Friends of Rizio Rizione

History! What sins of omission are committed in its name, what pivotal events ousted as unproven – as if lives obeyed the rules of a law-court instead of drifting like Lucretian atoms among the permutations of the possible.

To hear history tell it, I arrived in Rome early in 1570, somehow acquired the Certificate of Purity of Blood needed by a Spaniard for employment there and, through a distant kinsman, became chamberlain to a cardinal before going south (history offers no reason) to Naples, where I joined the Spanish Army of Italy in time to fight the Turks at the world-shaking Battle of Lepanto and lose my left hand – or at least the use of it – for the greater glory of my right. Note the symbolism. Even history acknowledges that, with only a wretched little sonnet and a pompous dedication behind me, I already dreamed of a career as a writer.

But if so, would I have spent almost two years in Italy, cradle of the Renaissance, without meeting the greatest poet of our time, Torquato Tasso? Or, come to think of it, almost two years in Italy, cradle of romance, only to leave as I had arrived: *virgo intacto*?

But that's history for you. No wonder that fiction, seeing the field abandoned, rolls up its sleeves and fashions its own sometimes serendipitous truth.

My distant kinsman Gaspar de Cervantes, a Vatican diplomat although not yet a priest, met me with a coach at Rome's port of Civitavecchia, and soon we were jouncing along the Via Aurelia.

'So you are Andrea Cervantes's brother,' he said.

'You know my sister?' I asked warily.

'Now that you mention it, I don't. But suffice it to say that a Certain Mutual Acquaintance . . .' With this ellipsis, he gave me a man-of-the-world smile for which his plump, pink, youthful face seemed unsuited.

Rizione, of course; what else could I have expected? The Genoese magnate seemed as omnipresent as God.

Cousin Gaspar, as if reading my mind, asked offhandedly, 'Do you believe in God and all that sort of thing?'

Coming from a Vatican diplomat, this shocked me. 'Of c-course I do.'

'So why are you stammering? I refer to the triune deity, divinely inspired parthenogenesis, Jesus as God's literal son, and so on and so forth.'

I said, with the loftiness of youth, 'There are no heretics in the Spanish branch of the family.'

'But virtually all Spaniards are the tainted spawn of *conversos*. Well, no matter – we'll soon get you a Certificate of Purity of Blood.'

'Those,' I pointed out, 'don't grow on trees, Cousin Gaspar.'

'Now that you mention it, they don't. But suffice it to say that a Certain Mutual Acquaintance . . .' With this ellipsis, he gave me a shrewd look for which his plump, pink, youthful face seemed equally unsuited.

Rizione again.

'Since the Certain Mutual Acquaintance can manage the Certificate, there's nothing to stop you beginning work at once. You know Giulio Acquaviva, naturally?'

'Who?'

'Giulio Cardinal-to-be Acquaviva. Of course you do. He represented His

Holiness in Madrid at the obsequies of the unfortunate Crown Prince, for which I believe you wrote a wretched little sonnet and a pompous dedication.'

'No, Cousin Gaspar. Those were for the obsequies a short time later of the equally unfortunate young Queen.'

'At any rate, Acquaviva was at the funeral of Don Carlos. Since your sister Andrea knew him . . .'

Believing that my kinsman referred to Don Carlos, I gave a vehement denial. 'She d-did not! They never met!'

'But my dear cousin. When Giulio Cardinal-to-be Acquaviva left Spain, he needed an export licence for the trunkloads of mementos he had acquired, and the same Mutual Acquaintance who will arrange your Certificate arranged his licence. And as your sister . . . I mean, considering the relationship . . . that is, I rather assumed . . .'

'Oh,' I said, relieved, 'you m-mean Ac-cqua-v-viva.'

The more he ellipsized, the more I stammered, and neither of us was displeased when we reached Rome and, at the doorway of Giulio Cardinal-to-be Acquaviva's chambers near the infamous Appartamento Borgia on Vatican Hill, parted. Not, alas, for the last time.

Giulio Acquaviva was an almost defunctly gaunt young bishop in the ascetic style made fashionable by Pope Pius V, who existed on a diet of boiled herbs.

'And who,' Acquaviva informed me smugly, 'has thrown all the Jews out of the Papal States, as you'll have heard.'

I hadn't, but thought it wise to nod.

Acquaviva then began my interrogation.

'Can you sing? Polyphonic madrigals of love? Motets? Cantatas?'

'Afraid not, Your Eminence-to-be.'

'Do you play some musical instrument then? The lute? Organ? Harpsichord? Theorbo?'

'Sorry, Your Eminence-to-be.'

'You might try that new thing da Salò's fiddling with – a variation of the lyre called a violin. A bit shrill and scratchy, but it shows promise.'

But I had to admit I couldn't read a note of music.

'Perhaps you act in plays? Italy sets the theatrical standards, you know. Sends actors all over Europe. Actresses too,' Giulio Acquaviva said, his mouth compressing into a smile that made his gaunt Pius-V-style face resemble a death's head. 'Except of course in England, where boys assume the roles of females. Can you?'

'Can I what, Your Eminence-to-be?'

'Assume the role of a female.'

Dismayed, I realized Cousin Gaspar had not indicated what sort of employment I might expect.

I told Giulio Cardinal-to-be Acquaviva firmly that I had neither thespian talent nor homosexual tendencies, and he said, 'That would seem to leave domestic service.'

This part of my life nettles those Cervantes experts who insist always on a macho image of me – if only the subtle one of benevolent machismo based chiefly on my exploits while a slave in Algiers.

There is nothing macho about a chamberlain. I turned down Giulio Cardinal-to-be Acquaviva's bed at night and brought him breakfast and vestments in the morning. I tended small-clothes; I kept my master's (for that's what he was) appointments schedule, day and night; I let his youthful male visitors out the back door at dawn, as well as the occasional female he brought in to maintain appearances.

That autumn, soon after Giulio Acquaviva got his red biretta, I was in the Vatican Library on one of my every-other-Thursday free mornings, catching up on the latest racy verses of the Neapolitan poet Giovanni Battista Colombina, when Cousin Gaspar sat down across the table.

'I see you like poetry.'

I almost blurted, 'Holy Virgin, it's to be my life!' I would have, before my service in the household of Giulio Cardinal-at-Last Acquaviva. But I had had to learn tact there, and taciturnity, *savoir faire* and *savoir quand ne rien faire*, without which no diplomat would be worthy of the name. So I said, 'A pastime for a morning off.'

'The poetry, for example, of Torquato Tasso?'

'Holy Virgin!' I blurted. 'He's the greatest.'

'Mmm. Did you know that this scribbler Tasso went to Paris last year as Cardinal d'Este's secretary and said such terrible things about the French king and court that d'Este sent him packing? Tasso's been here in Rome ever since, a patient at the Ospedale Sant' I——.'

'What happened to him?'

'Nothing at all. Sant' I—— is a mental hospital. Like most poets, Torquato Tasso is . . . mentally delicate.'

'You're speaking,' I said, 'of the genius who's writing *Aminta*?'

'Why, I suppose so.' Cousin Gaspar looked baffled.

And well he might. Historically, Tasso wouldn't produce his pastoral drama until 1573. But fictionally, part of the manuscript would shortly be read to me, now in 1570, at the Ospedale Sant' I——. This can be explained by what we know of the great Tasso. What we know is that, later in life, extraordinarily wary of critics, he sat five years on his other masterpiece *Jerusalem Liberated* before publishing it. Couldn't his *Aminta* have suffered the same fate?

'Tasso,' said Cousin Gaspar, 'will soon go to his family in Sorrento. For the arduous journey he needs a companion. A Certain Mutual Acquaintance believes you are ready for such a mission.'

The Ospedale Sant' I—— in the Via S——, originally a palace of the minor nobility, hid the usual luxury behind the usual drab stucco façade with its endless rows of windows (now unfortunately barred) like sightless eyes under the brows of their arched pediments. Inside was the usual courtyard bisected by the usual marble staircase climbing to the usual *piano nobile* with its reception halls and galleries, their walls covered by the usual pagan frescoes isolated by marble pilasters one from another (rather like Sant' I—— 's patients in their cells) so that, for example, Jupiter was spared the embarrassment of raping Leda with Mars and Venus eavesdropping from the next panel, where they lay fornicating in the toils of jealous Vulcan's net, fresco after fresco parading carnally into the dim distance.

I was directed to the floor above the *piano nobile*, where I found the nursing sister Suora Donatella seated at a refreshingly nondescript desk wearing a shapeless brown habit, her pale, pretty face animated as she read the manuscript of *Aminta*. Looking up, she said in melodious Latin, 'This is wonderful stuff, because Tasso is too clever to accuse the Spaniards outright, but everyone will know. Won't they? Listen – from the part that begins, "O lovely age of gold!"' Switching into Italian, she quoted:

> '. . . because that vain inane conception,
> Idol of errors and deception,
> That thing called Honour by addled masses
> Which o'er us plays the tyrannous lord,
> Had not yet come to sow discord
> Among the sweet joys – '

'Spaniards?' I interrupted. 'Accused the Spaniards of what?'

'Honour, that's what!' Voice melodious still, but censorious. 'Invented by Spaniards – if not by the Devil. Until you Spaniards came along with your ponderous protocol, your punctilio, your prickly points of honour – ' Here she picked up the manuscript again.

'Souls long used to liberty
Knew not any law so cruel,
But kept that gracious golden rule
With which kind Nature had endowed us:
"That which pleases, is allowed us." '

Face flushed, she repeated the final '*s'ei piace, ei lice*', then said breathily, 'So beautiful! I know I oughtn't even to read such pagan poetry. But since he's my patient, I must understand his art, mustn't I?'

Before I could answer, a voice from the doorway bellowed, 'How many times have I told you, you dumb Jesus-cunt, not to read my manuscript out loud?'

He was a man of thirty or so, dirtily barefoot, wearing baggy Turkish pantaloons and a black leather doublet, open to reveal a scrawny chest matted with hair and a protuberant navel ringed by a welted scar.

'Like it?' he asked her, almost shyly.

This change in demeanour did not seem to surprise Suora Donatella. 'It is absolutely magnificent, Torquato – though I sometimes wonder how any pastoral drama can idealize the very peasants who, in reality, work themselves into early graves to keep us in the usual luxury.'

'The point,' said Torquato Tasso testily, 'is that any age without the Spaniards was an age of gold.'

'Ser Tasso,' I said, 'the sister was kind enough to read me the part where – '

He roared wordlessly and slapped Suora Donatella's face. She staggered back against the desk, scattering the pages of his manuscript over the marble floor.

'How many times have I told you, you whore of the Son of Man, that for-your-eyes-only means for-your-eyes-only?' he asked her. Me he asked, 'What part?'

I told him.

'Like it? Subtle dig at Spaniards, eh?'

He had wild, red-rimmed eyes and a long mouth to which his unkempt, full-face beard gave an oddly lopsided look. Or maybe it *was* lopsided.

I assured him I did. Then, 'I'm thinking of making my way in the world as a writer,' I said diffidently.

'Got any of your stuff on you?'

As it happened, I did have copies of my wretched little sonnet and pompous dedication.

'You were not,' he said after a cursory glance, 'put on this planet to

70

be a poet. Which leaves prose. Though why anyone would want to write it, when every uncouth lout speaks it, I have no idea. What's that thing there?'

Tasso's dirty fingers yanked at the string around my neck, from which dangled my brother Rodrigo's toy soldier. 'This supposed to be a likeness of you? Symbolism's not bad. Soldier. Wounded in some decisive battle. Winds up with only one hand. Quite enough to write with – prose anyway. And you stammer too, I notice. So I can see how you'd want to be a writer. Compensation. Well, let me give you three pieces of advice.

'First, never try to be funny. Humour is out. Readers think reading's a serious business. Take Rabelais, he was bawdy and witty, so was Boccaccio most of his life, and who'll read *them* two, three hundred years from now? Or Ariosto – thought he could get away with lampooning perfect gentle knights and damsels in distress. Ha! Guaranteed way to the boneyard.

'Second, don't write in the language of the people. Petrarch's mistake, and Boccaccio's, not to mention Dante. So like a damn fool I got hooked on the vernacular too. Literary suicide. Vernaculars come and go, but literate folks'll always read Latin.'

'They'll always read you, Torquato. In whatever language,' Suora Donatella said loyally.

'Where's your lover?' he asked her suddenly.

Lover? She was a nursing sister, wasn't she, a bride of Christ, so how . . .?

'On a delicate diplomatic mission to the Signory.'

'He won't come back alive.'

'Oh dear,' said the suora. 'How inconvenient. We were supposed to summer in Capri.'

'Pull yourself together,' he told her harshly.

But she hardly seemed apart.

Remembering that conversation with the hindsight of professional experience, I'm certain it was in code. Note her unconcern at the prediction (which proved, curiously, correct) of her lover's death. As the English secret-agent-extraordinary and part-time playwright Marlowe always said, 'Scratch a writer and you'll find a spy.'

Consider Tasso. He was quite devoid of humour. Wouldn't the old-and-tired-and-sick-of-it-all syndrome, raging like the plague through the cynical half-world of espionage, do that to a man? And of course he travelled. How convenient. He travelled restlessly, incessantly, indefatigably. A writer could get away with that. A writer's always on the run from something or someone – creditors, or a wife, or perhaps the ultimate enemy, himself. Tasso's haphazard itinerary would include, before he was through, all the petty feuding feudal states of Italy. And when he needed protection from the pitiless noonday heat of poetry or the endless midnight cold of espionage, what better sanctuary than a bedlam like the Ospedale Sant' I——? Still – *was* he insane? Or was his recurrent insanity only another form of cover? Did even he himself know?

Tasso asked Suora Donatella, 'You really did like it?'

'Very much.'

'You're not just saying that?'

'She means it,' I said. 'Before you came, she – '

'Keep out of this, fellow,' he said menacingly, while Suora Donatella, delicately patting her puffed lip with a scented handkerchief, murmured to me, 'It happens every time he talks about his writing. Every time.'

'What else is there to talk about?' he snarled.

'He's fine when he talks about *other* writers,' she said.

'I cut 'em to ribbons,' he beamed.

'The problem,' explained the Suora, 'as with all great writers, is ambivalence. His work is both his sole delight and his everlasting despair.'

This evaluation made him look a bit smug, I thought. He said, 'Here's the third. Don't try.'

What with their strange behaviour and my ruminations about espionage and insanity, it took me a few seconds to realize that this was his third piece of advice for me as a would-be writer.

He shut his eyes, lost in bitter thought. 'My father Bernardo was a poet. Real poet. Knew all the pros and cons. Sent *me* to study law. But I got seduced by the muse, same as him. When he died, I had to borrow to put him in the ground. *That's* being a poet. Was your father one?'

'No sir. My father,' I said, forgetting, in my enthusiasm to elevate my origins, Tasso's abhorrence of Spaniards, 'is surgeon to the Italian community of Madrid.'

'*Madrid*? Then you're a Spaniard?'

There, I told myself glumly, goes my chance to learn from the great Torquato Tasso whatever he could teach me.

'Spaniard,' he repeated, darting red-rimmed eyes at the door behind him. 'You think you've got an Inquisition in Spain? Here in Italy the inquisitors masquerade as critics.' He sidled behind Suora Donatella's desk and peeped out of the window. 'It's all part of the cosmic master plan in which the Lord God delegated the archangel Raphael to imprison the Devil in the desert until Judgment Day. Gave the Devil all the time he needed to spew forth accursers, adversaries, imps, familiars, fiends, an archfiend or two, serpents, old clooties, demons, satans, even the Demogorgon, who taught man to make weapons and women to use cosmetics. The obvious intention being *to destroy me*. Donatella knows. Don't you, darlin'?' Abruptly he sobbed; she took him in her arms. 'There, it's going to be all right, dear,' she crooned, dulcet as a nightingale at unseen apogee, but he broke free of her embrace and cried, 'What makes you think I *want* it to be all right? If it's all right, how can I ever write again?' and he would have hit her a second time, but I caught his wrist.

'Spaniard, eh?' he said. Enigmatically.

Suora Donatella sat again at her desk. 'You must take him home,' she told me. 'Home to Sorrento. He trusts you, I can tell.'

'He does?'

'But the only one who can break the spell of his madness is – '

' – Cornelia,' moaned Torquato Tasso softly. 'I want my Cornelia.'

'Take him to her. Don't worry – he's far more suicidal than homicidal, despite appearances. In Sorrento just ask for Cornelia Tasso; everyone there knows her.'

The only noteworthy place we broke our journey was the Abbey of Monte Cassino, the great monastery founded by St Benedict (AD 529) on the mountain-top site of a pagan temple. Benedict's teens, it was said, had been spent in the wilderness as an anchorite because some Roman maid or matron, spurning him, had left him with a lust he could subdue only by stripping and plunging into the thick nettle bushes and briers growing handily near his cave.

I found Tasso that night, a solitary candle highlighting his lopsided mouth, using a dagger (or was it a bodkin?) to prise up a stone in the chancel floor and reveal an urn which he said contained the remains of St Benedict and his sister St Scholastica, who had joined her nettle-and-brier-scarred brother at his abbey. 'For Benedict couldn't live without his sister,' intoned Tasso, as he knelt before the urn in, I thought at first, pious genuflection. Only as he raised it overhead did I realize he intended to smash it on the chancel floor. I wrested it from his grasp and saw the glint of candlelight on his dagger. We began an uneven struggle, he with two hands and the dagger, I encumbered with the urn. But at least I could use it as a shield, blocking his thrusts and slashes. Soon I felt the stones of the chancel wall cold against my back. The point of the dagger touched my throat, scraped stone, searched for my throat again – and two cowled monks materialized out of the darkness. Tasso turned his maniacal rage on them, but they clearly had previous experience with him and he was soon quelled. Fury spent, he chanted:

73

'Lust, illicit concupiscence
Illimited by age-old bans,
Luring us in a doomed dance
To its endless chaotic ends
As Jocasta with Oedipus entoiled –

'No, better make that "Oedipus Rex" to rhyme with "sex". Then:

'... *dah dah dah* ... lewd,
Daughter to father, son to mother,
Yea, adored sister joined to brother
In sin perceived yet still pursued.'

I returned the urn with unsteady hands to its hole in the chancel floor and went to my cold cell. But I found neither sleep nor peace that night.

Leaving Benedictine hagiography, we stepped a few days later into Homeric myth. Starkly white against the blue of the bay of Naples in the summer sun of the *mezzogiorno* stood Sorrento, the village where tradition places blind Homer's sirens, those bird-women whose irresistible song lured sailors to their death on the rocks of the rugged promontory.

... ask for Cornelia Tasso; everyone there knows her.

I asked a young fisherman in a red Phrygian cap, and he smiled and, pointing to where a goat path rose steeply through a lemon grove, cried, 'Cornelia! *È bella, bella!*'

I asked bronzed, half-naked boys stealing lemons, and they too smiled and pointed upwards to where myrtle flowered out of season, and they cried, 'Cornelia! *È bella, bella!*'

And I asked a toothless old goatherd, and he smiled and pointed to a distant crag where perched a tiny white cube that might have been a cottage, and he cried, 'Cornelia! *È bella, bella!*'

Soon we were in a garden filled with blossoms that in some long-ago golden age might have scented Aphrodite's bower, while birds flashed by on ruby wings singing of love sacred and profane in sylvan glades that were old when Earth first began its endless journey round the sun. Sorrento! Was ever such splendour compressed between a sky bluer than the grotto of nearby Capri and a mirroring sea as shimmering as the lambent air itself? Sorrento! Home to that love called the thunderbolt, and how could it have been otherwise? Sorrento! But ruby-wingèd birds vanished as I carried poor exhausted Tasso the last few steps to an open door (there were no locks here; none was needed until I came) and into the cottage.

I deposited Tasso on a bed near the summer-cold hearth and, going out through a second door at the back of the simple room, heard again (or so I thought) the ruby-wingèd birds.

But I was wrong. It was a woman's voice I heard, a voice to rival Homer's sirens. Like one walking in a dream, I followed a path down to a swiftly flowing brook as the siren song grew richer and more radiant – as if music, soft air, *mezzogiorno* sunlight, all were one. At the edge of the brook I saw a naked child playing with a rag doll, the child my niece's age, hair all golden ringlets too, hardly less beautiful of face and clean of limb than dear postmature Constanza. Beyond her a woman bent over a rock pounding her laundry – as if blind Homer had found his Nausicaa at Sorrento too – garments of deepest magenta and cerulean, by no means colourfast, for as the woman pounded they beautified the brook with flowing ribbons of colour. It was this unknown washerwoman who sang, yet unknowing, for me.

'Mamma,' said the child, and the woman rose swan-graceful, her eyes widening in wonder while my own eyes took in a beauty the equal of her voice, bare as she was above the waist, her brook-damp skirt clinging to legs as long and slender, almost, as my sister Andrea's.

Neither of us could speak for a breathless moment, in which time expanded to become space, vast vaulted distances bending back on themselves like the perfect curve of her hip, or her breast. Then finally I could say, thick-throated, 'Cornelia,' and she could say, 'Costanza, go inside.'

Costanza! Minus an 'n' in Italian, but still . . .

The child Costanza took her rag doll and climbed obediently towards the cottage.

I took the first step, Cornelia the second. We touched, I her smooth bronzed arm, she my bearded face. At this first contact I came to climax instantly and, I am certain, so did she. Then our lips met – a tentative caress, no more – and it happened again. And I swear in that moment lost in space, in those vast, vaulted distances, the sky darkened for a single astounding instant, a natural *coup de théâtre*, to blaze with an awesome flash of lightning.

Soon the sun returned to find us splashing together along the brook to a dappled pool where jumped an iridescent trout, airborne almost as those ruby-wingèd birds, and beyond the pool I led her, as if I had known this unknown place, this other Eden, since before my birth or any mortal man's, to a mossy bank where we lay sleekly wet together.

'Who are you?' she asked when the sun hung low.

When I told her (but what was there to tell – Miguel de Cervantes? a Spaniard? a would-be writer?), her love-flushed face turned pale.

'You must go.'

Another hispanophobe, I thought, and sighed.

'It isn't that,' she said. Had I spoken?

'Then why?' I asked. 'Your husband in there, Tasso?'

'Torquato? He's not my husband.'

I smiled. Idiotically, I'm sure. 'He's not?'

But she only said, 'I must go to him,' and she went.

After a while the golden-haired child joined me on the embankment. 'Are you a friend of Signor Rizione?'

I almost fell into the brook. 'What makes you think so?'

'Practically everybody in the whole world is . . . here comes Mamma.'

'Go inside,' Cornelia said, and little golden-ringleted Costanza again obediently took her rag doll and departed.

Cornelia's cheeks were streaked with tears. 'I have to send you away,' she said. 'But how can I, if I can't?'

Heartened by these paradoxical words, I asked, 'Who is Rizio Rizione?'

And she said, 'A friend of your sister Andrea.'

And I said, 'How do you know that?'

And she said, 'I'll tell you after Torquato comes back from the isle of Tiberius.'

'Capri? He's going to Capri?'

'Soon. The Emperor Tiberius went there mad, some say, and Capri cured him of his madness. I've made arrangements to send Torquato.'

'The little girl?'

'Will go with him.'

When the thunderbolt has struck, what matter days, nights, autumn rains? What are the fingers of a cold wind exploring the chinks of our cottage wall, when we are warm in each other's arms? Time flees, we remain. Cornelia wears almond blossoms in her hair when the trees are winter-bare. We have no winter, winter we banish. I sip nectar from her navel, she paints me with honey and licks like a cat. Most days from our lofty crag we can see Capri, isle of Tiberius, who was Emperor in Rome when Christ was crucified, but she never speaks of Torquato and I never ask.

Oh, that I had never heard the siren song!

One day when we went down to Sorrento to drink, in banished winter, wine the colour of the summer sun, a gale blew out of the west and fishing boats raced for shore as the sea rose. I took my place trudging at the creaking winch as the boats were beached, so at first I did not hear the old man who came floundering through the surf, a small child on his shoulders, calling in a quavery voice for his Cornelia. But I saw her run to him across the strand, and I heard her scream. As I began running too, I saw her do a strange and startling thing, lifting away his drenched rag of a shirt to verify him by the welted scar that ringed his navel.

For it was Torquato Tasso, but he was old, his face lined, his red-rimmed eyes deep in their sockets, his back stooped, even the weight of little Costanza enough to bend it. Cornelia took the child, whose usually animated face seemed carved of wood as she clung to her mother, arms around her neck, small hands clasped piously. 'God,' she said, 'God, won't you please forgive Timberio?' Timberio was what the islanders still called Tiberius. 'It was ever so long ago. And he was surely possessed by the Devil, Uncle Torquato says so. A big black dog tried to bite me.'

'She's burning with fever,' Cornelia said, and carried the child to the village and the house of the blind old doctor who served the people of Sorrento. Three days and nights we stood vigil there at the bedside of little Costanza, and all that time a hard, cold rain beat down.

Once Tasso spoke, his manner so calm despite his quavery old-man's voice that he seemed quite sane. 'What the Devil has always aimed to convince us, you see, is not that he exists but that he *does not exist*. For unless a man believes in the power of darkness, it is hard to persuade him there is any need for God.'

'For shame, Tasso,' the blind old doctor admonished him. 'The child may be dying, at this very moment Father Nestore is with her, and you utter such blasphemy.'

'Blasphemy!' cried Father Nestore from the doorway. Young, he had the unworldly eyes of a child.

Tasso said at once, 'I am sure it is, Father. Confess me, I must be confessed.'

'Who is this old man?' Father Nestore asked.

Cornelia said, 'Don't you recognize my brother Torquato, Father?'

Inside, little Costanza cried out, and the blind old doctor hurried to her, Cornelia at his side. Which is why neither of them witnessed what happened next.

'Confess me, Father,' repeated the old man who was Torquato Tasso.

Here, I ought to point out, history is for once in total accord with the greater truth of fiction. All his life Tasso was tortured by a vacillating faith; even when it was strongest, he yet waited in dread for the times he knew would come when he rejected God, grace, redemption – everything which kept men from eternal damnation – and saw only a cosmos that mirrored his own disordered mind. At such times, he confessed compulsively to any priest who would shrive him.

Father Nestore lifted Tasso's rag of a shirt. In the priest's hand I glimpsed a surgeon's scalpel and I watched transfixed as he slashed at the welted scar that ringed the poet's navel as if to reopen the wound.

Tasso exulted, 'I feel nothing, there is no pain!' and the priest leaped back, his unworldly eyes wide with horror as he cried, 'It does not bleed, the knife pierced the flesh yet it does not bleed – who are you?'

Tasso laughed maniacally.

Just then the blind old doctor came out of the sick-room and told us, 'The crisis is past, the child will live.'

Father Nestore rushed from the house in terror.

The next morning I went with Tasso to the Church of San Francesco, but its doors were barred. Across the flooded piazza we found the caretaker. 'Father Nestore was called away,' she told us. 'They are sending someone in his place.'

On the fourth morning after Father Nestore fled, a dark but rainless day, I went again with Tasso to the Church of San Francesco. At the sight of the still-barred doors he grew paler and had to lean on me. But then I noticed that the churchyard gate stood open. As we entered, a man appeared at the far end and raised his arms in greeting. 'I am,' he called across to us in a familiar voice, 'the new priest.'

'Father, confess me!' Tasso begged.

'First,' said the new priest, 'I must exorcize you.'

He was my Cousin Gaspar.

The rites of exorcism are many and various, and a man need not be a priest to drive out evil spirits, if such things exist – and even less so, I suppose, if they don't. But still I couldn't help wondering why my not-yet-ordained Cousin Gaspar had been sent to exorcize Torquato Tasso.

I got the chance to ask him when we climbed the promontory on muleback to a place of stunted shrubs and strong winds where, the natives said, the entrance to the Infernal Kingdom was hidden and where brimstone could be found.

'Have you been ordained, Cousin Gaspar?'

'Now that you mention it, I haven't. But suffice it to say that a Certain Mutual Acquaintance . . .' With this ellipsis, he began to give me a look which either would or wouldn't have suited his plump, pink, youthful face.

'No, Cousin Gaspar. It will not suffice.'

'My dear cousin! You've changed! How pleased a Certain Mutual Acquaintance will be – as the purpose of the operation was, naturally, twofold.'

'What "operation" would that be, Cousin Gaspar?'

'Why, the unburdening of Torquato Tasso's soul, of course.' My cousin's eyes sparkled. He urged his mule towards an outcrop of sulphurous rock.

That very night Torquato Tasso, roped to a chair at the edge of a pit in which the brimstone smouldered, was given a concoction of holy oil, sach, rue and other ingredients. Drinking, Tasso swiftly convulsed and vomited. Cousin Gaspar, eyes shut, lips moving in silent incantation, pushed the poet's head down directly over the acrid smoke. The whole village had come to watch, and they muttered their disappointment at my cousin's lack of theatrics, for after a while, his face aglow with the ruddy light from the pit, he merely said, 'Cut him free, the man is no longer possessed.'

In the morning Tasso eagerly presented himself for confession and communion (alone: my not-yet-frocked cousin stopped short of offering the wine and wafer to others). Cornelia and I waited outside the Church of San Francesco in the sunlit piazza, the villagers crowding behind us. When Tasso emerged, a shout rose from every throat and Cornelia ran to her brother, her lovely face transfused with joy. For Torquato Tasso, who had returned from the isle of Tiberius a demon-ridden old man, was now young again, no more than three or four years older than myself.

I know this sounds impossible. But it is what I saw.

Cornelia I did not see for several hours after the miraculous transformation, for brother and sister went walking hand in hand on the beach. And as I watched from the belvedere high above, I swear they looked so like us they could have been myself and my sister Andrea. I turned away overwhelmed by emotion – and saw my Cousin Gaspar.

'We can talk in the churchyard,' he said.

'How did you make him young again?'

A careless wave of the hand. 'Was he ever really old?'

We strolled a while in silence. Finally he said, 'My dear cousin, you have a brilliant future.'

'But – but I've hardly written anything yet by which to judge,' I said. 'And anyway, in my wildest dreams I could never be another Torquato Tasso.'

'As to that, I wouldn't know,' said my Cousin Gaspar. 'Suffice it to say that a Certain Mutual Acquaintance . . .' With this ellipsis, he gave me a smile (part condescension, part approval) for which his plump, pink, youthful face proved perfectly suited.

'Stop calling him that. We both know his name. And it never suffices to say, because you never say sufficient.'

'Now that you mention it, I don't. But you *have* changed. Which will please a Certain Mutual . . . all right, all right, don't look at me like that. Suffice it to say . . . certain person . . . most grateful for everything you did.'

'But I didn't . . . at least, not with any intention of . . .'

By then he had *me* ellipsizing. My look of confusion, unfortunately, must have suited my broad-browed, proud-nosed, chestnut-bearded face just fine.

'By seducing his sister Cornelia, you drove Torquato Tasso to a degree of Satan-haunted madness he had never suffered before.'

'Seducing? But I . . . we both . . .'

'Such Satan-haunted madness, in fact, that his confession was more thorough than any previous. A Certain Mutual Acquaintance will soon know *everything* that Torquato Tasso ferreted out during all his years as an agent for, among others, the Holy League – which is to say the alliance of the Papal States, the Signory of Venice and your own King Felipe the Death-Loving against the Sublime Porte.'

'The Porte? But then, does our Acquaintance . . .'

'Spy for the Turk? My dear cousin! Consider – aware as he is that every decade since the discoveries of Columbus and Vasco da Gama and others has seen Mare Nostrum's pathetic little city-states become more and more, um, irrelevant as power shifts north and west from the Mediterranean to the Atlantic rim, yet equally aware that the Holy League must be given all possible encouragement to stop the Terrible Turk from further penetrating the West, such encouragement in no way preventing the inevitable reckoning to come when the brash new northern nations and the tired old city-states of the south . . . where was I?'

With my Cousin Gaspar, I began to suspect, suffice-it-to-say had definite advantages.

'You were telling me, I think,' I said, 'that a Certain Mutual Acquaintance is no Turkish spy.'

'Call him by his name, why don't you?' a woman's voice shrilled, and I saw Cornelia at the end of the churchyard. 'We all know who he is, this *Rizione*' – her words dripped the acid of impotent hatred – 'just as we have all been traduced by him, and always with the same weapon, sex. Like a fool

I bore his child, and like a fool I've done his bidding ever since, little things it seemed, but enough to demoralize an artist as sensitive and talented as my brother — for how well I know that no woman can ever make a writer happy but only herself will suffer sorely from the delusion that she can, not that that ever stops her trying, fool that she is, as who but I . . .'

Spluttering with syntax-destroying wrath, she crossed the churchyard and struck my face as hard as she could with a roll of parchment.

'You! Spaniard! Coming here with your thunderbolt to seduce me and push poor Torquato over the edge to become putty in the hands of this false-priest cousin of yours!'

'*My* thunderbolt? But – '

'Don't talk to me about your thunderbolt! The worst day of my life was the day the sky turned dark and your thunderbolt struck in a breathless moment in which time expanded to become space, vast vaulted distances bending back on themselves like some perfect curve or other while ruby-wingèd birds . . . Never mind! I hate you! I never want to see you again!' Once more she struck my face with the roll of parchment. My head rocked back, my eyes filled with tears, my ears rang, but I heard her say, 'Take that.' She meant it literally, for she gave me the parchment.

I unrolled it, and my eyes fell on these words: '. . . *none in his family back to the third generation having been Muslims, Jews,* conversos, *nor relaxed by the Supreme and General Council of the Inquisition to the civil authorities for punishment* . . .' and I knew it to be my Certificate of Purity of Blood.

'What will you do, now that you are at last pure?' my Cousin Gaspar enquired.

But I had eyes only for Cornelia as she crossed the churchyard and disappeared.

Was sex, I couldn't help wondering, power?

And I sought, in the time-honoured tradition, the waters of Lethe.

VII

How I Become a Parrot,

And Numerous Other Wonders Including

The Old Cypriot's Tale

Unrolling the parchment, I told the recruiting sergeant, 'And here's my Certificate of Purity of Blood.'

'Your certificate of *what*?'

'Purity. Purity of Blood. It certifies that I am a pure Spaniard of a pure Spanish family, or eight of them actually, back to the third generation.'

The sergeant, who wore a threadbare uniform under a magnificent cape of regal purple, tossed the parchment back at me. 'So who the fuck cares? In this man's army we got foot soldiers from the fuckin' Irish peat bogs and Swiss pikemen who washed out of the fuckin' Papal Guard, we got gypsies from Triana and Scandahoovian berserkers and some Germans I swear to Christ just climbed down from the trees, and you think anybody cares if you got pure Spanish blood in your veins or pure fuckin' piss? This is the army of the Holy League, son, and anybody that wants to fight the Terrible Turk is welcome. You know how to use a harquebus?'

'A what?'

'Like I fuckin' thought.' He rose wearily and shouted, 'Cervantes!'

'Yes sir?' I replied.

But he was looking past me to the doorway, through which strode a young soldier, tall and lean in leather doublet with short overcape, crimson shirt and hose, and slashed knee breeches in the Spanish royal colours, crimson and gold. His buckled black shoes had been spit-shined to rival the finish of his steel helmet, which was worn at a rakish old-soldier angle over a freckle-strewn face. He sighed. 'Another live one? Never heard of a harquebus?'

'You fuckin' got it, Cervantes. Lotsa luck.'

The young soldier looked at me and turned pale, his freckles standing out in bold relief.

'Miguel!'

'Rodrigo!'

'Sign here,' said the sergeant, and I signed, upside-down for all I knew, and then my brother and I fell into a manly embrace.

We repaired to a tavern on the edge of the Bay of Naples.

'So, baby brother,' I asked, 'how's military life?'

'I love the army,' Rodrigo said simply. 'Been in over a year and it's all I ever dreamed it would be.'

'I thought recruits had to be twenty. You're just twenty now.'

Rodrigo laughed. 'I could pass for twenty when I joined up, and in this life appearances are all you ever need.'

I asked, 'How's Papá? Does he still have his clinic near the Gate of the Moors?'

'Clinic? What clinic? He's got that little barber-shop.'

'Oh, sure. Barber-shop, that's what I meant. How is he?'

'He's dwindled. You'd be surprised how small he is — and deafer than ever. But his health's good.'

'And Doña Leonor?'

'Caustic. Definitely on the caustic side. Particularly when it comes to Papá.'

'And there still isn't anybody good enough to play with her children, right?' I smiled, remembering.

'Her grandchild, you mean. Constanza — that is one beautiful niece we have.'

'And Magdalena. I assume she doesn't pull wings off flies any more, being seventeen and all?'

'And all,' said my brother Rodrigo drily, for a moment reminding me of Doña Leonor. He moved his beer mug pensively on the table, leaving rings. 'You probably remember how Magdalena always used to say, "No, thank you, I would rather not." Last I saw, she was more inclined to say, "Yes, please, I'd be delighted." Especially if the fellow had a free way with money, if you take my meaning.'

I took his meaning and hastily enquired, 'How's little Juan?'

'Who?'

'Juan the Obscure.'

'Oh. He's around somewhere, I guess. In Madrid. I don't know.'

I waited a beat. Held my breath. Could feel my heart pounding against my ribs. Then, in as offhand a voice as I could summon, I asked, 'How's Andrea?'

After waiting his own, longer beat, my brother said, 'She misses you too.' He shifted uncomfortably on the bench. 'Last I knew, she was really into litigation. She hired this Picapleitos to sue the Pacheco Portocarrero brothers for not returning some family jewels – pearls and emeralds and rubies and things – they borrowed.'

'Where did Andrea get any "family jewels"? And who are the Pacheco Portocarrero brothers?'

'Bad news. The younger one, Pedro, is a killer.'

'Of people?'

'I didn't mean a *matador de toros*,' Rodrigo said. 'As for those alleged pearls and emeralds and rubies and things, they were this Picapleitos's idea. Suing for their return, provided she wins, is one way to get paid for . . . services rendered. Not,' said Rodrigo quickly, after a look at my face, 'that I mean to imply Andrea rendered them. I think Magdalena did. Probably.' He studied my face more carefully. 'I'm willing to bet on it. Absolutely. Andrea's just protecting her kid sister.' Rodrigo shifted on the bench again. It was obvious he wanted to change the subject. 'I had a short leave and went up to Rome to look for you. But our Cousin Gaspar said you never got there.'

'But – '

'So where have you been?'

I opened my mouth, then closed it. Had Cousin Gaspar already begun to obliterate all traces of my role in the Tasso confession, my first foray into the secret world of espionage? Since I wasn't eager to bring up my domestic service in Rome, I just shrugged and said, 'Sorrento.'

'Sorrento? Why would anybody want to – thunderbolt?'

'Her name was Cornelia.'

Rodrigo beamed. Even his freckles seemed to arrange themselves into smile-shaped clusters. 'So tell, bro! What was she like? Gorgeous, I'll bet.'

I sat there trying to picture a beauty the equal of her voice, bare as she was above the waist and her brook-damp skirt clinging to legs as long and slender, almost, as my sister Andrea's. But what did she *look like*? I hardly knew. A trick of memory? The merciful suppression of an image too painful to recall? Or had Cousin Gaspar exorcized more than just Tasso's madness?

Whatever, the image would not come. Disturbingly, the more I tried to picture Cornelia, the more I saw my sister Andrea.

'Well?' Rodrigo asked, after my long silence.

'What? Oh, sorry – I was, uh, wondering. A harquebus. Is it hard to get the hang of?'

'For some. But you'd better get the hang of it fast. We'll be shipping out soon. You can always tell. First the camp followers get kicked out. Then Jesuits and Capuchins descend like locusts. Plus, you hear the same Turkish-atrocity stories in every tavern in town.'

'You mean they're just propaganda?'

'I mean they're true. Very dumb of the Turks. Enough real atrocities and the so-called allies in our so-called Holy League will forget how much they hate each other. Come on, let's get you a uniform.'

At the supply depot, Rodrigo told the clerk, 'He's my brother. So make sure it fits, and make sure it's new, not something you stripped off a body riddled with French pox.'

The clerk tossed various items in my direction – crimson hose and shirt, stiff new leather doublet, gold overcape, and knee breeches stylishly slashed like Rodrigo's. The buckled black shoes pinched. The steel helmet, no matter how I angled it, looked, I was sure, unmartial.

Rodrigo surveyed me. 'How do you feel?'

'Colourful,' I said.

'That's the general idea. Would an army uniformed all in monkish brown strike terror into the hearts of an enemy? Not the way an army of iridescent parrots would. That's what we're called, by the way – parrots, the King's parrots. Come on, I'll show you our perch.'

High under the eaves of an ancient stone building near the Castelnuovo, the room was the size of two coffins.

'It's the size of two coffins,' I said.

'As much space as you'll have aboard ship if you're lucky – on a plank in the hold.'

'Aboard ship? I thought I joined the *army*.'

'Naval battles are fought by infantrymen, ship-to-ship,' Rodrigo explained. 'You have a lot to learn.'

The next morning Rodrigo led me and a dozen other bleary-eyed recruits, all shouldering harquebuses, up Vomero hill to meet the dawn. A harquebus weighs maybe twelve pounds and measures five feet from butt to muzzle, so in the half-darkness there was considerable stumbling and cursing and dropping of weapons, while Rodrigo shouted variations on this theme: 'You call yourselves men-at-arms? Babes-in-arms is more like it. Move those fat asses!'

Dawn found us on a weed-grown threshing floor. Below, the Bay of Naples and the city still lay in darkness pricked by tiny lights, as if sky and earth had exchanged places.

Here is my brother Rodrigo, down on one knee on the threshing floor, firing his harquebus.

Peers at target – man-sized silhouette in bulbous turban and baggy pantaloons, definitely Turkish-looking – nailed to gnarled trunk of olive tree a hundred paces away. Strikes flint on steel, ignites serpentine match. Loads

85

and primes with right hand, while left holds smouldering serpentine and somehow also shields priming powder. Pulls trigger, sending serpentine end into pan. Kneels rock-steady through flash of pan, roar of main powder charge in barrel, blossom of flame from muzzle. Then stands nonchalantly while recruits marvel at hole in exact centre of target.

And here am I, down on one knee on the threshing floor, firing my harquebus.

Wish they weren't all watching. Makes me nervous. How can harquebus weigh more now than when carrying up steepest part of hill? Breeches torn, must mend later. Remember: parrots frighten enemy . . . *Concentrate! Now!* Pull serpentine back, so. Hold in position with left hand, so . . . Holy Virgin! Will need three hands. At least. Where did powder flask get to? Wad hook, bullet extractor – ah, here. Spill powder into muzzle . . . Don't let go of serpentine! Wad after powder, ram ball in, so. Spill powder into priming pan, *not* on ground. Squeeze trigger. Gently. Serpentine end whips near cheek. Can feel heat. Beard on fire? Serpentine end hits pan, flash of priming powder . . . *Aim, clod! You're forgetting to aim!* BOOM! Embarrassed to find self flat on ground. Harquebus kicks like meanest mule in La Mancha. Shoulder dislocated? Or only badly bruised? Climb to feet. All examine target. Virgin but for single hole made by Rodrigo.

And here am I, down on one knee in my perch high above the deck of the galley *Marquesa*, loading my harquebus as this momentarily fear-banishing thought occurs: the sea really *is* wine-dark out here, but how did Homer know if he was blind? Here am I, an inviting, an irresistible target in this perch, a sitting duck (no, a kneeling parrot) as I put powder into muzzle (or maybe muzzle into powder, hard to tell with this vertigo, this *mal aria*, this fever not to be confused with the heat of battle). Here am I . . .

But where, that Homeric clue aside, is *here*?

I thought you might ask.

Now, if I were Lope de Vega – which sometimes I almost wish I were, but please don't tell him! – how orderly these events would appear. No confusion of points in time and moments in space, no jumping here, there, hill of Vomero to harbour of Lepanto (fortified town on the gulf of Corinth, Greek name Náfpaktos) in the turn of a page.

Lope wouldn't do it that way. Too disordered. Not that he could have done it any way at all, since he was a nine-year-old brat in Madrid when we fought at Lepanto (7 October 1571, for those who collect dates). His turn would come in '88 with the Invincible (so-called) Armada, and note this well: stricken with *mal aria*, wounded three times, I nevertheless (or all the more) tasted the glory of victory, the Grail my brother Rodrigo would pursue until it killed him, whereas Lope would taste only the bitter gall of ignominious defeat. Perhaps this accounts for a certain . . . emptiness in his work, cleverly concealed by a formula. Yes, *formula*, set down in his *The New Art of Writing Plays*, which he composed, hastily as usual, in answer to remarks I made in the first part of *Don Quixote* – clearly a digression on my part but, as you may have noticed, digressions are mother's milk to me.

Lope, meticulously avoiding all digressions, would have mounted his scenes on that well-tested formula of his. Two plays, I suspect, one as prelude to the battle, one the battle itself. What prodigality! But then, Lope in his long career ground out 1600, 1800, God-knows-how-many-00 plays, of three acts each. (Was three a magic number to him, or just an arbitrary part of his formula? See below.) Perhaps he structured his art so rigorously to compensate for a life so openly, so recklessly, so (I grant) romantically chaotic, what with all its elopements, marriages, assignations, a few abductions even. I, by contrast, was engaged in work *in addition to my writing* which, though chaotic in its own clandestine, dangerous way, must by its very nature be hidden from the prying eye of history. Am I jealous? A reasonable question. Lope Félix de Vega y Carpio would, with his quill-pen and his own extravagant life, hold Madrid in the palm of his hand while I, his senior by fifteen years, was still a virtual unknown. But a *formula!*

Here are the fundamentals of Lope's formula.

Divide all plays into three acts. Three – I'm suspicious of that number, so central to mysticism. Did Lope believe in numerology, wherein each letter has a value on a scale of nine (A=1, B=2, . . . I=9, J=1 etc.) and a name adds up to a single significant digit? Try L-O-P-E, which becomes 3+6+7+5 or 21, which reduces to 2+1=3. And if a person is a three, as Lope is? Numerologists tell us that threes are creative, versatile, bursting with energy. Threes are likely to succeed in anything they undertake. They are talented, lucky and carefree. They are often rich. Is this why Lope insists on dividing his plays into three acts? I myself am a four, which is to say suspicious, resentful, failure-prone, subject to unpredictable outbursts of rage, generally poverty-stricken . . . but all this, of course, is infantile superstition.

Limit each play's action to a single day. Indicates simply that Lope read the *Poetics* of Aristotle, whose dramatic unities I find stifling – in prose anyway.

Show life not as it really is but as the groundlings crowding the pit like to think it is. Meretricious, no? But Lope needed money for his extravagant life, and he wouldn't be the first writer to get it by pandering.

Always subordinate character to action, and action to message. Message? Pithy proverbs stretched into three-act plays! The sort of throwaway lines

I might put in the mouth of Sancho Panza to show his earthy origins, or Don Quixote to show his resistance to reality, taking precedence over real rounded characters! Still, I can forgive Lope that, and the whole tired, creaking apparatus of his formula (I mean, if he needed a crutch, he needed a crutch) except for one thing. I can never forgive the part of his formula that goes: *Avoid the impossible.*

Why, just to have been born and lived, against what astronomical odds, in an infinite universe of atoms randomly coalescing, isn't that the most wonderfully impossible of all impossibilities? Avoid the impossible? Might as well avoid breathing.

But you see the problem. You still don't know how I got to the Battle of Lepanto, 'The Naval', as we veterans would ever after call it, evoking with that one word two mighty fleets clashing on a wine-dark, soon a blood-red, sea with the fate of Europe hanging in the balance.

Points in time, moments in space, jumping here, there, Neapolitan hilltop to Aegean gulf in the turn of a page, why not? Fire when ready.

That's what war is like.

But Lope, formula firmly between his teeth as he gallops from play to play, would insist on beginning at a beginning.

Let's try it his way:

WAITING FOR LEPANTO

Act I

Naples Bay, aboard the Genoese galley Marquesa. *A morning in late August 1571.*

(Drums and trumpets. On deck, PARROTS *in flashy crimson-and-gold uniforms crowd the rail. Two,* RODRIGO *and* MIGUEL DE CERVANTES, *climb into the galley's skiff, suspended amidships, for a better view.)*

RODRIGO *(an eager grin on his freckled face)*: This is what a man lives for! The glory life! The mightiest fleet ever assembled, to defend all Christendom! See how the sun's making rainbows in the water sluicing off our oar-blades? Heaven itself smiles on us today!

MIGUEL *(glancing down into waist of galley)*: I see water sluicing off the slaves who man our oars. No rainbows, though. Just sweat, and some blood from the whips.

RODRIGO *(gesturing broadly)*: Look at that forest of masts, and banners flying from every one! There's the Lion of Venice, and the Cross of Malta, and our own red and gold, and over there on the flagship *Real* the blue and gold standard of the Holy League! Holiest of Virgins, did you ever see a ship of gold before? She's gold all over! And there in the prow, our glorious commander Don Juan . . .

MIGUEL: Don Juan the Bastard of Austria. (*Musingly*) You know what they say – 'Bastards and *conversos* are never brave.' What's he thinking now, I wonder?

RODRIGO: God, look at him – standing tall in the forecastle, the sun gleaming on his golden armour, and a golden halo over his head! Now he's waving – I swear to Christ he's waving at *us*! Oh, the glory!

MIGUEL (*softly beating the rail in time to the rhythmic slave-driving thud of the boatswain's mallet*): Glory . . .

(Marquesa's *sails catch the wind, and she swiftly passes a papal brigantine at anchor, on its deck the figure of*

Hold on, there could be a problem staging this. In fact, that's true of the whole of the Battle of Lepanto: special effects all the way. Well, let Lope worry about it.

a nuncio endlessly repeating, like some clever mechanical toy, the sign of the cross. RODRIGO *echoes the gesture.* MIGUEL *seems to; but winds up scratching himself.*)

MIGUEL (*plucking a louse from his stained and smelly uniform, and scrutinizing it*): I wonder, out there where the Sultan's fleet is, is some imam giving his blessing? If there's only one God . . .

RODRIGO: Glory!

Cut! Wrong approach. This is all characterization and description, which couldn't interest Lope less. Let's get to the message, or at least some motivation. A couple of characters will have to do some ship-jumping, but otherwise the unities will be respected.

WAITING FOR LEPANTO

Act I

Naples Bay, aboard the Holy League flagship Real. *A morning in late August 1571.*

(*Drums and trumpets. Atop the forecastle* DON JUAN OF AUSTRIA *stands with the crusty Venetian wing commander* ADMIRAL VENIERO, *the Spanish infantry captain* DIEGO DE URBINA, *and a* CAPUCHIN FRIAR.)

CAPUCHIN FRIAR: Glory! Glory to God Who will be our salvation as we face

89

Selim's heathen hordes! Glory to God Who will not suffer our churches to be razed for mosques! Glory to God Who will preserve our mothers and sisters from defilement by the janissaries of –

CAPTAIN URBINA (*dismissively*): Janissaries prefer to screw each other, not women. As for protecting Europe, God gets a little help from the likes of my parrots over on *Marquesa*.

ADMIRAL VENIERO: Protecting *Europe*, Captain? You're here to protect the Spanish empire, and we all know it. Or you'd have been here sooner.

DON JUAN: Admiral, you forget yourself! Today we stand together, ready to offer our lives under the banner of the Holy League, and you dare talk of provincial politics. The Ottoman *empire* we face stretches from the Indian Ocean to the Atlantic, and we must crush it for the purest of ideological reasons –

CIDE HAMETE (*interrupting*): Ideology! That word again! *Ráwi*, hand me my –

AUTHOR: How did you get into this scene? You're not here, you're not even now.

DON JUAN: – the defence of the Holy Faith.

CAPUCHIN: Amen!

VENIERO: Your pardon, Excellency (*stressing* DON JUAN's *title with syrupy venom, for all know that King Felipe the Death-Loving has denied his half-brother the use of the loftier 'Highness'*). Whoever wins, we Venetians will be ripe for plucking. Let the Sultan fight it out with King Felipe, and pray to God nobody wins – that's what they're saying on the Rialto.

DON JUAN: You sound like a Frenchman, Admiral, who'd gladly lose an eye if it meant we Spaniards would lose two.

VENIERO: The Spaniards, Excellency? Where were they when the Turk picked off our Aegean outposts one by one? Where were they when Corfu and Cyprus fell, when Marcantonio Bragadino was fla –

AUTHOR: Admiral, please! Not yet! I'm saving that for later.

DON JUAN: It's an Englishman you sound like now, Admiral.

VENIERO (*hand on sword hilt*): An Englishman! Now by God that's too much!

DON JUAN: An Englishman so terrified of Spain he'd sooner see minarets sprout all across Kent than grant the Pope sway over Canterbury.

VENIERO: But you yourself, Excellency, invoked ideological differ –

CIDE HAMETE (*interrupting again*): Ideology! That whore of a word! No relation to *idea*, just to isms (most often opportunism), and you know how I feel about isms. Whenever I hear the word ideology I reach for my scimitar.

AUTHOR: I thought you were a pacifist.
CIDE HAMETE: Careful. That's an ism.

Cut! The unities are taking a beating here. And we're swamped with more messages than any playwright can handle. Let's get back to something even Lope agrees is basic.

Let's tell a story.

WAITING FOR LEPANTO

Act I

On the deck of Marquesa *in Messina harbour, where the Holy League fleet has rendezvoused. Night.*

(The parrot MIGUEL DE CERVANTES, *sleepless, shaking with the first ague of* mal aria, *stands at the rail.)*

LOOKOUT *(from the crow's-nest)*: Sail ho!

(On the silver track of the full moon appears the enigmatic silhouette of an exotically rigged boat. A small dhow, it comes alongside. Its lone occupant, a skeletal OLD CYPRIOT *in rags, is hoisted aboard more dead than alive. His sunken eyes glare defiantly at the* SAILORS *of the watch as they, and* PARROTS *who have been sleeping on deck, drift towards him.)*

OLD CYPRIOT *(in a hoarse croak)*: Git your hands off'n me!

(MIGUEL DE CERVANTES holds out a wine cup; OLD CYPRIOT *swats it away and stands near the sterncastle hatch at bay, snarling and spitting.)*

FIRST PARROT: So let the old bastard die if he wants.
SHIP'S SURGEON: His desires in the matter, I assure you, are quite irrelevant. The man is moribund.
OLD CYPRIOT: Corfu . . .
SECOND PARROT: What's he saying?
FIRST PARROT: Said 'fuck you' I think.
OLD CYPRIOT: Fuck you too, the whole lot o' you. I said git your *hands* off'n me. Been in an open boat I don't know how many days, and I won't take shit from nobody . . . including you in the brown robe, brother, *git* your hands off . . . Sailing to rescue Cyprus, are you? Late, just a mite late. *(Spits at parrot* CERVANTES *who again tries to offer him wine cup)* I said git your hands *off* . . . Famagusta held out two months. That's my

91

town, Famagusta. Was. Good place to live. Was. Any woman survived, she'll wear black the rest of her life. (*Knocks cup from hand of persistent parrot* CERVANTES) Killed us thirty thousand Turks, and unlike some I could name we Cypriots don't lie. Git your *hands* . . . thirty thousand. But there was thirty thousand more. And thirty thousand after *them*. So finally, on the sorriest day since the beginning of the world, our garrison surrenders. Cut off by land, cut off by sea, dying of starvation. What choice was there? Turk commander, one of them watchacallit, pashas, Ahmed, Abdul, Ali, one o' them, he offers safe passage to Crete for the officers and men of the garrison. Sounds good. Too good, in what you call your reprospeck. Well, this here Marcantonio Bragadino, he's the garrison commander, a Venetian but a real gent, anyways he goes to this Abdul Pasha's tent to sign the watchacallit, articles of surrender. Walks in with full military honours, plus his staff officers. This Ahmed Pasha, he starts right in foaming at the mouth how Marcantonio Bragadino killed some Muslim prisoners. Lies. All lies. Then, this Ali Pasha has Bragadino's officers killed right before his eyes. *De*-captivated. Meanwhile the whole garrison's already embarked for their safe passage to Crete. But when the Turk commodore opens his sealed orders, he changes course for Constantinople with four, five thousand Christian slaves. But I was telling you what happened to Marcantonio Bragadino. First, right there in the tent over the bodies of his *de*-captivated dead officers, they slice off his ears. Then they slice off his nose. Then one by one over the next few days they break his teeth and when that's done they pull the stumps out of his head, also one by one. This brings us to the middle of August. Ahmed Pasha has the whole population of Famagusta that's still alive, by which I mean old men and them women that will wear black the rest of their lives, herded into the plaza to watch them flay Marcantonio Bragadino alive. *You* ever seen a man flayed alive? What they use, it's a real professional butcher knife they use, and it's a real professional butcher that uses it. Cut too deep, see, and the fellow'll bleed too much, and if he bleeds too much he'll die too soon and you miss all the screaming. Muslims, they got some good butchers – not of swine, mind you, they don't eat swine, but of sheeps and lambs, they eat plenty of sheeps and lambs, just dipping the old right hand into the communal stewpot, never the left because that's the one they use to wipe their – git your *left hand* off'n me! They eat plenty of sheeps, the eyes and the testicles being the delicacies. His testicles. That's how far they flayed Marcantonio Bragadino before he give up the ghost, peeling the skin off in one unbroken sheet, him not exactly quiet about what they are doing to him, until the knife reaches his groin, and that's when he dies, after which it is not the same, they are just skinning a carcass of meat. Git your hands off'n *me*, I'm almost through, can't you Venetian jellyfish tell when a person's almost through? Well, they stuff him, stuff his skin I mean because there ain't no *him* no more, strictly speaking, stuff the skin with straw, and when they finish, that straw man looks just like poor Marcantonio Bragadino again, minus the ears and nose o'course. Well, they hang the straw Marcantonio Bragadino from the mainmast of this Ali Pasha's flagship, and from that little boat of mine I seen it sailing up the coast, drums and cymbals banging away, pipes tooting, clappers sounding like gunfire, and that straw Marcantonio Bragadino dangling from the mast, twisting in the wind . . . Which is what I come here to say. Time was I mighta said it was God sent me straight to a Venetian warship, but what I seen, it took God right outa me, so I can't say who made you fish me from the water, but now at least you know what you gotta do if you don't want Venice to be next, or even the Pope in Rome, not that I give a flying fish's fart for the Pope in Rome, not no more . . . You in the brown robe! I said *git your hands off'n me*!

(*Dies*)

VIII

· Lepanto!

I lie on my plank without moving, harbouring the foolish notion that if I don't, the chill won't grab me. Which it has, every second day for – what? Ten days? The chill, followed by the fever and the sweating. *Mal aria*, bad air – Holy Virgin, I think, waiting absolutely still, if bad air is the cause of the disease, what better place to catch it than the foetid overcrowded hold of a war galley? But maybe the chill won't grab me. If I don't move.

It is due. How I know, I've been counting the changes of the galley's watch – Genoese galley *Marquesa*, Venetian wing of the fleet, Captain Sancto Pietro commanding, with Spanish infantry under Captain Diego de Urbina. Rodrigo comes every morning about this time. Brings salted fish, chick peas, sometimes a slab of good Manchego cheese. But this morning there's no Rodrigo.

Mal aria. Holy Virgin! Stink of bodies, of slop buckets. Stink of vomit, urine, faeces. Verminous blankets. Putrefying flesh. Does Hell, I wonder, smell like this?

The first chill grabs me and shakes me hard, the way a terrier shakes a rat to break its neck. Through the shaking I see in the darkness the eyes of a rat, one of the bold and numerous rats that share our hold, and as the next chill grabs me, in my mind I see a terrier (black and white spotted), and he has by the scruff of the neck a fat rat which he shakes as the chill shakes me, and the rat squeals and with a final shake (another chill), the terrier releases the corpse and barks excitedly, and the barking in my mind becomes the voice of my radiant-eyed brother saying *Oh, the glory . . .* and I see a ship of gold and on its forecastle in his golden armour Don Juan the Bastard of Austria.

Bastards and conversos are never brave.

No boatswain's stroke to be heard now, no rush of water past the hull. Except for the moaning in the darkness around me, silence. Then a thump, as if a small boat has come alongside. An abrupt shrill of pipes and an enormous cheer of '*Long Live the Prince!*' as boots march across the deck. More silence, and the fever comes at me, and I am instantly drenched with sweat. The piping again, and the boots, and again '*¡Viva el Principe!*' Then the rhythmic thud-thud-thud of the boatswain's mallet, and *Marquesa*'s banks of oars dip and pull, and soon she is juddering along on manpower, not sail, faster and faster.

Oh, the glory . . .

I find my padded leather jerkin, shrug into it, buckle up. Wobbly, I head in the general direction of the forecastle hatch. Rung by slow rung I climb. Light stabs my eyes. *Marquesa* is surging ahead through a moderate sea, oarsmen in dreadful toiling unison, boatswain's mallet echoing inside my head.

'Where's my gun? I want a gun!'

This shouting voice seems to be mine.

I find harquebuses racked near the forecastle companion. I take one. It weighs a ton.

A *gromete* – ordinary seaman – rushes past sprinkling sand from a bucket on to the deck. 'Gangway there!'

I slide-shuffle a few paces aft – into the path of a parrot rolling a gunpowder barrel towards the starboard rail, covered now with heavy leather bulwark.

Everywhere men are shouting, gesticulating, moving things which are aft forward and things which are forward aft. Nothing seems to be where it ought to be. I am no exception. I mean, I'm *here*, but where's my squad? Where's my squad leader Rodrigo? Something falls on my head, reminding me I am helmetless. I look down to see a pine cone at my feet, look up to see a parrot making his way out along a spar with a net of what look like earthenware pots. They look like pots, I tell myself, the fever coming in waves now, because they are pots – *piñatas*, potfuls of pine cones that will be ignited and hurled at the rigging of Turkish ships.

I start forward in my uncertain, boneless gait, for there seems to be a commotion up at the bow.

The beat of the mallet quickens. A boatswain on the gangway lays his bull-whip across an entire bench of turbaned oarsmen, a virtuoso performance. I quickly look seaward. The great battle fleet which has sailed line-ahead since leaving Messina harbour is now fanning into line-abreast formation, bow waves swirling white, spume flying from oar-blades. Coming through the fan of ships, towed straight ahead by galleys like teams of oxen, I see two of our Venetian galleasses, those floating fortresses with their mighty eighty-pound guns. Ahead, still a long way off, are grey rocky hillsides and a higher smudge of haze-blurred mountains. Between the land and our soon-to-be battle formation, another fleet is fanning out, bow waves swirling, spume flying from oars, a mirror image of us, and really quite beautiful in its sleek and functional deadliness.

A crowd of parrots at the bow, portside, is glaring at a crowd of *grometes* to starboard, who glare back, no love lost between army and navy. Between the hostile groups stand the Genoese ship captain Francesco Sancto Pietro and the Spanish infantry captain Diego de Urbina. The scene suggests a medieval battlefield in miniature, with the parrots and *grometes* the contending armies, and Sancto Pietro and Urbina their champions who will decide the issue, whatever the issue is, in single combat.

Sancto Pietro, arms going like signal flags, voice rising almost to falsetto, shouts, 'Nobody is going to saw off *my* battering ram!'

'It was an order, Captain. From the Prince himself.' Urbina with his resonant bass voice has no need to shout.

'He's a Spaniard, the Prince, and he's a bastard, the Prince, and she's a Genoese ship, *Marquesa*, and I'm a Genoese captain, me,' shrills Sancto Pietro.

'The Prince gave you a direct order, Captain.'

'I shit on Spanish orders! My ship! With no ram! Emasculation! Cut off my balls, why not, eh – eh? With no ram, what's to stop a Turk galley from splintering us into flotsam? Jetsam?'

'Artillery,' says Urbina in his resonant voice. 'With the ram off – you know the design of these ships as well as I do – we'll be less buoyant forward. And with the bow riding lower, our forward artillery can fire a flatter trajectory point-blank into the hull of any heathen ship that crosses our bow.'

'Nobody,' cries Sancto Pietro, 'is going to saw off *my* battering ram.'

For the first time I see, at the very prow of *Marquesa*, two ship's carpenters roped up and waiting to go over the side with one of those long two-handled saws.

Urbina gestures to seaward. Several battering rams, already sawn off Christian galleys, bob on the swells.

'Spanish galleys,' scorns Sancto Pietro. 'Show me a Genoese ram.'

'How can you tell?'

'Me, I can tell, that's how. Show me a Venetian ram. Show me a Papal ram. My ship, you will not emasculate her.'

Urbina gives a quick nod towards the crowd of parrots, which parts to reveal my brother Rodrigo down on one knee with his harquebus aimed straight at Sancto Pietro.

'You have ten seconds, Captain,' says Urbina calmly. 'If in that time your carpenters haven't begun removing the ram, you will be shot dead.'

Every pair of eyes except Urbina's is on the smouldering serpentine in my brother's left hand. The boatswain's mallet thuds, water gurgles in the scuppers, the bow rides high on a swell. Flame spouts through a billow of smoke at the prow of the nearest galleass, and a moment later the roar of an eighty-pounder is heard, the first shot of the battle we veterans will always call 'The Naval'.

'Seven,' counts Urbina. 'Eight.'

And Sancto Pietro screams, 'Saw it off, cut off our balls, emasculate Italy, emasculate the Pope!'

And the carpenters go to work.

'What the hell are you doing here?' This is Rodrigo.

'Me?' I say.

But by now it isn't just me. Several indescribably filthy, unbelievably smelly, half-clad, fever-flushed, boneless-legged spectres dragging harquebuses are making their unsteady way forward to where most of us parrots are cheering the removal of *Marquesa*'s ram. Whether it is a good thing we have no idea, but it represents a victory for our captain.

As these *inválidos* approach, I feel a sense of guilt. Are they following my own foolish example? But of what use will they be in battle?

'Get back below,' Rodrigo tells me.

But I can almost hear the Old Cypriot telling us what he had to, and only then allowing himself the luxury of dying. And if he had a tale to tell, haven't I a battle to fight? Hasn't every man a battle to fight in this life? And at the end of it a death to die, win or lose?

Bastards and conversos are never brave.

'You're going below if I have to drag you,' says Rodrigo, grasping my shoulder.

'Get your hands off me,' I shout. More a snarl.

Rodrigo pulls back.

I try a change of subject. 'Would you have killed him?'

My brother's eyes widen. 'What kind of dumb question is that? Of course I'd have killed him. Come on, I don't have all day.'

I shake my head. Sweat is streaming down my face, collecting under my padded leather jerkin.

'Get your hands off me!' Even more of a snarl. Rodrigo is using both hands now: he intends to carry me bodily.

Just then Urbina booms, 'Cervantes!' and we both turn.

He means me. 'Take these other invalids to the skiff. You're all crazy, but if you want to fight, you'll fight from there.'

'Emasculated!' cries Sancto Pietro as the drenched carpenters reappear on deck and *Marquesa*'s severed battering ram goes bobbing and banging aft along the hull.

Now that Urbina has given me an order, my brother Rodrigo is a changed man. 'I'll see that you have all the shot you need, and an extra keg of powder.'

He helps my squad of ten invalids up into the skiff. As I'm about to follow, he says, 'Not the safest position aboard. Higher even than the castles, exposed to fire. Plus, it's where enemy ships ram if they can – amidships.'

'Where will you be?' I ask, and watch with morbid fascination the line of Turkish galleys racing towards us.

This, from the look on my brother's face, is another dumb question. 'With the assault troops in the prow, naturally.'

His hand reaches out then and I feel a tug at my neck. For a moment he holds the one-handed toy soldier he gave me the night I left Madrid. 'Still wearing this, are you?' he asks, gruffly fond, before marching off to leave me in charge of my first and only military command.

My *inválidos* look at me expectantly. What they expect are orders. But I have none to give. So I pat a few backs and recite platitudes about Spain,

Santiago, Christ, God, of the sort that could fuel a Lope de Vega play for three acts and which now, with the enemy's swift approach, sound in my own ears less like platitudes and more like timeless moral truths temporarily true.

With the enemy's swift approach, something else sounds in my ears, an ululating 'Lelilii! Le-li-liii! LE-LI-LIIII!' – the blood-chilling Muslim battlecry.

A flash, and a puff of smoke from the galleass nearest shore, followed by a peal of thunder as she looses a salvo from her forward guns, those mighty eighty-pounders – and a Turk galley drops from the advancing line and goes precipitately down stern-first. Woefully premature shouts of 'Victory!' drown out that ululating Turk battlecry. My inválidos wave their harquebuses aloft in triumph, so I leave off my own shouting to manhandle them back into position, guns to seaward. By now both formations are dissolving as ship seeks ship in single combat, and I have just time to bawl, 'Light your goddam serpentines, you dumb fuck-ups!' sounding surprisingly like my brother Rodrigo on Vomero hill, when a shadow rushes at us and, yes, I tell myself with some degree of belief, that seems to be the prow of a galley about to ram us right here amidships. Turbaned assault troops crowd her prow, pikes and scimitars flash in the sun. I feel the kick of my harquebus just as one of my men falls, head crushed lopsided by the heavy iron fluke of a grappling hook which rocks the skiff before its line falls slack and the man I have shot tumbles from the passing Turk prow into the sea. Wood splinters somewhere further aft, oars snap, hulls collide. That whooshing sound is arrows, probably poison-tipped, and that fiery trail a piñata hurtling overhead as I load powder, wad, bullet, and again the harquebus kicks and we are so close, hull to hull, grappling hooks hurled both ways now, that I can see a Turk face explode to splatter me with blood, the blood of the second man I have killed, and, reloading once more, I look up to see a harquebus muzzle staring at me like an eye, a single eye, Princess Eboli I think giddily, and the eye winks redly as something smashes me flat on to a thwart and I spring right up to find my padded jerkin pierced by a roundball that has bruised or broken a rib or two, explaining why it is suddenly, strangely, frighteningly difficult to breathe, which may or may not be as important as the flames in the sails overhead or the inválido taking a swipe at me with a scimitar, which I parry with my harquebus as it dawns on me that the man beside me in the skiff is not one of my invalids at all but a turbaned Turk with fierce moustaches whose head I smash with my gun butt while one of us, possibly me, screams in . . . fear? exaltation?

Boarding lines fall away, decks swerve apart, our forward guns roar, a galley driving for us head-on becomes a torch and passes narrowly to starboard. Three of my *inválidos* are dead, three more including myself wounded. Gingerly I touch my chest. Someone cries out as I withdraw my hand and slump against a gunwale, everything spinning spinning spinning until another hull looms with other grappling hooks and other turbaned boarders, and I am hit again, same left side of the chest, and down again I go. Jerkin in tatters. Shirt blood-soaked. Bleeding to death? Where's harquebus? Serpentine still alight, good. Powder into pan, into muzzle, wad, bullet, good. Boarders swarming over bulwarks. Lines to grappling hooks again severed. Turk galley drifts off listing heavily. So this new wave of boarders – ululating, turbaned, scimitared, stranded – can do nothing but take *Marquesa* or perish on her blood-slippery deck. Fighting forward and aft, fighting down among oarsmen leg-ironed to benches, many hanging lifeless over oar-shafts while heathens and Christians run, strike, stab over their scarred sun-blackened backs. Big Turk there, scimitar a whirling blur over his bald turbanless head as he bounds towards forecastle roof where Captain de Urbina and a few parrots are holding off twice as many Turks. Shield pan, aim, caress trigger . . . Flame billows from pan. Harquebus explodes even as I rid myself of it with a frantic pushing motion.

Is that *thing* my left hand?

I collapse. Athwart a thwart. Know now what thwarts are for. How long there, no idea. Open eyes. See Turk face staring unseeing from under turban. See Turk hand death-gripping scimitar hilt. Pry it loose. Can feel blood pumping from own left hand. Whole side of chest numb. Can I stand? Absolutely. Even holding scimitar. *Git your hands off'n me!* Turk hands, under turbaned Turk head, this fellow very much alive. Experimental slash with scimitar. Turk hands leap from Turk wrists. I leap from skiff. Down briefly among oarsmen. Fall? Must have. Mallet goes thud-thud-thud. Some oarsmen miraculously still rowing. Climb out. See men rushing between castles. See desperate effort to keep fires in rigging from reaching powder barrels. See Rodrigo and Urbina at foot of sterncastle ladder. Turks between them and me, more Turks on castle roof. Running now. Me, that is. Left hand still pumping blood, right hand wielding scimitar blindly. Howl like a Turk, '*Lelilii!*' Gripping longsword now, acquired God knows where. Rodrigo closer, helmet gone, brow bloody, eyes slits, gleam of teeth. Above on roof a Turk leaning down, scimitar beginning its pendulum swing to *de*-captivate my brother. Parry, thrust up hard . . . '*Lelilii!*'

And abruptly, here at this point in time, now at this moment in space, a noteworthy occurrence occurs.

As I hack at the dead Turk's body, soon a body no more, deep inside

me something twists, writhes, turns with difficulty like a key in a rusty
lock, to reveal in the darkness behind the door of my soul a blood lust,
a joy, an obscene and terrifying joy in the act of killing, a glimpse into
the underself of the caged beast, the hell-hound, the demon, the ancestral
something lurking in us all – in dreadful euphemism ενθουσιασμος (the
Greeks have a word for it as for all things), not devil but god, 'the god
within' – and this vision, this knowledge of self in the dark chthonic world
behind the unlocked door of my soul, I must escape even as I find another
victim, this one as eager to kill me as I am to kill him, and begin flailing away
with my boathook (an estimable weapon, really) while at the same time I
slam the door on that darkness and rather unmiraculously (or so it feels)
rise out of my body and from a height of a few feet watch myself swinging
that boathook like a battle-axe, dead men piling up while I float higher to
see from the level of the crow's-nest the tiny boathook-swinging me, and
then I am higher still, a bird's view of ships, many ships, hundreds of ships,
of wakes criss-crossing, of battles fought by toys, of capsizings and burnings
and sinkings, and isn't that the Turkish flagship *Sultana* down there, eight,
nine hundred toy warriors fighting back and forth across her deck under
the wind-whipped flag bearing the name of Allah throwing shadows over
the sterncastle, and isn't that Ahmed or Abdul or Ali Pasha, isn't that his
head skewered on a pike, the toy pikeman presenting it to a toy officer in
golden armour who looks quickly away (I can taste the bile in his throat)
and orders the pikeman to throw the grisly thing overboard while I float
back to where *Marquesa* waits with this other grisly thing that used to be
my left hand, dripping blood now as I push through *grometes* and parrots
clamorous in victory to reach the port rail and stare out at spars, masts,
charred timbers, a sodden leather jerkin or two, a quiver with feathered
arrow shafts protruding, and bodies floating face-down, thousands of them,
with the sun blazing overhead – *is it still today?*

The next thing I remember is, I am looking up at the face of *Marquesa*'s
surgeon, a furrow of perplexity between his eyes as he peers first at the
broken-handed toy soldier on its string around my neck, then at what used
to be my left hand.

IX

In Which My Brother and I
Are Rewarded for Our Heroism

On a morning in late November I woke in my assigned position, second from the right, in an overpopulated bed in the Hospital of Our Lady of Charybdis in Messina, Sicily, to see to my left the Jawless Man trying to mount the Pregnant Woman With Leg Crushed By Wagon. The position to my right was empty, the Eyeless Burn having climbed down to use the already overflowing chamberpot between our bed and the next. The Pregnant Woman With Leg Crushed By Wagon whimpered beneath the Jawless Man as, weakly, I tried to roll him off her. This immediately made what used to be my left hand throb with pain. Patients in other beds shouted encouragement to the Jawless Man until a far louder voice thundered, 'Get that dead man out of that bed!'

The voice was my brother Rodrigo's. On his new parrot uniform he wore the silver medal of a *soldado aventajado*, a distinguished soldier. The dead man he referred to was poor Jawless, who must have rolled on to rather than tried to rape the Pregnant Etc. Still, despite Rodrigo's drill-sergeant voice, no one obeyed, so he draped the corpse over his own shoulder and stalked from the dying-in ward, to return dragging by one arm a fat little surgeon who seemed neither willing nor sober.

'While we're at it,' my brother thundered, 'this soldier here is a *soldado aventajado*, same as me' – as he spoke, Rodrigo was pinning a medal to my nightshirt – 'and if you don't get him a bed of his own I'll go straight to the Prince, who looks no more kindly on drunken surgeons than I do.'

Taking a guilty leave of Pregnant Etc. and Eyeless Burn (neither would survive the week), I was carried upstairs to a ward of only thirty one-man beds.

Charybdis hospital at that time still took civilian patients and was staffed by local barber-surgeons – too many, none of whom could be found when needed. Only one agreed with *Marquesa*'s surgeon that my fever came from *mal aria*. Another said it was hospital fever, meaning merely that patients who didn't arrive with a fever usually caught one. A third blamed it on

101

what used to be my left hand. This was swollen almost shapeless, was bright red, and oozed blood and pus and, occasionally, small particles of lead. The deep gouges on the left side of my chest seemed to be healing. Those oozed only good, healthy pus.

Rodrigo wangled daily passes from Captain de Urbina so that he could visit me. He brought food – fresh fruit, fresh-cooked fish, fresh goat's cheese – and strong red wine.

One morning he said, 'The Prince arrived today.'

'I thought he was here when you got me moved upstairs.'

My brother's face was innocent. 'Why, no. But he is today – and so is a surgeon-general who's to turn this place into a military hospital, so let's hope you'll get some decent care. Especially since I'll be gone a while.'

This alarmed me. 'Why?'

'Orders. I never ask why. Here, this ought to help.' It was a purse bulging with coins.

I began to protest.

'They're yours, three *escudos* a month bonus as *aventajado*. Plus all your back pay. Buy food, Miguel. What they give you here is garbage, and it'll get worse when the military take over. And stop trying to feed the whole ward.'

'They'd do the same for me.'

'The hell they would. Nobody here's bucking for sainthood but you. Dragging yourself around dressing wounds and things. Think I wouldn't find out?'

'I was Papá's apprentice,' I said. 'It's the least I can do.'

'Papá. Funny, I never think of him as a surgeon. A barber, he'll always be a barber to me.'

'Watch the surgeons around here and you'd realize he wasn't such a bad surgeon.'

'Maybe,' said my far-from-convinced brother. 'But if you keep it up, how will *you* get well? You're still not out of danger, you know.'

A few days later the new surgeon-general made his first rounds. With a large, dirty thumb he poked what used to be my left hand. I stifled a cry, but still he said, 'Amputate. First thing in the morning. At the elbow. Or perhaps at the shoulder.'

Even if he just took off the hand I would probably die. Amputation sent the mortality rate in military hospitals soaring.

'. . . but . . .' I said, sounding rather like my father in one of his moments of laconic astuteness.

'First thing in the morning,' said the surgeon-general. 'I always amputate first thing in the morning.'

Before dawn the next day I was at the dispensary, a dark cubby on the ground floor that smelled of turpentine and resounded with snoring. A jowly bloodshot face peered out when I knocked. 'Ain't open,' it growled.

I clinked my bag of coins. 'Clean cloth,' I said, 'beeswax, rosewater and hypericum oil.'

Fingers grabbed what used to be my left hand. I did not bother to stifle my cry of pain.

'What I figured,' said the new military dispenser of the new military hospital. 'They told me about you. The Maimed Hand. Thinks he's a surgeon.'

'I'll pay for the beeswax and all.'

'Sure you will, friend. But we ain't got no beeswax. We got eggs. White or yolk, take your pick.'

'White then. I'll be wanting supplies first thing every morning.'

I paid – double what the civilian dispenser had charged – and began my unofficial rounds.

That morning, as I moved from bed to bed, the story I told was how Luis the black slave got his freedom. Eyes turned towards me, moans subsided. Every day I tried to tell a different story, something to make my patients laugh. Laughter, my father used to say, was the best medicine. The next morning, after I told the story of how my grandmother Leonor's pet goat ate her wedding dress (remind me to tell you that one some time), I ran into the surgeon-general in an upstairs corridor, his arms bloody to the biceps and an apprentice trailing him with a wicked-looking collection of hammers, saws, knives. I hurried past. Another morning, I told how Rodrigo and his boy-army rescued me the night I rescued Juan the Obscure (I left out the part about how the two gypsies couldn't swim). I was spending so much on bandages, egg whites, rosewater and hypericum oil that I couldn't spare money for food, so I ate hospital rations, which had deteriorated as Rodrigo predicted.

The fifth morning, I encountered the surgeon-general again, his arms bloody to the armpits. Our eyes met. His narrowed, but he carried on down the corridor. A few mornings later he gave me a blood-spraying nod and almost smiled. Two weeks after he'd said he would amputate, we collided outside the dispensary. 'Morning, colleague,' he said, 'up early as usual, eh?' and we smiled our separate smiles and went our separate ways. He left bloody footprints.

The next time I saw him he was in spotless white, entering our ward at midday in the wake of Don Juan the Bastard Prince of Austria.

Don Juan – called His Excellency, you'll remember, not His Highness; he shared with King Felipe II the Death-Loving a royal sire (Charles V and I) but had unpardonably chosen a Viennese dancing girl for a mother – was a handsome man of my age, with pale blue eyes and hair almost the colour of my sister Andrea's wheaten mane.

The bloodless surgeon-general, a Capuchin chaplain and a single adjutant made up Don Juan's modest entourage.

'Where are you from, soldier?' – the time-tested common-touch question from commander to trooper.

'Th-that's hard for me to s-say, Highness.'

'Don't be nervous.' An easy smile. Don Juan was then at the apogee of his curve, though neither of us knew that.

Meanwhile the surgeon-general was studying my face.

'I'm n-not. It's j-just the way I talk. What I mean is, I'm from all over Spain. My family moved a lot.'

'*Aventajado*, I see.'

Then he saw what used to be my left hand, which I had been trying to hide from the surgeon-general by covering it with my right.

'Shouldn't that come off?' he asked the surgeon-general, in whose eyes I saw dawning recognition.

I stopped breathing.

'During my short time here, Excellency, I have already removed every life-threatening arm, leg, hand or foot left in place by the negligence of the civilian staff,' said the surgeon-general in a professional huff. 'And I'm pleased to report that only seven out of ten of the three out of ten who have so far survived the amputations remain in critical condition.'

'But this *soldado aventajado*?'

'Intact to the extent that he is, he has his uses as a sort of apprentice surgeon's assistant apprentice.'

I resumed breathing.

'We veterans of The Naval,' the Prince told me, 'will always have a bond. Are you making the military your career?'

Mutely I raised for his closer inspection what used to be my left hand.

'Yes, well,' he said. 'For now, you'll draw pay as an apprentice surgeon. But later? Would you perhaps like a place at court? I am not entirely without influence.'

But how could I forget my first, and last, disastrous few minutes on Liars' Walk? 'I wouldn't make much of a courtier, Highness.'

'Then what will you do with your life, soldier?'

Here a pause as I pictured a ward at dawn, the stronger patients sitting on the edges of the nearby beds and the others listening from where they lay, as I said, '. . . and then my sister – you have to remember we were very young at the time – told me, "Hit him Miguel," and I looked at this huge oaf twice my size, this disaster of a *picapedrero* who'd insulted Andrea, who happens to be the most beautiful girl in all Andalucía with her luminous blue eyes and her numinous walk and . . .' I remembered their rapt silence as I described the beauty of my sister Andrea and then resumed, to a chorus of encouragement, the tale of how I'd more or less accidentally beaten up the hulking Tomás Gutiérrez – a tale I interrupted with occasional digressions that provoked protests of 'But what happened?' or 'Go on with the story!' – closing with Juan Rufo's observation that the best of friendships, not to mention romances, often begin with a little altercation to clear the air (a message, I like to think, that even Lope de Vega would have approved).

Then what will you do with your life, soldier?

Tell stories, Highness, I might have said. But was that any way for a grown man to spend his life?

Literature, I might have said. But could I presume to cast my lot with Virgil, Dante, Boccaccio?

And if I had, Don Juan of Austria might have said, Literati are notoriously ill-paid; I still ought to do something for you.

But none of this happened. Instead I admitted, 'I don't know, Highness.'

'Well, you're young yet,' he said, which made me think: We're the same age and *he's* a *generalísimo*. But then, even if he was a bastard, his father'd been King of Spain, not to mention Holy Roman Emperor.

He told the adjutant to take my name.

'And my brother's name is Rodrigo,' I said quickly. 'He's *aventajado* too, and a far better soldier.'

In April I was released from the hospital, undernourished but relatively fit except for what used to be my left hand. It had shrivelled and was unresponsive to any plans I might have for it, sometimes manifesting a life of its own, quivering or jumping without warning.

Back in uniform, I served a period in garrison on the primitive island of Sardinia and a tour of sea duty as an apprentice surgeon in Don Juan's expedition to the Dragoniere Islands (where we skirmished with a Muslim fleet of green-timbered galleys whose terrified infantry, we heard, had to be whipped aboard). In time I learned a way of standing with what used to be my left hand behind my back, giving me a thoughtful, almost pedagogic, look. I ran into a streak of bad luck playing hundred-points in a Naples tavern, made worse when what used to be my left hand suddenly jerked, spilling face-up the only good cards I'd been dealt. '*Sinistra, sinistra!*' cried the Italians around the table when they realized the hand had its own perverse will. Penniless, I had to join the faded parrots begging (non-*aventajados* received no regular salaries in peacetime) on the Calle Toledo. Rodrigo, assigned to a different regiment, was always at sea when I was ashore, and vice versa.

I began to write poetry again. Such as:

> Love, you have raised me to such dizzying heights,
> Tumble me not into dark, remorseless depths.

Holy Virgin! I'll subject you to no more – but it does indicate why, when I had some leave time, I crossed the bay and returned to Sorrento.

. . . *ask for Cornelia Tasso; everyone there knows her.*

I asked a young fisherman in a red Phrygian cap, but instead of pointing to where a goat path rose steeply through a lemon grove, he dropped his net and ran away along the beach.

I asked bronzed, half-naked boys stealing lemons, but instead of pointing upwards to where myrtle once flowered, they bolted down the goat path crying, '*Diavolo! Diavolo!*'

Undaunted if surprised, I asked a toothless old goatherd, but instead of pointing to a distant crag where perched a tiny white cube that might have been a cottage, he made the sign to ward off the evil eye and chased his goats downhill, their heavy udders swinging as they ran.

Through a blighted garden, its exotic blooms withered and dying, I made my way, the smell of decay and lost dreams poisoning the air. Was ever a landscape so desolate – Dantesque almost? While gulls screamed in mockery overhead I kicked in the locked door of the cottage. Beyond the back door I followed a nightmare path thickly overgrown with weeds to a stagnant, evil-smelling stream. There at the edge of the foul water I found a rag doll, which I fondled for a moment, remembering what could never be again, and perhaps, I thought in fatalistic recognition of the uncertainty of life, had never been.

I returned to the now roofless cottage carrying the rag doll, sank on to the bed near the cold hearth, and slept the sleep of despair. When I awoke, a familiar voice said, 'I wondered how long you'd take to return.'

I looked into the plump, pink, youthful face of my Cousin Gaspar. He was twirling a cardinal's red biretta on one finger.

'Do you know where she is?' I cried.

'Now that you mention it, I don't. A Certain Mutual Acquaintance found it necessary to vanish her.'

I thought I had misheard. 'Banish her?'

'Vanish. With a V. Believe me, there's a world of difference.'

'Where have you taken her?'

'Nowhere. She isn't. She never was.

I held up the rag doll. 'Tell me she had no daughter Constanza. I mean Costanza.'

'Ah, but if the mother never existed . . .' With this ellipsis, he gave me a sardonic look that exactly suited his plump, pink, youthful face. 'You see, my dear cousin, if you were to canvass the inhabitants of Sorrento, no one, not a fisherman in a red Phrygian cap or a bronzed boy or a toothless goatherd, would have heard of her. No one.'

'But if . . . why would . . .'

With this ellipsis, I drew a grudging look of pity. 'Suffice it to say, Cornelia knew too much about your role in the confessions of Torquato Tasso.'

'*My* role? But I . . . we were only . . .'

'Stop ellipsizing, it makes me nervous. That's one reason I've retired from the profession. Now, tell me about the Battle of the Dragoniere Islands.'

Surprised, I said, 'There *was* no Battle of the Dragoniere Islands. Anyway, I thought you retired.'

'I am retiring slowly, a little at a time,' he said, twirling his biretta again.

'That's real? You're a cardinal?'

'So it would seem.' A smile lit his plump, pink, youthful face. 'Speaking of cardinals, it might interest you to know that Giulio Cardinal Acquaviva has departed this world.'

'Vanished?'

'Hardly. One cannot simply "vanish" a prince of the Church. As is usual in such cases, he died in his sleep. Poor fellow. Such a young man.' The smile faded. 'Now, about the Dragoniere Islands. What happened?'

I studied the plump, pink, now expectant face and pondered what went on behind it. Cousin Gaspar commanded limitless resources – he had power over the collective memory of a whole town, power over the creation and demise of cardinals – yet his appetite for minutiae, even concerning a minor naval skirmish, seemed insatiable.

Was knowledge, I couldn't help wondering, power?

I said, 'We had the Turks outgunned and outmanned. But when the wind shifted, our oar-propelled galleys and sail powered galleons got tangled up. So the Turks got away.'

As I spoke, I was pleased to see Cousin Gaspar taking notes.

'Lepanto marked the end of oar-propelled naval warfare. The next great battle,' I predicted, 'will be fought by sailing ships attacking each other broadside.'

'. . . galleons . . . broadside . . . A Certain Mutual Acquaintance will have much to digest, thanks to you.'

Heartened, I waited for some sign that I might be invited into the secret world of power I had as yet only glimpsed. But Cousin Gaspar merely said, 'We'll be in touch. Some time.'

He watched me leave through the blighted garden where once ruby-wingèd birds had sung. I still had the feeling he was watching when I boarded the boat for Naples.

My brother Rodrigo was pacing the dock when I got there.

'*Hombre*,' he cried, 'you almost missed the boat.'

'I was lucky,' I said as we pounded each other's backs. 'She left Sorrento late.'

'Not this tub,' he said. 'I mean the galley *Sol*.'

'No! We're finally pulling sea duty together?'

We stood grinning at each other. More than three years had passed since Rodrigo had left me to fend for myself at the hospital.

'Did they chop your hand off?' he asked.

I brought what used to be my left hand from behind my back. 'N-no,' I said.

'Let's have a look.' And, when he had, 'Seen worse. But it'll end your military career as soon as we get home.'

'Home? We're going back to Spain?'

What used to be my left hand jumped. My first thought was how hideous Andrea would find it.

'Man,' Rodrigo was saying, 'why didn't you tell me you were a favourite of the Prince? I dropped in at the palace in Salerno for the usual adjutant's letter of commendation, but when I gave my name Don Juan himself received me. Remembered you well – "that half-dead young hero who dragged himself around the wards helping others". Incorrigible!' said Rodrigo with one of those grins in which his freckles participated, and waved two sealed letters. 'Recommendations from the Prince to his royal brother. It will mean a commission for me and God knows what for you. Let's get your gear.'

On *Sol*'s maindeck grumbling veterans, many of them disabled, were packed aboard like herring in a barrel. As we made our way aft looking for a square yard of planking to claim for ourselves, a voice rang out.

'Miguel! *Dios mío*, Miguel de Cervantes!'

Tall, ramrod straight in a parrot uniform marginally less rainbow-hued than my brother's, right hand hovering over his rapier and a (probably cultivated) look of eagles in eyes narrowed from years of staring into the offing . . .

'Juan Rufo!' I shouted.

'What do you hear from Andrea?' he shouted back as we pushed through the crowds and met near the sterncastle.

'The last time I saw Andrea,' I said, 'was a few hours after you took me to Liars' Walk.'

Crestfallen, 'I thought maybe you'd heard something more recent than what Tomás Gutiérrez wrote six months ago.'

Meanwhile Rodrigo was asking, 'How long have you been here in Italy?'

'Since before Lepanto. I fought in The Naval.'

'But so did we!'

'It was a big battle,' said Juan Rufo impatiently, and returned to the subject closest to his, and not only his, heart. 'Then you've heard nothing? Not even out here, about this Figueroa who died a hero in The Naval?'

Blank looks from Rodrigo and me.

'Maybe I'd better start with the easy part,' Juan Rufo decided. 'It seems your younger sister Magdalena – who styles herself Señora Magdalena Pimentel de Sotomayor, according to Tomás – '

'She's married?' Rodrigo and I chorused.

'No. It's just the name she goes by. It seems she's still in litigation with the Pacheco Portocarrero brothers, one of whom is a known killer. Frankly, I'm worried, because Andrea, loyal sister that she is, is helping this Pimentel de Sotomayor slut – I mean, your sister Magdalena – when she has time.' Some throat-clearing here. 'Which isn't often. Also, thanks to this Picapleitos fellow's outrageous fees, your family is in dire financial straits.'

'What's taking up Andrea's time?' I asked, forgetting the family's dire financial straits for the moment.

'It's why I asked about this Figueroa. It seems that last year Nicolás de Ovando, with whom Andrea had, uh, well, that is – '

'He's postmature little Constanza's father,' I snapped out. 'What about him?'

'He sent somebody to the tall stone house near the Gate of the Sun – probably Pedro (Killer) Pacheco Portocarrero – to kidnap the child. Ovando's had her ever since. Andrea went right to this Picapleitos fellow, and your family's legal expenses immediately doubled.'

'You mean,' I cried, 'there's some chance Ovando will win custody of postmature little Constanza?'

'If he can prove in court he's, uh, well, that is – '

'The father,' Rodrigo supplied.

'Which is where this dead hero Figueroa comes in. Andrea claims *he* was, uh, well, that is – '

'The father,' Rodrigo resupplied.

'So that's where it stands. And this Picapleitos fellow is not particularly confident of the outcome.'

Sol sailed in convoy with the galleys *Mendoza*, *Higuera* and a third whose name is unrecorded in history, and which I forget. Unlike *Sol*, the other vessels were not overloaded. Our captain employed oars, sails and prayer in an attempt to keep them in sight, but by midnight of 26 September – this was in 1575, for those to whom dates matter – their stern lights had vanished. At dawn *Sol* was beating laboriously along the French coast as we sat down uneasily to a meal of *mazamorra*. Mark this well: so adverse had been the winds and so overcrowded was our ship that we had run out of cheese, fish, chick-peas and the like, and were reduced to this oddly named substance. And what was *mazamorra* but crumbled hardtack fried with garlic in rancid olive oil – the hated *migas* of my youth, the crumbs I'd been forced to eat or risk being kidnapped by Barbary pirates. And did I eat my *mazamorra* on the morning of 27 September? I did not. I sat back against an empty salt-cod barrel watching the others eat while I picked moodily at a particle of lead emerging from what used to be my left hand.

A cry came from the crow's-nest. 'Sails!'

Some optimist said, 'I knew they'd come back for us.'

But as the three ships closed with us, sleek and small and fast, one fired a warning shot.

Grappling hooks and *piñatas* were hurled, *Sol*'s hull shuddered, her canvas caught fire, pirates swarmed aboard. In a few minutes the battle had ended and *aventajados* were frantically getting rid of their silver medals – except for Rodrigo and me. 'Let them know what kind of soldiers we are,' my brother said, freckles bold against his pale face.

'You're crazy,' said Juan Rufo. 'They'll put a higher price on you. Get rid of those letters from the Prince too, they're even more dangerous than your medals.'

But Rodrigo would have none of it. 'They'll stand us in good stead,' he insisted.

An oriental carpet was unrolled amidships and a portly personage boarded.

He wore an aquamarine turban and tunic, a yellow scarf that streamed behind him in the wind, and a richly tooled leather shoulder strap that held his scimitar. He had a dark, curly beard and walked with a limp.

'It's Gimp the Greek,' whispered a soldier near us.

Most Barbary pirate captains or *re'is* were renegades, converts to Islam who bent over backwards to show cruelty towards their former coreligionists in order to avoid any suspicion of apostasy, which under Islamic law was punishable by death. Gimp the Greek, back in Salonika, had buggered and strangled one of the Metropolitan's acolytes before fleeing the Christian world.

Now he limped in our direction and, with an expressionless face and a swing of his scimitar, struck the head off the soldier who had whispered his cognomen.

'I am Dalí Mamí,' he said calmly as the headless body fell to the deck and the head into the sea. 'You will call me "Captain" or "sir" until we are ashore in Algiers, when, if you remain my property, you will call me "master" or . . . what happened to your hand?'

Morbidly staring at the blood still pumping from the neck of the headless body, I did not realize I had been addressed until Gimp the Greek took a step towards me and his scimitar flashed in a second backswing.

Rodrigo's face was so pale that all you could see were eyes and freckles.

'A b-battle wound,' I said. 'Lepanto. Sir.'

Deftly employing the flat of his scimitar, Gimp the Greek brought what used to be my left hand closer to his face for inspection. 'Maimed, you are of little use to anyone,' he said. 'Has your family money?'

What should I have said? Yes? No? Maybe? Would my life depend on my answer?

'They are poor, sir, but I am a surgeon.'

I spoke Spanish; Gimp the Greek was speaking the lingua franca I would hear everywhere in Algiers – a mixture of my own language with Italian and some Arabic.

Whether my answer had been wise I did not then learn, for Gimp the Greek turned and spoke to a lean, dark man with a Princess Eboli eye-patch, who shouted, 'All prisoners, form ranks! All prisoners, strip!'

Which we did, in a cold morning wind. Clothing was minutely examined, the size and quantity of Christian lice commented on, orders and other papers read.

'Open mouth! Tongue up! Turn! Bend! Spread cheeks! Wider! By Allah, you Christians stink like pig shit! Well, what have we here? A medal. Next!'

Before our turn came for this ignominy, Gimp the Greek called my brother's name and mine.

'You with the hand! You're which one?'

'Miguel. Sir.'

' "To His Royal Highness Don Felipe II, King of Castilla, León, Aragon, Flanders, Naples, Sicily 1 & 2 etc. etc. . . . from his most humble servant and affectionate brother . . . honour to present with highest commendation Don Miguel de Cervantes . . . bravery . . . skilled surgeon . . . outstanding display of – " What? What the hell does "benevolent machismo" mean?'

'I don't know. Sir.'

I didn't. But the words had a fine heroic ring, like something out of *Amadis of Gaul.*

'Jesus Christ – I mean, by Allah! Maimed hand or no, you're valuable.'

And Gimp the Greek scribbled the numeral '1' with a lot of zeroes after it.

'*Aventajado* too,' pointed out the man with the Princess Eboli eye-patch.

Two or three more zeroes were added.

I gave Rodrigo a reproachful look; I couldn't help it. With barely moving lips he muttered a stubborn, 'You'll see.'

An hour later, as the swift corsair ships raced south, we captives already were weighted down with leg irons.

X

In Which I Become a Slave in Algiers
And Meet Cide Hamete Benengeli
On His Deathmat

The softening-up process, though I did not recognize it as such, began the minute we reached Algiers.

As we clanked ashore, naked except for our leg irons, veiled, black-swathed women in their thousands mocked us, reviled us, shook fists, howled imprecations, chantingly railed at the baseness of us uncircumcised pig-dog Christians. If they could have got past the janissaries flanking us as we shuffled up Souk Street towards the dungeons, they would surely have torn us apart.

Urchins darted from behind the janissaries to hurl stones, pelt us with shit scooped from open sewers, jab sharpened sticks at our shackled legs. Upon hapless prisoners who tripped, the janissaries fell at once with their short clubs while the women and children shrieked approval.

From shadowed alleys the occasional face would gaze out in pity — a lipless, noseless or earless horror of a face. Lepers, I told myself, refusing to accept that they were Christian slaves disfigured for some probably unwitting infraction of laws we new slaves had yet to learn.

The higher uphill we toiled, the lower sagged our bodies and our spirits. Except for one man, we might have fallen under the weight of the chains, the women's implacable hatred, the urchins' volleys of stones, the lipless-noseless-earless evidence of our own future. But that one man was everywhere, his own chains clanking as he exhorted us to greater effort, shouting what sounded under the circumstances as much like derision as encouragement, cries of, 'Stand tall, you champions of Castilla and León! You parrots of Don Juan!' No janissary lifted a club against this man, for he eased their task by his quixotic (if I may use the word before I created the character) efforts. This, you'll have guessed, was my brother Rodrigo.

We were soon separated, Rodrigo led off to the royal *bagnio* or prison among those slaves claimed for their high ransom potential by the Dey's appraisers. How Gimp the Greek got to keep me, with my even more impressive letter of commendation, I never learned. Maybe he convinced the Dey's appraisers that what used to be my left hand offset my otherwise considerable value; maybe he bribed them.

A cell. Six feet square, deep beneath the cold earth of ancient Al-Djzaïr. Prisoner weighted with forty or fifty pounds of gratuitous chain, lying in damp, in muck, soon in own filth. Rats, lice, spiders, unidentified crawling objects unseen and unseeable in absolute dark.

Why, I asked myself, why solitary confinement? What have I done but be born (disputably, at that) a Christian?

Why, I asked myself, why why why?

Why was I born?

Why can't I be like Rodrigo who never asks why?

Why do I torment myself with this endless why?

Why! Who was I born – does this trouble anyone? What, where, when, how was I born – do these disturb the sleep? But *why*! That is the suicide's question.

I asked it and no one heard.

Time passed. I no longer reached eagerly for the daily bowl of rancid crumbs shoved through the door, but left it for the rats. More time passed, until at last the keeper entered my cell, torch in hand, and said, 'Your lucky day, slave. You're going outside.'

A tiled room where silent attendants doused me with bucket after bucket of water. A second room where another attendant gave me a pair of rope-soled shoes, underclothes (faintly bloodstained), a black-and-white-striped prisoner's burnous, and a blue hat rather like a sleeping cap – all in various sizes, none my own. Stairs next, circling up to a guard-room manned by two janissaries. One clamped leg irons on me. After the solitary cell, these shackles were freedom. The other janissary intoned, 'Cervantes Saavedra, Miguel de, Christian, property of Captain Dalí Mamí – may Allah reward his virtue – freedom of the city until curfew,' and thrust a paper into my hand, and I went clanking out.

Having stared endlessly into no future, how a man revels in (and is deceived by) the simplest things. Warm autumn sunlight. Whitewashed walls. A door opening on a flower-filled patio. Vendors hawking fruit juices. The decidedly *normal* look (despite turbans and burnouses) of the crowds in the arcaded streets. A city like any other city, I told myself, but ten, twenty times the size of raw, parvenu Madrid. It even had a festive air, as hooded Moorish natives and turbaned Turkish masters streamed noisily towards the harbour.

Did *hajjis* back from Mecca shave their heads, and zealots put their eyes out after beholding the *hajar-al-aswad*, the black stone in the *Kaaba*? Well, Christianity has its tonsured monks and its flagellants bloodying their bared torsos to make their sweethearts swoon. Customs vary, I told myself; far places hold countless wonders. Herodotus wrote of them; so did Sir John Mandeville, including headless men here in Africa (or was it the Orient?) with eyes on their shoulders. Travel broadens.

Did a janissary, accidentally jostled by an old man in a black-and-white burnous like mine, raise his club without breaking stride and drop the luckless slave with blood streaming from his ears, while strolling hand in hand with his partner? Brutish policemen, I told myself, are everywhere. It would be provincial to ascribe anything to the homosexuality of the pair. What is abomination in our world is normal in theirs. Think what Sir John Mandeville's men with eyes on their shoulders would make of heads.

And was the slave auction on this street corner inhuman – nude men and women, the unransomables, pinched and prodded by farmers shopping for field hands, thwacked with sticks to test reflexes, rubbed with spittle and donkey piss to reveal dirt-daubed scars? But Lisbon, I told myself, had a vast slave emporium too.

And what about that man in leg irons outside that tiny shop snipping at a customer's hair and talking his ear off, isn't that Christian slave a barber-surgeon like my father and my almost-self? At the sight my heart jumped. So substantial are the counterfeit wages of even a few hours' freedom that I could see myself taking my place in the life of this city, plying my trade until I was ransomed (conveniently ignoring my perennially impecunious family's inability to pay any ransom, however small).

The festive throngs bore me along to a large plaza open on one side to the harbour where I found myself beside a grizzlehead also in irons and black-and-white stripes.

'What's going on?' I asked.

A stage stood on the harbour side of the plaza, and upon it a maimed slave lay three-quarters spreadeagled, his one hand and two feet tied to stakes. Over him stood a Moor in a blood-red burnous and a black-swathed woman holding a long knife.

'Those are Mahmoud's brother and sister,' said the grizzlehead. 'Are you a simpleton that you do not know?' But then he took in my unkempt hair and beard, and my pallor. 'What dungeon did you just get out of?'

'Gimp the Gr – I mean, Dalí Mamí's.'

'This pair,' explained the grizzlehead, 'had a brother named Mahmoud who was captured years ago and made a galley slave aboard the   I think

115

she was Genoese – warship *Marquesa*. The galley slave Mahmoud collapsed over his oar and was beaten to death by a boatswain. Mahmoud's brother and sister saved up to buy a Christian slave they could retaliate on – a one-armed pauper, unransomable and unfit even for the galleys, so he went cheap. That's him you see staked up there.'

I also saw the grizzlehead glance at what used to be my left hand before returning his attention to the stage.

As the brother produced a whetstone from the folds of his burnous, the crowd erupted in a roar, and from that moment until the end of the retaliation it drowned out all other sound.

The sister sharpened the knife with gentle strokes, almost caresses, and passed it to her brother. The brother with a deft slash cut off the slave's left ear. He tossed it to the crowd and returned the knife to his sister. With an equally deft slash she cut off the slave's right ear. She tossed it to the crowd. The slave jerked convulsively, but the ropes that held him three-quarters spreadeagled were strong. The stump of his left arm pounded the stage like a boated fish.

The brother cut off the slave's nose; he tossed it to the crowd.

With a stick he pried the slave's mouth open and the sister cut out his tongue; she tossed it to the crowd.

The brother leaned over the slave and straightened, on the point of the knife the slave's left eye; he tossed it to the crowd.

The sister leaned over the slave and straightened, on the point of the knife the slave's right eye; she tossed it to the crowd.

The brother ripped away the slave's flimsy garment.

The sister emasculated him.

She studied impassively for a moment what she had removed; she tossed it to the crowd.

The brother slit the slave's throat, and with his sister stepped from the stage.

And then?

And then, if the retaliatory murder had been greeted by cheers and clapping and stamping and whistling, it might have been almost acceptable in all its horror – a death for a death and, though hideous, certainly less so than the ritual carnage at those Church- and Crown-sponsored autos-da-fé still prevalent in Portugal and hardly extinct in Spain. But there were no cheers. Instead, as luck would have it, from the hundred minarets of Algiers muezzins wailed the call to prayer, at which all but us Christian slaves and the few Jews in the crowd prostrated themselves, making it seem as if the gruesome death had been demanded not by revenge but by reverence, like an Aztec priest on a pyramid plucking the still-beating heart from . . .

But let me here say a few words in my defence.

Critics have accused me of certain prejudices, among them a bias against Turks and Moors and their religion. Do you blame me for losing no love on the people who enslaved and intermittently imprisoned me for five years?

Note that I haven't belittled their black stone. Have I pointed out that before AD 200 Maximus Tyrius said idolatrous Arabians worshipped it? This wouldn't be fair-minded. We too venerate questionable objects. Is there a city in Christendom that doesn't boast its piece of the One True Cross?

I have been accused of anti-semitism too, for that matter. 'Effeminate people, infamous and worthless' – so said a character in my play *The Dungeons of Algiers* (unstaged). But this was a character I didn't much like, and I don't think an audience would either.

The accusations of anti-clericalism trouble me more. What, some have asked, is *Don Quixote* but a thinly veiled attack on Holy Mother Church? Holy Virgin, why would I do that?! Am I the sort to harbour resentment, just because a blind bureaucracy excommunicated me? More than once?

As for the accusations of mocking the Spanish empire in its days of glory (*Don Quixote* again), I look at what used to be my left hand and wonder what further proof of patriotism is needed.

No, if Muslims say Adam built the *Kaaba* in thanks for Allah's pardon two hundred years after the expulsion from Eden, and Abraham rebuilt it after the Flood, who am I to argue? They know far more about it than I

Still, the call to prayer coming immediately after that retaliatory dismemberment was unfortunate.

My return long before curfew to Gimp the Greek's palace did not surprise the janissaries in the guard-room. They just said, 'Captain Dalí Mamí awaits you, slave.'

Several teenage male slaves hovered over him as he took his supine ease on a diamond-studded alabaster couch. One was giving him a pedicure, another kneading the doughy flesh of his bare thighs, a third reciting one of the tales of Sindbad the Sailor, a fourth holding a plate of sweetmeats. Gimp the Greek opened his mouth so the boy could feed him. Then he licked the boy's fingers. Then he said, 'Come in, come in, Miguel de Cervantes Saavedra. It is always a pleasure to converse with a rich and cultured man, even if he is a pig-dog Christian.'

I was waved to a bench covered in red-dyed camel hide. Gimp the

117

Greek clapped his hands, and four more youths entered bearing a low golden table.

I tried not to stare. But my empty belly rumbled as the aroma of roast lamb filled the room. A mound of couscous (a refined version of *migas*) steamed in a golden basin. Other golden dishes held stewed pigeons, a pilaf rich with dried fruits, a stuffed and baked eel, pungent relishes, pastries dripping with honey.

'Eat, eat!' urged Gimp the Greek, digging his own right hand into the platter of lamb.

Fortunately for me, the right hand is the eating hand in the Muslim world; men are turned into outcasts simply by lopping it off.

I ate. Piggishly, I'm afraid. Even pig-doggishly.

When the golden dishes were cleared away, a boy served persimmon sherbet in golden goblets. Then Gimp the Greek clapped his greasy hands, hot moist towels were brought, and all the slaves but me departed.

'Rich and cultured, yes,' said Gimp the Greek, eructing impressively. 'Not to mention a confidant of Don Juan the Bastard of Austria (may Allah send him the plagues of Job followed by the French pox). Shall we say, if for convenience we drop all those zeroes and talk gold ducats, two thousand?'

My own eructation, compounded by consternation, was even more impressive. 'Two thousand gold ducats?'

'You may call me master,' he reminded me.

'Two thousand gold ducats for what?' I asked. 'Master.' The word stuck in my throat like a fishbone.

'For a rich and cultured gentleman, a confidant of the Bastard of Austria (may Allah shrivel his penis and make all his women barren) and son of a renowned physician – two thousand ducats seems in no way an excessive ransom.'

Gimp the Greek spread a sheet of paper on the low table. 'Sign this, signifying your agreement to the magnanimous terms, and you'll have the freedom of the city – in leg irons, unfortunately, but I don't make the rules – until the ransom is paid.'

'The only time I met Don Juan of Austria,' I said, 'I was flat on my back in a hospital bed. My father's no physician but a common barber-surgeon who's never been out of debt in his life.'

'Then if two thousand gold ducats is a bit high, what value *do* you place on your freedom?'

I wondered suddenly if, at that very moment, my brother Rodrigo was being inflated to a military advisor to King Felipe II the Death-Loving in the rhetoric of *his* master the Dey. Was he bargaining right now too?

I suggested, 'Fifty ducats,' and hoped the family could somehow borrow that much for each of us.

Expressionless, Gimp the Greek said, 'Don't try my patience. You'd be surprised what people will pay for a maimed Christian slave to retaliate on. Also, it's common knowledge you were chamberlain to His Unholiness Fra Michele dell'Inquisizione, otherwise known as Pius V (may his ostensibly unused sexual organ precede him to Hell).'

I said I had briefly been second assistant chamberlain to a minor cardinal-to-be, since deceased.

But rhetorically he had made me the Pope's man, and the Pope's man I must be. 'Jesus Christ!' he shouted. 'I mean, by Allah! Surely someone of such worldly *and* churchly experience should be able to reach a simple business arrangement with the master whose only wish is to set him free. Shall we say, one thousand five hundred gold ducats?'

When I shrugged and suggested seventy-five, he called for the janissaries.

So began my second stay in solitary confinement, loaded down with more chains than before. But again, as the first time, a day came when, shackled and black-and-white-burnoused, I went outside. And again, as the first time, a festive crowd bore me to the plaza beside the harbour, where what looked like an exceedingly tall gibbet had been erected. From it a man was suspended in a harness directly above a huge, gleaming hook.

'What's going on?' I asked the same grizzlehead.

'This slave so balked at the ransom demanded by the Albanian renegade *re'is* Arnaute Mamí that in the course of their bargaining he foolishly struck his master. As punishment, he will be received by the hook.'

As the grizzlehead spoke, a man in green axed the rope holding the harness and the slave plunged, the hook catching him under one arm. He hung there, screaming.

'Bad luck,' said the grizzlehead, but I could hardly hear him for the crowd's roar. 'Caught at the throat or the groin, he would have died within an hour. As it is, the poor man is liable to dangle in agony for days.'

I returned quickly to the palace of Dalí Mamí a/k/a Gimp the Greek.

'So, Don Miguel,' he asked after he had gluttonized while I picked at the food, 'you have considered my offer?'

'How can I? My family is poor.'

'Your father is physician to King Felipe the Death-Loving and your sister is director of a school in a tall stone building near the Gate of the Sun — that's poor?'

119

'A school? What kind of school?'

'For one of the oldest and most remunerative of all professions,' Gimp the Greek said, and eructed.

What used to be my left hand jumped twice.

'Such a father and sister, Don Miguel, would have little difficulty raising, shall we say, one thousand three hundred gold ducats.'

'. . . b-b-b . . .'

'Unransomed, with what used to be that left hand of yours, you are of no use to anyone except – '

'I'm a s-surgeon.'

'A surgeon with a useless hand? Please.'

He rose from his couch, limped to me, slung a heavy arm across my shoulders. 'Don't force me to sell you, Miguel. It would pain me. To tell the truth, well, I'm rather fond of you.'

Uneasily I tried to move away, but he pulled me closer.

'A man wearies of pubescent boys,' he said in a hoarse whisper. 'Let me . . . care for you properly. I'll give you beautiful chains of silver and gold.'

What used to be my left hand jumped three times. He caught it in his own hand. 'This isn't at all repugnant, you know. In fact, it makes you seem appealingly helpless.'

My helplessness was real. I felt instant empathy for every woman who has ever been at the mercy of a lecherous man.

'Like a wounded dove. Let me . . . care for you until you're ransomed for, shall we say, one thousand ducats?'

Somewhere an unseen lutenist struck up a melody of love and the air grew fragrant with sandalwood and myrrh. My master's face, now flushed and sweaty, swam close to mine. His lips, greasy from the roast kid he had devoured, approached my lips.

I broke free and backed away. 'Five hundred ducats,' I heard myself saying.

'Done!' he cried with a simper of delight.

'And nobody . . . cares for me but myself.'

He misunderstood. 'Onanism in the dungeon, that I can understand. But here in my palace where I can shower you with undreamed-of delights – do you hate me so?'

The lutenist plucked an intricately seductive melody. Frankincense and jasmine mingled with sandalwood and myrrh – a fourfold olfactory attack I found rather cloying.

Gimp the Greek groped clumsily for my sex.

By a pure effort of will I heard not the lute but the words of the grizzlehead. 'This slave in the course of their bargaining foolishly struck his master.' And I saw not my would-be ravisher but the slave plunging on to the hook. And I told myself: Submit – haven't women always found strength, the strength of survival, in submission? The alternative is the final outrage from which no one ever returns.

While I stood motionless, resigned to letting him have his way with me, what used to be my left hand tingled with a spurious suggestion of life.

Then it levitated, raising the arm attached to it.

Then it struck Gimp the Greek in the face and sent him tumbling asprawl the couch, from which position he bellowed for his janissaries.

Loaded with chains (iron, not silver and gold), I languished again in the dungeon. But as before, a time came when I found myself on Souk Street in my black-and-white burnous following the festive crowd to the plaza beside the harbour, where, on a wooden platform, a naked youth was seated on a small pedestal.

'What's going on?' I asked the same grizzlehead. 'Why is he sitting on that pedestal?'

The grizzlehead gave me the sort of look reserved for mental deficients. 'Pedestal?'

I looked again. The pedestal was becoming shorter.

I felt the blood drain from my face.

'This slave,' the grizzlehead explained, shouting to make himself heard over the roar of the crowd, 'affronted and struck his master, and tried to escape. The punishment for these crimes is impalement. Your "pedestal" is a stake, upon which the fellow has been impaled since dawn.'

The victim by then seemed to be seated on the platform itself.

I turned away, retching drily.

The grizzlehead caught my arm and amazed me by saying, 'Take courage, stall for time, Juan Rufo has been ransomed and sails for Spain during the month of Ramadan.' Then he melted into the crowd.

I returned to Gimp the Greek's palace slightly heartened to know the world had not lost sight of me.

We sat in silence while our feast was spread, the renegade re'is studying me moodily. For the first time, tall janissaries stood impassively on either side of the low golden table while I watched my master eat.

'Sign here,' said Gimp the Greek without eructing.

I looked down at the ransom agreement. The number '500' had been written in before the words 'gold ducats'.

'As you see, Miguelito, I accept your figure.' Despite the diminutive, he said this grumpily.

Five hundred? Five hundred might as well have been all the gold ducats ever minted. But as it was I who had named the figure, what could I do but sign?

This time I caught Gimp the Greek's signal, a slight motion of the beringed little finger of his right hand, which caused the air to fill with seductive lute music and clashing fragrances.

'Meanwhile, we have months to wait, Miguelito. Perhaps years, who can say? Some men enjoy a certain ... asperity in their catamites. I am not one of them. I prefer acquiescence – or rape. So. Which is it to be?'

I pushed away from the low table and stood awkwardly. What used to be my left hand twitched, tingled, prepared (I assumed) to act as it, not I, considered appropriate. But the two janissaries grabbed my arms. In the shadows near the door I thought I saw a lean, dark man with a Princess Eboli eye-patch.

'To the couch with him!' cried Gimp the Greek, and they ran me there with my feet skimming the mosaic floor.

I landed face-down on a smelly gold brocade spread, to the clarion call of a trumpet – surely a vulgar touch, I couldn't help thinking, despite my plight. The doors burst open, the trumpet blasted another three or four peremptory notes, a squad of janissaries in the royal Ottoman green of Ramadan Pasha Dey stormed into the room. Their officer read in clipped tones from a scroll:

' "To the Dey's captains, may Allah fill your sails with a plundering wind, greetings! Be it known that the Dey's esteemed eunuch astrologer lies gravely ill and, unless Allah sends a miracle, will succumb before nightfall. All *re'is* are enjoined to extend medical assistance forthwith." '

'But my physician ran off to Rabat with a dancing girl,' protested Gimp the Greek.

'Noncompliance will earn the usual impalement prescribed for apostates,' said the Dey's officer indifferently.

'But Jesus Chr— I mean, by Allah! I'm no apostate.'

'You're a renegade, which is the same to me. Either send a healer or don't. But stop wasting my time, Dalí Mamí.' No title, just the Greek's renegade name, mouthed scornfully like a pair of four-letter words.

Gimp the Greek's eyes, perhaps in desperation, fell on me.

'While it's true that my physician is vacationing in Rabat,' he told the officer smoothly, 'I can still send my surgeon, Don Miguel de Cervantes

Saavedra, of great renown in the Christian world, formerly first surgeon to the duellists of Liars' Walk in Madrid.'

Which is how it came about that royal janissaries delivered me to the palace of Ramadan Pasha Dey.

A pair of eunuchs led me though corridors and courtyards of terracotta, porphyry and lapis lazuli to the harem with its virginal white marble walls, its richly carpeted floors, its halls crowded with women, all young, all pretty, all fat, all in deshabille – the usual segregation waived for mere eunuchs and a subhuman Christian slave in leg irons.

At last we reached the innermost court where, resting on the backs of four red stone elephants, a fountain spouted, its spray golden in sunlight streaming through a gossamer net, also golden, that stretched above the courtyard to cage doves, swallows and hummingbirds. The mob of lugubrious physicians and surgeons that filled the courtyard took not the slightest interest in any of this.

A hanging beyond the fountain parted and a grey-bearded physician, in black-and-white-striped burnous and leg irons like the rest of us, emerged from a dark alcove carrying a urine-specimen jug. He spilled the few drops it contained into the fountain, muttered 'hopeless!' and took his place among the despairing others.

'You're all Christian slaves,' I said, surprised. 'Aren't there any Moorish physicians and surgeons?'

Rending his garments and tearing his hair, one surgeon explained, 'It is bad form for a Muslim to shed Muslim blood. So we Christian slaves attend to their health needs.'

'But why are you all so distressed? Is this astrologer so beloved?'

'Beloved?' said a physician. 'What's love got to do with it? When he dies – and he will before nightfall – half a dozen of us chosen by lot will be impaled.'

'Which,' the surgeon pointed out, 'may also explain why no Moors practise medicine here.' Then he said, 'But who are you that you don't know these things?'

Another surgeon was making his funereal way towards the curtained alcove. Several physicians warned him: 'No more leeches! Not even the fattest man in Algiers has an inexhaustible supply of blood.'

'But these are albino leeches found only in an underground tributary of the White Nile.' And in the surgeon went, while I said a few ambiguous words about my time as a paramedic in Messina.

One by one my new colleagues entered the curtained alcove and emerged to pronounce the single word 'hopeless' before resuming their places in the death watch.

'What's wrong with him?' I asked.

'He is infinitely jaded with life,' a physician said.

'And infinitely curious about death,' said a surgeon.

I waited for the next physician or surgeon to trudge towards the alcove, but no one moved. Soon I realized all eyes were on me. Saying a silent prayer to SS Cosmas and Damian, patron saints of surgeons, I rose.

Sceptics immediately assailed me on all sides.

'Where's your specimen jug?'

'Where are your brass bowl and scalpels?'

'Your forceps, your trocar and cannula, your dilator?'

'Your jar of leeches?'

'FRAUD!' they all shouted, which of course I was, and as much to get away from their accusations as for any other reason, I hurried to the heavy hanging, parted it, and entered the gloom of the sick-alcove.

In the dim light of a smoking oil lamp I saw sprawled on a mat the dying man. A mountain of flesh, he filled a tent-sized silken gown. I leaned over him and smelled the acrid, feral stink of the unwashed sick, and heard shallow, uninterested breathing. I felt for his heartbeat, but either it was muted by intervening fat or he had none. His eyes were open but staring sightlessly from the dead-white full moon of his face. He was bald as any *hajji* and, I was startled to see, like my postmature niece Constanza he had a left eye of brown and a right eye of blue.

He is infinitely jaded with life. And infinitely curious about death.

What else did I know about him? I thought desperately, remembering that six of us would be dragged off for impalement if he died. What would *engage* him? What would make him say, 'But what happened?' and, 'Go on with the story!' like those wounded soldiers in the Messina wards?

Well, he was an astrologer and a eunuch. About astrology I knew next to nothing. But I could surmise this much about eunuchs: they are deprived forever of the delights of physical love, and more than likely have never heard a shot fired in anger. Love, then, and war. Love and war and . . . *think*! You'll want a protagonist not infinitely jaded but rather an innocent, prey to the vicissitudes of life, no more an artful lover than a mighty warrior, whose curiosity about death, especially his own, falls infinitely short of infinite.

And I pictured Cornelia Tasso crossing the churchyard to strike my face with a roll of parchment, and the image became a narrative, begun in classic Greek *medias res*, for with a dying man there was no time to begin like the Romans at the beginning, go on to the end and then stop.

'*She crossed the churchyard and struck my face as hard as she could with a roll of parchment.*

' *"You! Spaniard! Coming here with your thunderbolt to seduce me . . ."*

' "*My thunderbolt? But – "*

' *"Don't talk to me about your thunderbolt! The worst day of my life was the day the sky turned dark and your thunderbolt struck in a breathless moment in which time expanded to become space, vast vaulted distances bending back on themselves like some perfect curve or other while ruby-wingèd birds . . . Never mind! I hate you! I never want to see you again!"*

'*Once more she struck my face with the roll of parchment. My head rocked back, my eyes filled with tears, my ears rang but I heard her say, "Take that." She meant it literally, for she gave me the parchment.*

'*I unrolled it and my eyes fell on these words: ". . . none in his family back to the third generation having been Muslims, Jews, conversos . . ." and I knew it to be my Certificate of Purity of Blood.*

' *"What will you do, now that you are at last pure?" my Cousin Gaspar enquired . . .*'

Here I paused to stare intently at the moon face of the dying man. Would he demand 'Go on'? Or at least ask 'Who's your Cousin Gaspar'?

But his eyes just stared fixedly at the low ceiling as if I weren't there, and the only sound he made was his shallow, uninterested breathing.

Without much hope I resumed my tale.

'*But I had eyes only for Cornelia as she crossed the churchyard and disappeared.*

'*Was sex, I couldn't help wondering, power?*'

And would that question, I couldn't help wondering now, anger a eunuch, even a dying eunuch? If so, mightn't anger give him the will to argue, and therefore to live?

Apparently not.

I continued with even less hope.

'*And I sought, in the time-honoured tradition, the waters of Lethe.*

'New chapter:

'*Unrolling the parchment, I told the recruiting sergeant, "And here's my Certificate of Purity of Blood."*

' *"Your certificate of what?"*

' *"Purity. Purity of Blood. It certifies that I am a pure Spaniard of a pure Spanish family, or eight of them actually . . ."*

'*The sergeant ... tossed the parchment back at me. "So who the fuck cares? In this man's army we got foot soldiers from the fuckin' Irish peat bogs and ..."* '

And on I went, introducing Rodrigo and his parrots, sailing with Don Juan to Lepanto, etc. etc. So absorbed had I become in my own narrative that it was a while before I noticed in the dying man a profound change, indubitably for the worse. For, when I paused for breath as I climbed burning with fever into *Marquesa*'s skiff, I saw that his face, formerly dead white, was now red and sweaty, and his respiration came in loud, irregular wheezes.

Dare I continue? I wondered. If he died while I spoke, would I be held responsible, a scapegoat for the physicians and surgeons waiting outside?

Dare I stop? If he died while I just stood there doing nothing, wouldn't that be as bad?

I resumed my story, loud enough for him to hear – if he was listening – over his wheezes. Soon I was shouting.

'*And abruptly here at this point in time, now at this moment in space, a noteworthy occurrence occurs.*

'*As I hack at the dead Turk's body, soon a body no more, deep inside me something twists, writhes, turns with difficulty like a key in a rusty lock, to reveal in the darkness behind the door of my soul a blood lust, a joy, an obscene and terrifying joy in the act of killing, a glimpse into the underself ... I must escape even as I find another victim ... and begin flailing away ... while at the same time I slam the door on that darkness and rather unmiraculously (or so it feels) rise out of my body and from a height of a few feet watch myself swinging that boathook like a battle-axe ...*'

And the dying man's breath roared from his lungs, his face darkened to the colour of cordovan leather, his eyes strained from their sockets as I, caught up in my story, told a man with no interest in living of an obscene and terrifying joy in the act of killing.

The alcove suddenly filled with surgeons and physicians. Hands grabbed me.

'Charlatan!'

'Impostor!'

'Fabulist!'

Fabulist? Me?

Hands lifted me; the hanging parted to reveal the courtyard, the fountain, the swallows and doves and hummingbirds darting under their gossamer net, where more physicians and surgeons grabbed me, just as a bell-like tenor voice rang out.

'*Ráwi!* Where did you learn that part about time expanding to become space and vast vaulted distances bending back on themselves? Eh?'

This resulted in my being wheeled about at shoulder level and run back into the sick-alcove, where the obese patient was now sitting up, his huge bulk leaning forward as if poised for take-off, like a *jinni* on a flying carpet. His colour was normal, his brown eye and his blue eye clear.

I was deposited at his side while the physicians and surgeons prostrated themselves as if they were Muslims and he Mecca, and chanted:

> 'Deys may come and deys may go,
> Some of them even clever,
> But the royal astrologer, oh!
> The royal astrologer is forever.'

'From Cornelia,' I answered my patient's question, 'but she no longer exists.'

'Why the euphemism? If she died, say so.'

'She didn't die, she no longer exists. She was vanished.'

'*Was* vanished? Transitively? What a delicious conceit! In fact, the whole idea of the *ráwi* as healer ... Well! For a while *I* suspected them of using trance dancers, in my case the *last* thing ...' He looked past me. 'Speaking of whom, send her away, for pity's sake.'

A young woman, long-limbed and lithe in a world that liked its women fat, and wearing a variety of veils, all diaphanous, stood panting at the entrance to the alcove.

'I'm late,' she said.

'And quite superfluous, my dear Zoraida,' said my patient. 'As you can see.'

Physicians and surgeons laughed maliciously.

Zoraida the trance dancer said, 'Don't tell me any of *these* incompetents cured you?'

'No, it was the *ráwi* here,' said my patient.

Zoraida drew aside her uppermost veil to inspect me.

'You're one of those fellows who sit around the marketplace all day telling stories? *What* an easy life!'

I asked her, 'What exactly does a trance dancer do?'

'Dances herself into a trance, of course – drawing out of a dying man the poison that's killing him.'

'Primitive superstition,' scoffed a physician.

'Might as well put the bones of a saint in bed with him,' scorned a surgeon.

While physicians, surgeons and the equally superfluous trance dancer argued the merits of their respective vocations, my patient turned back to me.

'Now. About time expanding to become space and – '

'I'm just a storyteller,' I apologized. 'I really don't know much about such things.'

'Of course you do. Escaping your blood lust by rising out of your body – astral projection, it is sometimes called – would not be possible unless time *could* expand to become space, vast vaulted distances bending back on – ' But at this point his pachydermatous belly rumbled hugely and he interrupted himself in that tolling tenor voice: 'SOMEBODY BRING FOOD! I'M STARVING!'

Several physicians and surgeons left their argument with Zoraida the trance dancer and, in a surprisingly short time, returned with a basin of couscous the size of a baptismal font and another of stewed mutton swimming in grease.

They all hovered like anxious mothers while my patient plunged right in, forgetting himself in his eagerness and using both hands.

This gaucherie gave me an excuse to strike his laden hands, sending couscous and a neck of mutton flying.

'Eat that and you'll kill yourself,' I said flatly.

'But I've touched no food for days.'

'Exactly. So you can't gorge yourself now,' I said. And, to my new colleagues, 'Take this swill away.'

After a few moments my patient nodded, and the physicians and surgeons removed the two enormous basins.

'Mint tea, a dish of *cuajada*, *without* honey, some orange segments and one square of unleavened bread,' I said relentlessly.

His moon face made a face, but he nodded again.

When this meagre fare was brought, 'Eat slowly,' I admonished my patient, then added, 'assuming you know how.'

His moon face glowered behind a cloud of diminished self-esteem.

'What's the matter with you anyway? How could you let yourself get so fat? Obesity like yours can kill.'

'I'm a eunuch.' Defensively. 'Eunuchs put on weight if they even look at food.'

'Lucky you,' said Zoraida. 'I can eat and eat, but I just get thinner.'

'And after all, what's left to me but food?' My patient sighed and sipped his mint tea and nibbled a corner of unleavened bread. 'Is it so strange I lost the will to live when I began to suspect astrology was only a lot of 'mumbo-jumbo? Me, the esteemed eunuch astrologer to the Dey, losing faith in stellar and planetary prognostication!'

'Maybe,' I suggested, 'you decided astrology's a lot of mumbo-jumbo because it *is* a lot of mumbo-jumbo.'

'Oh? And what's wrong with it?' he demanded truculently.

'I don't really know much about it,' I said.

'Then let *me* tell *you*,' he told me. 'Everything's wrong with it. Everything! Twenty years of my life I gave to that false god before I saw the light. In my subsequently shrunken *amour propre*, I ate myself obese. I once, you know, cut quite a dashing figure – for a eunuch. What's your name?'

'Miguel de Cervantes.'

He studied me intently, so intently that I felt he looked straight into my mind. Presently he said, 'There's a child dear to you – a daughter? – who has mismatched eyes like mine.'

My spine tingled. 'Who are you?' I asked.

'Cide Hamete Benengeli,' he said.

Benengeli! You will remember, perhaps, that as a small boy I could not pronounce '*berengena*'; despite my sister Andrea's coaching, the closest I could come was '*benengeli*'. Cide Hamete's surname – twenty years and more before I ever met him! Mightn't I, except for that youthful mispronunciation of a favourite food, always have stood in helpless awe of this enigmatic presence, to my own peril? But sometimes merely thinking of him as Señor Aubergine or (better) Lord Eggplant almost let me see a fallible human, despite those extraordinary powers he would develop once he abandoned the constraints of astrology.

'Who's your master?' Cide Hamete Benengeli asked me. Again his eyes looked deep into mine. 'Gimp the Greek,' he answered his own question. 'That pederast! Has he molested you? Sometimes he wearies of pubescent boys.'

'He's tried.'

'He won't anymore. When word gets around – and in Algiers, it always does – you'll be celebrated as the healer who saved the life of the esteemed royal astrologer.'

'But I thought you said astrology's a false god.'

'You *are* an innocent! Don't you know, young *ráwi*, the world is full of priests and imams, monks and marabouts who serve gods they don't believe in?'

While he took another sip of mint tea and poked his golden spoon into what remained of his *cuajada*, Zoraida left us, trailing the longest of her diaphanous veils. Cide Hamete settled on his back on the mat, wheezing and blowing.

'Take heart, Miguel de Cervantes,' he advised. 'It is less bad than you imagine to be an innocent, prey to life's vicissitudes. And if my life has any value in the grand cosmic design that, sometimes, I almost believe I can see even while I doubt it exists, I am in your debt for saving it.'

I nodded as if I understood. I had entered the life of Cide Hamete Benengeli, and he, whether for good or evil, had entered mine.

XI

In Which I Rewrite a Scene

From an Unstaged Play

And Make My First Attempt to Escape

Even if I wasn't put on this planet to be a playwright, I still think *The Dungeons of Algiers* deserved production.

It was topical. It had real life in it, plus an exotic locale. It pitted good against evil, with good triumphing. Yet it remained forever unstaged, a play on paper only, like an unbaptized soul eternally in limbo.

Did I etch it too deeply with the acid of self-pity? But surely a man of flesh and blood, no less than my protagonist Something de Saavedra, would have railed at iniquitous fate for burying sixty-one months of his life in Algerian captivity.

Why did I leave my brother out? However autobiographical the play was, Rodrigo had no place in it. Some things a man doesn't write about. This needn't indicate ill-feeling. Until the day he fell in battle in the Low Countries, I loved my brother, although we rarely saw each other.

Betrayal? A harsh word. My brother was, first and always, a soldier. His honour was hierarchical, not personal. We didn't understand each other. Do brothers, ever?

Oh, I could put a scene on paper giving Rodrigo his role in those terrible events that would culminate in the Plaza of Atrocities. But I risk being misunderstood – Cain and Abel, brother versus brother. It wasn't like that.

With misgivings, then, a new scene for my unproduced play *The Dungeons of Algiers*, complete with a new cast of characters:

Algiers. The tavern of the royal bagnio *or prison, a cavernous room below ground level, dimly lit by oil lamps. An evening in 1570-something.*

(PRISONERS *sit at crude tables drinking beer. Enter* JANISSARIES, *swaggering to centre stage and occupying large table, hastily vacated. Noise of* PRISONERS' *conversation abates.*)

JANISSARY CAPTAIN: Innkeeper! Your special non-alcoholic foaming janissary-juice, quick now! (*Winks at his companions*)

GABRIEL MÚÑOZ, *the grizzleheaded taverner*: Coming right up, gents. (*Goes to tap and draws the same brew the others are drinking*)

(*Enter* MIGUEL DE CERVANTES, *neatly barbered and in a clean striped burnous. He peers anxiously into the dim interior.*)

RODRIGO DE CERVANTES (*waving from a small table, stage right*): Miguel! Over here!

MIGUEL DE CERVANTES (*joining him*): That grizzlehead's the taverner here? He's the fellow who was always explaining to me about the atrocities down at the harbour. I don't get it.

RODRIGO (*shrugging*): Everybody works out his own *modus vivendi* in Algiers. Look at yourself. You've come a long way   a room of your own at Dalí Mamí's palace, a career as a faith-healer –

MIGUEL: I just tell them stories. Still, faith-healing and storytelling aren't so different, are they. Both need a willing suspension of disbelief.

RODRIGO: Whatever, it works. You're hardly a prisoner these days, any more than I am.

MIGUEL: Hey, come on now! Talk about suspending disbelief! What about these shackles we wear? Have your ankles gone numb, along with your head? No wonder people are saying . . . Holy Virgin! Hardly a prisoner!

RODRIGO (*grimly*): People are saying what?

MIGUEL (*ignoring the question*): Hardly a prisoner! We can't go out of the city, can't go anywhere at night, can't look cross-eyed at a Turk without getting our brains bashed by the nearest janiss –

RODRIGO: Not so loud.

JANISSARY CAPTAIN (*loudly*): You call this mule-piss a fit drink for a man?

GABRIEL MÚÑOZ *the grizzlehead*: It is beer as she is drunk in my country, Captain. A superior brew to any you gents are familiar with on account of the law here, which I do not cast any aspersions on.
JANISSARIES (*in chorus*): Watch your tongue, slave, or we'll rip it out for you.
MIGUEL (*softly, to his brother*): And he's free, you'd tell me? Just like us? Hardly a prisoner . . . I'm going to find a way out.
RODRIGO: Not so loud, I said. And get this straight. Escape is impossible. And trying is machomaniacal. Worse, it's immoral.
MIGUEL: Im*m*oral?
RODRIGO: There are thirty-five thousand Christian captives in the city. You think maybe this is just a prisoner-of-war situation? They're holding merchants, lawyers, physicians. Priests. Women and children even. And with every fool who tries to escape, life gets tougher for all of us. Women and children, Miguel.

(*The* CERVANTES BROTHERS' *argument is overridden by two other conversations, separate but parallel, alternating at nearby tables. One is between three* YOUNG PRISONERS. *The other is between three* OLD PRISONERS, *all earless; the oldest,* ALONSO QUIJANO, *is missing his nose too. Behind the two tables, the chorus of* JANISSARIES *and their* CAPTAIN *range themselves, smirking and mimicking the speakers.*)

FIRST YOUNG PRISONER: Escape *is* possible. Provided you have the money.
SECOND YOUNG PRISONER: And patience.
THIRD YOUNG PRISONER: And *cojones*.
FIRST YOUNG PRISONER: On the coast . . .

> ALONSO QUIJANO: Yes sirree, boys, it was back in forty-seven – or was it forty-eight? Coast route to Spanish Oran. Practically got clean away.

FIRST YOUNG PRISONER: . . . regularly patrolled by janissaries, but at least it's a regular road you can't get lost on.
SECOND YOUNG PRISONER: Right. We can lie low during the day, travel at night.
THIRD YOUNG PRISONER: In the dark of the moon, right.

> ALONSO QUIJANO: Would've made it, except for that midnight patrol. Covered eighty miles, easy.

SECOND OLD PRISONER: Out of two-twenty.

THIRD OLD PRISONER: Eighty miles, that's the all-time record.

ALONSO QUIJANO: You bet. And it still stands. Came even closer on the *inland* route.

FIRST YOUNG PRISONER: Inland, they say the going's rough. All shale and sand.

SECOND YOUNG PRISONER: Right. I hear that shale can cut a man's feet to ribbons. We'd need good boots.

THIRD YOUNG PRISONER: And something to protect our faces, right. They say a man can suffocate in those desert sandstorms.

FIRST YOUNG PRISONER: As for the wolves and hyenas and lions, I figure those are just scare stories. Bounty-hunting nomads are the only animals to fear. We'd have to keep our ears open.

ALONSO QUIJANO: When was it we headed inland, boys?

SECOND OLD PRISONER: It was fifty-three, Quijano. I ought to know. That's when I lost my left ear.

THIRD OLD PRISONER (*musing*): Don't seem no twenty-three years. Where does a man's life go?

QUIJANO: I'd be back in Argamasilla de Alba twenty-three years, cultivating my vines, 'cept for those dern bounty hunters.

SECOND OLD PRISONER: It could have been worse than bounty hunters.

THIRD OLD PRISONER: *Was* worse. (*Shifts on his bench to reveal a peg leg*) Hyena did that. One chomp.

FIRST YOUNG PRISONER: Escape by sea might be best of all.

SECOND YOUNG PRISONER: If you don't make it, drowning's not such a bad way to go.

THIRD YOUNG PRISONER: Hey, the idea's to escape, not to die.

133

QUIJANO: Remember that time we hired a frigate? Back in fifty, wasn't it?

SECOND OLD PRISONER: Fifty-one. I ought to know. That's when I lost my *right* ear.

FIRST YOUNG PRISONER: It's expensive.

SECOND YOUNG PRISONER: Right. Because you're hiring professionals.

THIRD YOUNG PRISONER: Sailors who know this coast, right. And where to rendezvous and how to slip past the Dey's navy and . . .

THIRD OLD PRISONER: Friggin' frigate never showed.

QUIJANO: Wonder what scared 'em off?

THIRD OLD PRISONER: Maybe that ransomed prisoner just took our money and pocketed it. Maybe he didn't even *know* any friggin' frigate captain in Malta.

SECOND OLD PRISONER: Maybe the Dey's navy intercepted the frigate – if there was a frigate.

QUIJANO: There was! And there'll be another. I can't spend my whole life a captive. I have to see the world . . . Tordesillas . . . el Toboso . . . Provincio . . . We'll escape yet, I know we will. Don't lose faith, boys. God's on our side.

JANISSARY CAPTAIN (*looming over* QUIJANO, *taunting*): God, Grandpa? Which of your many gods did you have in mind?

QUIJANO: Which? What which? God – just God.

JANISSARY CAPTAIN: You mean your Father-god, perhaps? Or the Son-god he sent to die on a cross? Or the Ghost-god who knocked up the so-called Virgin-Mother-god, making the Father-god a cuckold and the Son-god plainly a bastard? Excuse me, a Bastard-*god*.

QUIJANO (*leaping up on spindly legs and cocking his fists in front of his missing nose*): The Devil take you, you blasphemer!

CAPTAIN: Ah, a Devil-god! That's five at last count.

(QUIJANO *hurls beer mug at* CAPTAIN, *who ducks easily*.)

CAPTAIN: Incredible how you people call yourselves monotheists. When the truth is so clear that –

JANISSARIES (*in chorus*): There is no God but Allah and Muhammad is His Prophet.

CAPTAIN: There. Say it, Grandpa.

(QUIJANO *stands mute.* YOUNG *and* OLD PRISONERS *cower at their tables.*)

JANISSARIES (*in chorus*): Heathen's lost his tongue.
CAPTAIN: Not yet. But since he seems to have no use for it . . .

(MIGUEL DE CERVANTES *half rises, but* RODRIGO *restrains him.*)

CAPTAIN: . . . you may as well relieve him of it.

(JANISSARIES *crowd* QUIJANO, *hiding him from view.*)

RODRIGO: Sit down, you fool! Or he won't be the only one.
MIGUEL: B-b-b-
FIRST YOUNG PRISONER: No, I don't know the one with what used to be a left hand. But the one with the freckles is Rodrigo de Cervantes.
SECOND YOUNG PRISONER: Oh.
THIRD YOUNG PRISONER: Oh.
SECOND YOUNG PRISONER: Right. The organizer.
THIRD YOUNG PRISONER: The rules and regulations man, right.
FIRST YOUNG PRISONER: That's him. Keeps the prisoners in line – supposedly for our own good.

(QUIJANO, *unseen in the tight huddle of* JANISSARIES, *screams.*)

MIGUEL (*struggling to break free of his brother*): . . . but . . .

You see the problem. It might reflect real life, but it can't be shoehorned into Lope's formula – with or without a suspension of disbelief.

Well, I lost some patients despite my storytelling, and I saved some, perhaps because of it. And as Cide Hamete predicted, Gimp the Greek no longer molested me. I slept alone and minded my own business and ran into Zoraida the trance dancer occasionally – always hurrying, generally breathless, trailing a diaphanous veil or two – as both of us were summoned to patients *in extremis* to work our magic, if any. I grew used to the clanking of my leg irons and almost to their chafing, and I dreamed of freedom. But freedom meant ransom or escape, and both were impossible.

One day I went to the prison tavern and asked Gabriel Múñoz, 'How do you stand it?'

'My beer?' He laughed. 'It is the only beer in town.'

'No, I mean doing your bit in the softening-up process down at the Plaza of Atrocities.'

'Give me a break, *compañero*. I just try to grease the wheels of bargaining. And the pay, it is not bad. Live among Moors long enough and you learn life is all money and rhetoric.'

135

'I'm looking for a Moor,' I said after a while.

'What Moor would that be?'

'One who knows the desert.'

Gabriel Múñoz glanced at what used to be my left hand. He was always doing that, but then, so were a lot of people.

'So that is the way it is,' he said. 'I would not get carried away by my own rhetoric if I were you. This could be fatal.'

'I know what I'm doing.'

'We are talking what kind of money?'

'Enough. Some of my patients are grateful.'

'I will see what I can do, but if I tell you I am glad this is not *my* kismet, I am only being honest, *compañero*.'

Ramadan that year of 1576 fell in February and early March. I mention this because escape, said to be impossible any other time, was merely wildly improbable during Ramadan.

To observe the holy month, pious Muslims avoid food, drink, sex, and smoking of hashish or of that new indulgence, tobacco, from dawn to dusk. Pious Muslims also pray for redemption. Not-so-pious Muslims sleep until the *iftar*, the meal served after dusk to break the daytime fast, then carouse all night long. Nominal Christians and Jews will understand.

Such nightly carousing alternating with daily abstinence made for a month-long state of communal lassitude that was the would-be escapee's best ally.

The second night of Ramadan, armed with papers provided by Gabriel Múñoz ostensibly permitting me to break curfew to visit a moribund marabout, I went to a farewell orgy for Juan Rufo and thirty or forty other ransomed Christians in the palace of the Albanian renegade *re'is* Arnaute Mamí.

Orgy! What a world of congenial depravity the word evokes! My curiosity was naturally high. But when I entered the vaulted hall with its central pool of bubbling crystal water, what caught my attention was a *ráwi* embarking on the Tale of the First Dervish – a tale I had declined to make part of my own repertoire or pharmacopoeia because (unlike the rest of the Scheherazadian canon, to which I helped myself at will) it made me stutter.

I looked around for the youth with oranges I'd come to find. I looked for Juan Rufo. Finding neither, I eagerly (I admit it) turned to what I could see of the orgy.

I could see couches of diamond-studded alabaster covered with pearl-embroidered red silk quilts on which couples disported themselves in positions that would have perplexed the Indian sage Vatsyayana, author of *Kama Sutra*, for at a quick glance the couples seemed exclusively male. To my considerable disappointment – for a man passes this way but once – visibility was poor. Not only were the alabaster couches strategically deployed in shadow, but an irritating haze of hashish and tobacco smoke hung in the air. I could hear, though, the usual (I assumed) orgiastic grunting, groaning and slobbering, and the occasional clank of leg irons, and I did see Arnaute Mamí himself, brandishing a cat-o'-nine-tails, chase from the vaulted hall an impenitent heterosexual couple with the scathing words, 'Out! Out! An orgy's no place for *that!*'

Still searching for Juan Rufo and the youth with oranges, I chanced upon a lighted *huqqa* or water pipe and, curious, puffed a while.

Presently I returned to the edge of the pool of bubbling crystal water, hoping the *ráwi* had finished the Tale of the First Dervish, but:

' "... *from their earliest youth,*" *said the King,* "*I knew that my son was in love with his sister, and she with him. So wisely I kept them apart.*" '

The *ráwi* was intoning in that rhythmic recitative I had never bothered to master, as it reminded me too much of poetry. I closed my ears to him and heard another voice, a familiar voice, at my side.

'... better off forgetting your sister, huh? Even when I used to propose regularly, she never really gave me a thought. By now – hell, she probably married somebody else long ago.'

It was Juan Rufo, blowing a thoughtful cloud of hashish or tobacco smoke.

The *ráwi*'s voice rose. '... *menaced with dishonour and death, yet yielded to the promptings of Shaitan. Secretly my son prepared this hidden chamber ...*'

On the eve of his release, Juan Rufo still wore the regulation stripes and leg irons. But when I blinked through the *huqqa* smoke I saw him bedizened in rich courtier's duds, his right hand hovering near the hilt of a rapier he seemed to be wearing at his side.

Conceding that he would make Andrea a good enough husband when he returned to Spain, I blinked him back into his black-and-white-striped burnous.

'... *brought down the scourge of Allah, and his avenging fire had burned their entwined bodies black as charcoal.*'

Who was I kidding? Juan Rufo would make Andrea a wonderful husband.

In a blink I turned him to charcoal. He looked at me, tall and handsome and no less a Spanish courtier for being coal-black. I let him fade to white.

Finally the *ráwi* finished the Tale of the First Dervish and, to faint applause, bowed off.

'Anyway,' said Juan Rufo, 'I won't believe I'm ransomed until I step ashore on Spanish soil.'

While he spoke, two eunuchs carried to the edge of the bubbling crystal pool a tight coil of hempen rope mounted on a sturdy frame, while a third eunuch placed on the marble floor a basket of blood oranges.

Disengaging from one another, hastily donning robes, men leaped off the diamond-studded alabaster couches shouting, 'The Maltrapillo boy – it's the Maltrapillo boy!'

I saw a beautiful youth stride to the hempen coil and take a stance before it, defiance in his disturbing amber eyes, hands on slender hips, the soft drape of his silk pantaloons emphasizing the perky curve of his firm young buttocks.

As we watched, a tall fat man appeared beside us in a robe of midnight-blue besprinkled randomly with stars, comets, signs of the Zodiac and assorted phases of the moon, all in gold.

'The boy is Michele Maltrapillo,' he said, his voice decidedly deeper than when we'd first met. But when we'd first met he'd been on his death-mat. He also seemed to have grown the wispy suggestion of hair on his bald pate.

I laughed. Blame it on whatever I'd smoked.

'Please! Don't ridicule the costume! Think of the little lace doilies your own priests deck themselves in. As for my apostasy – if I may speak so of mere astrology – remember, *ráwi*, a Christian priest need not be in a state of grace to administer the sacraments. If that were required, we'd all be out of business.'

'Who is he?' I wanted to know.

'You find him attractive?'

'He is rather – callipygean,' I said, blinking some more hair onto Cide Hamete Benengeli's fuzzy pate.

'Indeed, as you say, a cute ass. Which half the men in Algiers lust after. Unhappy lad! Wanted by many, forbidden to all. He calls no man master, yet any slave is freer than he to leave. The boy's life here and his father's trade are each conditional on the other.'

While Cide Hamete spoke those mystifying words, a eunuch was distributing bows and arrows to the orgiasts. Another balanced a blood orange atop the boy's dark curls, then quickly stepped back as the first archer took aim.

'He hasn't cared if he lived or died,' said Cide Hamete, 'since his father struck the deal that left him a prisoner without chains. Which is why he plays his dangerous games.'

'Maltrapillo, you called him?' asked Juan Rufo. 'Then his father must be captain of the ship that's taking us ransomees off to Spain tomorrow – or so they claim.'

'Stop worrying,' Cide Hamete advised him. 'It's foolish to worry about something you've no control over.'

Note the pompous platitude. Cide Hamete always saved his more astute metaphysical observations for me. Sometimes I have to wonder if others didn't find him just a run-of-the-mill apostate astrologer who dabbled in philosophy and preternatural powers to fill the void in his life.

'If Morato Maltrapillo doesn't show up, his son will be clamped in irons,' he told us. 'And if ever he smuggles an unransomed prisoner from Algiers, his son will die – provided he isn't killed first by one of these hopped-up, strung-out bowmen.'

'What kind of dangerous games?' I asked, although in my own hopped-up haze I was beginning to work it out; in the army I'd heard from Swiss pikemen about William Tell.

The first bowman let fly his arrow with a thrum and a whoosh, and at what seemed the same instant the orange burst on the youth's dark curls, blood-coloured juice running down his face while the arrow buried itself in the hempen coil behind him. He smiled, if anything more defiantly.

After considerable shouting, cheering and foot-stamping, a second blood orange was balanced on the boy's head.

'There's a frustration factor to take into account,' Cide Hamete informed us. 'Despite the boy's irresistibility, part of his father's deal is that no one molest him, not even Ramadan Pasha Dey himself.'

A second bowman let fly, resulting in the same burst orange, blood-coloured juice, defiant smile.

The third bowman was Gimp the Greek, 'whose yen for the boy and consequent resentment are particularly strong', said Cide Hamete.

As the portly renegade *re'is*, now only nominally my master, loosed his arrow, I glimpsed in the shadows behind him a lean, dark man with a Princess Eboli eye-patch.

Thrum, whoosh, a cry from Gimp the Greek of 'Jesus!' immediately corrected to 'By Allah!' – and the Maltrapillo boy staggered back against the hempen coil as blood, real blood, blossomed on the left side of his white silk shirt, from which the feathered shaft of an arrow protruded.

I reached him first, Juan Rufo right after me, Cide Hamete puffing and blowing behind. The boy had fallen to his knees, defiant smile incredibly still in place.

'Get back! This man is a healer!' cried Cide Hamete to the crowd. To me he whispered urgently, 'Pick the boy up, hurry! You can't do anything for him here!'

This made no sense, but Cide Hamete's voice compelled obedience, so I lifted the Maltrapillo boy and followed the apostate astrologer to a curtained alcove rather like the one where he himself had lain, not so long ago, on his deathmat. Gently I lowered the wounded boy to the floor while Cide Hamete returned outside to keep the crowd back.

The boy glared up at me. 'Molest me and you'll be executed on the hook.'

'I'll have to turn you on your side.' The white silk shirt, I'd seen, buttoned at the back.

The boy produced from somewhere a bodkin (or was it a stylet?). 'No you don't!' he cried.

I took the weapon from his hand and used it to cut the shirt away.

This revealed fair skin, much blood and a white silk sash binding the boy's chest, from which the arrow protruded. I eased the blade under the sash.

'Touch it and you're dead,' said the boy.

Finally I lost my temper. 'Listen, you miserable brat, I'm just trying to stop you bleeding to death. And if you hadn't been so busy playing your dangerous games I'd have said, "Castor and Pollux were twin sons of Leda," and you'd have responded, "Romulus and Remus were suckled by a she-wolf," and we'd have got down to the serious business of planning a desert crossing to Spanish Oran.'

'So that's who you are.'

'That's who I am.'

'Keep your hands off my sash!'

I wanted to use it to throttle him.

Instead, I used the bodkin or stylet to cut away the sash while his disturbing amber eyes skewered me with hatred.

I dropped the bodkin or stylet. On the floor, luckily.

'You'll get your guide,' the Maltrapillo child said, face colouring, eyes averted now. 'One who knows the desert like the palm of his hand. Just keep my secret, for the love of whatever gods you believe in.'

If, standing, she'd had a seductive derrière, supine her youthful breasts offered promise of the glorious woman she would become – if she lived that long.

'I *have* to masquerade as a boy,' she said. 'Girls have no value here.

As a girl, I couldn't be the hostage that guarantees my father's deal with the Dey.'

She said this without flinching while I pulled the arrow out. More blood welled. I wadded the white silk sash and tied it over the wound with a strip torn from her shirt. This left her breasts partly exposed.

By then the tumult outside the alcove was growing, orgiasts lewdly and loudly conjecturing what 'operations' I was performing on the helpless boy and clamouring to take their turn. (This, regrettably, would fuel debate about my sexuality in rumour-ridden Algiers.)

I called for a blanket, and a hand thrust through the curtain a pearl-embroidered red silk quilt from one of the alabaster couches. I cloaked the girl in it.

'Don't touch me!'

'Shut up. I'm just trying to keep your secret. How old are you anyway?'

'Twelve. And you needn't carry me. I know how to walk.'

It startled me to realize that my niece, postmature little Constanza, would be almost the same age; I felt my own youth fleeing.

I lifted her, the curve of her classic callipygean derrière cradled on my arm, her beautiful if angry face close to mine, her fair skin giving off a scent like new-mown hay mingled perhaps with musk-rose dew, her pearl-embroidered-red-silk-swathed breasts warm against me – all combining to make my voice censorious as I asked, just before Juan Rufo parted the curtain (Cide Hamete having disappeared as, I would learn, he had a way of doing), 'Doesn't your immunity kind of run out if you're caught helping prisoners cross the desert?'

'I'd never be caught. Anyway, since escape is impossible, Ramadan Pasha Dey encourages such enterprise – and takes his cut. He's lenient as deys go, but unfortunately he'll be gone in a year or so. They only buy the office from the Sultan for three years, more than time enough for any dey to set himself up for life.'

'Will this guide you're sending talk as much as you?'

'El Dorador? Hardly. He's a sullen boy, the bastard son of a black slave mother and a Moor from Melilla. That's on the other side of Oran.'

'I know where it is,' I said, and Juan Rufo led us through the crowd, calling, 'Make way, make way – the boy's seriously injured,' as I carried Micaela Maltrapillo outside to where in the pre-dawn light four Christian slaves waited with a palanquin.

'I'll see you home and mix you a sleeping draught.'

'And then have your way with me? How dumb do you think I am?'

'You're young enough to be my niece. Do you think I'd take advantage of her?'

'I live by one rule – trust no one in this life.'

'I'm not asking you to trust me. I'm just asking you to take something to make you sleep. You're overwrought.'

'That's my normal state.' By then she was settled in the palanquin. She slid the curtains closed.

'I'll just see you home and – '

'Sorry. Nobody knows where I live.'

'Wait!' But before I could tell her what folly it was to serve as hostage to her father's deal with the Dey, the slaves lifted the chair and trotted off into the dawn.

Was it any less folly, I wondered a few days later at dusk, for me and three other prisoners to follow the sullen mulatto teenager El Dorador boldly through the Bab-Azun Gate, even though we knew escape was impossible?

See us, leg irons removed, sentries bribed, haversacks crammed with biscuits and honeyed millet cakes, full waterskins at our sides, swinging along the dusty moonlit road past olive groves soon giving way to the desolate, rocky *hammada* where only stunted briers and brambles dare grow

FIRST YOUNG PRISONER: Ten days from now we'll be in Spanish Oran, free men – if we can do twenty miles a day.

SECOND YOUNG PRISONER: And if bounty-hunting nomads don't turn us in.

THIRD YOUNG PRISONER: And if wolves or hyenas or lions don't make a meal of us first.

I'd had no difficulty enlisting the Three Young Prisoners, but once *en route* they had a disconcerting tendency to sound more like the Old Prisoners from that new scene for *The Dungeons of Algiers*.

Was the guide El Dorador part of my folly too? Whatever, his own folly was to say something and mean only the half of it – but from El Dorador's viewpoint, was that so foolish? What he said was, 'I hear and obey.'

'Faster,' I would urge.

'I hear and obey,' El Dorador would reply. But his tortoiselike progress across the *hammada* never varied.

Or I would wake shivering in my burnous and tell El Dorador to put more briers and brambles on the fire.

'I hear and obey,' he would say, remaining huddled in his own burnous, and I would replenish the fire myself.

Dawn of the fifth day found us camped between the horns of a crescent dune, for we had left the *hammada* for the sand desert. Deciding which side of a crescent dune to camp on is a Hobson's choice since, pointing downwind, the crescents protect you from the wind but leave you in the path of the dune's advancing sands, which, that morning, had completely buried the fire and possibly El Dorador too. For he was nowhere to be seen.

(That wasn't a good example of a Hobson's choice. I would find out many years later exactly what the term meant, not that the knowledge would do me the slightest good.)

FIRST YOUNG PRISONER: He can't have been devoured by wolves or hyenas. They'd have left tell-tale gristle and bone.
SECOND YOUNG PRISONER: A lion can't have dragged him off. There's no blood spoor.
THIRD YOUNG PRISONER: The sand buried him. Tomorrow it could bury us.

But mutely, I up-ended my haversack; nothing fell out. I shook my waterskin; it made a depressingly empty sound.

The Three Young Prisoners' own haversacks and waterskins persuaded them I was right.

El Dorador had absconded.

FIRST YOUNG PRISONER: Only three things are certain in life.
SECOND YOUNG PRISONER: Death . . . and taxes . . .
THIRD YOUNG PRISONER: . . . and that no one ever escapes from Algiers.
THREE YOUNG PRISONERS (*in chorus*): Losing an ear is not the end of the world. We have two ears. Each. We're turning back.

I said, 'Nothing will ever make me turn back.'
If this surprised them, it surprised me more. The words just came out.

FIRST YOUNG PRISONER: He's mad.
SECOND YOUNG PRISONER: Stark and raving.
THIRD YOUNG PRISONER: Machismo – he's buying certain death with his own machismo.

Machomania, my brother had called it. As if he, a professional soldier, could talk.

143

'Macho – me?' I scoffed.

But could they be right? I asked myself, squinting westward at the endless sea of sand.

Was I fated, a victim of my own stubbornness, always to make wrong choices, Hobson's or otherwise, to reach that extreme of adversity on which – as Cide Hamete told me more than once – I seemed to thrive?

But no, I was not 'fated'. To submit to fate was the folly of the weak, and in those days I worshipped at the altar of free will, the folly of the strong.

The Three Young Prisoners turned and plodded east.

I loped west; trotted, now that I'd cast the die; ran almost, up the steep leeward side of a dune, floundering in sand to my knees, and then over the top to the gentler windward slope where a gust nearly knocked me down before I forged on with a spring to my step (no easy thing in sand), long, optimistic strides eating up the distance between me and Spanish Oran. The wind hurled sand in my face. And I laughed. With decision – the more difficult the better – comes freedom. Free, I climbed, crossed, conquered in my exuberance what I might more easily have skirted. Soon the sun was hot for February, or for any month, high in that brassy desert sky, and I loped on.

This is called depleting your resources, a folly of nations no less than of men.

A while before nightfall I tottered into the city.

Hallucination, of course. Or worse. Madness, stark and raving. And yet . . .

Dusk, then, an unnaturally long dusk it seemed, with that quality of light best described as crepuscular, as I made my way over the ancient paving stones of what had been a broad avenue, now flanked by ruins impressive as Marlowe's topless towers; but who had built this city and why, in the middle of a limitless desert, I could not say.

Wherever I turned I saw, in mythic bold relief on plinth or column or dolmen, likenesses of crocodiles and hippopotami, creatures sacred to Set, god of darkness and evil, who slew his son and brother Osiris by hacking him into fourteen (some say fifteen) pieces from which he somehow grew whole again to sit in judgment on the dead (was I dead?), yet another manifestation of the dying god or goddess reborn – Adonis, Dionysus, Tammuz, Persephone – in whose death is life, and in whose life death.

Hippopotami. Crocodiles. Beasts of the rivers of Africa, beasts of Set's Nile which brings to Egypt from its hidden source beyond the Mountains of the Moon life-giving water. But here? Why had long-vanished builders carved on every cornerstone these riparian icons? Why but that they had known, aeons ago, a mighty river of their own?

I stumbled wildly in the maze of time-abandoned streets, searching. Once, some subterranean stream had surfaced to make a city flourish in the desert — and if water had been abundant then, wouldn't a trace, a trickle, remain to keep me alive now?

The twilight was almost gone when I found the well. But in it I could see no glint, no gleam, only darkness. Feverishly, I prised loose a paving stone and hurled it down and listened as it struck, rock against rock, fainter and fainter. I had all but abandoned hope when the well hurled back the sound that meant life to me, muted but unmistakable, the splash of that paving stone into water.

The sound that meant life to me! O cosmic irony! Water there was, but how could I reach it?

I pounded the well enclosure until my fists were bloody. Hurled another paving stone to hurt that mocking water.

He's mad. Stark and raving.

I found a sheltered corner near the well and, huddled in my burnous against the sudden desert cold, watched the moon rise, distant and uncaring. Through the ruins echoed the cries of ravens and owls.

Sleeping at last, I dreamed not, and at midnight when the moon stood high over the city, I woke to see . . .

I know. I know what's bothering you. A lost city somewhere between Algiers and Spanish Oran, and I alone of those who ventured here saw it. But I did see it. I walked its streets. It was there. The unknown builders who passed this way (but once, like us all) did not leave their passing unmarked. And I? Were I to die in the ruins of their creation tonight, what monument would I leave? Almost thirty years of life, and it was as if I had never existed, as if the randomly joined atoms that eventually had to become Miguel de Cervantes had combined to no purpose. Nothing written on my forehead. Kismet nil.

To hell with kismet. I would make my own kismet.

Free will definitely at work here, I rose and in the ethereal moon-glow saw atop the well enclosure a wooden bucket, and attached to its handle a rope that coiled on to the ground where now I stood. I lowered the bucket hand over hand until the coil was gone. Close by an owl called, and I saw a moon-cast shadow dart across the wall beyond the well. Then I hauled on the rope. Was it heavier? Or did I feel only the weight of rope and bucket?

When most of the rope was coiled at my feet again, I heard the sloshing of water and saw its quicksilver shine, and I drank my fill, and the water was sweet, and when I had poured the rest into my waterskin, did the softest suggestion of an unseen hand touch mine? I gave the bucket, now empty, to whoever it was, to whatever phantom, whatever madness, and the bucket disappeared, and with it the well.

In the morning I walked swiftly from that city, nor did I once look back.

To the African and Oriental travels and fabulous adventures of Sir John Mandeville I've already alluded. Sir John was the first man since classical times (I exclude the Egyptians themselves) to see the Great Pyramids. He brought back no pyramidal stones as evidence, yet although his very identity is unverifiable, no one doubted him.

The great Arab traveller ibn Batuta, roughly Mandeville's contemporary, saw the ruins of Bokhara, Balkh and Samarkand. Ibn Batuta carried away no fire-blackened artefacts, but when he wrote that Genghis Khan had burned those fabled cities to the ground, people believed him too.

And almost two hundred years before them, a poor Spanish Jew named Benjamin from the ghetto of Tudela set out to see the world. He penetrated regions no Spaniard had seen before, and not many since, and when he wrote of resettlement of Galilean villages by the descendants of Jews expelled a century earlier by Crusaders, no one disbelieved him. Yet, conceivably, this Benjamin of Tudela might have had an axe to grind.

I had none. All I wanted was to live, and if I tell you my life was spared by the miraculous well in the lost city sacred to Set, god of darkness and evil, trust me.

On the fourth day after leaving the city, my waterskin empty again, I saw in the distance a cloud of dust and I had just time to scoop a hole in the sand and flatten myself when a band of men armed with ancient firelocks rode their camels towards me at an ungainly dromedary gallop.

I watched them drag their cloud of dust (sand, actually) across the face of the desert before making my plodding way west again. From then on I sensed that men were always close, bounty-hunting nomads who, more than likely, had run across my footprints before the wind obliterated them and now were quartering the desert to find me.

How long can a man go, with neither food nor water, at a lurching stumble that confirms what any year-old child would tell him if it could speak − that walking is a series of arrested falls? Soon I was crawling as much as walking, free will reduced to a vague awareness that death was not far off, death was waiting windward of the next dune perhaps, yet I struggled on with an absolutely private macho rage − for machismo is not all show – a rage against my self-betrayal by God-given (or not) free will, Algiers behind and Spanish Oran ahead, still seeking a freedom as illusory as the pool of clear water I saw then through the shimmering heat-haze in that man-killing expanse of blazing sand and rock, falling forward at the exact moment I realized it was no mirage and hauling myself to the lip, plunging my head into the coolness, drinking, drinking, then lifting my head to see reflected in the water four camels, and on the camels four men, and in the crook of each man's arm a firelock, and I thought without despair of my sister Andrea, whose hair was the colour of a wheatfield, my sister Andrea who moved with numinous grace and, smiling, I heard the shouts of the four riders, heard their leader cluck at his camel, the beast awkwardly collapsing its forelegs so he could slide from the saddle and, at a run, smash the stock of his firelock against my head.

XII

Meanwhile, Back in Madrid

'You're a remarkable woman, Doña Andrea.'

My sister's lawyer Picapleitos turned from the window of his chambers on San Vicente Ridge that overlooked almost condescendingly the Royal Palace. He sat and crossed his skinny legs, swinging a gold buckled shoe. His balding head rested on a mill wheel of a ruff. The tip of his inordinately long nose, which God or the Devil had pinched to a point, quivered.

Picapleitos stroked the nose, his clean hand somehow managing to leave an ink smear. 'Remarkable, lovely, and as young-looking as the day you first walked into my modest little chambers in – Sevilla, wasn't it?'

'I want my daughter,' Andrea told him.

'And you shall have her.'

'When? The District Court ordered Nicolás de Ovando to return her to me more than a year ago.'

'It is a sad fact of life, Doña Andrea, that the enforcement arm of the law, when confronting a man of substance, lacks teeth.'

'Substance? But he's a bankrupt.'

'I fear not.' With a sober stroke the nose was desmeared. 'The Royal Council acting in its judiciary capacity has determined that the estate of Ovando's uncle the Vicar-General, far from being insolvent, is impressively large. So large, in fact, that the District Court of Sevilla will hear Ovando's case against you.'

'*His* case against *me*?'

'Nicolás de Ovando is suing you in Sevilla for, ah, either defamatory damages or damaging defamation. You see, when you sued him there for, ah, breach of promise and he could not or would not pay, the court erroneously concluded that the Vicar-General's legacy was worthless.'

'But Ovando *made* them believe it was worthless so he wouldn't have to pay.'

'Still, you did initiate the suit, my dear.'

'I want my daughter.'

'And since Ovando is appealing – '

'*Appealing*? He's disgusting.'

' – the District Court's decision to grant you custody of the minor child Constanza de Figueroa, and since the hearing is already scheduled for late next year at the Tribunal of Appeals – '

'Late next year!'

'Believe me, we lawyers try to keep the case-flow flowing. You've seen my fifty-seven junior partners in the outer chambers, all burning their candles at both ends?' On went the smug ink smear again.

'She's an impressionable child, very young for her age. The Ovando mansion is no place for her, especially now that Pedro (Killer) Pacheco Portocarrero lives there.'

'To guard her from you, Ovando claims.'

'But he kidnapped her from me.'

'Be that as it may have been. Did I mention at our last meeting that Ovando was cross-suing you in the Tribunal of Matrimonial Tribulations?'

'Matrimonial? But we were never married.'

'When a child is involved, Matrimonial frequently claims jurisdiction. District naturally demurs. Its judges, clerks and so forth are entitled to make a living too.'

'But they *gave* custody of Constanza to me!'

'Their competence is also being disputed in the Tribunal de Hidalguía, where Ovando has challenged your father's gentility-by-repute on the grounds that the papers were not duly stamped when his lawyer registered them – '

148

'That was you.'

' – in Valladolid. It could not have been me, because I never make mistakes.'

'But it *was* you.'

'Or (I was coming to that) if it was me, then no mistake has been made. Of course, should Hidalguía rule, in the face of the facts, that the papers were improperly stamped, usage would forbid you to contest not only Ovando's petition but also his contention that the original court, whichever it was, was prejudiced against him.'

Andrea's mouth opened, but before she could speak, Picapleitos told her, 'However, you're in luck. Ovando is willing to concede your family's *hidalguía*-by-repute if you concede his guardianship of the minor child Constanza de Figueroa.'

'But – but why would any court grant him guardianship when all the courts concur that little Constanza's father is not Nicolás de Ovando but the late Captain Figueroa?'

'Precisely. So I suggest we counter-counter-sue at the Military and Naval Tribunal. Since the child's putative father was a hero of the Battle of Lepanto, killed in action and all that sort of thing – '

'But Captain Figueroa never existed. You advised me to pass myself off as the widow of some war hero.'

'Such legal fictions, my dear, once they become part of court records, have a life of their own far more, shall we say, vital than men of mere flesh and blood.' Again a swing of the gold-buckled shoe, again a quiver of the God- or Devil-pinched nose. 'At any rate, for all this expanded litigation, I shall need an additional retainer.'

'But just last week I gave you an additional retainer for my *sister*'s case.'

'The litigation of Señora Magdalena Pimentel de Sotomayor is costly because complex. But if she wins, the rewards will be great. Apparently she "loaned" the Pacheco Portocarrero brothers far more in the way of jewellery than you, my dear, could ever invent.'

'I only tried it the one time,' Andrea said. She refrained from adding, And it was all your idea.

'Given the proven resourcefulness of Ovando's counsel,' Picapleitos told her, 'the retainer must be substantial.'

'But the ship *Sol* carrying my brothers home from Italy last year was found abandoned off the coast of France, its decks awash with blood. So they are either dead or captured by Barbary pirates. How can I spare you more money if my family might receive ransom demands at any time?'

'If *Sol* were an ordinary merchantman carrying ordinary merchants,' said Picapleitos, 'the odds would favour capture. But *Sol* was transporting several companies of Don Juan's, ah, parrots I believe they are called, and those bloody decks bear mute testimony to how dearly and professionally they sold their lives. No, logic persuades me you will be troubled by no ransom demands.'

Andrea (as she told me long afterwards) would always remember with singular immediacy what happened next.

While Picapleitos dismissed my life and Rodrigo's, Andrea felt her world closing in: little Constanza kidnapped, Magdalena's endless litigation, Picapleitos demanding more money when she had none to pay the arrears of rent on the tall stone house near the Gate of the Sun or even to give to Doña Leonor 'so she and Papá might have food on the table – poor dear Papá, the barber-shop near the Gate of the Moors boarded up and him talking of going "on the old road again", but it was only talk, Miguel,' she would tell me, 'because Papá's spirit was broken. I knew he would never leave Madrid again – which was what *I* dreamed of doing, such a guilty dream, Miguel, just to leave it all behind, go somewhere, anywhere . . .'

And the next instant, even as she sat facing Picapleitos, a connection was somehow established through those vast vaulted distances where time expands to become space, for she remembers leaping from the client bench, knocking it over and clutching her head with both hands as, with no forewarning, she experienced intense pain. 'It felt,' she would tell me later, 'as if someone behind me, some invisible someone or some*thing*, struck my head a violent blow.'

(This had to be the precise moment the bounty-hunting nomad slid off his camel and smashed me unconscious with his firelock, but I never did tell Andrea that.)

Picapleitos barely had time to rid his nose of its tactlessly cheery ink smear before supporting Andrea with an arm around her shoulders. The lawyer was, for a moment, uncharacteristically at a loss for words.

Andrea, when the pain faded, felt a spurious (and short-lived) sense of well-being. 'A further retainer,' she said crisply, 'is out of the question. We don't *know* they're dead. If a ransom demand comes, we'll need every *maravedí* we have. Assuming we had any. Which we don't.'

'In that case' – Picapleitos found his tongue – 'you'll need someone who can influence the Mercenarians and Trinitarians who raise and allocate ransom money in God's name. I happen to have a cousin in minor orders who – '

'No,' Andrea began in what she convinced herself was icy self-control, 'it is premature to pre – '

'As any experienced attorney would assure you, it is never too early to prepare for so exigent a contingency.'

' – pare to meet ransom demands which have not been received and, perhaps, never will. Our priority – '

'But,' pointed out Picapleitos, 'I thought ransom demands were uppermost in your mind.'

Andrea shouted, 'Why is it that every time I talk to you I start sounding like a lawyer myself? Leave me alone – why can't you just leave me alone?' And, thoroughly belying those words, she went limp in Picapleitos's arms.

This was no weaker-sex-in-a-macho-world stratagem. 'I just couldn't take any more,' she would tell me.

Silently, she began to weep.

Picapleitos waited three beats of her heart against his narrow chest. Then he stroked her mane of wheaten hair and spoke, very unlawyerly.

'You're lovely when you weep. As lovely as when you smile. There doesn't,' he went on in a husky voice, 'have to be a retainer in the . . . normal sense of the term.'

She turned her tear-streaked face up in surprise.

His thin, pale, pettifogging lips touched hers. 'Madrid is a jungle,' he said. 'You need a protector.'

Once (she would remember thinking) she'd had one – Rizio Rizione. But she hadn't heard from him in years. Apparently no one had. The Genoese businessmen who no longer frequented her father's no longer open barber-shop believed that Rizione was dead.

Was Miguel dead too?

'. . . of mutual affection, but failing that, we could consider it a simple *liaison de convenance*,' Picapleitos was saying, his one free hand (thin, pale) daringly stroking her breast when it was not stroking his own nose. 'I'd represent you in any court in the land in return for – '

She brushed his hand away. 'I'll get the money,' she said.

Fifteen minutes later, Andrea stood in Toledo Street peering through softly falling snow at the Ovando mansion, invulnerable behind its stone wall, inscrutable windows aglow against the encroaching night like an enchanted castle (enchanted in the bad sense) in one of those knight-errantry stories Miguel used to read aloud when they were children. (Miguel! Miguel! Where are you now?) She imagined that at this very moment little Constanza stood at one of those inscrutable windows, her blue eye and her brown eye gazing forlornly out at the snow as she imagined, in her turn, that her mother would come to rescue her. Rescue her! Sometimes, sick with longing for her daughter, Andrea dreamed of it herself, a child's fantasy peopled with characters out of Miguel's stories – fearless heroes like Amadis of Gaul (whose face always was the dear familiar face of Miguel himself) and his brother Galaor, who between them could do any deed, anything.

As she reached this point in her reverie, picturing her lost brother rescuing her lost daughter, the old *sereno* came tottering along Toledo Street, ring of heavy iron keys jangling at his waist, heavy oak staff thumping the ground, and said in his kindly voice, 'Well, beautiful lady, I've let you tarry here longer than usual tonight looking up at those inscrutable windows and, you know, that's the kind of thing I'm paid to prevent, so I'll bid you a good evening, beautiful lady' – here a wink from his rheumy old eye – 'and hope to see you here again soon.'

Andrea returned the watchman's smile and, blowing a wistful kiss over the wall of little Constanza's prison, continued on her way to the Gate of the Sun and the tall stone house from which, unless a miracle happened, she and Tomás Gutiérrez would be evicted tomorrow.

Tomás opened the door for her.

'What are you doing here?' they both asked.

'I just wanted one last look around,' Tomás said.

'Me too.'

There wasn't much left to see in the Tall Stone House Players' School for Ladies. The furniture, carpets and wall hangings had gone over a period of months to the Monte de Piedad, with no hope they would ever be redeemed.

They went into the sitting-room, where a meagre fire glowed on the hearth.

'Last of the firewood,' Tomás said. 'Last of everything.' He put a foot up on the fender, his waxed date-coloured shoe reflecting the firelight. He always wore those shoes, every day; they set Andrea's teeth on edge. 'I was just thinking – when the eviction crew come in the morning to put all our stuff out on the street, it'll be kind of funny. Because we got no stuff.'

Andrea dredged up a wan smile. 'Where will you go, Tomás? What will you do?'

'Well, I got a friend of mine that's assistant producer at the Prince. No reason a drama coach can't do some acting himself, is there?' Tomás asked, somewhat defensively.

'Of course not. And you were a good drama coach too.'

'What will *you* do?'

'It doesn't matter. Live with my family, take in sewing maybe.' Or find a job. Shop girl, scullion, something.

How Andrea hated failure!

'Work your fingers to the bone for a few coppers? You're much too good for that, Andrea.'

She said, as surprised as he by her sharp words, 'Must you always wear those ridiculous shoes?'

'What? My shoes? What's wrong with them? They're broken in, comfortable as — as an old shoe. Ha, ha. And the wax keeps my feet dry when it rains.'

'They're hideous. The ugliest shoes I ever saw.'

Tomás's open, homely face took on an injured look.

Andrea had never realized how just plain *hulking* he was for a short man. And with his bull neck and earnest, close-set eyes, not exactly your suave theatrical coach. No wonder the school had folded.

'Maybe if you'd had a little *savoir faire*,' she said, and immediately hated herself for blaming their failure on Tomás. But she looked at the ridiculous shoe up on the fender and couldn't stop. 'If you'd known how to butter people up instead of insulting them, like the time Anica Villafranca was a shoo-in for the new Timoneda comedy, until you told Timoneda he should stick to being a printer.'

'Now wait a minute here! I found Ana Villafranca in a seedy tavern in German Street. I taught her everything she knows about acting. I taught them all. Except for me, little Anica would still be serving beer in German Street.'

'That's exactly what she's doing right now,' Andrea said coldly.

'And you? If you weren't always giving every ducat we earned to that Pimentel de Sotomayor bitch — '

' "That Pimentel de Sotomayor bitch" happens to be my sister, and I never gave her a *maravedí* she didn't desperately need.'

'For what?' shouted Tomás. 'For a twelve-pile velvet gown stretched over a farthingale as wide as a queen's?'

'A young girl has to keep up appearances to attract a suitable husband. Maybe Magdalena does live beyond her means, but — '

'The only suitable husband I can think of for that Pimentel de Sotomayor bitch is Pedro (Killer) Pacheco Portocarrero. And she don't live beyond her means, she lives beyond *our* means.'

'Oh, this is lovely,' said Andrea. 'I actually came here tonight feeling sentimental.'

'You started it,' Tomás told her.

'*I* started it?'

'Picking on my shoes.'

'It's a long way from commenting on a person's shoes to calling a person's sister a bitch and a — '

'Well, she is,' insisted Tomás, and Andrea wanted to fling something at that open, homely face, right between those earnest, close-set eyes. Instead, quite suddenly, she was laughing.

'Listen to us,' she said. 'We've worked together so long, we're bickering just like an old married couple.'

'I'm sorry,' Tomás said. 'For bickering and all.'

'So am I, Tomás. It was my fault.'

'I wish I knew how to say the right things, like Juan Rufo always used to. I wish I knew how to handle people. Especially women.'

Back on to the fender went a waxed date-coloured shoe.

'They're not so bad, Tomás, really,' Andrea said. 'I mean, if they're comfortable and keep you dry. What are shoes for, after all?'

'I was thinking,' Tomás said thoughtfully.

Andrea gave him an encouraging nod.

'What you said about bickering, you know?' He poked at a smouldering log, got another encouraging nod from Andrea. 'Just like an old married couple.' He listened for a while to the flutter of wind in the flue.

'The wax on your shoe is beginning to melt,' Andrea said.

Tomás withdrew his foot quickly from the fender and stared moodily at the last fire they would ever share in the Tall Stone House Players' School for Ladies.

Then he said, 'Andrea, will you marry me?'

Outside, a fierce gust lifted a few roof tiles and dropped them to shatter in the street.

Andrea said, 'Oh, Tomás! I don't know what to say after such a beautiful . . . beautiful . . .'

'You could try "yes".'

Andrea took his hand. Kissed him lightly on the cheek. Tears gathered in her pale blue eyes as Tomás stared raptly into them.

'I can't, Tomás,' she said simply, 'for I love another.'

'Oh well, sure. Juan Rufo. What lady wouldn't? A handsome, smooth-talking courtier with a brilliant future if he's still alive, and me with a mouth full of my own waxed date-coloured shoe. But — I wouldn't say this, believe me, except he's my best friend and I know he'd want me to — Juan Rufo's probably dead, Andrea. Or else he's a prisoner of the Barbary pirates, same as your brothers. They treat them like animals. Throw them in dungeons. Beat them. Torture them. The lucky ones die. You got to face reality, Andrea. Most prisoners never return from Algiers, never – what are you crying for?'

At that moment came the thud of the iron door knocker (Tomás's design: an elliptical ring in the mouths of side-by-side masks of tragedy and comedy), and Tomás, torn between concern for Andrea and curiosity, was only halfway to the door when it swung open to reveal a tall man, enviably handsome, with a twin-pointed beard. His right hand, in a remembered pose, hovered over the hilt of his rapier.

'Juan!' Tomás exclaimed. 'Juan Rufo!'

In another part of the city, Pedro de Isunza, once the ill-fated Crown Prince's bodyguard and now a petty functionary with the Investment Branch of the Supreme and General Council of the Inquisition, was hurrying through windswept streets, his black cape stiffly spread like the wings of a vampire bat, in the direction of the Inquisition processing centre located in the cellars (not the dungeons, for, like good wine, dungeons require ageing) of a nondescript building of that unweathered pine so ubiquitous in King Felipe II the Death-Loving's new capital. Cutpurses, footpads and other creatures of the night avoided Pedro de Isunza with an uneasiness they would have been unable to explain. A single obscure figure, however, followed him at a distance professionally adjusted to the emptiness of the streets, the darkness and Isunza's obvious hurry to reach his destination. When he did, the obscure figure slipped behind a stack of pine boards and scribbled for some time in a notebook, pausing only to reflect on the irony of his gathering information for a Certain Mutual Acquaintance (whom he had never met) at a time when insiders in the secret world had begun to suspect he was no longer even alive.

Pedro de Isunza spent most nights for the next four or five months in the cellars interrogating a gypsy-dark processee before returning to his spartan billet under the eaves of one of Madrid's few tall stone houses, very like the one where my sister Andrea and Tomás Gutiérrez were last seen. The obscure figure, hatless and, like Isunza, black-clad, filled notebook after notebook, writing in a code based on certain references to the summoning and employment of demons in the controversial Abbot of Sponheim's as-yet-unpublished masterwork, the *Steganographia*.

The gypsy-dark processee was now legally named Luis Blackslave – a name he had adopted by deed-poll with his sardonic sang-froid soon after he gained his freedom that long-ago night in Alcalá when the Crown Prince fell downstairs.

Luis (according to the entries my brother Juan the Obscure made in

155

what came to be called the Luis Blackslave Steganographic Notebooks) had arrived at the processing centre in response to the usual summons. A high-crowned silk hat covered his shaven pate, and he wore a flamboyant scarlet velvet cloak. He looked prosperous and menacing. He even flashed a smile displaying five or six wicked gold teeth when Pedro de Isunza made his appearance.

'What's this all about, anyway?' asked the unfazed Luis.

Here, at his first opportunity to establish rapport with the processee, Pedro de Isunza miscalculated. 'A minor matter, Señor Blackslave, which I'm sure you can easily clear up for us. No need to stand on ceremony, because I am as lowborn as you.'

'Lowborn? What the *hell* you talking about, man? My father is king-emperor of a vast archipelago stretching from the Yucatán coast to the Windward Islands and north to Bermuda, with a population three times Spain and England combined. With the Low Countries thrown in. When you say lowborn, man, don't speak for *me*.'

They glared mutual antipathy until the arrival of the torturer, who, according to custom and the Steganographic Notebooks, worked for the state, not the Suprema, which – rather like Muslim physicians in Algiers, if any could be found – seemed squeamish about shedding its victims' blood.

The torturer, when he learned that Pedro de Isunza worked only in Investment Branch, objected to his using processing centre facilities, but a gold coin exchanged hands and all adjourned to the torture chamber – Juan the Obscure apparently included, if unseen, as evidenced by verbatim dialogue in the Steganographic Notebooks.

Example:

'It's a well-known fact,' said Pedro de Isunza, 'that placing the processee *in conspectu tormentorum*, in sight of the torture instruments, is often sufficient to make him talk.'

'Avoiding unpleasantness all round,' added the torturer.

'But I have nothing to hide from anyone,' said Luis Blackslave with his habitual sang-froid. 'Ask your questions and I'll answer. Then we can all go home.'

'Impossible, I regret to say,' sniffed the torturer.

'Ever since the enlightened days of classical Greece,' explained Pedro de Isunza, 'a slave's testimony has been admissible only under torture. Here, for once, secular humanism is in complete accord with the Holy Office.'

Luis showed those five or six wicked gold teeth. 'But *I'm* no slave. I gained my freedom in 1564.'

On this seemingly innocuous statement, Isunza pounced. 'Wasn't it rather in 1562 that you gained your freedom?'

'Man! It meant a lot to me! So I ought to know when it happened. Which was in 1564.'

'You lie,' said Pedro de Isunza, and the door burst open right on schedule to admit six Suprema guards, all huge, who stripped Luis to his black – actually only a little darker than a gypsy – integument, but not before he laid three of them out flat.

'You'll agree, despite his protestations,' Pedro de Isunza asked the torturer, 'that he looks like a slave? The colour may be a bit off, but observe the musculature.'

'Plus,' said the torturer, 'he is hung the way black slaves are said to be hung.'

Luis, uninjured in the affray save for the loss of a pair of (natural white) teeth, lisped the single word, 'Jealouth?'

The three remaining guards bound Luis's hands behind his back and lugged their less fortunate comrades out, while the torturer commenced 'in conspectu tormentorum'.

'Here we have the garrucha and here the toca and here the potro.' He gestured at the pulley, the water-torture apparatus and the rack, respectively. 'All are capable of generating exquisite pain that reduces a man, even a well-hung black slave, to a blob of quivering cuajada.'

Luis Blackslave was unimpressed. 'I'm no slave.'

'Precisely how,' probed Pedro de Isunza, 'did you gain your freedom in – April, wasn't it? – 1562?'

'It was October. Of '64.'

(No resolution of this chronological disagreement is offered in the Steganographic Notebooks, but clearly the two men were viewing the same event in different time frames, Isunza in historical time and Luis Blackslave in fictional.)

'In conspectu tormentorum' having no effect, Luis was next hoisted by his bound wrists on the garrucha until his shaven pate touched the ceiling, a manoeuvre that threatened to dislocate his shoulders. Then an unprecedented thing happened.

Luis Blackslave momentarily lost his sang-froid.

The rush of terror at the first application of the torturer's art so humiliated him that, once he mastered it, he vowed that the eighth circle of Hell would freeze over and the ninth melt (even if this meant releasing Judas Iscariot from eternal torment, not to mention Lucifer) before he told these sadists what they wanted to know

According to other entries in the Luis Blackslave Steganographic Note-books, every night after torture had been suspended, Pedro de Isunza hurried home to his spartan billet to dream his recurrent nightmare, featuring 'a fantastically pulchritudinous virgin bearing an uncanny resemblance to [*name deleted*], who whipped him mercilessly with her long mane of wheaten hair'.

Though his billet was spartan, Pedro de Isunza's reaction to pain was not. At least half these nightmare whippings brought him to orgasm, and on several occasions he woke to find his skin covered with weals.

How Juan the Obscure learned the substance of the recurrent nightmares, and whether he actually saw the weals (which invariably faded moments after Isunza woke), is not spelled out in the notebooks.

Under Inquisition rules a processee could be tortured only once, so you may well wonder at the four or five months of questioning Luis Blackslave underwent. The Suprema solved this vexing limitation by a clever pretext: the end of any given session was classed as a suspension (the torturer had tired, the surgeon recommended a respite for the processee, etc.) rather than a termination.

An admirable solution. So admirable that I think I'll borrow it.

I mean, do you *really* want to witness all the grisly details of those four or five months of torture?

Squeamishness aside, wouldn't you rather hear what was developing (or not) between my sister and Juan Rufo, or how my family set about ransoming Rodrigo and me, or what happened the first time my father died, or even what happened to me when the bounty-hunters returned me to Algiers?

I'll get to all that right away.

But the processing of Luis Blackslave would have its repercussions. For if Luis, broken in body though not in spirit, had not bought a mule and headed for Andalucía to spend what was left of his life under the healing southern sun, then my own life would have unfolded as history records it and not as I disclose it here.

Let me just say, then, that during the time Luis Blackslave was tortured he steadily refused to answer Pedro de Isunza's crucial (if partly rhetorical) question, which Juan the Obscure transcribed as:

'Now tell me, while working in the Frenchman Pierre Papin's gambling den in Alcalá on the night of 19 April fifteen 1562, or, if you insist, some night in October of 1564, did you not see, losing recklessly at backgammon, a remorseless putative virgin, so lithe and long-limbed and blue-eyed that she might have leaped straight from the pages of Tacitus into the *cercle privé* with a go-to-hell look in her eyes and a deadly – a deadly – mane of long wheaten hair?'

One Thursday night when Pedro de Isunza entered the cellars, he saw that Luis Blackslave was fully clothed up to his high-crowned silk hat and was showing all those wicked gold teeth in a smile.

'What is this?' Isunza asked as the door opened to admit, he assumed, the torturer. Instead he saw a white-robed Dominican who demanded by what authority he, a petty functionary of Investment Branch, had been using processing-centre facilities.

Lacking an answer, Isunza lost his job on the spot.

Here, the Luis Blackslave Steganographic Notebooks end. But Pedro de Isunza and his implacable obsession do not disappear from these pages. For a time he buried himself in the ranks of Don Juan's army in the Low Countries. Travelling north with his regiment, he dreamed his recurrent nightmare every night. Somehow, he swore in his torment, he would find his wheaten-haired Nemesis and make her pay for destroying his life – for Pedro de Isunza believed with the moral certainty of a martyr (or a madman) that he would one day have walked the innermost corridors of power, the trusted confidant of the next king of the first empire on which the sun never set, except for the unknown virgin's murderous intervention.

The corridors of power were the objective of the budding courtier Juan Rufo too. But courtier-ing does not preclude courting, and in the first reliably balmy days of summer, Juan Rufo proposed marriage to my sister Andrea.

'I want to make you my wife,' were his exact words.

Andrea knew this was a more serious declaration than the ritual proposals Juan Rufo had made yearly, before his Algerian captivity, on the anniversary of their meeting.

'Oh,' she said, self-deprecatingly, 'you could do much better than me.'

'Let me be the judge of that.'

'I'm past thirty.'

'You don't look a day over twenty.'

(She didn't.)

'And there's my child, poor little Constanza who – '

'I'll give the child my name.'

They were strolling along the leafy banks of the Manzanares followed by two gypsy guitarists hired by Juan Rufo for the occasion.

'First,' Andrea suggested, and held her breath, 'it might be a good idea to get her back.'

'No problem whatever, my dear. I have merely to whisper your petition at the appropriate time in the ear of my patron Mateo Vázquez, newest of King Felipe II the Death-Loving's secretaries, and it shall be done.'

'Why wasn't last month appropriate? Or the month before?'

'Court intrigue, my dear; I thought you understood. For every word I can whisper in the ear of *my* patron, Nicolás de Ovando can whisper two to the senior royal secretary Antonio Pérez, lover of the one-eyed Princess Eboli, second most beautiful woman in Spain.'

'Does that,' asked Andrea, 'also explain why my brothers are still captive in Algiers?'

'We don't know that they are. I mentioned their case to Mateo Vázquez. They may be on their way home right now.'

(We weren't.)

At a signal from Juan Rufo, the first gypsy leaned over his guitar and coaxed a reluctant chord from it. The second gypsy gazed past Andrea, who was watching the play of sunlight on water, and uttered a flamenco wail acknowledging the illusion of human existence.

Sorely tempted though she must have been, Andrea did not agree to marry Juan Rufo if he used his influence to free little Constanza, Rodrigo and me. Later, when I asked her why, she told me, 'I'm not sure I wouldn't have. Most women marry for worse reasons.'

I felt obscurely offended. 'But the point is, you didn't.'

'I didn't have time.' The gypsy, she told me, had hardly begun wailing about the illusion of human existence when a messenger came galloping up with a letter for Juan Rufo. He read it, and his face turned white.

'Mateo Vázquez's faction has lost out at court,' he said.

'What will you do?'

'Keep a low profile for a few weeks. Or months. These things blow over.'

In the months that followed, Andrea had her hands full trying to keep the peace in the former Tall Stone House Players' School for Ladies, now the family home. Juan Rufo had settled the rent in the nick of time and had taken Tomás Gutiérrez into service as major-domo in his own modest twenty-two-room town house.

After my father died, my mother wouldn't let him outside. He spent most of his time polishing his old barber's basin, the last relic of his profession, until it gleamed like gold.

'*Ojalá* that it were,' said Doña Leonor. In the years her husband had dwindled, she had grown fat and moustached.

'No luck?' my father asked her one day, polishing and polishing.

160

'*Will* you stop that?'

'It gives me something to do.'

My father's demise disappointed him, for he soon found being dead no different from life as a retired barber-surgeon, except that his hearing had improved.

'Since when does a dead man need something to do?'

My sister Magdalena a/k/a Señora Pimentel de Sotomayor came in. She had no court appearances scheduled that day. 'It's beginning to look like Mambrino's helmet,' she said.

'You've read *Orlando Furioso*?' my father asked eagerly.

'I don't have to, you've talked about it enough. Such childish nonsense! A pure gold helmet that makes its wearer invulnerable. Really, Father.' Then, to Doña Leonor, 'Dotty. He's definitely dotty.'

'He's not dotty, he's dead,' said my mother, trying in exasperation to take the barber's basin from him. But he clung with a death grip, and when she put the basin up on a shelf my dwindled father, still holding on, went with it. Doña Leonor gave up and, on the shelf, my father resumed polishing.

After a while he held the gleaming basin at arm's length to admire it. Then he put it on his head. Then, embarrassed, he took it off and climbed down from the shelf.

'Being dead,' Andrea told me later, 'did make him a little dotty. But it was awful of Magdalena to say so.'

'Was that the day Mamá saw Prefect Olivar of the Order of Mercy?'

'It was.'

'How did she arrange Papá's death, anyway?'

'Picapleitos has a cousin, a physician who, for a small consideration, signs defunct-certificates. After that it was just a matter of a few *maravedís* for the government stamp.'

'And then she went to the Order of Mercy?' I asked.

The Mercenarians' most successful ransomer, Prefect Jorge del Olivar of Valencia, was then in Madrid seeking worthy candidates for release from Algerian captivity.

'One of my poor boys had his head cut off and the other is missing an arm,' my mother told him.

'His head?' repeated Prefect Olivar.

'Whose head what?' asked Doña Leonor.

Prefect Olivar waited philosophically for her to sort things out.

'Poor Miguel, as I was saying, had his hand cut off and poor Rodrigo is missing an arm.'

(Rodrigo, you will remember, was intact.)

161

'And as I am so recently widowed, they are, or would be if ransomed, my sole supports.'

'But,' said Prefect Olivar, 'how can they support you, disabled as they are? What do they do in life?'

'The one whose hand was cut off is a published poet.'

'Published or not,' the Prefect said with a sad shake of his head, 'poet is not on the approved list of widow-supporters.'

'The one who lost his leg is a professional soldier.'

'His arm.'

'Whose arm what?' asked Doña Leonor.

'I'm almost sure you said the other boy lost his arm.'

'It was his leg. Cut off at the shoul – hip!'

'Señora,' said the Prefect uncomfortably, 'arm or leg, I fear he has no future as a professional soldier. So he couldn't support you either.'

Desperate, Doña Leonor embroidered. 'Shortly before patriotically enlisting to fight at the Battle of Lepanto, which we in our family call "The Naval", the elder boy had some not inconsiderable experience as a courtier. For a time Liars' Walk was his second home.'

'Now that is something else again,' smiled the Prefect. 'The elder boy, you say?' Doña Leonor nodded. 'Because, other things being equal, we always try to ransom the elder son. It is part of his birthright. We cannot, alas, offer our assistance to more than one family member. At a time. In any given decade. The elder son's name is?'

'Miguel. Former courtier. Had his head cut off. Hand! Won a medal. *Aventajado*. For valour. A published poet. Sole support of his – '

'You'll hear from us, señora.'

'Which,' Andrea told me afterwards, 'we did. With the wonderful news that when the Mercenarians sailed for Algiers, one of the hundred and fifty prisoners they would ransom, if terms could be agreed, was you.'

'Didn't they find out what happened at Liars' Walk?'

'They might have, but Juan Rufo was able to misplace the records. Around then the Mateo Vázquez faction at court had found it expedient to misplace all official records concerning any of them.'

'I see,' I said.

'What I don't see,' said Andrea, 'is how you managed to switch things so Rodrigo was ransomed instead of you.'

'I had to. His life was in danger.'

'But you were the one always trying to escape across deserts and seas and so on.'

'Still, he was in more danger.'

162

'Miguel,' Andrea said. 'What used to be your left hand, it's starting to jump a little.'

It was jumping more than a little. But Andrea had a way of mentioning it that didn't make it worse. In fact, it restrained itself as I went on.

'He was in mortal danger from his fellow Christian prisoners. Including me.'

XIII

In Which I Save My Brother's Life
At the Peril of My Own

Emerging into pitiless sunlight after more than a year in the deepest (I was sure) dungeon in Algiers, I didn't have to be borne along by any festive crowds to any Plaza of Atrocities to run into Gabriel Múñoz. The grizzlehead was lounging against a wall right outside the gate.

'What's on for today?' I asked in a voice creaky with disuse. 'Hanging, impalement, the hook? A nice retaliatory dismemberment?'

'I do not do guided tours these days.'

We had fallen into step heading towards Souk Street and the bazaar, where Turks shoved Moors aside and Moors shoved Christians – except that there weren't any. Not a black-and-white-striped burnous was to be seen but ours.

'Where is everybody?' I asked.

'Down at the harbour besieging the Order of Mercy.'

'They've come?' My heart jumped into my throat, even though I knew my chances were worse than hopeless.

'Thirty-five thousand captives, thirty-five thousand reasons to be ransomed first. Will they ever learn? With the Order of Mercy it is all decided in Spain before the Prefect boards ship. Like kismet. But enough of a taverner's philosophizing. You will want your hair cut and that beard hacked back so you do not trip over it on the gangplank.'

I grabbed the arm that was steering me towards a barber-shop. 'What did you say?'

I stood still. I wasn't breathing.

He grinned. 'Congratulations, *compañero*. How your family managed it I do not know, but you made the list.'

Cuajada-kneed, I followed him into the barber-shop.

'Rodrigo is dying to see you,' Múñoz said. 'Especially on account of he does not get out much these days.'

'Why not?'

The barber asked, 'How may I help . . . ah, I see, sir. Please to sit.'

The barber, a small man with bright eyes and quivery pink jowls, didn't look Moorish. Yet no leg irons clanked as he positioned himself behind me and began to snip. His barber's basin, I observed, was a dull thing compared to my father's. Which didn't stop it from being beautiful. Everything was beautiful. Ransomed – me – ransomed!

'When do I sail?' I asked Gabriel Múñoz.

'Patience, *compañero*. A hundred and fifty ransomees make for a lot of paperwork. This Prefect Olivar and the new Dey will be at it for another week.'

'Hassan Pasha Dey the Venetian,' the barber groaned. His scissors nicked my ear. 'Known far and wide as the world's most sadistic man. Not,' he added hastily, 'that I have any complaints.'

Snip, snip.

'So you have been ransomed,' he said. 'You are a soldier, am I right?'

I looked at him in surprise.

'What used to be your left hand,' he explained, and attacked my beard. 'We Jews have had no military tradition since Massada. A decided short-coming in times like these. It's why I admired that Cervantes so much. A military man to the core. Spain must be told of his deeds.' He waved his comb emphatically. 'But from the look of it you've been in a dungeon or chained in a galley. So maybe you never heard of Rodrigo de Cervantes. It was a dungeon – you're pale enough for ten dungeons. But your friend here can tell you all about Cervantes.'

'You are not doing too bad of a job yourself,' said Gabriel Múñoz.

'Me? I mind my own business. I'm only a Jewish barber sometimes erroneously called the Wise, Suleiman Sa'adah by name. But I respect a real soldier and never mind his detractors. He used to have his beard trimmed here.'

'Cervantes?' I asked.

'The same. Outside would be an angry crowd. You think it's easy organizing thirty-five thousand captives along military lines? But it was good for them and good for Ramadan Pasha Dey. One hand washes the other, that's wrong?'

From the doorway a voice shouted, 'Pig-dog Christian! Out of that chair! Pig-dog Jew! My master desires a haircut and beard trim! You will use new scissors and comb!' These exhortations came from a eunuch who ushered in a portly fellow removing an aquamarine turban.

Suleiman Sa'adah the Jew bowed low. 'Captain Dalí Mamí,' he said, and I rose from the chair to face my master Gimp the Greek. Through the doorway I caught a glimpse of the lean, dark man with the Princess Eboli eye-patch.

'Miguel, dear boy!' the fat renegade captain cried.

I evaded his bearhug by saying that Sa'adah the Jew had found me infested with a remarkable crop of lice after my fourteen months in the deepest dungeon in Algiers.

Gimp the Greek said, 'What fun we could have had, you and I! Golden chains I'd have given you. Are you sure you wouldn't . . . no, all that's over now. I got your ransom papers yesterday – a clerical error, since I don't even own you any more. So I won't get the five hundred gold ducats. By Christ! I mean, by Allah, is that fair?'

'Who will?' I couldn't help asking.

'The new Dey, Hassan Pasha the Venetian. He's expropriated every remotely ransomable slave we pirate captains owned. I may have to mortgage the palace.' An epic sigh. 'But we all have our troubles, and I commiserate, dear boy, with you. Your poor brother, what ghastly kismet. But new régimes, new problems – as how well I know. Hassan the Venetian is no Ramadan Pasha, as your brother knows too, to his terminal regret.' Gimp the Greek eased his bulk into the barber's chair. 'Well, peace be with you, and may Allah the Compassionate and Merciful lighten the days which, with luck, remain to your brother.'

Outside, to my stammered questions, Gabriel Múñoz replied, 'Calmly, *compañero*. You will see him soon.'

It was one of those typically clandestine houses on a nameless narrow street in which faceless irrelevant people lead pointlessly inscrutable lives behind imperturbable whitewashed walls.

'You're supposed to identify yourself,' Gabriel Múñoz told me outside the door, 'by saying, "Everything the Laughing Philosopher knew he learned from Leucippus," and they must answer, "Demogorgon dwells in the Abyss with three fatal sisters or atop the Himalayas with elves and feys."'

As I knocked, he disappeared into the labyrinth of alleys between the bazaar and the Bab-Azun Gate. A peephole opened to reveal a disturbing amber eye.

I said, ' "Everything the Laughing Philosopher knew he learned from Leucippus," ' and a silver soprano voice cried, 'How did you find me?' and I turned to run, sure that something had gone amiss. But the voice called after me, 'Wait! "Demogorgon dwells in the Abyss with, uh, three fatal sisters or, uh, atop the Himalayas" – what comes next?' and I supplied, 'With elves and feys,' and came back.

In the doorway stood a small, slender figure all in white. Memory clicked into place – a blood orange on a head of dark curls, Gimp the Greek's wayward arrow, a callipygean child playing dangerous games.

'If nobody knows where I live,' she asked, 'how did you ever find me?'

'I wasn't looking for you.'

'Oh.' Did she sound deflated?

'I was looking for my brother. Is he here?'

'You're his brother? You? But *you're* like all the others, only interested in having their way with me – while he's the only man I almost trust in this life.'

'Listen,' I said, 'the only time I met you, the night of that orgy, you were injured and overwrought, and I just wanted to see you home and give you a sleeping potion.'

'How naïve did you think I was?'

'Micaela,' I asked, wishing she was still a boy so I could muscle her out of the doorway, 'don't you think you might let me come in?'

'I suppose. If you said Leucippus and so forth you said Leucippus and so forth.'

I followed the flouncing callipygean curve of Micaela Maltrapillo into an interior patio, off which impassive doors hid recondite rooms. On the mosaic floor was a creditable likeness of the fabulous cockatrice, whose very stare could shatter rock or burn a man to ash; I was reminded of my grandfather Juan the Patriarch.

Micaela exited through an archway at the opposite side of the patio.

Hearing a whisper of sound behind me, I whirled.

Breathless, trailing a diaphanous veil or two, long-limbed and olive-skinned and lithe in a world that preferred its women fat and white and tender, Zoraida the trance dancer hurried on to the patio. Her kohl-darkened eyes smiled.

'I remember you – you're the *ráwi*,' she said. 'What an easy life! Sitting around the marketplace all day telling stories. Lucky you.'

Dropping asprawl one of those ubiquitous diamond-studded alabaster couches, she clapped her hands to summon twin albino eunuchs bearing an awesome array of food in and on baskets and bowls, salvers, tureens, casseroles, crocks, panniers, punnets, canisters etc. etc., putting Gimp the Greek's remembered feasts to shame.

'I eat and eat, but I just get thinner,' sighed Zoraida the trance dancer. 'Speaking of which, you could use some flesh on your bones yourself, storyteller. Eat.'

I watched while she polished off plump partridges and ribs of fatted calf, hillocks of sherbet and ziggurats of cheeses. Overwhelmed, I finally settled on a modest earthenware bowl of couscous – upmarket Algerian *migas*. During my fourteen months in the deepest dungeon in Algiers, crumbs in rancid olive oil were my only link with reality, and from that day in Zoraida's patio *migas* became, as perversely they were fated to be, my favourite food.

I began to grow uneasy as Zoraida worked her way through that Gargantuan feast without bringing up the subject of my brother. Or any other subject.

'This is an opulent place you've got here,' I tried.

'I can't afford it any more. It's on the market. Ramadan Pasha Dey was a devout believer in trance dancing – he'd send for me if he so much as caught the sniffles – but Hassan the Venetian is a disbeliever in everything but astrology. Lucky Cide Hamete. Well, so you're Rodrigo's brother. I never even knew until yesterday that he had one. Ransomed! Lucky you.'

'Isn't he here?' I asked as drums and pipes sounded from the direction of the Dey's palace – the public hangman's musicians signalling curfew with the same dirgeful melody they played at executions, appropriately, since curfew-breaking was a capital offence.

'He ought to be starting for here right now.'

'After curfew?'

'*Only* after curfew. Micaela knows every back alley. She's taught him how to avoid janissary patrols.'

'What's wrong with before curfew?'

'Too many people. Somebody would turn him in for the reward.'

'Reward?'

'A new dey brings his own ideas to the job. Not that your brother had it easy before. He got a lot of resistance from his fellow Christian captives right from the beginning,' Zoraida said. 'How I met him, he was carried here more dead than alive after a beating by his own people. It took months and all my trance dancing skills to restore his health, not to mention his self-esteem.'

She cast her eyes down. 'If you're thinking what you're thinking, you're wrong. I'm talented enough at trance dancing, but no man finds a scarecrow like me desirable. Well, every profession has its drawbacks. Don't you find, as a storyteller, that people sometimes won't believe you when you tell the truth?

'There are other things in the world besides sex,' she said unconvincingly.

Having just devoured a brace of pheasants, she attacked the hind leg of a sheep. 'Organizing prisoners has its drawbacks too. Sure, your brother got them better working conditions and food distribution, but they saw him as a drill sergeant keeping them in line for the Dey.' She bit down savagely on the knee joint, splintering bone. 'He wasn't a martinet, really. More of a flawed altruist. But just when he was getting somewhere, along came this new Dey, Hassan Pasha the Venetian, and his first move was to return the prisoners to the anarchy they'd lived in until Rodrigo got here. Still, I see your point.'

I hadn't, so far as I could tell, made any point.

'Namely that, if the new Dey believes in only two things, astrology and the infliction of pain, an organized prison population is unwelcome and its organizer expendable. Or was it Cide Hamete who made that point?'

While the twin albino eunuchs were clearing the detritus of the feast, Micaela Maltrapillo returned.

'He's here.'

'How does he look?' Zoraida asked.

'The same,' said Micaela.

'How do I look?'

'Skinny,' said Micaela, who was not exactly fat herself. But since practically everybody believed she was a boy, corpulence would add nothing to her status as the most desired sex object in Algiers.

'Give me a few minutes alone with him, *ráwi*,' said Zoraida, and Micaela led me through the archway to a smaller patio with its own smaller mosaic cockatrice.

'She's in love with him,' Micaela informed me.

She stood in profile to me, her white silk pantaloons clinging softly to that classic callipygean curve.

'I look more noticeably like a girl, don't I?' she asked in a worried voice.

'Not necessarily,' I tried to reassure her.

'Oh? You *do* like girls? If not, you're hardly the one to ask. If I do look more female, steps will have to be taken. Drastic steps. Because that would be the end of my father's arrangement with the Dey, which just happens to be practically the only . . . only continuity between the régimes, so I ought to be . . . proud. Me! The sublime and supremely unattainable . . . the most beautiful boy in Algiers! I mean, a girl's pretty worthless, isn't she? In the marketplace, three . . . three teenage girls are only worth one mangy old camel,' she said, and suddenly broke into tears.

I put my arm around her and stroked her dark curls. Her scent was like new-mown hay and a touch of some oriental perfume, musk-rose dew perhaps.

'Keep your hands to yourself,' she said. 'You'd just love to have your way with me, wouldn't you?'

I pulled back. 'Micaela, I only meant to comfort you.'

'Turks and Moors want their way with the boy-me, and if you're any sample, Christians do too once they know I'm a girl. You're all the same, only different. Men! You're all after one thing – except Rodrigo. He's been a big brother to me and now . . . now they're going to kill him.'

As she spoke, a man came through the archway.

'Leave us, Michele,' he said, and Micaela did.

His hair was grey with, I saw, a single streak the colour of blood over the left temple; his eyes, pale blue like our sister Andrea's, looked bleak as a winter storm on a bone-bare plain in La Mancha. But when he spoke my name, shouted it almost, his harrowed face changed until I was looking at that remembered freckle-participating grin as we embraced, held each other off at arm's length, stared, laughed, embraced again.

'Home,' he said wonderingly. 'You're going home.'

I nodded. I could not speak.

He said, 'I'm living in a Jew's house. Would you believe it? I never even knew a Jew before, and now one's hiding me. A barber, Suleiman Sa'adah Sometimes Erroneously Called the Wise. He's Zoraida's uncle.'

'She's a Jewess?' I asked in surprise, relieved to have something – anything – to talk about. My brother had a price on his head, but I was going home. How could I talk about that?

'I don't know what she is. Sometimes I almost think she's a *jinnayah*. That would explain the trance dancing.'

'You believe in *jinn*?'

'Zoraida believes in nothing.'

'Everybody believes in something.'

'Not Zoraida. She's an – unusual person. She came here from Smyrna four or five years ago with her uncle.'

'As prisoners?'

169

'No, they just came. Algiers is no worse than Smyrna for a Jew. Besides, you see the way Zoraida lives.'

'I see the way you live. Going out only after curfew, and without leg irons. That's giving the janissaries a licence to kill you on sight, you know.'

Rodrigo shrugged. 'It got to be a habit when Ramadan Pasha was Dey. You don't think I spent all my time working for him, do you?'

'I never knew how you spent your time.'

'Ramadan Pasha had a list of prisoners he wanted killed. Malcontents.'

I wondered how any prisoner could not be malcontent.

'The new Dey, Hassan Pasha, *prefers* them,' Rodrigo told me. 'Any prisoner who pretends to be happy is up to something, Hassan thinks, so he beats the happiness out of them.

'But I was saying. One by one I took the men on Ramadan Pasha's death list to a cave on an estate outside the Bab-Azun Gate, where Zoraida knows the gardener. That meant going at night, and it's lucky I got used to it before Hassan Pasha came along. The first thing he did was break up our system of squads and companies, and the next thing was, he issued my death warrant.'

'But why?'

'His way of thanking me for teaching the prisoners discipline, maybe. But I'm a soldier. I can handle it. I had a pretty good run and, whatever they think, I helped our people. If I'm killed, that's my fate. Kismet.'

'Kismet's only an excuse for not staring your "fate" in the eye and telling it to get lost.'

'I won't argue,' Rodrigo said. 'Now that you're being redeemed, everything's changed. As soon as you sail, I'll join the others in the cave.'

'You can't hide in a cave forever.'

From his burnous, Rodrigo produced a wallet and tossed it to me. 'I won't have to – if you take these with you. They're notes from my cave-dwellers to a Valencia ship's captain named Onofre Exarque, guaranteeing him five thousand gold ducats if he sails here with a fast frigate crewed by men familiar with Algerian waters.'

'You're going to escape!'

'Onofre Exarque's the best sailor in the Mediterranean and he knows this coast like the back of his hand.'

'But it would be months before he even set out. And if you're found before he gets here, you'll be killed.'

'I told you. If I'm killed, I'm killed – that's my fate. Besides,' he brightened, 'they won't find us. Zoraida's practically the only one who knows about the cave and I'd trust her with my life.'

'Who else knows?'

'Not to worry. Only the boy who brings us food. And El Dorador is nothing if not loyal.'

'El Dorador?' I cried. 'A young mulatto from Melilla? A friend of Micaela's? Always says, "I hear and obey"?'

'A friend of whose?'

'Michele,' I said impatiently. 'A friend of Michele Maltrapillo.'

'That's El Dorador. "I hear and obey."' Rodrigo smiled fondly. 'And he does.'

'Rodrigo,' I said slowly, 'he's the one who abandoned me and those three young prisoners when we tried to escape across the desert. I spent fourteen months in a dungeon, thanks to your loyal, trustworthy El Dorador.'

'Now I see,' Rodrigo said. 'You think he can't be trusted. But what happened to you proves he can. If El Dorador hadn't abandoned you, you'd have kept going and died out there. As it was, you had to return.'

'I didn't. I kept going,' I said.

What used to be my left hand twitched.

'But you were caught and brought back alive. Can't I make you understand? You're my brother and I love you, and I entrusted your life to El Dorador.'

What used to be my left hand began to jump.

Rodrigo had actually ordered El Dorador to abandon us – for our own good, that was the horrible part. He believed that, and he was my brother who loved me, and it all added up to my having to forgive him.

What used to be my left hand saw things differently. It struck Rodrigo in the face.

My brother's nose spurted blood, and his legs skidded out from under him. Far from satisfied, what used to be my left hand darted after him, pulling me down to straddle him while it closed around his throat. His heels drummed on the mosaic cockatrice, his eyes bulged, his tongue began to protrude. Desperately I tried with my right hand to pull what used to be my left hand away from his throat, but the fingers only choked harder.

Micaela came at a screaming run into the smaller patio to launch herself on to my back, clinging like a rider to a bucking horse while she tried to pull my hair and beard out by the roots – all this activity serving only to divert my right hand from defending my brother against the homicidal intentions of what used to be my left hand.

A further diversion was Zoraida, who arrived on the scene shouting, 'Get off him so I can knock his brains out!' as she circled us looking

even taller than usual with her arms extended overhead gripping a heavy
ceramic bowl.

(Have you ever noticed how moments of high drama, in real life no less
than in a play or story, often degenerate into farce, almost as if God, like
a skilled playwright or storyteller, knows He must give the participants (or
the audience) a chance to catch their breath?)

Enter next the two albino eunuchs crying in falsetto unison, 'That bowl's
a priceless Sassanid antique!' as they tried to wrest it from Zoraida, who
was trying to smash it down on my head but could find no opening
because Micaela, leaning over my shoulders with her dark curls directly
above Zoraida's target, was still trying to pull my beard out.

High drama and low farce, then, and somewhere between (like every play
Lope de Vega would ever write), the melodramatic tempered by a touch,
possibly intentional, of buffoonery. Gabriel Múñoz, coming at an awkward
clanking run across the mosaic cockatrice, held that middle ground. Yanking
Micaela off my back, he hurled himself at what used to be my left hand,
giving Zoraida her chance. From the corner of my eye I caught a glimpse
of her rising high on those long dancer's legs as the twin eunuchs cried
in falsetto unison, 'Mistress, please – that priceless bowl dates from the
reign of Khosru Anushirvan!' Then the bowl descended, as forcefully as the
bounty-hunting nomad's equally antique firelock not too many pages back,
and there is only so much of that treatment a human head can take.

The first voice I heard when I woke was Micaela's: '. . . told you, trust
no one in this life.'

I opened my eyes warily.

Rodrigo said, 'You tried to kill me.'

How could I hope to explain that it hadn't been me, but only what used
to be my left hand? I said nothing.

Neither did anybody else for a while.

Then Zoraida told Micaela, 'You have to trust someone.'

Rodrigo said, 'That's what I used to think,' his voice hoarse, his eyes
bleak as he gingerly touched the purple bruises on his throat. 'Well, if I'm
to get back to Suleiman Sa'adah's place before curfew ends . . .

'Why?' he asked from the archway. 'Why'd you do it?'

I glowered at what used to be my left hand. And yet, some small part
of me couldn't blame it.

Also, my head hurt.

So at first it didn't sink in when Rodrigo said, 'I forgive you, Miguel,'
before turning to go.

I got up from where I'd lain unconscious on one of those ubiquitous alabaster couches and lurched towards him, choked by the effort to hold back unmanly tears.

He said, 'A kiss for Mamá and the girls, an embrace for Papá – and Juan the Obscure if you see him.' Then he went quickly, walking tall, his bearing military.

Shortly after the familiar pipes and drums signalled the end of curfew, I left with Gabriel Múñoz.

'I keep a special brew over at the prison tavern for my friends,' he said.

'You mean I'm one of them? After what happened?'

'*Compañero*, your brother forgave you. That is good enough for me.'

'You really admire him, don't you?'

'Let us say Algerian captivity can make people very protective of number one. Plus, in addition, they are far from public-spirited. This did not happen to Rodrigo.'

'Everybody thinks my brother's somebody different,' I said. 'Suleiman Sa'adah Sometimes Erroneously Called the Wise says he's a military genius. But if so, he'd be commander of a regiment in the Low Countries right now instead of an unransomed non-com in Algiers. Zoraida says – '

'Stop with the philosophy,' Gabriel Múñoz growled. 'It is bad enough when I do it. Let me tell you what your brother is. Rodrigo de Cervantes is a dead man, as dead as your poor father, unless – '

'My father? Dead? What are you telling me?'

'*Compañero* – I thought you knew.'

When we reached the royal *bagnio*, he led me to the list of ransomed captives posted on a wall of the prison courtyard. I found my name and read: '*Cervantes Saavedra, Miguel de, sole support of widowed mother, 500 ducats.*'

When I could speak I said, 'All he ever wanted for himself was to see a bit of the world.'

Gabriel Múñoz guided my steps towards his cellar tavern. 'You better have a stiff one,' he said.

'No. No, I . . .'

I went down past the Plaza of Atrocities to the deserted shingle beach sheltered by the mole that curved out to sea like a giant's scimitar. I walked at the water's edge, chains clanking, pebbles sliding underfoot. The sky was apple green with pre-dawn light. I picked up a flat stone and skipped it over the water.

On the old road again, my father's voice said, and when the tears came I did not resist them.

173

I sent another stone skipping across the water.

A family needed respect to get along in the modern world. Things were changing, changing fast. Just a century ago there wasn't any New World but once it was discovered the Old World never looked back.

What with debts and lawsuits and the kidnapping of Constanza, God knew the Cervantes family needed respect.

I looked down at the hateful thing that used to be my left hand. 'You!' I shouted. '*You* pick up a stone and throw it, why don't you?'

And I tried. But what used to be my left hand – which with near superhuman strength had almost killed my brother – couldn't even close around a pebble.

I was a cripple, and I had no career.

Rodrigo was sound of limb and a professional soldier, a noncommissioned officer decorated for valour. A respected figure.

Different things to different people.

To me he was my freckle-faced kid brother who, the night I fled Madrid, had given me his most prized possession, the little toy soldier. With its missing left hand.

Let me tell you what your brother is. Rodrigo de Cervantes is a dead man . . . unless –

Behind me I heard footsteps crunching on the shingle.

'Micaela. What do you want?' I asked her.

'Nothing. I often come here when the beach is deserted and pretend I can throw a stone clear to Spain. To Murcia.'

'That's where your family is, Murcia?'

'It's where my father's from. My mother died when I was born, and there's nobody else. I wish *I'd* had a brother.' She laughed, a rueful sound. 'Then he'd be the hostage. Instead – well, look at me. Neither fish nor fowl.' She skipped a stone across the water.

'Micaela,' I said, 'you're a lovely young woman.'

'Am I? Rodrigo still thinks I'm a boy – the little brother he never had unless you count this Juan the Obscure nobody ever sees.'

'It sounds like he's been telling you about the family.'

'Some. And Zoraida told me why you got so angry last night you almost killed him. I can see why you had to try to escape. *I* would, if it wouldn't ruin my father. But, well, I can also understand what Rodrigo did. If I thought my brother was going to his certain death, I'd stop him if I could. Funny, you and Rodrigo – sometimes it's as if you should be the soldier and he the – what are you?'

'I don't know,' I said. 'I'll find out when I get back to Spain. Maybe.'

'Until you go, can I . . . be your friend?'

Women! Girls too, even girls who masquerade as boys, how can anyone understand them? Until then Micaela had merely distrusted me on principle. But by attacking Rodrigo, I'd earned her hatred. And instead she wanted to be my friend.

'I'd be honoured, Micaela,' I said, and she flung her arms around my neck. Disengaging gently, I told her, 'You'd better be careful how you hug people. Especially men. Especially if you want to keep your secret.'

And as we stood side by side on the beach staring out at the immensity of the sea and the Lopean impossibility of everything, I knew that somehow, some way, I had to get Micaela Maltrapillo out of Algiers.

Avuncular concern in his pious voice, the Mercenarian Prefect Jorge del Olivar asked me, 'Are you quite certain this is no momentary whim inspired by a brotherly love even Our Dear Lord might find misguided?'

'I'm certain, Prefect.'

'It is *most* unusual. We of the Order of Mercy are no Trinitarian dilettantes arriving in Algiers with gold enough to ransom only a fraction of our candidates. We do not look on Algerian captivity as a real-life morality play in which the good are rewarded . . . By ceding the ransom right of the firstborn, you are dooming yourself to lifelong servitude here among the Godless. You *do* understand?'

'It has to be Rodrigo, Prefect. He has a profession, I have none. He's whole, I'm maimed. Look at it! Look at this thing that used to be my left hand!'

'Self-loathing is a terrible sin, my son, for we are all made in God's image. How did that . . . thing happen? Apart from being God's will, of course.'

'At Lepanto, Prefect, the battle we call "The Naval" — and I'm not sure God was even there.'

I hadn't meant to say that. Of course God was there; God is everywhere, I told myself. Then I thought of Zoraida. Zoraida, Rodrigo said, believed in nothing — as if 'nothing' were a something you could believe in. Even if those were just words, a semantic trap, surely belief, like love, required an object? But did that object have to be God?

'Of course God was there!' the Prefect said. 'Look at the score, man! Turkish vessels captured, one hundred and seventeen. Fifty more burned to the waterline or sunk. Turks and Moors killed, nine thousand, and even more taken prisoner.'

'Enslaved?'

'Of course enslaved; that's what Muslim prisoners are for. All that, all *that*, against our own loss of a paltry dozen galleys and a few thousand valiant men fallen under the banner of the Holy League and a few thousand others blinded or – ' A glance at what used to be my left hand. 'Well, you have to admit it was a lopsided victory.'

'Prefect,' I said, 'if Rodrigo stays and I go free, he'll be killed. Just show me where to sign.'

On tiptoe, Micaela tried to see over the heads of the crowd. 'That's my father there, the one on the poopdeck ostentatiously not looking at me.'

We stood on the mole that curved out into the sea like a giant's scimitar, watching the ransomed prisoners board the freedom ship *María de la Libertad*, Morato Maltrapillo commanding. At three hundred yards, I could see a half-dozen tiny figures on the frigate's poopdeck.

'Micaela, he couldn't pick you out in this mob if he wanted to.'

'He doesn't. He was very upset yesterday. He seems to think I can simply *stop* being a girl. Just try harder, he said! Of course I understand, he always wanted a son . . . but would it hurt him, for once, to show a little – ' She stretched on tiptoe again. 'There's Rodrigo!'

I caught a glimpse of my brother's freckled face and that blood-red streak in his prematurely grey hair as he turned to gaze shoreward before climbing aboard.

Gabriel Múñoz had helped me convince him he was the one slated for ransom all along, as he could see by the corrected official list. Rodrigo, good soldier that he was, did not argue with official lists. Nor with the uncaring fate that had taken our father from this life while we were captives across the sea.

'He was old,' Rodrigo said. 'Sixty-something.'

'Sixty-six,' I said.

'He lived a whole life and left a handful of kids. Which is more than I'll ever do.'

'Sure you will.'

'Uh-uh. A soldier has no time for kids. And I won't see sixty-something either. These are dangerous times to be a soldier.'

Rodrigo's intimations of mortality troubled me. He should have felt he was returning to life.

'I'll get in touch with Onofre Exarque the minute I set foot on Spanish soil,' he promised. 'I'll see you in Madrid by the end of the year.'

After watching the freedom ship clear the harbour, Micaela and I started uphill through sun-struck alleys towards Zoraida's house. We hadn't got very far before turbaned Turks, hooded Moors, veiled women, fly-specked children, laden donkeys and stray dogs melted into doorways, as if in response to some signal, so that I could see:

(SECOND *and* THIRD YOUNG PRISONER *approach along the alley. They seem larger and more muscular than* MIGUEL DE CERVANTES *remembers.* SECOND YOUNG PRISONER *is minus his left ear,* THIRD *minus his right.*)

SECOND YOUNG PRISONER: It's him! Cervantes!
THIRD YOUNG PRISONER: Whole, too, except for what used to be his left hand.
SECOND YOUNG PRISONER: There is no justice!

I tried sympathy: 'I'm sorry you lost your ears.'
I tried reason: 'Listen, I didn't exactly get off free. I spent more than a year in the deepest dungeon in Algiers.'
I tried being friendly: 'How's First Young Prisoner these days?'

SECOND YOUNG PRISONER: Died of wound-poisoning a week after they sliced off his nose – while you were lounging in a so-called dungeon.

(*In his hand a sharpened stake that can easily serve as dagger, poniard or misericorde,* THIRD YOUNG PRISONER *lunges at* MIGUEL DE CERVANTES.)

I shoved Micaela to one side and saw her stumble into a recessed doorway from which, a split second later, almost as if they had rehearsed it, Gabriel Múñoz came bursting out swinging a janissary's short, supple club (Allah knows where he got it), dropping Third Young Prisoner in his tracks.
As the three of us hurried up the alley I heard:

SECOND YOUNG PRISONER: Go on, run! You won't get far, not with a bounty on you large enough to ransom whoever collects it.

A bounty on *me*? Wasn't he confusing me with my brother? I looked a wordless question at Gabriel Múñoz.
'If Hassan Pasha Dey cannot have Rodrigo,' he told me, 'he will settle for any Cervantes he can get.'

XIV

Tameji?

Staring four daggers at me, as if *I* had smashed the priceless Khosru Anushirvan bowl to antique smithereens, the twin eunuchs cleared away Zoraida's eight-course brunch.

A surly-looking mulatto boy came in and, at a word from Zoraida, mumbled, 'I hear and obey,' and set to work with a pick on my leg irons. As they fell away, Zoraida said El Dorador would take me to the cave outside the Bab-Azun Gate before dawn the next day. 'During curfew, of course, since you've a price on your head.'

Micaela looked up at me, her eyes filling with tears, probably caused by some vapour from the ointment she was rubbing into the galls on my ankles.

'The last time El Dorador took me anywhere,' I reminded Zoraida, 'I spent fourteen months in a dungeon.'

'This is different. El Dorador idolized your brother. Rodrigo gave him his orders before he sailed.'

'I hear and obey,' said El Dorador as he left the patio.

'And once I'm in the cave? Fifteen men including me, that's a lot of mouths to feed.'

Zoraida gave me a warning look. She told Micaela, 'Why don't you get Miguel some nice mufti to wear?'

Micaela stamped a petulant bare foot and flounced out.

'Less like a boy every day,' I observed.

'You mean her classic callipygean curve? To an Arab, don't forget, that's youthful *male* beauty too. She has a lovely body, hasn't she? Not too skinny and not too long in the limb. Lucky her.'

'What happens if they find out she's not a boy?'

'How can they? Her person's inviolable. You worry too much, *ráwi*. As for the cave, it's my responsibility to get food for you, and El Dorador's to bring it.'

'What makes it your responsibility?'

'Sorry – that's all you need to know.'

This was said with an artful smile. But I'd had enough of artfulness.

'Who are you really? You're not just someone who dances to make Turkish hypochondriacs feel better.'

'My patients aren't all hypochondriacs. Trance dancing can cure the ill, if they believe.'

'Rodrigo says you believe in nothing.'

'I've lived too many places, with too many gods. They tend to cancel one another out. Or maybe, I don't know, maybe God's just a character dreamed up by some clever *ráwi*.'

I crossed myself.

Zoraida asked, 'Why'd you do that?'

'Habit. I guess.' Then I said, 'You still haven't told me what makes it your responsibility.'

After a purse-lipped silence she said, 'A Certain Mutual Acquaintance.'

'So *that's* what this is about. Ever meet him?'

'No.'

'What does he want from us all?'

'We each have our part to play.'

'In what?'

'Miguel,' she said, 'it's late, and we've had a long day, and you'll be going to the cave before dawn.'

'Late? It's not even noon.'

'I meant I have a long day ahead of me.'

(Notice how just talking about a Certain Mutual Acquaintance can confuse people. This had to be part of his grand design.)

After Zoraida left, I spent a restless day prowling both patios, staring back at the resident mosaic cockatrices, trying to make them blink. At dusk Micaela joined me.

'Where's Zoraida?' she pouted.

'Still out dancing. Where were *you*? I was worried.'

Her pout edged towards a smile. 'You were?'

'What do you do all day?'

'Just sort of sashay around the souks daring every Moor and Turk to touch me because they know if they do they'll be dropped on the hook. It's my favourite game.'

'You'd better stop playing it.'

She turned her back, cocked a hip, and gave me a heavy-lidded look over her shoulder. Then she stuck out her tongue and laughed. 'Actually I didn't feel like the game today, so I went down to the beach to our – to my place, you know? And just skipped stones. Here she is.' These last three words were said without enthusiasm.

Trailing a diaphanous veil or two, Zoraida hurried in. '*What* a day! Four patients *in extremis*, all from the old Dey's court, which meant four deathbed statements.'

'Four of your patients died today?' She didn't seem downcast.

'No, they all pulled through. But you'd be surprised what a person will say when he *thinks* he's about to die. State secrets are just the beginning. God, I'm starving!'

The twin eunuchs were not unprepared.

Later, it was I who found some excuse to send Micaela from the patio.

'We've got to get her out of Algiers,' I told Zoraida.

'But she's in no more danger than usual.'

'How long do you think she can get away with her masquerade? Besides, she's desperately unhappy. Why do you think she plays those dangerous games of hers?'

Zoraida shook her head. 'It's not Micaela I can't figure out. It's you, *ráwi*. Sacrificing yourself for your brother like that – I'm still not sure why you did it.'

Because he once gave me a toy soldier – but how could she understand?

'And then? Then you find out, not an hour after Rodrigo sails, that there's a price on *your* head – and what are you worried about? Getting *Micaela* out of Algiers! Don't you ever want something selfish? Something just for you?' Her voice softening, she asked, 'Did it occur to you that after tonight we may never see each other again?' and we both rose and melted into each other's arms. After a while she murmured, 'Hurry – in there.'

I groped my way to a bed, and waited in darkness.

Zoraida – what an enigma she is to Cervantes experts. Who was she, really? Were we lovers?

Zoraida – wouldn't a Zoraida in my unproduced *Dungeons of Algiers* run off with the heroic Don Lope (a common name, no relation to my rival playwright)? And in 'The Captive's Tale', which I wrote soon after regaining my freedom and would later slip into *Don Quixote* as a three-chapter divertissement after the Sad-Faced Knight waxed over-eloquent on warfare and pedagogy, wouldn't a Zoraida flee Algiers with the stalwart Captain Ruy Pérez de Viedma?

Wish fulfilment. *Ojalá*, as the Arabs say. But the real Zoraida never left Algiers.

Did she share my bed?

How diligently they build their case, those Cervantes experts who would see me less as a Don Quixote than as a Don Juan (not the hero Don Juan of Austria but Don Juan the legendary lover).

If they could lurk inside the door of that Barbary bedroom, what might they have seen? They might have seen the door open, and heard bare feet pad across the tiled floor to . . .

But how can they have this both ways? Ever since they read my fiction début *La Galatea*, the critics hounded me. Cervantes's words, they said, flow like a swift clear stream when he writes of warfare or a good brawl, or the roads of Spain (especially the roads, always the roads), but when he tries putting sex on paper he's a eunuch. Some would allude slyly to the three years Hassan Pasha Dey owned me, he of the notorious male harem that made his predecessor's look like a public school (as described by Marlowe). Well? Why should the burden of rebuttal rest on me? What is it they expect me to rebut? I narrated my Sorrento thunderbolt adventure *con brio*, didn't I?

As for that night in Algiers, how self-conscious I feel even now, writing about it.

. . . slip breathlessly into bed, feet like ice but the sleek smooth rest of her warm, fevered even. Her way of kissing was almost masticatory (well, Zoraida, I remember thinking), and as our bare bodies made first tingling contact, I sensed in her a disconcerting tentativeness, an inexperience, as if she had saved the lissome grace of those extraordinarily long limbs for the healing art of trance dancing, a touching (literally) awkwardness which surprised me in a woman so reflexively graceful. Not that this awkwardness inhibited desire. No: with each new bump and tangle and mis-fit, new cries of almost prenubile joy escaped her. Besides, I ascribed any gawkishness to her length of limb and expected, once I overlay her, this very length to add to our erotic delight. To this end I stroked her legs (not so exceptionally long, in the dark, as I had imagined) from ankle to thigh until my hand reached and then held the classic callipygean curve of her –

'Micaela!' I shouted.

And she gasped a frustrated 'Oh!' as I swiftly let go and sat up.

'Micaela, what are you doing here?'

'What do you think I'm doing here?'

'But you're just a child.'

'Did I *feel* like a child? Lots of women of thirteen are married.'

True; but they'd been raised as girls. Micaela, the motherless boy-impersonator, knew so little of what it was all about.

'Micaela,' I said, 'I'm more than twice your age.'

181

'Who cares? You're the bravest man in the world!'
See? That's how much she knew.
'And I'm *not* too young for you.'
'No,' I said, 'but, you see, I'm too old for you.'
She sat there in the darkness, just breathing. Then, 'Can't you have your way with me even a little bit?'
I sat there too, breathing and wondering.
How did I get here, caught in a fictive trap with a naked child-woman bent on proving that her boy-masquerade had cost her none of her femaleness (silly girl: quite the reverse!) in the bed where Zoraida should have . . .
'Where's Zoraida?' I asked.
'Asleep. She fell asleep.'
'Zoraida's asleep?' This was too startling to be insulting.
'Well, you know how she is. Before joining you she needed a pick-me-up, a baked sheep's head I think it was, and of course something to drink, so I just, well, it's easy to get sleeping draughts in Souk Street as you must know, and I always keep one handy in case anyone tries to have his way . . . Are you sure you don't want to?'
I was sure I did, and sure I mustn't, so I said, 'Micaela, where's El Dorador?'
'Outside waiting for you, but . . . then it *is* boys! That's the reason!' she wailed. 'You really like boys!'
What could I do? Convince her she was wrong by doing what she wanted – which I didn't want? That is, which I *did* want but . . .
I did the only thing I could. I left.
Crossing the moonlit patio I saw, on the alabaster couch, Zoraida recumbent in drug-induced rapture, on her lips a sated smile older than Eve, old as Lilith, as she lifted her long arms and purred, 'Oh, *ráwi, ráwi*, was it that good for you too?' So I stopped, stooped, lightly kissed that Lilith smile, and she murmured, '*Tameji, ráwi?*'
Are you leaving, storyteller?
And I told her I was, and I did, and there you have it. Or them. Zoraida of whom I would write more than once as a beautiful (and rich, why not?) Muslim woman who absconded from Algiers with a captive Christian (a captain, why not?); and Micaela of whom until now I have never written, knowing too well what my critics would say.

'*Tameji, ráwi?*' Are you leaving?
How this question came to taunt me!

When I mentioned it to Cide Hamete, his comment seemed a *non sequitur*.

'The present moment does not exist,' was what he said.

'Well, not for long,' I agreed.

'Not for short, even. As each so-called present moment comes into so-called existence, doesn't it disappear immediately and simultaneously in two directions – into the past and into the future? The function of the present, my friend, is not to *be* but only to *become*. Even astrologers, those charlatans, understand this. For don't they "predict" the worldly future by analysing the celestial past, bypassing the present altogether? No, my friend, the present moment, any present moment except one, is a contradiction, an impossibility, and a violation of the laws of nature.'

'Except one?'

'Consider poor Tantalus.' Again a *non sequitur*; he enjoyed them. 'Don't you imagine Tantalus wished that forever-looming boulder would fall and crush his life out so he wouldn't have to stand thirsting for all eternity in that lake whose waters dry up whenever he tries to drink? All eternity, also called forever, is the one exception – an endless present that becomes neither past nor future. Eternal damnation, for example, or eternal bliss. Both unendurable. No, don't ask me for sympathy when I've just learned' – Cide Hamete was always learning new things about himself – 'that I may well be immortal.' He groaned. 'You at least can watch the present recede into the past where, like pain itself, despair hurts less, while you stride into the hopeful future. Don't tell me of your piddling problems when I have all eternity to worry about.'

'Wait! Don't go! At least tell me why Onofre Exarque never came to rescue us.'

Cide Hamete, however, had already begun to disappear, as he had a way of doing, and I was alone in my solitary pit chained naked to a rock (where I would stay until Hassan Pasha had me thrown in with the general prison population, where I started hatching the plot that would result in my execution by hanging).

Were I writing a picaresque novel, a *Lazarillo de Tormes*, I would recount the entire sequence: my arrival at the cave with El Dorador; thumbnail biographies of my fellow fugitives; their disappointment on getting me instead of old-soldier Rodrigo; their edgy anticipation of our rescue culminating in stunned despair and (or did I imagine it?) distrust of me when the appointed night passed with no sign of Onofre Exarque; their frank hostility a few days later when loyal, trustworthy El Dorador failed to deliver the meagre fare that kept them alive. In a *Lazarillo* there would be a scene, *de rigueur* in the genre, in which the peripatetic (on the old road again) rogue of a hero outwits his fellow fugitives or the Dey or *someone* and makes his escape.

But this is no picaresque novel, just an account of my own death and life, so let's take it from the morning Hassan Pasha Dey, mounted on his gaudily gold-caparisoned stallion, led a company of janissaries (and a cringing El Dorador) to the estate outside the Bab-Azun Gate, where they surrounded the cave and fired a few shots. Out we stumbled blinking in the sunlight, to be searched, chained in two coffles, and marched back to Algiers.

Whether I might have faced recriminations or worse from the cave-dwellers I cannot say, for at the royal *bagnio* I was cut from my coffle and shoved into a large room with whitewashed walls on to which shafts of sunlight from four high embrasures cast disconcertingly fragmentary shadows of a whipping post, two torturers in loincloths, a captive wearing a physician's huge signet ring on his thumb – and Hassan Pasha Dey the Venetian himself, face painted with a lavishly decadent hand, eyelashes kohl-lengthened, and, tucked into the sash around his middle, a rhinoceros-sinew whip.

'So you're Cervantes,' he said, looking at what used to be my left hand. 'Remarkable that you didn't lose that thing. Hurt excruciatingly, did it?' His painted face took on a faraway, dreamy look. 'Must have swelled as big as a melon before suppurating, mmm? and no doubt plagued you for months with foetid splinters of bone and fragments of roundball surfacing, a not altogether painless process about which you must tell me some time, mmm? as I make a little study of such phenomena. Does a change in the weather hurt it still? Or if I were to strike it, mmm? like *this!* with the butt of my rhinoceros-sinew whip? No? Doesn't hurt? Pity.' Here another 'mmm?' followed by a wet white gleam in his henna-dyed beard that might have been a smile.

'Still' – cheerily despite his disappointment – 'if what used to be your left hand has hardened you to . . . discomfort, you and I will share some interesting times, for holding a man at a high level of pain without permitting him to slip into merciful unconsciousness is, I have often thought, the earthly mirror of the most perfect of the five heavens of delight, the pure and elemental fire that is truly empyrean,' said Hassan Pasha Dey the Venetian, known far and wide (according to Suleiman Sa'adah Sometimes Erroneously Called the Wise) as the world's most sadistic man.

Why do I go on so about this?

The simple answer is, the Dey did.

Believe me, I'm not catering to perverted tastes – who needs such readers? But so much has been made of my 'obscene servitude' to Hassan Pasha that I must speak now.

Obscene servitude! What did I know of his nefarious all-male harem with its ingeniously modified torture devices? I never even got a good look at the place. So how could it have been, to quote a critic (an admirer of Lope de Vega, I have no doubt), 'one of the twin headwaters of that bitter stream from which Cervantes's tragicomic worldview would flow. . . '?

Bitter stream! And what's the other headwater anyway? He never says.

Symbolism I can understand, metaphor and simile I am not a stranger to. And even if it's my own personal opinion that a writer attacks blank paper secretly hoping to change the world instead of just showing what it's like (which is hard enough), that needn't imply . . .

Twin headwaters!

My 'obscene servitude' was spent in a solitary pit chained naked to a rock. I hardly knew the depraved Dey.

At his signal the two loinclothed torturers bound me to the whipping post.

'You'll get nothing from me,' I vowed. Unoriginal but, all things considered, excusable.

'Fool! I already know everything,' said the Dey.

This was disquieting. Why bind a man to a whipping post if you don't plan to interrogate him?

I heard leather creaking. Was he taking from his sash that rhinoceros-sinew whip?

'Everyone dreams of escaping from somewhere,' he said. 'That's human nature, mmm? But here, Cervantes, here you are property, and an attempt to escape is an attempt to steal what I and the Sultan himself own, mmm?'

Have you ever found yourself, while trying desperately not to smile, perversely smiling all the more? This problem is common to children, but no one is immune. Fear can trigger it, or the incongruous. In my case, his manic hum.

I smiled. Worse, I tried not quite successfully to choke down laughter. This he took for machismo.

'Ah, the typical bravado of the Iberian male,' he purred. 'How delightful! For machismo raises the tolerance of pain almost as reliably as profound shock, a state in which you are about to find yourself, mmm?'

A hand ripped my shirt to the waist.

185

'Miguel de Cervantes Saavedra!' Hassan Pasha pronounced. 'For the attempted theft of the property of Sultan Selim II, the Degenerate, master of half the known world and claimant to the rest, you are sentenced to one thousand strokes of the rhinoceros-sinew whip and indefinite incarceration in a pit chained naked to a rock.'

Silence followed this sentence, a silence as significant to Arabs as words, before the two torturers could cry in anguished disbelief, 'One thousand? O mighty Pasha, no!'

'I do appreciate,' burbled the Dey, 'that no normal man – even two taking turns, mmm? – can deliver one thousand blows consecutively. I shall deliver them myself.'

The physician spoke. 'One thousand consecutive strokes of a rhinoceros-sinew whip are nine hundred more than any human has been known to survive.' Not that he seemed unduly concerned. I had recognized him as one of those who had attended the royal astrologer the day I saved his life.

I heard a deep intake of breath and watched the Dey's shadow rise on a whitewashed wall spotted with faded brown blood in a pattern strikingly reminiscent of the constellation Cassiopeia, that is, a connect-the-spots outline of a seated woman holding both arms high in supplication – not that it had done her, or would do me, any good.

I shut my eyes.

What was the Dey waiting for? Was delay part of the pleasure for him, like foreplay?

Strike! I wanted to scream. Whip me! Get it over with!

I heard footsteps, and metal clanging against stone. The Dey exhaled heavily. Then he said, 'Not now, may Allah turn your tongue to molten lead!'

'My master has urgent information, Pasha,' pleaded a servile voice.

In a whispered conference outside the door, an almost familiar voice said 'mansions', it said 'moon', it said incomprehensible things like Aratron and Phaleg, Ophiel and Och, which I write with capital letters because that's how it said them. It said Picatrix, at which mysterious (steganographic?) word Hassan Pasha gasped. I opened my eyes and saw that (miraculously?) the blood spots on the whitewashed wall seemed to have rearranged themselves. Connect them now, and you'd draw an old man with a long white beard riding a fire-snorting dragon past a juniper tree.

I heard footsteps marching away, the door clanging shut, and several men, one asthmatic, breathing.

Then I heard a bellow of pent-up rage and a whistling as of rhinoceros sinew slicing air. Again I braced for the first incandescent explosion of pain. But when the whip cracked, it was someone else who screamed.

Clanking and scuttling by the old man with a long white beard riding a fire-snorting dragon past a juniper tree, the physician fled Hassan Pasha's rhinoceros-sinew whip into and back out of my sector of vision. The whip continued to whistle and crack, the Dey to make circuits of the room, now chasing into my vision both torturers, on whose backs the rhinoceros sinew descended indiscriminately, eliciting impressive shrieks from one, while the other, the asthmatic, could manage only a pitiful wheezing whimper.

Again and again the whip whistled and cracked, striking flesh, the floor, the old man riding his dragon past the juniper tree – everything, I soon realized, except me – while Hassan Pasha Dey the Venetian, between snarls, whip-cracks and screams, could be heard to shout, '. . . did I ever do to deserve . . . Mars at seventeen degrees Pisces, and Mercury practically in the jaws of Leo, and the *sun* . . .' Here he whipped the non-asthmatic torturer through my sector. '. . . not in Sagittarius where it belongs, he *promised* me, but unaccountably off in Aquarius or some such house.' Here the physician went clanking frantically by. '. . . conjunctions could not possibly be less propitious . . .' Here the floor took a whipping, and then the old man with the long white beard riding the fire-snorting dragon past the juniper tree got his again. 'Saturn ascendant! Death! Destruction! Raising lost souls from Hell!' Then, with venomous sarcasm, 'An opportunity, he assures me, to recapture escaped prisoners! But with Mercury and Mars where they are, the inflictor of corporal punishment will suffer more than his rightful victim . . .' More snarls, whipcracks, screams. Then, 'Cut him down – the first part of the sentence is suspended. I said *cut him* DOWN!'

Janissaries, sidestepping the now wildly lashing Dey, unbound me. As they dragged me out, I caught a final glimpse of Hassan Pasha, puce with fury, rhinoceros-sinew whip aloft, chasing himself faster and faster around the room.

XV

Dangerous Games

Storytellers for millennia have got away with the 'pathetic fallacy' in which nature or inanimate objects echo our human emotions – like the supplicant connect-the-spots Cassiopeia on that wall. But no storyteller can get away with pretending his characters cease to exist when he isn't telling about them. Characters have a life of their own that continues behind the storyteller's back.

So, though this is the story of my death and life, other characters occupied the limelight while I, during my long incarceration chained naked to a ringbolt in a rock in a pit, was effectively offstage.

Oh, I ate (*migas*, what else?), fighting the rats for my fair share. And I pissed and shat. And my hair and beard and nails grew.

Also – this is embarrassing – I tried solo sex. What solitary prisoner doesn't? In the darkness I aroused myself by remembering Sorrento, Cornelia Tasso's siren song beckoning me into a breathless moment in which time expanded to become space, vast vaulted distances bending back on themselves as we stepped towards each other and touched, and the sky darkened for a single astounding instant, a natural *coup de théâtre*, to blaze with an awesome flash ... but as my excitement peaked I saw hair like a rippling wheatfield on a cloudless summer day in La Mancha and, assailed by guilt, I dropped what I was doing.

Also, I told myself stories, chiefly involving escapes from dungeons and pits. But the more I talked to myself – and isn't every storyteller, however large his audience, really talking to himself? – the more I stuttered.

This worried me. What if I went free but no one understood anything I said, ever again?

I saw myself in Madrid, running breathlessly to the tall stone house near the Gate of the Sun and taking my sister Andrea in my arms, more or less brotherly, and pouring out my joy at seeing her. But not a word was intelligible. And, cruelly out of character, she laughed at me.

In the lonely darkness, I made a superstitious pact with myself:

Conquer the stutter, and you'll go free.

I believed this fervently, even while I didn't believe it. (If you have

188

ever been chained naked to a ringbolt in a rock in a pitch-dark pit, you will understand.) It would work – if only I could master one supremely challenging sentence. But what sentence?

I found myself thinking with a smile of Micaela who, even though she could chatter like a jackdaw when she liked, had such trouble with the countersign the day she admitted me to Zoraida's house. So the sentence I chose was:

Demogorgon dwells in the Abyss with three fatal sisters or atop the Himalayas with elves and feys.

You wouldn't think that speaking those words I almost drove myself insane.

'Demogorgon dwells,' I began.

Dwells, that was a hard word for me. So was sisters. And the 'with three' combination was – well, fatal.

'Demogorgon dwells,' I repeated over and over, and then finally:

'Demogorgon dwells in the Abyss.'

I listened to the echo. I spoke the words again, cautiously. They came smoothly back to me.

Presently I had the five words up to nine.

At last the day arrived when in one breath I said, 'Demogorgon dwells in the Abyss with three fatal sisters or atop the Himalayas with elves and feys.'

I did it again, at almost indecent speed.

No stutter!

I was congratulating myself when the sentence began to disturb me. What was it all about? The three fatal sisters were easy – the Fates, those daughters of Night who control the destinies of men – but who was Demogorgon?

Where did the sentence come from, anyway?

Had it first appeared in the controversial Abbot of Sponheim's *Steganographia*? If so, why? Or was it chosen at random for one-time use? By whom? And come to think of it (for I did come to think of it), how random is random?

I also found myself wondering: why elves *and* feys? Was there a difference? And where *did* Demogorgon dwell? It was a long way from the Abyss in, say, Dante's *Inferno* to the top of the Himalayas.

Soon, trying to figure things out, I had repeated the words so often that they lost any meaning they ever had.

Try it, even if you're not chained to a rock.

Take a simple word like 'dwells'. Say it over and over. Dwells. Dwells dwells dwells. Dwellsdwellsdwellsdwellsdwells.

Has it any meaning left? Has it even a beginning and an end?

Sound without significance, like all words.

No wonder I stuttered.

Dwellsdwellsdwellsdwellsdwellsdwellsdwellsdwellsdwells.

Nobody ever really understands a single thing anybody else ever says. It's all pretence.

Demogorgon! I shouted. Are you here in *my* Abyss?

Eat your migas or the Barbary pirates will come in the night and get you!

He (or she) was coming – Demogorgon!

I hurled myself across the rock in which the ringbolt was embedded, and I howled.

Would I have gone completely over the edge if, just then, I hadn't pictured Micaela's disturbing amber eyes and remembered her silvery soprano voice trying to say, 'Demogorgon dwells in the Abyss with, uh, three fatal sisters or, uh, atop the Himalayas – what comes next?'

The image reminded me that only *I* was chained to a rock, only *I* was in the wings while Micaela and the rest acted out their fates. (The notion of free will, when you are chained naked to a rock, loses much of its force.)

I gave up on returning any time soon to the world and promised myself simply this:

Tell a single true story and you will keep your sanity.

Diminished expectations. But what could I do?

This is the story I told:

One morning not long after I was imprisoned, Micaela went sashaying through the bazaar playing that game of hers and happened to see El Dorador coming out of Tanners Lane just as he happened to see her. He ducked swiftly into Kettlemakers Lane, and she raced in pursuit.

Outside tiny shops strings of hanging kettles trembled like leaves in a storm – a thunderstorm, from the din they made – as first El Dorador, then Micaela, rushed by. Tall stacks of pots and pans swayed like belfries in an earthquake. Irate shopkeepers shouted. A crowd, including my former master Gimp the Greek, recently back in mean spirits from an unsuccessful raiding expedition, followed.

El Dorador, his narrow chest heaving, spurted at an awkward run from the far end of Kettlemakers and plunged into Potters Lane. Micaela plunged right after him.

Pottery both glazed and unglazed smashed and shattered.

'It's the inviolable Maltrapillo boy chasing loyal, trustworthy El Dorador,' cried a Moor.

'With murder in his disturbing amber eyes!' cried a Turk.

'And with a ripple of his classic callipygean curve!' cried Gimp the Greek, spirits uplifted as he charged with the crowd through an alley now ankle-deep in instant pot-sherds.

Before long everyone in the souks knew the Maltrapillo boy had vowed (with Arab hyperbole) to tear El Dorador limb from limb for betraying a maimed Christian called Zerbantes or some such. Betraying him twice, in fact.

El Dorador made his stand in the produce market. He hurled a melon. Micaela ducked. Then she was on him.

They thrashed about on the ground, now one gaining the upper hand, now the other, until El Dorador broke free.

Micaela launched herself after him like a cannonball and brought him down across a rickety table laden with ripe red tomatoes, which collapsed under their weight. Micaela's fist (or her elbow?) made blood spurt from El Dorador's nose. As they rolled over and over, tomato juice ran in rivulets across the hard-packed earth of the market, collected in puddles, was lapped up greedily by beggars. More affluent spectators wagered on the outcome of the fight. Soon no El Dorador money could be found. The battle had become one-sided, Micaela pitiless. El Dorador would struggle to his feet and she would knock him down and he would struggle up more slowly and she would knock him down again. Finally El Dorador begged for mercy.

Micaela stood over him, flushed, panting, hands on hips, white silk panta-loons stained a bright tomato-red clinging to that classic callipygean curve.

Gimp the Greek, breathless himself, was transfixed. Jesus! he thought – by Allah! he meant – how aroused the Maltrapillo boy looks! Almost as if it wasn't a brawl he'd just been in but a . . . no, Gimp the Greek warned himself, don't even think of it.

As the fat renegade captain sighed, a lean, dark man wearing a Princess Eboli eye-patch stood at the edge of the crowd observing the play of emotions on his face.

The Dey decreed the boy inviolable; the Greek found him irresistible. A situation worth watching.

Some months later, the niece of Suleiman Sa'adah Sometimes Erroneously Called the Wise visited him in his home above the barber-shop early one evening.

'I'm starving,' Zoraida said, reaching for one of the onions her uncle was packing in a crate. She raised it to her mouth before he could cry, 'Don't! That's no onion, it's a tulip bulb. I'm taking them to the Low Countries. I'll make my fortune.'

'Aren't there any tulips in Holland?'

Zoraida knew they came from somewhere out east, Persia maybe. They were common enough here in Algiers.

'These will be the first,' her uncle said, nesting the bulbs reverently in cotton wool.

Looking at his rapt face, its pink jowls aquiver, she felt a rush of affection.

'You really are getting out?' she asked.

'I'm fifty-nine,' said Suleiman Sa'adah Sometimes Erroneously Called the Wise. 'I gave thirty-five years to the secret world.'

'They say once it's in your blood . . .'

'I'm done with all that. Tulips will be my life now.'

The finality with which he spoke reminded Zoraida why she had come. She parted a few of her diaphanous veils and produced a sheaf of handwritten pages.

'The Confessions of a Trance Dancer,' she said. 'I'll feel safer knowing they're out of the country.'

Suleiman Sa'adah flipped through them. 'Astonishing.'

'I know,' Zoraida said modestly. 'It was a question of training myself not to forget what they were saying on their deathbeds as I danced myself into a trance.'

'If I were to leak even a fraction of this stuff,' her uncle mused, 'it would turn Constantinople upside-down.'

'I thought you were quitting.'

'I am,' said Suleiman Sa'adah firmly.

'You'll take the confessions with you?'

'Would a Certain Mutual Acquaintance approve?'

'I think so. Anyway, he could be dead.'

'Could be isn't is,' said her uncle testily.

Like so many in (or in his case, formerly in) the secret world, he rejected the possibility. When would they learn, Zoraida wondered. Not even a Certain Mutual Acquaintance was indispensable. And nobody lived for ever.

Both were silent a while. They had always been close. His ship sailed for Amsterdam on the morning tide.

'Would you consider taking a stowaway with you?'

'Child! You're in danger?'

'I don't mean me. I'm worried about Micaela.'

'What's to worry? She's inviolable.'

'She's not herself, hasn't been ever since Miguel de Cervantes was recaptured. She walks around with a vacant look. Once I had to pull her out of the way of a galloping horse. She asked me to teach her to read, and now she spends half the day reciting poems to herself. If I didn't know Micaela trusts no one, I'd say she was in love.'

'Since when has love required trust?' said Suleiman Sa'adah Sometimes Erroneously Called the Wise.

'Meanwhile half the men in Algiers want to have their way with the Maltrapillo "boy", but if they found out she's a girl, I hate to think what would happen,' Zoraida said.

'They'd stop wanting, those perverts, that's all that would happen.'

'They'd tear her apart. And they *will* learn before long unless . . . will you take her?'

Suleiman Sa'adah spread his hands. He had, she observed not for the first time, a long lifeline. Unlike hers. 'You know the rule, my darling niece: never meddle in internal affairs except for clear and obtainable benefit.'

Zoraida didn't plead. She did know the rule. It had been weakness to ask him to break it for personal reasons.

After a fortifying snack for the fifteen-minute walk home, she kissed Suleiman Sa'adah goodbye.

'Next year in Amsterdam,' he assured her. 'Your work will be finished here and you'll join me.'

'Next year in Amsterdam,' Zoraida echoed. But why did she feel a sudden premonitory dread?

At home, Micaela wasn't back. Probably still sashaying around. But when she hadn't returned the next morning, Zoraida hurried, trailing a diaphanous veil or two, to the tavern in the royal *bagnio*. Gabriel Múñoz knew almost everything of any importance that went on in Algiers.

'But I do not know where the Maltrapillo child is,' he said to Zoraida.

'Then find out. There's talk you're up for redemption when the Trinitarians come to Algiers.'

'Talk is cheap,' said Gabriel Múñoz evasively.

'I might be able to get you a few votes.' Redemption by the Trinitarians, everyone knew, was based on popularity.

'I will see what I can do,' Gabriel Múñoz said.

When Zoraida returned the next day, he told her, 'No one can say where she is. However.'

'Did you say "she"?'

'What else? I am in the grapevine business. So, to continue,' Gabriel Múñoz said, 'you will have heard some deathbed talk of a brisk trade in household goods stolen by Christian slaves in domestic service – zillions of *zianies* worth of gemstones, lustred tiles, bolts of Syrian damask, even full-size Persian carpets. How this contraband finds its way to European markets is known only to certain pirate captains who deliver it somewhere over the horizon to none other than our old friend Morato Maltrapillo.'

'Micaela's father? You mean that bastard left her here to guarantee his human cargo was legitimate, and all the time he's been up to his ears in smuggling?'

'A fellow I know who appraises stolen goods,' said Gabriel Múñoz, ignoring this outburst, 'says the current shipment will not make its rendezvous with Maltrapillo, since Gimp the Greek is still in port.'

'What's that got to do with Micaela?'

'This fellow I know says the fat pirate captain had an encounter the night before last with a reportedly intractable catamite in a warehouse used for storing the contraband.'

'A catamite? But – '

'This so-called catamite,' said Gabriel Múñoz, 'was heard to say, "Trust no one in this life." '

As Zoraida was returning from her uncle's the evening before his departure for Amsterdam, Micaela was making her way homeward too, through dark alleys, her amber eyes downcast and her lovesick heart fixed on one who, it discomfits me to say, was chained naked to a ringbolt in a rock. Discomfits because, though I had done nothing to encourage this crush of hers, it made her pathetically vulnerable.

'Psst! Michele!' A figure emerged from a side alley.

The lovesick look left Micaela's face. 'Out of my way, twerp,' she snarled at El Dorador, 'or I'll beat you up again.' Beating up El Dorador was the only thing Micaela could do for the man she loved.

'No, wait – I have a message for you. From Cervantes.'

Micaela shoved El Dorador against a wall and shook him. 'Where is he?'

'That's what I'm trying to tell you.'

I was, El Dorador said, hiding in a warehouse not far from the Plaza of Atrocities.

'Take me to him. Hurry.'

'I hear and obey,' said El Dorador.

The moment Micaela entered the warehouse, two of Gimp the Greek's pirate crewmen grabbed her. That was when she was heard to say, 'I trust no one in this life.'

The crewmen handed Micaela over to a quartet of eunuchs in an underground room where contraband was usually stored. It had been converted for the occasion into a love-nest for Gimp the Greek and the object of his desire. Tapestries depicting homoerotic acts covered the walls. The diamond-studded alabaster couch was twice the usual size and heaped with costly furs. Exotic birds from a hidden valley in the Hindu Kush sang of a freedom they would never know, fluttering forlorn wings against golden bars. All was suffused in the softly flattering glow of sperm-oil lamps.

Gimp the Greek looked at his prize, struggling in the grip of the eunuchs.

'Prepare him for a night of love that *râwis* will sing of for a hundred years,' the pirate captain instructed them, and took himself off to an adjacent room where, with shaking hands, he poured a cup of wine.

Acquiescence . . . or rape? Which would it be?

From the love-nest he heard sounds that suggested a roughhouse.

He sloshed more wine into his cup. Let the boy have his fun. He *was* a bit of a ruffian, as El Dorador could attest. But four experienced eunuchs could handle him.

A few minutes later Gimp the Greek drained the last of the wine and cocked an anxious ear. Not a sound from the love-nest now. He limped to the door. Nothing.

Impatiently he called, 'Hey in there!'

No answer.

'What's taking you nutless wonders so long?'

Still no answer.

He roared, 'Answer me or I'll tear your souls out through your assholes!'

The door opened a tentative crack. Gimp the Greek saw a pair of frightened eyes. The door opened wider, wide enough for the senior eunuch, a skilled cosmetician named Ma'aruf, to squeeze his bulk through. Both his cheeks were covered with scratches. He began to cry.

'We fear your wrath, master. We are not ready for the Annihilator of men.'

'What has happened?' demanded Gimp the Greek.

'We fear your wrath, master. We are not ready for the Leveller of mighty kings and humble peasants.'

'Tell me!'

'We fear your wrath, master. We are not ready for the Destroyer of all earthly pleasures.'

'You will *feel* my wrath if you don't answer.'

Ma'aruf dropped to his knees. 'We did not cause this thing, master. We did only as instructed, exactly. In order to anoint the Inviolable One with the seventeenfold fragrance that would make even a corpse rampant – '

'Ah!'

' – we stripped off the white silk pantaloons, overcoming considerable opposition – '

'Ah!'

' – and found . . .' Here Ma'aruf burst into renewed tears.

'During the struggle, did you damage him in some way?' Gimp the Greek demanded.

Unable to go on, the eunuch prostrated himself.

'Rise and speak or I'll cut off your balls and roast them before your eyes!' shouted Gimp the Greek, forgetting that was one threat he could not carry out.

Nevertheless, it loosened the terrified Ma'aruf's tongue. 'I unfortunately am bereft of balls,' he said, 'and . . . *and so is the Maltrapillo boy.*'

'Jesus-fucking-Christ, he's a eunuch?' roared Gimp the Greek, neglecting to convert the deity's name.

'Worse than a eunuch,' bawled Ma'aruf.

Gimp the Greek stepped over Ma'aruf's prostrate body and stalked into the love-nest. Emerging moments later, he hurled the empty wine jug at a wall. Then he sat with his elbows on his knees and his head in his hands.

For five minutes his mind was paralysed by disbelief. For five minutes more it was consumed by revulsion. For the next five, by rage.

That . . . *female*! Leading him down the garden path in the wake of a classic callipygean curve behind which (or in front of which) were hidden budlike young mammaries and a plump downy mound of Venus – how unutterably repulsive!

A groan escaped Gimp the Greek, and not just for what might have been. He couldn't even have the satisfaction of unmasking her – not without admitting his elaborate plans for a night of love so illicit it was punishable by death.

The Inviolable One! O mockery! O vile illusion!

He'd make the virago pay.

But how? Drawing and quartering was too good for that evil little hornswoggler who had hoodwinked two deys and the entire populace of Algiers, Gimp the Greek included.

He should pay her back in her own filthy coin . . . make the punishment fit the crime . . .

Sending Ma'aruf and the other eunuchs away, he sat brooding. He could hear his pirate crewmen pacing sentry duty outside, steadily, indefatigably. Able-bodied seamen, a lusty lot. Shipboard life required that. Why, even the lowest of the low, even galley slaves . . .

Gimp the Greek slowly raised his head and smiled a terrible smile.

He sent one of his crewmen to *Lela Marien*, his pirate command ship, to fetch his first mate Ajeeb, a lean, dark man who wore a Princess Eboli eye-patch.

'Give the crew a few days' leave,' Gimp the Greek told Ajeeb. 'We won't be sailing tomorrow.'

'But the contraband is aboard,' Ajeeb protested, 'and the galley slaves are already chained to their benches.'

'Before the night is out,' Gimp the Greek promised, 'I will give them something to keep them amused.'

On his way back to *Lela Marien's* berth at the lighthouse end of the mole, lean, dark Ajeeb assessed his good fortune. Had his opportunity finally come? Of course, he didn't know yet what the Greek had in store for his galley slaves. But whatever it was, if it gave him an excuse to interest the Dey's janissaries in the ship . . .

Ajeeb, a Muslim born and bred, a local boy in cosmopolitan Algiers, knew his chances for advancement were small. Hassan Pasha, like all deys, preferred apostate Christians as pirate captains. These new Muslims, eager to prove themselves, could be counted on to give a reasonably honest tally of the slaves and goods they brought in.

Outward-bound contraband, in which Gimp the Greek was the leading dealer, was another matter.

The Dey, Ajeeb knew, considered such smuggling the economic equivalent of anathema. Hassan Pasha, so depraved in other ways, was a veritable puritan on the subject.

If events proceeded as Ajeeb dared hope, his reward might be a pirate ship of his own – the very *Lela Marien*, in fact, on which he had served so long.

The appraiser of contraband, Haroun, burned with a secret longing.

It was not, like Ajeeb's, for command of a pirate ship – nor, like Gimp the Greek's, for forbidden erotic delights. Haroun yearned for peace in his tormented soul.

197

A young Spanish wool dealer whose former name was Géronimo Girón, he had accepted conversion two years ago. It meant a better life in captivity, and he knew his family could provide no ransom. But guilt consumed him. He would reconvert if he could. But apostasy from Islam was punishable by death, and Gerónimo Girón (as he still thought of himself) had no desire to die.

His religious troubles were compounded by the fact that, shortly after his conversion, as if in divine retribution, he had been stricken with the tertian ague. The Christian physicians of Algiers had given him up for lost. Then Zoraida the trance dancer had come, sent by his master the Dey, who took a paternal interest in new Muslims.

He remembered it still – how could he forget? – the sick-room with the single oil lamp in its niche casting upon the far wall Zoraida's dancing shadow, as insubstantial as her veils, serpentining on those long, sinuous legs like smoke, as if she were a *jinnayah* rising from the lamp. Her eyes soon showed white only, her mouth went slack, her olive skin gleamed with sweat and undulated with seismic hauteur through those diaphanous veils. Finally – the dying Gerónimo Girón would swear it – Zoraida *flickered*, becoming less substantial than the dancing shadow she cast. It was then that Gerónimo Girón half rose, felt the poison of the tertian ague drawn from his body, and knew he would live.

An apostate Christian, now an unwilling Muslim who owed his life to that *jinnayah* of a non-practising Jewess – why was it Gerónimo Girón's fate to be so bedevilled by religion?

Especially now, with Zoraida reminding him, 'When you said you could afford no gift, I did not press you, Haroun.'

Gerónimo Girón could only admit the truth of that.

'Now I have come to ask a service in return. Two nights ago, Gimp the Greek had an encounter in the cellar of a certain warehouse. What happened to the catamite?'

For a moment it seemed Girón would not speak. Then, 'He expected a catamite. But it was a girl.'

'I know *who* she is. I want to know where.'

'I don't know. How should I know?'

But looking at Zoraida brought back the instant when she had *flickered* – signifying that her own soul had almost been snuffed out? – and saved his life, and Gerónimo Girón knew that payment had simply been deferred.

'We'll have to wait until dark,' he told her.

*

A ragbag of characters thrown together by Fate in a will-less world (unless
the will is the author's): lean, dark Ajeeb who would betray his captain
to earn a command of his own; Gerónimo Girón the remorseful apostate
with a debt to pay; Zoraida the trance dancer who alone seemed to care
(I, you will remember, was still chained naked to a rock) that a teenage
girl had run out of luck and for two days and nights had been gang-
raped by several dozen sex-starved galley slaves; a sergeant of janissaries
named Al-Kuz still waiting offstage to play his small but deadly part –
given all these, who was I to disparage the plays of Lope de Vega as
melodramatic?

Isn't truth sometimes best served by melodrama?

The slave was huge, his face scarred and deformed, his massive shoulders
scarred too. He never spoke to her. Possibly he could not speak. He tried to
smile, unaware that this made his face even more fearsome. It also caused
a single tear to run down his twisted cheek. When he touched her she was
beyond screaming. But his huge callused hand was gentle. Was he protecting
her with his great bulk, holding her almost like a doll in the crook of one arm
while, with his free hand, he gathered the slack of his chain to use against
anyone who tried to take her from him? A score of men had her, and had
her brutally, before her arrival at his position beside the gangway in a tumble
of arms and legs – so small, so frail. Possibly he did not understand what
acts he was expected to commit upon her body. Possibly some wound or
illness had incapacitated him. But such conjectures would not account for
the – anguish? – that appeared on his until-then-expressionless scarfield
of a face. For a while his fellows watched the fearsome giant, eager to see
in what gross and monstrous way he would violate her. Ready to cheer,
they soon jeered instead, for he merely sat gigantically over her, tenderly
stroking her bruised face, her bare bruised arms and body. She was so
delicate and vulnerable in her nakedness that he unwound his headcloth,
the only garment permitted him, and draped it round her like a cloak.
Then, rousing from his distraction, he growled suddenly and swung his
chain, breaking the forearm of a man grabbing for her from the bench
in front.

The growl, strangely, did not frighten her. It was protective, like his
covering her with his headcloth, an intimate act somehow, almost loving.
Huddled in the warm crook of his arm, hurting, aware still of the flow of
blood (but it was slowing, she would not bleed to death), she wondered, for
the first time since she was tumbled and splayed and violated, whether she
might survive this night, and as wonder gave way to hope, she slept.

It was light and dark and light again, and once more dark on the ship

Lela Marien, and those on the nearby benches bided their time, for the giant could not remain awake for ever. Scratching their lice, catching and crushing and sometimes eating them, they waited.

His head lolled, slumped to one shoulder. His breathing deepened. Her eyes blinked open in the moonlight. A man on the bench in front reached for his chain.

They rowed to the lighthouse end of the mole in a skiff belonging to the harbourmaster, in whose office Gerónimo Girón worked when he was not moonlighting as a fence. Besides Zoraida, who insisted on coming, Girón had brought along two of his 'suppliers', both unhappy-looking as they shipped their oars and let the skiff glide the final few yards to Gimp the Greek's private jetty where *Lela Marien*, silhouetted against the backglow from the lighthouse, was moored. Gerónimo Girón awkwardly held a halberd, its spear- and axe-blades gleaming faintly. He would have preferred a firearm, but a lit match, let alone the sound of gunfire, was, of course, out of the question.

No such considerations hindered lean, dark, eye-patch-wearing Ajeeb, or the sergeant of janissaries Al-Kuz, summoned by Ajeeb to investigate 'alarming noises' coming from *Lela Marien*. Al-Kuz and his squad carried the usual truncheons, and Ajeeb a firearm which, as he explained to Al-Kuz, needed no match. It was a late-model wheellock pistol from Nuremberg, acquired in a pirate raid. Really too fine a weapon for himself, Ajeeb said. Perhaps the sergeant would care to borrow it?

The gesture, Ajeeb knew, would cost him nothing. The pistol would not be needed, for on the ship were only chained slaves and their naked, battered plaything – and some contraband which the janissaries would discover, to the definitive undoing of Dalí Mamí a/k/a Gimp the Greek.

Al-Kuz, flattered, hefted the pistol, testing its balance. A professional fighting man, his movements were economical, adroit. Yet there was about Al-Kuz something panurgic. Resourcefulness, as Rabelais well knew, needn't imply raw courage. Perhaps Al-Kuz survived in a violent milieu by striking first and asking questions afterwards.

Al-Kuz led his squad and the ship's first mate Ajeeb on to the mole. They were halfway to *Lela Marien* when they heard the shouting.

It is difficult not to see Gerónimo Girón as a villain of the piece. But that would be unfair. Girón was no man of action like the janissary sergeant Al-Kuz. Climbing on to the jetty, he asked himself what a normal person would ask – what am I doing here? – yet the question did not stop him. Halberd aslant his chest, he was first aboard *Lela Marien*, ready for confrontation. When no one challenged him, he proceeded along the gangway between the rows of benches, Zoraida close on his heels and his two rowers lagging behind.

Did the slaves sound unnaturally restive? On the gangway, Gerónimo Girón felt as if he were walking the plank. Would these dimly seen shapes drag him down among them? No, he assured himself, galley slaves were dumb brutes who did not look for trouble. Still, if these creatures, their appetite for sex newly whetted, knew a woman walked the gangway, even one as unfashionably slender and long-limbed as Zoraida. . . ? But she wore a shapeless cloak, its cowl hiding her face from the light of the torch she thrust to either side as they made their way forward.

His mood fluctuating between fear and assurance, he scanned the benches for the girl (a boy, according to the credulous Ma'aruf, transmogrified into a girl by some evil enchantment right before his eyes). Suddenly he heard a sharp intake of breath from Zoraida.

Gerónimo Girón would never forget what he saw in the torchlight. The slave was gigantic, his face an asymmetric nightmare. With one huge hand he was holding – trying to squeeze the life from? – the partially draped girl. With the other he wielded a length of chain, striking indiscriminately at his benchmates, laying flesh open, smashing bones.

As if this terrifying activity weren't enough, he rose abruptly and thrust the girl up at them, using her, it seemed to Gerónimo Girón, as a shield. Mother of God, the strength of the man! His shoulders bunched and Girón heard a ripping sound as planking came up with chains. One hand and one enormous foot appeared on the edge of the gangway. The giant rose higher, the girl's body shielding him so that Girón dared not strike. Then the giant, apparently losing his balance, shifted the girl's weight and stood her on her unsteady feet on the gangway so that for an instant his chest was exposed, and in that instant, with all his strength, Gerónimo Girón ran the spear of the halberd through the giant's chest up to the axe-blade. Afterwards Gerónimo Girón would always wonder why, as he plunged back down among the others, taking the deadly halberd with him, the giant seemed almost to smile.

Then Zoraida thrust the torch at Gerónimo Girón and herself supported the child as they returned down the gangway.

The janissary sergeant Al-Kuz knew survival involved respecting the odds. The odds told him, as he saw several figures scramble from *Lela Marien* on to the jetty, that the torchbearer was not their leader. And when Ajeeb whispered, 'Stop them,' Al-Kuz did not shout an order to halt the unknown men; they might be armed. Al-Kuz took aim with Ajeeb's wheellock pistol at the tallest of the figures, the one just behind the torchbearer, and pulled the trigger.

The tall figure staggered from torchlight into darkness and crumpled into my arms.

My arms? Me, Miguel de Cervantes?

What was I doing there, unexpectedly *in medias res* (but that's the idea of *medias res*, isn't it, to jump right in?) when, last you knew, I was chained naked to a ringbolt in a rock in a solitary pit trying to save my sanity by telling myself one true story?

This is where I enter that story – and re-enter the story of my own death and life, from which I've been absent through no fault of my own apart from trying to escape on Onofre Exarque's frigate that never came.

But apparently I had served my time for that.

Around noon, guards came into my pit to strike the chain attaching me to the rock and drag me up more spirals of stair than my confinement-weakened legs could manage. Sluiced off, and back in black-and-white-striped burnous and leg irons, I left the royal *bagnio* and saw Gabriel Múñoz leaning against the usual whitewashed wall.

He told me of his two meetings with Zoraida, and of Zoraida's with Gerónimo Girón.

'Then Micaela's a prisoner aboard Gimp the Greek's flagship? Help me get rid of these leg irons! Hurry!'

'Not so fast, *compañero*. Even a renegade like Girón knows things are safer after curfew.'

Micaela – and Gimp the Greek! My heart pounded with a hard, hollow thump. The sunlight was blinding. We started to walk. My knees wobbled.

'You better take a rest.'

'When does it get dark?'

'That usually happens after the sun sets,' he said. Then, when I did not smile, 'You won me some money, you know. There were not too many of us bet you would make it. You are the talk of Algiers, *compañero*, a genuine, bona-fide celebrity. How did you last that long of a time without either going crazy or defuncting yourself?'

'Telling myself stories. Dreaming of ways to escape.'

'You never learn, do you?' Maybe I was touchy, but I found the question patronizing.

I said, 'You've made yourself a pretty soft life here. That's your answer to captivity. Me, I want out. And I'll keep trying, no matter what they do. If they cut me off at the ankles, I'll crawl.'

'God help you, I think you mean that.'

'A mass breakout!' I heard myself say.

'What?'

I grew agitated. 'One man, four – even a dozen in the cave – they weren't enough. It's why I failed. I'll need fifty men, sixty! Bigger things are expected.'

'Expected, *compañero*? You get religion down there?'

I didn't know how to answer. Something had got me through my time in the pit, but could I say it was God?

Not unless God was just a way to fend off the dark and the silence and the nothing. Not unless religion was just trying not to stutter, and telling yourself stories, and dreaming of escape.

Although Gabriel Múñoz got me unshackled and unstriped by mid-afternoon, he did not know the details of Girón's foray. So I sauntered well before sunset on to the curving mole, attaching myself to one work party and then another, until I reached Gimp the Greek's jetty. I slid down among the rocks on the sea side, opposite. There I waited in my nondescript burnous, armed with nothing more than a stylet (or was it a dudgeon?), until dark. Then I slipped across the mole and under the jetty.

Moonrise, stars, moonset. At last (did I doze?) the thump of a skiff against a piling, footsteps overhead, a flare of torchlight guiding me up on to the jetty beside *Lela Marien* to hear shouting and a shot and to feel . . .

. . . Zoraida crumpling into my arms.

Carrying her, I felt a hot, pumping wetness soaking my burnous. At the end of the jetty the skiff rocked in the water. One man jumped in, then another, then the torchbearer. He reached a hand up for a youth oddly clad in – Micaela! She snarled and tried to bite his hastily withdrawn hand. Glared at me as I lowered Zoraida into the skiff, almost dropping her. Snarled again but, seeing Zoraida aboard, warily followed. I jumped after her, the skiff already moving. Micaela scuttled to the prow, where Zoraida was huddled. As we picked up speed, I crawled forward too. Micaela mewled, a feral sound. Zoraida raised one hand and I grasped it.

'*Ráwi*.'

I tore a strip from the hem of my borrowed burnous, wadded it, tried to stop the blood pumping from her side. No use.

'*Tameji, rāwi?*'

'No, I'm staying here with you.'

She spoke again, so faintly I had to lean close.

'Uncle Suleiman . . . tulips . . . Amst . . .'

What was she trying to tell me? In Turkish a tulip (*tülbent*) is both a turban and a showy, turban-shaped flower growing from a bulb. A code word? But how was I to decipher it? And what had tulips, or turbans, to do with angst?

'*Rāwi,*' she whispered. 'You never . . . saw me dance.'

'I will. When you're better.'

Did the ghost of a smile for what was not to be touch her face?

She made a little coughing sound, not much really, almost apologetic, but blood welled from her lips.

'Tell me . . . a story.'

'Once upon a time,' I began. But no story came to me.

'What time? Was it . . . very long ago?'

'Not very, no.'

'Only once . . . upon a time? Never twice? Can't a story ever . . .'

'Sure, but if it's a good story, no matter how often it's told, it should seem as if it's for the first time. So, "Once upon a time" is how *rāwis* sometimes begin.'

'And . . . Spanish storytellers?'

'They often,' I said, 'begin with a place, though they sometimes won't tell you quite where the place is, exactly.'

'Like . . . like a lost homeland you can . . . never find again?'

For an instant I saw a wheatfield, a sea of gold rippling in the breeze on a cloudless summer day in La Mancha.

'Yes,' I said.

'And even if you . . . can't find it . . . you have to keep looking or you'll die?'

'Yes,' I said.

'I'd like to hear . . . a story like that.'

And I began, for some reason I began, as I would again all those years later, so in a way it was as Zoraida wished, twice upon a time: 'In a place in La Mancha the name of which I don't care to remember . . .' but I said no more, because she made that little coughing sound again, not much really, almost apologetic, but the blood welled from her mouth and for a moment, for her final moment, she was in the past which, sooner or later, is the only time left for all of us, and she said, '*Ráwi* – sitting in the marketplace all day telling stories. What an easy life . . .'

When I looked up I saw that Micaela had disappeared from the prow of the skiff.

XVI

Damsel

Curfew over, daylight coming, and me with no leg irons, no captive's uniform. So what, I asked myself. So they'll throw you in the pit again, chain you to a rock. You survived that, didn't you?

Was I, at least until some distant April 23rd, a survivor? Zoraida wasn't.

And Micaela?

I wandered along the beach – her beach. Stared at nothing, kicked pebbles.

Then, far down the beach where the sun-track touched the shore like a bloodstain, I saw her. Stooping, rising, whipping one arm in a throwing motion. I started to run.

'Micaela!'

She did not turn, not right away. Down, up, throw. Down, up, throw. Stones skimmed the water, ricocheting, disappearing. Down, up, throw. Then she spun and hurled a stone that just missed my head.

Her face was dirt-encrusted except for the runnels of her tears. She was still wearing that odd strip of cloth. Her dark curls were lustreless, her nose bruised and swollen, her lips swollen too and split. Her eyes, those disturbing amber eyes, looked dead.

I stretched out my hand. She struck it aside and retreated into the surf, hissing like a viper.

'Micaela,' I called softly, entering the water.

Did those bruised lips form the shape of my name before her teeth snapped shut inches from my reaching hand?

Sometimes, I told myself, with a wary feral animal, if you pretend to ignore it, it will follow. So I turned and waded slowly to shore. At first nothing. Then I heard her coming, as slowly, after me. I walked, still slowly, at water's edge. Stopped. I could hear her rapid, shallow breathing. I walked again. She walked. I turned. She stiffened, stood at bay. I turned away and walked. In that way I led her in stops and starts into the city and up the hill to – where?

The barber-shop of Zoraida's uncle was shuttered. When I rapped on the adjacent door, Micaela almost took flight.

'What do you want?' A woman's voice, and old.

'I've come to see Suleiman Sa'adah Sometimes Erroneously Called the Wise,' I said, and the door opened.

'I only let the shop and rooms together,' she told me. She was a good eighty, with eyes starry white in the centres.

'Suleiman Sa'adah,' I enunciated. 'I'm looking for – '

Peering at me she cried, 'Why, it's Rodrigo! Captured you again, have they? Well, what Allah wills, will be. Leastways, that's what they say in these parts. Come in, boy, come in.' She asked, 'Is that dog housebroken?'

'I'm not Rodrigo,' I shouted as we climbed steep stairs. 'And she's not . . .' But what was the use? Her hearing was no better than her sight.

I followed her, and Micaela followed me, into a small, cosy room. Her face close, the old woman scrutinized me.

'What kind of fool do you take me for? You're not Rodrigo. Even if there is some slight resemblance.'

'I'm his brother.'

'Can't be. His brother's chained to a ringbolt in a rock.'

'Not any more.'

All through this conversation, imagine her peering and me shouting and Micaela cowering in a corner.

'What's that dog doing in that corner there?'

'It's a girl. Micaela. She's been hurt. She needs a place to stay. I thought Suleiman Sa'adah might help.'

'Might *have*. But he's gone. Time to get in out of the hot sun, he said. Too old to chase around being a spy, he meant. He thought I never knew, but I knew.'

She went to the corner where Micaela was trying to make herself invisible and crooned in an unfamiliar language. Taking the soon-docile Micaela's hand, she guided her through a door.

Moments later she came out alone with a broom and did her aged but furious best to break my head with it.

'Beast!' she cried. 'Monster! Asmodeus! How many times did you violate that poor child?'

Whack, whack, whack went the broom.

Desperately, I signalled my innocence and Ignorance.

'You trying to say you didn't do it?'

'Holy Virgin!' I managed, and started for the door through which she took Micaela.

Whack! 'Don't you dare go in there. Even if you didn't do it, this is no time for a *man* to come near her.' Never was that simple word uttered with such contempt.

'W-w-will she be all right?'

'If Allah wills it. Also, *I'll* be taking care of her.'

'Who are you?'

'The ex-landlady of Suleiman Sa'adah Sometimes Called the Wise.'

'Erroneously?'

'Hah! Wisest man I ever met – for a Westerner.'

'He's from Smyrna. Smyrna's not in the West.'

'Where *I* come from, it is.'

'Can't I help somehow? I could get a surgeon,' I suggested.

She raised her broom, then decided to try reason. 'What can a surgeon do that I can't? I'm a hundred and three years old at least, and I've seen my share of the world's folly. Besides,' she gritted, 'surgeons are men.'

'I'd still like to see her,' I said meekly.

'Not now. In a few days. I'll do what needs doing.'

'I have no money,' I said.

She took a final swipe at me with what was left of her broom – stick mostly. 'Money! The poor child's been raped and you say money! Out with you! Out!'

Fortunately it was Jum'a (Friday, the sabbath), so when I strolled in re-uniformed and -shackled, the prison guard-room was staffed by only one janissary, an aging veteran with one of those kinky beards that make you think of ancient Assyria. He scratched it.

'You were due back before curfew yesterday,' he said. 'Today is not yesterday. But Allah is compassionate and merciful – and so am I to anyone who won me several hundred *zianies*. How *did* you survive down in the pit that long?'

'Telling myself stories.' I omitted the part about thinking of new ways to escape.

In the prison yard, someone shouted my name and there was a smattering of applause from others who bet on my survival. But there was muttering from some who bet against.

'Probably had one of them ubiquitous diamond-studded alabaster couches.'

'A Persian carpet on the floor.'

'All the lamb he could eat, water to drink when all our wells are going dry.'

'What are you talking? He was in solitary!' said one of my supporters indignantly.

'There's solitary and solitary – if you've got a friend in the janissaries.'

Such insinuations were not the last I would hear.

'Forget it,' Gabriel Múñoz told me later in the tavern. 'Those bums are a minority.'

But how many rumours are started by majorities? So if you read anywhere about my having a janissary for a protector – let alone the Dey – you'll know what to make of it.

Gabriel Múñoz drew me a beer. 'You want a job? There could be an opening at the harbourmaster's.'

I jumped at it. The harbour meant boats, and boats meant escape. Also, working in the lower part of town, I'd be able to visit Micaela – if the Old Woman of the East would let me in.

At the harbourmaster's I spent my time logging out authorized freight, while Gerónimo Girón did the same with contraband to see that the harbourmaster got his cut.

We had a lot of slack time, but even so it was difficult to bring up the subject of escape with Girón because of his one-track-minded remorse.

If I began, 'Suppose a man, a renegade like yourself, could get hold of an armed frigate . . .' he would rejoin, 'A renegade like myself, could Christ ever forgive him?'

A frequent clicking sound came from Girón's side of the office. Turkish worry-beads, I thought at first. Then I realized it was a rosary. He hid it guiltily.

'Suppose this renegade,' I tried another time, 'wants to go into piracy – he needs a permit, right?'

'The Turks permit no apostasy. I can't even show my face in our makeshift little church. The penalty is death.'

'Is it difficult to get this piracy permit?'

'What's difficult is to pray alone in secret with no priest to intercede for a person or anything.'

'Lutherans do it all the time. Which comes first, the ship or the permit?'

Two monologues do not a dialogue make.

One day, when he was particularly remorseful, clicking like mad, I told him, 'Saint Peter himself would forgive any apostate who helped rescue fifty or sixty Christians.'

'Fifty or sixty?' he groaned. 'You're trying to tell me I have no hope, aren't you?'

'You do if you can get a piracy permit.'

His pessimism was reflexive. 'The permit is easy enough, but the frigate would cost a fortune.'

'You get the permit. I'll get the money.' Not that I had the faintest idea how, not yet. 'Trust me,' I said.

One afternoon as I was on my way to visit poor, mute Micaela, my irons began to drive me crazy. I stopped at a blacksmith's.

'Get these things off me.'

'You sure you know what you're doing?'

'That takes a wiser man. But get them off anyway.'

A crowd gathered. 'That's Zherbantay-Who-Survived-The-Pit having his leg irons removed,' they said.

They also said, 'The sacred fool! He'll be thrown in a pit again, chained to a rock. Then what?'

Then what? What did they mean, then what?

Chink-chink-chink went the blacksmith's pick and hammer.

'The sacred fool!' they said. 'What if he dies down there?'

What was it to these Moors if I died down there? And what was this sacred fool business? As if some divine spirit dwelled in me.

Dwells-dwells-dwells went the blacksmith's pick and hammer. The leg irons fell away.

The Moors chanted, '*Zherbantay, Zherbantay, Zherbantay.*' Some of them reached – to grab me, I thought at first. But all they wanted was to touch.

Without the irons I felt a curious, spurious sense of freedom. Exuberantly I cut a caper or two, as my father did the night I brought Juan the Obscure home from Triana.

In Tanners Lane a merchant rushed out of his shop and thrust a goatskin wallet at me. 'Take! An offering!' He darted a touch at what used to be my left hand.

Not long afterwards a *ráwi* named Shakashik, a lame old man with an off-key lute and a whispery voice, who was famous as Shakashik-Who-Sings-His-Own-Songs, sang one about me. I won't repeat it here;

it's embarrassing. Enough to say it was about a madly heroic veteran of The Naval who lost his right (*sic*) hand and survived 10,000 (!) nights and a night in the deepest pit in Algiers chained to a ringbolt – beginning on the first day of the Great-Drought-That-Is-Killing-Our-City. As if the drought were divine punishment imposed on those who imprisoned me!

In retrospect, I shouldn't have been surprised. Superstition flourished in this land where death was always close. But death was not merely close now, it was here. Months had passed without a drop of rain, though every marabout in Algiers prayed for it. The city's poor descended like locusts to strip suburban orchards of their withered fruits, and slaughtered on the spot any skin-and-bones beast still alive. Within the city walls, like a pillaging army, bands of janissaries ignored the corpses rotting in the streets and plundered the larders of the rich.

People with empty bellies craved signs and omens, wonders. If they couldn't have a comet or a two-headed calf, they'd settle for what they could get – me. My stutter they eagerly interpreted as the gift of tongues, glossolalia, that divinely inspired (if incomprehensible) communion with God. Their God, of course, not mine. But no matter.

Soon I heard Shakashik's song wherever I went.

Knowing a good thing by the way his coin-cup filled, Shakashik improvised new verses, some pretty far-fetched. The most ridiculous said that as long as Zherbantay-Who-Lost-His-Right-(*sic*)-Hand lived, the city would survive its time of troubles.

This particular nonsense I welcomed, of course. If my survival ensured the city's, the converse had to apply.

But while I, or Zherbantay-Who-Lost-His-Right-(*sic*)-Hand, was the talk of the souks, some of the talk was malicious. My special relationship with the Dey (I surely had one, since I went about without irons) was dissected. Some wanted to know, 'If he's such hot stuff, how come the Dey don't put him in the seraglio with his other playmates?'

But the Dey don't. That is, doesn't. Didn't. He just ignored me. He was busy worrying about the drought.

When people got the hand straight, Shakashik changed his evolving song accordingly. A crippled left hand – '*sinistra! sinistra!*' – rumoured to have a will of its own, a stutter that passed for glossolalia . . .

Signs and omens. Wonders.

The Moors began to ask, why *had* I been chained naked to that rock? Were they being punished for some mistake of their Turkish masters?

And what did the Turks make of all this, those wily inheritors of the Golden Horn with its Byzantine ways? Why, they were only too happy to encourage belief in the sacred fool. What better scapegoat, if one were needed?

Shakashik-Who-Sings-His-Own-Songs had never had a success like his *Zherbantay!* cycle. He soon disdained the Plaza of Storytellers and would sing only for large fees at Turkish orgies. The songs took on a sort of specious reality, and I achieved unmerited fame even among my fellow prisoners when the catchy tune reached the *bagnio*. Shakashik found himself scaling new heights to create exploits for the hero of his cycle, and it cheered the captives to sing of one of their own who righted wrongs, chastised the haughty, rescued damsels in distress, etc. etc.

In short, the sacred fool metamorphosed into a dismounted knight-errant in prisoner's stripes instead of armour, a practitioner of what Don Juan of Austria once called benevolent machismo.

But I had no time to live up to Shakashik's song cycle, even if I'd wanted to. In those last few months before my death I had more important things to do.

I slipped the harbourmaster's dudgeon (or was it a fish-scaling knife?) easily into the hull of the beached frigate.

'What about this?' I asked with a scowl.

Gabriel Múñoz, who knew far less about ships than I did, clucked his tongue.

Gerónimo Girón, who knew nothing about ships at all, clicked his rosary.

'A trifle. Hardly worthy of the name dry rot,' said the harbourmaster. 'Would I lie to you, Miguel?'

I shrugged. He was my employer, after all.

'She's a lucky ship, for a renegade just starting out in piracy.' The harbourmaster smiled at nervous Girón. 'A bargain at just half a million *zianies*. Brought in her share of Christian treasure, not to mention slaves – including six nuns who became the stellar attraction of a highly profitable travelling bordello that – '

'God! Say you're not serious!' cried Gerónimo Girón, clicking furiously.

'Oh, all right – for a newly licensed pirate like you, Haroun, I'll make it four hundred thousand and a percentage of first fruits,' said the harbourmaster, who assumed Girón was shocked not at the nuns' fate but at the price.

Gabriel Múñoz jumped in with, 'Three hundred thou,' just as Girón asked, 'What happened to the previous owner?'

'The late pirate Sindbad (the names these renegades choose!) was caught in reverse tergiversation,' said the harbourmaster. 'Praying at the makeshift church.'

'Oh, *that* Sindbad,' said Gabriel Múnoz uneasily.

'What happened?' persisted Girón.

'He was boiled in oil at the Plaza of Atrocities,' Múñoz admitted.

'You call her a *lucky* ship?' Gerónimo Girón screamed.

We calmed him and adjourned.

The Old Woman of the East shook her head sadly.

'Still just lies there, poor thing. But come in if you must. And I suppose you must, seeing as you're a protector of damsels in distress – or so they sing around these parts,' she said doubtfully.

Micaela lay with her face to the wall, that classic callipygean curve covered by a thin sheet. I opened the shutters and sat on the edge of the bed. Seeing her so still, so unaware, so living dead, I almost wished she'd turn those disturbing amber eyes from the wall and snarl and try to chew my hand, my sound right hand, off.

I started this time with the story of the night I rescued my little brother Juan the Obscure from the gypsies, and how Rodrigo saved us both.

Micaela's face remained to the wall.

I'd told her, these last few weeks, story after story. Some from my past, some from the *ráwi* canon, some just made up as I went along, like Shakashik-Who-Sings-His-Own-Songs. Every word was a plea for Micaela to react. I told her adventure stories, and stories of my travels with my father (on the old road again, road again). I told her of Odysseus and Aeneas, of the star-crossed Lovers of Teruel, of Amadis of Gaul. I whispered. I rhapsodized. I tried a sudden shout.

She never so much as stirred, and today was no different. She could have been carved from wood.

Gabriel Múñoz came to the harbourmaster's the next morning with the news that Micaela's father Morato Maltrapillo had dropped anchor in Algerian waters during the night.

'If he comes ashore looking for his "son", he's apt to get lynched,' I said.

'Who by, the Moors?' Múñoz shook his grizzled head. 'If they know he palmed off a girl, they are laughing up their sleeves. They love to see the Turks made fools of.'

'Anyway, Maltrapillo won't come ashore,' said Gerónimo Girón, looking up from his beads. 'This is a straight contraband run.'

'That still leaves Gimp the Greek,' I pointed out.

Múñoz nodded. 'True, the Gimp is mad enough to kill. But the other smugglers will keep him in line. They have a sweet set-up with Maltrapillo. The fix is in. Anybody makes waves, the Dey could get wise. In which case, I guarantee you for sure, Gimp the Greek will wind up at the bottom of the harbour wearing a surplus anchor for a medal.'

'I want to see him. Maltrapillo.'

Gabriel Múñoz gave me an uneasy look. 'Listen, *compañero*, I know how set you are on a ship and a mass breakout, but try to shake down Maltrapillo and you could wind up wearing that anchor instead of Gimp the Greek.'

'Actually, I'm hoping to get him to take his daughter back to Spain with him.'

'Her? But she is on the catatonic side these days.'

'It's no worse than a headache! Not even as bad as the common cold! She'll get over it!' I shouted.

'Miguel, be careful,' Gabriel Múñoz warned me. 'Extortion is no game for amateurs. Plus I would not mention the girl if I were you. What is so important about her?'

'Just tell me where to find him.'

The deck of the frigate rolled gently under my face.

I looked up to see a broad-shouldered man with a grey-streaked beard. He was vulgarly bedizened from the bottom up (which was how I viewed things at the moment) in purple cork-soled shoes, green ribbon-crossed garters at the knees of chartreuse trunk hose, and dark blue doublet, gold-braided to supply a nautical motif. Belted at his side was a short cutlass with jewelled hilt.

This was Captain Morato Maltrapillo, born Agi Morato Morato. His present surname (and Micaela's) was his sartorial biography: he'd spent the first twenty years of his life in rags and had been making up for it ever since. Maltrapillo is one of those double-duty Spanish words that can denote real rags or 'glad rags'.

'Let him up.'

A booted foot was removed from my back, and I stood.

The scene was the poopdeck of Maltrapillo's *María de la Libertad*, anchored in an inlet three miles east of the city – the very inlet, I realized, where Onofre Exarque should have landed to take us from the cave so many months ago. My skiff bobbed alongside.

'Who are you? What do you want?'

It jolted me to see Micaela's amber eyes staring at me from Morato Maltrapillo's masculine face.

Rowing out, I'd given some thought to the fine art of extortion. First: how much to hit him for. (Just the 300,000-*ziany* tag on the frigate? But what about the dry rot, plus a general overhaul? Figure another forty, fifty thousand. But odd numbers were for amateurs, so I'd round it up to 400,000, cash on the barrelhead, if Maltrapillo wanted the Dey to remain in the dark about certain activities.) Next: my approach. (A *quid* for a *quo*, very simple if I could get the tone right. I'd aim for a drawled understatement, even a shade bored because the conclusion was so foregone.) Finally: side issues. (On reflection, I knew Gabriel Múñoz was right. This was no time to mention Micaela. Why not be practical for once?)

The pair of crewmen who hauled me up the poopdeck ladder didn't shake my resolve. Even when they hurled me at Maltrapillo's purple-shod feet, I wasn't fazed. Professionalism was its own protection. I'd start with, *I've got a proposition, Maltrapillo, and unless you hang on every word you'll hang from your own yardarm.*

But with those amber Micaela-like eyes staring into mine, what I said was, 'You son-of-a-bitch, what kind of father are you?'

One crewman drew a cutlass (or was it a falchion?), but Maltrapillo made a brushing motion, like shooing a fly.

'You already destroyed her childhood,' I accused him, 'making her parade around as a pre-teen transvestite tease, and now that *that's* ended in d-disaster, you th-throw her away like a banana peel. Would it hurt you so much, you bastard, to take her back to Murcia?'

'Take her *back*? What for?'

'She's your daughter, flesh of your flesh.'

'So? Maternal instincts I can see, but *paternal*?'

'She's bright and beautiful and, in general, some kind of wonderful, and all she asks from you is – '

'A son, now, a stalwart son, that would have been – '

' – a little concern or even awareness of who she is.'

'If she couldn't make it as a boy, why blame me? What's so tough about being male? Being male's easy.'

'She's fourteen. It got harder and harder to hide certain developments, such as that classic calli – '

'Fifteen, and slim young boys also have curves like – '

'Not that kind. She's all girl, one hundred per cent feminine,' I said. 'And one hundred per cent loyal too. You asked the impossible of her, but she still loves you. She has so much love to offer, if only you'd treat her like a daughter. She's simply overflowing with love.'

'How would you know?'

'Take her back to Spain with you, that's all I'm asking. Put her in a convent or somewhere if you must, but get her out of here.'

'Why?'

So I began again. 'Because her life here is a nightmare. There's no way she can grow up normal after what she's been through unless – '

'In Murcia fifteen *is* grown up. And I don't believe in convents. Marriage, that's something else,' he mused. 'Of course, she'd have to live on the opposite side of Spain, say in the Basque country. Yeah, I could marry her off, why not? Some of her kids might even be boys.'

'Micaela could never face marriage,' I said. 'Not after what happened to her.'

'What happened to her?'

'Gimp the Greek's galley slaves gang-raped her.'

'Oh, sure. I heard about that,' he said.

The monumentality of his indifference shook me. I expected what used to be my left hand to twitch, jump – attack him even, as it attacked my brother Rodrigo. But it didn't.

It just followed along obediently as I struck Morato Maltrapillo with my *right* hand. Excruciating pain shot up my arm, a phenomenon I'd experienced before. Still, he was down and I was up, a reversal of how this all began, even if I had only a moment of satisfaction before I was grabbed from behind and the blade of a falchion (or was it a snickersnee?) dented my Adam's apple.

'Release him,' said Micaela's father, getting up and casually wiping a carmine smear from his lips.

'You've got *cojones*.' He looked me over, as if for the first time. 'Want me to take her back to Spain, eh?'

'*Or* the Dey will learn who is ferryman for a certain ongoing smuggling operation, and in case you should contemplate disposing of me I have confederates ashore who – '

He brushed off all this, which was not entirely true anyway, with that insect-shooing motion.

'Come with us,' he said. 'You could do a lot worse than marry Micaela and go produce grandsons in Bilbao or somewhere. You're not bad looking except for what used to be your left hand, and we know you've got *cojones*.'

'Marry Micaela? Me?'

215

'Of course you. It's as obvious as that hawk nose on your face – which is aggressive enough to breed true – that you're in love with her.'

This so surprised me that I gave it a moment's thought. 'Like a favourite niece, maybe. I'm thirty-three years old.'

'A good age to marry. Her dowry would be adequate.'

'Like postmature little Constanza,' I ruminated. 'If I love her, that's who I love her like.'

'Ample might be a more accurate word. Well? I leave in three days. Are you coming? I'll pay your ransom.'

'She's just a child.'

'I'm offering you your freedom, you fool.'

By now what used to be my left hand *was* twitching and jumping.

'Is that thing hereditary?' he asked in a new, less enthusiastic voice.

I can't marry Micaela, I told myself; she's practically young enough – *is* young enough – to be my daughter. Anyway, I also told myself, I can't marry anyone. Not that I could say why. It was just something I knew.

'Hereditary?' I said, seizing the way out offered me. 'Well, sort of – but only on the male side.'

'I see.' Decidedly unenthusiastic.

'In Spain,' I said, 'I'm sure you can find a husband who'll suit Micaela.' Saying it, I felt a sinking emptiness, as if the ship had just crested a mountainous wave.

Shielding his eyes, those Micaela-like amber eyes, he stared towards the westering sun, then said, 'I reckon I could find her somebody. A man of Galicia – they make the best sailors. Or a Basque, one of those rock-throwers with muscles between his ears, not smart enough to be mutinous but strong enough to give me some grandsons. I sail with Friday morning's tide. Get her aboard by then.'

I pictured Micaela lying with her face to the wall, hardly the marriageable young woman her father expected. Somehow I'd have to snap her out of it in the next two days. My mind already ashore, I put a foot on the ladder – and only then remembered why I'd rowed out here.

'Oh, one other thing,' I said. 'I have this friend who needs to borrow four hundred thousand *zianies* to buy a frigate and go into the piracy business – as a front for his real interest, which is a subject we touched on a bit earlier. Smuggling.'

By the next afternoon Gerónimo Girón's piety was interspersed with a nautical vocabulary little short of awesome.

'Rigging's trig, God be thanked, but the for'ard winch should be replaced,

216

and if the good Lord sees fit to try us with gale winds, I wouldn't put much trust in the for'ard hatch either. Binnacle's cracked and woodworm's been colonizing the hull starboard abaft the beam.' He consulted a list while I looked at our newly purchased frigate, its prow looming above us as we stood at the moleside. 'I'd prefer brazen guns, not iron – see that rust over there? – and if there's money enough, by the grace of God, a new powder magazine. And, Miguel, when you're finished at the sailmaker's, will you look into hiring us some galley slaves?'

'Gerónimo,' I told him gently, 'we don't need a new powder magazine. We're not outfitting *Land of Canaan* to go raiding. And we don't need galley slaves either. Captives making a run for freedom won't object to a little rowing.'

He gave his rosary a few nervous clicks. 'Maybe I was getting carried away,' he said sheepishly. Then he looked at the soft pink palms of his hands. 'Actually I wouldn't mind doing a little rowing myself.'

Half an hour later I was saying with rehearsed enthusiasm, 'Micaela, your father's come to take you back to Spain!'

Face to wall, no response.

'The only thing is,' I tried, 'the only thing is, he's come in secret and he has to sail in a couple of days. And he'll be wanting to see the spunky daughter he's always known. So, Micaela, can't you sort of sit up and practise smiling the way you'll smile when you board your father's ship?'

Apparently she couldn't.

'He's dying to see you,' I said. 'He's full of plans.'

She stared at the wall. I wanted to kick a hole in it.

Sixty men, sixty-five maximum, that's all *Land of Canaan* could hold. How would I pick them? Who was I to try?

'Afraid to play God, are you?' Gabriel Múñoz asked.

My answer was a grumpy, wordless sound.

'It comes with the territory. Leaders lead, make decisions of life and death,' said Múñoz. 'Kings, military commanders, knights-errant . . .' He grinned.

'Cut it out, Gabe. The only knight-errant in Algiers is in Shakashik's song cycle.'

He cleared his throat. 'It so happens I had some time on my hands, so I drew up a kind of preliminary list.'

He placed it on the table. The hour was late, the illegal tavern that the Turks wouldn't dream of putting out of business was closed for the night.

It didn't take long to realize that two men playing God were worse than one.

'No poets?' I protested. 'You left out poets?'

'Who needs poets? A poet does not build anything or fix anything or feed anybody.'

'The world needs poetry. Poetry stirs men's hearts.'

Múñoz sighed. 'Tell you what. Grant me a few more professional soldiers and you can have a poet or two.'

'Why should we give room to soldiers?'

'The frigate could sail into trouble, you know.'

Entries were weighed. Some were added, for talent, for value. Doctors and priests whose ransoms had been set unrealistically high. Promising university students. A few teachers, merchants. No lawyers.

Names blurred before my eyes. Torres, Pedrosa . . .

'There's not a woman on the list!' I cried suddenly.

'Of course not,' said Gabriel Múñoz. 'Women do not contribute. So we have nothing to measure them by.'

'It's not their fault. Men don't let them contribute.'

'Still, the fact remains. Besides, do you think we are just going to sail out of here? It could be dangerous. Would you want to expose a woman to that?'

'I couldn't live with myself if we excluded women.'

'And children? *Compañero*, there are whole boatloads of captive women and children in Algiers, and no way to choose except wealth and rank. The richest and highest usually get ransomed anyway. You want to make room for the dirtiest and lowest?'

Noah, I told myself, had it easy. Everything nice and quantitative, seven by seven, two by two. Well, not that easy – Noah's wife Waila was a problem. According to legends that didn't make the Bible, Waila refused to board the ark and tried to persuade the people that her husband, with his talk of a flood, was insane. Maybe he was. But did that mean he was wrong?

Feeling profoundly inadequate, I sat across the table from Gabriel Múñoz and stared at nothing. Like Micaela at her wall.

Micaela! I thought suddenly. If I couldn't get her in shape to sail with her father, why not take her with us?

But, I told myself, every male captive must know a woman he thought deserved to go. Only I was in a position to take mine. Playing God was bad enough. Playing a selfish God was worse.

'No women,' Gabriel Múñoz said firmly. 'No children.'
We went over more names.

Above the former barber-shop of Suleiman Sa'adah Sometimes Erroneously
Called the Wise, the Old Woman of the East showed me the robes and veil
Micaela would wear.

'Assuming she's going anywhere,' I said. 'But we're running out of time.
He sails in the morning.'

'Empires have been won and lost in a night,' said the Old Woman of
the East. 'A falling star splashed a hole in the ocean that swallowed the
continent of Lemuria – or Mu, as my Lemurian ancestors called it – in
an *hour*. You'll find the words to reach her, Miguel,' she told me, using
my name for the first time. 'I know you will.'

Her faith surprised me; was she a fan of Shakashik's?

'I've tried everything,' I said, looking at the door, that hateful door
behind which Micaela lay in thrall to an unendurable memory. I was
almost tempted to go back to the harbour. There at least my efforts were
paying off. A week, ten days, and *Land of Canaan* would be ready.

I saw myself at sea, the wind in my face, free – and Micaela still lying
silent behind that door.

I pushed it open and went in.

'Once upon a time,' I said to Micaela's rigid back, 'there was this
beautiful damsel – I don't remember her name, let's just call her Damsel
– who thought it wasn't fair that only men could be knights-errant. But
everybody in the kingdom where Damsel lived told her that if she tried to
be a knight-errant she'd only wind up a damsel in distress instead, the kind
knights-errant rescued. Ignoring these warnings, Damsel went in search of
adventure riding an ass named, uh, Picapleitos, because she wasn't really
a very big girl and would have found it hard to control a warhorse. Soon
she came to the frontier of a distant kingdom, but not before she'd found
a magic potion that could undo the work of evil enchanters.'

I looked at Micaela's unmoving back. *Ask me!* Why don't you ask me
how she found it?

But Micaela just lay there, face to the wall.

'It was a pretty lucky thing she found it,' I resumed. 'Not only had an
evil enchanter put the local prince into a deathlike trance that only the
magic potion could wake him from, but the whole kingdom was in dire
peril. Because unless the sleeping prince woke in time, the evil enchanter
would use his seventy codes of sorcery to raze every city in the kingdom

219

to the ground, and turn the land into a lake as deep and dark as the Black Sea and all its people into spiny fishes.

'Well, the frontier guards let Damsel pass, and she crossed hills and dales on her ass Picapleitos, knowing she had to hurry because the magic potion would work for barely three days every one hundred and twenty-eight years, when all five planets were lined up one exactly above the other in the western sky at sunset, and the time was almost up. Mercury, the swiftest planet, could tarry only part of one more day.

'At the royal city Damsel was welcomed with songs of praise for her beauty and songs of thanksgiving as well because she had the magic potion which could wake the prince who'd been in his drugged sleep ever since his return from the last crusade – or the Lost Crusade, I forget which. Damsel would have sympathized with my forgetfulness, because her own one shortcoming was, she didn't have such a good memory. Otherwise, she was practically perfect.'

Ask me, I pleaded. Ask me how the people knew Damsel had the magic potion, or how Damsel knew about the five planets. *Ask me, ask me!*

But Micaela asked me nothing.

'The knight commander of the royal city told Damsel: "You must ride your ass Picapleitos to the barbican gate of the gloomy castle where the prince lies sleeping." '

How did the knight commander know the ass was named Picapleitos? *Ask me!*

But Micaela asked me nothing.

' "Now listen carefully," said the knight commander. "The captain of the barbican gate will speak. What he says is extremely important and vital, Damsel. Also crucial," the knight commander warned her. "If he does not speak precisely the words I am about to tell you, you will know he is a false knight, and you must flee for your life. But if he speaks the words correctly, every syllable in place, then you in your turn must reply with certain other words, equally important and vital. Also crucial. And you must speak these words correctly, every syllable in place, for if you don't, the captain and his heavily armed horseguards have orders to kill you, in which case you cannot wake the prince in time to stop the evil enchanter from razing every city and turning the kingdom into a lake as deep and dark as the Black Sea.

' "Are you ready, Damsel? Here are the precise words the captain of the barbican gate must speak. On pain of death you must not forget them. The captain must say, 'Demogorgon dwells in the Abyss with three fatal sisters or atop the Himalayas with elves and feys.' I will repeat those words. You must engrave them on your memory." And the knight commander repeated the words.

' "And here are the precise words you must answer. On pain of death you must not forget them. You must say, 'An old man with a long white beard rode a fire-snorting dragon past a juniper tree.' I will repeat those words." And the knight commander repeated the words.

'As Damsel rode towards the crag where the gloomy castle perched, she kept going over the words because she knew how important and vital they were, not to mention crucial, and she also knew her memory was far from perfect.

'She urged Picapleitos across a windswept landscape where grew only stunted but fragrant shrubs of rosemary and thyme. As rosemary symbolizes remembrance, which is not so different from memory, and as thyme symbolizes courage, which a damsel as well as a knight-errant may possess, Damsel plucked a sprig of each.

'The captain of the barbican gate could be seen from a long way off, a giant at least nine feet six inches tall, and his horseguards on their warhorses were equally menacing. A pair galloped out to escort Damsel to where the gigantic captain was waiting. His helmet was as big as four barber's basins, his sword as long as a galley oar. Seventy or eighty horseguards on their warhorses immediately surrounded Damsel, levelling their lances at her. But the barbican gate was up, and Damsel knew they would let her pass as long as she followed the knight commander's instruction.

'In a voice that out-howled the howling wind and would put any thunder to shame, the captain of the barbican gate shouted: "Demogorgon dwells in the Abyss with three fatal sisters or atop the Himalayas with elves and feys."

'Damsel listened to every word as if her life depended on it – as it did – and to every syllable as if the fate of the kingdom hung in the balance – as *it* did. And with the help of that sprig of rosemary, she knew the words were correct, every syllable in place.

'Meanwhile, you can imagine with what anxiety the captain of the barbican gate and his horseguards awaited her answer. Depending on what she said, their kingdom would either survive or be destroyed.

'But Damsel sat astride Picapleitos, surrounded by all those heavily armed horseguards, and she said nothing.

'For she had listened so intently to every last syllable that came roaring from the giant's mouth that she had forgotten what *she* must say. And not just forgotten a word or two, no. She had completely forgotten the entire countersign on which her life, and the life of the sleeping prince (a very handsome and lonesome sleeping prince, by the way), and the fate of the kingdom all hinged. Not even sniffing the rosemary helped.

'At least, not right away.

'Damsel looked at the levelled lances and the impatient eyes of the captain of the barbican gate and his sword like a galley oar. Three minutes passed. Five.

'Then suddenly Damsel brightened. I remember, she told herself triumphantly; I remember. And in a firm and steady voice she said, "Everything the Laughing Philosopher knew he learned from Leucippus," and waited confidently for the horsemen to let her enter the city. Instead she saw the captain of the barbican gate slam his visor shut in disgust at the sound of those words (what made Damsel think they were the right words she would never know) and raise his galley oar of a sword, at which the horseguards lowered their visors too and couched their lances. In seconds they would spur their warhorses, and seventy or eighty steel lances would transfix poor Damsel.

'It was over, then – finished. She had failed herself, failed the sleeping prince, failed the kingdom. And all because she couldn't remember a few simple words.

'But suddenly, perhaps realizing that Damsel had never sallied forth to try her hand at knight-errantry before, the captain of the barbican gate raised the visor and repeated his words. "Demogorgon dwells in the Abyss with three fatal sisters or atop the Himalayas with elves and feys!" he roared, out-howling the wind, shaming thunder.

'Up went seventy or eighty visors, and seventy or eighty lances.

'But at this reprieve Damsel's face became even more anguished, and amber tears spilled from her despairing amber eyes. She couldn't remember! Not all the rosemary in the world could help her now, nor all the thyme.

'Down went the visors. The lances were couched again. Up rose the captain's galley oar of a sword.'

I held my breath.

Did Micaela move ever so slightly, a barely perceptible rearrangement of that classic callipygean curve?

I resumed: ' "An old ... m-m-m-man ..." stammered Damsel.' I did a very good job with the stammering.

Again I held my breath.

Did I hear something, the uncertain echo of a faint trembling in the air?

' "... with a l-long white b-b-beard ..." ' I resumed.

Once more I held my breath.

The silence, Micaela's silence, thickened, became a muffled *something*, the sound a butterfly's wings might make.

'Knowing all that was at stake, Damsel groped with her entire being for the next word. Yet it refused to come,' I said.

And Micaela's fingers fluttered, as if she wanted to grasp something.

I leaned close. Those dark curls brushed my cheek.

And her hand moved, as if she were trying to draw lines connecting unseen stars on a whitewashed wall.

A whisper of sound, then louder. Then words.

'. . . help her, Miguel. Can't you help her?'

And her head began to turn.

'I can't help her, Micaela. Only you can.'

And she said, ' "An old man with a long white beard . . . rode a fire-snorting dragon past . . . uh, past a . . . a . . ." '

Those lost amber eyes beseeched me. 'Tell me, Miguel. Please? *What comes next?*'

And, turning full away from the wall, she put her arms around my neck and clung.

I beached the skiff, watching dawn gild the minarets of the city and the palace of the Dey on its heights. How, I wondered, can evil be so beautiful? I turned seaward and waited to see the same golden light touch the sails of the ship, Micaela's father's ship, as it grew smaller and smaller until it was hull-down at the horizon, only a tiny golden gleam upon the blue. Then the golden light was everywhere, its beauty impartial, the city's evil an accidental irrelevance in a heedless world.

Was Micaela at the rail of the disappearing ship, watching the shore recede? But why should she be? She if anyone had seen enough of Algiers.

I gathered a pile of flat stones. One by one I scaled them over the water – down, up, throw, down, up, throw. They ricocheted from the unassailable sea and vanished.

There was a final glint of sail like a distant beacon at the edge of an eternity no one could envision, then only the four janissaries coming along the strand to arrest me.

XVII

The Death of Miguel de Cervantes

As Related by Himself

The midday sun casts a foreshortened shadow of the gallows erected for my hanging.

Perhaps, I think, the public executioner has already begun his funereal march down Souk Street, but if so, the dirgeful music of pipe and drum cannot be heard over the roaring of my name, 'Zher*ban*tay! Zher*ban*tay! Zher*ban*tay!' – so angry a sound that at first I believe the crowd would be pleased to do the executioner's work for him. But then I see the anxious knots of turbaned Turks and club-bearing janissaries among the cowled Moors, and I see the Dey's own pikemen uneasily surrounding the stage where I stand with my hands roped behind my back and a janissary on either side, looking not at me but where the pikemen are looking, which is at the crowd – for am I not a sign and an omen, a wonder, at whose death the already stricken city will also die? And if so, then the crowd's anger must be directed at those who would kill me, starting with Hassan Pasha Dey the Venetian – Hassan of the decadently painted face, Hassan of the rhinoceros-sinew whip, Hassan who (was it only yesterday?) in a room of whitewashed stone where shafts of sunlight from high embrasures cast disconcerting fragmentary shadows on a blood-spattered wall, asked me two questions with that manic hum of his, only two, over and over: 'Where did you get the money, mmm?' and 'Who are your confederates, mmm?' But how could I name Morato Maltrapillo, who is Micaela's father and who will return? And how could I, the sole author of the plot, name those sixty others who were no more than oarsmen who at my command would have rowed *Land of Canaan* north across the Mediterranean? So I could only wait for the whistling of the Dey's rhinoceros-sinew whip after the two questions I could not answer, the whip exploding across my back as I screamed what might have been Cide Hamete Benengeli's name – where was he, that erstwhile astromancer with his Aratron and Phaleg, Ophiel and Och, with his mysterious Picatrix that made the Dey gasp; where was my *deus ex machina* now that I really needed him?

224

'Got any money?' asks the janissary to my left. He looks familiar with that dense, kinky Assyrian beard.

I shake my head no.

'Pity,' he says. 'For a few *zianies* I could help.'

'How?'

'Pulling,' he says. 'See, when a person's dangling from a rope, he strangles slow. Takes half an hour or more. That's a lot of dancing on air. But if somebody who don't like to see his fellow man suffer was to pull on his legs, this would break his neck and put him out of his misery. You sure you don't have any loose change?'

Again I shake my head, the one that will soon be supported by a rope.

'Did they arrest anyone else?' I ask.

'I'm not allowed to answer that,' he says.

'Once I earned you several hundred *zianies*,' I remind him.

'I can say they confiscated the frigate,' he says, staring up at the crossbeam of the gallows. 'But I can't tell you a renegade named Haroun or Girón ran off in the direction of Spanish Oran. So that's the end of him.'

'Who betrayed us?'

The kinky-bearded janissary shrugs.

I shrug too. Will it help to learn the name of the resentful captive who, I assume, got back at me for not including him? Have I time to rage at bit players when Fate is to blame for my predicament? (I have conveniently forgotten that free will played its part in getting me into this mess.) What does Fate think she's doing? Three fatal sisters! I'd wring their necks if I could. I mean, failure I was prepared for — swarms of janissaries storming *Land of Canaan* as we boarded, or the Dey's ships overtaking us halfway to Spain, grappling hooks embracing us obscenely, and our outnumbered escapees selling their lives dearly on a deck (Gerónimo Girón's newly sanded deck) slippery with blood – but none of that happened.

There is something intolerable about not even getting to *try*.

I find myself thinking for the first time in years of my grandfather Juan the Patriarch, and how he died so abruptly, the first death in my life, the recollection of which I brush irritably from my mind. Standing under the crossbeam of the gallows, is death all I can think of?

I decide to think of Zoilos instead.

Zoilos was a literary critic, the first in recorded history, spiteful but shrewd and capable of the killing witticism. He lived in the fourth century BC and was called Homer's Scourge because he made his living tearing apart the *Iliad* and the *Odyssey* almost line by line, and blind Homer dead four hundred years by then so who was there to defend him?

Still, I'd rather have a Zoilos than nobody at all. In my short life what have I written to merit the critics working me over? I won't have even a Zoilos.

This realization hits me suddenly from another angle, far more wrenching. *A man is the son of his works.* Which means, literarily speaking, *I am about to die stillborn.*

I brood about this until it makes me wonder: What would I write if I didn't die? I'll never know.

This leads me to some seemingly unrelated speculation. Considering those numberless atoms of the Laughing Philosopher floating around in infinite space and endless time, considering all the permutations of the possible, is this world in which we live (and die) the only world? Why shouldn't there be another world somewhere . . .

(I hear music faintly, then louder, the skirl of pipes and bang of drums rising over the roar of the crowd.)

. . . almost exactly the same, but where a few billion atoms have come together differently so that there are minor changes, quite marginal really . . .

(An unremarkable-looking man in a green turban mounts the stage and gives the hempen noose a professional tug.)

. . . one of which is that I don't die today, which happens to be 23 April 1580?

April 23rd. To the champions of historical time, how can April 23rd be so sacrosanct when they've got *two* of them – indeed, thanks to English insularity, two whole rival time-frames on which historians drape their various versions of reality, me and this fellow Shakespeare dying on the same date *ten days apart*, as Cide Hamete was explaining when he let the date slip. You may remember . . .

(The unremarkable-looking man in the green turban shoves a crate directly under the dangling noose.)

. . . how pained he looked. His godlike omniscience was new to him at the time and he still had to feel his way. Or did he? Perhaps he *meant* to tell me the date of my death. Whatever, I said back then that he . . .

(The unremarkable-looking man speaks in a soft, apologetic voice, but I'm so busy thinking about Cide Hamete and his chronological conundrum that I don't hear.)

. . . would try 'long afterwards' to unscramble the confusion. 'Long afterwards' has come: it is the day of my death. So where is Cide Hamete? What's he . . .

('It is time for you to stand on the box,' the unremarkable-looking man is saying in his apologetic voice.)

. . . doing that's so important he's not here? What good will . . .

(I listen to the crowd roaring my name, or Shakashik-Who-Sings-His-Own-Songs's variation, and this gives me the strength – barely enough, for my knees are like *cuajada* – to walk the three steps to the crate and mount it. My cheek bumps the noose and sets it swinging. I recoil, as some people do from snakes and slugs.)

. . . whys and wherefores do me after my death?

Maybe, it occurs to me, he's not here because the Dey isn't. Maybe Cide Hamete is in the palace right now explaining to the Dey in astromancian terms (the old fraud) how, unless he spares my life, *his* life will go into one of those meteoric declines. At this moment I see . . .

(The unremarkable-looking man slips the noose over my head.)

. . . the Dey's own cavalry, the élite of the élite, clear a path through the crowd with whips and staves so Hassan Pasha the Venetian can ride his gaudily-caparisoned stallion to the foot of the stage, so close I can hear that manic hum of his.

Lord Eggplant is nowhere to be seen.

Though the sky is cloudless, bleached a brassy white by the implacable sun, thunder peals and a twin-pronged streak of lightning forks the harbour – the only implausible element in an otherwise straightforward account of my death – making the crowd of superstitious, Shakashik-quoting, miracle-hungry Moors prostrate themselves just as two burly members of the public executioner's entourage approach and, with a practised economy of motion, kick the crate out from under me so that I am left dangling eighteen inches above the stage.

Once when I went with my father to a cattle fair not far from the (to us) no longer great city of Cabra, a man came storming into our temporary surgery in the slaughterhouse, the hilt of a knife protruding from his chest, and ranted on and on about his former best friend who had stabbed him after he'd dallied with the former best friend's woman. In the heat of the moment (and the few additional moments left to him) the victim was so incensed at being stabbed that he felt scarcely any pain, nor even inconvenience, as he strode back and forth gesticulating wildly until in mid-sentence he opened his furious eyes a little wider and fell down dead.

I mention this because I had a similar experience at The Naval. Twice shot in the chest, my left hand shattered by an exploding harquebus, I felt no pain at the time of being wounded, though I did feel, when that first roundball hit my chest, a strange and frightening inability to breathe.

It is what, on the scaffold, I feel now. (Although, with a noose throttling me, a frightening inability to breathe is perhaps not so strange.)

Another thing reminds me of The Naval. Rather unmiraculously (or so it seems), I rise out of my body and from a height of a few feet look down at it. This I realize must be a part of dying, at least my way of dying.

I hover for a moment, then float above the unremarkable-looking executioner and off the stage. I pass just over Hassan Pasha Dey the Venetian, impulsively kicking him in the head as I go (he doesn't react in any way, but his turban falls off), and then experimentally swoop through the crowd (here a minor-key snatch of Shakashik's tune, there a wail for the death of the sign and omen, the Zher*ban*tay! I have become) and finally rise until I survey the whole vast Plaza of Atrocities centring on my suspended self.

Off to one side Gabriel Múñoz the taverner, still at liberty and apparently back at his old job, is briefing a prisoner obviously just out of his first softening-up in solitary. As I swoop in, I get the shock of my life (or death). The new prisoner is *me*, Miguel de Cervantes – but a me with a normal left hand and a maimed right hand.

'. . . looks an awful lot like me,' the new prisoner is saying uneasily.

'Way too far away to see,' scoffs Gabriel Múñoz. 'Plus, hanging distorts the features.'

'Look at his hand. The noose didn't distort *that*.'

'You are supposed to ask why they executed him,' Gabriel Múñoz says testily.

Past tense. I'm not wild about that.

'Holy Virgin!' cries the new prisoner. 'Now I get it. The man they hanged and me – we're mirror images! Is a m-mirror image the same as a D-Doppelgänger?'

'Why they hanged him,' says Gabriel Múñoz with, I think, a touch of admiration, 'he was organizing a breakout of sixty men. Bought a ship with stolen money – '

Stolen? This makes me angry. I extorted that money from Morato Maltrapillo with, I'd say, a certain flair.

' – and planned to sail her to Spain. Just like that. A funny guy. Always trying to tilt the world off its axis, but his intentions were pure and he had *cojones*,' says Gabriel Múñoz. 'I will miss him.'

'M-meeting your D-Doppelgänger means one of you is going to d-d-die,' says the new prisoner. What used to be his right hand has begun to jump and twitch.

'If so,' says Gabriel Múñoz, 'it is clear which one. Why are you worrying? Come on, I will stand you a beer.'

And off they go without a backwards look at me, the me hanging from the gallows, the dead me.

Or am I? I don't feel dead, just disembodied. I rise on an optimistic current of air and go soaring south to the mountains. High among jagged crags I spy vapour wafting from a fissure at the base of a scarp of abyssal rock. I drift down through the vapour (redolent of the springy floor of a rain forest, decidedly odd for North Africa) to a cavern where, floating on a pool of some murky green liquid, I see a head crowned with lush brown hair, eyes shut blissfully but opening at my approach to shoot sparks of rage as the body attached to the lush head bursts upwards, green liquid cascading from muscular shoulders, virile chest, narrow hips and powerful limbs, all of him ruggedly masculine except for the incongruously tiny, shiny pink genitalia which, nevertheless, sport an erection.

'What is the meaning of this intrusion?' he bellows basso-profundo, his blue right and brown left eye scathing me as he stands knee-deep in the pool looking for all the world like an ex-eunuch rampant.

'What is the meaning of you lolling here in a pool while they're hanging me?' I shout right back.

Cide Hamete says, 'I'm growing new genitalia. You think it's easy? You've set me back weeks. Months.'

'I'll be dead in *minutes*. Maybe I already am.'

With a profoundly selfish shrug he sinks back into the nurturing pool, eyes blissfully shut again.

'I saved your life when everybody else gave you up for dead!' I cry.

'And I saved you from one thousand strokes of the Dey's rhinoceros-sinew whip, of which one hundred are invariably fatal.'

'I gave you back the will to live.'

'You never lost yours, so I hardly need feel remiss. Goodbye and good luck.'

I have risen through the vapour almost to the fissure in the grotto's ceiling when I hear him call. Down again I drift, to see him burst forth a second time, an heroic male nude with that incongruously tiny, shiny pink erection. I look away, embarrassed.

'Why is it so important to you, this trifling little life of yours?'

'My life? *What* life? I barely get back on my feet from all my war wounds when I'm captured and slung into Algerian dungeons for five years. That's a life?'

'So you want five more years to replace the lost ones? How petty,' he drawls.

I wish I could grab and shake him, but in my incorporeal state, how can I? 'Not enough!' I shout. 'In five years I won't even be forty. I want to *live*.'

'How long?' he asks, not sounding enormously interested.

'I don't know how long. I don't want to know.'

Brown eye and blue eye shut, he begins to sink into the pool again.

I do grab him, not that he feels it. 'This Shakespeare, is he dying on either of the two April twenty-thirds this year?'

He shakes his head irritably but stops sinking. 'Why can't you let me nurture in peace?'

'Then it's the wrong April twenty-third, and I want every day I'm entitled to, until the right one,' I say. 'Why are you taking it away from me?'

'I? I'm taking nothing from you, although I suppose . . . I might give it back . . .' Despite his new basso-profundo voice he sounds puzzled, uncertain of his powers.

'Hurry,' I tell him.

'But isn't it customary . . . I mean, the rules set out by Trithemius, you know . . .'

'Never heard of him.'

'Never heard of Trithemius? How extraordinary. Born Johann Heidenberg, took his name from his birthplace Trittheim? A/k/a the controversial Abbot of Sponheim?'

'Author of the *Steganographia*?' I ask, surprised.

'Then you have read him?'

This is the sort of paradox Cide Hamete revels in, but there's not time to tell him I haven't read the *Steganographia* yet, even though I have signalled in these pages my future knowledge of it. More than once, as I recall.

With the sands of my life running out, I only have time for a curt 'yes'.

'And you don't find the terms he outlines troublesome?'

All this talk while I'm twisting at the end of a rope in the Plaza of Atrocities is driving me crazy.

So I just shake my head, no.

And without a ripple Cide Hamete ducks under the surface of that murky green nurturing liquid and disappears.

As fast as I get back to Algiers, Cide Hamete is faster. At least, I take the commanding figure standing with Hassan Pasha Dey beside the gibbet to be the erstwhile eunuch. I'm too high to hear, but I can see Cide Hamete raising a hand in a kind of plucking motion, as if he's trying to pull something from the sky. Rain is the proximate result, a hard, pelting rain that lasts perhaps fifteen seconds, the sky still brassy white, not a cloud in it, while Cide Hamete smiles somewhat smugly. The Dey, freeing the rhinoceros-sinew whip from his sash, jumps on to the stage to give the unremarkable-looking man in the green turban three quick lashes, directional rather than punitive, which send him at a sprint for the kicked-aside crate so that he can mount it and with one stroke of a scimitar (or is it a yataghan?) cut me down. I fall in a sacklike heap. That is, my body does. I myself am still hovering, watching Hassan Pasha Dey's pikemen hold the 'Zherbantay!'-chanting crowd back from the stage while his cavalry clear a path for a mild little man who clasps a crucifix just below a smile like beatitudes.

It begins to rain again. I drop quickly to the stage and re-enter me.

The next thing I'm aware of is a rocking motion. I get up and lurch towards the light, finding my sea legs as I go. From the hatch I see, under a darkening sky, the deck of a good-sized ship.

With tentative fingers, expecting the worst (such as that my head will fall off), I explore my neck. It feels in one piece. I turn my head. There's a crick, but nothing to make anyone scream.

I climb to the quarterdeck where the mild little man with a smile like beatitudes is listening to Gabriel Múñoz say, 'Sure, he has family. I know one brother – they get along okay – and I think he is very close to a sister.'

Gabriel Múñoz has been transformed. He wears scuffed leather shoes, a doublet missing its sleeves, a once-crimson cape and a flagging ruff. Good Christian clothing, in short, if a bit past its prime. The mild little man with the smile wears clerical robes. He says, 'Freedom makes its own demands, you know,' just as my head tops the ladder.

Gabriel Múñoz says, 'Here he is now.'

That smile like beatitudes is turned towards me. 'I am Juan Gil, Procurator General of the Trinitarians. On behalf of the Order permit me to congratulate you.'

231

'You got the most votes of anybody,' Gabriel Múñoz explains. 'Even though you were condemned to death.'

'A death sentence from the Dey of Algiers doesn't hurt a man's popularity,' says Juan Gil.

'You won a ticket home, *compañero*. Me too.' Gabriel Múñoz grins. 'I never knew my beer was *that* bad.'

To the south, thunder rolls like the executioner's drums. Under dark stormclouds Algiers suddenly appears two or three miles off, lightning-lit. And something inside me snaps. I slide down the ladder and across the spray-slick maindeck. I have one leg over the rail when Gabriel Múñoz grabs me and wrestles me down.

'What the hell is with you?'

I struggle to free myself. 'I've got to go back. The Dey will kill them all – sixty innocent men.'

'He cannot kill them without he knows who they are.'

'He has ways,' I rant. 'Informants. He'll find out.'

'Nobody could tell him but me and you,' Gabriel Múñoz says. 'And we are sprung, *compañero*. Free!'

'I was the author of the plot. I offered them freedom, and I failed them. Don't you see?'

'I see *you* have the rest of a life to live.'

How can I dispute that? It's the same argument I gave Cide Hamete.

'You can let go. I couldn't swim that far anyway.'

I stand. A few large drops of rain spatter the deck. Gabriel Múñoz watches me, wary. 'Usually, *compañero*,' he says, 'when you get upset like that, you are almost impossible to understand. But just now you did not stutter at all.'

'I didn't?'

'Not once.'

Suddenly I remember something. It's more than enough to make what used to be my left hand act up, but that doesn't happen either.

'Gabe, who was that new prisoner just out of solitary?'

'What prisoner?'

'In the Plaza of Atrocities. The one that looked like me.'

'I was not in the Plaza of Atrocities.'

'When they were hanging me, Gabe. Of course you were.'

'Not me. I was rushing around the dungeons all day electioneering. I figured if you got enough votes to be redeemed, the Dey would not dare hang you. As it turned out, everybody was voting for you anyway.'

'So after the voting you went to the Plaza, right?'

'I was heading there when the redemption team carried you out on a litter.' Múñoz shakes his head. 'Talk about the nick of time. Juan Gil got there the second they kicked the box out from under you.'

I stare down at what used to be my left hand. 'But the prisoner with the maimed *right* hand,' I say.

'The what?'

The bewilderment on Gabriel Múñoz's face is so genuine that I just shrug and stand with him at the rail in silence. We are running on a port tack, course NNW, the rain behind us now, the sky ahead blue, the bow wave foaming over turquoise water as we race towards lambent sunlight, every mile a mile closer to Spain.

It is later. We are below. The lantern has been extinguished, but I can't sleep. Water whooshes past the hull, timbers creak. I think of Micaela, two days' sail ahead, on her way to a new life in Spain, to breed sons with a Basque rock-thrower with muscles between his ears. *Tell me, Miguel! What comes next?* I hear feet thud on deck overhead, the changing of the watch, and Zoraida's voice, 'Tameji? *Tell me a story.* Tameji, ráwi? *Like a lost homeland you can never find again, and even if you can't find it you have to keep looking or you'll die?'* And the changing of the watch is followed by a silence as profound as the time before Creation, and in the utter darkness I see hair the colour of a wheatfield, a sea of gold rippling in the breeze on a cloudless summer day in La Mancha, and for the first time I really understand that I am going home.

Part the Second

THE LIFE
OF
MIGUEL DE CERVANTES

XVIII

The Snares and Disillusions of Love

I hurried from the Theatre of the Prince to the tall stone house near the Gate of the Sun without stopping in German Street at Taverna Múñoz. I could have used some of Gabe's beer, but not at the price of facing Anica.

At the theatre, my lunch at first had felt like a cannonball in my stomach. *The Naval* might as well have been my first play, for I'd suffered the same sweaty palms and dry mouth, the same urge to be somewhere, anywhere, else – not to mention the conviction that my absurd ambition to write for the stage would end in a disaster so resounding that I could never show my face in Madrid again.

In short, the standard first-performance jitters.

But as I stood at the rear of the corral in the deepening shadows of a late autumn afternoon – watching the audience watch the actors act out the roles I had created, listening to the rattles and clappers of the groundlings, assuring myself the catcalls were directed not at my play but at its Turkish villains – the inevitable moment came when I could relinquish my imagined world to these actors and this audience and, while still dreading the worst for my play, return to the real world with its real problems. Such as how to tell Anica I would soon be married.

How ironic that my play should be without a single female character, when plots traditionally revolved around who would bed whom and who be skewered on a point of honour, while my life was bedevilled by women.

Sheer perversity – reflected too in the single novel I'd published. Oh, there was plenty of amorous dalliance in *La Galatea*. But why had I breached novelistic morality by letting a murderer go unpunished? I'd been lucky to find a publisher.

That was in June, six months ago, and I'd gone to Taverna Múñoz to celebrate. Anica saw me that day for the first time (having seen me a hundred times before), and the next morning, when I came downstairs on shaky legs, Gabriel Múñoz cautioned, 'A man can get himself killed that way.' He shook his head, more white now than grizzled. 'Show pity for *me*, if you care nothing for yourself. Her husband is my partner, you know.'

Later that week, the royal censor Pedro Laínez had summoned me. 'Put an unpunished murder in a play and I'd lance it like a boil,' he told me. 'In a book? We have a bit more leeway, but whatever possessed you?'

'Most murderers in real life don't get caught.'

Laínez laughed. 'What's real life got to do with it?'

The next week, in real life, Pedro Laínez lay dead in the final connubial embrace of his wife Juana, who was young enough to be his granddaughter and had been about to leave him for an equally young ne'er-do-well, one Hondaro. It was Laínez's death that first sent me to Esquivias, the widow's native village near Toledo, where she'd returned after the funeral, taking with her a rough draft of Laínez's last work (like most censors, he wrote) which for some reason Juana thought no one but me could edit.

So it was through a misogynistic tract called *The Snares and Disillusions of Love* that I met Juana's childhood friend Catalina, who would be my bride.

Even after four years, I was impressed by the tall stone house near the Gate of the Sun. Not that it was exactly palatial, but the prodigally blazing fire in the hearth, the variety of wine on the sideboard, the many lamps lit though dusk had barely fallen – all spoke of easy circumstances.

I had asked my sister Andrea, shortly after my return from Algiers, where the money came from.

'Juan,' she said.

'Juan Rufo?' I felt a stab of jealousy.

'Juan the Obscure.'

'Oh. Where is he? What does he do?'

'Nobody knows. The bank drafts just come at irregular intervals. With a loving little note.'

'Don't you ever see him?'

'The last time was I think two years ago, but he only spent the night and was gone before breakfast.'

Andrea designed costumes for the theatre. Half a dozen seamstresses worked for her on the top floor of the tall stone house, supervised by her daughter Constanza, now twenty, and a beauty despite her disconcerting eyes.

'The child's enchanted,' my mother would say, and my sister Magdalena, if within earshot, would cross herself. 'What went on all those years she was in the Ovando mansion we'll never know. Her and that imaginary "friend" of hers.'

'She was practically a prisoner there,' Andrea defended her daughter. 'Until Miguel rescued her – '

'Well, I only – ' I began, but Doña Leonor ignored me.

'The children of Old Christians from La Mancha,' she said, 'have no need for imaginary "friends".'

My mother had continued to put on weight – in proportion, it seemed, as my father dwindled. Rodrigo de Cervantes was now a tiny, monkey-faced man of seventy-five who spent his days on the Bench of If-Only in the street where his barber-shop used to be, near the Gate of the Moors.

As soon as I got home from the première of *The Naval* I knew there would be trouble because Picapleitos was there, seated beside Magdalena.

Magdalena had not aged well. She tinted the premature grey out of her red hair but the effect was rather like cordovan leather. Her green cockatrice eyes glittered malignly, and lines of bitterness bracketed her thin lips. But she had a lush figure, overdressed now in a rose brocade gown.

I forced a cheery smile. 'Hello, all. Where's Papá?'

'Constanza's gone to get him,' Andrea told me and, brushing a stray strand of that wheaten mane back from her forehead, asked about the performance.

'Nobody left until the last line,' I said, and her smile was like the sunrise.

Doña Leonor turned her cheek from my kiss. 'You'll marry that Palacios girl over my dead body.'

'Mamá,' Andrea said. 'Miguel's a grown man of thirty-seven who – '

'And that Palacios girl is not yet twenty. Younger than Constanza,' huffed Doña Leonor.

Magdalena's cockatrice eyes glittered in disapproval of anyone who would marry such a child when Madrid was full of spinsters in need of husbands.

'And that,' said Doña Leonor, 'is not all. Counsellor!'

Picapleitos, his skinny legs crossed, swung one shoe bearing a tarnished buckle of some indeterminate alloy. His balding, undersized head rested on a greasy ruff. 'I don't as a rule do this sort of work,' he said, looking down his remarkable nose, 'but as a favour to a valued client . . .'

Picapleitos put on a brave front. We all knew he had come down in the world, though we couldn't have said why.

He stroked his nose, his clean hand leaving an ink smear, fainter than in his heyday but still an impressive trick. He produced a notebook, and read.

239

'Doña Catalina de Palacios de Salazar Vozmediano, the prospective bride, resides in the village of Esquivias with her widowed mother, also named Catalina. Aside from Catalina the younger, there is an eleven-year-old son, Fernando. An obnoxious little shit. Forgive me.' Picapleitos manipulated his nose. 'An uncle, Juan de Palacios, is parish priest of Esquivias and would join the couple in matrimony.'

'Over my dead body,' said Doña Leonor.

'The family, though in debt, clings to five hundred marginal acres of olive groves and vineyards, and a few dilapidated houses in Toledo that produce an average annual rent of three stewpot hens each. The wine, which I have had occasion to taste, is, charitably put, plonk.'

Picapleitos backstroked his nose. The ink smear did not quite disappear. 'There is a history of madness in the family. Worse, a taint of *converso* blood.'

'But no!' cried Magdalena in well-rehearsed horror; I was sure she had heard all this before.

'But yes. The girl's great-great-grandfather, one Alonso Quixada, read tales of chivalry incessantly until he lost his sight. He believed passionately that the heroes – the Knights of the Round Table, the paladins of Charlemagne, even Amadis of Gaul – were real, historical personages.'

Doña Leonor gave me a significant look.

'And why, in his declining years, did this same Alonso Quixada become a monk?' Picapleitos asked rhetorically, stroking a fresh, this time dark, ink smear on to his nose. 'To hide the fact that he was a backsliding *converso!*'

'How do they figure he was a backslider?' I asked.

'And who are we to cast the first stone at *conversos*?' Andrea asked. 'Our own family – '

'Not on *my* side,' said Doña Leonor.

'Amadis of Gaul,' said Magdalena darkly, just as my father and Constanza came in. 'Amadis' was the only sound my otherwise stone-deaf father could still hear. It always cheered him. 'When do we leave for Esquivias?' he shouted.

Esquivias wasn't far but, at seventy-five, it was as close to 'on the old road again' as he could get.

'We don't,' said Doña Leonor.

Constanza slipped her hand into mine. 'Not to worry, Uncle Miguel,' she said. 'Last night my friend told me it would be a beautiful wedding.'

Doña Leonor rounded on her. 'If you'd just say a Hail Mary whenever you saw that imaginary "friend" of yours, he'd disappear in a hurry.'

Constanza squeezed my hand and escaped, moving with her mother's numinous walk, to the kitchen. I followed.

'I know my friend's not real, Uncle Miguel,' she said, 'but I don't *want* him to disappear.'

My niece, though bright as a new *maravedí*, hardly seemed twenty. It was as if, during her years in the Ovando mansion, her growing up had been suspended.

'Why's Grandma such a horrible grump?'

I tried, as always with Constanza, to answer honestly. 'Most people's lives are so full of disappointments and frustrations that they have to lash out at someone. You shouldn't take it too personally.'

Andrea came in and got a roast joint of lamb from the larder. I took down a knife while Constanza filled three wine cups. I reached across the carving board as Andrea set the joint on it, and our hands touched. I dropped the knife. Andrea's pale blue eyes widened. Constanza picked up the knife. My hand was trembling when she gave it to me. She looked at her mother, then at me.

'To the bride and groom,' Andrea said, raising her wine. This turned out to be a mistake. She had to steady the cup with both hands and still spilled some. 'You *will* marry her, won't you?'

I think I intended saying, damn right I will. But what I said was, 'I've got to.'

Constanza blushed. 'Is Catalina in a family way?'

'Of course not.'

'Then why did you say "got to"?'

My hand tightened on the carving knife. I cut thick, uneven slices of meat.

Long ago I'd told myself I could never marry, not knowing why. Now I knew I must marry.

The reason was the same.

Eleven years I'd spent in exile, five of them captive in Algiers, then suddenly I was home.

I just walked into the entrance hall one summer afternoon and there she was, watering the plants. She dropped the bucket as, four years later, I would drop the carving knife. We reached for each other. Neither of us had time to plan any resistance. I held her against me hard enough to feel how every long curve of her fit my body. In seconds we were both gasping. Then she drew back. I did not try to stop her. But I cupped her face in my hands and kissed her lips. She moaned. Then she slapped me. Then she covered her face and wept.

I knew I didn't dare comfort her. Comfort meant touching and I could not touch her again.

It was weeks before we could act normal – whatever normal was – with each other.

When we could, she told me about Constanza.

At that time Picapleitos still had his impressive chambers on San Vicente Ridge with that condescending view of the Royal Palace, still employed fifty-seven junior partners all busily writing, writing.

He sat swinging a diamond-buckled shoe while he told me about the District Court here in Madrid and the Royal Council in its judiciary capacity, about the District Court back in Sevilla and the Tribunal of Appeals and the Tribunal of Matrimonial Tribulations and the Tribunal of Hidalguía and the Military and Naval Tribunal.

'You,' I said, 'have been fleecing my sister.'

'On the contrary, I admire Doña Andrea enormously. Even if she has seen fit to reject certain . . . arrangements that would obviate your need to pay further legal fees.'

'Me? I haven't been paying your fees,' I said.

He opened a small cabinet beside his desk. 'Why deny it? Since one of these comes with every payment.'

In the cabinet stood rows of little toy soldiers, dozens of them. Each missing its left hand.

Rodrigo? But it couldn't be. My brother was with the army in the Low Countries, and even though he'd been commissioned, a second lieutenant's pay was low, not to mention sporadic.

Picapleitos shut the cabinet. 'Now, where were we?'

'You were saying Andrea won in both district courts and at the Royal Council and all those others.'

'Just so. Ovando's final appeal was rejected almost two years ago. With, I may say, exceptional celerity.'

'So when does Andrea get custody?'

'She *has* custody. Your sister has in her possession stamped documents attesting that she is the sole legal guardian of the minor child Constanza de Figueroa. This is a matter of public record.' Picapleitos leaned forward, long index finger poised at the tip of his nose.

'Then where's Constanza?'

'Why, at the Ovando mansion on Toledo Street. I thought you knew.'

I asked, 'What takes so long between a custody award and the actual return of the child?'

'My dear Don Miguel. The function of the courts is to decide the legal issues in a conflict. This they have done. Justice has triumphed. What more can one ask?'

'For Constanza to come home.'

'But Nicolás de Ovando chooses not to surrender her.'

'Then it's up to the courts to take her from him.'

'The courts are already overburdened, without asking them to *implement* decisions which, in their wisdom, they have rendered. Moreover, courts are not kidnappers.'

'You mean courts don't enforce what they order?'

'Enforcement is a police responsibility.'

'Ah,' I said.

'In criminal matters, that is. The police have no role in civil suits – unless the losing party is a pauper. Then they jail him for failure to pay court costs.'

'So who enforces civil decisions?'

'No one.'

'Then what's to make Ovando or *anyone* obey a court order?'

'Nothing. The law, you see, is impartial.'

I caught Juan Rufo on his way home from Liars' Walk and explained the situation. He listened attentively, a studied look of eagles in his eyes, his right hand in the characteristic pose above his rapier hilt.

'No problem whatever,' he said cheerfully. 'I have merely to whisper at the appropriate time into the appropriate ear, and the child will be home in a trice. How's Andrea these days?'

'Andrea's fine,' I glowered.

A few weeks later, I asked what progress he'd made.

'Nothing yet. Nicolás de Ovando, alas, has the ear of the Princess Eboli, second most beautiful woman in Spain, and the Princess, even though she's under house arrest, is still a power, since death-loving King Felipe would forgive all if she came to the royal bed. You see the problem. I'll let you know when it's the appropriate time. How's Andrea these days?'

Andrea, I glowered, was fine.

For a week I watched the Ovando mansion, secure behind its stone wall on Toledo Street, its inscrutable windows aglow every night against the gloom like an enchanted (in the bad sense) castle, if you believed in that sort of thing.

On the seventh night, the old *sereno* who'd spoken kindly to Andrea came tottering along, ring of heavy keys jangling at his waist, heavy oak staff thumping the ground. His rheumy eyes studied me.

'You remind me of someone, don't you?' he said.

'I don't know,' I said, and tried to look as inscrutable as the mansion's windows.

'Seven consecutive nights leads a person to wonder. You wouldn't be one of Pierre Papin's boys, would you?'

This surprised me. According to Gabriel Múñoz, the Frenchman Pierre Papin now ran a string of gambling establishments all over the country.

'Assessing the competition?' the old *sereno* pursued.

'I don't work for Pierre Papin,' I said. 'But if I did, what's to assess? This can't be a gambling den. No one ever comes here.'

'Not by the front gate they don't.' The old *sereno* thumped the ground extra hard with his heavy oak staff. 'Got it,' he said in a now-kindly voice. 'You're connected to a beautiful lady with hair like a barley or millet field, am I right?'

'My sister.'

Clearing his throat portentously, he said, ' "Utnapishtim dwells with his wife beyond the Ocean of Death on an island where the plant of eternal youth is said to grow, but Utnapishtim is old, old." '

I said, 'What?'

The kindly old *sereno* repeated that business about Utnapishtim, and waited.

I waited too.

He gave me an exasperated look. 'The Abbot?' he said.

'Of Sponheim? The controversial Abbot of Sponheim?' Now, I thought, we were getting somewhere.

'Not the abbot of anywhere special. Just the *Abbot*.'

'Sorry,' I said.

He thumped the ground with his oak staff. He turned and stomped off. Then he turned and stomped back on.

'You sure she's your sister?'

'Positive.'

He thought about this and muttered, 'Could get my head handed to me if I do, likewise if I don't.' Then he told me, 'Tomorrow night at moonrise. I'll let you in the underground way.'

Interminable stairs going down, then a like number up. Long corridors dimly lit. Behind blank doors, an absolute silence – the silence of compulsive gamblers around gaming tables? A junction at which the kindly old *sereno* turned, thumped his staff three times, and stomped off. Another corridor. Great iron-studded oak doors with an unimaginative iron ring in a lion's mouth for a knocker. As the old *sereno* had instructed, I pressed a stud level with and two rows to the left of the lion's laid-back ears. The doors swung soundlessly into a vast room with seven or eight of those inscrutable windows I'd tried to scrutinize for a week from outside, then swung as soundlessly shut behind me. A single huge candelabrum with eighty or ninety branches lit that vast room as bright as full moonlight in the desert between Algiers and Spanish Oran. A figure, female, left the middle window and ran towards me. Her mane of wheaten hair told me whose daughter she was. Her blue right and brown left eye joyously reflected all that candlelight.

'You must be my Uncle Miguel, here to rescue me,' she breathed.

Feyness in her very first words. For how could she know?

'I'm all packed. My friend told me you'd come tonight.'

'Your friend?' I asked.

'The one who visits me in my dreams. I knew he would be my friend the very first time. Even before he told me you knew him. Because of our eyes.'

My spine began to tingle.

'He's got one brown and one blue eye, just like me.'

I expected what used to be my left hand to twitch, but it hadn't done that since they cut my body down from the gallows in Algiers.

'Did he tell you his name, this friend of yours?'

A nervous little laugh. 'It sounds like Lord Eggplant.'

If my hair stood on end, my niece Constanza did not remark it.

'Let's get you out of here,' I said, but before I could, the great double doors swung inwards to admit a giant of a man who, from descriptions current in Madrid, had to be Pedro (Killer) Pacheco Portocarrero. He came at me with a bladed instrument of some kind, indeterminate but lethal. Yet I felt no fear. I had already died one death, hadn't I?

I sidestepped while trying to shield Constanza, setting in motion a strangely elegant dance of death. I saw the impassive face of Pedro (Killer) Pacheco Portocarrero, the blade, an inscrutable window, the single huge candelabrum with its eighty or ninety branches, the double doors mockingly agape, then all over again the impassive face, the blade, a window etc., until Constanza cried out when, finally, Pedro (Killer) Pacheco Portocarrero cornered me, his blade glittering with the light of eighty or ninety candles.

As the blade began its downswing, I saw a swirling of cloth —

voluminous drapery? capacious cloak? – and the candles were all snuffed instantly. Through the blackness came a grunt, then the sound of metal – the blade? – striking the floor, and of a heavy object – Pedro (Killer) Pacheco Portocarrero? – falling with a room-jarring thud.

A voice said, 'Hurry,' and an uncertain point of light became the glow of a lantern.

He was of medium height and slender, though with broad shoulders. In the lantern-light his face, I thought, bore a strong resemblance to my own. But lantern-light is deceptive, and what man truly knows his own face?

Whoever he was, he obviously knew the Ovando mansion, for he led us swiftly through a maze of corridors, down interminable stairs and up again. Soon I felt cold night air and heard the distant thumping of a heavy oak staff.

'The kindly old *sereno* will take you home,' said the man with my face, in a voice rather like my own. But in the light of the full moon I saw that it wasn't quite my face. Gaunter, the nose perhaps more belligerent, the beard fuller.

He showed his teeth in a moonlit smile. 'Once when we were children, you saved my life,' he said.

'Juan!' I cried. 'Juan the Obscure! But . . . how . . .?'

'We haven't long, not this time,' he said. 'Just answer me one question, Miguel.'

'Anything.'

'Where are the Confessions of a Trance Dancer?'

'Confessions of a – you mean Zoraida wrote her memoirs?'

In the silence that followed I could almost hear her voice. *Tameji? Tameji, ráwi?*

'Think, man! You two were getting real close. That's why we decided to scrub your rescue by Onofre Exarque.'

'Holy Virgin! Are you saying you left me there chained naked to a rock, to rot forever for all you knew, on the off-chance I might be able to find her memoirs?'

'Plus, you were being groomed,' he said.

'For what?'

A silence, not exactly companionable, grew between us.

In a thin but true little voice, Constanza nervously sang a verse from the song about its being an ill day for Frenchmen at Roncesvalles.

'Maybe I don't want to be groomed,' I tried.

'What a simple world it would be,' he said, 'if the choice were yours to make. Well,' fatalistically, 'if you don't know where they are, you don't. It was our last hope.'

'I'm sorry, Juan. The Obscure.'

He pivoted, and disappeared into darkness.

Constanza and I became a familiar sight around Madrid, the promising playwright and his niece 'from the country'.

She saw the world with the unjaded eyes of a small child. Every avenue and alley, every street market and shop, she found entrancing.

'Didn't they ever let you out?' I asked.

'They let me sit in the courtyard for an airing every now and then, or up on the roof.'

'What did you do all day?' Andrea asked her.

'Nothing . . . much. I was usually pretty tired, days.'

These days Constanza did a lot of reading. There had been no books in the Ovando mansion.

'Put ideas into her head, books will,' grumbled Doña Leonor. '*Converso* ideas, Lutheran, Erasmian, God only knows what-ian. And you,' she told me, 'with your scribbling. Why would a Christian gentleman want to write plays?'

I said the only thing she, or most people, would understand. 'For the money.'

'Where is it then?' she asked, and turned to Constanza. 'Who was there for you to talk to? Was there a *dueña*?'

'There were the girls.'

'Serving girls? Not fit company for you.'

'And the men who came at night. But I wasn't supposed to talk to them.'

'Gamblers?' Doña Leonor demanded. 'What did they play? What did *you* play with them?'

'Mamá,' said Andrea. 'You sound like a Holy Office inquisitor. You're frightening her.'

Doña Leonor brooded. One day she came home from market with a bent, toothless crone in dusty black. This was old Zárate, the midwife who had delivered Constanza in Sevilla.

Old Zárate spent fifteen minutes closeted with Constanza. Then she drew Doña Leonor and Andrea aside and whispered.

In her thin but true little voice Constanza nervously sang a few of Ariosto's ambiguous lines on the indiscretions of the fair Angelica.

'Well?' I asked Andrea later.

'Old Zárate asked if Constanza's led an active life. Long journeys on horseback? Trampling grapes in village harvests? Streetwalking right here in Madrid?'

'But except for an occasional airing in the Ovando courtyard or up on the . . . streetwalking?'

'It isn't just that her maidenhead's not intact,' my sister told me. 'Old Zárate could find no sign she ever had one.'

So the refrain now became, 'What did you do all night?'

'Nothing . . . much.'

Constanza would ask me, 'Can't you make them stop?'

'They love you. And they're worried about you.'

'I know but . . . you're the only one I can talk to. Is Cide Hamete Benengeli your best friend?'

I had told her his real name. This may have been a mistake, encouraging her belief in an imaginary friend. Except that he wasn't imaginary.

'I never thought of him that way,' I said. 'I saved his life once. And he saved mine.'

Constanza nodded; her blue eye and her brown eye glowed. She said, 'That must be why he helped me. Because you saved his life. He could make me forget so *hard* it was as if the bad things never even happened.'

I didn't ask her what bad things. Instead I buckled on a rapier and went to Toledo Street.

The air was dense with smoke, the Ovando mansion ablaze.

As it collapsed on itself with a roar, I glimpsed in the crowd a man wearing the feather in his hat on the right, which is to say wrong, side.

No bodies were found in the burnt-out ruins, but we never heard of Nicolás de Ovando again.

To Catalina de Palacios, whose world was the village of Esquivias and an occasional trip to the (to her) great city of Toledo, my global misadventures – domestic/military service in Italy, near-fatal action at The Naval, captivity in Algiers – made me a romantic hero.

Even more impressive to Catalina, whose uncle Padre Juan had taught her to read, I could create such heroes. As a dramatist (four plays written, three produced) and novelist (my *Galatea* was then enjoying its brief notoriety), I was a celebrity.

Not that, literarily, my wife understood me.

'But he killed him,' Catalina said one afternoon, closing her copy of the *Galatea* while I sweated over editing *The Snares and Disillusions of Love*.

'Who killed whom?' I asked distractedly.

'Lisardo the shepherd killed this other shepherd Carino with a dagger still stained with the blood of Lisardo's lover Leonida who was murdered by her own brother Crisalvo the Cruel who was tricked into it by the dead Carino, but if – '

'He wasn't dead at the time,' I said, crossing out a few lines of her best friend Juana's dead husband's dead prose and wondering if I could contrive to lose the whole manuscript for the good of his memory.

'But if he's still free at the end of the story, after Timbrio and Silerio are reunited despite their rivalry for Nisida the Glory of the Guadalquivir – '

'Leonida was the Glory of the Guadalquivir,' I said, drawing a diagonal line through an entire Laínez page devoted to the moral failings of the fair sex.

'But Leonida died before the story began.'

'So? She was *remembered* as the Glory of the Guadalquivir. Nisida was called the Neapolitan. She was from Naples. That's in the south of Italy, the *mezzogiorno*.'

'You've been there,' Catalina sighed. 'You've been everywhere.'

'Not quite, Cat.' I may have sounded a shade condescending.

'It's wicked, him getting away with the murder. Wicked. I *love* it.'

'Umm,' I said, looking at her look at me.

'Would *you* kill if I made you jealous?'

'Don't make me jealous and we won't have to find out. Come here.'

A line of dark hair ran down Catalina's belly to the matted triangle of her sex, and when I traced it with a fingertip she would quiver. She was compactly built, with sturdy legs and broad hips and heavy breasts with nipples like dusky grapes. She smelled of yeast, of olive oil, of the cooking fire she tended in the patio of the Palacios house. Her long hair was so black it had blue highlights. Her arms were strong from carrying oil jars up from the cellar, from swinging a stick against the Palacios olive trees to knock the fruit off the branches, from breaking firewood across her knees. 'I'll do that,' I said. But, 'No you won't,' she told me. 'Let me do what I'm good at, I'm not good at all that much. And you do what *you're* good at. Such as writing your new play if I leave you any time after fucking.'

Catalina called a thing what it was – which isn't the same as being foul-mouthed, like one-eyed Princess Eboli, the second most beautiful woman in Spain. Catalina called a thing what it was, and what we did was fuck.

A country girl, she enjoyed 'country matters' (Shakespeare's term, not hers or mine). And when we weren't actually doing it, she liked to talk about it.

'They're like two walnuts in a soft leather pouch,' she said once. 'Funny, how they make all the difference between a man and a eunuch. Did you know any eunuchs in Algiers?'

'Sure. They handled most of the sensitive jobs. Like diplomacy and running the harems.'

'Harems. Hmph. Whorehouses, more like. How many women would a dey keep?'

'Dozens, if he was like Ramadan Pasha. But the last dey's harem was male.'

'You're joking. You mean he kept a palaceful of *pure*verts? Did you ever go in there?'

'As a healer. Perverts need healing too.'

'*I'll* say! And did you go in the female harems?'

'Same way, Cat, as a healer.'

'Uh-huh. Listen, would you stop talking and start – '

'You're doing the talking.'

'I'll bet you could make a whole harem happy. My friend Juana thinks so. She's really jealous of me. Because *conversos* have big cocks. Juana says it's known fact.'

I laughed and said, 'Listen, would you stop talking and start . . . fucking?'

Note the slight, self-conscious pause here. Though I tried, I could never match Catalina's frankness, which reflected her innate innocence. Catalina said what she meant and did what she thought right and hoped for the best but, like most dwellers on the high, hard plain of La Mancha, was prepared for the worst.

Did we love each other, my wife and I?

At the beginning Catalina said the words. And since she always said what she meant, she must have loved me.

At the beginning, the first time I felt those sturdy legs grip me and saw her eyes go narrow and her lips grow fuller, at the beginning, she wasn't the only one who cried out. But even then, even that first time, as her body drew that sound from my throat, I looked down at her face, that very first time, at the beginning, and I cried out in the silence of my soul that one day I would come to love that lustrous black hair spread on the pillow like a spill of ink, but I shut my eyes tight and I saw a wheatfield.

XIX

Learning to Cope with April 23rd

I wake with the annual sense of panic. In fact I have lain awake much of the night, listening to the healthy female purr next to me, not quite a snore. So get up, I tell myself. For all you know, this is the final day of your life.

Ritually I curse Cide Hamete. I do not doubt, much less forget, I'm to die on April 23rd. But which April 23rd?

I wonder about this Shakespeare in England. It still sounds like a made-up name. Shake spear! Does he know about April 23rd too? Has he woken with a vague sense of dread, afraid something – the sky maybe – will fall on him today? No, I remind myself. This Shakespeare's English April 23rd won't come until the week after next.

Catalina opens a sleepy eye and smiles. A hand brushes at a tangle of black hair. Another hand touches under the covers what she is pleased to call my cock.

'We've never fucked in Madrid,' says my wife.

We are in the top-floor bedroom of the tall stone house near the Gate of the Sun. The morning after our arrival, I still can't get over our welcome. Doña Leonor has been almost cordial to the woman she vowed I'd marry over her dead body. But should I be surprised? Doña Leonor's native Barajas – with its small plaza and parish church, its winter-muddy-summer-dusty streets, its swine and goats, its proud, stiff-necked, hospitable-to-friends, wary-of-strangers people – and Catalina's village of Esquivias (now my home, though not for much longer) might be the same place. My mother and my wife instinctively understand each other.

Was there a time, I ask myself, when words like fuck and cock came easily to Doña Leonor's now prudish lips?

Catalina rolls away from me. 'You're stiff as a board, all except the part that counts. What's the matter?'

I haven't told her about April 23rd.

I say, 'They'll hear us.' This makes me think: Andrea will hear us.

'So? What do you think they *think* we do?'

'Her seamstresses will be here any minute,' I say.

251

Catalina brightens. She gets out of bed, walks naked on those sturdy legs to the washbasin, splashes and gurgles. Through a towel she says, 'Three gowns! Made just for me, by seamstresses who sew for the theatre. I feel so rich. Will you help me choose the patterns?'

'Sorry, Cat. I have appointments all day.'

I do, including one with Juan Rufo, who wants me to puff a new edition of his *Austriada*. I have tried to explain this to Catalina, but she refuses to understand.

'Don't do it,' she says. 'Why help him sell *his* novel when you want people to buy *your* novel?'

'It's an honour to me that a courtier like Juan Rufo wants me to write a sonnet praising his work. It means my *Galatea*'s already a *succès d'estime*.'

'You get esteem and he gets money? Don't do it. How many copies has this *Austriada* of his sold?'

'Two thousand.'

'And *Galatea*?'

'Almost five hundred,' I say.

'Don't do it,' she says.

The light at the window fades, as if this April 23rd, the fifth since I was cut down from the gallows, has changed its mind about dawning. I hear thunder. Then I hear footsteps, and Andrea's voice. 'Anybody up?'

Catalina jumps under the covers and tells Andrea to come in, which she does, bearing three steaming cups of chocolate and a basket of just-fried *churros*.

'What a beautiful way to be awakened,' says Catalina, but gives me a darting look to remind me of another way that, through no fault of hers, hasn't been tried. My wife and my sister kiss each other's cheeks.

I dunk a *churro* in my chocolate and bite the end off. The two women talk, drink, eat, laugh, talk some more. The almost-cordiality that blossomed last night between my mother and my wife is nothing compared to how Andrea and Catalina have taken to one another.

After breakfast my sister and my wife get down to business. I might as well not be there.

'French cartwheel,' says Andrea.

'Shoulder wings,' says Andrea.

'With a green silk mask for riding,' says Andrea.

Catalina's eyes get wider and wider. The green silk mask makes her say 'Ooh!' though all she ever rides is a *burro*, and that rarely.

I wrap myself in a blanket and my offended dignity, and head for the washbasin.

The bookseller Blas de Robles shoves the untidy manuscript of *The Snares and Disillusions of Love* to the centre of the table. 'Poor Laínez,' he says. 'Couldn't you contrive to lose it?'

'The widow's convinced it's his masterpiece,' I say.

Robles, an indoor creature with faded eyes and faded moustaches, sighs. 'She's also convinced no one but you can edit it. She's half right. No one can, period. I often think, Don Miguel, that women never really *read*. Not the way men do. Can't she see that she herself is the target of this diatribe?'

'It won't help, but I'll ask my wife to have a word with her.'

There are only two of us for lunch, Juan Rufo and I. A footman hovers over my shoulder. He makes me nervous. Perhaps, I think, because it's April 23rd.

Juan Rufo sniffs at the glass he holds daintily to his nose. 'Italian,' he says. 'We Spaniards have never got the hang of sophisticated viticulture, have we. This white is Montefiascone. A surprising nose reminiscent of the scent of – currants, wouldn't you say? But *black* currants.

'Well, my friend, how respectfully the critics have received your *Galatea*. I congratulate you. And five hundred copies isn't bad for a first novel without the King's imprimatur. I was lucky. Timing. There our death-loving King Felipe was, out at the Slag Heap, swamped with the usual paperwork and desperate for diversion, especially with invasion imminent in the Low Countries – '

'Invasion?'

' – and his secretary Mateo Vázquez right there, bless him, with a copy of my *Austriada*. Invasion, yes. Seems that slut of a Virgin Queen will send an English Expeditionary Force to fight alongside the Netherlanders against our forces under Parma.'

I see my brother Rodrigo leading his company of harquebusiers through a flooded field east of Amsterdam, north of Deventer, somewhere like that, towards this new enemy.

'Well,' says Juan Rufo, 'we must be unyielding. Invade England one day, if need be. Singe the alleged Virgin Queen's hennaed beaver for her. Now, about that sonnet. Not overly flattering, Miguel. But if the author of the experimental *Galatea* can find something laudable in my modest mainstream *Austriada*, a critical success praising a commercial one . . . the mutual backscratching is rather like politics, isn't it. How's life with your little rustic wench? Diverting, I hope? And how is Andrea these days?'

Andrea, I glower, is fine.

I'm in the office of the player-manager Gaspar de Porres. I've brought an outline of *The Confused Woman* with me and will talk off the top of my head about *Life in Constantinople* and *The Death of Selim*. The player-manager Porres, according to his letter, is of the opinion that I should stick closer to home with my plays. Well, *The Confused Woman* has a Spanish setting.

Porres is telling me he can afford only forty ducats per play when a young man in a rain-spotted cloak swaggers in unannounced. He has thick dark eyebrows, heavy-lidded dark eyes, a Roman sort of a nose and a short beard trimmed to a careful point above the small wing-like collar he wears instead of a ruff.

'Forty ducats a play, old boy?' he repeats. 'I stand in awe of anyone who can write three plays in one day.'

Clearly this joker knows nothing about play-writing. I've sweated roundballs for ten weeks over *The Confused Woman* and I'm still far from satisfied.

He tosses a sheaf of paper on the desk. 'Next time you want a script overnight, old boy,' he tells Porres with a dazzling smile, 'make sure the author isn't already engaged. Did *you* ever try writing a play and bedding a temperamental actress at the same time?' he asks me.

'Overnight, you said?' I ask him. 'Surely you mean doing a clear copy. Or at most a final draft. With or without an actress.'

'I never recopy, and I never redraft. If it isn't coming right the first time, I know by the end of Act One, in which case I throw it away and start with a new idea. Can you really write three plays in one day? On a good day I can do two, but three's asking a lot.'

'I'm lucky if I write three *pages* a day,' I admit.

He looks at Gaspar de Porres. 'And you offer him only forty ducats per play? Slave labour, old boy.' He taps the script on the desk. 'You can call this *The Deeds of Garcilaso de la Vega*,' he says. 'No, make it *Tarfe the Moor*. Or both – why not? *The Deeds of Garcilaso de la Vega and Tarfe the Moor*. A play so full of action needs a double-barrelled title. And who might you be?'

Gaspar de Porres makes the introductions. 'Miguel de Cervantes Saavedra, Lope Félix de Vega y Carpio.' Then he steps back one step and watches us warily.

'Oh. Cervantes,' says Lope de Vega. 'I saw your *The Naval*. Or part of it.'

'I don't recall any performance being halted by rain.'

'I wouldn't know. I left.'

I say nothing. My cheeks are hot.

'It *was* the Battle of Lepanto you had in mind?'

'Don Miguel fought there,' says Gaspar de Porres quickly. 'Wounded three times. Won a medal for bravery.'

'Where is it then?'

'Stolen,' I say. 'By Barbary pirates.'

'Not the medal. The battle. In your play, old boy. You focus so much on the brother conflict, there's no room for any blood and thunder.'

'Action's convincing only if the characters are,' I counter, trying not to sound pedantic. But this Lope brings out the worst in me.

'Characters? Are you serious, old boy? Just make them talk according to type, that's all we playwrights need to know about characters. No cardinals talking like mule-skinners, no whores like princesses.'

'But people don't al – '

'Characters aren't people, old boy, they're types. The flatterer. The complacent cuckold. The easy lay. The . . . over-industrious drudge. Recognizable types.'

I keep the conversation almost civil, despite his last barbed example. 'Your characters, maybe,' I say.

'Take these brothers you invented – the dreamy poet type and the professional soldier type – '

'Not invented. I have such a brother.'

'So that explains it.'

I make the mistake of asking what it explains.

'Why I walked out in the second act. Know too much – *tell* too much – and you'll lose your audience. Tell just enough to make it seem convincing, old boy, that's the trick. Audiences don't want to learn anything. They want a lot of quick action, and confirmation of views they already hold. If you can sum a play up with a proverb, you won't go wrong.

'Plus,' he says, 'I couldn't swallow that dispute over hacking off the galley's ram. You mustn't ask an audience to believe the impossible.'

'I saw it at The Naval with my own eyes,' I say.

'Forty ducats a play.' He shakes his head. He tells Porres, 'Give him a pair of the best for the première of my – what did I call it?'

'*The Deeds of Garcilaso de la Vega and Tarfe the Moor*,' says Porres.

Lope de Vega smiles his dazzling smile again. It makes him look misleadingly likable, this cocksure young man only three or four years older than Catalina. 'Garcilaso de la Vega! Now there's a hero type, poet *and* warrior, straight out of history. No relation, but no harm in letting those fools out there believe I'm descended from him, is there!'

And, cloak flaring, he swaggers out.

'Didn't much like young Lope, did you?' Gaspar de Porres asks. 'Seen any of his plays?'

I admit I haven't.

'Don't say anything until you do.'

This being April 23rd, I have decided to see Anica and tell her I'm married. I'm even hoping, as I walk through the rain to Taverna Múñoz, that Gabe has already told her. But no such luck.

'Sealed lips, Gabe – you? That's out of character,' I tell him, immediately annoyed with myself because I sound like Lope.

'One thing an innocent bystander does not mess with, *compañero*,' Gabriel Múñoz says, 'is a woman scorned.'

He gestures to the far end of the room where, through a haze of cigar smoke, I see Anica removing the rind from a mountain ham with a butcher knife.

She shrieks when she sees me. 'I was beginning to think you was dead.'

'I got married,' I say – hardly the subtle approach but I want to get it over with.

My words seem to have no effect on Ana Villafranca de Rodríguez. She just lowers her head and continues cutting away rind and thick white fat, then slices the ham finely with swift, sure strokes.

Though Anica, the last pupil at the Tall Stone House Players' School for Ladies, has given up her dream of acting and married Rodríguez, she still idolizes my sister Andrea, still tries to emulate her. But no diet could slim Anica down to Andrea's unfashionable slenderness; indeed, she is now noticeably well padded. Her hair, bleached in hopes of achieving that glorious wheaten colour, looks more like straw. Andrea's beauty is beyond her. But with her heart-shaped face and big dark eyes Anica is an attractive woman.

'Anica, what's keeping that ham?' comes the voice of her husband Alonso Rodríguez the cuckold. The complacent cuckold, in fact; definitely a Lope type, I tell myself with more annoyance.

When she goes off with a platter, I pick up the butcher knife and twiddle it idly, unaware she's returned until she takes it from me. I feel a moment's alarm, this being April 23rd. But Anica just resumes slicing ham.

'Who is she, some little actress?'

'A country girl from a village near Toledo.'

She brushes nervously at a strand of strawlike hair, parodying my sister's mannerism. 'Well, "love and fancy blind the eyes of reason," ain't it the truth? Has she money?'

'Some, not much.'

'"An ass covered with gold looks better than a horse with a pack saddle."'

This unfortunately brings Lope de Vega to mind again.

'Will you stop mouthing those non-stop proverbs of yours and say what you really think?'

'I really think,' she says, drawling, 'since your worship says so, your worship must be married. And I really wonder, since your worship asks, why that has to change anything. My being married never stopped your worship, did it? But what does a barmaid what can't even write her own name know, compared to the likes of your worship? You're trying to tell me it's over between us, ain't you?'

Am I?

'Well,' I said, 'I'll be spending a lot of time in that village near Toledo, and my wife is – '

'I don't want to hear about her!' Anica shouts. Heads turn and eyes squint at us through the haze of cigar smoke. She points the butcher knife at me, a purple slice of ham impaled on it. 'What does your worship expect me to say – "God, who gives the wound, gives the remedy"?' Her hand is trembling. 'Ain't no wound, your worship. So ain't no remedy needed. And for all I know there ain't even no God. Now how about you leave me alone?'

I go, head down, past Gabriel Múñoz, who busies himself removing the bung from a keg.

The minute I leave, he corners Anica.

'Well?' he asks. 'Did you tell him?'

'You kidding? With him so high and mighty, it would of killed me. I've got my pride, I have.'

'But shouldn't he – '

'What for? He's married, I'm married. Who needs him? "What the eye don't see the heart don't long for,"' says Anica, and blows her nose hard.

At about this time I'm dashing through the rain to the tall stone house near the Gate of the Sun. The door swings open and Andrea comes running out.

'It's Papá,' she says. 'He's at the Bench of If-Only and he won't come home. He's got a sword.'

When we get there, dusk has fallen and it is raining harder. Still a crowd lingers, old men in black silently watching a dozen boys taunt a small figure huddled on the plank bench that girdles three sides of the large elm.

'If-only, if-only, if-only,' they chant. 'Tell us another if-only.'

'Tell us,' shouts one, 'how you'd have been Surgeon-General of New Spain, if-only.'

'Tell us,' shouts another, 'how you'd have been barber to the Pope, if-only.'

In the fading light I can see my father holding a rusty old sword in both hands.

One boy dances closer, waving a hat like a lure to a bull. My father takes a wild swing at him. The boy retreats, his hat sliced almost in two. My father himself is hatless, sodden and bedraggled.

Andrea calls, 'Miguel's here, Papá.'

He swings the rusty old sword again, a wild two-handed stroke aimed at demons only he can see.

When he speaks, his voice is a hoarse croak. 'Could've gone to Genoa with Signor Lomellino or Lomelín, that's the truth,' he says, rain or tears streaming down his monkey face, 'if only Doña Leonor was willing. Could've been barber to the richest bankers in Italy. But my wife doesn't hold with foreigners, and I'm a family man.'

Thunder crashes and the sky pulses with light.

My father's eyes look like two black holes in his face, and for a heartbreaking instant I can see him striding along a dusty road in Andalucía leading a donkey laden with saddlebags full of the instruments of his trade, a few clothes and a stained, dog-eared copy of *Lazarillo de Tormes* – can see myself half running at his side, him towering over me as we chase the horizon. And now? Now my monkey-faced father's world has dwindled to a bench girdling an elm tree in the middle of a thunderstorm on a small plaza where alleys intersect not far from the Gate of the Moors.

Every village in Spain, no matter how small, has its Bench of If-Only. Every Madrid neighbourhood has one. Here the old men gather to lament their lives' wrong turnings. Though the details vary, the litany is unchanging – the railing at fate, the reproach for unanswered prayers, the retrospective *ojalá* culminating in the invocation of if-only, the ritual self-exculpation for the regrets that must assail any man if only he lives long enough.

'. . . if only my sons had come home safe from The Naval instead of being taken by Barbary pirates and the older one a prisoner five years; if only my daughters hadn't got bad advice from that long-nosed pettifogger just when we needed money to ransom the other one who was adjutant to Don Juan of Austria, but he's dead; if only he'd lived until my boys returned . . .'

Thunder crashes, lightning strikes nearby, my sister Andrea's eyes beseech me, and I walk towards my father with my arms outstretched, but he swings his rusty old sword.

'. . . would have taken us all to New Spain and bought an estate next to the Duke of Veragua that's the direct descendant of Columbus in case you didn't know, practically a kinsman of ours, if only . . .'

'Papá,' I say. 'Papá, have you forgotten, first thing in the morning we're going on the old road again, so you'd better come home now and have a good night's sleep.'

'If only . . . what?'

'On the old road again,' I shout, not that I think he'll hear me. I start using the signs that replaced language when we travelled together all those years ago, but he surprises me by saying, 'I can hear you, Miguel. I could always hear *you.*'

'Let's go along,' I say, but he takes another wild two-handed swipe at the air with his rusty old sword.

'Papá,' I say, 'we're going to get us a brace of mules, and they'll know which road to take, and – '

'On the old road again,' whispers my father, and in those black holes that are his eyes I swear I can see a light begin to shine.

'And one night, one night after the campfire's burned down and we're lying close to the embers, a man will come out of the darkness, and we'll look up and see it's Juan the Obscure.'

'On the old road again,' whispers my father.

'And he'll be leading a string of four fine horses, their saddlebags filled with everything we'll need to cross all that France to the north because – know where we're going?'

'On the old road again,' whispers my father, praying as hard as he can for what can never be.

'We're going to Flanders, to the Low Countries to find Rodrigo. Juan the Obscure knows where, somewhere east of Amsterdam and north of

Deventer. Rodrigo, that's who the fourth horse is for. Then all of us, you and me and Rodrigo and Juan the Obscure, we'll – '

His head jerks up, and in the last of the light I see him smiling a terrible rictus of a smile, as if the stiff muscles of his face can turn a dream into a reality, and he springs to his feet almost like a young man, raising the rusty old sword overhead, and, as he does so, lightning descends and the sword clangs and vibrates and leaps from his hands, and in the aftermath of the thunderclap he falls and I catch him in my arms (how can a man weigh so little?) and with Andrea at my side I carry my father home through the rain to the tall stone house near the Gate of the Sun.

XX

In Which a Secret
Of Some Significance Is Revealed

- *Cervantes was probably in Madrid when his father died.*
- *There is nothing to suggest that Miguel was not at his father's bedside when Rodrigo de Cervantes died in Madrid at the age of seventy-five on 13 June 1585.*
- *We have no reason not to assume that Cervantes witnessed the final moments of his father's life.*

I have several pages of such quotes, courtesy of Cide Hamete, who can enter the future at will through the doorway of a present that does not exist.

... 'probably' ... 'nothing to suggest' ... 'no reason not to assume' ... Everything including a double negative. Two, in fact.

But how can they not hedge, these ex-post-facto tellers of my death and life? Until I became the son of my own works, I might as well have been another Juan the Obscure.

I also have several pages like this:

260

- *Excluding sonnets lauding other men's work, Cervantes would publish not a line for twenty years.*
- *Surely the central mystery of his life must be the reason behind his self-imposed exile in a spiritual and intellectual desert.*
- *To ignore the years he spent on the fringes of society, alien even to the rootless population he moved among, is to miss the essence of the man.*
- *The enigma of his career is that he could abandon it for so long and return like Christ out of the wilderness to write the most widely read book after the Bible.*

Like Christ out of the wilderness ... Holy Virgin! I'm only a simple storyteller.

I have this line too, which Cide Hamete would –

– Stop!

What?

– Would you kindly henceforth cease referring to me unnecessarily? It should be clear by now in the telling of your little tale that, whenever the ideas are at all original or come from a future to which you have no access, they can only come from me. It's been well established that, while others merely see backwards in time, I can see forwards and sideways as well.

Sideways?

– You'll see later. Meanwhile, no more according-to-Cide-Hamete. I have my own not-insignificant part to play in your story that transcends these trifling comments I make from time to time. Agreed?

Well ...

My father took to his bed the night I brought him home from the Bench of If Only, and except for once he stayed there until they carried him out six weeks later.

The family moved to the hushed rhythm of the sick-room routine and the physician's visits, but this was broken the night my father got out of bed and climbed to the attic to retrieve the rusty old sword he'd wielded at the Bench of If-Only. He got as far as the door before I woke and ran downstairs to carry him back to bed.

'He's in no hurry to die,' Doña Leonor grumbled, and resumed her habitual life. She spent her mornings at the small market near the Gate of the Moors (and even nearer the Bench of If-Only), where old women talked of what their lives might have been if only they hadn't married their husbands.

Andrea took Constanza to meet the theatre managers who commissioned costumes, as if preparing her daughter for when she'd be on her own. But how did Andrea know?

Catalina would ask, 'Why don't we ... sleep together any more, Miguel?' Note the self-conscious pause. Catalina considered euphemism more suitable with my father on his deathbed, but it didn't come easily to her.

'They'd hear us.'

'But it's normal,' said my wife. 'As normal as living and dying.'

Still we slept apart.

My sister Magdalena astonished everyone by taking over the nursing. During the final weeks of my father's life, I never once heard her say, 'No, thank you, I would rather not.' As the end approached, she jealously guarded her duties. She talked of taking vows. 'Minor orders,' she said, 'like this new Sisterhood of the Most Holy Sacrament. Chastity and obedience. Good works.'

'Chastity,' said Catalina. 'Ugh! I could never.'

In our bedroom on the top floor alongside the loft where the seamstresses worked, I began on *The Death of Selim*. If anyone told me it would be my last play ever produced, I'd have said he was crazy.

Picapleitos came to draw up my father's will. With a clean index finger he rubbed an impressive ink smear on to his long, pointy nose – something I would never see him do again.

My father named us children his heirs. Not that there was anything to inherit. He declared himself free of debt. He also returned to Doña Leonor the dowry she'd brought to the marriage, or what was left of it. Which wasn't much. But the gesture touched her, and my dour Manchega mother sniffled and wiped a tear from her cheek.

Forty-eight hours before the end, my brother Juan the Obscure came to the tall stone house near the Gate of the Sun wearing black riding clothes dusty from the road our father would never go on again.

'Am I in time?' he asked.

'How did you know he was dying?' I asked.

'I heard,' he said.

He took a dim view of Catalina, at least of my marrying her. 'She'll hold you down,' he said. 'You'll get mired in Esquivias.'

When he first saw the new Magdalena, he mistook her for a friend of Doña Leonor's. Magdalena was not offended. 'I don't mind looking my age,' she said. But she looked twice her age.

Andrea still looked half hers. On what would be the most important day in my life and Andrea's, we were sitting outside the sick-room when the physician and the priest came upstairs together. Andrea's head was bowed, her wheaten hair falling into wings on either side of her lovely face. She smelled of wild flowers, cinnamon and, I thought, lost dreams.

The priest opened the door and said, 'He wants Andrea.'

Half an hour later she came out and said, 'You almost had an older brother, did you know that, Miguel?'

I won't try to duplicate the many times Andrea's voice faltered as she retold my father's deathbed revelation. Nor will I try to explain how, even as I listened, I knew every word before she spoke it.

She said (and I knew), 'When her time came, Mamá returned to her people in Barajas because Papá was in debtors' prison. A boy was born, but he died before he could be baptized. The next night a royal equerry rode in from the capital and called on the priest. "Are there families in the parish whose lineage can be traced back five generations with no taint of *converso* blood?" the equerry asked. And the priest said many in Barajas were such. "Among these, are any as honourable as they are poor?" the equerry asked. And the priest said several were such. "Among these worthy families, has any lately lost a newborn child?" the equerry asked. And the priest said Leonor Cortinas's firstborn, God's will be done, had been buried that morning. "Is the mother healthy, able to nurse an infant?" the equerry asked. And the priest said she was. "Take me to her," said the equerry.

'The priest reflected, as they walked the silent streets, that he ought to tell the equerry that the husband was in debtors' prison, which some might not consider strictly honourable. But he did not speak. And as they neared the Cortinas house, the priest reflected that he ought to tell the equerry that, while the Cortinas family were pure as far back as parish records went, there was a disturbing rumour that Rodrigo de Cervantes Saavedra, the itinerant barber-surgeon to whom the blameless Doña Leonor was wed, had *converso* blood. But he did not speak.

'So the royal equerry said to Mamá, "If you will raise a girl-child to maturity as your own and never tell her otherwise, if you will raise her to love Holy Mother Church and become a bride of Christ, I am authorized to pay you — "

'Mamá demanded, "Who is the child?"

' "A well-formed girl one week old. You are permitted to see her before you decide."

' "But who are the parents?"

' "The mother was in service in . . . a noble house. The father is . . .

of that house. The money will be paid in one sum, and you will not hear from us again."

'The sum,' Andrea said, 'was more than enough to raise a girl from infancy until her novitiate. Mamá considered what else the money could do. It could keep Papá out of debtors' prison (as indeed it would do many times before it ran out six years later). So she agreed to the conditions and took the child home to raise as her own. It was baptized with the feminine form of the name her dead son would have had, which was Andrés.'

Andrea bowed her head, and it was as if a heavy door had shut between us (but silently, as a door in a dream can shut, the silence itself meaningful). The next thing I remember is, she toppled into my arms as I began to speak. Or, that is, tried to. But I could only make sounds like 'b-b-b' and 'y-y-y' while what used to be my left hand stroked and stroked that glorious mane of wheaten hair.

During the night Catalina cried out and I asked her, 'What's the m-m-matter?' She said crossly it was nothing, just a bad dream. My renewed stutter, unlike what used to be my left hand, bothered her. To Catalina, I told myself, the hand was intrinsic to me, and even something to be proud of, but the stutter was not. Unable to sleep, I told myself a lot of other things too, mostly inconsequential, to keep my mind off the one thing I dared not think of. Towards dawn I heard distantly in the streets of the city the wail of *cante jondo*, the sound of gypsy pain transmuted to contempt for all the things in the world that eventually must beat a man down. The singing came closer, so close I was sure the gypsies would pass right outside the house, but when I went to the window I saw no one.

In the morning, Andrea was gone.

XXI

The Deeds of Garcilaso de la Vega
And Tarfe the Moor

At first Catalina couldn't have been more patient.

'Tell me what I can do to help,' she would say. But I had no ideas, and none of her own worked either.

She asked me, when we returned to Esquivias, 'Is it too soon after we buried your father, is that why?' But it was five weeks. And then eight weeks, and then ten.

She asked me, 'Is it because you're working so hard, is that why?' I muttered something and left our bed and lit a candle at my writing table in the corner.

She asked me, 'Is it because you're worried about your sister, is that why? I'm sure Andrea's fine, wherever she is. She's a grown woman, Miguel, and it's her life.'

'It has n-nothing at all whatever in any f-form, shape or manner to do with my sister!' I shouted.

Once, when a sweaty roll in the hay (literally — we were trying in the barn, Catalina's idea) ended in my usual inability to perform, she said, 'Maybe you think about it too much. Animals don't think about it, they just do it.'

I *had* been thinking about it too much, certainly. But once she said that, I naturally thought about it even more, with the predictable non-result.

'Women have it easy,' she tried once. 'They don't need a hard-on to fuck, they just — '

'Will you stop using that kind of language!'

'It used to excite you. But now, nothing I do . . . Miguel, if it helped, I wouldn't mind if you went to a whore to straighten yourself out. As long as you paid her, I wouldn't be jealous.'

'I don't need any straightening out,' I said.

Catalina might have confided in her uncle Padre Juan. But she knew he was unworldly even for a priest, so she went instead to her friend Juana the widow Laínez. Juana, having lived in Madrid, was a worldly woman.

'You're just twenty years old,' she told Catalina after my wife unburdened herself, 'and you're saddled with a husband who might as well be a eunuch. Or worse.'

'What's worse?' Catalina asked.

And Juana told her.

The next day Catalina asked me, 'What was it like in that harem in Algiers?'

'I didn't spend much time in the harem.'

'The *all male harem*,' she said, each word a roundball.

'What are you t-trying to say?'

'Well, Juana said – '

'Juana? You mean you told Juana that you and I – '

'Me and Juana tell each other everything. We talked about *The Snares and Disillusions of Love* and I said how you wished you could lose the manuscript and – '

'You told her *that*? And then you told her we were having troubles in – '

'She told *me* that if a man was forced for five years to perform unnatural acts with Turkish – '

'I did *not* perform unnatural acts with T-Turks or anyone! Holy Virgin, Cat! Don't you know what a gossip Juana is? Now that you've told her my real opinion of Laínez's rotten manuscript, you think she won't g-gloat about my little p-problem all over Esquivias?'

'You think *I* want all Esquivias to know I married a pure-vert?' screamed Catalina, and we looked horrible deaths at each other, and she began to cry.

'I'm sorry,' I said, for what I couldn't do, and, 'I'm sorry,' she said, for the words her friend Juana had put in her mouth.

Then she said, 'But don't worry, Juana won't be telling anyone in Esquivias. She's gone back to Madrid.'

● *Was the central mystery of this tormented genius's life, then, sexual?*

I got this rhetorical question from a usually reliable (henceforth, at his own request, anonymous) source, who informed me it would be asked regularly by self-styled experts on me down through the ages.

Was it sexual?

I would eventually write a play called *The Kept Woman* (sometimes mistranslated as *The Dalliance*) in an attempt to exorcize whatever it was. The play, needless to say, was never produced, but those interested can read it.

The Kept Woman was not among the plays I delivered to the player-manager Gaspar de Porres the autumn after my father died.

'And I've something for you,' he said. 'As promised, two of the best.'

'Two of the best what?'

'Seats for Lope's *The Deeds of Garcilaso de la Vega and Tarfe the Moor.*'

'I only need one,' I said.

My intention was to return Lope de Vega's compliment. I would sit through his *capa y espada* melodrama just long enough for it to become ridiculous, then rise and ostentatiously leave. I intended doing this in the first act.

But the timing proved to be tricky.

As I expected, Lope had cavalierly mined the biographies of the soldier-poet Garcilaso and kept only the most swashbuckling aspects of a real life already noted for flash. Lope's Garcilaso, though a diverting cloak-and-dagger hero, was blatantly stereotyped. I could not willingly suspend my disbelief for as much as five minutes at a stretch. Not that Lope ever let a scene run that long. He piled derring-do on derring-done. And when that threatened to pall, he would remind the audience that Garcilaso could sit down and (almost with Lope's own speed) dash off one of those poems for which he was styled the Spanish Petrarch.

That's what I mean by tricky timing. I couldn't leave during the high action scenes – not if I hoped to be noticed. Too many spectators were jumping about and waving their arms, hissing at the villains, cheering the hero, as Lope kept his improbable plot aboil with complications piled on complications. (Verdict: Lope's formula stuck out like the bones of a dehydrated animal, say an ox, dying somewhere in all that desert between Algiers and Spanish Oran.) But neither could I leave when Garcilaso traded his sword for a pen – not if I wanted (for professional reasons) to check out Lope's approach to the problem of writing about a writer writing. (Verdict: Superficial if sprightly. Nothing here for the serious playwright. Or playgoer, for that matter.) And by then somehow the first act was over.

The reason I didn't walk out during the second act was a little different.

I wasn't caught up, of course, by the plot that seemed certain to lead to Garcilaso's death. But I was amused by Lope's conceit of weaving into his melodrama a pastoral interlude featuring characters of the writer-character Garcilaso's invention, a sort of play within a play. Nothing original, really, even if it had never been done before. (Indeed, Gaspar de Porres, without a demur from Lope, would remove it from subsequent performances.) But it was enough to hold my interest. For professional reasons. Briefly.

Anyway, it would be best to walk out just as the final act began, when my departure would be most noticed.

But again professional curiosity interfered. I gave myself a few minutes to see how Lope would use 'poetic justice' to give the audience what (he claimed) it wanted. I saw. Wrongdoers got punished, rightdoers rewarded, the action wrapped up in homily – all with a blithe disregard for reality.

When the last line had been spoken, and after rather more applause than seemed warranted, the audience took its euphoric leave.

I sat there. I sat there after the theatre was otherwise empty. I sat there until the afternoon light faded. I sat there trying to run *The Confused Woman* and *The Death of Selim* and *Life in Constantinople* through my mind, but I kept seeing Garcilaso de la Vega leap across the stage and hearing the audience shout Lope's name, and before I knew it cold moonlight bathed the corral and I went outside slowly and around the corner to Gaspar de Porres's office, where a light was still burning.

'These aren't half bad,' he said. 'Your Confused Woman is too low-key, Selim should be more villainous, and your Constantinople's a bit heavy on local colour, but there's nothing I can't fix.'

I reached for the neat stack of manuscript on his desk.

He said, 'I said nothing *I* can't fix.'

'They're my plays. I want them back.'

'They *were* yours. I bought them. Now they're mine.'

'I don't want them produced. I'll return your money.'

'I don't want my money. I want every play I can get my hands on. Madrid is theatre-crazy. What's got into you?'

'You wouldn't understand.'

But he did. 'You've just seen the Lope,' he said.

All I could manage was a nod.

Gaspar de Porres got up and put an arm around my shoulder. 'An army needs pikemen as well as generals,' he said.

'The usual?' Gabriel Múñoz asked, reaching for a jug of the house red. 'Where have you been keeping yourself?'

'Make it spirits. And no conversation.'

Gabriel Múñoz shrugged and left a bottle of *aguardiente*. I poured and drank, poured and drank. If only, I told myself. If only it were simple,

like with poetry. With poetry very simple. Wasn't put on this planet to be
a poem. Pikeman. Could've been worse. He could've said harquebusier.
'Harquebusier,' I said, giving Gabriel Múñoz the worldly-wise smile of
a soldier-poet. Who fought in The Naval. The trouble with playwriting
was, I wasn't bad. That made things complicated. Being a failure would
have been simple.

'Anica,' I shouted, making a grab for the empty bottle as it rolled along
the bar.

Gabriel Múñoz said, 'Upstairs with – look out!'

The next thing I knew, I was somehow on the floor. On my way down
I seemed to have collided with the corner of the bar. One whole side of
my head hurt.

'Pikeman,' I said, watching faces swim above me through a blue haze as
I was carried upstairs and deposited on something soft. A lamp flickered,
brightened. I heard either a cat mewling or a baby crying.

'Now that's a proper black eye, that is,' said Anica, giggling. 'Ain't never
seen your worship drunk before.' She slapped something cold and wet on
the proper black eye. This helped: I no longer saw two of her. She leaned
over me, her bleached hair brushing my face. I grabbed a handful of it
and held on tight.

The cat mewled or the baby cried. I made some overtures of an erotic
nature. Anica blew out the lamp and helped me off with my breeches.

' "While a person's laughing he ain't crying," ' she said.

I saw a few straw-coloured hairs on the pillow when I woke, but no Anica.
Saw a cradle in one corner, but no baby. Saw a washstand. I rinsed my
mouth and sloshed my face.

From the bar Gabriel Múñoz watched me wobble downstairs and slump
at a table.

'Don't you ever sleep?' I growled.

'Had a visitor. How is the head, *compañero?*' He set a steaming cup
of chocolate on the table.

'See the kid?' he asked.

'I heard it crying, that's all. Why?'

'Just wondering. A real cute kid. Your brother Juan was here.'

'Who?'

'Juan the Obscure.'

'Oh. And you didn't tell me?'

'I did not think you would appreciate a disturbance.'

'How is he?'

'Who can say? He looked the same. All dressed in black, dusty from the road, here one minute and gone the next.'

'You wouldn't happen to know what he does?'

'Me you ask, and you are his brother? Whatever it is, it keeps him on the move,' said Gabriel Múñoz, adding after a significant pause, 'Like a highwayman.'

'My brother?'

'*Like*, I said. For that matter,' Gabriel Múñoz told me, 'there was once a professional assassin who always dressed in black out of respect for his victims. Another profession where obscurity is an asset. Well, anyway,' said Gabriel Múñoz, 'your brother says a room is reserved for you at Tomás Gutiérrez's hostal in Sevilla.'

'Tomás is an innkeeper?'

'Best inn in the south from what I hear. But better you should call Tomás a hotelier, innkeeper he thinks is common.' Gabriel Múñoz tossed a black purse on the table. 'This is for on the road. Once you are down there, Pierre Papin will handle your expenses. And if you need your brother, leave a message at Papin's card shop in Sierpes near the royal prison.'

'Pierre Papin *sells* cards these days?'

'Sells, shuffles, stacks, shaves. That has not changed, *compañero*. His shop is cover for the biggest gambling den in Andalucía, among other things.'

'What other things?' I asked.

Gabriel Múñoz picked up and studied my empty, unremarkable cup. I got the impression he thought he'd said too much.

'I would not know,' he said. 'I am only telling you what your brother told me.'

'Did he tell you what I'm supposed to do in Sevilla?'

'Oh, that,' said Gabriel Múñoz. 'He said to tell you she has been seen with the gypsies in Triana.'

XXII

The Hostal in Bayona Street

I wonder if Shakespeare ever applied for a job on April 23rd. I did, in 1587.

The work was dangerous and poorly paid. But I hadn't a *maravedí* to my name, and in Sevilla, that illusive gateway to the New World, jobs were hard to come by. Someone had to send occasional bank drafts to the family in Madrid, and Juan the Obscure no longer could.

That April 23rd was a blustery day and the Commissary General of the Spanish Fleet, Andalucía, looked as if he might blow away as he paced the Patio of Orange Trees inside the cathedral precincts. He was lean to the point of emaciation, a starveling husk of a man who, when the wind gusted, would raise his arms to spread his cape like the wings of a bat so he seemed about to levitate above the businessmen, moneylenders, dispensers of influence and would-be colonial administrators, all in polychromatic costumes that made the Commissary General's black garb look blacker. His sepulchrally gaunt face was without expression except for the tormented eyes of a man gripped by some implacable obsession, quite possibly sexual.

'Why,' he asked me, 'do you want it? It's a Jew job, like tax farming. Generally only a *converso* will touch it.'

'I need the money to send north to my family.'

'How did your hand get like that?'

'The Naval. I was wounded three times. *Aventajado.*' I thought I slipped this in rather smoothly.

'A veteran. That's good, very good. Are you ruthless?'

'I don't think you could really say – '

'You will have to be. What brings you to Andalucía?'

'The usual. To get away from home.'

This was definitely misleading (to history, too, for according to Pierre Papin, the Commissary General was a compulsive keeper of records who wrote down everything). But to imply you are fleeing an unhappy marriage is much simpler than to say you came-to-find-your-sister-who-is-not-your-sister-and-who-ran-away-with-the-gypsies-but-after-almost-two-years-you-still-haven't-found-her.

'People will revile you,' predicted the Commissary General. 'They will lie to you, lock their doors to you. They might even do you violence. How old are you?'

'Thirty-nine.'

Thirty-nine. Doesn't that sound somehow older than forty, or forty-one? Those are the beginning of something, but thirty-nine is an end.

'. . . after her dispatch of troops to the Low Countries,' the Commissary General was saying, 'a Spanish invasion of England became likely. And with Fotheringay it became inevitable. Didn't it?'

'I don't know,' I said. I was thinking: how did I get to be thirty-nine?

'You never heard of Fotheringay?' cried the Commissary General. 'What did you *do* up north?'

'I wrote plays.'

'So that explains the unworldliness. It won't do. A commissary's got to have both feet on the ground ready to run. But you university types – was it Alcalá?'

I told him my family had been too poor to send me to university. Then I told him I knew that Mary Stuart had been executed at Fotheringay in February.

'Executed?' he exploded. 'Execution implies legality, whereas in fact the Queen of Scots was murdered in cold blood by that virgin whore on the English throne.'

'As you say. I don't want to disagree with the Spanish Crown,' I assured him. 'I just want to work for it.'

'As a fleet commissary you will not be a Crown employee, but rather a contractual agent accountable for any discrepancy between the amount of grain and fodder you collect and the amount that reaches Lisbon and Cádiz, where even now the Invincible Armada that will conquer England is assembling. The law requires a co-signer, a man of substance, to protect the government against malfeasance. Commissary work attracts the unscrupulous.'

I said that finding a co-signer would be no problem.

The Commissary General grunted. 'Then the job is yours. You will probably regret it. Most do.'

Watching me leave, the Commissary General felt the wind rise and quickly extended his arms. The batwing spread of his black cape gave him an uplift, more than merely physical, that tempered the debilitating effect of his nightmare, recurrent now for twenty-five years – or twenty-two and a half, depending whether you go by historical or fictional time.

For the Commissary General was of course Pedro de Isunza, one-time bodyguard-procurer to the ill-fated Crown Prince Carlos, one-time petty functionary of the Investment Branch of the Inquisition, one-time soldier in Don Juan of Austria's army in Flanders.

Isunza's military career had not ended, like his others, in disgrace. He remained a private (exceedingly private) soldier until Don Juan's death. Back in civilian life, he made a killing as one of the first tulip importers in Amsterdam, then returned to Spain and bought the post of Commissary General after a necromancer told him he would find in Andalucía what he most wanted. This prophecy, Nostradamianly vague, Pedro de Isunza interpreted to mean he would find there the 229th virgin (putative), who by mortally injuring the Crown Prince had prevented Isunza from one day walking the innermost corridors of power as the confidant of the future king of the first empire on which the sun never set.

It was so grossly unfair. Pedro de Isunza would make them all pay.

Don Juan of Austria already had, the Bastard. As one of Fortune's favourites who, early in 1562, historical time, had accompanied the ill-fated Crown Prince to Alcalá, why should Don Juan be allowed to live? Pedro de Isunza succeeded one night shortly before his demobilization in slipping into the Bastard's peppery stew a massive overdose of cantharides (a/k/a Spanish fly), the aphrodisiac favoured by the Bastard and, in quantity, a reliable poison. So it was that Don Juan of Austria, hero of Lepanto and commander-in-chief of Spanish forces in the Low Countries, died in October 1578 of a 'malignant fever' in Flanders.

Eight years, thought Pedro de Isunza. Eight years had passed, and then the necromancer's prophecy about finding in Andalucía what he most wanted. He knew he'd recognize her at once, that fantastically pulchritudinous virgin of his recurrent nightmare who brought him to orgasm with an ecstasy that almost compensated for the exquisite pain of the whipping she nightly administered with her glorious mane of wheaten hair. A man of limited imagination, Pedro de Isunza failed to consider that twenty-five (or twenty-two and a half) years had passed since the fateful night in Alcalá when the Crown Prince fell downstairs. It never occurred to him that she would have aged.

Still, is that so strange? As I could have told him, she hadn't.

'Co-sign?' Tomás Gutiérrez asked me. 'Why should I?'

We were sitting in the patio of Hostal Gutiérrez in Bayona Street, directly across from the cathedral. The marble and jasper fountain plashed, imported

South American birds cried raucously in the branches of the rare carambuco tree, half a dozen lissom Negresses skimpily attired in the green and gold Gutiérrez livery padded in picturesque silence through the patio on unknown errands.

'I know you are honest like I, Miguel. But a man of my standing, a hotelier of quality – I mean, supposing somebody rips you off. Whom is left holding the bag?'

The day was warm for April and Tomás Gutiérrez was sweating in one of his custom-made green sixty-pile suits.

'I wish I could help you, Miguel,' he said.

He'd said the same thing two years earlier, the day I arrived at his hostal to begin my search for Andrea.

'I wish I could help you, Miguel, but a man of my standing cannot have much to do with gypsies. But if you find the lady, tell her on behalf of I that . . .' He reflected, then smiled. His face was now jowly, and even his expensive tailor could not hide a substantial paunch. 'Tell her I still wear the same waxed date-coloured shoes. She'll understand,' he said. 'But she'd better hurry. She would make a good hotelière but a spring chicken she is not. How old is she anyway? She's older than you.'

'Andrea doesn't age,' I said. 'She's always been exempt from chronology. She's around twenty-two.'

Such poetic truth was wasted on Tomás. He plodded on.

'And how come your brother sends a scribbler like you to find her when he's the one that's got the means?'

'What do you mean, means?'

'Well, he knows Pierre Papin and them. Luis Blackslave. They've got big connections in the underworld that's called the *hampa* by we Sevillanos. And Luis Blackslave runs that secluded sanatorium of his or whatever it is up in the hills above Arcos. Which is what I mean by the means. So what is a naïve guy like you doing here?'

'I'm looking for Andrea,' I said.

'Well, if you find her, don't forget about the shoes. She'll understand. Twenty-two,' he said, shaking his head.

I'm looking for Andrea.

I looked in Sevilla's gypsy quarter Triana and in Granada's Albaicín, I looked in the gypsy cave-village of Guadix, I looked on the open road among gypsy caravans wandering from town to town.

It was easy to break down gypsy reserve by describing Andrea. For gypsies are great lovers of physical beauty. 'Her beauty,' I said, picking my words carefully, 'is like the caress of the sun on a windless winter day in high Castilla; or the silver track of a full moon on the sea bearing the enigmatic silhouette of an exotically rigged boat; or a pool of clear water in all that man-killing expanse of blazing sand and rock between Algiers and Spanish Oran at the exact moment the escaped prisoner realizes it is no mirage.'

'Has such a one ever existed?' they marvelled.

'If she whom you describe had walked among us, we would remember,' they assured me.

In April of my second futile year in the south, the flow of money stopped. 'But I can carry you myself a while,' Pierre Papin told me over the voice of a gypsy singing salacious *coplas* in the *cercle privé* of his gambling den. Then he said, 'Been meaning to ask you — what's that niece of yours doing these days?'

'She designs theatre costumes.'

'No money in it. She could name her salary, working for me. In my Madrid establishment or wherever she wants.'

'But Constanza,' I said, 'is one of life's innocents.'

Pierre Papin nodded enthusiastically. 'Look at that little gal over there.'

He indicated the dealer at the vingt-et-un table. She wore a perky cap of gold brocade on her blonde hair, and on her pretty face the look of a child ready to bolt at the first unkind word.

'Remind you of anybody?'

'You mean Constanza? Well, they're both blonde and sort of shy-looking, but '

'That niece of yours set the style ever since she was fourteen years old.'

'Constanza?'

'The best dealer in Spain. They all tried to copy her. Know why she was so good? Because when she dealt out the cards, it felt like taking candy from a baby. Plus whenever anybody had a run of luck, she'd look stricken, as if she was personally responsible for the house losing money. Total vulnerability. *And* it was no act. I dream about dealers like that.'

'All she did was deal cards?'

He took off the hat that had the feather on the wrong side, scratched his scalp through thinning hair, put his hat back on. 'What did you think? She was the star dealer at Ovando's place. And a world-class dealer like that doesn't just look untouchable, she *is* untouchable.'

I think I smiled. Then I looked again at the vingt-et-un dealer with the little cap of gold brocade whose slight resemblance to my niece Constanza ended at her two brown eyes. She was cowering across the table from a Fuggerman with a cannonball head and a neck like a fighting bull's. No one else was playing. The German bared his down cards – two aces – and with the blunt fingers of the typical Bavarian motioned for new down cards. Fuggermen, according to gypsies, had more money than God. This was a two-pointed barb. The travelling debt collectors of the Fugger banking family of Augsburg, merciless men who worked on commission, surely got rich. But God's money collectors didn't do badly either.

The frightened dealer looked at Pierre Papin. 'He's been winning and letting it ride. There's ten million *maravedís* . . . on each card.'

This was an awesome sum, even at 440 *maravedís* to the *escudo* (or ducat, the old name by which everybody called the new coin).

At the dice tables, at the monte table, even at the ever-popular *primera* tables (where face cards were of least value, mocking royalty) all action stopped.

Pierre Papin removed his errant-feathered hat and nodded.

Ducking her head so that only her little cap of gold brocade was visible, the dealer dealt a card on to each ace.

With the phlegm of the typical Bavarian, the Fuggerman turned them over. Both face cards.

'This,' he said, 'is not *primera* we are playing.'

Pierre Papin said, 'Gentlemen, the house is closed.'

As he shut his empty safe, the Frenchman told me, 'It seems I won't be able to carry you after all.'

I understood. But I didn't understand about Juan the Obscure. 'What happened to my brother?' I asked. 'It was his money I was spending, wasn't it?'

'He's up the street in the royal prison. They're holding him for murder.'

At the gatehouse they directed me to the *audiencia*, the local jail separated from the prison proper by an alley choked with wives, whores, guards and lawyers.

At the *audiencia* they wouldn't let me in.

'But I'm his brother,' I said, just as an intense little man bustled in. He wore a conservative black taffeta doublet and a neck-whisk, and carried a conservative beaver hat and a conservative briefcase.

'Good morning, Señor Zum,' they said respectfully.

'Picapleitos!' I exclaimed, for I recognized him even without his oversized ruff.

'I am counsel for Don Juan de Cervantes Saavedra a/k/a Juan the Obscure,' he said, ignoring my effusive greeting.

They said, 'If he's got you, Señor Zum, he'll be out in no time.'

'The brother,' said Picapleitos, 'is harmless. You have my word for that. Even if he is a playwright.'

Apparently Picapleitos's word was good enough, for they did not object when he led me into the jail where we could talk privately.

'What's going to happen?' I asked.

'The charges will be dropped. In two weeks, three tops.'

'Did he do it?'

'What an irrelevant question. You really haven't any idea what your brother does, have you?'

I admitted I hadn't.

'Just as well. Perhaps. For now.'

'What's this Señor Zum business?' I asked.

'Just that, business. No one could ever pronounce Iñaki Satrústegui Zumalacárregui except your grandfather. And me, of course. So – Señor Zum.'

'No more Picapleitos? I rather liked it.'

'Please! Such a name may have done at one time.' Picapleitos a/k/a Señor Zum reached up to touch his nose, the tip of which God or the Devil had pinched to a point, then dropped his hand guiltily. 'Old habits die hard,' he said, 'but such tricks are too . . . flamboyant for an attorney in my position. I am, you see, Iberian counsel to the Abbot and his . . . associates, with all that implies.' Again he reached for his nose; again he dropped his hand guiltily. 'But no, you do not see, do you? So we can trade no speculations on what will happen when the Abbot dies. He is desperately ill, you know.'

I didn't. I didn't even know who the Abbot was, since apparently he wasn't the controversial Abbot of Sponheim. Talking with Picapleitos a/k/a Señor Zum, I got the feeling I didn't know much of anything.

He said, 'If you are in need . . . certain contingency funds . . . a playwright can hardly be expected . . .'

'I'm applying for a job as a fleet commissary.'

'Dangerous work,' said Señor Zum. 'On the other hand, it is perfect cover for one of the Abbot's . . . associates.' Again that guilty motion of his hand. 'Could it be that I have been kept in the dark regarding ... no, not you. Well, if you need anything, just see Pierre Papin.'

'He's broke,' I said.

'Broke? A mere twenty million *maravedís*, my dear Don Miguel, well spent on cultivating the House of Fugger, who bankroll entire kingdoms even you can name.'

He waited. But I just shrugged.

He said, 'Could I have misjudged you?', which might have meant anything.

Tomás Gutiérrez agreed to co-sign my undertaking provided I wrote a poem.

I tried to point out that I hadn't been put on this planet to be a poet.

'All I need is an endorsement. A testimonial for my inn. I mean hostal. I'm having a broadsheet printed up that I want a known author – even if Lope de Vega you're not – to write a few verses for. You should put in how mules and mule-skinners get no welcome at Hostal Gutiérrez, but for folks of refinement I got six, almost seven thousand *escudos* – but call them ducats – worth of silver and crystal and furniture, not to mention six Negresses in two shifts for a total of twelve, all from Fernando Po. That's off West Africa. Parrots and macaws from Brazil. That's in the New World. Spring beds. That's in every room. Forty-two *escudos*, but say ducats, I paid for my personal horse. From Majorca. That's practically in Arabia. Class,' said Tomás Gutiérrez. 'We are talking real class.'

My questioning the use of poetry to publicize a business got me nowhere.

'No poem, no co-signature.'

I did it. But you will understand that it hardly fanned my enthusiasm to write poetry, what with its silver salt cellars and spring beds, its tapestry and damask, its cool upstairs chambers in summer and cosy downstairs rooms in winter (Tomás over the years would put me up in the reverse), all rhyming *abba* and ending with a crass pecuniary warning on which Tomás insisted:

> Should you consider it discreet
> To ask the price of room and board,
> 'Tis proof that you can ill afford
> The hostal in Bayona Street.

Tomás loved it, but can you blame me for sometimes thinking, in the months that followed, that it was Euterpe, the muse of lyric poetry, and not the Vicars-General of Sevilla and Córdoba, who called down on me the wrath of Heaven?

XXIII

In Which I Am Excommunicated
And Declared Anathema,
And in Which Worse Things Happen

Sweaty, grey with dust and fatigue, I dismounted in the plaza separating the town hall from St James's Church. News of my coming or the fearful heat of the early summer had driven the townspeople off the streets. Écija, fifty miles east of Sevilla in the Guadalquivir valley, is not called the Oven of Andalucía for nothing.

After pounding on the door for five or ten minutes with my staff emblematic of the King's justice, I was admitted to the town hall where, as it happened, the council of Écija was in plenary session. These are some of the things the councillors told me:

'Last year's harvest was a disaster.'

'Early flooding washed away the seed grain.'

'It didn't rain once the whole growing season.'

'Hailstones as big as oranges flattened the wheat just before reaping.'

'A blight destroyed the alfalfa.'

'When all five grain-storage barns burned down, the flames could be seen as far as Sevilla.'

'You really ought to go back there, fellow.'

Hoping that Holy Mother Church, owner of many grain-fields and much fodderland, might set an example, I crossed the plaza to St James's. This took more time than it should have, for hundreds of donkeys with bulging

279

paniers were being driven into the square from all directions, converging on the west portal of the church.

After pounding on the north transept door for fifteen or twenty minutes, I was admitted by the verger.

'You're in luck,' he told me. 'The Vicar-General of Sevilla is visiting.'

The Vicar-General looked as case-hardened as a Fuggerman. 'How large an example?' he boomed in an almost Bavarian voice.

'Well, the registers show the church holdings to be the most extensive in Écija, so I hoped – '

'The holdings in question do not belong to this humble little Church of St James.'

It didn't seem humble or little to me as I stood in the nave with the Vicar-General, his voice echoing from the vaulted ceiling and the *mudejar* windows looking down at us as if they could read souls. I asked him if the Church might urge the owners of those extensive lands, whoever they were, to show the way for their tight-fisted brethren. Fifteen hundred bushels, I suggested, would get things rolling.

'The holdings,' boomed the Vicar-General, 'belong to the dean and chapter of Sevilla Cathedral, and therefore to God. I, as Vicar-General, have a minority interest. The *burros* gathered outside will, as soon as they are blessed, transport their fifteen hundred and twenty-five bushels of wheat direct to the cathedral storehouses.'

And he turned to march westward up the nave.

'But the wheat,' I called after him, reasonably I thought, 'is required in Lisbon by the Crown.'

'The wheat will be sold to the highest bidder. The Church is not in the farming business for its health. Profit, Señor Commissary. Profit's the thing.'

I might have pointed out that the profit motive, so linked to Lutheran heretics, hardly suited a Vicar-General. But I said nothing until he suggested with unctuous ecclesiastical cheer, 'Come, we may be in time to watch the blessing,' to which I responded, 'B-blessed or not, that wheat's going nowhere but to the K-King's Invincible Armada,' at which the Vicar-General boomed, 'There will be no rendering unto Caesar here,' and continued up the nave.

Church and State, your classic confrontation.

While the priest was blessing the *burros*, I ran through the church to the door where I'd hitched my mule and got an official form from my saddlebag. I filled it out and signed, then ran back up the nave in time to hear, 'Amen.'

The first laden *burros* began to move out of the plaza.

I raised my staff of justice on high.

'This wheat, under the power vested in me by the Crown, is hereby embargoed.'

For I had the power, and the Vicar-General knew it.

He raised his crucifix on high.

'This man, under the power vested in me by the Church,' he said, 'is hereby excommunicated.'

I tried to thrust the embargo notice into his hand, but he recoiled and said, 'Plus, he is anathema. Anyone having contact with him commits a mortal sin. This includes accepting official papers.'

Standoff.

I broke it by nailing the embargo notice to the west portal of St James's Church (an impulsive act that, in hindsight, may have invited the persistent charge that the Lutheran heresy informs my works).

Riding north into the province and diocese of Córdoba, I met an itinerant toothpuller headed for Sevilla and gave him a letter asking Pierre Papin to retain Picapleitos a/k/a Señor Zum to represent me in the ecclesiastical court there. Then I rode on to the town of La Rambla.

After making me cool my heels for several weeks, the town council said, 'The promissory note the Fleet Commissary gave us before the Battle of Lepanto has never been redeemed. The King will get no more La Rambla wheat, no matter how urgently he needs it for his Invisible whatsis.'

'Armada. Invincible Armada.'

'Not to mention the wheat requisitioned in '78 and '82, also unpaid for, and there was no Lepanto then and no Invisible Armada nor any France to invade neither.'

'England. Invincible.'

Just then Pedro de Isunza arrived in a cloud of dust upon which his black cape was spread batlike as he dismounted from a lathered stallion.

He took me brusquely aside. 'How do you expect to do business if you're anathema?' he growled. 'On your very first assignment! Fortunately the eminent lawyer Señor Zum promptly got you *un*-excommunicated. But you can't count on Señor Zum representing you if you're excommunicated again.' (He was wrong, but neither of us could know that.)

'Stop sisyphussing around,' he admonished me. 'Let me show you how a commissary does business.'

Leading me back to the council chamber, he removed the black leather gloves he always wore on the road. He had small, neat, pink hands.

'Your quota is two thousand bushels, at market prices, less twenty per cent patriotic discount,' he told the council, 'payment by official promissory note.'

The president of the town council reviewed the Battle of Lepanto promissory note and the rest. 'So why should we accept another one now?' he asked. He did, however, agree to retire to the next room with Pedro de Isunza to discuss the matter privately.

After twenty minutes the door opened and Pedro de Isunza called for a jug of wine, which was brought.

After a further twenty minutes the door opened and Pedro de Isunza called for a physician, who was summoned.

The physician hurried inside in a swirl of red physicianly robes and soon reappeared to say, 'The end was sudden, he did not suffer.' He produced a certificate of defunction, filling in the cause of death as apoplexy.

Pedro de Isunza came out and commiserated with the town council of La Rambla while replacing his black leather gloves finger by finger on his small, neat, pink hands which, I thought, smelled faintly of some exotic fruit.

Except for his implacably (quite possibly sexually) obsessed eyes, he looked inordinately pleased with himself.

The president, Pedro de Isunza informed the council, had agreed before his fatal seizure to nineteen hundred bushels of wheat and a like amount of fodder. If, Isunza suggested, the surviving councillors had any qualms about ratifying this contribution to the Invincible Armada, he would be pleased to discuss the issue privately with their new president. But this proved unworkable because no one would place his name in nomination until Pedro de Isunza had definitively departed La Rambla.

Agreement secured, Izunza and I went outside together and walked over to where we had hitched our mounts, Isunza lifting his arms to catch a hint of breeze and let his black cape spread like bat wings.

'A commissary,' he said, 'must never evade responsibility for failure by pleading good intentions. Good intentions, I am convinced, are the root of all difficulties. That is why I never harbour any.'

In Castro del Río the sacristan of the Church of Our Lady of the Good Milk professed the best of intentions.

He said, 'You want to see the wheat, I'll show you the wheat. It's in that barn over there beyond the *arroyo*.'

By then it was high summer, and when the sacristan and I walked across the baked, bone-dry field and over the cracked, stone-hard clay bed of the dry gulch, it was as if we two with our intentions – mine to get the wheat, his to keep it; and in this world of absurdities did God or Anything Out There care? – were the last two humans on the face of an earth that, in the new heretical heliocentric scheme of things, had drifted too close to a hostile sun.

As we entered the barn, a rectangular shaft of light penetrated the open door. The stinking gases exuded by rotting wheat and the poisonous dust stirred up by our feet seemed enough, quite apart from the superheated air, to asphyxiate any two men. But when I examined with an educated eye the sheaved wheat filling the barn and said, 'Eleven hundred bushels, wouldn't you say?' the only reply was the creak of the door shutting. Had I any doubts about the intentions of the sacristan, they were settled by the narrowing to nothing of that rectangular shaft of light.

I shouted, groping blindly through head-high stacks of sheaved wheat to where I thought the door was, but in the darkness my outstretched hands encountered only more wheat.

Don't panic, I tried to tell myself. But the stacked sheaves blocking me no matter which way I turned, the nefarious heat, the toxic silage stench all told me that the sacristan's intentions would triumph over mine – an outcome not necessarily more absurd than the reverse, but more permanent. How long I groped in sightless desperation I cannot say. Surely it was only by the greatest good fortune that what used to be my left hand at last encountered the door.

I pounded as hard as I could, but to what avail? Who would let me out? (I would become a statistic. People die every summer of asphyxiation-by-silage. Accidents happen.) I began kicking the door with my stout travelling boots. (People die of apoplexy too; my own grandfather Juan the Patriarch had died right there in his own house in Córdoba of an argument. And the corpses floating in the sea at Lepanto were without number. What's so special about dying?) I kicked and kicked at the door. (Unless you happen to be the one that's doing it, with no erstwhile royal astrologer to rescue you.) The door shook in its frame. I kicked. I heard in the darkness what I took at first for a scream. This was the sound rusty nails make when prised reluctantly from wood. I saw light. I kicked. The door screamed. I kicked again and it gave.

Back in town I went to my mule and drank a skinful of watered wine and filled out a warrant for the sacristan's arrest for interfering with a government functionary in the performance of his function. I took the sacristan from the Church of Our Lady of the Good Milk to Castro del Río's *juzgado*. Then – this required several frustrating months, for the

Castro del Ríans were in no hurry to part with their grain – I personally saw to cleaning, drying, winnowing, and loading upon requisitioned *burros* 2500 bushels of wheat. This done, I visited the morning shape-up in the town plaza and hired half a dozen unemployable farmhands to help me drive the *burro* train to Lisbon.

By then the jailed sacristan had succeeded in getting a message to his Vicar-General in Córdoba. Once more I was an excommunicate and anathema.

But I didn't know this, and it was with some pride that I led my *burro* train west along the Guadalquivir valley on what I thought was the first leg of my journey to the sea.

The brigand Aurelio Ollero stood in driving rain on an outcrop of rock halfway up Fat Hill in the Bald Mountains and watched the *burro* train approach the defile far below. A short, broad man with a tall, broad-brimmed hat, drooping moustaches, and a leather lanyard he always wore for no known purpose, the brigand Aurelio Ollero, unlike Robin of Locksley or Roque Guinart of Cataluña, inspired no legend about taking from the rich to give to the poor. He took from each according to his ability to be taken from, and it was said that after the three great ducal families he commanded the largest fortune in south-western Spain. With any luck he would shortly be richer to the tune of 2500 bushels of wheat.

The brigand Aurelio Ollero ruled the countryside almost into Sevilla itself, exacting tribute from every town and hamlet. The only exception was a mysterious complex of buildings east of Arcos de la Frontera that seemed not built upon but carved from the living rock of the rugged mountains – rumoured to be a community of religious fanatics, Lutheran or worse, or (the view of a vocal minority) the Rest and Rehabilitation Centre for some nameless organization that spread its sinister web from England to Transylvania and beyond.

The beauty of it, the brigand Aurelio Ollero told himself as he settled his weather-slung musket more comfortably, was that attacking the *burro* train would be no crime. The courts had long since determined that a man anathematized was fair game, and Aurelio Ollero had known that the commissary in charge was anathematized ever since the *burro* train started out from Castro del Río ten days ago. The brigand had his scouts everywhere. So he also knew when four of the drivers deserted, leaving the commissary Cervantes with two old men with three teeth between them. Only Cervantes was armed – with an ancient flintlock pistol (picked up at the *venta* atop the Pass of the She-Wolf) wildly inaccurate beyond five paces, and his heavy staff emblematic of the King's justice. Which was a joke here in these mountains where the brigand Aurelio Ollero dispensed the only justice there was.

When the last of the *burros* had slogged through the mud into the defile, the brigand Aurelio Ollero waggled his musket, whereon two teams of his men, using young poplars as levers, sent boulders tumbling down to close the trap.

Only then did Aurelio Ollero, with a lazy grace belied by his plumpness, mount his roan filly and at a slithering gallop lead his dozen men down into the defile, shouting and shooting off their muskets.

When he thought about it afterwards, which wasn't often, the brigand Aurelio Ollero reluctantly had to admire the bravery, however futile, of the commissary Cervantes. Instead of surrendering, as the two old *burro* drivers had done, and as anyone else *would* have done, the commissary Cervantes somehow managed to get his ancient pistol to fire despite the rain (the roundball ricocheted with a cranky whine off a rock) and then flung it at Aurelio Ollero with his left hand. He was left-handed, it seemed. Funny, the things you remember. In the brief but intense struggle, he fired with his left hand, threw the pistol left-handed, hunkered down behind his mule (killed by the first fusillade of musketfire) and threw stones, also southpaw, unseating three of Aurelio Ollero's less skilled riders. And then, evidently out of stones, the commissary Cervantes rose behind the riddled carcass of his mule and, wielding his staff of office left-handed, tripped (and broke the leg of) Aurelio Ollero's lieutenant Lombrizcacha's valuable black warhorse.

'I kill the cocksucker!' screamed Lombrizcacha. And he would have, if the light had been a shootist's light. But rain and encroaching darkness contrived to spoil his aim, and the roundball, instead of drilling a third eye in the commissary Cervantes's head, passed through his left shoulder. At this, Cervantes, illumined momentarily by a bolt of lightning (rather like the one that had struck the rusty sword from his father's hands that night at the Bench of If-Only, not that Aurelio Ollero knew that), threw down his splintered staff emblematic of the King's justice and ran, upon which the remainder of Aurelio Ollero's gang raised their muskets as one and awaited the next flash of lightning, but before they could perforate the fleeing commissary, Aurelio Ollero gave the signal to cease fire. A single musket discharged, and Cervantes fell and rolled over and got up and, as darkness re-encroached, disappeared towards the boulders blocking the western end of the defile.

'Let him go,' said Aurelio Ollero.

This was no night to pursue a foolhardy commissary who, doubtless, would bleed to death anyway. No, back to the hills above the village of Whore's Hut and the warm, dry comfort of his cave with its Persian-carpeted floors and tapestried walls, where waited Aurelio Ollero's gypsy woman Pilar, Pilar of the pure coloratura voice and never mind that the village had been named for her. Aurelio Ollero was not one to hold eponyms against anyone – after all, people change, don't they?

'Look at him,' said Juan the Obscure admiringly as dawn touched the rimrock.

'So he's up with the dawn, so what?' Luis Blackslave said with his habitual sang-froid.

It was rare for Juan the Obscure and Luis Blackslave to venture together from the mysterious complex of buildings that seemed not built upon but carved from the living rock in the rugged mountains east of Arcos de la Frontera. Juan the Obscure, ever on the move, was seldom there. And Luis Blackslave hadn't left the complex for years. Why should he? It was his life.

'Why did he climb all that way, half bleeding to death? You suppose the roundball got him in the ass, where he keeps his brains?' Luis Blackslave said with a flash of his eight or ten gold teeth.

'Instinct. A man climbs or he's nothing. Up from the primordial mud,' said Juan the Obscure, trying to keep the brotherly pride from his voice.

Miguel, he knew now, could be one of the good ones.

Standing in his stirrups, Juan the Obscure imitated the distinctive scream of the eagles of the Serranía de Ronda, and three horsemen on the next ridge forced their mounts up towards the rimrock. Then he told Luis Blackslave, 'We'll go now. I don't want him to see us yet.'

'Why not?' Blackslave asked. Not that he wasn't eager to get back to the R&R Centre. Rest and Rehabilitation – that was a laugh; it was the least of what they did there.

'I don't want him to join up out of some sense of family obligation,' explained Juan the Obscure.

A reasonable worry. Even if it often miscarried, Miguel's sense of family remained strong. Particularly for their sister Andrea. The irony did not escape Juan the Obscure: Andrea was no blood of their blood.

Well, she had served his ends, the bait that had lured Miguel from his stultifying bourgeois existence in Esquivias and Madrid.

The three recruitment specialists riding up towards the rimrock could be counted on to get the wounded man safely to the R&R Centre. For when something mattered to the Maimed Man, it got done properly or else.

This was especially true since, these days, there was so little one could be sure of – a daunting situation for those whose business it was to *know*. Of course, they could not hope to know everything in the vast territory they covered, from England to Transylvania and beyond. But what they did not know they had persuaded themselves, in the pragmatic tradition of the organization they served, they had no need to know. They did know, however, the two riders descending and the three men coming to my rescue as dawn climbed over the rimrock, that in his secret headquarters a thousand leagues from everywhere, the Abbot lay dying. What direction the Nameless Service took – it had been under his stewardship since the death of a Certain Mutual Acquaintance – would be determined by his successor, who would not emerge from the shadows at once. Power struggles were to be expected in the Nameless (and correctly so) Service. Until the Abbot died and the identity of the new Innominate became known, anything might happen.

These were perilous times.

XXIV

More Dangerous Games

Some days after I was pronounced out of danger – if such can be said of anyone entering the Nameless Service – and turned loose in the top-secret archives of the so-called R&R Centre (more properly Base Iberia) in the rugged mountains east of Arcos de la Frontera, the Marqués de Santa Cruz, Commander-Designate of the Invincible Armada, died in Lisbon. The date on the Gregorian calendar was 9 February 1588 and the cause of death was overwork at the prodding of his master King Felipe II the Death-Loving. The once-cautious monarch of the first sun-never-sets empire had fallen prey to the illusion of accelerating time and felt he must hurry if he were to make his mark. (He was wrong; he had ten more years.) Making his mark meant dumping England's virgin whore off her throne as once he had dumped her half-sister Mary Tudor on her back, and for the same reason, to guarantee Spanish domination of the New World. And dethroning Elizabeth meant war. Which meant the usual call on the House of Fugger for financing.

From Augsburg to Lisbon had come Baron Hasko von Nacht zu Nebel to supervise the conversion of strong German *gulden* into weak *escudos* at a rate advantageous to Fugger. A tidy profit would have been assured had the Baron not tithed the *gulden* as they arrived from Augsburg, diverting ten per cent to Pierre Papin's new Lisbon gaming establishment. Von Nacht zu Nebel, a steady if unspectacular winner at *primera* and vingt-et-un, lost everything one drunken night not long before Santa Cruz's death at, of all things, the old shell game. After the Captain General's funeral no more was seen in Lisbon of the Fuggerman, but he was not missed in the clamour of the arrival of the new Commander-Designate, the Duke of Medina Sidonia.

'Who has impeccable ancestry but *no* naval experience whatsoever,' Luis Blackslave observed to my brother Juan the Obscure one day in the situation room of Base Iberia in the rugged mountains east of Arcos.

The walls of the situation room were covered with large world maps, all wildly inaccurate. The two men studied them in professional camaraderie, until my brother told Luis Blackslave, 'One of W's agents is on his way from England to find the Fuggerman.'

W was, of course, Queen Elizabeth's espionage chief Sir Francis Walsingham, officially Principal Secretary of the Privy Council. But my brother and Blackslave, bound by the punctilio of the Nameless Service, named no names.

'We chill him when he lands in Lisbon or what?' Blackslave asked with his habitual sang-froid.

'On the contrary. We help him find the Fuggerman.'

'You joshing me?'

'Luis,' my brother chided gently.

Blackslave managed an embarrassed gold-toothed grin. 'Sure. The first priority of the Nameless is – '

'Infiltration,' the two men chorused, almost devoutly, and my brother went on, 'We turn up the Fuggerman, the only one outside the Admiralty who knows the order of battle of the Invincible Armada, and we help this English agent *ex*filtrate him and – who knows? – this Englishman might just become our means of *in*filtrating W's service.'

'Not bad,' Luis Blackslave said. 'Except. The Fuggerman has dropped off the face of the earth.' Blackslave glanced in frustration at the wildly inaccurate maps.

'We've just had a make on him. In Záhara of the Tunas.'

'Holy Jesus,' said Luis Blackslave, almost deserted by his habitual sang-froid. 'Even my father the king of kings who has agents-in-place all the way from frigid Tierra del Fuego to doomed Roanoke Island and beyond – '

'Never mind that father of yours,' said Juan the Obscure with an indulgent smile.

' – would hate to send any agent he valued into Záhara of the Tunas.'

'That's why W's man needs our help. Who've we got down there?' Though my brother was commandant of the Nameless Service's Base Iberia, he was rarely there, and Luis Blackslave handled day-to-day operations.

'Mnemosyne,' Blackslave said.

'Good. Mnemosyne's rash enough to walk into anything.'

'But,' said Blackslave dubiously, 'maybe not cautious enough to walk back out.'

'If you mean what terrifies most people about Záhara may be what turns Mnemosyne on, it's time we found out,' said Juan the Obscure. 'And, since it's Záhara, we'll also need a gypsy expert.'

'Your brother?' Blackslave suggested.

'Záhara's a stiff assignment for a raw recruit,' Juan the Obscure said. 'He doesn't even have a code name yet.'

Blackslave seemed to change the subject. 'What's this English agent's background?'

'Young. Not long out of Cambridge,' my brother said. He doodled along the South American coastline on one of the New World maps, not altering it for the worse, before reciting moodily:

'See, what a world of ground
Lies westward from the ... *something something* ... line
Unto the rising of this earthly globe,
Whereas the sun, declining from our sight,
Begins the day with our Antipodes.'

Luis Blackslave said, 'Your brother write that? I didn't know he had that kind of poetry in him.'

'He doesn't. The English agent wrote it.'

'The quarry's in a gypsy lair *and* the agent's a scribbler? Then it's obvious Miguel's the man for the job.'

My brother doodled some more. 'Could be he's the unluckiest playwright that ever penned a line. That play of his I was quoting from, it got every theatre in England closed by royal edict. All the other playwrights would like to slit his throat.'

'That must have been some seditious play.'

'Not at all,' said my brother Juan the Obscure. 'It was something to do with special effects. Whatever, they say it haunts him still.'

'Miguel,' said Luis Blackslave, 'has his ghosts too.'

I sat cross-legged on the floor in the archives, reading, with one of those inexplicable shocks of recognition, about a German scholar and necromancer named Georg Faust (?1479–1538) who, in exchange for experiencing everything life could offer (and some things it could not), sold his immortal soul to the Devil. I had found his story in one of the manuscripts of the controversial Abbot of Sponheim, whose *Steganographia* could be read either as a treatise on the summoning of demons or (justifying its place in the archives) as the definitive work on cryptography in our time.

I read slowly, for my command of Latin was not superb and the controversial Abbot wrote a cramped hand.

Those who dismiss Georg Faust as a mere braggart ignore his considerable success as a necromancer in his native Wittenberg and the esteem he enjoys at various lay and ecclesiastical courts. Already it becomes impossible to distinguish the legendary figure from the real man, and some have begun confounding him with *Johann* Faust, an earlier necromancer of lesser renown (although perhaps greater integrity). Whether Georg Faust can achieve his goal of mastering all knowledge, and whether in return for such mastery he has indeed pledged his immortal soul to the unholy spirit Mephistopheles/Mephistophilis/Mefistofele/Mephostophilus, must of course remain a matter for conjecture. But I submit that 'all knowledge' is here meant not in the encyclopedic sense but rather in the context of Adam's expulsion from the Garden, when God feared that the first man would become 'as one of us' – incidentally conceding with His words that He was hardly the only deity at the time. *Sed non est his locus.* Faust, in seeking, in striving, in becoming a pawn in the cosmic struggle between forces he but dimly comprehends, must be viewed as both protagonist and victim of his own tragedy. For –

So absorbed had I become in the history of Georg Faust in the faded ink on the brittle yellowed pages of the Abbot of Sponheim's eighty-year-old manuscript, that it was some time before I noticed Juan the Obscure standing over me.

I asked him, 'The Abbot – if he's not the controversial Abbot of Sponheim, would he be his son or maybe grandson?'

'The Abbot of Sponheim died celibate in Würzburg in 1516,' Juan the Obscure said, 'while *our* Abbot lingers on his deathbed at Nameless Main Base a thousand leagues from everywhere.'

'You mean a thousand leagues from Base Iberia?'

'A thousand leagues,' repeated my brother, 'from everywhere.'

I tried, 'Then if he's not Sponheim, who is he?'

Juan the Obscure told me I had no need to know.

'But I *do* need to know ... everything!' I shouted, much to my own surprise. The influence of this Georg Faust? I mean, it wasn't like me at all, was it?

With a philosophic shrug, Juan the Obscure told me the dying Innominate's name. 'Onofre Exarque.'

I gasped. Exarque – Greek for super-abbot! How could I have missed it? 'Only ... when Rodrigo paid him to sail to Algiers and rescue me, why didn't he?'

'That wasn't Rodrigo's decision to make.' Then, apologetically, 'Nor mine. Enough. Your investiture's tonight. You leave on your first assignment tomorrow.'

'Unless you answer some questions, I'm not going on any – ' Again I gasped. Because suddenly, I don't know how, I knew. One revelation for another? An association of ideas too tenuous to comprehend? Whatever, I blurted, 'Uncle Suleiman! Angst! Only it wasn't angst, it was Amst – Amsterdam. Zoraida's confessions. She sent them to Amsterdam with her uncle Suleiman Sa'adah Sometimes Erroneously Called the Wise for safekeeping.'

'We-ell now,' said Juan the Obscure with one of those lazy, fond grins I would get to know. 'So leaving you there finally paid off.'

His delight was contagious and I found myself grinning too. Which didn't stop me from saying, 'About those questions.'

His grin became wry. 'Dogged too,' he said. 'Such as?'

'Such as your sending money to Picapleitos or Señor Zum for our sisters' legal bills, always accompanied by a toy soldier with a missing hand. That's your code name, isn't it – the Maimed Man? What's going on?'

I expected anger, but the look Juan the Obscure gave me was uncharacteristically vulnerable. 'Yes, it's my code name,' he said. And said no more until I asked him, 'Why?'

'Listen, all the time we were kids, when you and Rodrigo used to play together, I was there watching from some dark corner wishing I could play too but afraid to ask.'

'I never realized,' I said.

'Then the night you fled, and Rodrigo gave you his treasured toy soldier, I cried myself to sleep. You were so close, you two. But I was only good for hiding in corners. Prowling around in the dark. For me that toy soldier became a symbol of all I could never be. So when I needed a code name, I chose the Maimed Man. Maimed signifies ugliness to most people. But not to me.'

He turned his back and busied himself straightening a few volumes on the archive shelves.

I asked gently, 'What do you do it for? Spying?'

He faced me. 'Because somebody has to do it. Somebody has to watch them. Unseen. Unsung. From the dark corners of history. I know you don't give a damn for history,' he said, 'but it has its uses – a place with convenient dark corners, if nothing else.'

'But who do you watch from those dark corners?'

'Kings, queens, knaves the lot of them!'

'Then the Nameless Service is not in the employ of any one government?' I asked, relieved.

'Autonomous. Not for sale at any price. Knowledge! Secret knowledge! Of the sacred and the profane. Shake the tree of history, and see what forbidden fruit falls from its branches! Obscurity's a small price to pay.'

Was obscurity, I couldn't help wondering, power?

'Never abuse it,' said Juan the Obscure, as if he could read my mind.

Encouraged to find my brother in an almost talkative mood, I asked, 'Who did you murder?'

'We live in violent times,' he said. Defensively, I thought.

'Who,' I persisted, 'did you murder in Sevilla?'

'When?' he asked. A discomfiting response.

'Just before I went to work as a commissary.'

'Señor Zum got me off with self-defence. Which was the truth. For once.'

Did he mean truth was rarely used by Señor Zum? Or that he rarely killed in self-defence? I decided not to ask.

'You see, ever since you rescued our niece Constanza from the Ovando mansion with a little help from me, Pedro (Killer) Pacheco Portocarrero was laying for us. He caught up with me in Sevilla. I was quicker,' Juan the Obscure said simply. He added, 'Now I've got his baby brother to worry about, but luckily that doesn't concern you.'

Of my investiture I can say almost nothing, for I swore secrecy in the name of the Nameless Service. The torchlit ceremony occurred at the edge of a *barranca* in a wild, craggy landscape; the words of the oath I took left me with a profound, quasi-religious awe, as the oath of a knight in the age of chivalry must have done, almost as if the Nameless Service in its endless quest for knowledge . . .

But I have already said too much.

My conversation the next morning with Luis Blackslave is not covered by the Nameless Service oath.

'Where's Juan?'

'Who?'

'My brother Juan the Obscure.'

'He left right after your investiture for . . . somewhere,' said Blackslave. 'Now, about your assignment, Amadis.'

Amadis – what else could my code name have been?

'As far as the world knows, you're still a commissary. Señor Zum's got a nephew who's filling in for you. There's a superficial resemblance, and our make-up specialists did the rest. By the way, Zum's got you un-excommunicated again. Not that anybody in Záhara of the Tunas will give a damn.'

Blackslave next told me what I needed to know about the Fuggerman von Nacht zu Nebel. Then, 'The English agent coming to exfiltrate him is a playwright, Quillpusher by code name. You'll have a lot in common. That's a big plus.'

Playwright, I wrote. Naïvely, I was taking notes.

'Give me those,' Luis Blackslave said, and, red-faced, I watched him burn them.

'You'll be working with one of our people already in place in Záhara. Code name Mnemosyne.'

'Von Nacht zu Nebel, Quillpusher, Mnemosyne, right.'

'Your job's to use your gypsy connections to help Quillpusher and Mnemosyne exfiltrate the Fuggerman. Any questions?'

I had none.

'To identify yourself to Mnemosyne you say, "When Inanna penetrates the underworld to rescue her dead lover Dumuzi, she is stripped of her robes and ornaments and brought naked before her terrible sister Ereshkigal, who kills her with a single glance and hangs her from a stake." And Mnemosyne must answer, "At the southern end of Gehenna lies the valley of Tophet, where Sennacherib's army was destroyed in the night, and sacrifices to Baal and Moloch are still cast into the perpetual fires." '

I committed sign and countersign to memory, and left for Záhara and Operation Weltschmerz.

The gypsy was as old as the inevitability of sin and as slender as the hope of salvation.

'Come to have thy Tarot read?' he asked me. 'Or maybe a fish's entrails? This being a seaport, icthyomancy's popular here.

'Wasn't always a seaport. Used to be what lies back of the back of beyond, until one moonless night with a whiff of sulphur in the air the Devil rolled his dice here. Come morning, he left those dice behind as the town of Záhara, right on the edge of *the* most diabolical sea this side of the Sargasso. Sooner or later there washes up on the Sands of Terminal Despair, not a mile from where thou art standing, the detritus of every wasted life and every lost dream.

'Everything that can be, is, in Záhara. And everything that is, is bad. Unless thou art wise enough to know that when a beast is slain the slaughterhouse profits.'

'Were I so wise,' I said by rote, 'I wouldn't be here.'

'Whom dost thou seek?'

Choosing my words with great care, I described her.

'Dost thou not see that such as she cannot exist?' said the gypsy. 'For if she did, the world would cease all else to worship at her feet.'

'But she does exist,' I said. 'She's my sister. At least, for a long time I thought she was.'

'The unsullied sanctuary of a flawless love,' the gypsy said softly, reverently. 'To be envied, for even if thou never find it, the seeking keeps thee young. Whom else dost thou seek?'

'Mnemosyne,' I said.

'Sullied,' he said. 'Flawed. But at least Mnemosyne exists.'

It was the prototype of every dive in every sinistrous back alley in all the world's *verso* seaports, the sort of joint where you could buy whatever you hadn't come to sell, and steal whatever you hadn't come to beg or barter. It was, like the town of Záhara itself, margin-as-centre, a place (as I wrote in 'The Illustrious Serving Wench') of clean dirt, instant hunger and too-abundant satiety, a place where violent death rid the world of excess *picaros*.

Two brutish figures came at a tumbling roll out of the doorway, punching, kicking, biting, butting, gouging and otherwise trying to tear one another limb from limb. In the light from the doorway I saw a ripped doublet spill forth a plump breast, and realized at least one combatant was a woman. A handful of spectators jadedly watched the brawl: an everynight occurrence.

Why would Mnemosyne frequent a place like this?

Foolish question. All places in Záhara were like this.

The barman was drawing wine so fast he didn't even pretend to listen to an existential monologue delivered by a pockmarked pimp. A large woman, one of the brawlers, came in and without a word stuck a knife between the pimp's ribs. As he fell, 'Jug o' red,' said the large woman, who was cheered perfunctorily by two or three customers but otherwise ignored.

'Yours?' the barman asked me.

I dropped a couple of ducats on the bar. He bit one. Then he bit the other.

'Mnemosyne,' I said, and he jerked an indifferent thumb in the direction of a low door beyond the last wine cask. I opened it and found myself in one of those innyards I would later immortalize in *Don Quixote*. A horse whickered. A commotion, obviously carnal, shook the hayloft. A gaunt old man in a chamois shirt and nightcap stood guard over some unidentifiable objects next to the horse trough, muttering as I passed him and approached a door of stout oak, its wrought-iron knocker a miniature Durandel crossed over a miniature Olivant. I lifted this elaborate device and let it fall with the expected reverberation.

A peephole opened to reveal a disturbing amber eye.

I said, ' "When Inanna penetrates the underworld to rescue her dead lover Dumuzi, she is stripped of her robes and ornaments and brought naked before her terrible sister Ereshkigal, who kills her with a single glance and hangs her from a stake." '

The peephole widened. So did that disturbing amber eye. An equally disturbing contralto voice said, 'And the story just ends there? She's really dead?' and I turned to run, sure that something had gone amiss. But the voice called after me, 'Wait! "At the southern end of Gehenna lies the valley of the prophet – " '

'That's Tophet,' I said, returning and starting to smile. 'And no "the".'

' "Tophet, where a sunny cherub's army – " '

'Sennacherib's army.' My smile broadened to a grin.

' " – where Sennacherib's army was destroyed in the night and sacrifices to Ball and" ... uh ... "are still cast into" ... uh ... isn't that *enough* already?'

'Yes, Micaela, it's enough,' I said, and she flung open the heavy oak door and just sort of flowed into my arms, which just sort of flowed around her.

After a while I stepped back and looked.

She was dressed as a youth, in breeches of green cloth-of-gold and a matching coat hanging loose over a rapier and masking the undeniably female form I'd felt flowing against me. Under her dark curls her face was one big grin, matching mine.

'What are you doing here?' I asked. 'I thought your father was going to find you a Basque rock-thrower to marry.'

'He tried. He found the best rock-thrower in all Guipúzcoa, complete with ear-to-ear muscles. But I ran away to Madrid hoping to find Rodrigo, but I found your other brother Juan instead, and when he saw how I liked dangerous games he took me back to Base Iberia and, well, that's how come I'm Mnemosyne.'

While she brought me up to date I have to admit I couldn't take my eyes off her. Odd, isn't it, how dressing as a boy makes a sexy woman look even sexier?

She said, 'Come inside where I can see you.'

Inside, there was more of that flowing into and around, and my hand, my right hand, slipped down to trace, to verify sentimentally, that classic callipygean curve. No reason to feel guilty, not in the Nameless Service, for whose operatives stolen moments are the only respite from a drear life of shadowing potential perpetrators of God-knows-what, their whereabouts known only to Nameless Service traffic control. What time for regret, when at any moment (or no moment at all, if the present did not exist) you might become a brief line in a ledger of the fallen, steganographically incomprehensible to all but the cognoscenti?

She had grown taller. I could tell by the way her dark curls didn't snuggle against my throat now but tickled my nose while I breathed her scent that was like new-mown hay and a touch of some half-forgotten Algerian perfume, musk-rose dew perhaps. It was natural, I told myself, perfectly natural after those months of frustration with Catalina, to find a woman as sexy as Micaela sexy – especially since she was clinging around

296

my neck and kissing me now – wasn't it? On the mouth. But then I thought of those even more frustrating months of not finding my sister Andrea who wasn't my sister, just as Micaela murmured against my lips, 'For a long time I used to dream about you every night, but I forced myself to stop because I knew you'd have your own dream like every captive in Algiers, and once you got free you'd start to turn that dream into a career and a place and a family of your own, wouldn't you.'

It was one of those moments that I with my stutter am most poorly equipped to handle. If I could have said something Liars'-Walk-glib like, 'My wife doesn't understand me,' it might have eased us past an awkward situation. But if you got right down to it, Catalina was pretty good at understanding me. So I just said, 'Yes, I'm m-married.'

Micaela withdrew from my embrace and I think she tried to smile. At least, she showed her teeth. They were even and white. I expected her to say, Trust no one in this life, but what she said was, 'Well! We have a lot of work to do. Don't we.'

The room was small, but then this was not exactly Hostal Gutiérrez. Micaela flattened herself against the wall beside the window, raised the sleazy curtain, peered out suspiciously, let the curtain drop.

'Anyone out there?' I asked.

'Of course. In Záhara there's always someone.'

'Quillpusher here yet?'

'He arrived yesterday. You'd like him – *if* you could understand him. He's a playwright.'

'So am I.'

'You are?'

'Why are you surprised? I was a *ráwi*, wasn't I?'

'Quillpusher speaks four languages fluently. He's young and handsome. He *looks* like a playwright.'

'What does a playwright look like?'

'I don't know. Like Quillpusher, I suppose. His play was so successful that anybody else's would have been redundant, so they shut down all the theatres. In London.'

'That's not exactly the way I heard it.'

'Whatever happened, he doesn't like talking about it. He's very self-effacing as well as a genius. He'd *better* be self-effacing. After the way El Draque pillaged this coast last year, they'd draw and quarter anyone they even suspected of being English. Especially since Záhara was spared. They think they have to prove themselves.'

(History tells us – and fiction has no reason to contest it – that in the spring of 1587 the privateer Sir Francis Drake struck the Atlantic coast of Andalucía, raiding the naval base at Cádiz and putting to the torch every village but Záhara, which, at the urging of Sir Francis Walsingham, was left untouched. W, no less than the Nameless Service, needed a listening post in that corner of the continent, and Záhara was it.)

'I left him with von Nacht zu Nebel this afternoon. On a wrecked tuna boat on the Sands of Terminal Despair. Von Nacht zu Nebel's so sure the House of Fugger's sent someone to kill him, he's hired himself a bodyguard.'

'It's not entirely unlikely,' I said.

'It's more likely they'd use local talent. There's a glut of killers for hire here,' Micaela said. 'So we'd better exfiltrate him fast. What's the plan?'

'Nothing to it. Punt across the swamps to Mazagón and a gypsy caravan up the coast to Huelva. Then they join a Hanseatic merchant – from Lübeck, I think – who takes them by mule as far as Sevilla, where they board a . . . but why don't we hold the details until Quillpusher gets back? He'll want to know.'

Micaela nodded. 'Listen, sometimes if somebody's surprised to see somebody, they get demonstrative. It doesn't have to imply anything, my kissing you like that.' A brittle-bright smile. 'I mean, I'm not the same teenage kid wet behind the ears who drugged poor Zoraida and slipped into bed with you. I have my career now, dangerous enough even for me. I'm not the type to settle down. At all. So it's not of the slightest significance to me that you're married. See?'

A key turned in the lock. He walked in, the smile dropping from his face when he saw me, and reached for his rapier. He was surprisingly young for a successful playwright (but so was Lope de Vega, I reminded myself peevishly). He wore green cloth-of-gold like Micaela, was no taller than she, and moved with the same quick grace. Between his thick auburn hair and fiery red beard was a handsome face dominated by dark blue eyes that gleamed with what I can only describe as benign wickedness.

Micaela went swiftly to his side, linked her arm in his and – I thought to his surprise – snuggled against him. 'It's all right,' she told him.

Her disturbing amber eyes stared at me defiantly. 'See what I mean? Doesn't he look like a playwright? He took two degrees at Cambridge. That's in Oxford, England. Then he wrote two plays about Attila the Hun.'

'Tamburlaine,' said Quillpusher.

'Well, he was the grandson of Attila,' she said.

298

'Great-great-grandson, actually,' said Quillpusher. 'Of Genghis Khan. I take it,' he told me, 'that you are a colleague of Mnemosyne.'

Suddenly his dark blue eyes changed from benign wickedness to wide-open wonder. Shoving Micaela aside, he crossed to me and, to my intense embarrassment, dropped on one knee and, grasping what used to be my left hand, cried, 'It's you! It's really you!'

I tried to free myself, but he clung like a drowning man to a rope.

'Never in my wildest dreams did I hope to meet a legend such as you,' he said passionately. 'In person.'

'Let go of the hand,' I suggested.

But he held on and looked at it raptly, like Galahad at the Holy Grail. 'You're him! You're the Maimed Man!'

I ought to say here that my brother *was* a pretty legendary character by then, a leading contender to be the new Innominate and certainly Base Iberia's choice.

'Let me explain,' I said. 'The fact is – '

But I could explain nothing. My brother might be Juan the Obscure to me, but in the perilous world where the Nameless Service operated, he was the Maimed Man, his true identity unknown, a safe harbour when needed.

'Yes?' said Quillpusher, still holding on.

'If you don't let go of the hand,' I said, 'I'll kick your teeth out.'

He released it abruptly. Over his head I could see Micaela staring at me, doing her best not to look impressed. Quillpusher rose.

'Forgive me. But this is only my second assignment and I hardly expected I'd be working with the Maimed Man.'

'Forget it,' I said in a blasé tone, as if this happened all the time. 'You get anywhere with von Nacht zu Nebel?'

'He was terrified – until I gave him one of your toy soldiers with the missing hand.'

'Where'd you get it?' I demanded.

'We forge them in England by the dozens. They can make quite a difference, believe me. Von Nacht zu Nebel's bodyguard was all set to carve out my liver and lights. But the moment I dangled that toy soldier in front of him, the Fuggerman agreed to put himself in our hands.'

Rain began to rattle on the window.

'When do we go?' Micaela asked.

'At first light,' I said.

'We're waiting?' Quillpusher shot me a surprised look. 'But they say you can see in the dark, Maimed Man, so . . .'

I debated demonstrating my non-existent night vision, but he'd just think I was shamming. So I let it go with, 'The arrangements are for first light.'

An uneasy silence followed, broken by Micaela. 'Amadis says he's a playwright too.'

Another surprised look from Quillpusher. 'The Maimed Man finds time to write? How extraordinary.' Then, thoughtfully, 'Still, scratch a writer and you'll find a spy. Are you a three-unities man? Aristotelian?'

'The only unity Aristotle really cared about was time: one day per play. The rest, at least according to Tasso – '

'You know the great Tasso?'

'Did some travelling together. The rest was Aristotle as misinterpreted by an Italian named, uh, Castelvetro,' I said, and we were off and running, I touching on Lope and his formula, Quillpusher on Kyd's bloodily staged tragedies (with the observation, not amplified, that special effects were dangerous), I on not avoiding the impossible, he on writing about what you don't know – all this in quick bursts, half-completed sentences, and an instant affinity that left Micaela staring at the ceiling and repeating her ritual at the window until Quillpusher said, '. . . by law in England female parts are acted by boys, which can get confusing when a boy plays the role of a woman disguised as a man,' at which Micaela ran her hands over her cloth-of-gold breeches and said wryly, 'I can relate to that. It's practically the story of my life.'

The next time she flattened herself against the wall and raised the sleazy curtain – Quillpusher and I were debating Greek *medias res* versus Roman begin-at-the-beginning – all of us could see the dirty pewter false dawn.

We left separately through the rain at five-minute intervals. This was Quillpusher's plausible suggestion, and he even volunteered to go first.

Only afterwards when it was too late did I realize that, while making much of what used to be my left hand and of our shared interest in the theatre, Quillpusher had shown not the slightest curiosity about the arrangements for his and von Nacht zu Nebel's exfiltration.

The north-easterly breeze freshened and the galleon *Elizabeth Bonaventure* tacked once more to hold her position. The privateer Sir Francis Drake, friend of that other Sir Francis, Walsingham, paced his quarterdeck back and forth, back and forth, as if harmonically attuned to the motion of his ship. Sea flat under a cold drizzle, so when dawn came, he told himself, the pinnace could ride that offshore breeze like a highroad straight back to *Elizabeth Bonaventure*. If nothing went wrong.

Francis Drake hated espionage. Pull all the bloody spies out of bloody everywhere and you wouldn't *need* spies bloody anywhere, if you took his meaning. But espionage was W's addiction. What could Drake, a loyal son of England, do?

Francis Drake craved action. Been around the bloody world, Plymouth to the Straits of Magellan (hateful name; bloody scandal to let the bloody Portugee get there first), up the west coast of both Americas (claimed New Albion for the Queen but the Spaniards moved in and called it San Fran-bloody-cisco), and across the Pacific to the islands named for death-loving King Felipe, damn his eyes, and finally home via the Cape of Good Hope to be knighted aboard his only surviving ship, *Pelican*. The whole three years at sea, attacking every Spanish vessel he met, was easier than this bloody waiting.

Good men aboard the pinnace he'd sent in to the Sands of Terminal Despair (bloody weird these bloody Spanish names), but even that was a worry. Good men, men the Spaniards would love to capture, wouldn't they just! Still, one doesn't say no when W wants a favour, does one. He'd just have to hope that playwriting fellow could pull it off. Go right in, do what you went in to do, come right out – first rule of everything from love to war. But Marlowe was young, and anyway, how could a playwright be a man of action? One either did things or wrote things. No time in this bloody life for bloody both.

The drizzle became a hard, lashing rain. Francis Drake peered towards the shore he could not see, towards invisible Záhara, the one village on this coast not for burning, then turned his back on what he did not understand and looked at the familiar glow of the binnacle light, and waited.

The gypsy Anselmo, as old as the inevitability of sin and as slender as the hope of salvation, found the woman called La Gitana in her hut, draping her showstone with a fringed shawl. How rare, the old gypsy thought, not for the first time, that she was called La Gitana when, of all who lived in the *gitanería*, she alone was no gypsy.

Anselmo stood in the doorway and watched her in the light of the hut's tallow lamp. What a beauty she must have been. Even lined as her face was now, one could see the delicate bone structure. Hair a faded silver that in the lamplight gleamed like spun gold. And those forget-me-not blue eyes, what secrets they must hold! La Gitana was one who had lived, known many men, suffered. And she had done this unlikely thing: had become an interpreter of dreams to the gypsies themselves, the gypsies who so cynically read the future in the dreams of gullible Spaniards – green figs meant embarrassment, anemones love, pomegranates happiness, yellow flowers jealousy. La Gitana spurned all this symbolism learned by heart that had nothing to *do* with the heart, and found meaning in dreams as if they were dreamed in a language only she could understand. Could she truly see the future, as many in the *gitanería* believed? Anselmo himself at unexpected moments glimpsed things with a second sight that frightened him. It was such an experience that had brought him here now.

The other dreamtellers lost no love on La Gitana. Who is she, they asked, and how comes she among us? Tales were whispered. La Gitana was an infant abandoned by the Devil the night he rolled his dice and left them behind to become Záhara where everything that can be, is, and everything that is, is bad. But La Gitana was no Devil-spawn. The old gypsy Anselmo had lived long enough almost to sense the ineffable aura of good that sometimes came from those rare people who had been touched by the old gods whose names men no longer dared speak, and in La Gitana's presence he almost sensed it most of all.

'Good evening, Anselmo my friend,' said La Gitana as Anselmo came in out of the rain.

'Good evening to thee, thee of the forget-me-not eyes – '

'Oh now,' said La Gitana. But she was smiling.

' – that hold visions others cannot see.'

After this *piropo* – for what else was it? – they made small talk in the way of gypsies until she said, 'Something troubles thee, Anselmo my friend. What is it?'

'A stranger came today seeking the woman of whom thou hast spoken, the one of such perfection that she cannot exist. For, if she did, the world would cease all else to worship at her feet.'

'Was he who sought her maimed in any way?'

'His left hand was deformed.'

La Gitana looked long at Anselmo with those forget-me-not eyes. The lamp flickered and dimmed, eradicating the wrinkles on her fine-boned face, eradicating the years.

'Where is he now?' La Gitana asked.

'He sought also a German with a rare name who hides in a wrecked tuna boat on the Sands of Terminal Despair.'

'Hides? There is danger?'

302

'There is much danger.'

La Gitana got her cloak, but Anselmo said, 'Not yet. With first light, I will take thee.'

On the roof of the hut, the rain beat harder.

Pepe (Choirboy) Pacheco Portocarrero was of two minds about the rain.

As a bodyguard, he hated it. A moonless night was bad enough, but in this pre-dawn downpour anyone stalking Pepe (Choirboy) Pacheco Portocarrero's client could approach the beached tuna boat not only unseen but unheard.

As the younger brother of the late Pedro (Killer) Pacheco Portocarrero, he welcomed the rain. The foreigner called Quillpusher would soon return with an unnamed Nameless agent who figured to be the Maimed Man. The downpour would diminish their professional watchfulness and give Pepe (Choirboy) Pacheco Portocarrero the chance he'd waited for ever since the Maimed Man had murdered his brother in cold blood. Granted, it was the Maimed Man who had been walking and Pedro (Killer) Pacheco Portocarrero who had been lurking in an alley. But it was still cold-blooded murder, and the murderer must pay.

Choirboy fondled, in the darkness, the little toy soldier with the missing hand. He smiled, a deceptive smile. Unlike his hulking late brother, Choirboy was slim and angelic-looking and moved easily in polite society; he had been taught to eat with a fork by no less a lady than the one-eyed Princess Eboli, second most beautiful woman in Spain, for whom he'd done several jobs. He had Cupid's-bow lips, eyelashes a girl would envy, a beardless skin and the nicest hazel eyes. His older brother Pedro (Killer) Pacheco Portocarrero, before his untimely demise, had notched 417 proven victims. Choirboy's own score had reached 416 and he expected to draw even not long after first light. Then he could sleep easy. Killer had taught him all he knew and Killer was dead and Choirboy was a very sentimental sort.

'How much longer must we wait?' cried von Nacht zu Nebel in an angst-laden voice.

'First light. Nothing will happen before first light.'

Von Nacht zu Nebel gave a weltschmerzy groan. 'It's easy for you to say. Nobody hired a killer to kill *you*.'

Pepe (Choirboy) Pacheco Portocarrero said, 'No, but I have my reputation to consider. If you die, I lose points.'

'Losing points is not losing your life; that's the thing in itself,' wailed von Nacht zu Nebel categorically.

Crouched against a bulkhead in the tuna boat's cramped hold, Pepe (Choirboy) Pacheco Portocarrero said nothing.

'You can't let me die!' screamed von Nacht zu Nebel imperatively.

Clients. They were all alike. Wrapped up in their petty little problems.

Choirboy waited for first light, that dirty pewter false dawn in which the Maimed Man would meet his fate.

Like his captain aboard *Elizabeth Bonaventure*, the leader of the half-dozen black-clad seamen in the pinnace anchored off the Sands of Terminal Despair was an impatient man, and when the dirty pewter false dawn was still no brighter than the phosphorescence of the rain-flattened surf, he raised his hand. His black-clad crew, knives between their teeth, slipped over the side and swam for shore.

When Quillpusher reached the Sands of Terminal Despair the dirty pewter false dawn had faded into the darkness that precedes true daybreak. Even so, he maintained a fast trot, hoping the phosphorescent gleam at water's edge would keep him from running head-first into the wrecked tuna boat. He had five minutes' start on Mnemosyne, ten on the Maimed Man. Would it be enough?

Would he really outwit the legendary Maimed Man? There seemed at least a chance – and could one ask more, with Night's terrible daughter Nemesis breathing down one's neck?

W had not put it that way, of course; W was too urbane. But he knew. For in certain London circles, the only circles that counted, everyone knew that Quillpusher had written (with what overweening pride!), in the very play that had brought him down:

> Over my zenith hangs a blazing star
> That may endure till heaven be dissolv'd.

Not that Quillpusher believed in Nemesis, really, any more than he believed in God with a capital G. But the myth had a compelling resonance.

What W had said, in his low-key way, was that he had another mission for Quillpusher, perhaps a trifle more arduous than his recent pleasure-jaunt to Rheims to vet a school of English dissidents, and would Quillpusher oblige?

And so here he was. At twenty-four Quillpusher or, to use his real name, Christopher Marlowe (or Marlye, Marlin, Marlyn, Marly, Marley, Marlen, even, for God's sake, Merling: couldn't anybody in Cambridge spell?), was driven by the youthful ambition that made Elizabethan England so exuberantly deadly a place. Marlowe, Kit to his friends (of whom not many remained among theatrical people after that bizarre special-effects misfire in Part II Act V of *Tamburlaine* last November: bad luck, and she was pregnant too, poor thing), hurried now across the Sands of Terminal Despair feeling pretty chipper, all things considered.

The girl Mnemosyne (code-named by what mad irony?) was so pathetically eager to prove herself in a man's world. And she might have done, except that her career would be aborted this very dawn by the man she knew as Quillpusher. Mnemosyne at first, with her innate whore's sense, had been wary of Kit Marlowe. But on the arrival of the Maimed Man she had changed completely; Marlowe remembered how her breast cuddled his arm while they both faced the legendary spy. No, Mnemosyne would be no problem. But the Maimed Man, if he knew that Marlowe had his own exfiltration plans (and not only for von Nacht zu Nebel), with a galleon waiting just over the horizon, would snuff him out as lesser men snuff a candle flame.

Thus preoccupied, Marlowe was just five paces from the beached tuna boat when something grabbed him roughly from behind and a knife dug into his gullet.

Micaela, second to leave the inn, toyed with the idea of dawdling so I would catch up with her. Stolen moments? A premonition? But her restless pursuit of danger got the better of her, and she had almost overtaken Quillpusher when, as the false dawn faded, she discerned vague movement, a more concentrated darkness, that suddenly rose between her and the Englishman. Whipping out her rapier with a practised motion (practised, in fact, only desultorily at Base Iberia), she ran to Quillpusher's aid.

So intent was she on penetrating the darkness ahead that she failed to see behind her, emerging from the surf's phosphorescence, a line of crouching black-clad figures.

What with Pepe (Choirboy) Pacheco Portocarrero attacking Quillpusher, and Micaela rushing towards them with drawn rapier, and those half-dozen (seven, counting their leader) black-clad seamen from *Elizabeth Bonaventure*'s pinnace gliding over the beach to intercept Micaela, we have the makings of a classic free-for-all – even forgetting for the moment von Nacht zu Nebel cowering in the beached tuna boat, not to mention the woman called La Gitana and the old gypsy Anselmo now nearing the Sands of Terminal Despair with the latter's three strapping grandsons.

But it will have to wait. The critics are restless; I can all but hear them.

It's bad enough when, in relating Don Quixote's story, you keep interrupting yourself to tell what other characters are doing, but to be guilty of the same lack of focus in your own death and life is positively absurd.

What can I say?

In writing about a (possibly) self-deluded old man wandering the face of Spain as a knight-errant, I found it necessary to do some narrative wandering as well.

For my own story — well, you remember how confused things got at Lepanto and, even more, at the Plaza of Atrocities on the day of my execution. Floating free of my body lent perspective, but I can't do it at will. It happens or it doesn't.

It didn't happen that morning on the Sands of Terminal Despair, but I still think you should know what was going on, even if at the time I myself knew nothing at all of Francis Drake pacing the quarterdeck of *Elizabeth Bonaventure*, and nothing of the gypsy Anselmo bringing his intimation of danger to the woman called La Gitana, and nothing of Pepe (Choirboy) Pacheco Portocarrero waiting to kill me (but happy to take out Quillpusher first), and nothing of Quillpusher's own exfiltration plans.

I could only go by what I saw.

I saw Micaela smoothly whipping out her rapier as she raced ahead.

I saw (peripheral vision against that phosphorescent surf, so it took a while to register) seven black-clad figures bearing down on Micaela's seaside flank.

I saw (peripheral vision, other side, first indication that a bleak true dawn was at last lightening that drenched morning) an old gypsy and three strapping young gypsies approaching to landward, and behind them a caped woman.

Finally I saw a man leap, bellowing, from the prow of a beached boat. This was von Nacht zu Nebel, crazed with fear, who ran a zigzag course through the rain pouring down ever harder on the Sands of Terminal Despair. His panic changed everything.

Micaela swerved in pursuit of him.

The seven black-clad seamen swerved in pursuit of her.

Pepe (Choirboy) Pacheco Portocarrero raised his knife to dispatch the struggling Quillpusher so he could pursue Micaela pursuing von Nacht zu Nebel when, with his own peripheral vision, he saw me.

By then, less smoothly than Micaela, I was reaching for my rapier without breaking stride, but the rain-slick hilt squirted from my fingers and, weaponless, I collided with Pepe (Choirboy) Pacheco Portocarrero, whose left arm encircled Quillpusher's throat and whose right hand was about to plunge a knife into his heart.

All three of us tumbled to the sand.

Micaela simultaneously left her own feet and tackled von Nacht zu Nebel around the middle, bringing him down.

Quillpusher went on hands and knees to recover either his own rapier or mine.

I straddled Pepe (Choirboy) Pacheco Portocarrero and tried to immobilize his knife hand. But with a convulsive heave he overturned me and reversed our positions, though I still managed to retain my desperate grip on his wrist.

Von Nacht zu Nebel meanwhile – convinced his tackler was an assassin sent by the House of Fugger – had similarly overturned Micaela and was proceeding to strangle her.

It was then that the seven black-clad men from *Elizabeth Bonaventure* arrived on the scene.

It was also then that the old gypsy Anselmo with his three strapping grandsons got there, but I, with a convulsive heave like Pepe (Choirboy) Pacheco Portocarrero's earlier one, chose that moment to reverse our positions again, hindering two of Anselmo's grandsons from getting at him and leading the third to conclude that *I* was Choirboy.

Quillpusher chose the same moment to return with his, or my, rapier. Taking the gypsies for allies of Pepe (Choirboy) Pacheco Portocarrero, he attacked them with a series of awkward cuts and thrusts.

The seven black-clad men meanwhile carried the biting, kicking and screaming von Nacht zu Nebel and the dazed Micaela towards the pinnace.

Belatedly catching sight of this activity, Quillpusher, with a final wild backswing that just missed decapitating me, left off his attack and sprinted for the surf.

Anselmo's third strapping grandson, his misidentification confirmed by Quillpusher's parting rapier stroke, lifted me off Pepe (Choirboy) Pacheco Portocarrero and tumbled me on the sand nearby, freeing Choirboy long enough for him to lunge at me with his knife.

By then, their human cargo aboard, the crew of *Elizabeth Bonaventure*'s pinnace were setting off in the direction of Sir Francis Drake.

Realizing their brother's mistake, Anselmo's two other strapping grandsons dragged Pepe (Choirboy) Pacheco Portocarrero off me and subdued him with such methodical abuse that, after a months-long period in which his survival was in doubt, he changed vocations to become an angelic-looking shill (in the usual priestly vestments) at gambling dens all over Spain.

It was Anselmo who extracted the knife from the right side of my ribcage, his face indicating that he didn't like the look of the wound. I heard cloth ripping and felt deft fingers bind a bandage in place, and just before losing consciousness I saw – or thought I saw, for how could it be? – droplets of rain like beads of mercury on a glorious windblown mane of wheaten hair and, shimmering as she leaned down to kiss me on the lips, silver tears in the luminous pale blue eyes of my sister Andrea.

XXV

In Which Mnemosyne Is Forgotten

And I Receive a Letter from Home

After more Rest & Rehabilitation than anyone ought to be subjected to, I got out of bed one summer morning against doctors' advice and made my way down some staircases in the mysterious complex of buildings in the rugged mountains east of Arcos de la Frontera to the situation room, where I found Luis Blackslave and an insecure-looking young man studying one of those wildly inaccurate world maps.

'The Lost Continent of Lemuria,' Blackslave said, tracing with a pointer a great grey landmass connecting Madagascar, India and Sumatra. 'That's where you're going – if it exists.'

Lemuria. Where had I heard of it before? I remembered: the Old Woman of the East. Had she been an agent of the Nameless Service?

'And if it doesn't exist?' the insecure-looking young man asked in an apprehensive voice.

'That won't be held against you. When *I* was a brand-new agent, they sent me to find Atlantis.'

'Ah,' said the insecure-looking young man, and left.

'Where's Juan?' I asked Luis Blackslave curtly.

'Who?'

'You know who. My brother Juan the Obscure.'

'Not here. Nobody knows where he is.'

With Juan the Obscure that was easy to believe.

I jabbed an accusing finger at Blackslave. 'What steps have been taken to rescue Mnemosyne?'

'You're overwrought. First-mission blues,' Luis Blackslave diagnosed knowledgeably.

'What kind of absurd "mission" was – '

'That fellow who just left is on his way to Lemuria and *you're* talking absurd?'

' – Operation Weltschmerz anyway? To possibly – just possibly – win Quillpusher's goodwill we sacrificed Mnemosyne.'

'If you feel better calling it absurd, go ahead. Most of life is absurd, not to mention harsh and capricious. That's what my father the God-Emperor of the Western Hemisphere always said.'

'You can't just forget Mnemosyne.'

'Oh, we'll keep her on the books. You never know. But I'm not inclined to trust an agent who re-defects.'

'Re-defects? She didn't defect. She was shanghaied.'

'A marginal distinction, Amadis,' Luis Blackslave said with his habitual sang-froid, and turned back to the map. 'Since the lost continent of Atlantis *doesn't* exist,' he mused, 'couldn't it be, in a kind of diametric antipodality or antipodal dialectic, that Lemuria *does*? . . . Are you still here? You belong upstairs in bed.'

But I went to the stables and signed for a mule.

Two days later, in Pierre Papin's card shop in Sierpes Street in Sevilla, a clerk asked me, 'Help you, sir?' but his heart wasn't in it. Nobody's heart was in anything that day in Sevilla.

I shoved the clerk aside and kicked open the door to the *cercle privé*. It was like a morgue. Dice stared at one another mournfully; cards lay scattered on green baize like corpses floating face-down on a broad expanse of water. Such as the English Channel.

I had heard most of the calamitous news at the inn where I'd broken my journey. 'Unfavourable winds,' I heard, and, 'If such a storm comes, it is sent by God.' I heard place names like 'Isle of Wight' and 'Calais Roads' and 'Gravelines' and 'Firth of Forth' mangled almost beyond recognition. I heard Medina Sidonia and Parma, and I heard Lord Howard of Effingham, the Lord High Admiral, and Hawkins and, of course, Drake, pronounced Dra-que. Small, swift English men-of-war, I heard, and fireships. I heard that death-loving King Felipe had taken to his bed/bier in his room/crypt in his palace/mausoleum in the mountains north of Madrid.

The débâcle was utter, the defeat worse than the one we inflicted at Lepanto. Our Invincible Armada was no more.

The gypsy singer contemplated in lugubrious silence the guitar on his lap. The vingt-et-un dealer, who wore a little cap of gold brocade and whose slight resemblance to my niece Constanza ended at her two brown eyes, sang a few lines from canto 38 of *Orlando Furioso*, set to music for his own amusement by the painter El Greco, but a look from Pierre Papin made her stop.

I yanked the Frenchman's hat off and jammed it back on his head with the feather over his heart, Spanish style.

'Where's my brother?' I said.

'He hasn't been in for a while.'

'Tell him I need to see him. The usual place.'

I found Tomás Gutiérrez seated on a black-draped alabaster bench in the patio of his deluxe hostal. The marble and jasper fountain wept, the birds imported from South America sang dirges in the branches of the rare *Carambuco* tree. Not a single skimpily-liveried-in-green-and-gold Negress from Fernando Po was to be seen.

'Life sucks, am I right?' Tomás said, face woebegone.

I thought he was alluding to the tragic fate of the Invincible Armada, but he next said, 'The Brotherhood of the Most Holy Sacrament of Sagrario – what kind of a dumb name is that for a social club? Which I told them.'

'My brother been around?' I asked.

'What's your brother got to do with the Brotherhood? I've been black-beaned by Sevilla's most exclusive club. There goes my last chance for social standing. Even if I own the classiest deluxe hostal in all Spain, to those snobs I'm still an innkeeper.' He asked suddenly, 'Do I look like a New Christian?'

'I don't know what a New Christian looks like,' I said.

'A *converso*. Of Jewish ancestry. Like a Jew. *You* could pass for one,' Tomás said, studying my face in a way he never had before. 'Were your people New Christians?'

'It's possible,' I said.

'And I was fool enough to let you write that poem of endorsement,' Tomás groaned. 'If they connect you and I, I'll never be able to apply for membership in Sagrario again. Listen, we're all full up, no room at the inn. I mean hostal,' Tomás corrected himself, still studying my face in that new way. 'You got to understand, we get a lot of ecclesiastical trade here, being right across from the cathedral. I hear you been excommunicated. Twice.'

I told him I'd been un-excommunicated. Twice. I also told him that when my brother came to town he'd expect to find me right here at the hostal.

'Can I help it,' Tomás asked plaintively, 'if Gutiérrez is a suspicious name? Is Cervantes a suspicious name too?'

'I have no idea,' I said.

'I'll give you a room downstairs. Use the back way when you come and go, and try to go more than you come. If anybody asks are we friends, you're just a paying guest.'

The small, windowless room was emptied of its garden tools and tubs of potsoil by one of Tomás's lissom Negresses and I settled in with the lingering smell of fertilizer to wait for my brother.

Before dawn on the fifth day I woke to Juan the Obscure's voice. 'You wanted to see me.'

'Once you told me, "Shake the tree of history and see what forbidden fruit falls from its branches,"' I reminded him. 'Well, you shook, and I saw. You used me.'

'Everybody's used all the time by somebody who's used by somebody else,' said my brother. 'But if you think Operation Weltschmerz was a calculated plan to scuttle the Armada, you don't understand the purpose of the Nameless Service.'

'Tell me.'

'I already have. Knowledge. Secret knowledge. Of the sacred and the profane. For starters.'

'For starters? What else is there?'

'There's always something else. Anyway, does it really matter to you if Elizabeth keeps England or if Felipe II the Death-Loving adds her throne to his sun-never-sets empire?'

'Not really, but – '

'And besides, isn't it naïve to think *we* sank the Armada? Felipe made the usual mistake of planning this war with lessons learned in the last one. The Armada was doomed before a shot was fired. But if the English want to think secret intelligence sank the Armada, and Quillpusher provided it – a Quillpusher with a debt to us – what's to object? What is Quillpusher

311

but a philosopher's stone to transmute the base metal of English intelligence into the gold of knowledge stored by the Nameless?'

'What do you store it for?'

'Why do preachers preach? Why do warriors war or painters paint? Why do kings king? Either you have the calling or you don't. Sure, motives vary,' he acknowledged. 'Me, I always had to poke into dark corners. Luis Blackslave has to thumb his nose at authority, all authority everywhere. Mnemosyne can trust no one in this life, so she has to play her dangerous games. And you?'

'I don't know. I don't even know if I've got this calling.'

'Tell me you don't have to *know*.'

Instead, I said, 'Did you have to sacrifice Mnemosyne?'

In the darkness my brother sighed and said what could have been 'Juan-O' with, I thought, a dopy smile on his face. I couldn't see him, of course, but that's how he sounded. 'I used to love it when she called me Juan-O in those few stolen moments when . . .'

'This is Micaela we're talking about?'

'Mnemosyne, yes. Believe me, it was no part of Operation Weltschmerz to get her kidnapped. But now that it's happened, what are *you* worried about? She's a bit on the scatterbrained side, so when they debrief her it can only confuse them. Besides, she's loyal. It wouldn't surprise me if we wind up with *two* philosopher's stones in England. Or moles, as W calls them.'

'Luis Blackslave told me the Nameless Service doesn't trust re-defectors. Even if she could escape.'

'Don't believe everything Luis tells you,' said my brother. Then, after a long silence, 'And don't believe everything *I* tell you.'

Juan-O, I found myself thinking – why had she called him Juan-O? . . . *those few stolen moments* . . . A term of endearment?

If so, why did it trouble me? My brother Juan the Obscure was a lonely man.

'You could,' he said, 'do us both a favour, cut the moralizing and come back to Base Iberia. The state the world's in, there's more than enough work for you.'

Of my months of research in the archives of Base Iberia and of the assignments that followed, in Spain and abroad, I shall not write, for they have no bearing on the events in these pages. Eventually I passed through Sevilla again – leaner, bronzed, with a hairline scar on my left temple, and, possibly, wiser – and found a letter waiting for me at Pierre Papin's. It was datelined Madrid:

Esteemed *compañero* Miguel,

      Recently, having nothing better to do, I went up German Street for a brew at Taverna Isabel. This is a new place that is In with a capital I. Every out-of-work actor – and there are lots, *compañero*, times are hard – every would-be artist, every soldier on leave, every scrounger, confidence man and whore, all the usual *hoi polloi* go there. Taverna Múñoz is like a tomb, and not just on account of because my partner Rodríguez died. Which he did.

This is the thanks I get for buying out your old friend Anica, the widow, who uses the money to open up Taverna Isabel and practically put your old *compañero* out of business. But I am not complaining.

You are probably dying to know how an old established establishment like Taverna Múñoz can lose its business to a joint like Taverna Isabel where all the serving wenches have cleavage down to their navels and in a room downstairs women perform acts which your correspondent shall leave to your imagination to imagine. With donkeys even.

But that is not the only reason your old friend Anica is that big of a success. You should see her. I do not mean your old friend Anica. I mean that gorgeous little daughter of hers after which the taverna gets its name. She has got this long hair down to her navel (but no cleavage as she is only a child of 6) and she sits on the bar swinging what promise to be a good pair of legs and laughing at all the dirty jokes, plus the innuendo, which I do not think is such a hot environment for a 6-year-old child. Also, she sees too much of what is going on and your old friend Anica, who I cast no aspersions on, is not the sort of mother to send her kid to school to learn how to read and write, which genteel girls are learning to, nowadays, if they want to rise in the world, which I know you would wish for lovely little Isabel if only you could see her, so it is a shame you are down there in Sevilla instead of here in Madrid, that taverna is no kind of a place for a child of 6, believe me.

How the trouble started was, I have all this time on my hands and this big room downstairs, where you will not catch me putting on any circuses. With or without donkeys. So what I do, I decide to go into the gambling business, first clearing it with Pierre Papin who owns joints all over Spain as I am sure you know, *compañero*, being as you are in with that crowd including Juan the Obscure

313

who I am giving this letter to. Pierre says it is okay, he only wants a cut of the action, which is fair enough. But he happens to mention your niece Constanza who is the best dealer of 21 in Spain but not working these days, what a waste he says, and who am I to argue. So I go around to the tall stone house near the Gate of the Sun and see her. Well, *compañero*, on account of business being slow in the theatre she is not overflowing with orders for costumes, plus the little she does earn she gives to her aunt, your sister that calls herself Doña Magdalena Pimentel de Sotomayor, who gives it to the poor in distant places since she (Magdalena Pimentel de Sotomayor) has seen the poor in Madrid and has not liked what she saw, maybe they are not so criminally lazy elsewhere, you know that type of thinking, but I am only being honest, *compañero*.

Well anyway, your niece Constanza comes to work for me as a dealer of 21 and she is everything Pierre Papin says and we are really raking in the *maravedís*, and it looks like I will give Anica the widow Rodríguez a run for her money, when it happens. I wish, *compañero*, that I did not have to be the bearer of bad news, but what are old friends for?

                       aunt   niece

Like ~~mother~~ like ~~daughter~~ they always say, and I am getting this wild crowd of people who used to be hangers-on of Antonio Pérez and that one-eyed Princess Eboli, once the second most beautiful woman in Spain but she is getting long in the tooth, until they were arrested for murder and the Princess I hear is going nuts under house arrest in the tower of her palace whereas her lover Pérez managed to escape.

But I was telling you about this wild crowd of people which is how the trouble started.

His name is Pedro Lanuza Perellos with a couple of de's in there somewhere, the younger brother of that Viscount Rueda that got himself decapitated from his head recently for hiding Antonio Pérez. So by the time young Lanuza Perellos meets your niece Constanza and falls for those eyes of hers that you will remember she has two of them of different colours and they tumble into the nearest bed, King Felipe II the Death-Loving has confiscated all of his family's wealth in its entirety, but how is your niece to know that?

Well, *compañero*, she retains this lawyer Señor Zum who, except

314

that he keeps his nose clean, reminds me a lot of another lawyer I used to know named Picapleitos to represent her in a suit for breach of promise and of course she is too upset to deal 21 so to pay Señor Zum's fees which are not small she takes up fortune-telling (I will live to be 91, ha ha), and some people that I believe are confederates of the Rueda Lanuza Perellos clan are accusing her of witchcraft which what with those eyes of hers she is already suspected of especially in these troubled times. This is a jam Señor Zum cannot get her out of.

Your compañero from the old Algiers days,
Gabriel Múñoz

XXVI

In Which I Visit the Bench of If-Only

Andrea, who must have had her own sources, got to Madrid shortly before I did, and when she couldn't find Constanza she went straight to the law offices on San Vicente Ridge.

The former Picapleitos was turned out in conservative Señor Zum black from head to toe except for the white neck-whisk he wore instead of a ruff. His nose, which God or the Devil had pinched to a point, was dull from disuse.

'I can spare only a few moments, my dear Doña Andrea,' he said. 'A certain organization which must remain nameless has me on permanent retainer, which leaves little time for *pro bono* work.'

'*Pro bono*? You call it *pro bono*, the fees you charge?'

'To defend someone accused of witchcraft – '

'But that's why I'm here. You're encouraging her to keep on fortune-telling so she can pay you for trying to get her acquitted of the very activity that got her charged with witchcraft in the first place.'

'Your reasoning,' criticized Señor Zum, 'is circular.'

'Mine?! She didn't hire you because of the fortune-telling, she took up fortune-telling because she hired you!'

'My dear Doña Andrea, you are begging the question.'

'What question?'

'If you don't know what question, why ask it?' said Señor Zum. 'Your daughter needs me. She stands accused of witchcraft before both the Royal Council in its judiciary capacity and the Supreme and General Council of the Inquisition, in its. You see, as long as witchcraft is viewed merely as heretical belief, the Suprema can claim jurisdiction. But if witchcraft is viewed as reality rather than illusion – or *de*lusion – then the civil authorities are entitled. So the Suprema must either renounce exclusive jurisdiction or deny that witchcraft truly exists, options which stick equally in the Grand Inquisitor's craw. In my opinion, if we can encourage this jurisdictional confusion over the next few years – '

'Where is she?'

'In seclusion. Until this blows over.'

'But you said years.'

'The mills of justice grind slowly but they – '

'Tell me where she is.'

'I regret that I cannot. Privileged communication.'

'But I'm her mother.'

'I must respect my client's wishes. She is an adult woman, in her legal majority.'

Andrea's thoughts alternated between maternal anxiety and repugnance for the man in whose office she sat. She said, 'Once you suggested there didn't have to be a retainer in the . . . normal sense.' A pause. 'You said you'd represent me in any court in the land if I would . . .' Another pause, perhaps a blush. 'Now I'm just asking you to tell me where my daughter is. And in return . . .'

For a few seconds Señor Zum did nothing. Then he stood and looked down his long, dull nose (reaching for and withdrawing his hand guiltily from it), and told my sister coolly, 'I'm so sorry, Doña Andrea, but your time is up.'

Imagine how humiliated Andrea felt as she made her way past all those junior partners writing, writing, to the reception room where, as Fate or free will would have it, the son-in-law of the late Genoese businessman Lomellino or Lomelín, who had sped me from Madrid after my one disastrous visit to Liars' Walk, was pacing. A widower of about fifty, Santi Ambrosio by name, he had been waiting over a decade for various Spanish courts to confirm him as heir to his father-in-law's Spanish estate.

Meanwhile he had earned a fortune of his own in Tuscany as advisor to the last of the Medici grand dukes.

Santi Ambrosio was a comfortably padded man with a round face and a fringe of still-black hair that, along with his merry eyes, gave him the aspect of a benevolent confessor. He was known in Livorno (which under Grand Duke Francesco he had made a free port) as well as in Florence as a man of gentle temperament whose trustworthiness was equalled only by his modest demeanour.

'Madonna, are you unwell?' he asked my sister, who was dismayed that her humiliation showed.

A clerk said, 'Señor Zum will see you, Signor Ambrosio, on the matter of the Lomellino or Lomelín estate.'

Andrea turned with her hand on the outer door. 'Signor Lomellino or Lomelín? You knew him?'

'He was my father-in-law.'

Andrea smiled a wisp of a smile. 'My father used to cut his hair.'

'Then you must be the beauteous Andrea.'

'He was *such* a nice man, we all loved him.'

'The finest human being I ever knew except for my sainted wife.'

'I'm sorry,' said Andrea.

A philosophical shrug. 'She died many years ago.'

The clerk said, 'Signor Ambrosio, Señor Zum is waiting.'

'But forgive me,' Signor Ambrosio told my sister with a shy smile. 'I am Santi Ambrosio, at your service.'

And he offered his arm. And my humiliated sister took it. By then I'm sure Santi Ambrosio was drowning in those luminous pale blue eyes.

'Signor Ambrosio,' the clerk called, and might have heard the following exchange just as the outer door shut behind them:

'What troubles you, then, Doña Andrea?'

'It's a long story.'

'I have time, dear lady. All the time you'd care to give me.'

I got to San Vicente Ridge a few minutes later, dusty from the road and badly in need of a night's sleep.

Because Santi Ambrosio had walked out on his appointment, Señor Zum could squeeze me in.

'Have you been excommunicated out in the boondocks again?' he asked. 'I can't drop everything every time you have a skirmish with God. And if you're worried about how my nephew who filled in for you as a commissary has affected your reputation, I can assure you – '

If only I'd had the patience to hear him out! But my concern about Constanza was only just less than Andrea's, so I cut him off. 'Where's my niece?'

'Her whereabouts are what here in the shop we call privileged communication, as I've just told your – '

Again: If-only-I'd-etc. But no, not me.

'I'm her uncle.'

'It would not matter if you were her father. She is an adult woman, in her legal majority.'

'You don't know her.'

'Ah, but I do. Too well. Like mother like daughter.'

I recalled Gabriel Múñoz's letter with its crossed-out 'mother', which I'd taken as a mere slip of the quill-pen. But Señor Zum used words precisely, if profusely.

'Release me,' he managed, for what used to be my left hand had grabbed his neck-whisk, yanking his face within an inch of my own.

I released him. In fact, I shoved him back into his chair. 'Explain!'

'I don't do breach-of-promise work any more except as a favour to valued old clients, but there was a time when I kept a separate filing cabinet just for your sister.'

'Surely you mean my sister Magdalena.'

'Her too. But the . . . *modus operandi* was not exactly unfamiliar to your sister Andrea back when – release me!'

This time I had jerked him out of his chair with both hands and shaken him. 'You're lying.'

'*My* veracity,' Señor Zum said, 'is hardly the issue. Whether any promises were in fact breached, who can say? An attorney's clients always lie to him, and I gave up years ago trying to sort truth from falsehood – let go of me! I'll shout for help.'

I locked the door and pocketed the key.

'Where's my niece?'

His face again an inch from mine, he shouted as promised.

Came a thudding at the door, but it held.

'Where?' I said.

And Señor Zum told me, and I unlocked the door and stepped over what was left of a heavy bench and pushed my way past his assembled junior partners and out.

At about this time Santi Ambrosio and my sister Andrea were seated in a cosy private room of a *bodega* in Cava Baja, sipping vintage Cazalla wine.

'Your distress, my dear Andrea,' he said, 'is my own. Perhaps I can help. I have important friends here in Madrid.' Embarrassed, he added, 'I hope that doesn't sound crass,' then went on, 'Who is the young man?'

'Pedro Lanuza Perellos.'

'Good heavens – the brother of the viscount who was beheaded for treason? He and your child planned to marry?'

'Well . . . I wasn't here, but . . . one assumes . . . that is, it was all quite sudden.'

'I understand.' Santi Ambrosio gazed into Andrea's eyes until she looked away. He asked, 'But then this fellow's friends denounced her to the Suprema? Because she'd broken off with him?'

'Well . . . not exactly. What she'd done was sue him. For breach of promise.'

Santi Ambrosio's gentle face looked dismayed. 'She must have had dreadful advice. Suing never helps.'

Andrea winced. 'That's true. But sometimes it's all a girl can do. I myself . . . before Constanza was born . . .'

For about thirty heartbeats no more was said. Then, 'You may tell me, dear Andrea – or not, as you wish. None of that matters. From the instant I saw you in Zum's reception room, I had no past. And neither did you.'

Across the table he placed his gentle hand on hers. She let it rest there.

'Even in my youth,' he said, 'I never cut a romantic figure. And never in my wildest dreams – not that I ever had any – did I think I could be struck by the thunderbolt of love.' A shy laugh. 'But there it is. Of course, I hardly dare hope that you feel it too.'

'No, but it's no reflection on you, Santi. It's just that it can never be like that for me because . . .'

'Was it Constanza's father?' Santi Ambrosio asked. 'One thunderbolt in a lifetime, they say.'

Andrea bowed her head and did not speak.

'Whoever, it no longer matters. All I ask is that I be allowed to help you. Tell your daughter she can drop her breach-of-promise suit. Money's nothing to me.' Santi Ambrosio sighed. 'But that sounds crass too, doesn't it? Parvenu. I don't mean it that way.'

'I know you don't. But her lawsuit isn't the real problem. Young Lanuza's friends have accused her of witchcraft.'

Santi Ambrosio's gentle face hardened. 'I know how to deal with defamers and such scum.'

'But, you see, Santi . . . you see, it's possible they're not exactly defamers, because . . . because my daughter . . .'

And Andrea began to weep.

Through a steady snowfall I followed Señor Zum's directions to a hovel on the Riverbank of the Tanners near the city's southern edge. No river flowed there now, if any ever had, and hides these days were tanned elsewhere. The area had been taken over by the more reputable sort of gypsies who brokered horses, or sold second-hand what others had stolen, or told the future for those foolish enough to spurn the blessing of not knowing what tomorrow – or some April 23rd – would bring.

The door, chewed jagged at the bottom by rodents, rattled in the wind. I knocked; no answer. I pushed, and it opened on a room bare except for a rude table and chair and a pile of straw. Something dark streaked past me and outside. I flinched, then told myself lots of nice, ordinary non-witches are fond of cats, including black ones.

My niece Constanza stood near a dead fire, her wheaten hair usually so like her mother's matted and tangled, her cheeks smudged, her bare feet blue with cold.

'Hello, Uncle Miguel.'

We exchanged kisses; then she hugged me hard.

The black cat crept back in, a struggling something between its jaws. 'Benengeli,' Constanza scolded, 'must you always bring them inside?'

'If you need any money,' I began, wishing I didn't sound so avuncular. Besides, I had no money. 'You're not starving or anything?'

She sat on the straw and waved me to the chair. 'I get by. I don't charge much, but I tell a lot of fortunes.'

'Still? Are you trying to prove their case for them?'

'It's all right, Uncle Miguel. Gypsies don't believe you're a witch just because you tell fortunes.'

'Are you saying you tell *gypsies'* fortunes?'

'Uh-huh. The same as my mother did in Andalucía when you couldn't find her.' She said this matter of factly.

'Who told you that?' I was immediately sorry I'd asked: I was pretty sure what the answer would be.

'He did.'

I cast a glance, almost furtive, at the black cat.

Constanza laughed. 'Not Benengeli. He's just a cat.'

Benengeli had finished his meal. He licked his paws and stretched and looked up at me with one blue eye and one brown eye. Then he curled up in Constanza's lap and started purring. She stroked him and said, 'As for me, I always give good value when I tell the future. You see, I always tell the truth.'

'But,' I asked, 'how do you know what the truth is?' Another question I immediately regretted.

'He tells me.'

I changed the subject with, 'If you dropped your breach-of-promise suit against this Lanuza, his friends would drop their witchcraft charges.'

'Well, I won't.' Stubbornly.

'Constanza, I can see how, if you once thought you loved him, you might be reluctant – '

'*Me* love Pedro La*nuza*?'

'But if you didn't love him, why did . . . uh . . .'

'Because the money stopped coming from Uncle Juan.'

'Who?'

'Uncle Juan the Obscure. So, when the money stopped, I just thought, okay, the easiest way to get some is to seduce a man into seducing me and then sue him.'

Well, I'd asked.

'Don't look so censorious. I earned that money. It's no different from fortune-telling – I gave good value. Just like my mother always did.'

'Constanza! You don't know what you're talking about.'

'I do so. Everybody knows but you.'

Her head jerked to one side and she cried out. My hand stung; I wish I could say it was what used to be my left hand.

Benengeli leaped from her lap and yowled.

'I'm sorry,' I said. 'I'm sorry, Constanza.'

A just-perceptible nod at my apology. A waggle of her fingers to bring Benengeli back.

'What else could she do?' she asked. The whole left side of her face was red. 'My father'd put her out of business by telling everybody her seamstresses were really whores, and it was a long time before she and Tomás Gutiérrez started the Tall Stone House Players' School for Ladies, not that *that* was a success. She did what she had to do. And so have I. And in case you have any lingering doubts, *tío mío*,' she said, lips trembling, 'that makes me neither a whore *nor* a witch. I could never have gone through with . . . what I did with Lanuza . . . if I hadn't shut my eyes and imagined what it might be like with . . . with my lover who comes to me in my dreams.'

'Cide Hamete?' I asked, appalled.

'Oh no! My lover's this romantic older man whose face I never see, but I know he's handsome even though there's always something to tear at my heart, a scar maybe, or a limp or . . .'

Benengeli hissed in alarm and darted out through the door.

'Aunt Magdalena says I *am* a witch, but who cares, she's not really my aunt, is she. No more than you're my uncle.'

She turned away, but not before I saw tears gleaming on her cheeks. I held her, the most avuncular embrace I could manage, and smoothed that tangled mane of wheaten hair. 'Sometimes,' I said, 'when the world seems to be closing in on all sides, the best thing is to get away. Just leave where you are and let someone else worry about things. Go to work for Pierre Papin, maybe.'

She drew a ragged breath against my shoulder. 'What kind of work,' she asked, 'could *you* do for Pierre Papin?'

'I meant you.'

But could I blame her for thinking I meant me? I could hardly expect her to see me as I wished I was – someone who took charge, a righter of wrongs, another Amadis of Gaul. Still, I felt a pang.

'No,' I said lightly, 'I don't see myself dealing vingt-et-un in a little gold brocade cap.'

I tilted Constanza's face up to mine and coaxed a smile from her. But as I tried to comfort my wayward non-niece and digest what I'd learned today, my world did seem to be closing in on all sides.

It would be some time yet before I understood that living was a lot like telling stories – life and fiction two different versions of some greater reality, perhaps. And if there were no greater reality? Then life and fiction became even more important, didn't they? You had to live, or write, one event at a time, and try your best, and hope that with luck it would all come out right.

'. . . not my uncle,' Constanza was saying. 'At first it was as though you'd died. Then I tried to tell myself you could still be. My uncle. Even if you weren't. Only I was wrong, because I remembered how I felt when . . . when . . .'

She turned away again. Went to the door. Reported it was snowing harder. Came back. Stared at the dead ashes. Returned to the door. So I went there too and stood behind her in avuncular silence and, seeing the goose flesh on her slender arms, removed my cloak and draped it over her.

'I remembered how I felt,' she said, looking through the dusk at the falling snow in a world unpeopled except for me and this fey child who wasn't a child, this niece who wasn't my niece, who now said a third time, 'I remembered how I felt,' and her voice wavered, 'the day you got married. That's how I knew you couldn't be. My uncle.'

Well, what can I tell you? Sometimes when I'm writing – when it's going really well, how's that for paradoxical? – I'll want a character to do a simple thing like, say, go a few paces along a snow-covered road, but it refuses. Just digs in its heels and won't budge. Or sometimes it does the opposite of what I want. Or sometimes a third thing, an entirely unexpected thing right off someone else's Bench of If-Only – like Constanza flinging her arms around me and kissing me, hard, her mouth opening under my mouth while I stood there foolishly, a character in a story I would never write, not knowing what to do until my treacherous body decided for itself, just like a character coming alive under my quill-pen, and I could feel the goose flesh on her arms as I pulled her against me, and the enormity of this particular moment of reality, if there was such a thing, hit me, and the next moment I tried to break away but she clung, and it just might have looked, to anybody who chanced upon the scene, as if she were trying to break away from me – a young female helpless in the clutches of an older male – it just might have looked that way, in the dusk in the doorway where we turned in a slow dance of desire that one of us wanted to end; it *did* look that way to my sister Andrea who wasn't my sister standing in the snow beside a balding man, outrage on her beautiful face and a gentle smile freezing on his.

We broke apart and Constanza cried, 'It isn't what it looks like, it isn't what you think.' Which could have sounded, couldn't it, like her way of saying this latest indiscretion wasn't *her* indiscretion when she was really trying to say I was quite blameless?

And I? Anything I said would be wrong, so I said nothing. Didn't even stutter. Just stood there looking at them look at me.

And then my sister Andrea entered the space between me and her sobbing daughter.

And I put my head down and brushed past Santi Ambrosio and walked away through the falling snow.

If this were only fiction, I could write here that they were married on April 23rd. But this is the story of my death and life, in which fiction and that lesser truth, history, from time to time form a seamless whole. And truth constrains me to say the wedding took place on a blustery day earlier in the month.

In the crowd outside the church I spotted Juan Rufo.

'Well,' he said, stroking his grey-flecked, twin-pointed beard, 'we are none of us getting any younger.'

Had he always been so sententious? Or was it my mood?

A coach pulled up, and there were the usual oohs and ahs as my sister Andrea who wasn't my sister alighted, gowned in ivory, her eyes luminous through her veil as, with that numinous walk of hers, she entered the church.

'A man can't go on forever,' said Juan Rufo, 'living on his own private Bench of If-Only, can he?'

It took me a while to understand he meant himself.

'Besides, *she* couldn't go on forever, though for a time she did age rather well. Like good wine. Ha ha ha.'

What was this fatuous greying fool talking about? Andrea looked twenty-two, the way she always did, the way she always would. She didn't get older like other people.

'Your sister seems to have done very well for herself,' Juan Rufo said. 'I salute her. And I thank her for freeing me. There's a lass I have my eye on, just fifteen, connected to the Chinchóns, and I don't have to tell you *they* – '

I walked rudely away and, while my sister who wasn't my sister became Doña Andrea de Cervantes Saavedra de Ambrosio, I stood among strangers and heard snatches of conversation.

'. . . chance of a shower? You know – "Happy the bride the rain falls on." '

'Hmph! Raindrops won't bring *her* any babies. She's long past that.'

'. . . mystery man in her past, so they say. It's why she never married.'

'. . . so well preserved, though, she could pass for forty. On a good day.'

My numinous, luminous sister Andrea? Where were their eyes?

The bridal couple stood a moment in the church door, comfortably padded Santi Ambrosio looking almost tall in his white ruff and well-tailored doublet and short cape, and my sister Andrea who wasn't my sister looking regal in an even larger ruff and an ivory silk gown with wide velvet bands of jewel embroidery, her glorious mane of wheaten hair upswept in a cloud of veiling held by a tiara studded with . . . And why do I go on at such length when ordinarily, if you asked me what someone I'd seen five minutes ago was wearing, I couldn't have told you? Why? Because the ceremony was over, my sister was married now and, her veil thrown back, moving through the crowd towards the coach that would take the couple on their honeymoon, and I, after my stalling scrutiny of their wedding finery, had finally to look at her, to look at my sister, who was waving to the well-wishers in that happy way of brides, in the noonday sunlight that nestled those undeniably pale blue but hardly luminous (were they, in fact, washed-out?) eyes more deeply into their crowsfeet and etched more firmly the lines around her smiling mouth as she passed, not seeing me, her walk endearingly self-conscious as she clung to her groom's arm, a rather lithe and long-striding walk despite the cumbersome gown, but hardly what you could call numinous; who ever heard of a numinous walk anyway?

Seeing her like that, seeing my older sister Andrea who wasn't my sister, seeing her truly as she looked on her wedding day (had it been April 23rd, would I have fallen down dead?), I turned and pushed through the crowd and ran to the Gate of the Moors and the one place I had to go.

The great dead oak spread its branches over the stone bench where old men in black passed a wineskin from withered hand to withered hand, each toothless mouth awaiting its turn to receive the purple stream before, consecrated, it would emit its ritual lament.

'. . . *still would've owned the shop, if only . . .*'

'. . . *never run off with that sweet-talking Sevillano, if only . . .*'

I edged closer, and one of the men on the bench said, 'Ain't a day over fifty, what's *he* doing here?' and another said, 'Too young for a codger, or even a galoot,' and another said, 'Well, you never know, old comes to some before others,' and another said, 'If you need the bench, you need the bench,' and the wineskin returned on its rounds, and I was thirsty from running so I edged closer still, no intention of staying, just a quick reviving squirt of wine and I'd be off; I wasn't fifty or even forty-five, I had my whole life ahead of me and no place in it for a dead oak tree girdled by a stone (if comfortable-looking) bench on which, now, two ancient fellows moved apart to make room and a withered hand held out the wineskin just as I heard the clip-clop of hooves and saw my wife Catalina leading two *burros*, and she said, 'You're coming home with me,' and, mounting, I turned my back on the Bench of If-Only.

But I had no home.

Catalina set me to work whitewashing the already white walls, a job that had to be done after a death in the house. Her mother had died, as it turned out intestate, but Catalina was sure there would be no problem about the small house, the rocky vineyards and olive groves, the few head of livestock, for she was not one to believe what everyone said, that her eighteen-year-old brother Fernando was an obnoxious little shit, not even after he hired a lawyer to protect him from the sister who felt her fair share was half.

At first I thought it was this dispute with her obnoxious little shit of a brother that kept my wife Catalina from our nuptial bed. Then I thought it was reaction to her mother's death, rather like my own to my father's. Then I noticed Catalina had a habit of disappearing for hours on end, which would have made a more suspicious man than me suspicious, but I knew it wasn't anything like that because if it was, Catalina being Catalina, she would have told me.

One day a fortnight after Andrea's wedding we were discussing her brother and repairing the barn door a neighbour's bull had demolished trying to get at the milk cow. It happened to be April 23rd. I was ready for anything.

I said, 'I feel the same about lawyers as you. More, even. But you ought to get one.'

'To set against Fernando? I'm his big sister and I have to look out for him.'

'You *bet* you do,' I said.

'I'll be all right.'

I spat a nail, set my hammer aside, and took her guileless, trusting face in my hands. I kissed her.

'Please, Miguel. You mustn't do that.'

'Why not?'

'I was beginning to wonder if you'd ever ask. I thought maybe you didn't want to fuck.'

Catalina, you'll remember, called a thing what it was.

'I'm asking. Right now,' I said, and grabbed for her.

She fended me off. 'I'm glad you want to. A woman likes to feel wanted. But . . .'

'But?'

She looked at my face, which was over hers because she lay on her back on a hayrick where I had shoved her.

'Off,' she said. 'Get off and go and see my uncle.'

Padre Juan was sitting in the tiny vestry of the parish church mending the hem of his soutane.

He said, 'That obnoxious little shit Fernando says he just saw you and his sister Catalina in the barn well on your way to . . . ah, fornicating.'

'Fornicating? She's my wife.'

'Dear me,' said Padre Juan. 'Hasn't she told you? Why do you think she wears rough fabrics, fustian and such, all the time? Next to her skin.'

I mentioned poverty, and her mother's estate (such as it was) being tied up by that obnoxious little shit Fernando.

Padre Juan said, 'Today, the twenty-third of April, is the final day of her novitiate. It is typical of Sister Catalina to be hard at work on the family property instead of here in church praying, but she is, for all that, no less Sister Catalina of the Tertiary Order of St Francis. The vows she took are strict, my son. *Not*, I hasten to add, that you must part. The Order encourages its members, many of whom are married, to live with their husbands as sister and brother.'

'How soon can she get released from these vows?'

'I fear, my son, in the eyes of the Church such vows are as unbreakable as the holy sacrament of marriage. They *are* a kind of marriage. You will learn with God's help, I am sure, that there are satisfactions in sibling love.'

I found Catalina on the patio carding wool and asked, as reasonably as possible under the circumstances, 'Why the hell did you invite me home to this one-horse hayseed town if you'd become a virtual nun, for Christ's sake?'

Her answer seemed an almost Cide-Hametesque *non sequitur*. 'My friend Juana's broken off with her Hondaro and she likes sex more than any woman I know except me.'

'Then if you're so goddamn crazy about sex, what in God's creation made you take vows of celibacy?'

'You think *I* like it, now that you're home a whole man again?'

'No, but – '

'You think *I* liked it when your Señor Machismo hung down like a hound's tongue on a hot day no matter what I tried?'

'No, but – '

'You think *I* liked it after you went south and every time any man between fifteen and fifty came near me I wanted to grab him because, in my all-too-short married life, I found I *liked* fucking?'

'No, but – '

'No buts! It was driving me crazy. The only thing I could do was take the habit. How was I to know you'd get better? Or even come back? At least it stopped me from committing adultery. Juana says she's got a real talent for around-the-world.'

'Catalina! You're my wife, not my procuress.'

'I just want you to be happy. And you don't have to worry about me. I have my animals.'

'Catalina!' I shouted again.

'I mean to take care of. Strays.'

As if on cue, one of the household's three almost-wolf-sized dogs barked and snarled outside the door.

Her obnoxious little shit of a brother Fernando came in waving a piece of paper.

'The first thing that goes are those filthy hounds. The place is mine – lock, stock and barrel. The second thing that goes, since you don't need a husband any longer, sister dear, is this fellow who calls himself a poet.'

Catalina snatched the paper and read it.

'Lock, stock and barrel,' she said.

'The third thing that goes,' shitty little Fernando told her, 'is you. The big sister! Always ordering me around! Married herself a crippled wreck of a war veteran who thinks he's another Lope de Vega to feed her literary pretensions, and now she's married God and St Francis too to satisfy her spiritual ones. You're just a – '

She slapped his face. He slapped hers.

I knocked him down.

There was more barking at the door and Juana the widow Laínez came in, dressed seductively in a lot of décolletage. She saw what was to be seen and said, 'I like a masterful man.' Silence. She tried, 'I've got this real talent for . . . but surely Catalina must have mentioned . . .' but my wife gave a decisive negative headshake, and Juana the widow Laínez shrugged and went out, and I heard a horse galloping off. I wouldn't see Juana the widow Laínez for more than a dozen years, not until Lord Howard of Effingham arrived in Valladolid (once more Spain's capital, Madrid having been temporarily tossed on to the rubbish-heap of history with such as Nineveh, Babylon and Lemuria) to ratify the treaty between England and Spain outlawing war in our time.

Shitty little Fernando got to his feet and pointed an imperious finger doorwards. 'Before nightfall,' he said.

Later, while she was packing her stray animals, I asked my wife Catalina, 'Have you anywhere to go? There's lots of room at the tall stone house near the Gate of the Sun.'

'You mean we could live with your family?'

'I mean you could. There's no place for me there.'

'Just because you tried to fuck Constanza? What's so terrible? She's not actually your niece and she's had a thing for you ever since I've known her.'

'I didn't try to – '

'Really, and her such a beauty? It'd be perfectly normal. Might even straighten her out. That Lanuza business must have been a turn-off. Are you sure your family won't take you in?'

'I wouldn't want them to. Since I got back from Algiers I've done everything wrong. Maybe I don't understand how to deal with people any more unless I'm dragging leg irons around and plotting escape. Maybe trying to be a hero isn't good training for living in the real world.'

'What's so hot about the real world? In the real world I've just been dispossessed by my shitty little brother. The world is what you make it, they say. No more fucking for me, so I guess I didn't make it what I wanted. And you think *you're* a failure?'

'What I think is, I have to go away.'

'Where?'

'Away. I don't know where.'

Forty-eight hours later our rented galley passed through the Gate of the Sun. Catalina's three almost-wolf-sized dogs came barking along behind, and the cages of birds and rabbits and fieldmice in various stages of recovery from various mishaps swayed with the swaying of the wagon.

'You sure you won't come, just as far as the door? Your family will want to see you.'

'No they won't.'

'Miguel, you're wrong. Even that Manchega mother-in-law of mine has a soft spot for you. I never met a woman yet that didn't — except maybe Magdalena. But you know Magdalena when it comes to men.'

When she saw I wouldn't change my mind, Catalina reined up and I got out.

'Well, if you feel . . . You wouldn't be going off to war?'

For the first time in I don't remember how long, I thought of my brother Rodrigo; I could see the rapt look on his freckled face as his lips formed the word glory.

I said nothing, just waited alongside the galley. In a hurry to go, I stood without moving.

'Why is it that when a man's life gets out of hand he starts right in thinking of war?'

I denied I was thinking in that direction.

'The last time you went to war you spent five years in Algiers a slave of that pure-vert dey.'

I almost smiled. 'Pervert.'

'Whatever.' She leaned down from the galley to kiss me. 'I'm not even permitted to do *this*,' she said.

Her sturdy arms held me. She didn't want to let go and for a few moments neither did I. But then I felt the pull of the old road again, like an invisible hand, the hand of my dead father maybe.

She said, 'Once when you were away Juana and I went to the theatre. Of the Prince? We saw a play by Lope de Vega.'

'Like it?'

'Well, I'd never seen a play before. I liked it. But . . . I mean, this Lope sailed with the Invincible Armada and it's said his beloved brother died in his arms on the deck of a warship. So, I mean to say,' groped Catalina, 'if he suffered like that and he's such a great playwriter he should be able to make a person . . . feel things more. *You* could, Miguel. If you wanted to. So why are you going off to war instead?'

'*I* didn't say I was going off to war, you did.'

'Well, while we're at it, you've been everywhere and seen almost everything, so tell me – why did God let those English sink the Invincible Armada, if we're in the right and they're in the wrong?'

'What makes you think we're in the right?'

'What? Because we're here and we're us and they're there and they're them,' said Catalina.

'To them,' I said gently, 'it's the other way around.'

'I never thought of that.' Catalina looked pensive. 'Then there's no reason for you, there's no reason for anybody, ever to go to war again, is there?'

Looking at me, she took a turn of the reins around her strong hands.

I reached up to touch her cheek, but she cried what sounded like 'Grawr!' and the galley lurched forward.

It was late afternoon when my sister Andrea saw the galley pull up. She raced outside and embraced Catalina.

'Where is he?'

'He got off near the palace. He's leaving. Leaving Spain, he said. I think he's going off to war.'

Andrea turned and ran towards the palace. She plunged into the crowd starting their evening *paseo* in the shadow of the bluff. She pushed past people, looked at faces, called my name. But it was no use. The shadows under the bluff deepened, the moon brightened, the first stars came out, faces blurred.

I might have seen Andrea as I stood on the edge of the crowd and watched the *paseo*, but how would I know if I no longer knew what my sister who wasn't my sister looked like?

And what if not only my vision of Andrea was imperfect (but how can perfection be imperfect)? What if all these people in the ambulatory crowd, searching for a returned glance, for a confirmation of the uniqueness of themselves – what if they bore no resemblance to what I in my faulty way of seeing (who ever heard of a numinous walk?) thought they looked like?

Would it matter? Would the world be any less, or more?

Darkness fell, wind rose, dust swirled through deserted streets. I walked, aimlessly I thought, but not quite to my surprise I saw ahead the tall stone house near the Gate of the Sun, and I wondered what would happen if I went in.

Would Constanza have told them the truth about that night on the Riverbank of the Tanners?

Would Andrea tell me that the truth about her birth had come when she was least ready for it, a truth that might have meant a new life when she had (we all had) prepared for a death? Would she then ask, what difference can this truth make, you were my brother for so long that you are my brother still and you have a wife, here with me now, here in your place, Miguel? Oh, Miguel, where are you going?

But none of this was said because I did not go in.

I walked then to German Street, where my old friend Gabriel Múñoz might have said, 'Nobody comes to Taverna Múñoz any more,' as he poured two cups of red. 'They all go to Taverna Isabel where the proprietor is your old girlfriend Ana Villafranca who has this real doll of a daughter, you have really got to see her.'

And I might have said, curtly, 'Where's Juan-O?'

'Who? I do not know any Juan-O.'

'My brother Juan the Obscure. If you see him, tell him I'm looking for him.'

But I didn't go into the taverna either, so none of this was said.

I walked. Just walked until I saw near the Gate of the Moors in the moonlight the Bench of If-Only, deserted now so I could linger and remember the night I ran through the downpour with Andrea who doesn't look like Andrea any more to find my father, that dwindled, kismeted man huddled on the plank bench that girdles three sides of the large elm that, when Catalina found me there not long ago, I thought was an oak, a dead oak tree, and the bench not wood planking but stone. Was my vision defective? Or was my memory just playing tricks on me? My memory which now brings my father back to life to swing his rusty old sword at demons only he can see. My father's eyes look like two black holes in his face, and for a heartbreaking instant I can see him striding along a dusty road in Andalucia, myself half running at his side as we chase the horizon, and I say, 'Papá, have you forgotten, first thing in the morning we're going on the old road again,' but he takes another wild two-handed swing with his rusty old sword. 'Papá,' I say, 'know where we're going?' And my father whispers, praying as hard as he can for what can never be, 'On the old road again,' and I tell him, 'We're going to Flanders, to the Low Countries to find Rodrigo,' and my father's head jerks up and he springs to his feet almost like a young man, raising the rusty sword overhead, and lightning descends and the sword clangs and . . .

And I hear behind me what sounds like the clink of coins in a bag. Whirling, I expect to see Juan the Obscure standing in the moonlight watching me. But it's Luis Blackslave, who tosses the bag of coins and a letter negligently in my direction and says with that sang-froid of his, 'You'll need these to get where you're going.'

XXVII

On the Old Road Again

Crossing France I wore out three *burros*, then numerous pairs of boots; my feet blistered, then callused hard as horn; an incipient paunch, I'm glad to say, melted away.

I even got the urge to write again one morning when I woke from a dream, a rather graphic dream of an erotic encounter with a woman.

Not Andrea. I wouldn't admit to myself who she was.

Lighting a candle a safe distance from my straw pallet, I wrote a love poem:

Adrift on the Sea of Love

A sailor on the sea of love,
Its depthless depths I roam
Without a hope I'll ever reach
A port to call my home.

A star I follow, spied afar,
More splendid and more beauteous
Than guided him for love of whom
Fair Dido died, Aeneas.

I do not know where I must go
But choose a random bearing.
To find her is my soul's sole care,
For all else I'm uncaring.

Constraints, impertinently coy,
Modesty meant to pique,
Are clouds behind which she obscures
What I most frankly seek.

O bright unwinking amber light
In whose flame I pale!
If you hide yourself from me
Then death shall close my tale.

Yes, well. I know. I wasn't put on this planet to be a poet – but considering all those years when I'd written nothing, *Adrift* didn't entirely displease me.

Leaving the inn that morning I chanced upon a Sicilian *giravolo* or wandering healer, a specialist in snakebite *en route* from a disastrous season in Ireland to Madrid where, he claimed, he had connections at court. He agree to deliver my little effort to the player-manager Gaspar de Porres who, I hoped, might find a spot for it in some love-poem-deficient comedy.

I would think no more of it until, on my return to Spain in 1594, I was flabbergasted to hear . . .

But first, the Netherlands.

At sunset on one of those late November days so cold the road rang like iron under my boots, I reached Spa. The town had lately become a health resort famous for its restorative waters; it had also become a Spanish army replacement depot.

I found the personnel office in the former town hall.

'I'm looking for Second Lieutenant Rodrigo de Cervantes,' I told one of those big, burly, health-exuding noncoms who always seem to get desk jobs.

'Why?'

'He's my kid brother. The last we heard, he was in combat somewhere east of Amsterdam and north of Deventer.'

'Lieutenant Cervantes is your *younger* brother?'

'That's right. Know where he is?'

'Come on, fellow. This is a security area, especially now. You got any ID?'

'No, but I know whose brother I am.'

'You have nothing to prove who you are? There's nothing anywhere in the world to confirm your identity?' This was hardly a question. It was, almost, an accusation.

I mulled it over. It was unsettling. 'Well, no. But p-people know me. Quite a few people.'

'They know who you *claim* to be. But babies are switched at birth. A blow to the head can cause amnesia. People assume new identities to escape retribution for nefarious crimes. So don't stand there and tell me who you are.'

'My brother could identify me,' I suggested hopefully.

'There's a war on, you know. We can't be too careful. Why don't you tell me about your brother – like the last time you saw him or something.'

'It was in Algiers,' I said. 'We were p-prisoners.'

'Try to be a little more specific.'

I tried. 'I tried to choke him to death.'

The health-exuding noncom shot to his feet and bellowed, 'Drempel!' and a servile little man with prognathic jaws hurried in tugging his forelock. I thought I was for it, but at a word from the noncom, Drempel tugged his forelock at me too.

Drempel escorted me through the dusk to what might have been a whorehouse. An ornate sign said *Pap's Place*. As he left me at the door I did not see the look of distaste on the little man's face. 'Consensual crimes,' I did not hear him mutter, 'in that they imply free will in a world where all, *all* is preordained, are the worst crimes of all. Among the Elect. . .' And brushing back the servile forelock he so loathed, Drempel contemplated the conversion that would change so many lives.

Inside, I saw baize the young green of a pasture after spring rain, crisp new playing cards with faces eager to be smudged, backgammon boards bright as mirrors reflecting the light of candles strategically deployed to help Pierre Papin's experienced dealers fleece parrots *en route* to or from the battlefront.

Pierre Papin himself, for once, was wearing the ostrich plume on the Spanish side of his hat.

'A patriotic gesture,' he explained.

'What are you doing in Spa?' I asked.

'Those who are about to die need diversion more than they need ducats,' he explained.

I told him I was looking for my brother.

'I know. Your briefing starts right after I close shop at dawn. Without the right cover you'll never make it through enemy territory alive.'

This didn't surprise me. The letter Luis Blackslave had tossed me at the Bench of If-Only had alluded to a briefing to be set up by one 'Pap', who figured to be Pierre Papin. The letter was obscure, but reading between the lines (with Juan-O this was often easier than reading the lines themselves) I gathered the death of the Abbot was imminent, as it had been for years, and the leading contenders for the new Innominate of the Nameless were my brother and a mysterious Persian named (code-named?) Bādindjan rumoured to have magic powers; also, Juan-O was counting on me to help him get elected.

But if precedent held, the moribund Abbot would hang on a while longer, and I wanted to see Rodrigo. Indeed, by now I'd convinced myself I'd promised our dying father I would.

'Actually, it's my brother Rodrigo I'm looking for,' I said.

'Well, they didn't tell me that, but need-to-know is all I ever *want* to know,' said Pierre Papin, and I followed him into the *cercle privé*.

At the vingt-et-un table a lone officer stood facing the young dealer who wore on her blonde hair a little cap of gold brocade and whose resemblance to my niece Constanza ended at her two brown eyes. She was singing in a thin, true voice a few snatches of *The Ballad of Sir Philip Sidney* (who since his death in combat six years ago had become a beau idéal to both sides). The officer ran a hand through his shock of white hair and studied his two cards.

'Hit me,' he said, and downed the contents of a goblet.

'Brandy-wine,' said Pierre Papin. 'Drinks it every night all night long. There's no tomorrow.'

'". . . of that kidney,"' sang the blonde dealer nervously and flipped over a card: a five.

'Bust,' said the white-haired officer indifferently.

'Why must you always draw to seventeen?' the blonde scolded him.

'Well, that cleans me out,' he said, turning from the table to look for the first time in my direction.

335

Under that shock of white hair (no vestige of any blood-red streak) he had the haunted eyes of my father during his Inquisition days. In fact, except for the tic in his gaunt left cheek, he could have been my father in his early dwindling period. He even had a tracery of fine wrinkles that might, in time, become a wizened monkey face.

'Miguel!' he cried.

'R-Rodrigo?'

We embraced, pounded backs, held each other off at arm's length to look, embraced again. The blonde vingt-et-un dealer bit her lip and dabbed her eyes. And all the while I kept remembering my freckle-faced kid brother who used to play soldiers. His freckles had all become liver spots.

'You haven't changed a bit,' he said. I stuttered a 'you too' and pounded his back again.

He picked up a full bottle of brandy-wine and took me to his billet, a fifteen-room villa not far from Spa's town hall.

'A far cry from that coffin under the eaves in Naples, eh?' he said, and began, old-soldier-fashion, to reminisce about our now-halcyon-seeming youth.

'Remember how ill you were at The Naval? Jesus! I had to hoist you into that skiff, which didn't stop you winning a medal for bravery,' said my brother halcyonly. 'Remember that Zoraida with the unbelievably long legs who trance danced me back from the edge of the grave?'

I did not tell him Zoraida had died in my arms.

'Remember her uncle Suleiman Sa'adah Sometimes Erroneously Called the Wise but nobody could ever figure out why? Remember El Dorador who always said "I hear and obey" and always . . . uh, maybe we'd better skip that one?'

I said it didn't matter, no hard feelings.

'Remember that spunky kid Michele with those dangerous games of his – what's so funny?'

'Micaela,' I said. 'She was a girl.'

'No! So *that* explains the classic callipygean curve. I used to wonder why it excited me so. Cynical kid, always saying . . . what was it?'

' "Trust no one in this life," ' I quoted.

'*Now* what's funny?'

'You mean why am I smiling? Thinking about Micaela always makes me smile. Not just me, Juan-O too.'

'Juan-O? Who's Juan-O?'

'Our brother. Juan the Obscure.'

'Oh. He knows Micaela? But he wasn't in Algiers. Was he?'

'He met her later. After all of us went to work for the Abbot – her, me, Juan-O, Luis Blackslave – '

'The Abbot?' This obviously meant nothing to Rodrigo.

Caught up in the heady role of insider, I persisted, 'Onofre Exarque?'

'Hey, I remember Exarque! I paid him good money to rescue you but . . .'

'Never mind, he's in a different line of work nowadays. What kind of work are *you* doing? Combat days over?'

'Very Important People,' said my brother Rodrigo. 'I'm in Very Important People. A soft assignment usually. But this week, Jesus! The *generalísimo* himself, the Duke of Parma's coming to Spa to recuperate. I've been putting in sixteen-hour days and – '

'And you hardly have time for me any more.' This was the blonde vingt-et-un dealer, who came in with a new bottle of brandy-wine. Good timing: my brother had emptied, with scant help from me, the one he'd brought along from Pap's Place.

'You staying?' he asked her.

'I wish. But I've got to get back. Later?' She kissed his cheek and was gone.

'Well, you know, wartime,' Rodrigo told me, and blushed. It made him look almost young.

He uncorked the brandy-wine and saluted me with the bottle and the single word 'Glory!' Then he said, softer, 'Jesus, how I used to sing and dance to that tune. But what happens to glory when . . . I don't know, the things I've seen . . .' in a bewildered voice, my brother who had gone from youth to premature old age in a blink of missed maturity, my brother who all his life had followed orders without once asking why, his free will buried on how many battlefields, drowned in how many bottles of brandy-wine?

'The things I've seen,' he said again. 'I tell myself it's the Others. It always is, isn't it?' he pleaded. 'It's always the Others who commit the atrocities, the horrors, only . . . only . . . aren't we the *Others*' Others?' he asked, and tic went his cheek, and the reminiscing he began then was something else entirely.

Meanwhile the blonde vingt-et-un dealer, returning through the night to Pap's Place, was almost run down by a black-clad rider on a black stallion. Though a starveling husk of a man, he was an expert horseman and reined

337

up inches from the blonde. She screamed. Dismounting, the horseman removed black travelling gloves and let the wind that always seemed to spring up at such times spread his black cape like the wings of a bat. As the blonde entered the spill of light from the door, he grasped her arm with one small, neat, pink hand. His face, expressionless except for the tormented eyes of a man gripped by an implacable obsession, quite possibly sexual, made her shudder.

'Were you in the casino in Alcalá de Henares,' he asked, 'in either April of 1562 or October of 1564?'

His hand tightened; pain and fear left her mute.

'But you're too young, aren't you,' he said. 'Could it have been an older sister? Your mother? Alcalá – well?'

'My family's from Córdoba,' the blonde vingt-et-un dealer managed. 'They don't travel much.'

'It's a long way,' the black-clad stranger accused her, 'from Córdoba to Spa.'

'Pierre Papin always brings me to the grand opening of his latest casino.'

Pierre Papin. He rolled the name around in his mouth like a wine taster trying to identify a vintage. Pierre Papin, he tasted, and the lingering finish of the first name on his palate, the pronounced nose of the second, stirred something in the cellars of his memory.

A mad gleam touched his obsessed eyes. This encounter had to be more than mere chance. His number-two priority had brought him to Spa – and had landed him squarely on the trail of number one.

'This Pierre Papin,' he asked the blonde vingt-et-un dealer, 'is he here in this whorehouse? Is that what you are?' He backed away. The French pox had changed, perhaps forever, relations between the sexes, not that he had any.

'It's a casino, I told you. I'm a dealer.'

In the *cercle privé*, the man in black told Pierre Papin, 'Your dealer here reminds me of a woman I met in Alcalá on the night of 19 April 1562 or on a night in October 1564.'

'Well, which was it?' the Frenchman asked.

'You should know I seek a murderess,' said the stranger. 'Were *you* in Alcalá de Henares on either of those nights?'

'It was one of my first establishments in Spain,' said Pierre Papin, not unsentimentally. 'I don't recall any murderesses. Care to try your luck at vingt-et-un? Hundred points? Backgammon? *Primera*?'

'I never gamble,' said the black-clad stranger. 'Only fools – backgammon!' he rasped. 'She was losing recklessly at backgammon! She was with a young man . . . a student . . .' He collapsed into a chair. His gaunt face, normally abnormally pale, had gone the colour of a wall recently whitewashed to honour the dead. 'He called her . . .'

But the name eluded him. Curses! So close, yet it would not come.

'A hundred joints like mine all over Spain, and every night a hundred blondes losing recklessly at backgammon,' said Pierre Papin. 'Lots of them come with students. Students have money. You expect me to remember her?'

'He made good her losses. He called her . . .'

The name continued to elude him. As it would until after I'd written the first part of *Don Quixote*; as it would until Lord Howard of Effingham came to Spain to ratify the peace treaty; as it would until an inept gentleman bullfighter died under mysterious circumstances unrelated to the taurine art . . .

But for the first time Pedro de Isunza was sure he would find her.

Meanwhile he had his number-two priority to attend to – Alexander Farnese, Duke of Parma, the only survivor of the three gilded youths, Fortune's favourites, who had come to the University of Alcalá to study early in 1562.

Damn it all, he *knew* it was 1562!

Some time after midnight my brother passed out. I'd just hauled him up to bed when I heard light footsteps on the stairs. The blonde vingt-et-un dealer came in.

'Did he tell you about the old woman, and how they slit her grandson's throat and made her drink a cup of his blood still steaming in the cold?'

'Yes,' I said.

'Did he tell you how they hung a deserter over a fire and slowly roasted him alive?'

'Yes,' I said.

'And how they tied fifty prisoners in pairs back to back and sewed them into sacks and threw them into the Ijssel and how desperately those *sacks* tried to stay afloat?'

'Yes.'

'And how – '

'Yes.'

'And how it's always the Others who do it, only . . .'

'Yes,' I said. 'He's got to get out of the army.'

'Out? He couldn't live. The army's all he knows.'

339

'I could get him work with an international organization that functions along roughly military lines, but no combat.'

'But combat's what he's good at, combat and discipline. He's the most decorated soldier in the Spanish Netherlands, you know. He's a fine company commander – as long as orders come down from above. He needs someone to tell him *what* to do before he can work out *how*. He couldn't make a real decision if his life depended on it.'

She kissed my sleeping brother's forehead. 'Plus, in combat he has no time to dwell on what's tearing him apart. Combat's better than killing himself slowly, a bottle at a time. Brandy-wine – burnt wine. It's burning his insides out. But give him an enemy stronghold to take, and he'll be chasing "glory" again. When he has to die, let it be like that.'

'Glory?' I said. 'Glory's like a flag or a sermon. It's what they give us to fight their wars for them.'

'But don't you see, even if this glory of his is only a dream, he's lucky. At least he *has* a dream. And I'm lucky too. Because when he goes into battle he takes another dream with him, a dream of me, and in it I'm not Aldonza the dumb blonde vingt-et-un dealer, I'm a fabulous beauty, elegant, mysterious even, like that Princess Eboli with her eye-patch. Me! Don't you see? Your brother didn't ask to be born and he doesn't like having to die, but at least he has this dream to face death *with*.'

I wanted to tell her that if a man did the things he had it in him to do, then all life was like a dream, a good dream, and death held no terror for him, but because I had done none of those things myself, and maybe never would, I said nothing.

'So you're Lieutenant Uh! Wounded eleven times! Eleven citations for valour! A splendid example of the younger officers' – here Alexander Farnese, Duke of Parma, must have regarded dubiously my brother's raddled face – 'pumping new blood into the glorious Spanish Army of the Netherlands. What is your current assignment, Lieutenant Uh?'

'You are, Your Grace,' said my brother, and an aide whispered, 'His name's Cervantes, Your Grace,' as snow began to fall on the parade ground and on His Grace, resplendent in the uniform of a *generalísimo*.

In his swarthy face the Duke of Parma's eyes burned feverishly. Parma was recovering (it was hoped) from a roundball wound in the left thigh. He was also suffering from the flux. His state of general exhaustion (or *generalísimo* exhaustion, ha ha ha, said the Lord Mayor of Spa, lately dispossessed of his town hall) would be alleviated by Spa's medicinal waters, his rheum and ague by drinking good Breda ale spiked with belladonna and by avoiding like the plague all pagan spices such as cinnamon.

'Well then,' said the Duke, 'I expect you to take good care of me, Cervantes.' Rodrigo would always remember how that sounded, despite the warmth of the Duke's tone, rather like an order.

After the formation was dismissed, my brother made his rounds. The baths first: thermal room, steam room, drying-out room all in order, no discernible problems, no decisions necessary, thank God. Rodrigo met the new masseur in the massage room. His predecessor, poor fellow, had slipped on the ice the day before and broken his neck. The new man had small, neat, pink hands, not at all usual for his trade, but his credentials were good.

Rodrigo hurried through the snow to the guest-house. No problems there either, no decisions necessary, thank God. In the ducal bedroom a coverlet of swansdown with the Duke's own crest, and in the adjoining bedroom a virginal-looking (Parma was, after all, Italian) whore from Delft nibbling caramel-coated *poffertjes* to keep her strength up. A professional trained in minding her own business, she remained silent about the new assistant valet-de-chambre whose venereally obsessed eyes she didn't like the look of; who knew what the Duke's tastes were?

To the banquet kitchen next, where Rodrigo wandered aimlessly, acquiescing to a wholesale confusion from which would somehow emerge a feast for five hundred people. Three dozen cooks raced frenetically about the two central banks of great iron stoves. Glaring faces luridly reflected the glare of ovens. Rodrigo sidestepped an animal corpse that came gliding by at head level. He could smell woodsmoke and sweat, hotchpotch and roasting pig, offal and rotting fish. The air was dead, the heat homicidal. He saw feathers plucked from fowl and meat pies plucked from ovens. He saw two small dogs fighting over the skeleton of what might have been a hare (the final atrocity from the hare's viewpoint, a valuable perspective for one who pondered atrocities, even if the hare was past caring). He saw naked scullions climbing into cauldrons to scour them. He saw two stokers fighting in grim silence until one fell. It was all quite Tartarean and it pleased Rodrigo because he wouldn't have recognized a problem here if he tripped over it, no decisions necessary, thank God.

He was about to leave when a stridulous voice cut through the din. 'Name of a turd of a sub-cellarman, get that Rhenish vinegar and French piss back below and have up the oxheads of Montefiascone red and Cinque Terre white before I drown your useless carcass in a ton of Esquivias!' And the sub-cellarman sidled past Rodrigo and opened the cellar door, letting into that stultifying place a cool draught in which he lifted his arms almost as if he wanted to spread a cape he wasn't wearing.

History informs us that Alexander Farnese, Duke of Parma, died on the night of 2–3 December 1592, of wounds and exhaustion.

Fiction can add only that he ate sparingly at the banquet and did not avail himself of the Delftware in the bedroom adjoining his, but that it was she who found him in the morning lying lifeless under the Parma crest, a faint smile on his cold blue lips and a book clutched in his death grip – a collection of plays by Lope de Vega.

Rodrigo was inconsolable.

'I must have done something wrong,' he said.

'How could it be your fault,' said Aldonza the blonde vingt-et-un dealer, 'if he died of wounds and exhaustion?'

'They say,' said Rodrigo.

'Why don't you get dressed?' Aldonza asked him, as she had done the day before. And the day before that.

'I can't decide what to wear,' he said.

'Wear your wool cape. It's cold out.'

'The brown or the blue? I don't know if the brown or the blue is more respectful.'

'I'll fix you some lunch,' Aldonza said. 'What would you like?'

'I don't know,' said Rodrigo, and got up quickly and quickly sat down again. Then he got up again.

That was when I came in. I had spent most of the past three days being briefed at Pap's Place on the cover that would get us safely across the hostile United Provinces to equally hostile Amsterdam, where Juan-O was. That finally accomplished, I had spent this morning in Personnel.

'It's all arranged,' I said. 'They've agreed to waive the last few months of your current enlistment.'

'Oh,' said Rodrigo. Then he said, 'But.'

I glanced at Aldonza; her face confirmed that Rodrigo was no better.

'How about grabbing a bite to eat at the officers' mess?' I suggested. 'Then we'll get started for Amsterdam.'

'They always have three or four things on the menu,' said Rodrigo. 'To choose from. For each course. Besides, I'm not sure I'm hungry.'

'Baby,' said Aldonza, 'you haven't touched a thing since the funeral. Not even brandy-wine.'

'I don't know if I want anything,' said Rodrigo. 'Or if I don't,' he added, to be certain he made himself clear. He hoped. He got back in bed and pulled the covers up under his chin.

Aldonoza told me, 'Maybe you can bring us all back something to eat?'

Evidently she had an idea. And evidently it entailed being alone with him.

'I'll get some *broodjes*,' I said.

As soon as I left, she got into bed with Rodrigo. 'Want to?'

'Maybe. Let me think about it.'

She ran her fingernails along the inside of his thigh. His physiological response was encouraging. But he said, 'What if I can't . . . I mean, sometimes a fellow . . .'

She straddled him.

'Maybe,' wondered Rodrigo, 'with me on top?'

She rolled off him. He climbed on her. 'Or maybe not,' he said. He climbed off her.

'Or from the back,' he wondered, 'or you on my lap, or if you could grab hold of my ankles . . . but maybe the problem is . . .'

'There's no problem, Rodrigo, at all.'

'. . . we ought to be more spontaneous and just throw that sheepskin on the floor and tumble on it and whoever's on top's on top and, uh . . . listen, maybe you were right and we ought to do it the way we started because, uh . . .'

His encouraging physiological response had fizzled.

They sat for twenty minutes side by side, neither one speaking. Aldonza held his hand. Then she dressed and went to the window and looked out at the sunlight glittering blurrily on the snow. Then she brushed away her tears. Then I came in with a variety of *broodjes*, tiny loaves of bread stuffed with assorted foods, a neat Netherlandish idea, not that Rodrigo could decide between the roast pork and the smoked eel and the cold omelette and the salt herring, so although at Aldonza's insistence he held various *broodjes* in his hand, he didn't take so much as a bite of any.

I decided to put our departure off a day. This at first relieved Rodrigo. Then he wasn't so sure.

That night I must have slept soundly, and as usual Aldonza was over at Pap's Place, working. Rodrigo got into his parrot uniform and packed two bottles of brandy-wine in his haversack and hurried outside, all his movements decisive. Without a backward glance at the fifteen-room villa or at Pap's Place, he quick-marched on the road north out of Spa all night, and he slept in a barn the next day and quick-marched the next night, and a few nights later he walked out of wooded hills to where the terrain stretched flat as far as he could see in the moonlight and the sails of windmills silhouetted against the night sky looked like the wings of great black bats. Finally a day came when he saw horsemen galloping distantly atop a dike beside a canal and heard dimly the crackle of harquebus-fire, and he ran towards it, ran faster and faster until he found himself among parrots running too, and one of them cried, 'It's the lieutenant!' and he smiled a real Rodrigo sort of a smile, even his freckles participating, and shouted at the top of his voice, 'Oh, the glory!' somewhere east of Amsterdam and north of Deventer.

XXVIII

Concerning Various Unexpected Developments
Found in This Story and No Other

Often as I sit, paper before me, quill-pen in my ear, elbow on desk and chin on hand, wondering what untapped inspiration will help me fill a blank page, I fume at the critic (an admirer of Lope de Vega, no doubt) who wrote so knowingly of the 'twin headwaters of that bitter stream from which Cervantes's tragicomic worldview would flow'.

One 'headwater', he said, was my 'obscene servitude to the Dey' — insinuating some aberrant sexual behaviour in which I played an ignoble role. Holy Virgin! As if the ownership of one human by another isn't obscenity enough.

Granted, the creative impulse has to come from somewhere. I'm no Lope who, with his formula, can dash off ten plays a week and once, or so he claimed, one before breakfast. But did the critic, falling back on the old standby Repressed Sexual Tension, have to assume it could be found in my Algerian captivity and smugly look no further?

Somebody should have told him that every fiction writer has inside his head a Bench of If-Only from which to contemplate the world — not merely the world he's forced to live in but the one he's free to invent. And, come to think of it, why just one? With all the permutations of the possible, can't a writer invent any number of worlds?

Somewhere, isn't there one where Andrea and I didn't grow up sister and brother? Human nature being contrary, would we have been indifferent to each other in that world? Or even hated each other?

And somewhere, isn't there one where all my ancestors had pure Rusty Old Christian blood? There, would I have wished my great-grandfather had a great friendship with Christopher Columbus even if it implied tainted blood in his veins? Or would I have become just another fashionable anti-semite?

You see, now, where we're heading — upstream to that other, unidentified 'twin headwater'.

And where better to look for it than in that city of waters, Amsterdam?

On a bridge over a canal, not long after dark on a night in late winter, a foreigner was accosted by an Amsterdam night-watch. The foreigner spoke Spanish but claimed to be a Jew. Dragged roughly into an alley behind the Herengracht's stately new townhouses, he was interrogated by the watch officer in his own language.

'Name?'

'Miguel de Torreblanca.'

'Where from?'

'Originally, Córdoba. I come from a *marrano* family there.'

When the watch officer looked blank, he added, 'That's Jews who pretend to accept Catholicism. Spaniards call us *marranos*, "swine".'

'You talk Spanish like a native,' the officer said.

'Of course. I *am* a native. Our Sephardic language,' explained Miguel de Torreblanca patiently, 'is called Ladino, but except for the occasional word it's the same as Spanish.'

'You look like a Spaniard too.' The officer grinned. 'C'mon, boys, let's see if he's really a Jew. Strip him.'

Miguel de Torreblanca's arms were pinned, his breeches yanked down. The watch officer examined him, back and then front, saying in that order, 'No tail,' and, 'Big one, ain't it? But it ain't docked.'

345

'Jews practising in secret,' said Miguel de Torreblanca, again patiently, 'have had to forgo that covenant with God.'

'Covenant, crap. Size don't signify. You ain't circumcised, you ain't got a tail, you ain't a Jew.'

'I was on my way,' said the Jew or Spaniard Miguel de Torreblanca, 'to visit the leader of Amsterdam's Jewish community. He'll vouch for me.'

'The leader of *what*?' The watch officer hooted.

'He lives quite near. He's called Solon Wise.'

'The tulip king? You telling me you know Mynheer Solon Wise the tulip king?'

Miguel de Torreblanca answered, not entirely truthfully, 'He's expecting me.'

The officer deliberated only briefly. Solon Wise was one of the richest men in Amsterdam at a time when wealth and godliness were, if not indistinguishable, at least blood relations. It would be foolish to risk offending him.

They went to the back door and, after being passed from servant to servant, found themselves in a large foyer where a crone with the milky white eyeballs of apparent blindness stood leaning on a broom.

'How should I know if he's a Jew?' she asked. 'Or even if he's expected? Mynheer's off in Haarlem seeing to those tulips of his. Red-golds. Rarer than roc's teeth.'

The officer started to speak, but the crone wasn't finished.

'If you expect me,' she said, making vigorous sweeping motions on the spotless parquet floor in the direction of the officer, 'if you expect *me* to inspect his pizzle, you've got another expect coming.'

'Begging mevrouw's pardon, I already looked. He ain't circumcised,' said the officer. 'Got no tail neither.'

The Jew Miguel de Torreblanca cleared his throat and recited: ' "Before He created man and woman the Lord God naïvely intended to mate Behemoth and Leviathan. But realizing that their gigantic coupling might crack the very foundations of the Earth, He kept Behemoth on land and sent Leviathan to dwell in the depths of the sea." '

To this, the crone with the milky eyeballs responded: ' "Adam ordered his first helpmate Lilith to assume the recumbent position, but Lilith refused, saying, 'Why should you surmount me if the Lord God made us of the same primordial dust?' And, leaving Eden, she went to dwell on the edge of the Red Sea in prolific cohabitation with three hundred priapic demons." '

'What?' said the watch officer. 'What?'

'Fairytales known to Jews from earliest childhood,' the old crone assured him, 'and to no one else except – '

'You're no Jewess.'

'Let me finish. Known only to Jews *and* the descendants of survivors of the lost continent of Lemuria, which it so happens I happen to be.'

It was obvious the officer wasn't entirely persuaded, but he decided he'd done his duty and left.

'You're not, are you?' the crone asked.

'No,' said Miguel de Torreblanca.

Her apparently blind eyes narrowed. 'I know you, don't I.' This was no question, so I did not reply. 'Well, I don't care how-all-many signs and countersigns you know, you're wasting your time. He's finished with the secret world.' The crone smiled then, the white flash of a young woman's teeth. 'I knew it'd come to me! You're the one who told that poor little girl who was gang-raped the story of Damsel and the sleeping prince where she couldn't remember until almost too late that business about the old man with the long white beard riding his whatever past a whatzit tree.'

'You're the Old Woman of the East,' I said. 'But you were already a hundred and three years old when we met in Algiers.'

She glanced around the foyer, considering how to answer. The room was understated by Spanish standards of opulence, with just one Venetian crystal chandelier and not much gilt apart from the frames of the paintings by a lot of up-and-coming artists mostly named Breughel.

'We descendants of the survivors of Lemuria,' said the Old Woman of the East with pride, 'enjoy a kind of rejuvenation in our eleventh decade. Don't let these eyes fool you, I can see like a gryphon and hear as well as you.' With her broom she indicated a door. 'Wait in there. You can keep the Dominie company, he's waiting for Mynheer too. Oh, and since you're supposed to be a Jew, Mynheer'd appreciate your making a good impression. It might incline him to help with whatever brought you here.'

I entered a large room, its walls hung with more Breughels where they weren't covered floor to ceiling with books. A narrow man dressed in sober black and white turned from contemplating a canvas and began an eager greeting in Dutch. His voice fell on seeing who I was, or wasn't, but at my diffident smile and stammered apology he switched to Ladino. I was impressed that a Protestant preacher would speak the language of a (presumed) Jew. Then I reminded myself Ladino was Spanish, and the rebellious United Provinces had until recently been part of the first sun-never-sets empire.

The narrow man asked, 'Are you off the dogger?'

Not knowing what 'off the dogger' meant, I tried a no.

'I am Dominie Dweepziek. *Aaron* Dweepziek. A good Old Testament name. Yours?'

'Miguel de Torreblanca.'

'Miguel. Michael.' The Dominie nodded approval. 'A pan-Biblical name. Prince of all the Angels, after Lucifer fell. General of the Celestial Armies. Wielder of the sword of the Lord through all eternity. "And there was war in heaven: Michael and his angels fought against the dragon . . . And the great dragon was cast out, that old serpent called the Devil and Satan which deceiveth the whole world: he was cast out into the earth." '

'Pity they didn't cast him some other place,' I murmured.

'Verily. Revelations 12:7–9. A stirring climax to the only Book worth reading.' He waved dismissively at Solon Wise's library walls, then pointed to the Pieter (Hell) Breughel beside him, a vividly depicted apocalypse, and said, 'Pestilence, fire, persecution, famine, boils – might be a history of your people. Hard to see why you're called the Chosen People. Besides, how can you be, if *we* are?'

'Different models?' I suggested mildly.

He elaborated on that. 'I always say, there's Chosen and Chosen. The original experimental Chosen and the improved final-version Chosen. That's no put-down of you Hebrews. But even the Lord God can surpass Himself – indeed, the Lord God most of all, if the truth be known, and it is.'

The door opened to admit a small man dressed, like Dweepziek, in sober black and white. The newcomer wore gold-rimmed spectacles over bright eyes. Strands of silver hair were brushed carefully across his gleaming scalp, and when he spoke his pink jowls quivered.

'You should forgive my keeping you waiting, my dear Dominie and my dear co-religionist. Any word of the dogger?'

'I was hoping, mynheer,' said Dweepziek, 'that you would bring news of it.'

'But I've come directly from Haarlem where my new red-golds are thriving, thriving! Such firm base plates, such healthy tunics and bulb coats, and the leaves already – '

'Mynheer, the things of this earth are not idolized by the Chosen, new *or* old, now are they?' A finger waggled in reproach, then, 'It's true the dogger's long overdue. But God has spoken to me more than once of His plans for a Jewish community here in Amsterdam. So, they are bound to come. And I,' said Dominie Dweepziek in his resonant voice, 'shall be there, yea! at the very dockside to welcome these Children of a previous Covenant with God in the name of the Children of the current Covenant with God, to live in harmony among us. Provided, of course, they understand that they may seek no converts but must heed the suasion of us *predikants* in the shared hope of speeding the arrival of the Last Days. *And* that they may not, on pain of death, slander the Christian faith (except insofar as they are encouraged to revile the Papist antichrist) but are otherwise free to publish, except in the Dutch language. *And*, oh yes,' said Dominie Dweepziek, drawing fresh breath, 'that to punish sins of the flesh committed by any male Jew upon a Christian female, the pain of death will be preceded by unpleasantnesses that to this day even the Inquisition has eschewed. Contrariwise, the red-blooded Christian male who yields to the temptations of a Jewess merits indulgence, for his actions have been predestined by the only free will that ever did or ever can exist, which is to say God's. Well, do let me know when the dogger makes port.'

And with a stiff little bow the Dominie left us.

For a while we regarded each other, me in the gaberdine of Miguel de Torreblanca, itinerant Jewish merchant, he in the quasi-Calvinist garb of Solon Wise, the Jewish tulip king of Amsterdam. His bright eyes looked wry.

'Do the terms sound draconian to you, my dear non-co-religionist?'

I fingered the gaberdine. 'I meant no disrespect.'

'Of course you didn't,' said Suleiman Sa'adah now called Solon Wise. 'But what choice *do* we Jews have? Thrown out of most countries of Europe, locked in ghettos in the rest – compared to that, Dutch sanctuary is a Promised Land.' His pink jowls quivered. 'Now, how may I help you?'

I intended to ask about Juan-O. But what I asked was, 'Those papers Zoraida gave you for safekeeping before you left Algiers, where are they?'

'I destroyed them years ago,' he said with a regretful smile. 'My poor niece had compiled countless deathbed revelations from a world that, I assure you, is as Byzantine as people say. Had they been disclosed, they would have imperilled the whole precarious, paranoid hierarchy in Constantinople. Power would have shifted by default to our – that is, my – people on whom the Turks already depend to run their civil service. But I could not let this happen.'

I said I didn't see why not.

'For some time to come,' said Suleiman Sa'adah Sometimes Erroneously Called the Wise, 'humanity's future will be dictated by developments here in Europe. And this contentious little so-called continent would self-destruct without a strong Other, an Adversary to hate. Fortunately that role is filled by the Turk. And so I had to destroy poor Zoraida's papers to keep the peace here by keeping the Sublime Porte strong.'

'It's not exactly peace we have these days in Europe,' I pointed out. 'Spain against England, the United Provinces in revolt against Spain, Frenchmen against Frenchmen – '

'Believe me, compared to what could be, it's peaceful. Europe needs an Adversary just as – some say – God needs the Devil. I don't say *I* believe such claptrap, I merely draw the analogy. But you've come about your brother, haven't you – the soldier Rodrigo? My housekeeper remembered him with fondness.'

'Actually, it's my brother Juan I've come about.'

'Who?'

'Juan the Obscure. The Maimed Man.'

'You're *his* brother too? Well, now – that one just might be the next Innominate of the Nameless. Now that the Abbot is dying.'

The Abbot had been dying for years, but I let that go. 'How do you rate Juan-O's chances?'

Suleiman Sa'adah Sometimes Erroneously Called the Wise thought it over. 'Dicy. Times are changing. For decades we had a Certain Mutual Acquaintance, a Renaissance humanist if a trifle Machiavellian. Then came the Abbot, a retreat from reason to faith, the predictable swing of the pendulum. But your brother,' said Suleiman Sa'adah, 'doesn't seem to fit anywhere in that pendulum swing. No ideology. He's simply the consummate professional, the techno-crat, to coin a word, convinced that information clandestinely obtained is the key to overseeing what he calls "kings, queens, knaves the lot of them". But frankly, my dear Cervantes, such derring-do is *passé*. Despite the Renaissance we are seeing a retreat from rationalism back beyond faith to a superstitious fundamentalism in which the supernatural (whether real or sham) seems far more vital to the achievement of Nameless objectives, whatever they may be, than old-style espionage, for all its sentimentalized heroics.

'But since my retirement I'm just a tulip grower, so I could be wrong.'

Having got more of an answer than I bargained for, I kept the next question simple.

'Where *is* Juan-O?'

'With the Abbot, but precisely where the Abbot lies dying is something they no longer tell me,' said Suleiman Sa'adah, and just then a man walked in through the wall.

I mean this literally. No bookcase pivoted into the room, nor did a door concealed as panelling slide open. He just came right through the wall (his head on a level with the complete works of the controversial Abbot of Sponheim, I couldn't help noticing), looking somewhat insubstantial for perhaps half a second and then every bit as corporeal as Suleiman Sa'adah or me.

It was probably some clever trick, I tried to tell myself. I'd understand it if I saw it a few more times.

At least I knew right away beyond the shadow of any doubt who he

---

ERRATUM: Several manuscript pages of chapter xxviii were found to be unaccountably missing on arrival at the printing works. The publisher regrets the inconvenience and asks the reader to proceed with the story.

---

charming little legend about some Sephardic crypto-Jews fleeing the Portuguese Inquisition, bound for Amsterdam in an overloaded two-masted fishing boat of the type known as a dogger, one source says in 1592, another in 1597. Like many such legends, it is based on fact. The actual year was 1593. Blown off course, the badly listing dogger was sighted one morning by the English frigate *Roebuck* and towed up the Thames to Deptford Strand, where no one at the naval arsenal would take responsibility for the 127 unspeakably filthy, starving *marranos* aboard, until one night a crypto-Jew with Nameless connections named López Pereira or Núñez, depending on which version of the legend you read, slipped overboard, swam ashore and made his way to Chislehurst, reaching the grounds of Scadbury House before dawn.

In the Scadbury kennels Ingram Frizer found Micaela scratching her favourite's ears. Frizer, a charmless man serenely confident of his appeal to the fair sex, held his torch close to her face and said, 'Couldn't sleep, eh, dolly? But why cuddle up to Irish wolfhounds when you could have an English man, hah?'

'It's part of my training,' Micaela said, straight-faced.

'Seems there's an intruder in the grounds,' said Frizer.

The kennel man and dog handlers came in behind him and the hounds began to bay and leap about their runs.

'I'll take Brian Boru,' Micaela said and, anticipating Frizer's objections, added, 'It's part of my training.'

It was she – or her favourite wolfhound Brian Boru – that found López Pereira or Núñez at the south-east corner of the property. While she just managed to hold the lunging wolfhound, López Pereira or Núñez, hoping against hope, gasped out the latest Nameless sign. Micaela, reciting the countersign, omitted 'leaving Eden' and numbered the priapic demons on the edge ('shore', she said) of the Red Sea as 400, but López Pereira or Núñez wasn't about to quibble.

He outlined the problem.

By now the other wolfhounds and handlers were close, and so was Ingram Frizer, factotum and chief bodyguard to Thomas Walsingham, master of Scadbury House.

'I'll take care of this,' Micaela said, again cutting short Frizer's protests with, 'It's part of my training.'

She had been old W's pet pupil, as anyone with a need-to-know knew. And W's cousin Thomas Walsingham, apparent heir to his late cousin's service, was loath to change anything. So Frizer could only accede.

'It's not Nameless business, you know,' Micaela told the *marrano* when they were alone.

López Pereira or Núñez waited anxiously.

'But I know how it is to have no one in this world you can trust. Once I had someone, a Jewish woman in Algiers, but she was killed. So I'm doing this for her, see?'

Micaela appropriated from Scadbury House a gold-embroidered doublet, its taffeta canions fashionably wrinkled, and silk trunk hose. (After five years of advanced training she was well drilled in burglary. Also in certain other talents she didn't care to think about.)

'How's your English?' she asked while López Pereira or Núñez dressed in the borrowed finery.

'Lousy. All I speak except Ladino is some French.'

A problem – to which the *marrano* found the solution. For, while they decided on an identity for him (a French refugee, not an English baronet; the charming legend was wrong on this count too), it was he who suggested her role.

'You're pretty,' he said. 'And with those dark curls and those Egyptian cat's eyes of yours, you could pass.'

So Micaela helped herself to a pair of Walsingham horses and they proceeded to Deptford Strand. Word soon spread that 'a well-born young Huguenot immigrant' had fallen in love with 'an attractive little Jewess off the dogger'. There, his role played, López Pereira or Núñez leaves the legend – which then takes another wrong turn.

Elizabeth Tudor, Queen of England, France (*sic*) and Ireland, Defender of the Faith, was nearly sixty and beginning to look it, a vain woman whose red hair (like some of her teeth) was removable, so she was not likely to parade around London in an open coach with the 'attractive little Jewess off the dogger' at her side, as legend has it.

Exactly how Micaela contrived to be drowning in the Thames just as the Queen's barge made its stately way down river to Greenwich, the sun reflecting off the great gilt crown on the royal purple canopy, I have no idea.

But there she was on the barge, dried off and wishing she had a mirror so she could see herself wrapped in that royal hand-me-down cloak with its face-framing silver fox collar, while the Queen was saying, 'You *are* an attractive little thing, aren't you,' in an ambivalent voice. 'Are you fond of dancing? Masques and mumming? Gambling? Gambolling? Playing on the virginal?' (Note the symbolism of the Queen's favourite musical instrument: she always played on her virginity for all it was worth.)

If Gloriana (as her courtiers called her after Spenser's Faerie Queene) seemed entranced by the 'little Jewess off the dogger', she was also thinking politics. A philosemitic gesture like installing a Jewess at court – one who had *voluntarily* (as presumably Micaela had contrived to tell her) spent years in Algiers – might promote her hoped-for alliance with the Turk against Spain.

'I'm not very good at games and things, your Majesty.'

'We should enjoy teaching you.'

'I'd have little heart for it, ma'am.'

'But we are offering,' the Queen said, surprised, 'royal permission to leave the dogger and even, if you are quite set on it, to pursue your little romance with your Frenchman.'

'You don't understand, Your Majesty,' Micaela said.

'Then perhaps you might explain,' said Gloriana coolly.

Just then the Queen's Master of Revels had the misfortune to stick his head under the royal purple canopy unbidden to announce the musical programme: some Mateu Fletxa the Elder, a pavane by Milà. The Queen, who rivalled one-eyed Princess Eboli in the use of colourful invective, roared, 'God's death, can't you see we're busy? Get that jug-eared pisspot you call a head the fuck out from under the royal canopy.'

The Master of Revels did, but not before Gloriana hurled a cushion at him. Accurately. Micaela hid a smile.

'Well, we *are* the Queen,' the Queen said. 'And,' she reminded Micaela, 'we told you to explain.'

'There are a hundred and twenty-seven more of us aboard the dogger, Your Majesty, all longing as much as I to reach a new home.'

'Only a hundred and twenty-seven? So what's the problem? We'll let them *all* off their wretched boat.'

With admirable poise Micaela said, 'That's not what they want, Your Majesty.'

'God's blood, we ought to throw you back like an undersized fish, you ungrateful Jewish twat!' screamed the Queen. Then she apologized.

So did Micaela. 'But you see, ma'am, they'd find only grudging acceptance here. In Amsterdam, where they're bound, they've been invited to start a Jewish community.'

Pensively, the Queen toyed with the festoons of emeralds and diamonds (real) in her red hair (false). England and the United Provinces were allies, of course. Sir Philip Sidney, that beau ideal, had died fighting for the Dutch. His widow was W's only child. Connections – how well Gloriana knew their importance.

'If you help my people go, ma'am,' Micaela told her, 'your kindness won't be forgotten.'

'It never is.'

Micaela said boldly, 'They'll need fresh water, good English food, proper clothes to replace their rags.'

'No, let them wear rags,' suggested the Queen. 'If the Dutch Calvinists are anything like our own smug Puritans, a doggerload of pitiable refugees can only confirm to them how very Chosen they themselves are.'

'I begin to see, ma'am,' said Micaela with a grin at once impertinent and admiring, 'there's more to being Queen than throwing cushions.'

Back at Scadbury, she found Quillpusher going through one of his crises.

'No sooner dare I show my face again after that ghastly business during *Tamburlaine*, Part II – as if it were *my* fault the musketfire onstage killed that poor spectator – '

'But, Kit,' Micaela interrupted, 'whose idea was it to use loaded guns?'

' – which promptly closed both parts of *Tamburlaine* for good and looked like ruining my career *utterly* – no sooner dare I mount another play than *this* has to happen!'

'What had to happen?'

'At the dress rehearsal – the dress rehearsal, mind you, we're on the point of *opening* – we'd arranged for half a dozen cloven-hoofed demons to come galloping across the stage and disappear in a puff of sulphurous smoke. Lovely special effects, you say? But in the event there were *seven*. Where did the seventh demon come from? Afterwards there were just six boys and six costumes. Thanks to that weird visitation, the authorities have revoked *Doctor Faustus*'s licence indefinitely.'

He didn't quite weep, but it was a large snuffle and a near thing.

'Listen,' suggested Micaela briskly, 'maybe that trip to Amsterdam on the dogger's just what you need to take your mind off things.'

But he was in too much of a funk, so he charged her with getting the crucial Three Thomases Dossier to my brother Juan-O.

Dealing as it did with that always vexatious period of interregnum in an espionage service when no one trusts anyone, the dossier was complicated – and made more so by its leading players' names.

Thomas Walsingham, perhaps out of family feeling, aimed to keep his late cousin Francis's team together in his own hands. He had tradition and inertia going for him – plus friends in high places, including Secretary of State William Cecil, first Baron Burghley, and his rising-star son Robert.

Thomas Henneage had no objection to keeping the late W's team intact, but reasoned that he, Henneage, as second-in-command for years, had earned the right to captain it. He had ability and seniority going for him – plus friends in high places, including the Bacon brothers, although young Francis was so busy trying to curb the impetuosity of his ill-starred (but how could he know?) friend Robert Devereux, second Earl of Essex, that he could afford little time for his own protégés, even if he was William Cecil's nephew.

Thomas Phelippes, the late W's cryptographer, far from wanting to keep the team together, was secretly bent on raiding it to staff the world's first freelance intelligence network, Phelippes Espionage & Esoteric Knowledge, or PEEK, which would sell its services to governmental or private clients. Phelippes had no friends in high places, but he did have the allegiance of W's erstwhile chief enforcer, the Welshman Maliverny Catlyn, the notorious Butcher of Clynnogfawr Llanllyfni, who had more kills to his credit than Pedro (Killer) Pacheco Portocarrero and his brother Choirboy combined.

Thomas Walsingham's wife of two years, née Audrey Shelton, was thought to be sleeping with at least one other Thomas, but which one Quillpusher hadn't been able to determine. Audrey, related through the Boleyns to the Queen and a ruthless beauty with an eye for the main chance, would be the brains behind whichever Thomas prevailed. She did not expect it to be her husband.

Quillpusher, judging that he had no future in any of this no matter *which* Thomas prevailed, and still idolizing the Maimed Man, meant to establish his Nameless bona fides by presenting them with the Three Thomases Dossier.

'You'll have to memorize it, of course,' he told Micaela.

'Of course,' she said.

The day the dogger sailed with Micaela aboard, there were two sightings of Maliverny Catlyn, the notorious Butcher of Clynnogfawr Llanllyfni, near Chislehurst.

The day after, Ingram Frizer was found outside the kennels severely concussed. All thirty-eight Irish wolfhounds had been poisoned.

Doctor Faustus sabotaged – and now Maliverny Catlyn stalking Scadbury House . . .

Putting out from Gravesend in a small boat in the middle of the night, Quillpusher fled for his life.

We'd left me in the library of Suleiman Sa'adah now called Solon Wise, watching a man walk in through the wall, his head on a level with the complete works of the controversial Abbot of Sponheim. As you'll recall, he then tossed his *erratum* into my story, probably thinking that with so much else happening I'd forget I'd realized who he was. But I realized.

Well, he made his grand entrance, which Suleiman Sa'adah had presumably seen before, for he said, unsurprised, 'Ah, my dear Bādindjan! I was just telling my friend here, the Maimed Man's brother, that Europe needs an Adversary just as some say God needs the Devil.'

'Harmless myths, both of them, for the gullible masses,' said Bādindjan with a condescending smile.

He was a strikingly handsome man, tall, swarthy, with an aquiline nose, coal-black hair and a spade-shaped beard. He wore a robe of green the colour of the pool where Cide Hamete Benengeli had regained his manhood.

I couldn't help thinking what Lope de Vega with his avoid-the-impossible dictum would make of walking through walls. Absurd, he'd say. But isn't it the absurd that gives life its savour?

I said to Bādindjan, 'Good trick. How'd you do it?'

'Really, *ráwi*, you of all people should know I don't resort to "tricks",' said Cide Hamete Benengeli. (You'll have guessed by now that's who Bādindjan was, even if you don't know – as I didn't – what his name meant in Persian.)

'I could say,' he told me, 'it's only a matter of infinitesimal atoms adrift in infinite space. To walk through a solid wall – an *apparently* solid wall – simply requires a trifling effort of will to line up your trillions of atoms with *its* trillions of atoms so they'll slip through.

'I could say that,' Cide Hamete went on, 'but though it generally satisfies people it wouldn't be the truth – which, incidentally, often *doesn't* satisfy people.'

'I'll take my chances with the truth.'

'Easy to say, *ráwi*, but you won't be entirely reconciled to the perils of the truth until a certain April twenty-third.'

Here sweat ran into Bādindjan's brown left and blue right eye, and he blinked. 'What is this I see?' he exclaimed, and shut both eyes tight to see it, whatever it was, more clearly in what he would later sometimes refer to as the showstone in his head. 'How awesome!' he cried, either in terror or in unholy delight. 'One of those seismic encounters that produce epic poetry or a new religion out of the desert of the soul. Yes, *ráwi*, I'll surely be there on the right April twenty-third even if, to my intense chagrin, I cannot as yet envision the scene clearly – but never mind, how dull if one always could.

'Now, the truth about walking through walls.

'As I've told you often, no present moment except one can possibly exist. If it did, no one, not even I, could pass through solid matter. But just before you saw me, where actually was I? Outside the wall. And just afterwards, I was inside. So, what transpired? One present moment transpired. But if that moment did not exist, then neither could any *thing* capable of occupying space exist during that non-existent moment. This wall here, for example. At the non-space-time to which I refer, it *wasn't*. So what I walked through was absolutely nothing. Anyone can do it – if he knows how. Here, I'll show you.'

He launched himself with force head-first at the wall (doubtless a theatrical gesture where walking would have done as well), to become insubstantial, then disappear.

We waited in uneasy silence, but he did not return. Perhaps he was still a bit taken aback by whatever he'd almost seen in that showstone inside his head.

'Your brother – Juan-O? – faces an image problem,' Suleiman Sa'adah told me. 'What can he do to impress undecided delegates as much as walking through walls?'

'Cide Hamete Benengeli's running for Innominate of the Nameless?'

'Cide Hamete Benengeli?'

'Sorry. Bādindjan.'

'Indeed he is. Your brother will need all the help he can get.'

My first stop on the campaign trail was the open-air stock market behind the Oude Kerk, where I found the French alchemist Denis Zachaire

357

transacting some business, probably illegal. When I introduced myself, he spoke bluntly.

'The Maimed Man's a pro, sure, with a solid rep. But all we hear these days is Bādindjan, and no wonder. What's so special about your brother compared with walking through walls?'

'He can see in the dark,' I said, but Denis Zachaire only shrugged.

'He can see in the dark,' I next told the kindly old *sereno* who (rather than Luis Blackslave, who was conspicuous by his absence) led the Spanish delegation.

But jangling his keys and thumping his staff once, he said, 'I've been a night watchman so long *I* can see in the dark, but nobody'd want me to be Innominate of the Nameless.'

'He can see in the dark,' I told the English delegation chief John Dee.

Doctor Dee, a veteran spy of sixty-five ostensibly in W's sole employ – also a geographer, astrologer, mathematician and showstone gazer (outside his head) – was a pioneer in applying the paranormal to espionage. He'd fallen afoul of the law in England in 1555 for practising sorcery (apparently successfully) to make Mary Tudor barren – for which they should have been grateful, as it thwarted her husband King Felipe II's scheme to control, virtually, the whole world. By the time the Invincible Armada sailed to defeat, Dee was in Cracow, where by arcane means he obtained for W corroboration of von Nacht zu Nebel's naval intelligence. But lately Dee, who had coined the term 'the British Empire' during a conversational lull at a Whitehall lunch, was in such demand in upper-class drawing rooms that he had little time left for the supernatural.

Stroking his silky silver beard, he said, 'If seeing in the dark is all you claim for your brother, I believe you're an honest man. But honesty won't help him. Mind you, Bādindjan isn't a shoo-in. Rather too theatrical, don't you think? But it'll be hard for the conclave to resist a candidate who, it is rumoured, can not only walk through walls but transport himself instantly to the ends of the earth – even if it's only a charlatan's trick.'

History and fiction agree on this: Onofre Exarque a/k/a the Abbot died peacefully in his sleep at the age of seventy-four on Friday 16 April 1593.

A few nights later Juan-O walked into my lodgings near the Leidseplein and, obviously miffed, demanded, 'What's this business you're handing all the delegates about my being able to see in the dark?'

'What's wrong? You can, can't you?'

'I can hear in the dark too. So what?'

'Well, I just thought – in the spy business, it has a nice symbolism, being able to see where other people can't. Maybe it's not quite walking through walls, but – '

'You mean other people can't?' said Juan-O. 'See in the dark? I always thought, since *I* could – '

'No. It's a definite paranormal talent.'

'A paranormal talent. Me!' Juan-O marvelled. 'How's the vote shaping?'

'It'll be close,' I hedged. 'Where's Luis Blackslave? He should be electioneering.'

'Nobody knows where he is.'

'The campaign could use some of his flamboyance. Could use some glamour too,' I said. 'Now if only Mnemosyne . . .'

Juan-O got that dopy look on his face he always got when we talked about Micaela.

'She's still in England.' He sighed. 'I wonder if we'll ever see her again.'

'Luis Blackslave says the Nameless never trusts an agent who re-defects.'

'He also says,' Juan-O pointed out, 'that his father is God-Emperor of the New World.'

We didn't sleep that night. Juan-O filled me in on the mechanics of electing the new Innominate of the Nameless. The ninety-nine delegates would meet in conclave in a huge old house on the dunes outside Haarlem until a majority backed one candidate. Juan-O smiled. 'According to local myth, Amadis of Gaul once slept there.'

'In a house on the outskirts of Haarlem? Come on.'

'Mythical heroes get around, you know,' said Juan-O.

'What do you know about mythical heroes?'

When we were boys Juan-O spent so much time in dark corners he couldn't have read the books I'd read. But I reminded myself he could see in the dark.

'What anyone knows, I guess. Heroes always go off to some distant kingdom on a mission, and when they've found the Grail or slain the dragon or whatever, they're rewarded, usually with the king's daughter. This,' said my brother Juan-O, 'is enough to make your average mythical hero forget the girl back home. But then, your average mythical hero almost never *goes* back home, does he. Could the point of all the journeying in those myths be for the hero to bring some faraway kingdom new blood?'

Night talk from my brother Juan-O. He was full of surprises, and if sometimes I wasn't sure he knew what he was talking about, long afterwards in some far place his words would come back to me and I'd think, so *that's* what Juan-O meant.

Soon after dawn I was telling him how Rodrigo had gone back to combat when there was a rap on the door.

'Messenger,' gasped a breathless urchin. 'From the Old Woman of the East. My job's to tell you the dogger's tied up in Het Ij and they're disembarking right now and you'll want to be down there.' Then, catching his breath, he added, 'Which I have just did,' and left.

'Coming?' I asked Juan-O, but he said, 'I've got to get over to Haarlem. You too, Miguel. Anybody not sequestered by nightfall tomorrow misses the conclave.'

'Don't worry, I'll be there.'

I hurried towards the waterfront, so full of that false sense of energy that comes after staying up all night that I didn't even consider it strange that I was running.

In the estuary of Het Ij a lot of things were happening at once.

The dogger had rolled on to her starboard side and was slowly sinking, her mission accomplished.

Scores of unspeakably filthy rag-clad refugees milled about the pier, on their faces the stricken look of people who have squandered all their courage to get where they are only to find they don't like what they see there.

Sailors and dockers, an average waterfront crowd from the taverns that Dominie Dweepziek had been trying for years to close down, stood on the quay raucously cheering the dogger as she settled into her grave with her barnacle-encrusted keel visible through the shallow water like the flipper of a dead whale.

A young woman in a silver-fox-collared cloak that looked fit for a queen moved purposefully among the milling refugees speaking words I couldn't hear.

Dominie Dweepziek, using a barrel for a pulpit, was just reaching the peroration of a sermon-cum-welcoming-speech, lifting his resonant voice above the raucous crowd.

As I stepped on to the pier, a girl of ten or twelve bolted from among the refugees, heading straight for me. The young woman in the fox-collared cloak ran after her.

Half a dozen militiamen stood to one side on the quay, watching everything with disinterested interest.

'. . . pursuit of good works, yea though it weigh not in the balance since all, all is predestined . . .' resonated Dominie Dweepziek in Dutch, then translated his words into Spanish for the refugees.

I caught the fleeing child and held her. She struggled to break free.

'Both her parents died on the voyage,' said the young woman in the fox collar in a familiar voice.

The orphan tried to bite my hand, giving me an eerie sense of *déjà vu*, which became the poignant memory of Micaela feral on the beach at Algiers.

'. . . nor ever defame the Son and Saviour of Man . . .' resonated and translated Dominie Dweepziek.

By then the sailors and dockers had approached the foot of the pier, giving the possibly unintentional impression of blocking the refugees' way off. The refugees retreated, huddling together and showing the first signs of panic.

'Juan-O!' cried the young woman in the fox collar, her disturbing amber eyes widening. 'Oh God, am I glad to see you!' She reached for the feral child with one hand and hugged herself to my side with the other.

'. . . but if some red-blooded local Calvinist lad . . .' resonated and translated Dominie Dweepziek.

Even as I recognized her, Micaela recoiled, fending me off with the hand that for an instant had held us close. 'What is this?' she said. 'You're not Juan-O.' Her face turned red. 'You're Miguel.'

The feral child, that *déjà vu* Micaela, tugged at the real Micaela's regal cloak.

Twice I stuttered the beginning of Micaela's name.

Micaela said, 'Tell Juan-O I've got to see him. Three W's – I mean Thomases. He'll understand.' Then, taking the child's hand, she walked right through the crowd of sailors and dockers now on the pier to where the refugees cowered with their backs to the sunken dogger.

What was Micaela doing here? She couldn't have come off that wretched boat with the others, surely. She was no Jewess.

I noticed that many of the sailors and dockers were eyeing her too, especially the suggestion of that classic callipygean curve under the flowing cloak.

The rest were eyeing me.

No, not me – this crowd, I realized with a jolt, were eyeing Miguel de Torreblanca, Jew. The me inside, a 100% standard (except for what used to be my left hand) Christian gentleman of Castilla, was annulled by a skullcap and a gaberdine robe. Unconsciously I gave a touch, a reassuring pat, to the slight bulge in my breeches that was my uncovenanted maleness.

Inspection by the sailors and dockers made me inspect them back – and this in turn made me inspect the refugees.

Did I look more like them, or more like *them*?

I didn't look very Dutch, admittedly, but in the waterfront crowd there was a mix of types, and I thought I could blend. But these bedraggled Jews huddling near their sunken dogger, even with Dutch haircuts and clean Dutch clothes, could they ever blend into this average sort of a waterfront crowd? Didn't their demeanour set them apart? Did they have to look so – well, furtive?

But perhaps, I reproached myself, furtive was unjust. Frightened might describe them better.

Their noses, then, the characteristic noses so many of them had, wouldn't those set them apart?

Would mine?

My high-bridged hawk nose, proud and plenteous, was of a sort seen all over Spain. Aggressively masculine, quintessentially Iberian. A Spanish nose.

Certainly I didn't look frightened, though I had reason to be: this was no time to be a Spaniard in Amsterdam.

But nobody would take me for a Spaniard, let alone a Dutchman. At least in the garb of Miguel de Torreblanca, I obviously looked more like them than like *them*.

If so, it was hardly surprising. I'd picked the cover name Torreblanca from my own family tree.

I hated that name suddenly, as if it were responsible – as, in a way, it was – for my no-longer-Spanish nose, maybe even for a certain bearing, a way of holding my head (of looking at the world?) which I'd never noticed before.

All these thoughts culminated in a flash of loathsome empathy for the average waterfront crowd which behind its averageness could hide an age-old belief, based on nothing so banal as truth, that Jews were poisoners of wells, ritual slaughterers of gentile children, Christ killers . . .

Did I hate that crowd more, or myself?

What happened next wasn't my fault, even if Juan-O (despite his frequent assurances) never quite forgave me.

Whose fault was it? Who do *I* blame?

I blame nobody. The refugees, fleeing the Inquisition, homeless, now even shipless – how could they not look furtive or at least frightened? As for the waterfront crowd, they'd been drinking all night (beer laced in the Dutch manner with thornapple or black henbane seed) and they had in mind only a little harmless ridicule, not of Jews in particular but of any foreigners; it's normal to ridicule foreigners (you remember, don't you, the Greeks used the same word for foreigner or barbarian as for stutterer, so believe me I could relate to all this). It's human nature, right? – the crowd bellying up to those cowering refugees like thirsty men bellying up to a bar – and it might have simmered down, as such situations usually do, had not two sailors who looked alike except for their size, one being merely huge and the other humongous, planted themselves like trees in Micaela's path, Micaela who with her swift grace would easily, despite their reach, have evaded them but for the feral child tugging at her hand, and God knows nobody can blame that poor orphan either, and nobody can blame the white-bearded, white-faced, emaciated elder who tried to insert himself into the decreasing slice of space between Micaela and the two sailors only to be sent flying by a casual swat of a huge or humongous hand, nor can anybody blame any individual on that waterfront, one moment embarrassed by the excesses of the violent sailors, the next metamorphosed into a mob, individuals no longer but a single body of boon companions, *compañeros*, good-old-boys that needed to identify with what had, an instant before, embarrassed them, that's human nature, right? And surely nobody could blame those militiamen for not rushing in to break heads but looking on with vigilant detachment so next time they could predict exactly how and when a crowd ripens and bursts into a mob pulling the rags off some of those panic-stricken, barbarian (stuttering), alien-looking men (and women and children), those Others who can retreat no further, *hey, you drowned rats, you reeking vermin* says the merely huge sailor *what you ought to do, you ought to patch up that old tub and sail her to Cathay where they maybe got room for you* and the humongous sailor is saying *I heard somewhere their hair their women's hair comes off but this one's hair don't seem to come off at all* and soon he is not the only brave soul yanking at hair and then not just hair while the cowering refugees, by the incontrovertible fact of being Others, are inciting to riot, they don't need any horned hats yellow badges *let us pray* Dominie Dweepziek resonates and translates but no one does even if in the crowd now a mob some still feel uneasy but not for long as they persuade themselves they really didn't start anything since in these types of situations it's a well-established fact that the victims always start it *first*.

What am I doing all this time that seems such a long time but can't have been more than a few minutes?

Not much, really, just watching those pale, dirty, shaken, defeated people and, I don't know why, thinking of my father – my father on the old road again, the midnight departure preferable to debtors' prison; my father trying always to put a good face on it for us children no matter how failure and flight must have hurt him, degraded him, *dwindled* him; my father fleeing the Inquisition (but remember, *he* condemned *them*) to go on the old road again, road again; my twice-dead father in Madrid, lightning striking the ancient sword from his hand, *If-Only!* – and these people here, one step ahead of the Inquisition, cursed wherever they go, these Jews who are at once themselves and all the rejects and outcasts who ever lived, fleeing in the night (two minutes' notice, no problem, what's to pack?), these Jews on the old road again, seeking for their children a better life somewhere, anywhere, chasing the horizon, on the old road again ever since the last fall of Jerusalem fifteen hundred years ago.

Well, they marched away from the sunken dogger without looking back (I'm told) and along the Herengracht to that miracle of a canalside townhouse where Solon Wise would and did (I'm told) provide everything needed for their new lives, but I didn't see any of that because by then I was seated, head down, painful hands dangling between my knees, on a hard bench in a cell in the *tuchthuis* in Heiligeweg. My cellmate assured me that the nine resident magistrates could meet in special session to review whatever offence had brought a new evildoer, ne'er-do-well, vagabond or stutterer to the *tuchthuis*, though they did not do it very often because the sheriff liked to handle things himself, even if he didn't get around to them any sooner than absolutely necessary.

They *marched away*?

Obviously, I'm getting ahead of what happened.

What happened was, after the crowd ripened into a mob the merely huge sailor turned his attention back to Micaela who, in evading him, lost her grip on the hand of the feral child who could have been Micaela herself, Micaela on the beach at Algiers, Damsel – and the feral child bolted a second time and ran straight into the arms of the humongous sailor, who lifted her, lifted Damsel and held her at arm's length with one hand while with the other he parted her from the rag-dress she wore and bared Damsel's almost-woman body and pawed it (drunk on black henbane seed, blame nobody) while Damsel just hung there in his grip, Damsel with her face to the wall but there was no wall, Damsel opening her mouth to scream but she had forgotten how to scream, forgotten Demogorgon, Demogorgon dwells, dwellsdwellsdwellsdwellsdwells, and what used to be my left hand jumped.

The next thing I remember, I was standing between the merely huge sailor and the humongous sailor, both of whom seemed to be stretched out on the pier, and my right hand and what used to be my left hand both seemed to be swollen and throbbing with pain. (*What happened to your hands, Miguel? – My what? Nothing. Happened to them.*) The crowd, in the way of crowds that have unripened back from being mobs, were discussing technical aspects of the fight with a dispassionate expertise not surprising in Amsterdam, a port city, a tough city, where the arts of fisticuffs and self-defence, the Most Admirable Arts they were called, had an enthusiastic following.

The crowd was in general agreement. The Jewish fellow (not the Jew: this was a slight step up for the refugees off the dogger) had a truly amazing left hand. An absolute brute of a left hand. Not that he hadn't absorbed a certain amount of punishment too, they said, expertly appraising me, but with that left hand the outcome never really was in doubt, was it, despite the one sailor being merely huge and the other humongous.

I became aware, as they spoke, of that 'certain amount of punishment'. The way I was breathing, for example – through an open mouth, since my nose was occupied for the time being by blood. Blood dripped from my ear too, which can happen to an ear when it is clamped between humongous or merely huge teeth. A few of my own teeth felt loose. Further punishment would manifest itself presently, an assortment of abrasions, contusions and lacerations that only confirmed what I should have known: I was getting too old for this sort of thing.

But when a man who is writing of his own life lives in violent times, what can he do? Turn to fiction for escape? But bodily injury, often fatal, is the essence not only of chivalric romances (in Ariosto even women are warriors) but of those picaresque novels like *Lazarillo de Tormes* so dear to my father's heart. And who can say whether fiction imitates life or life fiction? No, there was no escaping those Most Admirable Arts (or weapons for that matter), and if lingering aches and pains reminded me of my age, think of poor Don Quixote whom I would send forth, ten years my senior, in the glory of his madness (and a rusty suit of armour) to right the wrongs of the world.

Hearing their post-mortem, I knew the mob was just a crowd again, an ordinary waterfront crowd that liked a good fight and was not displeased that those who had turned them into a mob had received their comeuppance.

By then, Micaela and the refugees were nowhere to be seen. Micaela, remember, was Chislehurst-trained and knew how to make use of a diversion, so (I have it on good authority) while the mob was absorbed by my splendid display of the Most Admirable Arts she got the refugees off the pier and moving across the quay and into the city to that miracle of a townhouse on the Herengracht.

Just as they were leaving, my good authority Solon Wise arrived on a lathered mule, his tardiness (he would tell me after my release from prison) occasioned by snags in housing arrangements for all 127 refugees.

'That girl,' he would remember with a quiver of his pink jowls. 'Stand tall, she told them, and they stood like ramrods. March, she told them, and they could have been an army on parade. Smile, she told them, if it kills you, and they smiled and it did not kill them. Who would have thought, when she was an impudent boy in Algiers playing dangerous games, that she would become a young woman of such serene selflessness, holding that wild little girl's hand in hers and never looking back, as if nothing else in the world mattered.' And Suleiman Sa'adah now called Solon Wise would sigh. 'But if nothing else mattered, can you please tell me, my dear Cervantes, why did she leave?'

But I'm getting ahead of myself again.

The crowd dispersed, still discussing the finer points of my use of the Most Admirable Arts.

Even the militiamen said I'd handled myself well.

This did not stop them from placing me under arrest. I was, after all, a foreigner.

XXIX

In Which the New Innominate of the Nameless

Is Named

Juan-O saw a new tenderness in Micaela's disturbing amber eyes. 'Maybe that's the problem,' he said.

'There is no problem,' she insisted.

But then why was there a dopy smile on her face, so like the one Juan-O wore whenever he talked about her? Understandably misunderstanding, he tried to kiss her.

She jumped to her feet and put the width of the table between them. 'Sex,' she said, 'has no place in my life.'

But her eyes still overflowed with tenderness as she stared past Juan-O at a Pieter (Hell) Breughel canvas or, probably, right through it. 'They trusted me,' she said. 'Refugees who had no reason to trust anyone in this life, and they trusted *me.*'

'Try to concentrate,' Juan-O urged.

'Will they be all right?'

'Suleiman Sa'adah's found them homes, and he'll find them jobs too, eventually. The children will go to school. It's all taken care of. Stop worrying about it.'

'I'm not. I'm worried about Miguel.'

'Look, it's not exactly a capital offence, punching out a pair of drunken sailors. Suleiman Sa'adah can fix it. Now please, just *concentrate.*'

Micaela tried. 'If only they weren't all named Thomas.'

'Start with one. Any one you want.'

'Thomas Walsingham then. I don't like his wife,' Micaela said.

'Why not?'

'I just can't stand her, that's all.'

'What about him?'

'He's all right, I guess.'

'I mean what does the dossier say about him?'

'Uh, he wants to keep W's team together. Unless he's the Thomas that wants to break it apart.'

Juan-O's ears perked up. 'No, he couldn't be. But one of them does, eh? What Thomas is that?'

'Thomas Butcher?'

'There's no Thomas Butcher that I know of.'

'I'm sure there was something about a butcher. And bacon, maybe?'

My brother Juan-O's forbearance was remarkable. 'How does Francis Bacon fit into this?' he asked Micaela.

'Did I say he did? A butcher with a long name,' Micaela said suddenly. 'There was definitely something about a butcher with a long name.'

'Would that be Maliverny Catlyn, the Butcher of Clynnogfawr Llanllyfni?' my brother asked her.

'Thomas Catlyn!' she cried. 'Maybe that's it!'

Juan-O waited. Saintlike.

'Unless it was Catlyn Thomas?'

Juan-O sighed.

It went on like this until there was a knock at the door and the Old Woman of the East came in.

'Fellow outside says he's looking for the Maimed Man. Why you call yourself that when your *brother* should is none of my affair, but I sometimes can't help wondering.'

'Who is he?'

'Didn't know Behemoth, Leviathan, and then you say Lilith. We had to go clean back to Inanna, Dumuzi, Ereshkigal, and then you say Gehenna and Tophet.'

'That's five years out of date,' Juan-O said.

'As I told him. So then he said to tell you Mnemosyne.'

'I'll see him,' Juan-O said.

Entering, Quillpusher demanded, 'Who the hell are you? There may be a resemblance but the Maimed Man is – well, maimed. That thing that used to be his left hand.'

'It's something a girl hardly notices,' said Micaela, but they didn't hear her.

'You're confusing me with my brother. *I'm* the Maimed Man, fellow,' said Juan-O, the impatience he'd suppressed with Micaela finding a target in the newcomer. 'So maybe you ought to get around to telling me who *you* are.'

'I can tell you,' said Micaela. 'He's Quillpusher.'

'*This* is Quillpusher?' said Juan-O, looking at Kit Marlowe, as draggled as any refugee off the dogger after his North Sea crossing in an open boat and, at his best, just a slender young man no taller than Micaela, his most memorable feature a fiery red beard, now scraggly. Well, writers, thought Juan-O. And yet they always had an affinity for the secret world, didn't they.

'So you're the Maimed Man,' Quillpusher said doubtfully, shaking Juan-O's reluctantly offered hand.

'I'm having a little trouble,' Micaela dropped into the ensuing silence, 'with the Three Thomases Dossier.'

And Quillpusher began to talk.

In the *tuchthuis* in Heiligeweg I'd about given up hope of reaching Haarlem before sequestration of the ninety-nine delegates to the conclave in the house where legend said Amadis of Gaul had slept, when I heard the warder's footsteps outside my cell. My cellmate observed this wasn't his day for the drowning torture, an unnerving observation, and the cell door opened.

'Torreblanca!'

I was taken to the sheriff, who said, 'You've been released on the recognizance of Mynheer Solon Wise the tulip king,' and gave me a paper to sign, and two minutes later I was walking out through a main hall so bustling with arrivees and departees that I failed to notice a servile little man with prognathic jaws who, however, noticed me.

Drempel had just done a week for vagrancy. (You may remember him as the walk-on who'd taken me from the personnel office in Spa to Pierre Papin's gambling den.)

On seeing me in the *tuchthuis*, Drempel's first impulse was to rush to the nearest warder, tug his forelock, and say, 'I must tell you, sir, that the brother of the most decorated soldier in the Spanish Army of the Netherlands is walking around loose in this very building.'

But Drempel hesitated. His luck had not been good lately. After years as a flunky in Spa he had woken one morning with the shattering conviction that he was of the Elect. No more forelock tugging, ever, not to any man, no matter in Whose image he was made. Slipping into the United Provinces and converting (not that, strictly speaking, he had to – if you've been elected, you've been elected), Drempel tugged his forelock only to God and eagerly awaited his new, improved life. It failed to materialize. He couldn't even find work. Soon, much against his will (not that the Elect had, or needed, any), he was the same old servile Drempel, tugging his forelock to *tuchthuis* warders even as he wondered why this should trouble him since it had been preordained long before his time and possibly God's as we know Him.

Drempel's hesitation, unfortunately, did not last long enough. Overcoming his distaste for warders, he persuaded himself this must be the turning point he'd awaited, and hastened to tell what was to be told.

Two steps this side of freedom, I felt a heavy hand on my shoulder.

This, for date sticklers, was one week to the day after the death on 16 April of Onofre Exarque a/k/a the Abbot.

Dutch tulip fanciers did not protest when polite but firm guards kept them from gawking through the barred gate in the high brick wall enclosing the Amadis of Gaul house. Outside for them to marvel at were regimented beds of striped and flamed varieties, some already in exuberant bloom, developed by Mynheer Solon Wise from outgrowths of his Algiers bulbs. It was no surprise that, Mynheer Solon Wise excepted, no Dutchmen were attending the convention. The Dutch were tulip tiros, and the few capable of truly original work with outgrowths were (as Suleiman Sa'adah had made sure) busy elsewhere. Someday the exotic tulip would assume its routine place in Dutch life, but for now its fanciers could simply speculate about those mysterious foreigners convening at the Amadis of Gaul house. Could Mynheer Solon Wise have achieved the ultimate, the *princesse lointaine*, the Holy Grail of his *métier*, the elusive Black Tulip?

Speculation was terminated by the polite but firm guards who, under a German named Rosencreutz (a descendant of that fourteenth-century Rosencreutz only just less controversial than the Abbot of Sponheim), sent the gawkers on their way.

For it was dusk on the eve of the Nameless conclave.

My brother Juan-O, standing inside the main portal, peered anxiously through the fading light. Still no sign of me. Could Suleiman Sa'adah have been wrong? Might bail have been delayed too long for me to reach the Amadis of Gaul house in time? In minutes all doors would be barred and tardy delegates excluded by Nameless tradition.

Juan-O had first-round commitments from half the delegates in the house. But for an absolute majority of those present and voting, he was still one short. And momentum, he knew, often turned against a frontrunner.

With sinking heart, he watched Rosencreutz returning to the house, in his hand the traditional black and white threads purchased no one knew how many conclaves ago from a mendicant in front of Hagia Sophia in Constantinople when it was still a church. Juan-O knew that, in the gloom, only he could distinguish between those threads. Nightfall – and with it the dashing of his hopes. Until he heard in the distance the unmistakable sound of a horse at full gallop.

It wasn't me, of course. I was, as you know, somewhere else. And right now I wish I were also somewhere else in this book, say two chapters along. I mean, I *said* it wasn't my fault but I'm still concerned nobody will see it that way.

So I asked three experts for advice.

'Lie to your readers,' Cide Hamete urged. 'Divert them with unrelated but riveting adventures.'

But I promised myself when I began recounting my death and life that I'd keep unrelated adventures strictly out.

'Tell your readers the truth at all times,' said Spain's greatest historian Juan de Mariana de la Reina.

But Mariana, who steadfastly told the truth himself, also steadfastly condemned the theatre for stimulating lust and depravity, so I was disinclined to follow his counsel.

'Since when has literal truth meant anything to *you?*' asked Lope de Vega, one of those rare times we weren't feuding. 'It didn't when you sent your Sad-Faced Knight down into Montesino's cave for three days while in the real world only an hour or so passed. And it didn't when you sent him flying through the air on that ludicrous wooden horse Clavileño. You litter the pages of *Don Quixote* with impossibilities, Cervantes – and now you scruple over a possible fib?'

Lie to your readers. Tell them the truth. Stop being a hypocrite.

Holy Virgin! If only I could skip to something like:

On my return to Spain in 1594, I was flabbergasted to hear on every street corner . . .

But being me, I have to tell how Juan-O bounded from the Amadis of Gaul house to welcome me, his face registering at first disappointment, then renewed relief as he beheld not me but a more imposing personage, as imposing as his flamboyant rival Badindjan, with a shaven head more gypsy-brown than black, despite his name, and the rest of him swathed in a satin cloak coruscating with vibrant colours even in the first dark of night. This personage, prosperous and menacing, smiled to reveal a mouthful of dazzling gold teeth, and with his habitual sang-froid asked, 'Any truth to the rumour they're homing in on a black tulip?'

'Luis Blackslave!' cried Juan-O. 'What kept you?'

More sang-froid. 'Run-in with the corsair El Draque, but he got away. Well, there'll be a next time.'

Since Luis Blackslave's vote would, it seemed safe to assume, give Juan-O his first-ballot majority, delegates began whispering 'the Maimed Man' to one another. But when the results were tallied, my brother remained, as before Blackslave's arrival, one vote short.

'What is this?' Juan-O asked.

And Blackslave said, as he had that night so long ago when my father's toss of the dice had won him his freedom, 'I owe you Cervanteses nothing.'

I got the news in the exercise yard from a newly incarcerated Englishman named Richard Baines, a disreputable-looking fellow doing time for counterfeiting.

'Goldfang,' he said while covering a feigned cough with his hand. Talking in the exercise yard was forbidden.

I thought he'd said goldfang. 'Goldfang?' I asked.

'Goldfang. Three hundred and forty-second ballot.'

I said out of the side of my mouth that I, or he, didn't know what he was talking about. We were communicating in Dutch, after all, a language neither of us spoke well.

'Listen,' side-mouthed Richard Baines, 'I saw the Maimed Man enter your lodgings shortly after the Abbot died, so there's no use pretending you're not who you are.'

It was a hoary espionage device, to plant an informer in prison to gain a fellow inmate's confidence, and I said so.

He took it well. 'Of course I'm an informer. I'm informing you Goldfang's the new Innominate of the Nameless.'

I remained sceptical.

'Your brother peaked early, Bādindjan was too ostentatious, and Suleiman Sa'adah Sometimes Erroneously Called the Wise withdrew when he became frontrunner on the two hundredth ballot. I hear you're being held because your other brother's the most decorated soldier in the Spanish Army of the Netherlands. How long are you in for?'

'Indeterminate. They can't figure what to charge me with.'

Richard Baines clucked his tongue in shifty sympathy – another informer's ploy to gain confidence, I was sure.

'Who,' I asked, 'is Goldfang?'

But a warder snarled, 'Move along there!' and we could not resume the conversation until work brought us together in the sawhouse, where brazil wood was processed for eventual pulverization and use in the *tuchthuis* dyeworks – a highly profitable, labour-intensive monopoly which encouraged the handing out of indeterminate sentences.

'All I know about him,' said Richard Baines, 'is that his father the

God-Emperor of the New World, in his spare time, developed the fabled Black Tulip.'

A few days later Baines moved in as my cellmate.

I waited for him to ask one of those innocent-sounding informer's questions, but he just stretched out on his planks and contemplated the ceiling in shifty-eyed silence.

So I asked him, 'How did you learn about Goldfang?'

'It was soon after the election, when the goldsmith Gifford Gilbert – or was it Gilbert Gifford? – was teaching me and Morley how to counterfeit a Dutch guilder from pewter. Marley was on the point of nervous collapse. Not only is the Maimed Man not the Maimed Man (he says), but no Maimed Man was elected at all. And Marling can't go back to England and write plays because if he does the Butcher of Clynnogfawr Llanllyfni will kill him. So, Merling says, he's going to give up the spy business *and* playwriting to be a counterfeiter. You should have seen him in that cramped workshop at the back of the goldsmithy looking at his first pewter guilder and imagining it was thousand, thousands, and whispering, "Infinite riches in a little room."

'Then Merlin asks how much it would cost to have his reputation destroyed.

'Mind you, I'm a destroyer of reputations by profession, but still the question shocks me. Lots of people will pay to wreck someone else's reputation. But their own?

'Well, I name a price, and Marlen wants to know would a conviction for counterfeiting help. I don't have to tell you how naïve this is. Sex and religion: it's always sex and religion that destroys reputations. Well, Marlye pays me to do the necessary but there's a slight hitch because he's already informed on himself (not to mention me and Gifford or Gilbert) for counterfeiting, in order to get his reputation-destruction underway.

'We run for it – right into the arms of the night-watch just coming in the back way. Gilbert or Gifford and Marlow are deported but I'm caught with the pewter guilder burning a hole in my pocket, so here I am.'

Richard Baines shifted his eyes from the ceiling to me. 'If it's the last thing I do,' he vowed, 'I'll make Marlowe pay. I'll destroy his reputation until there's nothing left but a few names even his friends won't dare utter.'

'But that,' I pointed out, hoping it might do Quillpusher some good, 'is what he *wants* you to do.'

As the months rolled by I learned, in a time-killing exchange of language lessons with Richard Baines, a fair amount of the Queen's English. Apart from that, prison life was the usual limbo. So once again my story is saddled with a protagonist indefinitely sidelined, while all the action belongs to other characters.

Facing this narrative problem the first time I was in prison – or maybe it was the third or fourth time but anyway it was the first *place*, Algiers – I filled the hiatus with a story, *ráwi*-style. This time I offer a synopsis of developments in the free world:

JUAN-O. Returns by a circuitous route to the mysterious complex of buildings in the rugged mountains east of Arcos de la Frontera. Drowns his disappointment in work, chiefly an attempt to disentangle the Three Thomases Dossier.

LUIS BLACKSLAVE a/k/a GOLDFANG. Travels by an even more circuitous route to Nameless Main Base, said to be a thousand leagues from everywhere. Receives a message, encoded in a cipher keyed to the controversial Abbot of Sponheim's *Steganographia*, which so startles him that his famous sang-froid deserts him for only the second time in his life.

CIDE HAMETE BENENGELI. Abandons Bādindjan and begins building a new identity.

SULEIMAN SA'ADAH SOMETIMES ERRONEOUSLY CALLED THE WISE. Receives, in exchange for outgrowths of an impressively deep purple, almost black, tulip, a sapphire on which are incised, in Aramaic, aeons-old cosmic secrets dealing with the nature of good and evil. Becomes expert on same.

PEDRO DE ISUNZA. Compulsively records interrogations of all known to have been at Alcalá University when the 229th virgin destroyed his life. Returns to Madrid. Still seeing danger everywhere, takes rapier lessons from the Catalán master Agulla de Espadón.

QUILLPUSHER a/k/a CHRISTOPHER MARLOWE *et varii*. In England, is accused by Her Majesty's Privy Council of:

(a) believing religion was 'invented' to keep men in awe;

(b) saying any man who does not love tobacco and young boys is a fool; and,

(c) suggesting St John the Evangelist was used by Christ as the sinners of Sodom used their catamites.

MICAELA. Micaela . . .

The night she left, Micaela stood a long time with a candle in her hand looking down at the formerly feral child she still thought of as Damsel.

I have to go away, Damsel, she said silently. I'd tell you why, honestly, if I knew why myself. It's not that I wasn't happy. I was. For a while I was happier here than I ever thought I could be, but –

But. What was left here for her to do?

How quickly Solon Wise's refugee community had established itself, like a field of well-tended tulip bulbs. The children most of all, already slipping effortlessly from Ladino to Dutch and back as they learned to be both Dutchmen and openly practising Jews. Micaela could help with neither. In their exciting new lives, which she had helped make possible, she was superfluous.

Lying abed until mid-morning in her room in the townhouse on the Herengracht, she would daydream herself back to those dangerous games of hers, longing guiltily for the exhilaration of flaunting herself in the souks of Algiers, or facing a drunken bowman with a blood orange balanced on her dark curls, or cruising the lowest dives of Záhara on a Nameless mission . . .

One night she went back to the waterfront. There, where garish light and laughter spilled from the taverns, she slowed to a walk, that taunting walk she had taught herself in the souks, and in no time men drunk on black henbane seed were demanding, hey, you with the classic callipygean curve, how much you charge? She fled, but no faster than she absolutely had to, letting them think they could catch her while she stayed just the merest half-step out of reach.

But it wasn't any fun.

In the candlelight Micaela looked down at the sleeping child's face.

Damsel, don't you see, I can't stay. There is a life for me, but it's in another place, a place where dangerous games are normal. It's not only that I learned all those things at Scadbury House that I haven't had the chance to use yet. It's that, you could almost say, I was trained my whole life to play dangerous games.

Micaela watched the sleeping child a moment longer, her disturbing amber eyes shimmering in the candlelight. Then she went swiftly downstairs and into the night.

I left Amsterdam suddenly myself, not long after a six-month supply of brazil wood for the dyeworks was hijacked from the 2000-tun Dutch merchantman *Til Uilenspiegel* in the North Sea.

In a labour-intensive industry deprived of raw materials, employees are laid off. But we dyehouse workers were convicts, and to lay us off meant the state would pay our upkeep and get nothing in return. What to do?

The nine magistrates who ordinarily didn't meet, met in special session to review all indeterminate sentences. Foreigners were easiest. Foreigners could be deported instead of being held at state expense.

The felony of being brother to the most decorated soldier in the Spanish Army of the Netherlands was, since the kinship had been preordained before the Creation, reduced to a misdemeanour. My sentence was commuted, and a friendly deputy sheriff gave me a few hours in Amsterdam before carting me to the border. I walked into Antwerp and worked my passage to Santander on the north coast of Spain aboard one of those two-masted fishing boats called, as you know, a dogger.

XXX

Adrift on the Sea of Love

And Elsewhere

The blonde vingt-et-un dealer whose resemblance to my niece Constanza ended at her two brown eyes was singing in her thin, true voice,

> 'A sailor on the sea of love,
> Its depthless depths I roam
> Without a hope I'll ever reach
> A port to call my home,'

when I walked into Pierre Papin's new gambling den in German Street a few doors from Taverna Múñoz, which was boarded up.

Ever since setting foot in Spain I'd heard nothing but that song. It was sung by gypsies. It was sung in chorus at village wells. It was sung by itinerants of every stripe including the motley group of travellers I'd fallen in with, but when I asked where they'd learned it, they just said, 'Everybody's singing *Adrift on the Sea of Love*.'

Evidently Gaspar de Porres had received the lyrics I'd entrusted to the Sicilian *giravolo* or wandering healer. I became hopeful some money would be waiting for me.

A rosy-cheeked barmaid at the inn in Quintanaortuño said, 'This song? They say the Saviour wrote it.'

Before I could question her bizarre attribution, she sauntered to the far end of the taproom, singing as she went,

> 'I do not know where I must go
> But choose a random bearing.'

When word reached our motley group that highwaymen were abroad, we detoured through Linares the Little, where an old man sat under a willow tree at the edge of a lake. Strumming an out-of-tune guitar, he sang off-key,

> 'More splendid and more beauteous
> Than guided him for love of whom
> Fair . . . fair . . .

'Damn! Can't never remember his name.'

'Dido,' I said. 'She's a her.'

'Ends in "o" so it's a him, but thankee anyway,' the old man said, and resumed,

> '. . . fair Dido died, uh . . .

'Damn! Lost it again – *her* name.'

'Aeneas. But he's a him.'

'If Dido's a him, follows that Aeneas is a her. But thankee anyway.'

'Listen, oldtimer,' I said, 'at the inn in Quintanaortuño they told me the Saviour wrote that song.'

'Oh well, Quintanaortuño,' he said, and strummed his guitar, and the motley group became impatient and we left.

At Upper Cherry we chanced upon a goatherd singing, as he searched for something among copses of wild cherry trees,

> 'Are clouds behind which she obscures
> What I most frankly seek.'

'Would you happen to know who wrote that?'

'Folksong, I reckon. Seen a herd of goats hereabouts?'

'They say the Saviour – '

Crossing himself, the goatherd vanished among the trees.

By the time I heard Pierre Papin's blonde dealer Aldonza, my question was automatic.

'Words and music by whom?'

'Miguel! Miguel de Cervantes!'

'Only the lyrics,' I said, with modesty.

'When did you get back to Madrid?'

'Who wrote the music?' I persisted.

'*Adrift on the Sea of Love*? Isn't it a catchy tune? *And* it came along at exactly the right time for me. You see, I lost my innocence. A love affair will do that, you know? And if a girl loses her innocence, Pierre says, she doesn't look like a frightened fawn when she deals, so her value – '

'The music,' I begged her.

'I never remember authors' names, but I've got a copy of the sheet music here somewhere.' She found it folded in a little purse of gold brocade that matched her little cap. 'Words and music by Luis Salvador, Chapel and Chamber Singer to His Royal Highness Felipe II the Death-Loving. I'll be forever grateful to this Salvador. *Adrift* has such a quality of lost innocence *found*.'

'Are you telling me this Salvador claims he wrote it all, music *and* words?'

But she was singing my song again in her thin, true voice.

Pierre Papin came over. 'Most popular number to hit Madrid in years,' he said. 'Decades.' He shook his head admiringly, the wrongly placed feather in his hat swaying. 'It saved Aldonza's career. Salvador's first-ever try at secular lyrics. You've got to hand it to him.'

I said, '*I* wrote those lyrics.' I was mad enough to yank the feather out of his hat, which I did.

'Hey! You think I wear that on the wrong side to insult my adopted homeland? Not on your life. It's to draw attention. Like that Princess Eboli who nobody's seen for years but everybody remembers her because of the eye-patch. It'll do it every time. You should know, with that thing that used to be your left hand. So can I kindly have my feather back?'

I gave it back to him and he replaced it in the wrong side of his hat.

'Did you really write the lyrics?'

'Shortly before I got to Spa.'

'My advice is, forget it. Why do you think I had to close up in Spa and come back here? Rank. They outlawed *primera* because the officers thought the face cards being lowest was a slur on themselves. And you can't run a gambling den without everybody's favourite game.'

'What's that got to do with song-lyric credits?'

'There are officers and other ranks in this life. Luis Salvador the Royal

Chapel and Chamber Singer is definitely an officer. Do yourself a favour and forget it.'

From Pierre Papin's I went, my heart in my mouth, to the tall stone house near the Gate of the Sun.

My sister Magdalena, her hair faded to rust, answered the door singing,

> 'To find him is my soul's sole care,
> For all else I'm uncaring.'

My man-hating sister Magdalena! It was the last straw.

'Where does this Luis Salvador hang out?' I shouted.

'Not even a word of hello,' said Magdalena coldly. 'How like a man.' Her cockatrice eyes, more than ever the eyes of our grandfather the Patriarch, withered me.

Then she said, 'Mamá's dead.'

'Mamá – '

Magdalena said, 'The way I'll always remember her best is ordering Papá to die.'

A voice an octave or so higher than Magdalena's misandrous growl said, 'It was last year. She just went to sleep and never woke. No pain. She hadn't even been feeling poorly,' and I saw this woman with tawny-grey hair coiled at the nape of her neck, crowsfeet at the corners of her pale blue eyes, and fine vertical lines on her upper lip – a pleasant-looking matron, though thin compared with still-voluptuous Magdalena.

'Andrea,' I said, and all at once, I don't know why, somehow I found those signs of age on her pretty if not perfect face endearing, and something, grief for our mother maybe, welled up in me, and for the first time I saw Andrea, really saw her, as my sister.

My brother-in-law Santi Ambrosio was very good about everything. 'Take as long as you need,' he said, an embarrassed smile on his round, gentle face. 'I know this sounds vulgar, but I've got plenty of money, so don't feel you have to accept the first thing that comes along.'

I was embarrassed too: employment hadn't crossed my mind. Except for military service (for which I'd paid with my left hand and five years in Algiers) and civil service as a commissary (which got me twice excommunicated), I'd always been a part-time man of letters and part-time agent of the Nameless. Somehow I'd assumed I always would be.

'Or,' said Santi, 'I can find you something if you'd like.'

'I'm not even sure I'm staying in Madrid,' I said.

From upstairs came a blood-curdling howl to which no one paid the slightest attention.

'If you decide to go abroad, I could get you work with one of our affiliates in Italy.'

Did he stress this? Was it a hint that shortly after saying my hellos would be a good time to say my goodbyes? The family was used to doing without me. And I wasn't such a great family man anyway. Something always seemed to go wrong. Maybe I'd be better as an occasional visitor, like Juan-O in the old days. But I wasn't such a great occasional visitor either. My visit to Spa hadn't done my brother Rodrigo any good, unless returning to combat was an improvement. And my visit to Amsterdam had cost Juan-O what he most wanted in life.

Again came that blood-curdling howl to which nobody paid attention. It was followed by a pounding on the stairs, all the way down from the top floor, punctuated twice more by that howl before Catalina came hurrying in on her sturdy countrywoman legs. She was wearing black fustian, and a hairy creature with a long tail perched on her shoulder.

It's funny the way people can just melt away sometimes. That's what they did – Andrea, Santi, Magdalena – disappeared like Cide Hamete Benengeli a/k/a Bādindjan walking through a wall, leaving Catalina and me alone. With a glad cry (and a tentative yelp from whatever perched on her shoulder) she gripped my arms and kissed both sides of my face, a show of matrimonial affection apparently permitted by the Tertiary Order of St Francis.

'Well,' we both said, and she told me, 'It's a howling monkey, from Colombia,' and on cue it howled. 'Got its hand chewed teasing the lynx cub with the broken ribs. You're looking well, Miguel.'

So was she. Probably the only one in damp, late-winter Madrid who looked as though she led an outdoor life.

For someone who spent her time with howling monkeys and battered wildcats and God only knew what else, she had a remarkably tranquil smile.

I asked, 'Menagerie been keeping you busy?'

'Sure. They're my work, Miguel, just like you have your playwriting. And they're my friends. The way they were for St Francis. But I have to say *he's* been a big disappointment. When I first joined the Tertiary Order, I prayed to him all the time to help me forget fucking. But I guess it's not his department, him being a man.' She said this without rancour, not at all like Magdalena. 'Since I switched back to the Virgin, I don't miss fucking at all. She's so understanding, we're so close, it's like we're hardly two separate people.' Catalina blushed. 'I'm practically a virgin myself again.'

The howling monkey howled. Catalina tapped it gently on the unbandaged hand. 'No, I have a good life.'

'You look as though you're thriving on it. How's Constanza? Where is she?'

And Catalina answered, 'Come upstairs and I'll show you the menagerie.'

The next day I asked Magdalena where Constanza was, but she just crossed herself.

I asked Santi Ambrosio, 'Where's Constanza?'

He answered, 'People change.'

'Same or changed, where is she?'

Red crept up Santi's neck to his round, gentle face. 'Out. She's generally out.'

'Doesn't she live here any more?'

'I'm out a lot myself. Tuscany, Liguria. I'm the wrong one to ask about other people's comings and goings.'

I asked Andrea.

'She's no child, Miguel. You'll be glad to know nobody accuses her of witchcraft any more, and since her first love affair she hasn't dreamed once about that imaginary friend.'

'Her *first* love affair?'

'Lanuza. I only meant,' Andrea said quickly, 'when a woman has a love affair she loses her innocence, and if she *had* an imaginary friend she no longer needs him. You know?'

'So where does she live?'

'You'll also be glad to know she told me what really happened that time on the Riverbank of the Tanners.'

'It wasn't her fault.'

'It was. But it was a long time ago.'

I asked again, 'Where does she live?'

'Constanza's getting on for thirty, you know,' Andrea said.

'I guess she is. So's Catalina. Which means Micaela must be, almost.' I smiled, thinking that Micaela didn't look anywhere near it; she looked around twenty-two.

'Who's Micaela?'

'Oh, just someone Juan-O knows a lot better than I do.' What used to be my left hand gave a tiny twitch.

'And who's Juan-O?'

'Our b-brother Juan the Obscure.'

381

And we spent some time talking about Juan-O, and after Juan-O Rodrigo, and she never did say where Constanza was.

The next evening I said, 'Listen, my interest is purely avuncular. It always was.'

'I know, Miguel. Well, I've got to run.'

She ran upstairs, and soon I heard the clear tones of the cembalo that Santi Ambrosio had had shipped back from Genoa for her. Playing *Adrift on the Sea of Love.*

I went out and found myself walking along German Street. A chill drizzle was falling. To my surprise Taverna Múñoz was no longer boarded up, but inside I saw a man in the plumage of a colonial seated forlornly at a plank table beside a wall decorated with feathers, masks and what might have been a fair facsimile of a calendar stone.

'See the glories of New Spain?' He launched an impressive pitch about silver, gold, and Aztec maidens. Cortés on a peak in Darien, he said.

I told him that was Balboa.

He held out paper and dripping quill-pen. 'Five years over there and you'll come back a rich man.'

'They have to recruit for New Spain now? They used to turn people away in droves.'

'Times have changed.'

Another dream shot. Who was it said, every night you go to sleep a wiser man, not that it does you any good, and every day you wake a sadder one, not that that seemed possible the night before? Me, I guess. In my down phase, which despite my latest prison release didn't seem over yet.

'You wouldn't happen to know,' I asked, 'where I can find the fellow who used to run the tavern here?'

Taverna Isabel was so crowded it took me a while to work my way to the bar. Gabriel Múñoz was drawing wine and beer as fast as a man could. The snowy hair on his formerly grizzled head was lank with sweat and there were wine-dark sweat stains at the armpits of his white shirt.

'*Compañero!*' He flashed a huge welcoming smile.

But flashed is the word, because it was gone just as quickly. He peered anxiously through the tobacco haze at the door. Then he looked at the single vacant table, large and set spectacularly for two. Gold flatware and candelabra, Venetian crystal.

'If,' he said, 'you have finally come to see that gorgeous little child Isabel, you are too late. She is living these days with her mother down in Hundred Wells who is retired, which is how come I am manager here.'

He drew a cup of red for me. 'One on the house before you go, *compañero*.'

'I have nowhere to go.' How true that was.

'Some people,' he sighed, darting another look over my shoulder, 'are not as big of a success as they dreamed of back in Algiers. If they cannot make a go of their own place. But at least I am working, *compañero*.'

He didn't mean that the way it sounded.

'If you are wondering' – with another glance at the resplendently set empty table – 'how come I lost my place, it was on account of just when I got the hang of running a gambling den Pierre Papin closes his joint in Spa and opens up right here in German Street, and you do not compete in competition with Pierre Papin unless you want to carry your head around like that Mary Queen of Scots.'

Another sigh. Another glance at the door.

'Listen, *compañero*, I have got rid of the circuses downstairs, with or without donkeys, I serve good food, and I try to avoid trouble, so – '

The door opened, and suddenly he and everyone else in the tavern fell silent as a couple made a studiedly casual entrance. She wore ermine, satin and voile, plus a few yards of pearls, he a blue satin cape on which was stitched a great white Cross of Malta. Her blonde hair was pulled up into the shape of a heart and surmounted by a topknot held in place by a moonstone. She smiled up at him, a stiff smile because her face was stylishly whitened with almond paste.

As a phalanx of waiters escorted them to the resplendently set table, people on all sides whispered, 'It's Lope.'

He was so much the centre of attention that no one seemed to notice his companion had one blue and one brown eye. But maybe they already knew.

'. . . dead end in gongorismo,' he was saying, his tone suavely lethal, his volume calculated to be just overhearable. 'But then, my dear, who *is* this Luis Góngora but the mortician of modern verse, burying art in artificiality, euphemisms and epithets, antitheses and upside-down-isms . . . Don Miguel! What a splendid surprise, old boy!' His black pointed beard underscored the white of his large anthropophagous teeth. 'Waiter! A chair, a comfortable chair for the retired playwright Miguel de Cervantes.'

Gogglers and gawpers at other tables watched me plant an avuncular kiss on Constanza's bare shoulder. I heard, '. . . Lepanto . . . Algiers . . . disappeared for ages . . .'

I expected Constanza to look flustered; instead she basked contentedly in her escort's fame. My ears felt red. Retired playwright? Well, yes, what other sort of playwright was I? And as her mother had implied, Constanza was old enough to decide who would play Pygmalion to her Galatea, and, for that matter, whose bed she would sleep in.

But why, of all the men in Madrid, did it have to be Lope de Vega?

Wine was decanted, sipped, approved.

'Poor old Luis Ponce de León,' Lope told my niece and all within earshot, 'never did master the distinction between courting and raping Euterpe, muse of lyric poetry.'

'But weren't we discussing Luis Góngora?' asked a confused Constanza.

'Finished,' said Lope, not specifying whether he meant his critique or the poet's career. 'Now that we have the pleasure of Don Miguel's company, how much more appropriate to discuss someone of his generation.'

I was tempted to suggest that a-play-a-day Lope hardly went in for long courtships of the muses either. But my old friend Gabriel Múñoz wanted to avoid a scene. So I said nothing.

'Ponce de León – that *converso* professor of Christianity who recast the Song of Songs into a pagan eclogue so impious,' pontificated Lope as his audience leaned closer, 'that it earned him five years in prison – one almost suspects just so he could reoccupy his chair at Salamanca with the quip, "As we were remarking when last we met." Of course, prison does encourage some *marranos* to produce the occasional pearl – rather as a grain of sand encourages an oyster.'

I was tempted to point out that Lope himself once fled Madrid to avoid a term of 'encouragement' for libel. But Constanza looked so worshipful that I said nothing.

'But then, prison is the closest the *marrano* comes to stability,' said Lope. 'It must be quite a handicap, always a bag packed by the door, ready to flee with no idea where. The artist, in order to get anywhere, must know exactly where he is going. God knows I always have.'

I was tempted to say that anyone who always knew exactly where he was going was unlikely to go far. But Gabriel Múñoz arrived with an anxious look and the silver-salvered fish course, grilled tails of that incomparably ugly, unexpectedly edible creature known on various coasts as angler-fish, monkfish, lampfish, snitcher and (I smiled) all-mouth.

I gave Gabe a not-to-worry wink and said nothing.

When the all-mouth was succeeded by quails in grape leaves, Lope informed me that he and Constanza were celebrating his 500th play.

I congratulated him; I didn't have to like him to be impressed. I was not even tempted to point out (as Luis Góngora once had) that Lope's works were more handwriting than playwriting.

'Why, who knows,' he asked, in a tone indicating that *he* did, 'I might write another five hundred before I'm through. But I was lucky. A man must hone his talents while young.' Those anthropophagous teeth beamed at me. 'You, Don Miguel, despite all those years wasted as a parrot and a slave and so on, still turned out how many plays in your day, old boy?'

I wasn't sure whether closed-after-one-performance counted. To be on the safe side, I said half a dozen or so.

'Not to be belittled,' Lope allowed. 'Particularly if, as you mentioned in Porres's office, you might produce three pages on a good day. Believe me, we whom the muses have favoured with facility are the first to respect, as I then said, the pertinacious plodder.'

I was half tempted to correct him, as the words he'd used all those years ago were 'overindustrious drudge'. But his alliterative memory amused me, and I said nothing.

When roast suckling pig had given way to dessert, Constanza turned her adoring gaze from her escort and, pleased the encounter had gone so well, bestowed a smile on me.

'Lope,' she breathed, 'is a real playwright.'

Did that hurt? Did I pause to wonder what sort of plays an unreal playwright might aspire to write?

'Or a *thousand* more,' said Lope. 'Why not? The formula's the thing, and there are only four essential ingredients. Character types the audience knows. Plot elements the audience expects. A moral the audience approves. And a picture of the world that asks them neither to see life as it is, God forbid, nor to swallow the impossible. Four essentials anyone can learn, it's that simple.'

'To be a genius like Lope,' appended my niece Constanza.

I looked at her spellbound face. And I said nothing.

Lope gave her hand a pat before settling into an attitude of reposeful narcissism, complete with cigar.

I watched him blow a smug smoke-ring and poke a smug finger through it. And I said nothing.

It was Constanza's humming a few bars from *Adrift* that, finally, made me enquire, 'Aren't you forgetting your fifth and most essential essential?'

Lope chuckled, 'What might that be, old boy?'
'I was thinking of headlong complacency.'

Constanza returned home a few weeks later when Lope abandoned her for an aspiring actress not quite seventeen named, of all things, Micaela.

'You insulted him, you ruined my life, I hate you,' my niece accused me tearfully.

Magdalena came unexpectedly to my defence. 'Don't blame your uncle,' she said. 'Men always trade up to younger women.'

Constanza howled like my wife-in-name-only Catalina's howling Colombian monkey.

I spent a lot of time roaming the neighbourhood in search of nothing in particular, which, not surprisingly, is what I found.

Summer came and, for the first time in decades, plague. Half Madrid fled to the country, the other half stayed home behind shuttered windows and barred doors. Doctors recommended leather clothes and abstinence from sex. Everybody was always scratching: there were a lot of fleas that summer. Every day the dead-cart came creaking past the tall stone house near the Gate of the Sun. Santi Ambrosio took Andrea on a visit to Genoa, Livorno and Pisa. Constanza remained red-eyed until autumn, when the plague abated. (It would return the next summer, and the summer after that.) Magdalena counted her beads as much as our sister Luisa ever had, and speculated on what sort of world it would have been if God had been a woman.

In late autumn Andrea and Santi returned and I emerged from the tiny room next to Catalina's menagerie, half deaf from months of the howling monkey's howling. I took the two plays I had written to Gaspar de Porres's office behind the Theatre of the Prince. The former player-manager, now manager, was not in, so I left the manuscripts with a note.

When a few days passed I told myself Gaspar de Porres had probably forgotten where I lived, so I returned to the theatre. I walked through the corral where two actresses were trilling some tentative notes of *Adrift on the Sea of Love* and along the alley to the manager's office. I could hear them talking before I got there, Porres in a voice that still had its stage-trained timbre, and Lope de Vega.

'Well then, maybe *The Go-Between*,' Lope was saying, naming one of my two plays.

'Comedy, tragedy, you tell me,' said Porres, sighing. 'I don't see what to do but give it to him straight.'

'How about the provinces?' Lope asked. 'Doesn't some theatre manager somewhere owe you a favour?'

'There's a limit,' said Porres, 'to what's a favour.'

'That bad?'

'We're not talking bad, good. We're talking audience.'

'Could I rework them? I have part of the afternoon free,' said Lope.

'First, he wouldn't go for it. Second, what could you do to rework what's already his own reworking of *Life in Algiers*? Or a "comedy" in which this character has a thing about his sister, for God's sake? But I'm curious,' said Porres. 'Why do you want to help? He doesn't exactly like you, and I gather it's mutual.'

'It is. But his niece . . . pleased me for a time.'

I stepped back into the shadows as they said their goodbyes, and watched Lope swagger towards the theatre corral. Faintly I could hear the actresses still singing my song. Then Lope's voice, one of those untrained but pure baritones, belted out, 'Two stars I follow, spied afar!' and the two actresses laughed and clapped their hands. 'In whose flame I pale!' Lope sang – a line, I thought, out of harmony with the singer. Then I felt small for scorning someone who'd wanted to help me, whatever the reason.

Back at the tall stone house near the Gate of the Sun, I asked Santi Ambrosio for a word in private. All the way home I'd been thinking about his offer. I would ask him to find me a brother-in-law sort of job in the backest back country of the Abruzzi, some place where nobody would know my life had been all downhill since Lepanto or, if there was any basis for it, Shakashik's *Zherhantayl* cycle.

But when we were alone I found myself still hearing Lope belt out my song in that damnably effortless baritone, and what I said was, 'I have to take a little trip, Santi. I wonder, could you spare some, uh . . .'

My mule floundered in a snowdrift, scrambled out, plodded uphill – and there it was, rising through the swirling snow, half-seen spires and towers flanking the great grey dome of the church and finally the bleak black stone façade of the mausoleum/palace called the Escorial or Slag Heap (after the hills of scoria from nearby iron works) or, properly, the Royal Site of San Lorenzo.

In the courtyard, royal lackeys rushed to my mule, I thought to help me dismount. Then I realized they were yanking peremptorily on the bridle and shouting, 'Not here!'

I said if they would direct me, I would willingly dismount elsewhere.

But my mule, exhausted, began just then to keel over. To avoid being crushed, I flung myself from the saddle, knocking down an elderly fellow in homespun robes.

The lackeys rushed to his aid, but the elderly monk waved them off, brushed snow from his robes and asked me, 'Did you get that left hand with the Invincible? In the Azores? The Naval? Flanders?'

'It was The Naval,' I said, still sitting in the snow. The elderly monk offered his hand and I hauled myself up. When I put weight on it, my right ankle throbbed with pain.

'Can you walk? We can get a litter and take you to the hospital.'

But by leaning on his arm I was able to hobble along.

'Now, what brings you to the Slag Heap on a half-dead mule?' the elderly monk asked.

I told him.

'*That* song? Da-da-da-*dee*, da-da-da-*dah* . . . it's all we ever hear around here except for plainsong. And you say our chapel singer stole it?'

We proceeded across the courtyard, both of us limping (my companion, I later understood, suffered from gout), and up a staircase to an austere whitewashed room with an interior window that overlooked the high altar of the church, adazzle with gold, agate and porphyry.

'Are you the sexton here?' I asked.

'One way of looking at things,' he said, and led me through four stark cells devoid of decoration except for four versions (all by Hieronymus Bosch, he said) of the Devil tempting St Anthony in the Egyptian desert. A fifth and last cell, windowless, would be mine for the night.

From the doorway, as the elderly sexton lit a lamp, I saw that my cell too contained a Hieronymus Bosch canvas, this one of a hay-ride. On the hay were a girl singing and a youth playing pipes, a pair of lovers embracing and a kneeling angel; on billowy clouds above, the figure of Christ; on the ground below, an evil-looking charlatan selling nostrums, a procuress tempting a country girl into prostitution, a murderer stabbing his victim, some emaciated nuns paying off a fat priest, drunken revellers being crushed under the hay-wagon's wheels – and in case any doubt lingered about Hieronymus's intention, at one side of the canvas a mob of demons dragging sinners off to the flames of eternal damnation.

'Hay-ride, sleigh-ride,' said the old sexton. 'That's s-l-a-y. Bosch knew that good Christians as well as bad ones have nightmares like this. Don't go in there!'

I was still standing in the doorway. I thought he meant the cell.

'Stay out of that painting, I mean,' he warned. 'I recognize a lot of faces in there. Dead men. There's old Medina Sidonia, and that one's Alba, to mention just two. You think it's a kind of purgatory?'

He didn't seem to expect an answer. He turned to leave and said, 'Well, we'll find Salvador for you. And we'll send in some supper. Good night.'

It wasn't.

The Bosch painting bedevilled me. I lay unable to sleep – or dreamed I was unable to sleep. All night I heard the rumble of the hay-wagon's wheels and felt the hay swaying beneath me. I blew the pipes, looked at the girl on the hay next to me. Why hadn't I notice her strange, protean beauty in the lamplight – that mane of wheaten hair (head of dark curls), those luminous pale blue (disturbing amber) eyes? In a thin, true voice (Constanza's? Aldonza's?) she sang, 'If you hide yourself from me/Then death shall close my tale.' I blew again on the pipes, a bell-like sound that became the ringing of the angelus.

I rolled off my pallet and stood on my left leg. Tried the right ankle and found it could support me. The painting was just a painting, the girl just a girl.

The sexton came in with a steaming bowl of gruel. 'An hour from now, you'll find Luis Salvador in the gallery above the Courtyard of the Masks.'

In the gallery a chubby man was making faces at the masks below, shouting one perfect tenor note at each in turn. He heard my footsteps and said, 'Listen, the *giravolo* told me he wrote those lyrics himself. How was I to know?'

'Where is he?'

'Wherever *giravoli* go for the winter. I paid him ten thousand *maravedís* for those lyrics.'

'For my song. That's all?'

'He was hard up after a season peddling snakebite cures in Ireland. Ten thousand – for all rights.' Sweat was streaming down his chubby face. 'How was I to know?' he asked again, mopping with a silk handkerchief between his neck and ruff. 'How about fifty thousand *and* you get proper credit for the lyrics?'

Not knowing what to say, I said nothing.

'All right, all right. A hundred thousand.'

I raised my eyebrows.

He settled for 225,000 *maravedís* – a good 500 ducats – and handed me a pouch.

'You drive a hard bargain,' he said. 'At least promise you'll tell the King it was an honest mistake.'

'How can I do that?'

'But it *was* an honest mistake.'

'I believe you.'

'Then tell him. Plagiarist, he called me. "You'd better come up with a good explanation, Salvador," he said, "or you'll wind up chapel singer to some bumpkin baron down in Murcia." And he meant it, you know the King, probity's his middle name.'

'Old man in monkish robes, about my height, with the well-known royal gout?'

'Well, sure. Did you expect something out of an official portrait? How did a drifter like you meet him anyway?'

'I just bumped into him,' I said, and returned with my pouch of gold to the King's apartments but couldn't get past a fourth assistant secretary. I left a note and rented another mule at the Slag Heap stables and went home, where I repaid the money Santi Ambrosio had lent me. This seemed to surprise him. I bought a beret toque with a band of semi-precious stones for Andrea and a striped silk mask for Magdalena, who only went out these days with her face covered. For Catalina, who couldn't accept finery, I hired a metalworker to construct roomy animal cages and some swings for the howling monkey. For Constanza I bought a chest-shaped embroidered handbag, the very latest style, and put inside for luck a few ducats. She threw her arms around my neck and said she hadn't meant it when she said Lope was a real playwright, at least not the way it sounded. He might be the biggest celebrity in Madrid, she said, and I might walk unnoticed through our own neighbourhood, but she was sorry. I wasn't sure what she was sorry about but figured she meant well.

Presently I checked with the royal printing office and confirmed that I was the official author of the lyrics of *Adrift on the Sea of Love*. For a while I followed strangers in the street who were humming Salvador's catchy tune, but pretty soon such people became harder to find. *Adrift* lasted more than most popular songs, but more than most is hardly forever. Even at home it was seldom played on the cembalo or sung over kitchen chores.

Madrid's two seasons – winter and hell – alternated, the annual plague moderated, silver crept into my copper beard, I wrote and tore up a dozen songs. The gold in my pouch dwindled, though I still could stroll to Taverna Isabel evenings for a convivial cup with Gabe.

One day a magistrate's clerk brought a summons to the tall stone house near the Gate of the Sun, ordering me to appear in Sevilla to answer charges of defalcation as a commissary at various places in Andalucía. Since my career in the civil service had begun and ended almost a decade ago, this was palpably ridiculous.

My brother-in-law urged me to demand an audit right here in Madrid, but the royal auditors told me the records were all in Sevilla, and to Sevilla I must go.

I had enough money for the journey, and for the lawyer I would probably need to unscramble an obvious bureaucratic mess. As I turned my latest rented mule's head south on the old road again, I whistled a few bars of a song that wasn't *Adrift on the Sea of Love*.

XXXI

The Birth of Don Quixote

And the Death of Christopher Marlowe

A corpulent horseman on a white stallion galloped into the patio of the deluxe hostal in Bayona Street across from Sevilla Cathedral. The marble and jasper fountain plashed, an imported South American bird in the branches of the rare carambuco tree cut off a madrigal in mid-trill to sing a martial air, and three lissom Negresses from Fernando Po scantily clad in the familiar green and gold livery rushed up to take the bridle, hold a platinum stirrup, and deftly catch the sombrero the horseman tossed negligently aloft as he dismounted.

I rose from a marble bench as the horse was led away.

'What do *you* want here?' my old friend Tomás Gutiérrez greeted me.

'A room. I can pay.'

'What a novel idea,' he said.

A lissom Negress brought him a tall cool drink. 'Nothing's more refreshing than tigernut milk,' said Tomás, and drank. Then he grinned, a self-satisfied grin that took years off his face. He fingered the broad purple sash he wore diagonally across his chest. 'The Brotherhood of the Most Holy Sacrament of Sagrario,' he said. 'I've been elected to provisional membership.'

'How did you manage that?' I asked, remembering his being black-beaned the last time we'd met.

'Convention facilities. They needed a place to meet, and here at the inn, I mean hostal, I've got this banquet hall that holds two hundred easy. The Gold Coast Room. Decorated with eighteen-carat gold leaf, discreetly of course. Remember that ditty you wrote about the hostal? It really caught on after I had it set to music.'

I said, rather curtly, that I wasn't interested in any verses of mine that had been set to music.

But Tomás sang anyway:

> 'Should you consider it discreet
> To ask the price of room and board,
> 'Tis proof that you can ill afford
> The hostal in Bayona Street.'

Eyeing Tomás's empty tigernut-milk glass, I went to the fountain and drank.

'What if one of my Sagrario brothers walked in and saw you slurping water from an ornamental fountain?' Tomás reproved me. 'Of marble and jasper. What if he knew you were a friend of mine? Funny, how people change. The same background produced you and I, but we've gone our different ways. One the owner of the number-one classiest deluxe hostal in all of Spain, the other a drifter – '

This was the second time I'd been called that. Why it should have surprised me, I don't know.

' – who even took a Jew job to keep on the move. Do *I* look like a New Christian?' he asked, suddenly insecure.

I tried to place this overweight innkeeper among the ragged and starving refugees off the dogger. 'No,' I said.

Tomás beamed. Then he scowled. 'There's no room at the inn. I mean hostal. Unless you'd settle for that room downstairs I gave you last time, and use the back way when you come and go, and try to go more than you come . . . Hey, remember my old pal Juan Rufo?'

'Sure.'

'Coming up in the world, just like I. Got a royal appointment as Chief Magistrate down here. How come his office is making enquiries about you?' Tomás asked.

Tomás being Tomás, I didn't know what to say. I decided on, 'Time for the usual audit. You know bureaucracy.'

'I told them it's been four, five years at least since you've been here, because if you'd been here I'd have known because you'd have been *here*. Sponging,' said Tomás.

'I said I can pay,' I bristled, then realized what he'd said. 'You mean the auditors think I've been here recently?'

'Actually it was a couple of investigators for the Chief Magistrate, the most powerful man in Sevilla, my old friend Juan Rufo.'

'I'd better go and see him,' I said.

Juan Rufo kept me waiting three hours. After the minimal embrace demanded by etiquette, he said, 'I hear Andrea's marriage to that shifty Medici travelling man seems to be working out.'

'He's a fine husband and a decent human being.'

'Aren't they all if they're rich,' said Juan Rufo. His twin-pointed beard had gone entirely silver. The look of eagles in his eyes, so assiduously cultivated, had become the look of the giant Andean condor, largest raptor of all.

'I have a warrant for your arrest,' he told me.

'No need for that,' I said. 'I'm here voluntarily.'

'I'll have to arrest you anyway. Any Chief Magistrate who bends the law for an old . . . acquaintance is taking that first step over the line of corruption. And after the first step it becomes easier.'

'The charges are nonsense. I haven't been anywhere in Andalucía in years.'

Juan Rufo opened a bulging file. 'Embezzlement . . . royal funds to purchase grain and fodder for the Invincible Armada . . . Écija in 1590 . . . Vélez Málaga, La Rambla and Castro del Río in 1593 . . . Almuñécar and La Herradura in 1591 and again from 1594 to the present . . .'

'Now wait just a minute here!' I cried. 'It's all obviously some kind of stupid mistake. You said funds for the Invincible Armada. But it sank in 1588. So how could I or anyone have embezzled funds for it years later?'

'A typical laymanly misconception,' said Juan Rufo. 'The military didn't stop collecting provisions for the Invincible Armada just because it was sunk. Military procurement is an end in itself. Quotas are, if anything, larger than ever before.'

I tried, 'I wasn't *in* any of those places any of those years. Part of the time I wasn't even in the country.'

My old friend Juan Rufo's condor eyes narrowed. He whipped a paper from the file and turned it around so I could see it right-side up. The bottom line was my signature.

'What is this?' I shouted.

'Your signature,' said Juan Rufo. 'Do you deny it?'

'No, but ... that is, it *looks* like my signature, but how can it be my signature if I never signed any' – I scanned the paper – 'official document acknowledging receipt of an illegible sum of *maravedís* from the Commissary General for payment to the village of La Herradura as – '

'But you did receive that illegible sum if this is your signature.'

The more I looked at it, the more it looked exactly like my signature.

Juan Rufo pulled more papers from the file. 'To continue: from 1588 to the present, if we include your work as a tax farmer as well as a commissary, that is, funds paid over to you *by* the various townships as well as funds entrusted to you *for* the various townships – '

'I was never a tax farmer, not for five minutes! That's a Jew job!' I said, and immediately added, 'I take that back.'

'Then you admit defalcating as a tax farmer? I'll go as easy on you as the law permits, Miguel.'

'I'm guilty of nothing.'

'A magistrate soon learns everyone is guilty of something. You, specifically, are guilty of embezzlement to the tune of two million five hundred and fifty-seven thousand and twenty-nine *maravedís*. Three embezzling tax farmers were hanged last year.'

'The whole thing's ridiculous,' I said. 'That file of yours could pass for a brief by Señor Zum.'

'You want him? He's good.'

'I want Juan-O.'

'Who?'

'My brother Juan the Obscure.'

When Juan Rufo just shrugged, I blurted, 'Pierre Papin's gambling den! That's the answer!'

'You mean you *gambled away* two million five hundred and fifty-seven thousand and twenty-nine *maravedís*?'

'I mean I could get word to Juan-O through Papin.'

'As Chief Magistrate I've closed all the gambling dens in town until certain ... arrangements can be made between them and this office,' said Juan Rufo.

'But I've got to get word to Juan-O. A note care of Tomás Gutiérrez might work.'

Juan Rufo agreed to have the note delivered, and I wrote it and was hustled off to the royal prison in Sierpes Street, where Juan-O himself had been incarcerated for a time after killing Pedro (Killer) Pacheco Portocarrero and where, watching the gates thud shut behind a coffle of prisoners when we were young, my sister Andrea had gone into a trance of second sight and murmured, 'Dear God . . . Miguel . . . so many prison cells.'

My detention pen in the *audiencia* contained forty or fifty jailhouse lawyers, and they all agreed the thing to do, if you could, was get Señor Zum – so it was a pity he was so busy with nameless business (nameless, to them, with a small 'n'). But finally one day a respectful-looking warder led me out to the prison alley where, among the usual wives, whores, guards and lawyers, Señor Zum was waiting.

His long nose which God or the Devil had pinched to a point was duller than ever from disuse. During our conversation he didn't once touch it, not even after it bled the second time.

'My hearty congratulations, Don Miguel,' he said. 'There'll be no trial.'

This hardly surprised me. It had all been just one of those maddening bureaucratic cock-ups so common in the first sun-never-sets empire.

'Any formalities, or can I go now?'

'You'll be transferred today,' said Señor Zum, 'from the *audiencia* to the prison proper.'

'But I'm innocent. I didn't embezzle anything.'

'Only two people in the world – or three, including yourself – know that, and there is absolutely no way I could have proven it, not if I intended to honour the promise I made to my dear sister on her deathbed. I therefore acceded to an administrative session instead of a trial, at which you could have been sentenced to hang.'

'But I'm innocent.'

'I entered an administrative plea of guilty to the lesser charge of embezzling funds of and for the towns and villages of Écija, La Rambla, Castro del Río, Vélez Málaga and Almuñécar.'

'Lesser charge!'

'During plea bargaining, charges of embezzlement of funds of and for La Herradura were dropped, reducing the amount embezzled from two million five hundred and fifty-seven thousand and twenty-nine *maravedís* to two million three hundred and forty-five thousand four hundred and twenty-two *maravedís*, reducing your sentence from ten to nine years.'

I hit him. You can guess with which hand. He fell down. Guards grabbed me, pinning my arms.

'I want Juan-O,' I shouted.

Señor Zum picked himself up. His nose was bleeding but, as I've said, he didn't so much as touch it. Despite everything, I found his willpower admirable. He said, 'He isn't here.'

'Then who sent you?'

'He did. That's why it took so long. He's in . . . Quillpusher country.'

Señor Zum pointed the tip of his bloody nose at what used to be my left hand. 'Can you control that thing?'

When I promised to try, he waved the guards away.

'I want Goldfang,' I said.

'I wouldn't. If I were you. Strange things are happening a thousand leagues from everywhere.'

'What kind of strange things?'

'I, alas, have no need to know. But one can know that things *are* strange without knowing *how* they are strange. Take your signature, for example.'

'It wasn't my signature.'

'Of course it wasn't. My nephew Fortuny has a clever way with a quill-pen.' Señor Zum exuded familial pride.

'Then you admit it?'

'Nothing to admit. In the world of documents, known by the legal profession to have greater reality than the real world, an authentic signature is an authentic signature.'

'Not if someone else signed it.'

'But you did not make that claim at the administrative hearing where you were sentenced.'

'I wasn't even there!'

'You were represented by counsel, which is the same. Really, Don Miguel, you're a most difficult client.'

I searched desperately for some way out. 'Commissary General Isunza!' I cried. 'He can testify that I haven't worked for him since before the Invincible sailed.'

'Perhaps he could have, had he not died in 1593.'

Señor Zum was not trying to deceive me to shield his nephew. History does indeed record the death of the implacably obsessed Pedro de Isunza from natural causes in 1593. *Ojalá* that it were so!

'Still, with four off for good behaviour, you might be incarcerated just five years, during which the influential new Commissary General for Andalucía, who happens to be my nephew Fortuny, will see that your accommodation and treatment are the best available.'

I hit him again. You can guess with which hand. And again he fell down. But his willpower was unshaken. Through the blood flowing from his nose, he said, 'You're overwrought. Clients often are when, despite my best efforts, they are found guilty. My promise stands. Fortuny will get you preferential treatment.'

Fortuny did, though it took a month or so before he could grease the wheels, a month in which I occupied floor space (all the bunks were taken) in a dormitory for drifters like me who could count on no help from the prison chapter of the *hampa*. Manacles and fetters chafed my limbs. But whereas in Algiers they were badges of honour, here they were marks of degradation. I was the lowest of the low, and would have sunk even further into the slough of self-pity (which is often a life sentence) except for Señor Zum's nephew Fortuny – who was responsible for my being here instead of himself. One of life's ironies, this, but I was unable to think ironically (or any other way; I simply subsisted; to be is to eat *migas*) until guards struck my irons and escorted me upstairs to a private cell with a narrow slit of a window and two shelves crammed with books. There I found *Orlando* in his many emotional states and *Amadís de Gaula* and an anthology I never saw before or since containing the exploits of such knights-errant as Sir Gawain and Sir Lanval, Guy of Warwick, Ogier the Dane, Roland and Oliver, Pierre of Provence, the McLaughlin of Scotland, the Red Knight, the Green Knight, and other colourful heroes. I read these books, and reread them, and re-reread them until they fell apart. And the more I read them the more rational their world seemed and the more absurd mine (and yours). Can you wonder? In Amsterdam I'd been imprisoned (and still would be, if that shipload of brazil wood hadn't been hijacked) for having a brother with a chestful of medals, and here in Sevilla I'd been imprisoned for crimes committed in my name by my own lawyer's nephew. Faced with such absurdity I had to do something or, like not a few prisoners, go mad. So I asked the guard for paper, an inkhorn and quill-pens. Then for days I stared at them, thinking.

I thought about the family's Columbus connection and its *converso* origins. I thought about my father in debtors' prison, and the death of the Patriarch, and the first twinges of an illicit attachment to my sister Andrea who wasn't my sister. I thought about Picapleitos a/k/a Señor Zum, and about Luis the black slave, later Luis Blackslave, now Goldfang. I remembered rescuing Juan-O, who wasn't Juan-O yet, from the gypsies in Triana. I remembered the birth of postmature little Constanza, and my duel with Nicolás de Ovando's hulking stand-in Sigura, and my flight to Italy, and Cousin Gaspar and poor crazy-brilliant Tasso and his sister Cornelia ('*è bella, bella!*'). I remembered my brother Rodrigo pursuing glory like the Holy Grail, and I relived The Naval and our capture by Barbary pirates. I met again Cide Hamete Benengeli on his deathmat and Zoraida the trance dancer and her uncle Suleiman Sa'adah Sometimes (how Erroneously?) Called the Wise and Michele-Micaela of the classic callipygean curve (are you still playing your dangerous games, Micaela?). And I remembered Shakashik-Who-Sings-His-Own-Songs and what he sang about me, and how could I forget my own death in the Plaza of Atrocities? I remembered my poor dwindled father off the old road for ever, defending himself at the Bench of If-Only with an ancient rusty sword. I remembered Catalina as a bride, and Andrea. I remembered Gabriel Múñoz and Pierre Papin, and the Sands of Terminal Despair and the Fuggerman Hasko von Nacht zu Nebel and Kit Marlowe a/k/a Quillpusher and the brigand Aurelio Ollero whom I never met, and all the people and places that had gone by but also *into* me, and I looked at that stack of paper and that full inkhorn and those quill-pens, and I wrote about none of that.

It takes a bigger ego than mine to write only about what you know, as some (not Lope, I grant) always urge. 'Write about what you know' is dumb advice, if you ask me. Painters don't paint only what they see on the street corner (not unless Hieronymus Bosch's streets were very different from mine), so why should writers be trammelled by firsthand knowledge? Writers, when they're at work, become solitary and downright dull. If every writer wrote about what he knew best, books would be filled with writers crossing out lines, crumpling pages in disgust, staring bleakly at empty paper, hurling inkhorns in frustration – but only at the wall and not, as Martin Luther did, at the Devil.

Write about what you know? It's not just bad advice, it's backwards. A writer *must go beyond* what he knows. And when he does, if he does it in the right way, a strange and wonderful thing happens. When he does, if he does it in the right way, the things he's *not* writing about, the things he knows firsthand, nevertheless by some inexplicable alchemy are there lending their truth to what he *does* write.

Well, I stared at all that blank paper brought by the guard Fortuny had bribed, and suddenly I dipped one of the quill-pens into the inkhorn and wrote the word *ingenioso*, I didn't at first know why. In fact, I crossed it out and substituted *ingenuo*, then crossed that out and wrote *ingenioso* again. Can someone think he's ingenious when really he's ingenuous? Sure; happens all the time.

I started on a fresh page.

THE BIRTH OF DON QUIXOTE

EL INGENIOSO
HIDALGO
DON QUIXOTE
DE LA MANCHA

Following the title I wrote the traditional *ráwi* beginning 'Once upon a time', but somehow that didn't seem quite right, so I crossed it out and started over with a variation of a common Spanish way to begin a story which is supposed to tantalize the reader by setting the scene without actually saying where. I wrote:

En un lugar de la Mancha, de cuyo nombre no quiero acordarme,

and I smiled because '*no quiero acordarme*' had a touch of mystery which the more common '*no recuerdo*' or '*no me viene a la memoria*' would have lacked. Pleased, I continued:

no ha mucho tiempo que vivía un hidalgo

and I smiled again, but sadly this time, remembering how much it had meant to my father to become an *hidalgo*, and I dipped the quill-pen, and pretty soon I was writing that this ingenious *hidalgo* (who, for me, would ever after also be ingenuous even though I'd crossed that word out, because crossing a word out isn't the same as never having written it) became so addled by all the stories of chivalry he read that they grew more real to him than the real world, which, anyway, could stand some improvement, so he decided to become a knight-errant himself, righting wrongs wherever he found them (benevolent machismo personified, you might say).

It was growing dark when I wrote that the first thing he did on making this decision was climb to his attic where he found a rusty suit of armour that had belonged to his ancestors and had stood gathering dust in a dark corner since time out of mind.

As I laid my pen aside, I couldn't help wondering about the battered old suit of armour, which I could see as clearly as the rusty sword my father had wielded in defence of his dreams of If-Only. Was it supposed to stand for something? Even if I didn't think so, readers might – a common problem for a writer who deals not in symbols but only in suggestions. Was this ancestral armour meant to protect a thin-skinned individual, which my Sad-Faced Knight certainly was, from attacks on the purity of

399

his blood? If so, it didn't work. Wouldn't my knight soon be unhorsed and laid out flat, so encumbered by his armour that an irate mule-skinner was able to beat him senseless with his own lance? Or was the armour something entirely different – inadequate protection, perhaps, against his own darker impulses? Why, come to think of it, was he *really* going on the old road?

I do not answer; asking is enough. To ask a question is like crossing out a word, the word 'ingenuous' for example: just as something of the word remains, so the answer to a question is inherent in the asking.

I wrote, and the pages began to pile up, and the seasons turned, and my cell became stultifyingly hot, and between quill-strokes I was scratching madly because the fleas were bad that summer (so were the rats), so bad my first warder said they must have come down from Madrid like all evils, like the plague itself, the plague which soon sent dead-carts through the streets, according to my next warder (the old warder had 'gone away' he said, crossing himself), a very nervous young man who fled screaming the first time the dead-cart came inside, rumbling along piled high with inmates felled by fever, vomiting, delirium, purple-black swellings in the armpits like poisoned fruit, and soon that cart rumbled past every day, and I kept writing, and the next new warder looked like a gypsy, and the next was a foreigner, a deserter off a ship in the now almost empty harbour (from which my great-grandfather's great friend Christopher Columbus had sailed), who would sing in a half-crazed voice over and over, 'I am sick, I must die, Lord have mercy on us!' and who scrawled this dirge on the doors of cells in which prisoners had perished until when he took me out for my daily exercise I saw it on almost every door I passed, so I went back to my writing and lost myself in attacking giants who turned out to be sturdy Manchego windmills, and by the time that episode was finished I became aware that no one had been around with my daily bowl of *migas*, nor had the dead-cart rumbled by, nor had a next new warder opened my cell to take me out for exercise, so I shouted, 'Hey out there, ¿que pasa?' which got no answer but a spooky silence which made me bang on my cell door, which obligingly swung open, and I stood a long time listening to nothing until a cannon boomed from the harbour and all the churchbells of the city began to toll, and I shut the cell door and went back to finish the fight between the Sad-Faced Knight and the so-called gallant Basque, who reminded me a lot of Ovando's hulking stand-in Sigura, before gathering up the manuscript and walking out past all the doors on which the last warder had scrawled, 'I am sick, I must die, Lord have mercy on us!' which were all the doors in the corridor but

mine, and down to a corpse-filled courtyard and through a gateway to
Sierpes Street where I saw a few gypsies scuttling past dressed in black,
and a string of *burros* shrouded in black, and a pair of horsemen, horses
and riders alike in black, and all the shopfronts draped in black cloth, the
city seemingly in mourning for itself, and I walked towards the cathedral,
its bells tolling louder and louder, and banged on the door of the hostal in
Bayona Street which was immediately opened by one of Tomás Gutiérrez's
lissom Negresses from Fernando Po wearing, instead of the usual G-string
of hostal green-and-gold, a breechclout of black silk, while Tomás, in a
black thirty-pile velvet suit, his broad purple Sagrario Brotherhood sash
bordered in black too, came puffing up making shoving motions with both
fat, dimpled, manicured hands and shouting, 'Out! Out of here, you bum!
You trying to ruin me?'

Imported South American birds sang sorrowfully from the branches of
the rare carambuco tree, and water so dark it looked black flowed from
the marble and jasper fountain.

'Tomás, I just want to clean up and get a decent night's sleep before
I – '

'I said out! The plague's bad enough, I don't need an ex-con or escaped
fugitive or whatever you are showing up with the Brotherhood assembling
here in a few minutes for the memorial mass. If they see you and I together,
I could still be black-beaned, I'm only a provisional member, all my life
I dreamed of this, what did I ever do to you, out, out, out, after today I
never even heard of you, any son of a bitch wearing stripes, *stripes!* while
King Felipe II the Death-Loving lies dead in the Slag Heap from a
horrible death, ulcerous sores all over his body, they say, and his bones
crippled by – '

'The King is dead?'

'Long live the King,' responded Tomás, almost as if it were a countersign.
'Long live Felipe III the Inglorious!'

Instead of shoving air with both fat, dimpled, manicured hands, this
time he shoved me. 'Out! Out of my life forever, you freeloader, you
chiseller, you niggard!'

I walked a few steps, acutely conscious of my prison stripes. Even in a city
paralysed by the plague, how far could I go without being apprehended?

'Psst! Don Miguel!'

I whirled. Side door. Lissom Negress from Fernando Po in black silk
breechclout.

'I always took you for a white man,' she said.

'Well, uh – I am.'

'I thought he called you a Negro,' she said. Her open, pretty face began to close. So did the side door.

'Niggard. He called me a niggard.'

The door edged open again. 'Sounds awful close if you ask me. You won't get fifty yards dressed like that. Here.' She handed out a black satin cloak.

I took the cloak and, not knowing what to do with my manuscript, gave it to her for safekeeping.

'Put that cloak on, man!' she said. 'You look like Siena Cathedral.'

'You've been to Siena?'

'You'd be surprised the places I been, the things I seen, before I went to work for this niggardly *innkeeper*.'

'So you do know what niggard means.'

'The way he always treated you, that little shed for a room and come and go the back way and go more than you come – you couldn't possibly be a whitey. Though you're pretty pale in the epidermis for – here they come!'

A troop of *caballeros*, their black thirty-pile crossed by black-bordered purple sashes, rode black-caparisoned horses slowly along Bayona Street chanting, 'The King is dead, long live King Felipe III the Inglorious!'

'Go,' said the lissom Negress from Fernando Po, and as she cast a last doubtful look at my pigmentation and shut the side door, I went.

At about this time, an hour or so past noon on a day in late September, the brigand Aurelio Ollero was having his doubts about black and white too. The one with the mouthful of gold teeth or fangs who used to call himself Blackslave troubled Aurelio Ollero. Not that the brigand wouldn't take the man's money. He would take any man's money, by force or otherwise. But what, he couldn't help wondering, was Blackslave up to? Why would he pay important money to destroy his own secret headquarters carved from the living rock in the rugged mountains east of Arcos de la Frontera? And why had he given no instructions for the disposition of Base Iberia staff who, to a man, when offered the choice of death or membership in Aurelio Ollero's band of brigands, had chosen the latter and were even now making their selections from the *remuda* while Aurelio Ollero's lieutenant Lombrizcacha appraised them on the basis of how they appraised horseflesh?

For all that, Blackslave-Goldfang was no harder to figure than the one called the Maimed Man, who was not maimed in any way Aurelio

Ollero could ever see. That one was gone now, like Goldfang. That one, according to Base Iberia staff, was in Quillpusher country (wherever that was) while Goldfang was on his way back to somewhere a thousand leagues from everywhere.

Striding briskly through the situation room, Aurelio Ollero slashed, randomly thorough, at map after wildly inaccurate map with an old cavalry sword, a gift from his gypsy woman Pilar for whom the village of Whore's Hut had been named, but Aurelio Ollero was not one to hold eponyms against anyone – people change, don't they? There came an instant when, slashing haphazardly at a map ostensibly depicting the northern coast of South America, Aurelio Ollero cut away all the inaccurate bits so the map became a perfect two-dimensional representation (scale 1:100,000) correct to the tiniest detail of every wrinkle of coastline, but the instant proved as transient as any other present moment, and when Aurelio Ollero slashed again the map was no more accurate than all the others.

The cipher room, which was next, meant nothing to Aurelio Ollero, and he left deputies to demolish the cluttered tables, the strangely archaic-looking device of concentric wheels (which made him think of the prophet Ezekiel), the stacks of manuscripts in which, had he been literate, Aurelio Ollero could have found keys to many things he didn't know he didn't know. To his expert *incendiario* Ollero left the archives – *abacus, Abbadon, Abbot . . . Zohar, zutano, Zwingli,* secret knowledge of the sacred and profane down through the ages (shake the tree of history and see what forbidden fruit falls from its branches) – but the *incendiario* did not shake, merely set fire to the thousands of books and manuscripts hauled outside and dumped close to the *barranca* where I had received my investiture into the Nameless.

Aurelio Ollero returned outside to watch the bonfire, pale in the mountain sunlight, then went to the *remuda* and gathered his men for the zigzagging descent from Base Iberia. They had reached the bottom of the scarp when Lombrizcacha looked south, shaded his eyes, and reined in.

'A lone rider. There on the rimrock,' he said.

Lombrizcacha's eyesight was phenomenal, almost the equal of my brother Juan-O's, though not in the dark.

The lone rider, in fact, *was* Juan-O.

'A moving target,' rhapsodized Lombrizcacha, and reached to his right for his musket.

Juan-O might have seen the brigands far below, despite the deep shadow, had he looked in their direction. But, unaware of Goldfang's inexplicable treachery, he trotted confidently along, secure within the perimeters of Nameless territory.

When the others could just make out a horse and rider, Lombrizcacha could see my brother's face.

'*Jefe*, it is the Maimed Man who is not maimed. I shoot his fucking head off.' And Lombrizcacha raised his musket.

Pensively Aurelio Ollero quoted, "A man climbs or he is nothing." The Maimed Man who is not maimed lives by those words. They are good words.' And he shoved Lombrizcacha's musket aside.

The brigands waited, motionless in the shadow of the scarp, until Juan-O had passed in brightness high above. Then they resumed their journey.

Juan-O saw smoke ahead. He urged his horse to a gallop.

Twenty-four hours later, mounted on a mule – stolen, I confess – I got there to find Juan-O camped out beside the ash-filled *barranca*.

No brotherly embrace. Juan-O just looked at me disconsolately, then asked, 'Why? Can you tell me why?'

Unlike our brother Rodrigo, Juan-O was not one to avoid that question.

'Knowledge of the sacred and the profane, for starters,' he brooded. 'Collected at what risk to how many Nameless agents over how many centuries, only to go up in smoke just hours before I get back? The most accurate maps the science of cartography can produce, slashed to shreds. The code-room a shambles. And here's what's left of the archives.' He tossed me a partially burned manuscript. 'The only survivor.'

It was, I saw, a work of the controversial Abbot of Sponheim, and when I caught it, it opened to a badly charred page on which I could make out these word groupings:

> e legendary figure from the real man,
> him with *Johann* Faust, an earlier necr
> lthough perhaps greater integrity). Whether
> goal of mastering all knowledge, and wheth
> y he has indeed pledged his immortal soul to the
> pheles/Mephistophilis/Mefistofele/Mephostophilus,
> a matter for conjecture. But I submit that 'all knowl
> ot in the encyclopedic sense but rather in the
> expulsion from the Garden, when God feare
> uld become 'as one of us' – inci

My hands began to shake. I dropped the charred manuscript.

Why had it opened to that particular page? And why was it so easy for me to quote the next few lines, which were burned to illegibility? And why did the passage give me now, as when I first read it, an inexplicable shock of recognition?

'What is it?' Juan-O asked.

I wanted to say:

Faust, in seeking, in striving, in becoming a pawn in the cosmic struggle between forces he but dimly comprehends, must be viewed as both protagonist and victim of his own tragedy,

But Juan-O had his own problems, so I said, 'Nothing. I heard you were in England.'

'Quillpusher country,' Juan-O said, even more disconsolate. 'Ironic we still call it that. Quillpusher's dead.'

'Quillpusher dead!' I couldn't believe it.

'A stupid death in a stupid tavern brawl at Deptford Strand. Way back in ninety-three.'

In moody commemorative silence we gazed at the ashes filling the *barranca*. Then I asked, 'Did you find whatever you went to England for?'

'When I heard you were in prison, I dropped everything and came back here. The usual circuitous Nameless route.'

'How did you hear?'

'The usual circuitous Nameless way. But I gather you arranged your own release this time?'

'All the warders left. Because of the plague,' I said. 'What do you mean, this time?'

'I mean,' said my brother, 'I wouldn't know how to arrange an epidemic of plague, but I'm pretty good at hijacking a shipload of brazil wood.'

'That was *you*?'

'It seemed the simplest way.'

'And you left England because I was back in prison here?'

Juan-O looked embarrassed. 'Forget it. I wasn't getting anywhere. I was about ready to give up.' He stared again at the ash-filled *barranca*; I was sure he could taste those ashes in his mouth. 'But this,' he said, 'changes things. Somebody named Thomas is responsible for this. Hiding in a dark corner in Quillpusher country. I'm going to find him. I'm going back.'

Everything in me cried out to return to Sevilla, reclaim my manuscript

from the lissom Negress from Fernando Po and finish writing *Don Quixote*.
But the last time my brother needed me, in the house where legend said
Amadis of Gaul had slept, I'd failed him. This time, no matter what, I
had to help.

'Is Mnemosyne there?' I asked.

Juan-O's face got a stricken look instead of the dopy smile I'd come
to expect. He said, 'She'd have been one of the great ones. She was
already good when she was with us, and after her training at Scadbury,
particularly' – he laughed, a sound as desolate as the ruins of Base Iberia
– 'particularly the . . . specialized skills they taught her, she was in a class
by herself.'

I didn't like the way Juan-O was speaking in the past tense. 'Juan-O,
wh-what happened to her?'

'Funny,' he said, evading my question, 'how she was nothing but
a classic callipygean curve and a pair of disturbing amber eyes, but
suddenly it all came together, the dangerous games, the distrust, the
frenetic energy . . .'

'*What happened to her?*'

'For a couple of years,' said Juan-O, as if I hadn't spoken, 'she was the
toast of London, a bluestocking and *femme fatale* rolled into one. Well,
that's finished.'

'You mean – the same as Quillpusher?'

'Worse.'

I didn't want to know, but of course I had to. 'How?'

'The usual way,' Juan-O said.

'There is no usual way,' I said.

'How can you quibble about a thing like this?' he said.

'I'm not quibbling,' I said.

We glared at each other.

'If you want to split hairs,' Juan-O said, 'sure, the Church of England
rite isn't exactly the same, but it's closer than you'd think to the real
Catholic Christian ceremony. Not that I was invited, but they tell me,'
said my brother with a ghost of that dopy smile, 'it was the event of the
London season when Mnemosyne got married.'

XXXII

The Extraordinary Events at Loose Chippings

Shortly after Easter, when the cruel unpredictability of early April yielded to the balm of a tentative spring, Sir Gawayne and Lady Waynescote gave their annual fête for several hundred of their best friends and not a few strangers.

The scarcity of exotics this year worried Lady Waynescote, who liked to surprise her guests – even shock them. Still, the variety of entertainment scheduled would divert attention from the closed-door colloquium that, it was rumoured to be a well-known fact, was the Waynescote fête's real *raison d'être*. Fortunately old Doctor Dee would be coming; and Solon Wise was bringing a genuine Lebanese magus, though Lady Waynescote hadn't met him yet.

The fête was a recent tradition, dating only from the remarriage three years ago of Sir Gawayne, scion of Dutch immigrants (original name Wagenschot) who had made their fortune in wood panelling. For decades a widower, Sir Gawayne had quietly divided his time between business and birdwatching. His country manor (palace might have been a better word) between Kew and Richmond on the south bank of the Thames was just a place to sleep.

The second Lady Waynescote soon changed all that, making extensive renovations and buffing up the old family crest, including a motto Sir Gawayne hadn't known he possessed: '*Vita Jocus Periculosus Est.*'

Lady Waynescote got the idea for this year's illicit colloquium from a sapphire said to be owned by her guest the Amsterdam tulip king Solon Wise (what kind of Dutch name was that, people wondered), on which were incised aeons-old cosmic secrets dealing with the nature of good and evil. Good *per se* was a bit of a bore, so the topic would be: 'The Existence of Evil in a Benevolent Deity's World'.

Young Lady Waynescote, Em to her intimates, was an enigma even to them. Although a certain amount of dalliance prior to her marriage was rumoured to be a well-known fact, she could not be called *demimondaine* nor *déclassée* since she had no (known) social position to fall from. Some detected in her enticing accent, with its voluptuous vowels and castanet-like consonants, a hint of Spanish. Others, Quincy Purslayne for one, detected a more bizarre element, perhaps Arabic.

Lady Waynescote was an accomplished chatelaine with her ear to the ground for the *dernier cri* in household innovations. Her first, a gravel-surfaced circular drive, had given the great house its new name, Loose Chippings. Her latest had her guests agog; Lady Waynescote had installed the first John-Harington outside London.

Crowding the passage leading to the candlelit closet, they entered – one at a time, for propriety's sake – and either used the contraption or not, but certainly pulled the chain that emptied the cistern in a swirling rush, cleansing the bowl below and refilling in an impressively short time. In the queue it was rumoured to be a well-known fact that the Queen would confer on John Harington a knighthood for his invention. Only Lady Walsingham, that bitch Audrey, emerged from the closet unimpressed.

Lady Waynescote was beginning to think the damn John-Harington would send her fête, so to speak, down the drain. The entertainers – puppeteers, players, merry-andrews, jugglers, tumblers and a reputedly gifted hocus-pocus man – attracted few spectators. And hardly anyone was in the music-room listening to the lute virtuoso John Dowland play his *Songes and Ayres* when Lady Waynescote was joined there by Quincy Purslayne.

'Who the devil's this Dasim Zalambur?' Quincy asked. He looked pale and frightened, though perhaps no more than usual.

'A Lebanese magus. Came with Solon Wise.'

'He reminds me of someone, I can't put my finger on who. But when I do, I know I won't like it.'

Quincy Purslayne was a smallish man of about thirty-five (Lady Waynescote's own age, though she looked far younger) who would have been handsome except for his crooked nose and the misalignment of his cheek-bones, the work of Ingram Frizer's talented fists which, Lady Waynescote knew, Quincy himself had paid for. His hair was mousy brown, no colour anyone would have chosen, yet it *was* out of a bottle. His blue eyes, which before he was called Quincy Purslayne had gleamed with benign wickedness, now stared at the inimical world with a permanently haunted look.

'Dear Quincy,' said Lady Waynescote, 'you do worry so.'

'I need to worry. If I want to stay alive.'

Thunder crashed directly overhead and, as if that were a signal, two dozen select guests began to make their separate ways towards the upstairs withdrawing-room. Quincy Purslayne offered Lady Waynescote his arm.

Downstairs, meanwhile, after prestidigitating for some twenty minutes (one trick, in which a full-grown swan disappeared up his sleeve, was not unimpressive), the hocus-pocus man sat through a rather dull melodrama by Chettle, Day, Dekker, Munday and, possibly, a few others. Then he sought out the company's manager, one Philip Hinchlo.

'He here?' the hocus-pocus man said.

Hinchlo was a semi-literate who owned the Rose Theatre at Bankside, Southwark, and a louche brothel. He was also moneylender to ninety per cent of the playwrights in London.

'He's here,' Hinchlo acknowledged, and fell silent.

'Well?' prompted the hocus-pocus man from behind his clown's mask.

'I changed my mind, maybe, like,' Hinchlo said.

The hocus-pocus man did something to a nerve on Hinchlo's elbow, and Hinchlo blanched but did not cry out.

'One of your troupe?' the hocus-pocus man asked.

'No.'

'Some other entertainer? Household staff?'

'No.' Twice.

The inside of the elbow again.

Members of his troupe were all around them. Still Hinchlo did not dare cry out.

'If it's not a performer and not staff, that leaves the guests, doesn't it,' reasoned the hocus-pocus man.

'He's worth a lot to me in one piece,' whined Hinchlo. 'Blokes like Chettle, Day, Dekker, Munday couldn't write a play to save their arses but for him. He's the best script surgeon in London.'

'So he *is* one of your merry little band?' said the hocus-pocus man, squeezing again. 'You lied to me.'

Hinchlo would have crumpled this time but the strong hand gripping his elbow supported him.

''sblood, I didn't! He ain't in my employ, he's a free lance! Anonymous, like.'

'But he does doctor unplayable plays for you? In sterling terms over, let's say five years, he's worth how much?'

Hinchlo named a preposterous sum and waited for pain.

But the hocus-pocus man merely said, 'I will double it if you identify this person.'

So, finally, it wasn't the fear of more pain, nor of dying. Hinchlo began to feel better. It was a transaction he could understand. Just a matter of money.

As Lady Waynescote stood to open the colloquium, her eyes by chance met those of the Lebanese magus Dasim Zalambur; she knew at once who he was. But how could Quincy have known him?

He was a tall man of indeterminate age whose broad shoulders bulged a tight-sleeved robe of some sleek leathery material, possibly the hide of a Komodo dragon. His face was rather lupine, with a slight flare of the nostrils that conveyed confidence and power, and such an intensity of gaze that one might not have noticed one of his eyes was brown and the other blue.

I wish I could set down here verbatim Lady Waynescote's introductory remarks and the discussion that ensued. But of the two Torreblanca brothers (Portuguese wine merchants and political refugees from the Spanish occupiers of their country), only Juan was present that evening at Loose Chippings. And instead of paying attention, he alternated between his dopy Micaela-smile and glum reminders to himself that she was now married to one of the richest men in England. So I can only indicate the general drift of the colloquium, which anyway terminated prematurely when the Welsh hook was thrown and the body hit the floor.

Lady Waynescote addressed the question, 'What actually *is* the supernatural?' with the observation that in the beginning was the myth, and if enough people believed, it was called religion, and if enough debated, it was called philosophy – but how she got from there to the topic of the colloquium, evil in God's world, I can't say exactly, for my brother was then at the dopy-smile stage.

The first speakers were English. What they had to say Juan-O doesn't remember, but afterwards everyone seemed to agree that regarding evil the English were witty but not very profound. The best received was old Doctor Dee who, Juan-O was able to tell me, began with an obligatory trotting out of his well-loved coinage 'the British Empire' (shouts of 'Here! Here!' but Juan-O looked and could see nothing) before invoking the Old Testament twice (Genesis 6:7 and another verse Juan-O forgets) to prove that evil exists because God, while well-meaning, just happens to be incompetent.

Solon Wise the tulip king went a bit easier on God, saying that general incompetence was unproven, and the presence of evil might be the result of one unfortunate mistake, the sort anyone could make. It seems that originally all space was filled by God Himself and His various attributes – goodness, beauty, truth and so on. But then God decided, without researching the project thoroughly, to try His hand at Creation, so He made the universe and everything in it in six days of God-time (with a seventh off for good behaviour) – and ran smack up against the unforeseen. All that space formerly filled by God Himself was now crammed with everything He had created, ironically leaving no room for its Creator. He had forced Himself and His attributes into exile. And what is evil if not the lack of God's presence?

The next speaker, one Dasim Zalambur (whom Juan-O did not connect with Bādindjan the Persian), looked as if he would steal the show, but my brother couldn't elaborate much because (a) the Lebanese magus's discourse was filtered through his preoccupation with Micaela, and (b) before it got very far the Welsh hook was thrown and the body fell (in reverse order, actually) and Juan-O went out the window.

Dasim Zalambur asked why, if a Holy Trinity is so weighty a part of our creedal baggage, we persist in ignoring its necessary opposite, the Unholy Trinity collectively called the Devil, consisting of:

Satan the Antagonist,

Lucifer the Light-Bringer, and

Mephistopheles (from the Hebrew *mephitz*, destroyer, and *tophel*, liar), their agent.

Dasim Zalambur then said something about evil, like beauty, being in the eye of the beholder, but my brother had trouble following because the man next to him, the man with the crooked nose and misaligned cheekbones, had begun to squirm as he stared at the Lebanese magus, who was now suggesting that we'd had it all backwards ever since the better-known Trinity's earliest publicists persuaded us that good was really evil and vice versa — that, in short, we'd been worshipping the wrong Trinity. Were we to look at the matter (or antimatter) under discussion, said the magus, with the rigorous objectivity of our colleague Francis Bacon, who, I note, is not with us tonight, we would see that the relationship between absolute good and absolute evil is startlingly parallel to that between matter and antimatter themselves, which coexist harmlessly if kept apart but on contact totally destroy each other and their surroundings. So we need not, after all, trouble ourselves over which is which, for neither good nor evil is intrinsically harmful, but only the meeting of the two, the sudden intolerable interfacing that always results in annihilation.

Here, Juan-O says, is when it happened.

The man with the broken nose and misaligned cheekbones jumped up, pointed a trembling finger at Dasim Zalambur and cried, 'I know who you are, you're . . .' and got no further because he fainted dead away, just an instant before Juan-O heard a *thunk* as the steel head of a Welsh hook embedded itself to the haft in the wainscoted wall directly above the fallen man. This was followed by the sound of broken glass and the usual screams. Of the two dozen men and women present, most would later say they had no idea who the first man out the window was, while the rest would be divided, some testifying that he was the hocus-pocus man and others the actor-playwright William Shakespeare who, though, was in London earlier that day, watching from the pit (while waiting unhappily for me) a return engagement of his *Titus Andronicus* with major surgery by Quincy Purslayne, and could not possibly have reached Loose Chippings in time to almost murder Purslayne.

The second man out the shattered window was my brother Juan-O. Landing in a boxwood hedge, he regained his feet and heard the crunching sound of the would-be killer running across loose chippings. Juan-O set off in pursuit and might have overtaken the hocus-pocus man, who was none other than Maliverny Catlyn, the notorious Butcher of Clynnogfawr Llanllyfni, had not the hedge, by bad luck, been part of Loose Chippings's famous boxwood maze. In the time it took Juan-O to extricate himself, Maliverny Catlyn made his escape.

Upstairs in the withdrawing-room, a remarkably composed Lady Waynescote revived Quincy Purslayne. After a few eyeblinks and, some said, the traditional, 'Where am I?', he cried out, 'Mephistophilis! *My* Mephistophilis in the flesh!'

But by then, of course, the Lebanese magus Dasim Zalambur had quite disappeared.

XXXIII

'That Time May Cease
And Midnight Never Come'

Earlier that same day. The Rose Theatre, Bankside, Southwark, a few hundred yards from London Bridge.

Groundlings pushed their way from the pit, commenting noisily on the performance. There'd been a few eggs and apples thrown – but also a fair amount of applause at Lucius's hopeful closing lines about similar events never ruining the state again.

In cape and black doublet with a Señor Zum kind of starched white collar instead of a ruff, a man approached me: lank hair, broad unfurrowed brow, vague eyes. He looked at the book I was carrying, Spenser's *Faerie Queene*, its title facing outward.

' "Me seemes the world is runne quite out of square,/ From the first point of his appointed sourse,/ And being once amisse growes daily wourse and wourse," ' recited the man with the vague eyes.

' "For from the golden age, that first was named,/ It's now at earst become a stonie one," ' I recited back.

'You like his stuff?' he asked.

'Well, I'm a foreigner,' I said.

'Bit didactic,' he dismissed, and looked at the empty stage. A light rain began to fall in the pit, emptied now of stinkards. 'And the play?' he asked me.

'A lot of thud and blunder,' I said frankly.

'Audience demands it.' He sounded defensive.

'Ten murders, or was it eleven? *And* the captive queen's three sons sliced up, baked in a pie and served her for dinner? You English don't show much restraint, do you.'

'They added that scene. Munday and a few others. Purslayne, for all I know. Don't blame me.'

'You're Shakespeare?' I said, surprised.

'Well,' he said.

'Call me Amadis.'

'I'm yclept Dromio,' he advised. 'For a character – two, actually – from *The Comedy of Errors*. Ever see it actured?'

'What?'

'Performed. Have you ever seen it performed?'

'Ah. Sorry, I haven't. As I said, I'm a foreigner.'

'Amadis, eh? Know you by reputation. Bit of a sheep-biter.'

I didn't know what that meant. I didn't know what a lot of what he said meant.

'But I always godded your brother. Pity, him not getting the big one. Well, what sort of bale's your pleasure?'

'I'm looking,' I said, 'for Henneage.'

Henneage, you'll remember, was one of the Three Thomases. He'd gone into hiding, it was said, in fear of his life.

'You trying to wind me in cerements?' Shakespeare asked, clearly agitated.

'Huh?'

'I know what our departed shepherd always said, scratch a writer and you'll find a spy. But I no longer have the stomach for it. It's got me on the allicholy side. In short, I want out. You don't know what it's been like.' Shakespeare wrung his hands, a broad theatrical gesture – well, he *was* an actor. 'Essex up to God knows what and my patron Southampton thick as thieves with him. What can I do?'

'You can take me to Thomas Henneage.'

'I have things to write. I want to live to write them.'

Silence from me.

'They'll emboss me,' he said.

More silence from me. Sometimes, I had learned, a dialogue of one works best.

'Irregulous they are. A bodkin in the back's the thanks I'd get.'

It started raining buckets and we ran for the gallery.

'Try to understand my position,' Shakespeare pleaded. 'But how can you? Only another writer could.'

I might have raised an eyebrow.

'I don't want to leave you with the impression that I'm being cautelous.'

'Umm-mm,' I contributed.

'The best I can do is accite someone further up the line. Tomorrow. There's a revival of poor Marlowe's *The Tragicall History of the Horrible Life and Death of Doctor Ffaustus*. Worse than moving his bones, what Hinchlo's done to that play. Carry your Spenser, open to Book One, Canto Four. Your contact will say, "Here will be an old abusing of God's patience and the King's English," to which you must respond, "Why, then the world's mine oyster,/ Which I with sword will open."'

I repeated sign and countersign.

'Not bad, those lines, eh?'

'They'll serve.'

'I mean, if you heard them from that stage there, would you *like* them?'

' "The world's mine oyster," that's got a nice ring to it.'

'From *The Merry Wives of Windsor*. Wrote it year before last, not a decade ago like *Titus Andronicus*, so Hinchlo's script surgeons haven't had much time to beslurber it with gallimaufry. Well, I aim to live long enough to write a few more plays. So make sure you tell 'em this is the last bit of intelligencing I do.'

The rain slackened then and Shakespeare said, 'I'd better fetch off,' and went splashing away.

I remembered the spy Quillpusher with mixed emotions (likable, yet he *had* got Micaela shanghaied and me almost fatally knifed), but I didn't know the work of the playwright Marlowe (however spelled). So I returned to the Rose the next day as interested in the play as in the contact Shakespeare had set up.

When two trumpet blasts signalled the start of the performance, I saw that the late Marlowe's Doctor F(f)austus was, as I'd surmised, none other than the controversial Abbot of Sponheim's Georg or Johann Faust who, in exchange for superhuman power and knowledge, sold his soul to the Devil. And from the moment the actor playing Faustus opened with,

> 'Settle thy studies, Faustus, and begin
> To sound the depth of that thou wilt profess,'

I felt my interest quickening to excitement. Who wouldn't be stirred by Faustus's temptation?

It should have been the stuff of high tragedy, Faustus not getting what he bargained for: his paranormal knowledge used for nothing more impressive than playing magic tricks on the Pope, his godlike power never giving him control of as much as a single *barataria* of an insignificant island. Oh, he did embrace (if you used your imagination) the legendary beauty of all time, Helen of Troy. Or was this just another bit of Luciferian legerdemain, the so-called 'face that launched a thousand ships' really some minor devil in drag? Faustus's subtle line dropped in the middle of all this Helen-idolatry, 'Her lips suck forth my soul: see, see where it flies!' – wasn't this a hint to the perceptive playgoer? Poor old Faustus, duped into the most horrendous of all sexual transgressions, demoniality.

But except for this artful touch, the play ploughed ahead with little indirection and less irony, propelling the audience along by the hypnotic effect, rather like African war drums, of the incessant beat of Marlowe's blank verse.

Soon I found myself paying less attention to the plot than to the special effects: the white-robed Good Angel descending to the stage on a pulley, a Bad Angel in black rising via a trapdoor, drumroll thunder and fireworks lightning to remind the audience it was in the grip of terror.

Early in Act II, scene ii, a dishevelled fellow who stank of horse took his place at my side. His clothes were dusty, his face grimy; he had the smashed nose of a pugilist and his cheekbones were misaligned. His running commentary on the play was disconcerting.

'What happened to Wagner?' he muttered. 'Who are these Robins and Ralphs?'

(Wagner was Faustus's servant who suggested in Act I that Mephistophilis dress as a Franciscan, which he obligingly did to satisfy the Catholic-baiting authorities.)

'What *is* this?' through clenched teeth. 'The will to power, reduced to growing grapes in January?'

Between his muted protests, however, he out-cheered and out-hissed the most vociferous stinkards. Minutely he scrutinized the actor, a bit on the podgy side, who had been miscast as Mephistophilis, before heaving a sigh of relief. When a troop of demons cavorted across the stage he counted them carefully and heaved another, louder sigh. And when the doomed Doctor Faustus, knowing that Mephistophilis would soon come for him, cried,

> 'Stand still, you ever-moving spheres of heaven,
> That time may cease and midnight never come,'

tears streamed down my neighbour's face, some diverted earward by a misaligned cheekbone. Nor was he alone. Here Faustus *was* at once protagonist and victim of his own tragedy, as in the controversial Abbot of Sponheim's manuscript: here Faustus appeared almost to take on his shoulders the death we all must face, so that every man and woman in the audience (or so my neighbour must have felt, to judge by the rapture in his tear-filled eyes) was momentarily immortal.

Except me. I felt not the exalting presence of a scapegoat but an inexplicable dread, as if those mighty lines foreshadowed my own future, and not a distant one.

On stage, time didn't and midnight did. Mephistophilis led poor Faustus to Hell with more thunder and lightning and even a whiff of sulphur. As the stinkards left the pit, the man with the misaligned cheekbones looked at the Spenser in my hand and said, ' "Here will be an old abusing of God's patience and the King's English," ' to which I naturally responded, ' "Why, then the world's mine oys − " ' when he grabbed what used to be my left hand and shouted, 'Maimed Man! It's you!'

'Quillpusher!' I shouted in my turn, recognizing his voice, not to mention that delusion of his. 'But you were killed in a tavern brawl back in ninety-three!'

'Hardly. It was a Dutch sailor got stabbed to death in Deptford Strand. A superficial resemblance. We didn't waste any time, believe me, Maimed Man. Smashed his dead face beyond recognition, bought witnesses for the coroner's hearing. I'd already got that Baines fellow to wreck my reputation, so to polite society it was good riddance to bad rubbish. Which left only the rather messy business of altering my phiz, which was accomplished with perhaps more enthusiasm than strictly necessary because Ingram Frizer had got a bit of a scare before they pardoned him for killing me in self-defence . . . but what brings you here, Maimed Man?'

'I'm not the – '

'No, of course not,' said Quillpusher with a conspiratorial wink. 'You know, if it hadn't been for that damnable boxwood maze at Loose Chippings, your brother actually would have taken out Maliverny Catlyn, the Butcher of Clynnogfawr Llanllyfni.'

He was easier to understand than Shakespeare, but not much. He next asked, 'Who *is* this Dasim Zalambur?'

'Dasim who?'

His face fell; his voice rose. 'I've got to find out or I'll go crazy. You're a playwright, you'll understand. Here I was creating a character who was the embodiment of evil, yet I knew he had to be, in his way, attractive. For if evil were hideous, who'd be suaded by it? Follow?'

I followed.

'And before I could write a part an actor could sink his teeth into, I had to know everything about my Mephistophilis, had to imagine his every telling little detail, down to the slight nostril-flare that conveyed confidence and power. Follow?'

I followed.

'And then . . . then at Lady Waynescote's colloquium – on evil, what incredible irony! – I saw the so-called Lebanese magus Dasim Zalambur, and recognized *my own character, the Mephistophilis I had created, in the flesh – oh God! – right down to his one blue and one brown eye!*'

I think I drew a sharp breath, then exhaled a long slow one. I think Quillpusher started to say something more, then let his voice trail off. I think I shut my eyes.

Why was I so upset?

It wasn't news that Cide Hamete Benengeli could change his appearance at will. Nor was it news that, since giving up astrology, he'd wielded increasingly powerful magic. But looking different could be accounted for by nothing more mysterious than a good make-up kit. And how much, really, did I know about this magic of his? My niece Constanza dreaming about him I could accept as a (admittedly hackle-raising) coincidence. The walking through walls he could have done with mirrors or something.

But this –

It was staggering that the Mephistophilis Marlowe had imagined, the embodiment of evil he had committed to paper who would only thereafter appear to him in the flesh as a Lebanese magus, happened – just happened! – also to be my sometime mentor, my saviour (twice, in fact), the Cide Hamete Benengeli I'd first met on his deathmat in Algiers when Marlowe was still a child here in England.

Quillpusher assumed the distress he saw on my face was a sharing of his own.

'You'll be seeing 'em, Maimed Man,' he said. 'Tell 'em I've lost my nerve, I've got to get out. This Dasim Zalambur on top of the Butcher of Clynnogfawr Llanllyfni is more than I can handle. Espialls, intelligencing – I'm saying goodbye to all that.'

'You and Shakespeare,' I said.

'Oh, well, Shakespeare.'

I asked, 'What will you do?'

'Run for my life. Let 'em know. Purslayne's on the run.'

'So that's what you call yourself these days. First name Quentin, something like that?'

'Quincy, actually, but how – '

'Q.P. Quill Pusher. Funny how often they do it.'

Dark clouds hung heavy over the Rose Theatre. His face swam towards mine in the gloom. 'You don't miss anything, do you,' he said. 'You're uncanny, Maimed Man.'

He reached for what used to be my left hand. Then he appeared to stumble against me, grabbing my arms to regain his balance, pulling me close to himself, chest to chest (he was up on tiptoe), his breath coming in excited little gasps as without warning he kissed the angle of my jaw and then tried to get at my lips. I stepped back awkwardly, nonplussed. Quillpusher flinched as if from a blow, but I had only raised what used to be my left hand in a wordless suggestion that he stop.

We stood in silence, contemplating nothing much. A smile of infinite sadness softened Quillpusher's battered face. 'I could claim,' he said, 'that that was just my over-theatrical way of saying goodbye. But the truth, Maimed Man, is that everything this Baines fellow said to wreck my reputation wasn't entirely cock-and-bull. I felt . . . attracted to you from the moment we met, down there by the Sands of Terminal Despair.' A harsh laugh. 'Terminal despair – that seems to sum up my current situation.'

'At the time I almost thought you and Mnemosyne . . .'

'Friends. Just friends. She's a lady now, you know.'

'She was always a lady.'

'You'd never recognize her,' Quillpusher said.

I heard myself say, 'I'll always recognize her.'

Our eyes met; he nodded. 'Yes,' he said, 'I believe you would. Well,' brightly, 'what can I do for you, Maimed Man? As, you might say, my swan song.'

'I'm looking for Thomas Henneage.'

'If you want to see him while he's still alive, better hurry. The Cross Keys in Gracechurch Street. Same sign and countersign. Can you make it no later than cockshut?'

'Maybe. If I knew when that was.'

'Twilight. Carry the Spenser.' Another sad smile. 'Damme, Maimed Man,' he said, 'damme,' and his voice broke, and as Shakespeare had, though with far more feeling, he said, 'I'd better fetch off.'

And off he fetched, a courageous little man with big problems, and not untalented. I never saw him again.

At cockshut the innyard of the Cross Keys not far from London Bridge was far more crowded than the pit of the Rose a few hours earlier. What held the attention of the spectators four or five deep around the half-timbered walls was a dancing horse named Clavileño (after the mythical flying steed that had galloped its way from the *ráwi* canon into European folklore) prancing to the music of a hurdy-gurdy.

To my surprise I saw a familiar face in the front row on the south-east side of the innyard: Shakespeare-Dromio.

I greeted him and asked, 'Where is he?'

'Do I know you, fellow?' Shakespeare said.

So I gave him, ' "Here will be an old abusing of God's patience and the King's English," ' and he declaimed, ' "Why, then the world's mine oyster,/ Which I with sword will open." Upstairs, second-floor rear. You'll be sure to tell 'em I'm finished as an intelligencer? Two years I signed on for – two years too many they were. Two years to the day since, in a weak moment, I let 'em recruit me for espialls and intelligences, forraine and domestick. Twenty-third of April in '98 it was. Might as well have let 'em rip out my chaudron and tie horses to my four quarters.'

'What?' I said. 'What did you say?'

'Chaudron. Entrails. I referred to evisceration.'

'No, I mean the date.'

Trying to make sense of the Three Thomases Dossier, I'd been so busy following false leads (other Thomases confused the issue: Kyd, deceased; Nash, still alive; but they're part of Marlowe's story, not mine) that I'd lost all track of time. Anyway, *my* April 23rd had passed while Juan-O and I were *en route* to England.

'April the twenty-third,' he said. 'So?' It meant nothing to him. What bliss it must be, I thought, to live in ignorance of that fateful date!

Again Shakespeare reminded me to tell 'em he was finished with espialls, and fetched off past Clavileño who was ramping gracefully in the fading light to a sprightly ayre or aire by William Byrd or Birde.

When no one answered to my knock, I spoke that line about abusing the King's English, and a morose voice inside the room told me not very convincingly that the world was its oyster. Also that the door wasn't locked.

I went in to the twin stenches of unwashed male and stale beer. The shutters were open. A man wearing only his underwear was stretched out on the narrow bed staring up at the low ceiling, smoke-blackened by countless candles like the one now burning on the ewer stand.

'They send you to kill me?' he asked. 'Don't I even rate the Butcher of Clynnogfawr Llanllyfni?'

If he expected someone to kill him, I asked, how come the unlocked door and the unshut shutters?

'Why bother?' he said. 'No locks ever kept death out.'

'You're Henneage, Thomas Henneage?'

'Soon to be the late Thomas Henneage.'

'Who wants to kill you?' I asked, and he said, 'As if you didn't know,' still staring ceilingwards as if he saw his own death there. Maybe he did.

'Who destroyed Base Iberia?' I asked him.

'Base Iberia? They destroyed *every* Nameless base except the one a thousand leagues from everywhere.'

'But why? Who are they?'

He said, 'As if you didn't know.'

In this abject state he was useless to me. So, perhaps prompted by Marlowe, I suggested, 'Why don't you make a run for it? Fetch off to the New World or somewhere?'

'He'd find me.'

'Who?'

'Maliverny Catlyn, the Butcher of Clynnogfawr Llanllyfni, with that bloody Welsh hook of his.'

420

Where had I heard that name? From Quillpusher, yes – something about Juan-O and a boxwood maze. Were my brother and I close to fathoming the Three Thomases Dossier?

'What's a Welsh hook?'

'A kind of battle-axe. The Butcher of Clynnogfawr Llanllyfni's weapon of choice. When he can't get his hands on a stone-bow. Which is a crossbow converted to fire not bolts but stones or bullets, as if you didn't know. Now just leave me. I'm a dead man. RIP.'

He looked at me dismissively, and saw what used to be my left hand. 'The Maimed Man. So that's who you are.'

Best not to disabuse him. But how to keep him talking? I tried, 'I'm supposed to tell 'em Dromio's finished with espialls. Forraine and domestick.'

'You know 'em, do you?'

'Actually, no. I figured you would.'

He sat up. A knife with an iniquitous seven-and-a-half-inch blade materialized in his hand. So he was armed after all. 'Leave 'em alone,' he snarled. The knife blade traced glittering morris-dance patterns in the candlelight.

'I'll leave 'em alone if you tell me who destroyed those nameless bases,' I said, wondering why he cared about *them*, whoever they were, since he didn't seem to care about anything else, not even himself.

Back went his eyes to the ceiling. 'There are three of us Thomases – Walsingham, Phelippes, and me. Me, I had this pipe-dream of becoming the new W, even though Walsingham had the blood relation and Phelippes controlled the codes. But one of us was going to, see? Walsingham, he was always a joke. Maybe he doesn't fear easy like me, but can you deny he's an unroosted spaniel?'

I said I couldn't.

He continued. 'He's coyed, but where's his power? With that wife of his, that Audrey, mankind and riggish, and him all wittolly? She knows Her Majesty won't live for ever, and Essex, for a man who would be king, is not only knot-pated but a geck, *and* little Audrey's never been moonish on the subject of James of Scotland, now has she. Which takes care of Thomas Walsingham, it does.'

I said, 'It does?'

But he just continued. 'Which leaves Thomas Phelippes. If he weren't an idiot savant at ciphering and didn't have that Maliverny Catlyn to do his dirty he'd be a nullity right out of one of his own codes. But that doesn't stop him from going freelance with this Phelippes Espionage and Esoteric

Knowledge firm of his. Wouldn't have got off the ground except for his forraine associate with that sang-froid of his. So if they can eliminate – '

A sharp rapping interrupted him. He put the knife away and sagged kismetically back on to the bed as I went to the door, which had already opened a crack to reveal a disturbing amber eye.

' "Here will be an old abusing of God's patience and the King's English," ' she shot at me impatiently, and nudged me aside with a riding crop. I heard a glad shout of what sounded like 'Mistress Em!' from the bed while I tried to adjust to her presence and still get the countersign right.

' "Why, th-then the world's m-mine – " '

' "Oyster which I with sword will open," ' she rattled off even more impatiently, and told Thomas Henneage, 'He's here, he's crossed the bridge, he's been seen in Gracechurch Str – ' before she whirled and gasped, 'Miguel!'

Had she appeared in her Lady Waynescote finery and her Lady Waynescote persona, cool and poised and aristocratic, I never would have dared take her in my arms. But dressed as she was as a stableboy or groom, she could have been the tomboy I'd first seen in Algiers with a blood orange on her dark curls – and take her in my arms I did. Her response in kind was fleeting, terminated by a few taps of her riding crop on my shoulder and the words, 'What do you expect me to do when you come back into my life once every few years, usually at the *most* inopportune moment – babble that I've loved you ever since I was fourteen and roll over with all four feet in the air because you've magnanimously granted me some of your precious time when Maliverny Catlyn, the Butcher of Clynnogfawr Llanllyfni, has been seen in Gracechurch Street? Get off the bed,' she ordered Thomas Henneage.

'What's the use?' he kismeted.

To rally him, she said, 'You had it right about the Three Thomases including yourself, except it was no Thomas that Audrey Walsingham's been cuckolding her husband with.'

'I can tell you it wasn't this Thomas, more's the pity,' said Thomas Henneage wistfully.

'You're *attracted* to that bitch?'

'Sexy. She's a sexy bitch,' said Henneage.

'It's obvious the Butcher of Clynnogfawr Llanllyfni thinks so,' said Micaela frostily, 'since it's with him that Audrey's wittolling Walsingham. Get dressed.'

Soon Henneage's muffled voice came from under the bed. 'Where're my shoes, I can't find my shoes.'

She found them for him. That callipygean curve was as classic as ever.

I said suddenly, 'Em! He called you Milady Em! They didn't tell me to tell 'em, they told me to tell *Em*.'

'Who told you to tell me what?'

'Shakespeare-Dromio and Marlowe-Quillpusher-Purslayne. They're both getting out of the spy business.'

'Poor Quincy has no choice. He knows almost as much about that bitch Audrey as I do, and she knows he knows. But don't worry about Will. He's just a go-between who gives himself airs. He was never *in* the spy business.'

'If you're the one they wanted me to tell, does that mean you're the new W?'

'Nobody is, not yet. The Queen favours me, but she *is* sixty-seven and her interest in espialls isn't what it was. And that bitch Audrey's got the ear of the likely successors. Well, I'll get it or Audrey will. Whichever, England won't be big enough for the two of us. All this, you can imagine, has been pretty hard on dear old Gawayne.'

'Oh,' I said. 'Sure. Gawayne. Juan-O told me you were m-married.'

'A husband of a certain standing makes an ideal cover.'

'I understand perfectly,' I said.

'He's a very sweet man and practically old enough to be my grandfather,' she said.

'Of course,' I said.

'We have our arrangement,' she said. 'He's free to birdwatch and I'm free to . . . But my private life could be of no possible interest to you, even if it and my professional life have to a degree overlapped since my special training at Chislehurst cured me of a certain traumatic childhood exper – why am I telling you all this? For God's sake get a move on!' she shouted at Thomas Henneage, who was stumbling around near the bed trying to climb into a pair of out-at-knee breeches. 'Torreblanca's downstairs with the horses. You might try,' Micaela said, 'taking your shoes back off,' and I said, 'Juan-O's here?' and Micaela said, 'I'm not wild about him not knowing what Maliverny Catlyn looks like, but then so few people do,' and Henneage complained, 'My hat, I can't find my hat,' as Micaela prodded him through the door with her riding crop.

Hurrying Thomas Henneage downstairs, Micaela wondered whether she and I always said the wrong thing to each other simply because there never was a right thing, then reminded herself she had more pressing worries.

She heard music (the tune was *Cherry Ripe*) and saw by torchlight the hurdy-gurdy man turning the crank of his lute-shaped instrument while the dancing horse Clavileño bowed to the crowd. She whistled the first four glorious notes of an upward-soaring skylark, hoping Juan-O would hear them despite *Cherry Ripe*. Apparently he did, because soon he was entering the innyard leading three horses. Just three, but now there were four of us. Imagining herself swinging up behind me and clinging to my waist as we went galloping off, Micaela savoured for an instant the unfamiliar role of helpless female.

Outside, Thomas Henneage's indifference to his own demise was replaced by an extreme of caution that made demise the more likely. He found a place where instinctively he felt safe and, like a fighting bull in its *querencia*, would not budge until Micaela's riding crop prodded him into renewed forward motion. By this time Juan-O had almost reached us, and Micaela steeled herself for the moment of maximum danger when four people mounted three spirited stallions, exactly the sort of moment Maliverny Catlyn knew how to turn to his instant and permanent advantage.

Was he here?

The crowd streamed from the innyard through the backlit doorway of the public room, continuing a sentimental sing-along of *Cherry Ripe* even though the hurdy-gurdy had fallen silent. The hurdy-gurdy man could be seen (as many witnesses would later testify) bringing the lute-shaped instrument up to his shoulder (an odd position for it) before turning the crank again. In the torchlit shadows, the hurdy-gurdy now seemed curiously to resemble a stone-bow.

Micaela saw all this – too late by what fraction of a split second to avert disaster? Was she thinking that I, crossing the innyard at her side, might be in danger? Or was she even then beginning to suspect subliminally, as I was, that the real danger was to herself? Did it occur to her that she'd walked right into it, duped no less than Doctor Faustus by that miscast Mephistophilis – for what would the death of a ha'-penny hero like Thomas Henneage matter to Audrey Walsingham? What was he but a decoy to get Micaela within range of Maliverny Catlyn's stone-bow? Did she even, as awareness dawned that the hurdy-gurdy stone-bow was pointed not at Henneage but at her, admire her adversary's cunning?

She saw me leap at the hurdy-gurdy man just as he fired the stone-bow, driving a roundball into the left side of my chest and plunging me into an oblivion distinguishable from death only by a thready heartbeat that, it could be assumed (and was assumed by one Dr Duguid, summoned hastily by the proprietor of the Cross Keys), would cease at any moment.

Did she cry out as I went down? Try to ease my fall?

No, being Micaela, she jumped astride the bay stallion just as Juan-O mounted the roan to race in pursuit of Maliverny Catlyn, who had taken off at a furious bareback gallop on Clavileno, north along Gracechurch Street to Bishopsgate and thence to Norton Folgate and finally Hog Lane where eleven years earlier Marlowe had fought the duel with one William Bradley that started him down the path to Quincy Purslayne and where, now, the bay stallion stumbled in the deceptive mooncast shadows and bolted so that, by the time she regained control, the Butcher of Clynnogfawr Llanllyfni and my brother Juan-O had disappeared into the night, Lamb Street or even Worship Street and Curtain Road, who could say?

Returning to the Cross Keys, Micaela entered the public room to see me stretched on the bar, the doctor with the encouraging name Duguid holding a compress over the entrance wound immediately below my left nipple even as he told the innkeeper, 'It doesn't matter,' sounding rather like Thomas Henneage.

'Maybe not to you but I won't have him cluttering up my bar and him not even a paying customer,' the innkeeper said, which was when she rushed over and (according to several witnesses) spilled tears on my face as she kissed me.

Dr Duguid gave her a sympathetic pat. 'Your father?'

(Whoever has been on the verge of death knows that one doesn't look one's best or most youthful then.)

'My . . . friend,' she said. 'He's so cold – can't you do something?'

'Staunch the bleeding, but I've already done that.' A headshake, and a prognosis couched as conditional-contrary-to-fact: 'Were he not dead by midnight it would be a miracle.'

'I want this corpse off my bar right now,' said the innkeeper.

'I,' said Micaela with hauteur, 'am Lady Waynescote of Loose Chippings. We require a room.'

The innkeeper looked dubiously at her stableboy attire until a gold coin rang on the bar near my inert body.

Since I was moribund anyway, Dr Duguid had no objection to my being moved and, for the price of a pint, volunteers carried me across the innyard and upstairs to the room where Thomas Henneage had awaited the death that had come for someone else.

Henneage was back on the bed, in his underwear again, staring up at the smoke-blackened ceiling.

425

Micaela shouted something and, after the usual fumbling and a few fatalistic words, he left.

To her surprise Dr Duguid did not leave with him. 'I've never seen anyone hang on like this,' he marvelled.

She bathed my face, now flushed and feverish, with water from the ewer.

'Midnight,' said Dr Duguid firmly. 'He'll be dead before midnight.'

Murmuring a line from *Doctor Faustus*, Micaela began her vigil.

XXXIV

The Fateful Adventure

Of the Flying Horse Clavileño

And Other Impossibilities

It's often been said that at the point of death a person's whole life passes in review before his eyes.

I used to wonder why no one ever carried this notion, which for all I know is true, to its obvious conclusion. Which is that there *is* no conclusion.

Here's this person dying, say with a roundball embedded in the left side of his chest, a hair's-breadth from his heart. And he discovers that his whole life *does* pass before his eyes – finally reaching the point where (or when, depending on whether you give precedence to space or time) he's dying and his whole life passes before his eyes, his whole life up to the point where (or when) he's dying and his whole life passes before his eyes, again reaching the point where . . .

Is space-time, with its vast vaulted distances bending back on themselves, elastic enough to accommodate this *ad infinitum*? If so, is that all that's meant by immortality? And wouldn't the quality of a person's life determine whether this eternal return is Heaven or Hell?

426

Intriguing questions, but how could I have answered them? None of this had happened to me. At least, not yet.

I walk up from the river where a ferryboat lies sunken and along a cobbled street flanked by pale stone buildings inspired by Gothic cathedrals to a dusty road on the edge of a city where over a livery stable I see the sign

T. HOBSON
HORSES FOR HIRE

and a man, presumably Hobson, leading a stunted, superannuated mare with long donkey ears past a black Arabian stallion hitched outside the stable doors.

'Not Dapple again,' groans a dumpy fellow clutching his hat who waits anxiously near the horse trough.

'You know the rules. First horse inside the door's the horse you get, or you get nothing.'

'Yeah – and a man's worth just what he's got and gets just what he's worth,' says the dumpy fellow.

'Take it or leave it,' says Hobson.

'Cover a donkey with gold,' observes the dumpy fellow, 'and he'll look better than a horse with a pack saddle. But a nag is a nag is a nag.'

This off his chest, he hands over some coins, mounts, and rides Dapple past me at a dispirited walk.

'What are *you* standing there for?' Hobson demands.

After some reflection I say, 'I think I need a horse.'

'Going far?'

'Just . . . on the old road again.'

A suspicious look from Hobson. 'You've no intention of returning this way, have you?'

'*T. Hobson*' – I'm willing to bet the 'T' is for Thomas. It's a troublesome name. T. Hobson turns his back to curry-comb the black Arabian stallion.

I trudge a few steps away before he calls, 'Hey, you! What road was that you said?'

'Just the old road again.'

T. Hobson disappears into the gloom of the stable. I can hear a healthy whicker – first horse inside the door, I hope. But T. Hobson leads out an equine disaster, mane straggly, muzzle aquiver over too-long teeth, knees knobbly, back swayed, rump and stifles all but fleshless, hooves cracked.

'What about the black Arabian there?' I ask.

'You know the rules. First inside the door. Anyway, you'll find this old boy here's got enough life in him yet to get you . . . where you're going.'

I don't like the sound of that; as if he knows something I don't.

And I don't like the look of T. Hobson, or of the nag that was first inside the door.

But before I can say, 'Thanks, I'll try elsewhere,' a cold wind howls in from somewhere north of infinity, obscuring the livery stable with swirling dust, obscuring T. Hobson and his nag, obscuring the sign I can hear swinging on rusty hinges.

As quickly as it came, the wind blows itself out. The dust settles, the sign hangs by one hinge, T. Hobson and the nag and the black Arabian are nowhere to be seen. The horse trough is dry, the dusty road overgrown with weeds.

I shout a tentative 'Hello?' that startles a crow on the stable roof. The stable doors stand agape.

'Anybody home?' I call. No sound within. No smell of horses, fodder, manure. I go inside.

The only thing I see, standing just inside the door of that otherwise empty stable, is a wooden horse.

I know at once the way you know things in a dream that it's Clavileño. Not the dancing horse at the Cross Keys but the real Clavileño of mythical fame in the flesh – or wood. Painted in bright primary colours – blue mane and tail, red hide, yellow saddle – Clavileño is a wingless flying horse steered by means of a stubby peg in his forehead like the horn of an underendowed unicorn. In Spanish, 'clavo' means nail. And Clavileño? Spike, more or less. I'll call him Spike.

I mount and fiddle with the stubby unicorn horn in his forehead. Clavileño or Spike walks out through the stable doors but evinces no aeronautical skills.

This perplexes me. The great wingless flying horse Clavileño came to me straight from the *ráwi* canon, a tale not far behind Ali Baba or Aladdin in popularity, and Clavileño's claim to fame is that he flies. But Spike apparently can't. Maybe he only looks like Clavileño.

Outside, I feel a prickling at the back of my neck. The livery stable, the dusty road, the Gothic-cathedral-inspired buildings of the city – all have vanished. *Been* vanished, like Cornelia Tasso?

I see a potted tree and a not very realistic boulder, like the props used to denote countryside at the Theatre of the Prince in Madrid, or the Rose right here in London. Except that right here doesn't seem to be London. Or anywhere.

Foreground, background, middle distance, all are obscured by something I have to call fog, but it's not fog exactly, more just the colour grey. And not exactly grey either. A sort of no-colour colour.

Nothing could be less like the fabulous geography of troubadours and trouvères, of the Knights of the Round Table and the Paladins of Charlemagne, of the *ráwi* canon and Ariosto, where Lombardy is hard by Denmark and Cologne misplaced on a Mediterranean fjord, yet I have a feeling I'm embarking on an adventure no less extravagant than those of Peredur of Wales (or was he Breton?), Sindbad the Sailor, even Amadis of Gaul.

I try my luck with Spike's undersized unicorn horn again, but all he does is walk sedately past more props – a cottage painted on a scrim, a steeple and altar proclaiming a church – before stopping at a solitary tombstone that does duty for a churchyard. The property tombstone is papier-mâché, the letters cleverly painted to give the impression of engraving in stone:

MIGUEL DE TORREBLANCA
(? – 23 April 1600)
RIP

I cry out in alarm and slap Clavileño's or Spike's hard bright-red shoulder. He gallops past a one-sail ship that conveys a sea, then a minaret for a faraway city, and another potted tree, a palm, I assume for a desert.

By then I've calmed down. So Miguel de Torreblanca is dead, so what? Isn't he the part of myself I've been fleeing ever since my grandfather died so abruptly in that icy room across the river from the cathedral-spawning mosque? Doesn't his death mean, in some way I'm not certain I understand, that I can finally go home?

But, I have to remind myself, I have no home.

Am I supposed to? Has a mistake somehow been made? Will the death of Miguel de Torreblanca rectify it, even if Miguel de Torreblanca never existed?

It begins to rain. I try my luck once more with the stubby horn in Clavileño's or Spike's forehead.

And skyward he leaps in one of those gigantic bounds so beloved of *ráwis*, swiftly soaring through rain and rain-clouds into brilliant sunlight, while I cling to his mane (there are handholds in the bright blue wood that I hadn't noticed before). Getting over my fright, I experiment with the control horn or spike, soon mastering the simple technique: pull for up, push for down (I get a second drenching), tug left for a left turn, right for a right . . .

I ought to say, as Spike and I skim the cloud-tops at great speed, that I never had any particular interest in the supernatural. I could, in the words of T. Hobson, take it or leave it. But this time I haven't even a Hobson's choice. Because, for the rest of that year and the first three years of the seventeenth century, I seem to have disappeared.

I'm not talking about relegation to unhistory: that's happened to me before. But this time I vanished from the story of my death and life too. And relegation to unfiction is more difficult to take. I went missing even from myself.

Historians, puzzled by my disappearance, would search for me rather like astronomers looking for an overdue comet.

What they managed to find is not enlightening:

• That on 2 May 1600, when one Agustín de Cetina petitioned to become a resident of Sevilla, my signature supported his petition. (Señor Zum's nephew Fortuny is known to have been in Sevilla at the time.)

• That on 19 August 1600 Catalina's little shit of a brother, unaccountably finding God, entered the Franciscan monastery in Toledo. Required to leave a valid will, he again unaccountably named Catalina and me his executors. (Historians eagerly seeking their comet would offer this as proof of my presence in Toledo on that date.)

• That during the entire year 1601 I did not surface.

• That as of 14 September 1602 the authorities in Sevilla had not closed the books on my defalcation (sic), even if no new summons was issued. (A few historians insist this proves I was still incarcerated in that city!)

• That on 14 January 1603 a new investigation of my defalcation (sic) was undertaken, but I was not interrogated as my whereabouts were unknown. (No conclusion drawn by any historian, but I'm glad to say it was the last such investigation.)

And that's it.

As Cide Hamete would say, history has more than its share of off-days, so its non-sightings don't trouble me. But for *me* not to know where I was during those almost four years *is* disturbing, and I want an explanation, no matter where I have to look.

Well – once I get the hang of Clavileño's control horn, we leave the bad weather behind to go streaking through clear skies and occasional cottony clouds high over hills, dales, rivers, streams, plateaus, massifs, savannahs, drumlins, heaths, bays (and a haff or two), firths, a crater lake, lowlands, uplands, badlands, three or four moraines and a mangrove swamp, escarpments and coastal plains, numerous ravines, a long meander belt, and a rain forest where no rain falls. The faster Clavileño flies, the more my confidence soars, until I'm certain I'll reach my destination in minutes, whatever my destination is, as fresh as when I started out and ready for the heroics always associated with Clavileño's rider. But as overconfidence generally leads to a fall, without warning Clavileño banks steeply left and plunges earthward so swiftly that I barely manage to cling to the handholds in his bright blue mane.

Nothing in the *ráwi* canon or any chivalric romance has prepared me for the landscape rising to meet us. Stretching from horizon to horizon is a dazzling white plain, utterly flat and lined with parallel rows of what I at first take for saplings. But when Clavileño levels off again, I see we're racing over a vast printed page, not topography so much as typography, the words whizzing by too fast to read.

Clavileño slows into a landing glide, and ahead, like a monolith come to life, looms a powerful male figure wearing nothing but a printer's apron as he hacks words away with a huge scimitar like a forester clearing undergrowth.

'Have a good death?' he asks as I dismount. 'Nothing messy, I hope?'

He examines me as if searching for indications of a messy death. 'But of course, one leaves such blemishes behind. It was a stone-bow, wasn't it?'

'What are you talking about?'

'The death weapon,' the man in the printer's apron says patiently. His face is rough-hewn as if from abyssal or plutonic rock – harsh quartz and feldspar angles and planes of broad cheekbones and imperious nose, granite ridge of brow (obsidian black hair slicked back from arrowhead-sharp widow's peak), cleft boulder of jaw – a face impervious to the ravages of emotion, except for the eyes. Right eye blue, left eye brown.

'Maybe we'd better begin at the beginning,' I suggest. 'Is it customary to ask, "Where am I?" '

He takes a warning swipe at air with his scimitar. 'Careful. I've been pruning clichés.'

'But if I'm dead,' I say, 'I wouldn't be – '

'You're not going to be one of those wearisome creatures who dispute their demise, are you? So many do. Though I find it strange that you would, *ráwi*, since this is April the twenty-third.'

'Not *my* April twenty-third. That was ten days ago. Besides, last I knew, Shakespeare was alive.'

431

'The last he knew, *you* were alive. Which you no longer are. Dead is dead. Terminated. No sequels. As for Shakespeare, I might have got his year wrong, since I have no arrangement with him.'

'No what? Arrangement?'

He takes from his printer's apron a paper yellow with age. 'This *is* your signature?'

The signature on the document is indubitably mine. But so too were those signed by Señor Zum's nephew Fortuny.

'It looks like my signature,' I allow.

'Then it's time to live up to your end of the bargain, isn't it?' says Cide Hamete.

I try to read the document, but it's written in some unfamiliar language with odd diacritical marks. 'I'd never have signed something I couldn't read,' I say.

'You don't remember my translating for you? Verbatim?'

'Absolutely not.'

'In a pool in a cavern in the mountains inland from Algiers? Green pool. You were overwrought at the time, but I still find your lapse of memory terribly convenient.'

'What does it say?'

'The usual, of course. That in return for certain advantages, you cede your soul to the Devil for all eternity. Signed in your own blood, too – a tasteless touch, but mandatory. One day I'll get them to eliminate it along with other excesses . . . well, do come along.'

We fall into step between two rows of words. At ground level the vast page is three-dimensional; the lower-case letters are shoulder high, the capitals a foot taller. Seen side-on, they can't be read. Occasionally, with a flick of his scimitar, Cide Hamete slices off a superfluous serif.

'What is this place?' I ask.

A thoughtful squint from his blue right eye. 'If I said the Egyptians of pharaonic times cultivated a much smaller and depressingly pedestrian version unimaginatively called *The Book of the Dead*, intended as a guide for the journey through the underworld, would you understand?'

'And you're the . . . author?'

He puffs his chest out but says, 'Don't go jumping to conclusions.'

'Are you trying to suggest you're the Devil?'

'Please! Surely as a man of learning – or at least erudition – you must know the Devil for what he is, the invention of clever medieval ecclesiastics whose purpose was to terrify people into turning to God.'

'Then if he isn't real, I didn't sell my soul to anyone.'

'*Ráwi!* Really! That's too casuistic, even for me.'

'What did I allegedly sell it *for?*'

'Oh, the usual foolishness about godlike knowledge and power. You should have known better. That sort of thing used to work, but not any more. Until the Renaissance, which, thank God, seems to be winding down, a bold man actually could aspire to all knowledge. But that's impossible now. There's simply too much to know. Well, you did sign, and you did get a bonus which was not only of immediate and lasting value but, so far as I know, unique.'

'I did?'

'Never,' says Cide Hamete, 'did the seller approach the bargain from a position of such abject weakness – which you must admit death by hanging to be. The bonus was your life. I saved it when you signed, giving you twenty additional years. The fact that you frittered them away in nameless adventures, many of them clandestine, instead of writing *Don Quixote* and other exemplary fictions, is regrettable but no concern of the buyer. You got your life, and the usual godlike knowledge and power, and now it's time to live up to your end of the bargain. Just step right in here.'

'Here' seems to be an etching the size of a village plaza, black and white like the rest of this weird printscape. Dead centre stands a hay-wagon. A youth seated on the hay plays pipes to accompany a girl serenading a pair of embracing lovers. I have the notion there ought to be an angel in there somewhere, and possibly an etched Christ, but I can see neither. I *can* see, close to the wagon, an evil-looking charlatan selling nostrums and a procuress tempting a country girl into prostitution. Quite stylized and unreal, all of it, including the nuns paying off the fat priest, the drunken revellers about to fall under the wheels of the hay-wagon, the murderer with his knife poised above his victim's breast and, a bit further off, a mob of appropriately horrible-looking demons dragging presumed sinners off into a black-and-white approximation of the lurid flames of eternal damnation.

'A bit off-putting, isn't it?' says Cide Hamete. 'But it really is quite painless. Or so I've heard. Now, in you go.'

I fold my arms. 'You won't catch me going in there.'

'But you must. Haven't you read what the controversial Abbot of Sponheim's written on the subject?'

'Maybe you did save my life – '

'You know I did.'

' – but before you did, I saved yours.'

433

'And claimed your reward when the Dey hanged you. Twenty extra years are nothing to sneeze at, not to mention the usual godlike knowledge and power.'

'But you said that doesn't work any more.'

'Is that my fault? They'll get around to rewriting the basic contract. One of these days.'

'If I was deceived, the contract's not binding.'

'You were no more deceived than anyone else. We're quits, and I'm busy. I've got a field of stubborn isms to weed. That's hard work, unlike clichés. Isms send their roots deep. Now, in with you.'

He shoves me, and I stumble over the black border of the etching. The procuress now has her arm about the country girl's shoulders, the fat priest is pocketing the nuns' coins, the hay-wagon's wheels have crushed the drunken revellers, the murderer is withdrawing his knife from his victim's chest, the demons are dragging someone who might easily be me into those black-and-white flames of damnation.

Regaining my balance, I flee, a row of words on one side, the etching on the other.

Black-and-white flames lick at my heels.

'Fascinating,' observed Dr Duguid, standing at my bedside in the room at the Cross Keys, candle in hand.

Seated on the edge of the bed holding what used to be my left hand in both of hers, Micaela was thinking, Trust no one in this life.

Trust someone and they die.

Dr Duguid found a vantage from which to peer around her. 'Observe the eyes,' he said.

His dispassion infuriated Micaela. 'I can't observe "the" eyes because "the" eyes are closed. "The" eyes are closed because "it" is unconscious.'

Insulated by professional curiosity, Dr Duguid missed the sarcasm. 'There is eye movement, m'lady,' he said, 'rapid eye movement. I've never heard of anyone in a terminal coma dreaming, but this man evidently is.'

'Then mightn't it mean it's not a terminal coma?'

'M'lady, a man can dream his own death – and never wake from the dream.'

'But if it's only a dream . . .' Micaela said hopefully.

'Oh, it's real to him. This man is fighting desperately for his life. But there is no hope. He cannot win.'

Micaela squeezed what used to be my left hand, and imagined she felt it squeeze in reply.

*

434

The point of his scimitar pricking my sternum, Cide Hamete corners me with my back to what might be a capital 'M' seen side-on; it might also be a 'W'.

'I could dispatch you myself,' he says, 'but to be quite honest, that would be frowned on. Why won't you be sensible, *rāwi*? You haven't any choice but to live up to your end of the bargain.'

'Will you stop saying "live up to"?'

'It *is* deliciously inappropriate, isn't it.' He smiles, genuinely amused, a charming smile. No one ever claimed the Devil lacks charm. Not that he *is* the Devil. At least, he said he wasn't. But he hasn't denied being Lucifer, Son of the Dawn, who was replaced as God's archangel-in-chief by my namesake St Michael after a heavenly power struggle.

He hasn't denied being Mephistophilis either, who so terrified poor Marlowe that he fled to God-or-the-Devil only knows where. If he *is* Mephistophilis, I could handle that. What's Mephistophilis but a flashy agent dealing in human souls? What's in it for him, anyway? You can't take a percentage of a soul as commission.

'What's in it for you?' I ask.

With the point of Cide Hamete Benengeli's scimitar pinning me to that capital 'M', you must be wondering how I have the nerve to ask. But consider, I've known him since he was an unsexed mountain of blubber whose name reminded me of aubergine. Benengeli! How can anyone called Lord Eggplant cast me irrevocably into whichever circle of Hell my misdeeds may have earned me?

The scimitar jabs; a trickle of blood runs down my belly.

'Fool that I was, I signed my own bargain. You think I like doing Satan's work – to give the Devil the name he prefers – when I'm not even sure there *is* a Satan?'

'I don't concede that *I* signed any bargain. And even if I did, I was not advised that you represented the forces of evil.'

'Represented. . .!' The point of his scimitar nicks my throat. 'By the Five Books of Moses, the Ten Commandments, the Four Gospels and the One Hundred and Fourteen Surahs, your soul is in your teeth!'

'Wherever it is, you can't have it.'

He lowers his scimitar and in a put-upon voice admits, 'There *are* provisions, in the extraordinary event that someone refuses. At least, I think there are.' From a pocket of his printer's apron he produces a small volume. He blows on it; the puff of dust makes me cough.

'The rule book,' he says, flipping through pages, his blue right eye shut, his brown left eye tracking.

'I always wondered about that door,' he mumbles, and I let out a long breath. Doesn't a door imply a way out?

He snaps the rule book shut. 'Listen to me, *ráwi*. I liked you. Truly I did. So, sentimental old fool that I am, I urge you to take your place in that etching.'

'You listen to me,' I tell him. 'I've seen the Bosch original. The man who showed me it recognized some old friends in there. All of them dead.'

'Everyone tends to recognize people in there. And if they weren't dead, they wouldn't *be* in there. Don't let that door delude you. Nor anything else in the rule book. There is no way out, only ways further in. Before you're through, you'll wish you'd died in your dream.'

He shakes me; I wake. Nothing has changed.

'I'm only trying to make it easy for you. Why must you resist me, *ráwi* – you who have never walked through walls or slipped sideways through time to glimpse the divergent futures fanning out from every routine choice made in the present – which is the only justification for the alleged existence of any present moment save one.'

Concerned as I am with my predicament in the here and now (even if there is no here and now), I don't pay much attention to these strange words.

'But how can you possibly understand? Like everyone else who ever lived, you are locked into a single version of reality, unable to remember those other futures except as a vague nostalgia for what can never be. Unless . . . Didn't you write once that living was a lot like telling stories – life and fiction two different versions of some greater reality?'

We have resumed walking between rows of words. Peering anxiously ahead and hoping to see a door, I acknowledge with a distracted nod that I wrote that somewhere.

'Then you know there is a virtual infinitude of possibilities in every story idea. Take boy-meets-girl.

'Boy falls in love with girl but girl does not return his love.

'Or vice versa.

'Or they are mutually smitten but star-crossed by:

(1) the implacable enmity of their families (ask Shakespeare about this one);
(2) his being married and misguidedly believing he must cleave to his wife;
(3) her being married and misguidedly etc.;
(4) a third party of either sex;

436

(5)   a guilty secret;

(6)   a secret guilt (not at all the same as (5));

(7)   war;

(8)   disease;

(9)   a sense of inadequacy;

(10)   financial problems; or

(11)   any combination of the above.

'You see my point. Infinite possibilities – but limited, if not by the storyteller's imagination, at least by the time at his disposal. So he must constantly make choices. Isn't life similarly restricted?

'Yet the greater reality, of which fiction and life are but two versions, is free to unroll itself with limitless imagination through infinite time to include all possible versions of what was and will be.

'So there can be – and therefore *necessarily is* – a world in which each version of reality is the only reality. Do you see?'

I say, 'Just show me that door.'

'We're almost there. But it won't help you. How can it, if the only reality for you is the version in which you die *this* April twenty-third? Now. One reality to a customer. That's a natural law, like gravity. It's what they mean by kismet. Think of the chaos if we could all choose divergent realities whenever we didn't like the one we're stuck in. Count your blessings, *ráwi*. There are numerous realities in which you were never even born. Here we are.'

I see a door. A plain wooden door with a rusty bolt.

'Now what are you waiting for? This is what you wanted, isn't it? What are you afraid of – cataclysms, a tsunami or a whirlwind or a *zalzalah*, so-called acts of God? It's not like that at all. As a matter of fact, the terrain won't be . . . unfamiliar to you.'

With a flourish he steps back and disappears. The world has been reduced to that most unremarkable door and me. I pull the rusty bolt, and go in.

Cide Hamete returns to the Hieronymus Bosch etching.

Not for nothing, he thinks, is his boss often called the master of illusion. The etching always does its job. Seeing it, who wouldn't go peacefully, even eagerly, through that door instead?

Cide Hamete opens a panel alongside the etching and winds the crank that will reset the tableau, but nothing happens.

He wonders if he dare try to repair the mechanism. But his powers here,

437

he knows, are distressingly limited. He'd better move the figures by main strength, as he did the last time there was a breakdown.

The Renaissance! So much to keep track of, and every branch tagged with an ism. Have to weed them later, he reminds himself as he rolls the hay-wagon back, returns the revellers to their un-run-over postures, removes the procuress's arm from the country girl's shoulders, gives the coins back to the nuns and repositions the murderer so that when Cide Hamete's next client arrives, the victim can be knifed anew.

Cide Hamete crosses the little plaza and finally turns his attention to the demons dragging the condemned into the black-and-white flames of eternal damnation. These figures, for reasons of perspective, are smaller than the rest, only eighteen or twenty inches tall. Stooping, he returns each to its original place, until only one demon and one sinner, their backs turned, remain. He tries to pry the demon's claws from the sinner's shoulders, but the small demon holds fast. Cide Hamete pulls harder. He begins to sweat. His abyssal rock face goes a deep red, like a cliff at sunset. Has the demon turned his head – just enough for the eyes to glare at him? Has it moved to one side – just enough for Cide Hamete to recognize the victim as himself?

He hurries out with his scimitar.

Whenever things go wrong, uprooting isms makes him feel better.

I find myself in what looks like the tiring room of a theatre. There are the usual benches around the walls, costumes hanging on pegs and a couple of oaken chests.

I seem to be wearing a suit of soft chamois leather, the sort worn by knights of old under their armour. I'm also wearing a worried look on my face. In the far corner of the room I see the components of several suits of armour. Outside, a horse whickers; from further off comes the blood-lusty roar of a crowd.

My squire enters, dressed in loose white shirt and white pantaloons with flaring knees but tight enough at the hip to display a classic callipygean curve.

'He won again.'

'À outrance?'

'The Knight of the Mirrors only fights à outrance,' says my squire.

'Who is he?'

This earns me an odd look from my squire. 'Nobody knows who the Knight of the Mirrors is, sir.'

My squire selects helmet, gorget, breastplate, tasse and so forth, all of a dazzling white – like the armour of my patron Saint Michael, I tell myself with what optimism I can muster. Michael leads the celestial armies in battle, and do celestial armies lose?

But this is to be single combat.

The archangel Michael is a comforting analogy, but the Knight of the Mirrors is the real thing. And, since he fights only to the death, simple logic forces me to conclude he has never been defeated.

The door bursts open and my brother Rodrigo hurries in. 'I'll bet you gave me up for lost,' he says as he swiftly removes his parrot uniform to reveal a soft chamois suit like my own. 'I was unavoidably detained in the Low Countries – a place called Nieuport.'

He's not the Rodrigo I saw at Spa, defeated by the very grail of glory he sought; he's the freckle-faced Rodrigo of Lepanto or even before. I realize I'm young again too, a pre-Lepanto me, except for what used to be my left hand.

Rodrigo removes the string with the maimed toy soldier from my neck and hangs it around his own.

When I object, he says, 'You took my place in Algiers, didn't you? Besides, I'm being selfish. Think of the glory I'll win for defeating the Knight of the Mirrors.'

'No one's ever defeated him.'

'I know. Get me some armour,' he tells my squire.

Soon Rodrigo is smiling at me through his open visor while my squire hurries out to saddle my warhorse Spike, whose platings and housings match the red, blue and yellow of the legendary wingless wooden flying horse Clavileño.

Outside, Rodrigo embraces me, turns, vaults into the saddle with a cry of, 'Oh, the glory!' and raises a gauntleted fist as Spike snorts and gallops off.

Before long a groan of disapproval comes from the unseen crowd and I can hear the distinctive hoofbeats of Spike returning. I rush out to see Rodrigo climbing slowly from the saddle. Brushing my helping hand away, he goes at a slouching clank into the tiring room and lifts off his helmet. His hair is white, his face pale, all his freckles have become liver spots, a tic jumps under his eye, his skin is wrinkled as a monkey's.

He sits in a slumped daze while my squire unfastens his armour, which, by the way, is black. Read no symbolism into this.

'What happened?' I ask.

Rodrigo takes a long, shuddering breath. 'I yielded.'

Crouching to remove Rodrigo's greaves, my squire says, 'Trust no one in this life.'

'I couldn't fight him!' shouts Rodrigo.

Since when has Rodrigo avoided a fight?

I check my own armour, then tell Rodrigo, 'Better let me have the amulet.'

The tic jumps all over my brother's face. 'The Knight of the Mirrors took it as a prize. It was either that or fight, and how could I fight him?'

Rodrigo sounds so defeated that, despite everything, I pat his arm – fortunately I'm not yet wearing my gauntlets – and say I understand.

All I understand, though, is that I'll be lost without the amulet that's seen me through so many adventures, the little toy soldier with the missing hand.

Rodrigo comes outside with me.

My warhorse Spike is a bay (like fabled Bayard), white blaze on forehead, thick mane spilling over arched neck, chest swelling with muscle, a huge stallion seventeen and a half hands tall. He turns his great head, dragging my squire who clings to his bridle, to sniff my scent through the armour. He nuzzles my gauntlet.

The blood of battle pounding in my throat gives me the strength of two, almost making me forget that the Knight of the Mirrors wears my amulet. Or that my armour weighs more than I do. I go clanking a few paces behind Spike, turn ponderously, lumber forward and vault into the saddle as easily as Rodrigo did.

My squire puts the butt of my lance in the rest; I take the shaft in my gauntleted right hand. Battle-axe is looped at saddle bow, sword hangs at my side. I gather the reins.

'Please, sir – wait!' My squire sounds diffident. 'You've lost your amulet and you wear no colours. Would you wear this?'

The silk scarf my squire holds up for my inspection is of a disturbing amber colour. I fasten it between pauldron and breastplate. My squire hands up my shield.

Then I dig my heels into Spike's flanks and he surges into full gallop.

At a stylish canter – Spike's idea – I ride past the tents pitched on the north side of the jousting field, then up the west end, before turning alongside the grandstand on the south side. Galleries, terraces, balconied towers slim as minarets go jouncing by, all bedecked with colourful swags and aflutter with bright pennants, and all empty. Yet as I glance across at the deserted campgrounds the unseen crowd roars again, a perfervid sound that boils over when the Knight of the Mirrors and I meet before the empty royal pavilion with its black bunting – read into this what symbolism you will – to salute the unseen sovereign.

I face my adversary. Hundreds of tiny mirrors that overlap like fish-scales cover his armour from helm to greaves, reflecting sunlight, bright blue sky, deserted galleries, empty royal pavilion, and my own self. Especially my own self – hundreds of miniature white knights mounted on miniature Spikes.

I try for a look at my adversary's eyes through his raised visor, but he jerks his reins and his smoky grey warhorse rears, making those tiny mirrors flash with movement. This gives me the eerie impression of seeing in each one a different image of myself, from the childhood me to the me of middle age, so that, if I assembled them all, I could see in those overlapping mirrors the story of my death and life until in one final mirror I would inevitably see myself mounted on Spike before the empty royal pavilion with its black bunting, lance dipped to salute the unseen sovereign as I see reflected in the Knight of the Mirrors's armour the story of my death and life until in one final mirror . . .

I tug the reins (too hard, from the angry toss of Spike's head) and wheel away from my adversary.

We take our positions at opposite ends of the field. Spike ramps high with vast equine impatience. A charger, he wants to charge. I bring him under control and lean forward to stroke his neck (gently: those steel gauntlets) just as unseen trumpets blare their peremptory call.

I lower my visor, severing my final connection with my clement, human self. Anyone who has ever fought in full battle armour will understand.

Already the hard hot sun has heated the steel so that I feel as if I am cooking in my own sweat. As Spike charges downfield, I see pennants whipping in the wind but feel no breeze; my armour isolates me. With my visor down, it no longer matters that grandstand, galleries, towers, royal pavilion, all are empty. I can see only straight ahead, and not very well at that, through a half-dozen peepholes. I am, in short, disoriented. I have been transformed to something less, and something more, than human. I am one component of a centaur, my purpose to separate the two components of that other centaur now swiftly closing with the creature of which I'm part. If successful I will dismount, and if not I will be thrown (either way my centaur-self sundered), and on foot, enclosed in the carapace that has nullified my humanity, try to kill the Knight of the Mirrors before he kills me.

Spike hits his great stride. I couch my lance, taking the weight of it in my steel gauntlet, and raise my shield. The amber scarf streams over my shoulder. I see a glare of captured sunlight, a many-faceted gleam as the smoky grey warhorse carries the Knight of the Mirrors full-tilt towards me, those tiny reflections bearing down on me until all is shattered by impact and I feel myself teetering, stirrups flapping but knees still gripping Spike, and see with my limited vision the Knight of the Mirrors listing to his own right. Both lances have shivered cleanly.

I canter to my end of the field where, after my squire hands up a new lance, I wheel and again give Spike free rein as I crouch low behind my shield and see through the peepholes in my visor those tiny reflections of myself galloping at me until they explode in a second shivering of lances and an abrupt shift of my armour-burdened weight as I'm almost tilted from the saddle before wheeling again amid a surf of crowd-roar.

At my end of the field my worried squire has trouble giving me a third lance, for Spike ramps nervously before surging into a charge again, mirror-glint of sunlight closer and closer, and then the weight, the weight of my own shield, the leather-covered wood pierced squarely by the tip of my adversary's lance as I slide to the right, too far, leaning, tilting, my own lance shivered. As I tumble, my sword flies from me and I have just enough time, and life-preserving instinct, to grab for my battle-axe and swing my greave-heavy left leg over Spike's broad back, so that if my luck is good I may land on my feet.

Assuming I do, some seconds must follow in which through peepholes I scan the field desperately for mounted or dismounted knight, possibly seeing neither until he delivers my death. Tradition says I must not raise my visor. A raised visor signals surrender. And once combat à outrance has commenced, there can be no surrender without disgrace.

I land heavily on steel-shod foot and kneepiece, battle-axe jarred from gauntleted hand. In blind, giddy panic I grope for it on the turf while a blood-lusty roar washes over me like the ebbing tide of my own life. I hear hoof-beats, muted, fading – one horse being led from the field, or two? I blunder in armour-slowed circles, not seeing the Knight of the Mirrors, not finding my battle-axe. Finally my steel-shod foot clangs against something hard. I bend awkwardly and retrieve my battle-axe from turf torn up by pounding hooves. Is this where we met, that third time? Where is he now? The crowd roars on a higher note. Is this a cheer? Signifying that my adversary is bearing down on me at a gallop, bringing my death? Or that, obeying the tradition of chivalry instead of the more compelling dictates of self-preservation, he has dismounted and will meet me on foot?

My scanning picks up a glint to the left. I turn, and see the Knight of the

Mirrors coming at a ponderous run, battle-axe already on the downswing. I parry. Sparks fly from the two broad blades. The impact numbs my hands, my arms. He swings his axe again, sideways now, and I close with him inside the blow and with my axe-haft shove him away. Three backward steps he takes, and falls. If I want, it is ended now, for before he can rise, I can cleave his helmet. But he dismounted for me, and now I wait for him to regain his steel-shod feet. Would he have given me such quarter, a second time?

His mirrors flash those tiny images of myself at me, and again we close. Axe-blades clang and spark; we circle slowly, ungainly in our steel carapaces. The flat of his blade strikes my cheekpiece and I reel away. Frantically, I search for him. I see only sky, turf, tents, flapping pennants – but I can hear him, or think I can, and in that direction I turn to take the expected death blow not on my helm but on the left side of my breastplate. He is too eager, again it is the flat of his axe-blade, but still it sends me in a clanking stagger to one knee, and he looms huge, axe overhead to deliver now the killing stroke that thunderously in mid-swing meets my own axe as he comes clanking down, both of us down now under his weight, down weighted by armour, down and rolling heavily apart only to seek each other anew, I on my knees now and wielding my axe wildly, and hearing the clang as shards of shattered mirrors flash past my visor, and again, and again, until through the peepholes I see broken glass, splinters of it everywhere, and the Knight of the Mirrors, mirrorless, on his back, left gauntlet shielding his visor from the sun as he tries to find me, right gauntlet ripped away and, scrabbling on the grass like a thing separately alive searching for his axe, his bare right hand, *what used to be his right hand* . . .

I grasp his visor and raise it. Then I raise my own.

Do his eyes, unfocused now as death approaches, yet try to smile? A quizzical sort of shared smile which reflects the death-imparted knowledge that only the easy questions are ever answered, or even asked? And does he say, or do I only think he says, 'But when I was newly captive in Algiers, *I saw them hang you, I saw you die*,' and, saying this, die himself?

These questions I cannot answer, for when I remove the toy soldier with the missing hand from inside the dead man's gorget, the weight of armour goes from me, and the dead man goes, and the jousting field and those deserted galleries and the empty royal pavilion draped in black, and I see stretching from horizon to horizon that dazzling white plain utterly flat and lined with rows of words, that vast topographical page where looms the powerful figure of Cide Hamete plying his scimitar to uproot words, in his blue right eye and brown left eye a fierce joy.

He is so engrossed he doesn't see me. Each word he wrests from the bright white earth ends in an 'ism' of a taproot, and each he sends flying with an ecstatic *envoi*.

'Relativism and absolutism, globalism, regionalism – and so much for solecism!' he cries.

'Intellectualism *and* anti-intellectualism!' and off they go.

'Optimism, pessimism, classicism, romanticism, diabolism and deism and theism, and why not yahooism? Militarism and pacifism. Truism (does a false-ism lurk somewhere?). Obscurantism, negativism and positivism, atavism, anachronism, away with you all!

'Quixotism . . . but I'll miss the *ráwi*.'

Here he stabs his scimitar into the earth and rests his weight on the hilt. Pensively he stares at the wingless wooden flying horse Clavileño, patiently waiting.

He rouses himself and resumes. 'Alarmism, defeatism, and to the Devil – if there is a Devil – with historical revisionism!' More flinging.

'Creationism and cretinism (adjacent by no accident) – away, away! Sexism, but also feminism – off with you!'

Rapturously he extirpates, and a wind springs up and hundreds of uprooted isms blow away like tumbleweed.

He is poised before 'aphorism' when I step forward and say, 'Once you told me to avoid all isms except the one good one. But you never said which it was.'

He thrusts downward with his scimitar and screams the outraged scream of a peacock.

Or is it outrage? It's hard to tell with screams; a peacock's sounds utterly apoplectic, yet he's only displaying the splendour of his tail.

I see that Cide Hamete in his surprise has taken an inaccurate jab at 'aphorism', leaving the word intact but, apparently, doing damage to himself.

He drops his scimitar and collapses into a sitting position in the shade of some remaining isms, his rough-hewn face of abyssal or plutonic rock eroding even as I watch, like a landscape weathered by time, harsh quartz and feldspar angles and planes giving way to a soft curve of hummocky cheek, a bland drumlin of brow, a deforested pink pate.

When he speaks, it is in a wondering voice that rises, bass to baritone to tenor. 'Have I really inflicted this ultimate indignity upon myself, all unknowing? I who can remember the future as lesser men recall the past?

Auto-orchiectomy, is that not the final irony? Must I spend the rest of my days asking, why me? Unless . . .' and a tear rolls from his blue right eye. '. . . could it all have been a dream? Everything since I met you, *ráwi*, only a dream?'

His new-old voice, countertenor now, is plaintive, but I have no answer for him. Who am I to say if he was dreaming, or what dream he dreamt?

'Only a dream that I forsook astrology, that queen of sciences, and left Algiers to seek devilish power God knows where? A dream that I became first Bādindjan then Dasim Zalambur – what ludicrous names, ask any Persian, any Muslim! A dream that I almost became . . . what you with your hopelessly limited understanding assumed I was? No, *ráwi*,' and a tear rolls from his brown left eye. 'No, the prosaic truth is that I was born under so disastrous a conjunction of astrological signs that I could only, in compensation, become an astrologer myself. All the rest . . . the rest I dreamed and now, now I am awake . . .'

And this figure formerly hewn from abyssal or plutonic rock becomes before my eyes softly plump, then stout, then obese, his burgeoning bulk now draped in a robe of midnight-blue silk besprinkled randomly with stars, comets, signs of the Zodiac and assorted phases of the moon, all in gold. He cocks an ear and smiles, world-weary but smug. Faintly, I hear music, and far off I see figures which approach at a stately march, revealing themselves to be half a dozen eunuchs robed in costly cloth-of-gold. Reaching us, they ignore me (one actually steps without awareness on my foot) and raise Cide Hamete to their shoulders to bear him off, singing:

> 'Deys may come and deys may go,
> Some of them even clever,
> But the royal astrologer, oh!
> The royal astrologer is forever.'

Looking back once between rows of what might be, after all, no more than saplings, he seems about to speak, but shakes his head resolutely and says nothing.

I mount Clavileño and pull back hard on the spike.

Dr Duguid slumped in the doorway of the small room under the eaves of the Cross Keys in Gracechurch Street, his face drawn with fatigue.

Micaela rose from the edge of the bed, her own face pale but radiant.

'Mind, I can't promise,' the doctor said. 'I'm too old for miracles, m'lady.'

445

Outside the window a faint smear of light touched the eastern sky.

'Everything I know about medicine tells me he should have died hours ago. But his heartbeat's stronger and the fever's broken. Well, I need my sleep. Send the boy if there's any change.'

Impulsively, Micaela threw her arms around his neck.

'Please, m'lady. I did nothing.'

He was just starting downstairs when she cried out. He hurried back to her side.

The bed was empty.

XXXV

Fifty Pounds of Raisins

And Three Bushels of Wheat

Over the city hung a full moon, white and wintry, casting deep shadows. My boots crunched on glittering hoarfrost. I was bundled to the ears in sheepskin. No window gleamed with welcoming light, nor, except for the wind whistling through the deserted streets, was there a sound – no voice, no footfall other than my own, no horse's hooves. Then I heard the howl of a wolf. And what was a wolf doing, in the heart of the city? I hurried through the moonlight to the tall stone house near the Gate of the Sun.

When I pounded on the door, a dog inside barked ferociously. I imagined my wife-in-name-only Catalina coming downstairs with no howling monkey on her shoulder but trailed by the loudest-barking dog in Madrid, probably limping or one-eyed. Or would it be my sister Andrea who wasn't my sister opening the door to me, or my niece Constanza with her one blue and one brown eye, or my sister Magdalena, complaining about the hours men kept?

Waiting in the cold, I felt for a moment the sweet anticipation of coming home. Even if I'd never been much good at staying.

The ferocious barking ended on a slurping gurgle, and paws beat the door so hard it shook in its frame. This was a serious watchdog. Definitely no part of the picture I had of my family.

In the door a small grilled window opened where I remembered no window before. 'Who are you? What do you want?' A man's voice, unfamiliar, unfamilial.

'I live here.'

'The fuck you do.' And the grilled window slammed.

I was about to knock again when I heard a rhythmic jangle and thump. Turning, I saw the kindly old *sereno* tottering towards me with his heavy ring of keys and oaken staff. His face was old. But then, his face had always been old. He probably could have given the Old Woman of the East competition.

I expected him to say, as he ritually did, that I mustn't tarry. But he said, 'Squatters – it's a regular progression, caves to hovels to houses to mansions, not that I include this tall stone house in that category, even if Santi Ambrosio did make improvements before the family left for Valladolid. They should've hired a house watcher. I told them.'

'They've gone to Valladolid?'

We fell into step, the jangle of his keys and thump of his staff companionable sounds.

'Where else? Practically everybody went, once the Valladolid city fathers bribed King Felipe III the Inglorious to move the capital back there. Needed three hundred bullock carts. The night of the ninth of January in sixteen-ought-ought it was. Snuck out of Madrid like a pack of thieves.'

I was trying to imagine three hundred bullock carts sneaking out of Madrid when we turned into German Street.

The New Spain recruitment office that had replaced Taverna Múñoz was boarded up. So were all the other buildings I could see; German Street had gone into hibernation.

'What happened to Pierre Papin's gambling den? Did he move it to Valladolid?'

'Sure didn't. When the capital left Madrid he hightailed it back to France so he could spend his declining years wearing the feather in any side of his hat he pleased.'

Taverna Isabel was boarded up too.

'Did Gabriel Múñoz go to Valladolid?'

'Was planning to. No clientele here, and then the owner-lady died. But it pains me to tell you, he was stabbed to death by a drunken sheepman from Segovia. It was shortly before Christmas, as I recall.'

The wind howled. So did the wolf.

After a minute I said, 'And Anica's dead too, you say? What happened to the child?'

'That gorgeous little Isabel? I don't know where she went after her mother died. Well, here's home.'

It was a building boarded up like all the others. He moved some boards aside to reveal an opening. 'You aim to tarry a spell? Madrid's dying. It needs real folks. Spend what's left of the night here, then in the morning we can find you a house to watch – sufficiently downscale so the criminal element'll leave you in peace. Took me most of three years to learn what's safe.'

I grabbed his arm; the heavy ring of keys jangled at his belt. He looked alarmed.

'It took you *how* long? What year is this?' I asked.

'Sixteen-ought-three. The third of December.'

And there you have it. I lay dying in Gracechurch Street in London towards midnight on 23 April (local time) 1600. The next thing I knew, I was walking the deserted streets of Madrid the night of 2–3 December 1603.

I wish I could ascribe this to loss of memory stemming from my almost fatal wound. Or could say, later in these pages, I was permitted to disclose that those years had dropped into nothing more recondite than a top-secret mission for the Nameless. But was there any Nameless left? Every base except the one a thousand leagues from everywhere had been destroyed. I didn't even know if Juan-O, last seen in hot pursuit of Maliverny Catlyn, the Butcher of Clynnogfawr Llanllyfni, was still alive. No, I'd gone on no Nameless missions.

But I'd gone somewhere. A person has to be somewhere every second of his life, doesn't he?

We went inside. The kindly old *sereno* lit the stove, lit candles. He sliced sausage and cheese, poured wine. I took off my heavy sheepskin coat.

'Only ever saw me a coat like that once before,' he said, impressed. 'Where'd you get it anyways?'

'This old sheepskin?' I tried to remember, couldn't.

'That ain't just sheepskin, that's genuine karakul. Met a trader once wearing karakul, said he got his coat gambling with a spice merchant who said *he* got it in one of those mountainous countries on the far side of Persia where nobody with any sense in his head would want to go. On account of the cold.'

'It gets pretty cold winters in Madrid too,' I said, just to be saying something. Then I thought, just to be thinking something, that if my karakul coat had come from the far side of Persia, maybe I had too. Was that where I'd spent those missing years? I would never learn; I would never learn a lot of things, and they would haunt me even if I could not say what they were.

'Ironical, ain't it,' the old *sereno* said as he speared a chunk of cheese – sheep, not karakul – 'how often folks get credit for a thing, and I don't exclude kings, when the credit belongs to nobody? Like the peace that's being signed between Felipe III the Inglorious and that James in Britain. Heck, Felipe inherited an empty treasury he emptied worse with his love of pomp and circumstance, so Spain's too broke to fight any more. And that Stuart fellow's so busy trying to unite his kingdoms he plain don't have time left over for war. But they'll get the credit.'

'What happened to Queen Elizabeth?'

'Died last March, plumb wore out from reigning forty-five years. Where you been?'

'I don't know,' I said, and without undue concern he said, 'That's what I figured,' but it wasn't his life that had a hole in it.

Micaela, I remembered, had felt her fortunes were tied to Elizabeth's. Was she at risk right now? Had her dangerous games finally caught up with her? Maybe she was dead, and maybe I'd never know.

I moved closer to the stove, but that didn't stop a chill from penetrating me. I could feel my grip – tenuous to begin with – slipping from whatever version of reality I happened to be in, almost like poor Torquato Tasso, fighting insanity all his life, creating madly while he heard devil-voices and saw spectral beings come in the night to steal his manuscripts, Tasso who spent his final years on the old road (without his sister Cornelia, who'd been vanished, mea culpa, mea maxima culpa!), Tasso famous all over Europe but not a copper in his pocket, dead at fifty-one. And I? If it was true this was 1603, I'd be fifty-six, and I had no manuscripts for anyone, spectral or otherwise, to steal – nor any faith to take refuge in either. At least Tasso had had that always, a compulsion to confess indistinguishable, possibly, from a compulsion to write.

I asked the old *sereno*, 'Who else died?'

He said, 'Your whole family up there in Valladolid is fine. Your sister Andrea and her daughter have their own little *modista* shop. Keeps them busy, with Santi Ambrosio on the old road so much. Your wife's fine too, though it's not the best place for an animal-lover to live, seeing as they're across from the municipal slaughterhouse. And your sister Magdalena, apart from her disposition, she's also fine.'

449

The old *sereno* said nothing else for a while, just stared down at the table.

Which one? Which one was it?

'I'm sorry to have to tell you,' he said, 'your brother Rodrigo fell in battle at a place called Nieuport back in sixteen hundred.'

I stood at the boarded-up window, light now filtering through the cracks, a new day beginning in the dying city, and saw Rodrigo's freckle-participating grin. But the voice I heard belonged to the blonde vingt-et-un dealer with the little cap of gold brocade: *Don't you see, even if this glory of his is only a dream, at least he has a dream to face death with.*

The old *sereno* poked at the coals in the stove. 'You wouldn't happen to know a lissom Negress who hails from Fernando Po near Africa?' His face coloured. 'Who, weather permitting, don't wear an especially large amount of attire?'

'There were some women from Fernando Po,' I said, 'who worked at Tomás Gutiérrez's hostal in Sevilla.'

'The one I mean, you'd be surprised the places she'd been, the things she'd seen before she went to work for that niggardly innkeeper,' said the *sereno*, and I remembered the Negress in the black mourning breechclout who'd given me a black cloak to wear over my prison stripes.

'When she passed through Madrid last year on her way to see a few more places, a few more things, she gave me something that belonged to you. She'd planned on giving it to your family, but of course *they* were gone, so ... oh, one other thing. She said if I saw you I was to tell you it's not half bad, you should finish it.'

The manuscript was bundled in green and gold silk. I unwrapped it and saw my handwriting on the title page:

EL INGENIOSO

HIDALGO

DON QUIXOTE

DE LA MANCHA

I spread the pages on the table, nine chapters up to the epic battle with the huge Basque who reminded me of Ovando's stand-in Sigura in Liars' Walk, despite how careful I'd been to avoid writing about what I knew.

The Sad-Faced Knight!

How clearly I could see him, tall, gaunt and far from young, a barber's basin for a helmet, an old nag for a warhorse, so nostalgic for a Golden Age that never was that he sallied forth like a knight of old, serenely determined to right wrongs, rescue maidens and succour widows with the kind of benevolent machismo some people once imputed to me.

The Sad-Faced Knight!

Waiting with the patience of a saint (or at least the stoicism of a knight-errant) to sally forth again from my manuscript . . .

Mine? No, not exactly. I smiled.

The kindly old *sereno* nodded, encouraging me to speak, but I said nothing.

What made me smile was the notion that I, a mere storyteller, could persuade readers to believe in adventures as absurd as Don Quixote's. What I needed was an authority to lend his imprimatur, a bona fide historian with one of those confidence-inspiring foreign names like – well, like Cide Hamete Benengeli (roughly, in Arabic: Cide, señor or lord; Hámed, he who praises or glorifies; and Benengeli, which you've seen doesn't stand up to scrutiny but never mind).

Yet, I went on thinking, if *Don Quixote* was the supposed work of a foreign historian, how would I, the storyteller-once-removed, have got the manuscript? A lissom Negress from Fernando Po was just too improbable. Could I have come across it accidentally, say in Toledo, that ancient city where Arabic wasn't the only venerable language spoken behind closed doors? I'd be walking along the Alcaná, perhaps right here on this page in Chapter IX (it wouldn't need much revising), and see a boy selling old parchments and papers; and since I'm one of those people who, as you know, if he sees old parchments (or even new papers) has to read them – that's how I'd find this history of the ingenious or ingenuous knight-errant Don Quixote de la Mancha written by that flower of historians Cide Hamete Benengeli.

I laughed (the old *sereno* gave me an odd look: what did I have to laugh about?), thinking how Cide Hamete, who so scorned history and historians, would bellow if he knew how I intended using him. But he had it coming.

I'd also need somebody, probably a *morisco*, to translate, since the Arabic I'd learned in Algiers was hardly up to reading that flower of historians Cide Hamete Benengeli. This *morisco* would have, like practically all *moriscos*, a passion for raisins. So, for translating the whole work into crisp Castilian Spanish, I'd give him fifty pounds of golden raisins – and, since he'd have not just a sweet tooth but a family to feed, three bushels of wheat.

The best part of all this is that, if any reader objects to anything in *Don Quixote* on grounds of inaccuracy or flat-out lying, I need only point out that the historian was an Arab – for every Spaniard knows that an Arab, even an Arab historian (perhaps most of all an Arab historian), would as soon lie as tell the truth.

Cide Hamete had it coming, all right.

As Dr Duguid said, a man could dream his own death and never wake. And if I hadn't, whose fault would it have been but Cide Hamete's? Moving right into this dream in which I'm fighting for my life, complicating it with his Hieronymus Bosch etching and his unremarkable door (death's door: hardly what you'd call original) and his Knight of the Mirrors. He could have killed me! And when he failed? When he failed, he retreated into his own dream inside mine. Auto-orchiectomy! Without a drop of blood! Holy Virgin! Right before my eyes he turns back into that fat falsetto fraud of a royal astrologer complete with fawning attendant eunuchs and that fatuous song, no more able to walk through walls than I am, nor to remember the future.

Or have I misunderstood? Missed the point?

What if he existed in no one's version of reality, not even his own, and never would, unless someone gave him one to inhabit?

Was that why he'd saved my life in Algiers and then bowed out of it after the death of the Knight of the Mirrors, disappearing into that dream within a dream knowing I'd write him into *Don Quixote*?

Maybe he wanted all along to be known as the flower of historians.

I laughed again, or started to; but outside, the wolf howled, and I was suddenly afraid, not knowing whose dream I could escape into – or from – so that, like Cide Hamete, I could live.

It was a one-room hovel on the north side of a small plaza where alleys intersected not far from the Gate of the Moors. No one had bothered to board it up, so I moved right in. A cold rain was falling, the roof leaked, water poured through the hole in the ceiling that served as chimney, table and bed were one, a single rickety stool completed the furniture. Primitive, but it would do.

I hurried to the shop I wanted, smashed the lock and went in. There were paper, ink and quill-pens enough to write a dozen *Don Quixotes*. In a dying city these were not prized commodities. As I returned to the small plaza near the Gate of the Moors, the intersecting alleys fell into place in my memory, and I was sure if I turned that corner, just there, I would see the Bench of If-Only where my father had defended his lost dreams with a rusty old sword. I turned the corner, but saw only a great fire-blackened oak that had been struck by lightning, one huge branch jaggedly down.

Coming closer, I saw what was left of a stone bench under the dead tree. No one was there. I told myself the rain kept them away, but the next day was cold and clear and still no one came, not even at dusk when dreams die hardest. No one ever made use of the Bench of If-Only. I'm sure, because I passed it daily on my way to the small market where my mother had congregated with other old women to talk of what their lives might have been if only they hadn't married their husbands. The market was still open – three old crones who got food from God knows where and sold it to God knows whom. Their customers, old women too, came and went in a swirl of black shawls along dark alleys and down narrow staircase-streets, looking back to make sure no one was following them to the secret places they lived.

For a few days I went to the market just to look at the food – withered winter apples and root vegetables, coarse loaves, some eggs, salt cod, dried meat that looked like black leather. Then on a Monday I managed to steal an apple and a loaf of bread. It was that or starve. On the Tuesday I made off with a few eggs, or almost did. But one of the crones saw me. Running, I lost my footing and the eggs flew from my cupped right hand and smashed on the ground. I didn't go back until the Friday, when my hunger was too much to bear. I waited in the shadows until all three crones were busy, then made off with apples, bread, eggs and a few paper-thin slices of that suspicious-looking black meat, which proved delicious.

This went on for some time, but early in the third week one of the crones looked up again, and I ran and the eggs flew from my cupped hand as before. Again I didn't go back until my hunger was too much to bear. To my surprise, one of the crones thrust a bundle at me.

'What's the sense of running?' she said. 'Eggs don't grow on trees.'

'I can't p-pay you,' I said.

'Most folks in Madrid can't pay these days,' said the second crone. 'Barter's the coming thing, and it already came.'

'Can you find us some firewood?' asked the third crone. 'Firewood don't grow on trees neither, not when all the trees it used to grow on have been cut down.'

'We're old, we need warmth. Bring us firewood and you can take all the food you need,' said the first crone.

They gave me a small, rusty axe.

I went straight to the lightning-blasted oak where the Bench of If-Only used to be and chopped from the huge fallen branch as much wood as I could carry in my sheepskin or karakul coat.

Soon I didn't supply just the three crones; I became wood merchant to the neighbourhood squatters, who came out of hiding when they learned what I had to barter.

I never learned why I was the only one who cut firewood at the former Bench of If-Only. It was close to the Gate of the Moors and in plain view – if you knew where to look. But I *was* the only one. Even the ringing of my axe drew no spectators. But pretty soon, thanks to that firewood, my one-room hovel became a well-furnished, snug, dry-roofed, chimney-instead-of-ceiling-hole, one-room home. Sometimes I worried that I'd run out of wood and have nothing to trade for food, but no matter how I hacked away at that lightning-blasted oak, it never seemed to dwindle.

But enough about the quotidian. I've been procrastinating. Anything to avoid the One True Subject, writing.

The One True Subject – as if writing were a religion. I would hear that sort of nonsense in every tavern near the Plaza Mayor in Valladolid, Spain's new-old capital. (This was after *Don Quixote* was published and I became an instant celebrity.) The act of Creation! They called it that, young Quevedo and Góngora and Lope and the others, Creation with a capital C. The writer as God. But I always shunned such hyperbole, maybe because as a mere prose-fiction writer instead of a poet or playwright I felt less entitled to an opinion, let alone deification.

I didn't boast about my output either. (Does Lope expect a medal, *aventajado* or something, for writing his play a day and, once, one before breakfast? I have to wonder about the link between 'prolific' and 'prolix'.) Oh, I wrote. I was no dilettante. One and a half million words in all (excluding this book) – some three thousand pages, most of them written after I returned from my lost years. Why? I don't know why. But as I learned when I began *Don Quixote* in prison in Sevilla, to ask is enough. Asking a question is like crossing out a word or even a whole scene: something of the word or scene yet remains, just as the answer to a question is inherent in the asking.

Here's an example:

Not too many pages back, I wrote a long paragraph ruminating on what could have happened to me during those lost years. I began by suggesting that, by killing the Knight of the Mirrors when he was supposed to kill me, I might have tampered in some inexplicable way with whatever laws of nature keep the various versions of reality separate, and spent those years in God-(or the Devil or Cide Hamete)-knows-how-many alternate worlds, an exile from this one. Cide Hamete even gave me some useful vocabulary, about subatomic particles jumping from one energy state to another without passing through space *or* time. (Here I parenthetically mentioned a dream in which a badly frightened Cide Hamete said, 'The knowledge of mere atoms was enough to make the Laughing Philosopher put out his own eyes, and Lucretius kill himself. What's to happen to me with my quarks, my bosons, my quantum jumps? Lucifer was hurled into Sheol.') So, I ruminated, there I was lost in a maze of alternate realities, like Theseus in the Minotaur's lair without Ariadne's clew of thread to guide me back to here, and I probably had some adventures that would seem absurd in our own workaday reality. How else account for my writing about a glass man, talking dogs, a cave where time sped up (according to Don Quixote) and a wingless wooden flying horse that really flew (according to Sancho Panza), not to mention enchantment (in the bad sense), signs, omens, wonders beyond counting – and even folly as salvation from the twin absurdities of death and life?

But then, deciding all this was too much to ask you to swallow, I crumpled the page and tossed it into the stove (which I got in exchange for some If-Only firewood), figuring that even if I omitted it from this book, once I wrote it the idea would remain for you to ponder.

And it did, didn't it.

Well, I wrote, and as in Sevilla prison the pages piled up, and nine months of winter rolled around to three of hell and back again, and one morning that second winter I walked outside the Gate of the Moors and got chased by a pack of hungry wolves, but I won't go into that because it's no part of writing about writing, which I'm expected to do now, even though I'd rather get on with the story of my death and life, revealing the sorry fate of the inept gentleman bullfighter Gaspar de Ezpeleta and how Pedro de Isunza, that compulsive keeper of records, finally found his 229th virgin.

What I learned about writing, mostly, was this. The first thing writers of fiction have to do is willingly – and not just willingly but joyfully – suspend *their own* disbelief. Then everything else follows. It's harder, of course, if you're a writer who worries a lot, telling yourself that even if what happens in imagination is as intense as the real world, still, you could be doing everything wrong; that writing about a hero who tries to impose on the world an impossible reality, a hero who must forever fail, is all a mistake, hopeless, irremediable. What if, pretty soon, you do more worrying than writing? There's a solution. I found it by accident while writing *Don Quixote*, and I'll pass it along. If you want to stop worrying, you must make so much go wrong for your hapless hero that there's no time left to agonize over your hapless self.

Which is a long way from the writer as God – the view Lope's circle took of themselves – God on a smaller scale, perhaps, a modest God, but God nonetheless, moulding clay into people, breathing life into them, controlling them.

Holy Virgin! How could they be so wrong? Nobody is less like God than a storyteller because, when a storyteller is lucky enough to write the story he or she wants to write, a marvellous thing happens, something the storyteller could never consciously make happen: it just does if everything works, one chance in I don't know how many (and no chance at all if you write to a formula), what happens is that the story, with all the people who live and die in it, love and hate, fight and fornicate, hope, despair, dream in it – the story becomes part of the world that *is*, becomes more real than the writer, becomes so real that everything that happens in its pages would have happened in exactly the same way if the writer had never even lived.

Late in 1604 I went to the former Bench of If-Only to cut enough firewood for my last night in Madrid, but to my surprise all that remained of that lightning-blasted oak was a stump, ringed by stone-hard gall. I hit it one blow with my axe; the handle split, the head flew off. Hoping the three old crones might spare a log or two, I went to the marketplace, but it was deserted. I returned to the plaza where alleys intersect not far from the Gate of the Moors and spent a cold night in the hovel, snow sifting through the ceiling-hole and disturbing my sleep.

In the morning, bundled in sheepskin or karakul, I walked north across the dying city through the snow and set out on the road to Valladolid with my manuscript.

XXXVI
The 229th Virgin, Found At Last

My wife-in-name-only Catalina didn't like the parts about the animals.

'Just because crazy Don Quixote thinks windmills are evil giants a knight has to attack, does that mean his poor old horse Rocinante has to have his poor old shoulders practically dislocated?' she asked, stroking the silver-black skin of the baby anaconda that was draped around her neck staring at me with its cold, accusing, reptilian eyes.

'Or those flocks of innocent sheep he mistook for armies, did he have to attack so blindly with his lance that he killed "more than seven" of them?' she pursued. 'What's more than seven, anyway – twelve, a hundred?'

My sister Magdalena didn't like the parts about women. 'Not just Aldonza. That Maritornes, you made her nothing but a whore, sneaking up to the hayloft to . . . you know . . . with that mule-skinner.'

'The word,' said Catalina, 'is fuck. But,' smiling, 'things surely did get complicated when she wound up in the sack with Sancho Panza.'

'Things,' said Catalina's friend Juana the widow Laínez (now recently also the widow Hondaro), 'always get complicated when it comes to the snares and disillusions of love.'

Brandishing a new copy of her first husband's last manuscript, the widow urged, 'When Robles comes, everybody *please* be nice.' She was still hoping, after twenty years, to find a publisher for *The Snares and Disillusions of Love*.

Juana the widow Laínez-Hondaro had a room on the top floor of the building where we lived across a noxious stream from the municipal slaughterhouse. On the ground floor was a tavern patronized day and night by meatpackers who crossed on a rickety footbridge, so you must imagine all conversation in our first-floor parlour conducted at the top of our voices.

My niece Constanza didn't like the parts about Don Quixote's niece. 'Where'd he get that kind of niece?' she asked. 'I'm the only niece you have, and *I'd* never tell the priest to burn all your books.'

'She thought it was for his own good,' I said, staring at Constanza, still disconcerted by her eyes, both exactly the same pale blue as her mother's. Nobody ever commented on this, so I never did either.

'But to make a bonfire of books!' cried Constanza.

'What's such a big deal about books?' demanded Isabel from the window, where she was watching the comings and goings on the rickety bridge.

My sister Andrea didn't like my not taking sides in the tug-of-war between Don Quixote and Sancho Panza.

'Characters in a book,' I shrugged, though I knew that wasn't what she meant. 'Why do I have to take sides?'

'I mean in real life. The old Miguel wanted to change the world, same as that knight of yours. But these days, sometimes you almost seem inclined, like Sancho, to just let life roll by.' Despite words like 'sometimes', 'almost' and 'seem' this sounded like a criticism, but before I quite decided not to defend myself (thus conceding that Andrea was right), she patted my hand and said, 'How well I know the feeling, dear. It comes with growing old.'

This was hard to deny, the growing-old part. Even my wife-in-name-only Catalina and my niece Constanza with the two pale blue eyes like her mother's were both forty. Still I said a gallant, 'Who's old? Certainly not you.'

At the window, Isabel snickered. It was a rude sound, coarse. I didn't like it. Isabel knew I didn't.

'Well,' Andrea said briskly, 'I'll be sixty-two my next birthday.' She pushed at the fine silver hair coiled at the nape of her neck. 'Which makes you fifty-eight, dear. That's not exactly *young*.'

She didn't look sixty-two. Nothing like it. Not that she looked twenty-two either – I was long over that. For me it was now Micaela who looked forever twenty-two. Sometimes I found myself talking about her to Andrea. Dangerous games – it seemed another life. But talking about Micaela was talismanic: it meant she was still alive.

'Fifty-eight,' I said. 'That's funny. That's Don Quixote's age.'

Andrea smiled. 'Is it?'

'And he'll be older at the end of the sequel,' I said.

'Of course,' said Andrea, still smiling. 'The age *you'll* be when you finish writ – what sequel? The book's only just been published.'

'It needs a sequel. See, the knight used to believe the truth was not in real life but in all those tales of chivalry he read. But now he knows better.'

Andrea gave me a bemused (also a loving) look. 'He does? This *is* Don Quixote you're talking about?'

'He knows now that the place to look for the truth is in his own story that's just been published.'

'But if a man starts by rejecting reality for a set of illusions and then, uh, rejects those illusions in favour of *a story about them* – is that what you mean? – that leaves him further adrift than ever. Doesn't it?'

It did. But so what? It was just a book. The important thing was, there was no place for illusion in my life. None! Zero! I was finished with all that; had become a man, put away childish things etc. etc. What good had illusions ever done me? Let Don Quixote have the illusions! And not just the *ingenuous* illusions he had in the novel recently published (664 pages, paperbound, price 290 *maravedís*, typos on every page and a glaring omission on the cover, never mind), but, in the sequel I'd write, *ingenious* illusions based on the story of his earlier adventures while under the influence of illusion – an illusory snake eating its illusory tale. (Ouch!) Compensation for my own loss of illusion? Possibly. I'd even abandoned my weird notion of various versions of reality. They put people away who believe things like that. (I thought of Tasso.) The night I was wounded in the innyard of the Cross Keys and almost died, I had the sort of wild, crazy nightmare you could expect on your almost-death bed. (I thought of Cide Hamete.) There was a rational explanation for everything. (I thought of Dr Duguid.) In fact, I just gave it, didn't I?

So, over to you, Don Quixote!

At the mention of a sequel, my niece Constanza clapped her hands with almost childlike enthusiasm. 'Oh, good.'

Isabel shouted from the window, 'Why all the fuss? It's only a *book!*'

Except for my brother-in-law Santi Ambrosio, Isabel had no use for anybody in the family, and, I fear, it was mutual. I can't say whose fault it was. Isabel had joined the household before it moved to Valladolid. As soon as Gabriel Múñoz told Andrea the child's mother had died and the child's father was me, my sister had hurried down to Hundred Wells. Isabel, shrugging, had observed, ' "When one door shuts, another opens," ' and gone home with Andrea.

When I met her, Isabel was a girl of nineteen with glossy black hair and a heart-shaped face that reminded me of her mother's. Except for the sneer that perpetually curled her lips, she would have been pretty. But, in a family of readers, Isabel was illiterate. My own daughter. When I got over the shock, I tried to teach her, as Andrea had before me, but it was no use.

'Who needs books?' Isabel would sneer. 'My old lady got along without them and so will I.'

I'd say, 'I promise you, reading will change your life.'

'Promises, promises. "One gift is worth two promises," Mamá always said. If you're really my old man, never mind learning me to read. Give me a proper gift, huh? Like Uncle Santi does whenever he comes home.'

Santi Ambrosio was always bringing gifts back from Italy, as if to apologize for all the time he spent away.

Right after the bookseller Francisco Robles, Blas de Robles's son, bought *Don Quixote* (for 148½ ducats, hardly a fortune, and it was Catalina who talked him up from 125), I got gifts for everyone too, for all the women in the family and Juana the widow Laínez-Hondaro.

Isabel, unwrapping silver drop earrings, had smirked. 'You got a thing going with the Laínez broad or what?'

My denial was vehement. (Also true. If Juana courted the snares and disillusions of love, it wasn't with me.)

But Isabel said, 'If you didn't waste money on her, these earrings might have been of gold,' making what used to be my left hand twitch.

Now Constanza asked, 'In the sequel, will Sancho finally get an island to govern?' and Catalina said, 'If he does, don't let him mistreat the livestock,' and Isabel rolled her eyes and said, 'A *sequel*! Can you believe? I'll be downstairs' – meaning the meatpackers' tavern – 'if anyone should happen to want me,' and flounced out.

My publisher Francisco Robles arrived a few minutes later. 'Here he comes,' said Juana the widow Laínez-Hondaro from the window. 'Everybody be nice. Please?'

Francisco Robles had faded eyes and faded moustaches like his father, and always wore worn grey serge. (Publishers tended to the view that they should appear to be hurting for money.) He was carrying a copy of my book.

It actually said *Don Quixote* on the cover. I mention this because the copies we already had only said

EL INGENIOSO

HIDALGO

DE LA MANCHA

although Francisco Robles swore the error was the fault of the printer Juan de la Cuesta.

'Third printing,' Robles beamed. 'Fourth on the way.'

The women all shouted, except Catalina.

'If you're selling so many copies,' she asked, 'why don't you give Miguel some more money?'

'Señora, please! Your husband only had to write the book once, but for every copy I print, think of my risk, my expenses. I had to sell five hundred just to break even.'

'How many have you sold?' Catalina asked.

'Nine thousand,' said Francisco Robles.

'And what expenses?' pursued Catalina, holding up a volume for its publisher's inspection. 'You call this cheap pulp paper expenses? The Jesuits practically give it away. Real paper made from linen, that's expenses.'

I was surprised by Catalina's knowledge. Catalina never ceased to surprise me. She stroked her baby anaconda. It glared reptilianly at Francisco Robles, its tongue flicking. Robles stepped hastily back.

Juana the widow Laínez-Hondaro bit her lip.

'Or the covers,' said Catalina. 'Paper! Why not parchment?'

'The risk in the added cost of parchment – '

'Nine thousand copies sold, and you talk of risk? My Miguel will make you a rich man, señor. What will you do for him?'

'That's one reason I'm here. Don Miguel, I have decided you are exactly the man to write a feature story: local colour, the crowds, the sights and sounds and smells' – here Francisco Robles glanced at the window; it was a hot day and the stream flowing sluggishly past the slaughterhouse was particularly noisome – 'of history being made right here in Valladolid, Spain's once and future capital.'

'I doubt that,' said Catalina. 'Before you know it, the city fathers of Madrid will offer a bigger bribe and back to Madrid the court will go.'

'Whatever. Meanwhile, the peace treaty with England *is* being ratified, there *are* over six hundred Lutheran heretics in town including the official ratifier, that Lutheran archfiend Lord Howard of Effingham, the same who as Lord High Admiral sank the Invincible seventeen years ago and – *and*, my dear Don Miguel, I want a famous author such as yourself to write it all up for my news sheet, which, to be quite frank, is a far less risky undertaking than publishing novels.'

'How much,' Catalina asked, 'will you pay?'

'Ten ducats,' said Francisco Robles.

'Fifty,' said Catalina.

Juana the widow Laínez-Hondaro's face was purple.

'I never even asked Lope,' protested Francisco Robles.

'Then if you admit Miguel is a better writer than the great Lope de Vega,' said Catalina, 'fifty's cheap.'

They settled on twenty-five plus a firm option giving Robles the right to be the first to refuse my next book.

Juana said, after some impressive throat-clearing, 'It never ceases to amaze me how it holds up.'

'How what holds up?' said Catalina, co-operating. The baby boa had wrapped itself in three coils around her neck but didn't appear to be constricting.

'My late husband's *The Snares and Disillusions of Love*. As timely as if he wrote it yesterday. Or tomorrow.'

Robles gave me and the door a significant look.

'The war between the sexes,' said Juana, 'is no passing skirmish. Don't you agree, Don Francisco?'

'Why, ah, I . . .' said Robles at the door.

'Have you read it, Don Francisco?'

'Not personally, but my father did, just prior to his early retirement,' said Robles, mopping his brow.

'It so happens,' said the widow Laínez-Hondaro, 'that I have recently copied a copy of the original copy of the reworked copy of the final draft.'

'We're more in the market these days for picaresque novels,' said Francisco Robles on the landing. 'Or poetry. Like the caustic verses of Baltasar del Alcázar.'

'Nobody can possibly be named Baltasar del Alcázar,' I heard someone, I think Constanza, say. By then I was descending the stairs with Francisco Robles.

'How bad *is* it, actually?' he asked me.

'She's a very determined lady.'

'That's what my father said, his last day on the job. He was too soft. A publisher,' said Robles, 'must have "no more soul than a pitcher, a heart of cork, and bowels of flint and pebble". Have I got that right?'

He was quoting the silver nymph in *Don Quixote* who railed at Sancho Panza for his reluctance to lash himself 3300 times to cure Dulcinea del Toboso of the enchantment that had turned her into an uncouth peasant.

I nodded, and we both laughed as we stepped on to the rickety footbridge that crossed the noxious stream to the municipal slaughterhouse and the road to the town centre.

'Just sort of wander around,' Robles suggested, 'ear to the ground. You journalists know all the tricks.'

'I'm not a journalist and I don't know any tricks.'

Bloody-smocked meatpackers passed us, heading for the tavern on the ground floor of my family's house.

'It would definitely be advisable to keep your distance from Lope de Vega for a while,' Robles told me. 'He's livid.'

'You didn't give Lope a free copy, I hope?'

'No, but presumably one of your mutual friends lent him one. Whatever, it seems he read the prologue.'

'Well, that's the place to start,' I said.

'Don Miguel, that part where your unnamed friend tells you not to worry about finding authors to supply quotes praising your novel, because you can always write them yourself and attribute them to Prester John of the Indies or the Emperor of Trebizond – you remember that part?'

'Sure I do. You didn't find it amusing?'

'Oh, I did. I did. But Lope always writes the puffs for his own works, you know.'

'You don't say!' I said.

Robles looked at me. He almost smiled. 'You go your own way, don't you.'

'It's the only way I know,' I said, and a woman's voice called 'Señor!' There was a clatter on the rickety bridge we had just crossed, and I saw Isabel running towards us.

She never called me Papá; we both would have been uneasy with that. She never called me Don Miguel or even plain Miguel, which I would have liked. She rarely called me anything. (Try this with someone you see every day: it imposes a strain.) When she had to call me something, it was invariably 'señor' – as if to put as much distance between us as she could.

Now here she was in front of the municipal slaughterhouse, scuffing her shoes on the bare earth and looking down at them as if hoping to find the words she never found anywhere else. (How often do any of us, the exactly right words?) She mumbled, '. . . real dumb of me . . . I know I'd like him, your knight . . . if I could read . . .' And she scuffed her shoes some more (Italian shoes, a gift from Santi) as I awkwardly reached to stroke her glossy dark hair; then she turned and ran back across the bridge.

Why do I mention Lope's fury over my gibe at him in my prologue and, almost in the same breath, Isabel's out-of-character apology?

Because it was typical of that day.

Because even if something was overdue to go wrong, it wouldn't be today. Today belonged to me. What was this citywide fiesta anyway, even if no one else knew it (making it all the sweeter), but a celebration of me and my book?

I walked with Francisco Robles to his bookshop (*Don Quixote*, his name on the cover now, on prominent display), then followed Robles's advice and wandered around, employing no journalistic tricks because I knew none, but jotting notes for the feature story I would write for his news sheet, which duly appeared and was duly swallowed up by time. For those interested a truncated translation into German can be found (minus my byline, alas) in the appropriate number of the *House of Fugger Weekly Newsletter*, giving the exact time and place of ratification of the peace treaty, a brief description (see below) of the bullfight in the Plaza Mayor, and a briefer one of the new royal palace (stucco painted to look like brick) where, that afternoon in the gardens under a striped canopy, a performance was staged of *The Gentleman of Illescas*, a play in three acts (what else?) by Lope de Vega (who else?), but never mind.

A lot of my jottings didn't get into the *Fugger Newsletter*, since Valladolid was not the centre of the Augsburg universe, just as a lot of what went on that day didn't get into my jottings, since I couldn't be everywhere at once.

Here are some of the things I did and did not witness:
• Streets mobbed. No fewer than nineteen tall skinny men greeted in my hearing as Don Quixote, and short fat ones numbering at least twelve as Sancho Panza.
• Sentry in red-gold sentry box outside royal palace removed from same for reading on duty. Book *Don Quixote*.
• A Quixote in cardboard armour, fourteen feet tall on stilts, entertaining crowd in Plaza Mayor before bullfight by reciting lines from guess-what-book. This line especially appeals: 'Can we ever have too much of a good thing?'
• Not counting *The Gentleman of Illescas*, no talk anywhere in Valladolid that day of Lope.
• Bullfight. First bull – named El Invincible; touch of irony? – *manso* and weak in forelegs. Bullfighter, one Gaspar de Ezpeleta, gentleman of Navarra, falls from horse while trying to drive lance into *morrillo* (neck muscle) of bull. (*Due to circumstances beyond his control, your correspondent unable to report on rest of bullfight.*)
• Same Gaspar de Ezpeleta, after treatment of injuries, pays official visit to house across noxious stream from municipal slaughterhouse.
• An ambitious young scribbler whose name is not Alonso Fernández de Avellaneda lunches that afternoon with Lope de Vega in back room of tavern called the Liars' Coterie.

'You understand what I want?' I do not hear Lope ask.

'No sweat,' says the young scribbler whose name is not Fernández de

Avellaneda. 'Only, see, I've got some commitments and I don't write as fast as some people.'

'There's time,' says Lope. 'I'd as soon hit him with this when he's even older. You're *sure* you understand?'

'Like I said, no sweat. The knight winds up in some loony bin, and the squire becomes a hopeless drunkard. You want I should make one of them a child molester?'

'Let's not get carried away,' I don't hear Lope say as he hands over the first of many payments. By the time the man whose name is not Fernández de Avellaneda is finished, he will have milked Lope for three times the 148½ ducats Francisco Robles paid me for *Don Quixote*. But Lope will get what he paid for.

● A prosperous- but not menacing-looking elderly Negro gentleman rides at full gallop into Valladolid on an exhausted stallion. Urgently, he asks directions to house across noxious stream from municipal slaughterhouse.

● A starveling husk of a man, of some sixty winters, is seen (but not by me) to enter meatpackers' tavern on ground floor of house across noxious stream from municipal slaughterhouse. All in black, including black-hilted rapier (graduation gift from Catalán rapier master Agulla de Espadón), he has habit (compulsion?) of lifting arms to spread black cape, giving appearance of bat (vampire bat?) and diverting observers' attention from eyes, those of man in grip of implacable obsession, quite possibly sexual. He removes black gloves one finger at a time, revealing small, neat, pink hands. Drinks no wine, no beer. Sips water (polluted, from stream, who drinks water?). Surveying tavern, reflects that citywide fiesta, no less than war, is ideal environment for undetected murder – not that snuffing out life of 229th virgin would be regarded by any fair-minded person as murder, for if ever a human since Abel had it coming (did Abel have it coming? no matter), she does. Sees sitting on corner of bar (legs crossed, dress scandalously hiked up), young female, sluttish-looking (aren't they all?), flirting with bloody-smocked meatpacker she calls Rafa.

Asks, 'Are you from around here, little girl?' averting obsessed eyes from bare knees.

Isabel, probably, sneers. Little girl? Her?

'Little girl? Her?' laughs meatpacker Rafa who, not too many years later, when she is married to someone else, will impregnate Isabel.

'I live upstairs,' says Isabel in a bored voice.

'I seek,' Pedro de Isunza tells her, 'a certain Doña Andrea de Cervantes de – Ambrosio, is it? What kind of name is that?' You can't be too careful. Of anything.

'Italian. He's nice. He brings me gifts.'

'You know him?'

'He's my uncle, more or less. What do you want his old lady for?'

'Official business,' says Pedro de Isunza. 'A routine matter.'

'That's a coincidence,' sneers Isabel. 'There's someone with her right now. They said official business too. A routine matter.'

Some hours earlier, Gaspar de Ezpeleta dug his sparrow's-beak spurs into the flanks of his beribboned piebald gelding, directing it, he hoped, tangentially into the line of El Invincible's charge. But the bull, more *manso* than invincible, swerved, forcing Ezpeleta to lean too far from his saddle while trying to plant his lance, also beribboned, in El Invincible's fear-swollen *morrillo*, the lance barely piercing the bull's hide before both lance and horseman fell to the sand-covered floor of the Plaza Mayor, the latter landing hard. Other, more skilled horsemen rode out to distract El Invincible long enough for Ezpeleta to make his ignominious escape, at which the privileged spectators in the grandstand rose with a collective animal sound that could have been either concern for Ezpeleta or disappointment that he had vaulted to safety. We standing spectators meanwhile surged noisily forward, our weight breaking the makeshift fence and causing an interruption of the spectacle.

All this activity explains why I failed to see a lady dressed in mourning (black silk alleviated by a gold brooch at the throat, dark curls peeking from under a black hood) scrambling down pell-mell and never mind ladylike from the block of seats reserved for the English (no fraternization at the bullfights).

Bumped and shoved by that milling crowd, I didn't pay much attention to the hand on my arm until it became obvious it had no intention of letting go. Irritably, I turned.

I think I shouted her name.

I think she shouted mine. Contralto voice. It said, 'But five years ago in Gracechurch Street I saw you disappear practically before my eyes. I would have thought I was going crazy or something if Dr Duguid hadn't seen you disappear practically before *his* eyes. So how can you be here in Valladolid or anywhere? You're not even real, you're just an illusion. That's a false conception or idea, as you may know, and I had to get over it, Dr Duguid said, if I hoped to lead any kind of normal life – which was a laugh anyway, wasn't it.'

She swayed forward.

I caught her in my arms and kissed her on the mouth.

And I heard myself say something which, when things calmed down and I had time to look back over my life, I knew I'd never told anyone before. I heard myself say, 'I love you.'

Then I kissed her on the mouth again. Though her scent was like new-mown hay and a touch of some half-forgotten Algerian perfume, musk-rose dew perhaps, she tasted salty.

I said, 'What are you doing here?'

She said, 'Running for my life. That bitch Audrey won, I lost, she's the new W. The Nameless is finished in England.'

I said, 'You were working for the Nameless?'

She said, 'Just because I was shanghaied doesn't mean I was disloyal. And sometimes I wonder about the shanghaied part. The longer I know your brother Juan-O, the more I think his obscurity's just a cover for lateral thinking, if not serpentine. But of course nobody could figure Luis Blackslave would yank the rug from under us all by selling out to Thomas Phclippcs, so – '

'Where's Juan-O? Is he all right? I didn't even know if he was alive. Or you.'

'I'm alive,' she said, or rather purred, and kissed me. 'And so is Juan-O. But I'm glad to say Maliverny Catlyn, the Butcher of Clynnogfawr Llanllyfni, isn't. His horse stumbled in a chuckhole in Hog Lane, Norton Folgate, and he was thrown headfirst into a stone wall. So, once Luis Blackslave underwent his remarkable re-conversion, Juan-O was able to use the very funds that earlier had corrupted Blackslave to start rebuilding Nameless bases.'

I said, 'What remarkable re-conversion of Blackslave's?'

She said, 'You know Luis and his need to thumb his nose at authority, all authority everywhere? It was inevitable, after he became Innominate of the Nameless, that he'd have to thumb his nose at the biggest authority figure of all, himself. But ultimately he came to realize – I hate that phrase, but what else is there? – that by going into espialls and intelligences for profit with Thomas Phelippes he had perverted the ideals of the Nameless, which, as you know, is autonomous and not for sale at any price. It just shakes the tree of history to see what forbidden fruit falls from its branches.'

I said, 'Sure. Secret knowledge. Of the sacred and the profane. For starters.'

She said, 'It took Luis Blackslave almost three years to come to realize – *don't* you hate that phrase? – that if you sell it, you lose it. Anyway,

Juan-O's begun rebuilding Nameless bases with Luis's ill-gotten gains, and I'll be helping even though I'm on the run. For all I know I'll be on the run the rest of my life. I got this far because Lord Howard of Effingham owed my late husband Sir Gawayne a favour, so he let me join his entourage to get out of England alive. You might know I'd be the only woman in the entire group, and I had to argue him out of making me dress like a man. Kiss me again.'

I did. And said, 'We have to go somewhere and talk.'

She said, 'What do you think we've been doing?' Then her face became thoughtful. She said, 'A while back, somewhere along in there, did I hear you say something that may have sounded a little like "I love you"?'

I said, 'Yes.' Then I said it again. I said, 'I love you.'

She said, 'Why don't we go talk at my place?'

Some time later, on the first floor of the house across the noxious stream from the municipal slaughterhouse, Luis Blackslave flattened himself – no mean feat, for he had grown stout – against the wall beside the window, raised the curtain, and peered suspiciously out. This stylized routine was reminiscent of Micaela's all those years ago in Záhara during Operation Weltschmerz, and no wonder. It was one of the first bits of tradecraft recruits at Base Iberia learned.

Blackslave shook his head to indicate no untoward traffic on the rickety bridge, just the usual bloody-smocked meatpackers.

'So that's about it,' he said. 'Isunza kidnapped the Rufo children in Sevilla and returned them alive only after Juan Rufo revealed the identity of the girl who refused to be seduced by the Crown Prince of the first sun-never-sets empire, either on the night of 19 April 1562 or some night in October 1564.'

'It was October '64,' said Andrea. 'The twelfth, to be precise.'

'I knew it!' said Luis Blackslave. 'October sixty-four. But try to tell them something, even when they're torturing you.' His eyes swept the parlour. 'My, what a lot of copies of one book,' he said. 'For code use, or what?'

Andrea, Constanza, Catalina, Magdalena and Juana the widow Laínez-Hondaro all began to explain at once. Blackslave, unaccustomed to being in a houseful of women, waited until their voices ran down before he said, 'He can't be far behind me. He could even be ahead of me. And I don't want to alarm you, Doña Andrea, but he's the worst kind of deadly. We now suspect he murdered Don Juan of Austria and the Duke of Parma.'

He did not say who 'we' were, nor why they suspected, and no one asked. 'So, we've got to hide you until this blows over.'

'But how can you expect it to blow over if he's a homicidal maniac who's been trying to find me for forty-three – no, forty-one – years?'

'I expect it to blow over,' said Luis Blackslave with his habitual sang-froid, 'if I find him before he finds you.'

'Where can you hide me?' Andrea asked.

'Oh, there's a place, a bit dilapidated now, in the rugged mountains east of Arcos de la Frontera, that could use a woman's touch,' said Luis Blackslave, and showed a mouthful of gold.

But it was not fated that Andrea go there, for just then the door burst open, its lock proving no match for the heavy boot of Gaspar de Ezpeleta's page, nineteen years old, six feet six inches tall and almost as wide, one Paco Camporredondo.

'No reason to get alarmed, folks, this is official business, a routine matter,' announced Camporredondo in a booming voice that alarmed everyone but Luis Blackslave, and presented a card stamped not with the usual three keys of the Royal Treasury (run these days, like the rest of Felipe III the Inglorious's government, by the Duke of Lerma) but four keys, the fourth off in one corner so it could easily be hidden by covering it with a thumb. But not this time.

'The Fourth Key Bureau,' said Luis Blackslave, his habitual sang-froid intact despite the smashed door.

Gaspar de Ezpeleta limped in, favouring the knee wrenched when he mislanced El Invincible and glaring at his page Camporredondo (possibly for kicking down the door), while Blackslave explained to the women that the fourth key of the bureau's name was a play on the popular name for the Royal Treasury, the Chest with Three Keys (which, under whatever name, was running a colossal deficit). As Camporredondo had boomingly announced, nobody here had reason for alarm, since the Fourth Key Bureau dealt with fiscal malfeasance, peculation and similar policies of the Spanish bureaucracy.

Gaspar de Ezpeleta, eyeing all those copies of *Don Quixote* scattered around the room, asked, 'Isn't that extravagant? Thirty copies of the same book – even if it is *The Ingenious Gentleman of La Mancha*?'

'I can explain,' all the women of the household offered at once, while Ezpeleta's page Camporredondo boomed, 'If we decide to confiscate those books, along with anything here of real value, not that I see any such, you will all be the first to know.'

'Camporredondo, how many times must I tell you there's a certain order in which things are best accomplished?' said Gaspar de Ezpeleta testily, and his page went sulking out to the landing where a woman named Carmen Ceballos was waiting.

'It is, as you know' – except for Blackslave, they didn't – 'the function of the Fourth Key Bureau to reclaim for the Royal Treasury government funds wrongfully spent. While cases of misappropriation do crop up from time to time, we thrive on technicalities, as bureaucrats have since the Chou Dynasty in China. Now then. Which of you good women is Doña Andrea de Cervantes Saavedra de Ambrosio?'

'I am,' said Andrea simply.

'You were baptized in 1544 in the village of Barajas?'

'Yes.'

'Adopted child of Rodrigo de Cervantes Saavedra, barber-surgeon, no fixed abode, and of his wife Leonor Cortinas?'

'Yes.'

'And a certain sum was paid to said adoptive parents to provide for your care with the understanding that when old enough you would take the veil?'

'Yes.'

'Yet,' said Gaspar de Ezpeleta, 'we have no record of your having taken the veil, and in fact you *did not*.'

'*Did you*,' boomed Camporredondo from the landing.

'Shut up, Camporredondo, I'll handle this. So therefore your parents – '

'My parents intended to honour the agreement, señor,' Andrea said. 'They even paid my dowry to the Carmelites. But I ran away.'

'Ah,' said Gaspar de Ezpeleta, limping to the window and back. 'Then it is my duty to demand the return of the sum paid for your upbringing – with interest compounded annually, two thousand two hundred gold ducats.'

(This was, a careful reader will note, exactly the sum my sister Andrea once sued Nicolás de Ovando for. Having noted it, the reader should disregard it as no more than one of those coincidences in which life abounds.)

All the women of my family except Andrea began to talk at once, and the widow Laínez-Hondaro chimed in. When they finally fell silent Andrea said, with an hauteur Luis Blackslave mistook for sang-froid, 'If such a debt is owed, señor, my husband Santi Ambrosio the well-connected Florentine will settle it on his return.'

Despite the bruises and contusions on his face, Gaspar de Ezpeleta looked a happy man. Cases usually didn't go so smoothly. He said, 'Then it remains only to confirm your identity, señora.' And he summoned the woman Carmen Ceballos from the landing. Small and square, she was built along the general lines of the brigand Lombrizcacha, her dowdiness relieved by the stylish pink-dyed ostrich plume waving over her green beret.

'The infant in question,' she gushed, 'the child of a uniquely prominent, the *most* uniquely prominent man of his time – I shall say no more – is known to have had . . . But come inside with me, dear.'

Curious, Andrea withdrew into one of the bedrooms with Carmen Ceballos.

They came out in no time at all. Carmen Ceballos had a surprised look on her face. So did Andrea.

'She doesn't have it,' said Carmen Ceballos, her pink ostrich plume swaying in emphasis.

'She doesn't have the birthmark in the shape of the Habsburg eagle on her right hip?' said Gaspar de Ezpeleta.

'No sign of it,' said Carmen Ceballos.

'But the child is known to have had it. So this woman cannot have been that child,' said Ezpeleta.

'So it would seem,' said Carmen Ceballos.

'Then who is this woman?' asked Ezpeleta.

But neither Carmen Ceballos nor anybody else knew.

A worried frown split the scab on Gaspar de Ezpeleta's right eyebrow and he dabbed distractedly at the oozing blood with a silk handkerchief in one corner of which a discreet fourth key was embroidered.

'I very much fear,' he said, 'that we shall have to take you in for further questioning, señora.'

'Of a purely routine nature,' boomed Camporredondo from the landing.

Andrea looked at Luis Blackslave, who nodded. He was thinking that temporary custody in the well-guarded headquarters of the Fourth Key Bureau in the east wing of the palace might, all things considered, not be such a bad idea.

Some time earlier, somewhere in the labyrinthine streets between the College of San Gregorio and the river, on the top floor of a house whose stone façade was carved in the same motif as the college itself (a plethora of naked New World savages hidden in intertwined thorn branches, the work of the prolific Gil de Siloé or one of his many apprentices), Micaela and I lay on an enormous canopied bed, naked as the stone savages, with our limbs as intertwined as the thorn branches, a living facsimile of all that Isabeline architecture outside.

I traced lightly her classic callipygean curve. Her dark curls were mussed. Her disturbing amber eyes regarded me with demure lechery, an unusual juxtaposition. She said, 'Do you know any more juxtapositions?'

'Not right now. I'm not as young as I once was.'

'When you were younger we didn't do this. Not with each other. Through no fault of mine. So we have a lot of time to make up for.'

Did I detect pique in her voice? Never mind. We linked mouths and found another juxtaposition, this one her idea.

So afterwards – how's this for stupid? – I asked, 'Where did you learn that?'

She sat up and turned her back. Shapely back. 'Scadbury House, Chislehurst, Kent. Perfected in field work.' Coolly. 'A lot of field work. Once I got over a certain . . . childhood trauma, I became very good at what I did.'

I touched her arm. She pulled away.

'Micaela, listen, I . . .'

'Don't worry, I'm leaving in the morning,' she said. 'First thing. This was just one of those stolen moments they taught us about at Base Iberia.'

'Leaving? But we – '

'I told you, I'm on the run. Rebuilding Nameless bases as I go. Venice, Ragusa, a place called Vaduz. Constantinople, Trebizond. Around. I'll be around. If you should ever want to find me. For another stolen moment.'

'Micaela, stop it.'

'Why should I stop it? I like doing it.' For we had found another juxtaposition.

'I mean, Micaela, I know I'm too old for you, but – '

'And after Trebizond, there's this unconfirmed rumour that Prester John himself can be found out there somewhere, in the north of India maybe – did you know he's a direct descendant of the paladin Ogier the Dane?'

'My publisher and I were talking about the Emperor of Trebizond and Prester John today. Coincidence? Or . . .'

'There are no coincidences in this life,' said Micaela as we finished juxtaposing.

'But Prester John lived in the twelfth century,' I said, helping her get her right leg down off my right shoulder.

'According to Doctor Dee, centuries are closer together than people think. Did you say you're too old for me? You're the youngest man of fifty I ever met. Or juxtaposed with.'

I didn't disabuse her about my age.

'. . . with seventy kings for vassals in a land called Teneduc, which I hope to find,' I next remember her saying.

Small-talk, even if mythic. To avoid discussing what we both knew could never be.

But finally Micaela, pivoting slowly one final time as she climbed off me, said, 'It's late. I suppose you'll have to be going soon. You still have a wife, don't you?'

'Not really. I mean I do, but I don't. She has her animals.' Hastily, I added, 'I don't mean that the way it sounds. Didn't Juan-O ever tell you?'

'Tell me what?'

'Catalina took vows. Celibacy. The Tertiary Order of St Francis. So if I asked her, she'd let me go.'

'What are you saying?'

'A woman alone on the run,' I said, 'hasn't much of a chance.'

'I don't need your sympathy.'

She stood. Went to the window. Did not do that tradecraft with the curtain. Just stood there, pensively naked, gazing over the rooftops of Valladolid.

'She's probably a very nice lady.'

'Who?'

'Your wife, even if she's not really your wife any more.'

'Catalina and I have spent a total of maybe four years under the same roof, in the twenty we've been married. So if I went away with you it would hardly change her life.'

Micaela stood silently watching echelons of swallows or swifts soar in formation against a blood-red sunset. I came up behind her. Blew on the nape of her neck. Ran a finger down the tiny bone-knobs of her spine. No response.

In her imagination, I thought, she was already on her way to wherever she was going. Trebizond, Teneduc. Had I lost her? There was probably no returning from Teneduc, wherever Teneduc was.

She said, 'A few stolen moments and you think everything's changed. I know nothing has. What do you expect me to do when you come back into my life every five or ten years, invariably at the most inopportune moment, tell you I've loved you since I was fourteen and never stopped, just because it happens . . . happens to be . . . the truth?'

I held my breath.

Pensively naked, watching those soaring swallows or swifts, she said, 'Trust no one in this life.'

'Trust me. You can trust me.'

In a fierce whisper, 'Don't you think I want to?'

'Micaela, I'm not getting any younger and I want to go on the old road again, and those places you named are on it. Plus, I love you.'

Less fierce, more a whisper, 'The arrangements are made for me to leave from here at first light. You'll need to get your things, say your farewells.'

My heart bounced up against my Adam's apple.

'First light,' I said. 'I'll be here. Nothing can stop me.'

'Of course,' she said. 'Of course you will. What a lovely dream.' Without turning away from the window.

The last I saw of her she was silhouetted against that blood-red sunset. The swallows or swifts flew past again. We didn't even say goodbye.

Isabel got down from her perch on the bar, flashing a few inches of thigh. Bloody-smocked meatpackers gave her hungry looks. The man in the black batwing cape was putting his gloves back on, smoothing the leather over one small, neat, pink finger at a time.

'Who is this other . . . official person?' he asked.

'Three of them,' said Isabel. 'I don't know who.'

'And they are with this Cervantes woman?'

'She's my aunt,' said Isabel. 'So to speak.'

'And where would I find her?'

Isabel held out a businesslike hand, and Pedro de Isunza inverted a drawstring purse from which copper coins showered, Isabel catching most of them. Second time today. That Camporredondo was nice. She wished dear old Aunt Andrea would have more visitors.

'Come on,' she said, and they went out into the blood-red sunset.

As Isabel would later testify to the magistrate Cristóbal Villaroël – the Duke of Lerma's creature, but what Valladolid magistrate wasn't? – she'd led the man in the batwing cape no further than outside when she saw, coming down the stairs with an elderly Negro gentleman at her side, her Aunt Andrea, followed by that nice Camporredondo, his limping boss, and the dowdy woman with the ostrich feather.

'That's them,' Isabel said, and without a pause to . . .

But here a pause *is* necessary.

Write about what you know. Does anyone, ever? Can anyone, really?

Do witnesses testify about what *they* know? Witnesses are notoriously unreliable. She wore her silver hair in a coil at the nape of her neck. Her mousy brown hair in a bun at the back of her head. She was dowdy. She was stylish in a green beret sporting an ostrich plume. An eagle feather.

What are magistrates to make of all this? Should we naïvely expect the magistrate Villaroël to write a report for the Duke of Lerma based on what those unreliable witnesses testified, which was all he, Villaroël, knew? Rather, wouldn't Villaroël's report say what he thought Lerma wanted to hear? And Lerma, what notes would he jot in the margins before passing the report along to scribes who would draw up the document that would take its place in the archives of the Royal Academy of History? Surely not what he knew, but what he wanted the world to think had happened. And the scribes, reading these notes, what would they write? Surely not what *they* knew, which was at best third-hand. No, the more you have a responsibility to anyone, including yourself, let alone the loftier responsibility to the idea of truth, the less you can write about what you know. Like Lerma, you can only write about what the world will, once you have written it, think you know, which may or may not resemble what you do know, if you know anything.

So, the curious reader will find in the archives of the Royal Academy of History one version of what happened in those next few harrowing moments.

I offer another, somewhat closer to the facts.

I crossed the rickety bridge from the slaughterhouse walking on air. At least, I didn't hear the usual clatter of loose boards underfoot, so light was my step.

But I did hear the clash of swords and a voice booming, 'Constable! Someone get a constable!' The owner of the voice, six feet six inches tall and almost as wide, lumbered on to the bridge and probably would have found a constable himself, had the bridge not given way under his weight just as I stepped off it and saw (the setting sun behind me, no problem), of all people, the ex-Commissary General of Andalucía, Pedro de Isunza, batwing cape and all, crossing rapiers at the foot of our stairs with a much younger man who looked like the injured gentleman bullfighter Gaspar de Ezpeleta. I also saw a crowd streaming from the meatpackers' tavern, none of whom, to judge by the archives, was ever called by the magistrate Cristóbal Villaroël to testify.

Although Ezpeleta had the advantage of youth, he handled a rapier no more adroitly than a bullfighter's lance, and, moreover, was forced to favour his wrenched knee. So Pedro de Isunza easily drove him back until the unfortunate Ezpeleta tripped over the body lying to one side of the stairs, from which a groan then escaped, and as easily ran Ezpeleta through twice, thrusts which, as the surgeon Sebastián Macías testified, penetrated deeply Ezpeleta's left thigh and his lower abdomen.

Gaspar de Ezpeleta collapsed next to the prostrate body of Luis Blackslave, who moments earlier had taken through the chest the rapier-thrust meant for my sister Andrea, who now knelt at his side.

This was when I reached the scene, just in time to pick up the fallen Ezpeleta's rapier and whirl with it to confront the ex-Commissary General of Andalucía who, according to Señor Zum, had been dead since 1593.

Parrying Isunza's first thrust, I felt the unfamiliar weapon almost fly from my hand. This did not trouble me. Had it flown from my hand, I'd have caught it in mid-air. Naturally. For I experienced then a strange sense of invulnerability, like a wearer of Mambrino's helmet. Knowing no more of rapier fighting than I had all those years ago on Liars' Walk, I yet felt that my every move must necessarily be the right move. How could it be otherwise? The sunset was a deeper crimson than I'd ever seen, the air clearer, every movement of Isunza's practised wrist one I could unfailingly predict. Might this have been the self-delusion of the doomed creature facing death without terror? Perhaps, but when Isunza followed a forestroke with a backswing, either capable of decapitating me, I seemed to have all the time in the world to duck. I could even remark that the whoosh of the madman's blade over my head was not unlike the sound of Hassan Pasha Dey's rhinoceros-sinew whip as he chased himself around and around the torture chamber after Cide Hamete's astrological mumbo-jumbo (but was it?) had saved me from a first horrible death.

Isunza pressed forward, I retreated, it did not matter, for whatever he did I was ready, and surely soon the irrelevance of his superior skills must unsettle him.

Someone – Andrea, I believe – screamed.

And the spell was broken, the sunset was only a sunset, the air was air, Mambrino's helmet, had I been wearing it, only a barber's basin. Isunza's deft rapier forced me to retreat until, back literally to the wall, I saw Camporredondo come dripping from the stream, shedding slaughterhouse offal as he called in his booming voice for a constable. Positioned as we were, Isunza could not have seen him, but he could hear. Did the booming voice distract him? I certainly lacked the skill for what followed, though had Andrea not screamed I might have gone to my death believing I would prevail, not a bad way to die if only death did not outlast wishful thinking. As it was, I pushed myself off the wall with what used to be my left hand, and Isunza yielded a step, the cup-shaped guards of our rapiers clattering together, blades skyward-pointing, those eyes so long obsessed with my sister Andrea bulging inches from my eyes until he yielded a second step as Camporredondo's voice boomed again for a constable. (They're never there when you need them, are they, Camporredondo was young. He would learn.)

By the time two constables did arrive – according to the archives Constables García and Vicente – Pedro de Isunza was down on his back, dead from a thrust I had no recollection of delivering (my rapier, however, was bloody to the hilt), and I was down on one knee, the dying Luis Blackslave smiling a mouthful of gold up at me.

'When my daddy's time came,' he said, 'the whole New World from Baffin Island to Ushuaia went into a year of deep mourning, but I want a simple burial, no fuss, hear?'

(In the event, Blackslave's and Isunza's bodies were, later that moonless night, carted off to some unknown place, so he got his wish. Gaspar de Ezpeleta could not so neatly be swept under the rug of history. He took thirty hours to die, on the thin mattress where Magdalena under normal circumstances slept the blameless sleep of the lay sister Magdalena de Jesús. The surgeon Sebastián Macías visited three times, a priest administered the last rites, young Camporredondo was a stubborn presence, as was dowdy-stylish Carmen Ceballos, and we even have the unfortunate Ezpeleta's last will and testament, dictated to and witnessed by the surgeon Macías. Given all this, the archives had to acknowledge Ezpeleta's death by foul play. Only his occupation and the identity of his killer were omitted from the account.)

Blackslave's mouthful of gold was flecked now with red.

'Kind of looks . . .' he said.

Less gold, more red.

'. . . like I owed . . .'

All red.

'. . . you Cervanteses . . . more than I reckoned.'

Just as he breathed his last, the magistrate Cristóbal Villaroël arrived. More decisive than Constables García and Vicente, who stood inspecting the carnage, two men dead, a third mortally wounded, Villaroël saw the bloody rapier still clutched in my hand and said, 'Arrest this man.'

Here is what a curious reader will find in the archives:

• That shortly before eleven p.m. on Monday, 27 June 1605, a gentleman bullfighter and man-about-town identified as Gaspar de Ezpeleta was fatally wounded outside the door of 1A Slaughterhouse Street – later Fleamarket Street – by an assailant or assailants unknown.

(Shortly before eleven p.m. How clever. Sunset was at 9.07 that night. Why move the hour back? The night was moonless. Towards eleven it would have been completely dark. The testimony of witnesses, if any, who saw a prosperous-looking elderly Negro gentleman die with sang-froid or a black-clad man in a batwing cape die with a look in his eyes of implacable obsession, quite possibly sexual, could be ignored. Equally, the late hour and the darkness made it easy to deny that *a certain person* was anywhere near Slaughterhouse Street that night.)

● That the victim Ezpeleta was rumoured to have a mistress, a married woman who lived near – but not too near – 1A Slaughterhouse Street, and that her name was either Hernández or Fernández or Galván or some other name, not quite legible.

● That testimony had duly been taken from all residents of 1A Slaughterhouse Street, namely, Don Miguel de Cervantes, Doña Catalina de Palacios de Cervantes, Doña Magdalena Pimentel de Sotomayor a/k/a Cervantes and her personal maid Isabel Saavedra (*sic*), Doña Constanza de Figueroa, and Doña Juana the widow Laínez-Hondaro.

(*No testimony was taken from Doña Andrea de Cervantes de Ambrosio, nor is she listed in the archives as resident at that address.*)

● That just before dying, Gaspar de Ezpeleta bequeathed a silk gown to the woman who nursed him in the last hours of his life, Doña Magdalena Pimentel de Sotomayor, a lay sister in her fifties. As she would have no need for such a gown, it was therefore presumed intended for the Pimentel de Sotomayor woman's twenty-year-old personal maid Isabel Saavedra (*sic*).

● That the investigation would continue.

(It did not.)

Villaroël interrogated me until well past midnight. He could accept, he said, no part of my story.

'But I admitted I killed Isunza,' I said.

'But the archives will show that Isunza died of natural causes in February 1593, so you could not have killed him tonight.'

(Note how easily history can be rewritten retroactively. Señor Zum told me in the late 1590s that Pedro de Isunza had died in 1593, even though the date, a quite arbitrary one, was chosen only in the pre-dawn hours of 28 June 1605.)

'Isunza killed Luis Blackslave who was protecting my sister Andrea,' I tried.

'Your sister Andrea could not possibly have required protection here in Valladolid because, at this very minute, she is living with her husband Signor Santi Ambrosio, the well-connected Florentine, in Livorno.'

'But I just saw her.'

'Your illusions, my dear Don Miguel, need form no part of the record.'

'I'm telling you I killed Isunza!'

Señor Zum arrived, and Villaroël left us alone.

'Isunza died in February 1593,' Zum said.

'Tell me Luis Blackslave died in 1593!' I shouted.

'In the interests of Nameless anonymity, any mention of Luis Blackslave in tonight's unfortunate events must be suppressed.'

'What's really going on?' I asked.

'What's really going on is that unless you co-operate, the magistrate Cristóbal Villaroël promises to do everything in his power to smear your daughter Isabel's reputation, which, I hardly need point out, is already as smearable as, shall we say, my nose once was.'

'But why?'

'To encourage you to forget some . . . details of what happened.'

'I mean *why*?'

'They seem to have thought your sister Andrea was someone of . . . elevated antecedents, but now they don't know what to think. They probably never will. Listen to me, Don Miguel. Villaroël's an ambitious man, and he has his orders. Unless you agree you didn't kill Isunza, so Andrea can be kept out of it, you'll spend the rest of your life rotting in jail.'

Did it matter, really matter to me, whether history would know me as the man who killed Pedro de Isunza, who died of natural causes twelve years before I killed him?

It was more than an hour after Señor Zum left before Villaroel returned.

The arrangements are made for me to leave from here at first light.

I'll be here. Nothing can stop me.

Of course. Of course you will. What a lovely dream.

Villaroël came in. 'If you have Zum, I imagine you won't be with us long.'

'I didn't kill him.'

'Ah,' said Villaroël.

'I'll swear that I didn't kill him. Right now.'

'You're being sensible. A statement will be prepared for your signature.'

'I can write it. I'm a writer.'

'We must go by the book. A statement will be prepared.'

'When?'

'Tomorrow. When the statement-preparers are on duty.'

'I can't wait for tomorrow.'

'Any sooner is impossible.'

'Then I must get a message to a house in the *barrio* between the College of San Gregorio and the river.'

'That won't be any problem, since you didn't kill anyone. What's the address?'

'I don't know.'

'Can you describe the place?' I have to give Villaroël this: he really did seem to want to help.

'Stone façade. Complicated carving. Naked savages hiding in thorn branches.'

'That describes virtually all the buildings in that *barrio*. Can you be more specific?'

I couldn't. 'If you take me there, I can find it.'

'There are limits to what we can do for a man being held on suspicion of murder.'

'But I couldn't have killed him if he died twelve years ago. I recanted my confession.'

'You *will have recanted* when your statement is prepared.'

'But it's a matter of life and death.'

He said he was sorry, but rules were rules.

Write about what you know . . .

And what did I know?

I knew it was the longest night of my life and yet, in a blink, in a heartbeat, dawn streaked the eastern sky outside my cell window. I knew she would not wait. She had said first light. First light she meant.

Does writing about what you know include writing about what you can't have? This would be poignant, the stuff of good fiction, good theatre. Poetry in its rightful place, ascendant over history. Cide Hamete once told me more than one critic would call *Don Quixote* the first existential novel, whatever existential means, because the Sad-Faced Knight created himself (as God might have created him, if the world were absurd) out of his own illusions. And once self-created, Don Quixote tries to impose those illusions on the real (or absurd) world, an attempt doomed to fail. But if he abandons it, will the world be any more real (or less absurd)? In an absurd real world I buried Ezpeleta's rapier to the hilt in Pedro de Isunza's body either a few minutes after nine or a few minutes before eleven p.m. on 27 June, even though history says he died a dozen years earlier. Which part of that is what I know? And which the truth? Is there some point where what I know and the truth converge, or do I only think there should be?

Write about what you can't have.

I would have gone with her to find Teneduc, if there was a Teneduc, if only.

If only I hadn't saved my sister Andrea's life.

Who wasn't my sister. Unless she was.

The night was long. Dawn came in a heartbeat.

She stands at the window, pensively naked, watching echelons of swallows or swifts, up with the sun, soaring past. They fly a circular pattern to a distant belltower and back, crying shrilly, happily. Are birds, she wonders, capable of happiness? She is happy. She knows, for a few moments more, she knows I will come. But I do not come. The sun is up, the red-streaked sky pales to yellow, the sky is blue. The swallows or swifts fly no more. She turns from the window, her disturbing amber eyes unable to see for a moment in the dimness of the room. Is she smiling? Why is she smiling? At some picture she sees of what might have been? Or – is it a cynical smile, then? – at the knowledge, confirmed by me this morning, that she was right all along. Trust no one in this life.

I'll be here. Nothing can stop me.

There is a soft knock. She runs, but as she reaches the door a voice she recognizes as that of Effingham's secretary calls, 'Are you awake, m'lady? The sun is up.'

The sun is up.

She opens the door just wide enough for the secretary to hand a bundle through. She knows him, a youth with a bright smile and blond hair and a beardless face that reddens whenever she speaks to him. Clearly he finds her attractive – for an older woman. What would happen, she wonders, if she were to open the door wider and take his hand and lead him into the room? There are things she has learned that the boy would never forget. Would that be a kind of immortality, his not forgetting, his passing the things she has learned to some woman younger than himself, who will teach them to some man younger . . .? She finds the idea intriguing. And it would serve me right, wouldn't it, if she were to take the boy into the bed where yesterday we spent a few stolen moments, she and I. Which, she now knows, is all they were for me. Trust no one in this life. But how would it serve me right if she were to take the boy and do those things with him she can do so well (why be modest? so spectacularly) and I were to come, late, but come, while she was doing them? Besides, admit it, wouldn't the boy be only a token of what, from now on, she might do too easily, with any man who caught her fancy (and after a while too many would, trust no one in this life, not even yourself).

She thanks the boy and shuts the door and undoes the bundle and dons doublet and knee breeches of the kind called venetians (she will go to Venice first to help with the Nameless base there), and boots with rounded toes, and a broad-brimmed traveller's hat and a silk lion-coloured cloak, and when she has finished dressing she looks like a boy no older than the secretary now returning to the great house on the river where Effingham is lodged, wondering perhaps what it would have been like if that beautiful lady who could make him blush just by talking to him had opened her door and led him in by the hand and, in case there was any doubt, she wasn't even wearing anything . . .

She leaves, half an hour late. In a few days she will be in Barcelona, then at sea. Then? Then she will find Teneduc, alone, if there is a Teneduc.

I signed my statement without even reading it, and as soon as I was released went to the *barrio* between San Gregorio and the river. I thought – but how could I be sure? – I found the house, but it was empty and looked as if it had been for some time. Swallows or swifts nested under the eaves.

The next January the city fathers of dying Madrid said they would pay King Felipe III the Inglorious 2,500,000 gold ducats if he moved the capital back. The move required more than the three hundred bullock carts it took to move the court in the opposite direction. I do not know where the city fathers of Madrid got the money, but there is no record of King Felipe or the Duke of Lerma complaining, so they must have received it.

Catalina said, I told you so.

In February, when most of Andrea's and Constanza's wealthy customers followed the court, the family returned to Madrid. Constanza left the couture business to her mother and created a successful line of small jewelled perfume boxes of the sort known as pomanders that fashionable women dangled from their girdles. Pomanders not only smelled good – half-forgotten Eastern scents like musk-rose dew were not uncommon – but were believed to protect against infection and, some said, ward off bad luck.

XXXVII

A Thousand Leagues from Everywhere

For my birthday some time after the family settled in Lion Street in Madrid not far from the Theatre of the Prince, my niece Constanza hired a painter to do my portrait.

'What would anybody want with a portrait of me?' I protested.

But it was a present and I couldn't be churlish, so the painter Juan Jáuregui soon established himself in my work-room to do preliminary studies at a time when I craved solitude: Part Two of *Don Quixote* was coming slowly.

Jáuregui was half Basque, half Sevillano, and had the natural pig-headedness of the one and the irrepressible loquacity of the other. Also a braying voice.

He had opinions on everything and I tried to listen to none of them. But one day I heard him say 'Tasso'.

I stopped what I was doing. (What I was doing was Chapter XXV where the aldermen bray like asses. Write about what you know.) I put my quill-pen down. 'Are you *that* Jáuregui? Hombre, why didn't you say so?'

He *was* that Jáuregui, and from that moment his braying didn't bother me at all. Jáuregui, poet as well as painter, was recently back from Italy and already famous for his Spanish translation of Tasso's *Aminta*.

For a few days I didn't even try to write. The braying aldermen of Chapter XXV could wait. Jáuregui was young, not yet thirty, and I liked to hear him talk about Italy. He had never known Tasso, of course. Tasso had died when Jáuregui was twelve. But he knew the Italian literary scene.

One day as Jáuregui was lamenting how ill-paid translators are, I countered by telling him what Robles had given me for Part One of *Don Quixote*.

'A scandal!' he said. 'Outside Spain you're more famous than Lope de Vega. You're being translated everywhere.'

'Maybe I'll get two or three hundred for Part Two,' I said. (I wouldn't.)

'Know the most I ever got for a portrait? I'm not boasting, just showing you how underpaid writers are.'

'I couldn't guess,' I said.

'Six hundred ducats. I won't deny the sitter was rich. Advisor to the Medicis. Made Livorno a free port.'

'Santi Ambrosio? You painted Santi's portrait?'

'In Florence. You knew him?' Jáuregui asked.

'He's my brother-in-law.'

Jáuregui looked surprised. 'You mean your wife, the one with all the animals, is his sister?'

'No, I mean *his* wife is my sister Andrea.'

Jáuregui stopped painting. 'Maybe there are two Santi Ambrosios.'

But we both knew there weren't.

'This brother-in-law of yours had a family in Florence. Italian wife. A dozen children, two grandchildren that I know of,' Jáuregui said, then told me, 'Ambrosio died last December a few days after I finished his portrait.'

I saw Señor Zum. His hair was white now, like his neck-whisk. He stood at the window with its condescending view of the Royal Palace. Office and palace had been spruced up. Madrid was a thriving city again.

I told Zum what Jáuregui had told me. Zum said he had a colleague in Florence, not to worry, we would get to the bottom of this.

At home, I told Andrea nothing. But I had to tell someone.

As I entered the attic, Catalina's large spotted cat Magnificat pounced from the rafters on to my shoulders with a playful growl. Magnificat was a sleek, healthy beast, a cat and a half in size.

'I found her in the streets,' Catalina had said. 'Not a cat, a margay. From New Spain. Probably abandoned as a kitten by some sailor.'

Now she said less. She said, 'What?!'

I repeated the salient details.

Catalina swiftly got over her shock. 'You might not understand, not being such a family type yourself. But Santi, he was the most complete family man I ever met. He could take care of two families, easy. And on the old road so much, dividing his time between Spain and Italy . . . I can forgive his being a bigamist, or at least understand his need.' Catalina looked at me. Magnificat leaped from my shoulder into the rafters.

'This leaves you in charge,' Catalina said. 'Can you handle it? A house full of women, and the way Isabel's marriage is going, she'll probably be back soon too.'

'I can handle it,' I said.

'What will you do for money?'

'Zum has a colleague in Florence who'll find out about Santi's estate.'

A few weeks later Zum sent for me.

'According to what my colleague could learn, Ambrosio died intestate,' Zum said. He perched gold-rimmed spectacles on the tip of his versatile nose and read from a letter. 'Leaving an estate worth, um, 97,300 ducats, *escudos* or Florentine livre, take your pick, they're at par.'

'Why wouldn't he have made a will? He was no young man, and he cared about his family.'

'Families. I didn't say he didn't. I said according to what my colleague could *learn* he died intestate. Probably the Italian family destroyed his will because it made provisions for your sister.'

'Wouldn't he have left a copy with a lawyer or a banker or someone?'

'My colleague can search for a lawyer or banker. But.'

'But?'

'By Florentine law, the widow Costanza Ambrosio – '

'Costanza?'

'One "n", correct. Costanza. By law she may apply, and she has applied, to have the estate of her intestate husband, after deduction of taxes, paid over to her.'

Ninety-seven thousand ducats. What part had Santi intended for Andrea? Even a fraction would give her lifelong ease.

'What happens to such an application?'

'It is routinely granted unless challenged. My colleague in Florence proposes filing such a challenge – for a fee, payable in advance, of forty per cent of whatever he recovers.'

'But how can we know in advance what he'll recover or even if he'll recover anything?'

'My colleague is aware of the problem. Therefore, before taking action, he would require a retainer in the amount of three thousand ducats or livres.'

We looked at each other.

'I'm sorry,' Señor Zum said. It almost sounded as if he meant it.

As gently as I could, I broke the news – or as much of the news as I intended breaking – to my sister Andrea.

She was weeping softly when I got to the part that went, 'But you see, he had reverses over there in Italy, the Medicis haven't been doing that well lately . . .'

I gave Andrea a handkerchief and she blew her nose. Why do women so rarely have them when they need them?

'Poor Santi,' she said. 'Family meant everything to him. I only hope to God he didn't know he died penniless.'

'Not p-penniless,' I said quickly. 'The will got lost in the bureaucracy over there in Florence. That can happen. But according to Señor Zum's colleague, Santi left everything to his b-beloved wife Andrea.'

And I gave her the eighty ducats Francisco Robles had recently paid me for the Aragonese edition of *Don Quixote*.

Andrea blew her nose harder. 'A man who handled millions for the Medicis, and this was all he had left at the end of his life.'

'Oh no,' I heard myself saying. 'This is just the first instalment before taxes. There'll be more.'

'He was a provider, my Santi, I could always count on it. That's a good thing now, because my fingers aren't as clever with a needle as they once were, and pomanders were just a passing fancy.'

I dropped Part Two of *Don Quixote* and wrote day and night to finish a collection of short stories and novelettes for which Robles had agreed to pay a hundred and twenty-five ducats. My own favourite was 'The Little Gypsy Girl'. But you know me and gypsies.

I gave Andrea all but five of the ducats.

'The rest of Santi's estate,' I told her, 'unless there's more later,' and she wept again, and blew her nose in my handkerchief again.

One morning a week or so later Robles walked into my workroom and said, 'Look at this.'

It was a book. I looked and immediately sat down.

SECOND VOLUME
OF THE INGENIOUS DON QUIXOTE
DE LA MANCHA
by
Alonso Fernández de Avellaneda

Robles had already cut the pages. I flipped through them.

'Who is he?' I think I said.

'I don't know. I'll try to find out.'

(He tried but couldn't. No one ever did.)

I browsed through enough of the book to see that this Avellaneda had turned my Don Quixote into a gross lunatic, and Sancho Panza into a sly alcoholic. The humour was coarse, the story vulgar. It might appeal to marginal readers.

(It did, including some critics who'd prefer it to the original, according to Cide Hamete. Cide Hamete – does it surprise you, my still mentioning him, after what happened? But how can I help thinking of him? Once he asked me, 'Are you sure, *ráwi*, that I'm anything more than that disordered, irrational, left-hand side of your brain, a kind of *jinni* trapped in there from which the creative impulse comes?' But if that's all he was, then how could he tell me about my death and Shakespeare's, and what critics would write, and those quarks and bosons of his and – I almost left this out – that while I was writing Part Two of *Don Quixote*, Lope de Vega lived in a nearby street that would eventually be named Cervantes Street? Seeing into the future like that, and walking through walls, and then he goes back to being the fat fatuous astrologer to some dey? Don't expect me to explain it. But he was real.)

'I don't care who Avellaneda is,' I told Robles. 'Lope put him up to this.'

'Whoever, he's within his legal rights.'

'But I created Don Quixote.'

'And, once you did, he no longer belonged to you. Anybody can write a sequel to anything.'

I slammed the Avellaneda on the table, where it fell open. I read a few paragraphs.

'It says here Don Quixote accuses Dulcinea of faithlessness. The unsullied sanctuary of a flawless love, faithless? He'd never. Never!'

'Well then,' said Robles, 'write what really happens.'

But I had a long way to go and we both knew it.

That afternoon I couldn't concentrate. The gall of this Avellaneda! I took the five ducats remaining from the so-called balance of Santi Ambrosio's so-called estate and went to the intersecting alleys not far from the Gate of the Moors that used to lead to the lightning-blasted oak tree that once had been girdled by the Bench of If-Only. It wasn't there, of course. I knew it wasn't. I often walked in that part of town. I went into the gambling den that had replaced the Bench of If-Only and over to the *primera* table. There was a lot of action and the crowd was young. The proprietor, a man too casually dressed in a faded leather jerkin open at the throat revealing an Aurelio Ollero lanyard to affect a toughness he didn't have, asked me what I wanted to drink.

His actual words were, 'What's yours, gramps?'

What used to be my left hand quivered, but I managed to decline a drink. Then I played a few hands of *primera*. I lost them all. I got mostly face cards which, as you know, are worthless.

I went outside and in the fading light saw Micaela.

She was dressed as an English milady and was climbing into a four-horse coach. A footman shut the door and took the step away. I called her name, but at the same instant the coach started up with a jerk and a rumble. I ran after it. Actually began to gain. Then without warning my legs gave under me. I rolled over and over and when I came to a stop I could hardly move. My body didn't seem to work. People ran towards me. A man leaned over me saying something. Another put a folded cloak under my head. I said, take me to Lion Street. They asked my name and I tried to tell them. I was breathless. Also thirsty. I had never been so thirsty. (*What's yours, gramps?*) Someone brought water. I drank and drank. I drank a whole bucket. They asked my name again. Someone helped me up. I said, Miguel de Cervantes, and the man who had helped me up looked at what used to be my left hand and said, 'You're him all right, how about that?' Then they took me home.

I couldn't get over how the man had verified who I was. Even though I could hardly stand, it made me feel something I'd never felt before, a special kind of power.

A physician came and diagnosed the thirsting sickness. Some diagnostician. Rodrigo de Cervantes the surgeon could have done as well without sniffing urine.

The physician said I was all skin and bones. He told Catalina she had to fatten me up.

She made a big bowl of *migas* twice a day after that, and served it to me with a big jug of sweet red wine.

By the time I went back to my work-room, weak as a kitten or a newborn margay, I could tell myself it was a good thing Micaela hadn't heard me calling her because, when you got right down to it, how could I have gone away with her? The family needed me. I sharpened quill-pens and wrote. With Santi dead I was in charge. Whenever I reached a difficult place in Part Two of *Don Quixote* I'd remember how the man who'd helped me up looked at what used to be my left hand to verify who I was, and I could get over the difficult place. I wrote every day all day, and I was always thirsty. One day Constanza brought in a large draped canvas and all the women came in behind her making a big fuss. They wouldn't let me look until they hung it on the wall I faced when working. Then they undraped it. It was Jáuregui's portrait of me. Holy Virgin! Was that ancient, bald, eggheaded apparition, with its wispy mandarin beard resting on a ruff bigger than any Señor Zum ever wore when he was Picapleitos, me?

(Possibly. The portrait would hang for a long time in the Spanish Royal Academy, not far from the archives containing the file on the death of the gentleman bullfighter Gaspar de Ezpeleta.)

Nights when I felt strong enough I went out, carrying a big flask of water, just in case. Sometimes I went to the gambling den where the Bench of If-Only used to be. '*Here comes gramps.*' After the portrait, how could I object to their calling me that? '*Remember that golden oldie, Asea on the Drift of Love?*' '*Adrift on the Sea of Love.*' '*Right. He wrote it.*' That really was a young crowd they got in there. I couldn't help wondering if they'd maybe lowered the legal gambling age. Sometimes those youngsters sat around and listened to what I had to say on the Big Subjects. Love. War. Life. Death. Enchantment. The Old Road.

Sometimes I caught myself thinking of her. I tried to stop, but how could I?

One midday it was Andrea instead of Catalina who brought my bowl of *migas* to the work-room. Some *cuajada* too. That's rennet pudding, for anyone who hasn't guessed by now.

'Going well?'

'They aren't having much success disenchanting Dulcinea,' I said. 'But that's what I had in mind.'

Andrea studied the floor. 'Remember how you had to carry poor Papá home from the Bench of If-Only?'

I said I remembered.

'Must you go there so much? Who'll carry *you* home?'

'What are you talking about?' I don't remember ever having been angry with Andrea before. Who did she think she was, Avellaneda?

When I calmed down, I saw she was wearing the same coarse homespun as Catalina.

'What's with the homespun?' I said.

'I'm a sister of the Tertiary Order of St Francis, same as Catalina.'

'How long has this been going on?'

'I completed my novitiate last week. You know,' she said, 'very few men who take lay orders wind up at the Bench of If-Only. It's a statistical fact.'

I studiously sharpened quill-pens until she left.

My niece Constanza told me about the Congregation of Unworthy Slaves of the Most Holy Sacrament a few days later. 'They don't wear hair shirts or anything,' she said. 'It's an intellectual brotherhood. The simple life and . . .'

'. . . abstinence from fucking, but that won't be any problem at your age.' This was Catalina. 'And they . . .'

'. . . visit hospitals,' Magdalena told me, 'and write songs for religious festivals . . .'

'. . . safe from the snares and disillusions of love,' said Juana the widow Laínez-Hondaro.

Andrea came back with, 'It's a Trinitarian order. The Trinitarians, you know? Who ransomed you from Algiers?'

What can I say? Soon I was wearing the scapular of the Congregation of Unworthy Slaves of the Most Holy Sacrament. One year I won a prize for a song I submitted through the brotherhood for Corpus Christi. Dressed in my best suit, I climbed the hill to the palace to receive my prize from the Duke of Lerma. It was a small inscribed silver bowl. Given the family's circumstances, I would have appreciated money more, but you don't tell the Duke of Lerma that.

The day I won the prize Lope de Vega joined the Unworthy Slaves. He never won a prize but attended all the meetings and became Brother Superior.

There's no way to write what comes next, except the simplest way I can.

My sister Andrea came down with a fever one night and was dead before dawn.

They had to help me dress when we went to the Church of San Sebastián for the funeral. We followed the coffin to the cemetery, where it was put into the wall. From then on it was a different world. It was the wrong world. But I had no idea where the right world was. For a long time I didn't write. Magnificat no longer came to curl at my feet. I went to the attic to find her, but she wouldn't come down from the rafters. I could see her eyes glowing there. Luminous pale blue eyes. I went that night through a driving rain to the intersecting alleys near the Gate of the Moors where, if I turned that corner, just there, I would find the gambling den. I was carrying an old harquebus. The match wouldn't light in the rain, but I didn't care. The gambling den wasn't there. It began to thunder. A lightning bolt speared the ground in front of me and I saw the Bench of If-Only. Stone bench girdling an old oak. I took my place on it with my old harquebus. I sat there. I sat there all night. I half expected me and Andrea to come and take me home, but nobody came. The storm passed, the moon came out, the moon faded, it was dawn. I got up and went home. I was feverish. I think everybody expected me to die. Lope was so sure I would die that he sent some Unworthy Slaves around to be on hand when it happened. But how could I die when I hadn't even got to the place in Part Two where Don Quixote is unhorsed by the Knight of the Moons who called himself the Knight of the Mirrors in an earlier chapter when Don Quixote unhorsed *him*?

So I got well enough to sharpen all the quill-pens I could find and go back to work. I got so engrossed in the story that I thought the book I was writing was the right world, the one I had to find. But it turned out not to be, it couldn't be, because Don Quixote went home to die, after all the adventures he'd been through, in bed.

Francisco Robles came for the manuscript, and I waited for the book to be published. The thirsting sickness grew worse. I rarely got out of bed. Most days Magnificat curled at my feet, purring, those luminous pale blue eyes watching me wait for April 23rd.

... By the time I went back to my work-room, weak as a kitten or a newborn margay, I could tell myself it was a good thing Micaela hadn't heard me calling her because, when you got right down to it, how could I have gone away with her? The family needed me. I sharpened quill-pens and wrote. With Santi dead I was in charge. Whenever I reached a difficult place in Part Two of *Don Quixote* I'd remember how the man who'd helped me up looked at what used to be my left hand to verify who I was, and I could get over the difficult place. One day Constanza brought in a large draped canvas and all the women came in behind her making a big fuss. They wouldn't let me look until they hung it on the wall I faced when working. Then they undraped it. It was Jáuregui's portrait of me. Holy Virgin! It made me feel good. My beard was golden, not silver, I was haughty as a Roman emperor and fifteen or twenty years younger than I pictured myself. But does anyone really know what he looks like?

(The same Cervantes expert who said I wrote the first nine chapters of *Don Quixote* in prison – as, you've seen, I did – believes the portrait to be a good likeness. Who am I to argue?)

More and more I spent my nights at the gambling den where the Bench of If-Only used to be. '*It's Miguel de Cervantes. Wrote* Don Quixote.' The proprietor with the Aurelio Ollero lanyard would grumble when players left the gaming tables to hear me tell about the Man of Glass or the Illustrious Serving Wench or the Jealous Extremaduran or Damsel or what really happened (I changed the names to protect the innocent) the night Gaspar de Ezpeleta died. But telling stories didn't stop me from thinking about her.

One evening Andrea asked me how my day's work had gone.

'I finally got Sancho off his island. He wasn't really happy as a governor.'

Andrea studied the floor. 'If you stopped to consider it, you'd know it's in the blood.'

'You mean that we're *conversos*? So what?'

'I mean love of gambling. Our grandfather Juan the Patriarch left most of his money on the gaming tables.'

'So?'

'So we don't *have* that kind of money.'

'Who do you think you are – Avellaneda?' I said, but I was smiling. I could never be angry with my sister Andrea.

'You've been seen there a lot.'

'Andrea, I just go to tell them stories. Being a storyteller, that's gamble enough.'

Catalina told me that the Trinitarians were starting a new chapter of a lay brotherhood called – are you ready? – the Congregation of Unworthy Slaves of the Most Holy Sacrament.

'They don't wear hair shirts or anything,' she said. 'They're more like an intellectual brotherhood. They write songs for religious festivals. The simple life, and of course no fucking, but that won't be a problem at your age.'

'What's all that got to do with me?'

'Well, you know, at your age – '

'Will you stop saying "at your age"? I never felt younger in my life.'

'Well, if you examined your conscience every night, the way an Unworthy Slave's supposed to, you wouldn't have any time left for that gambling den.'

'All I do is tell them stories.'

'Don't forget it was the Trinitarians who ransomed you from Algiers,' Catalina persisted.

'Catalina, maybe you won't understand this, but it was a song by an old *ráwi* named Shakashik that ransomed me from Algiers.'

Catalina didn't understand, but she didn't bring up the subject again.

A while later Lope de Vega joined the Unworthy Slaves. He wished to atone, he told anyone who would listen, for his rakehell life. With Lope a member, I knew I'd been right not to join.

Andrea died that October without warning. Just came down with a fever one night and was dead before dawn.

The one who took it hardest, at least outwardly, was Constanza. Catalina had to help her dress. She leaned heavily on my arm as we followed the coffin from the Church of San Sebastián to the cemetery.

Write about what you can't have.

For a long time I couldn't write. I felt as if I were living in the wrong world, though I had no idea where the right world was. I went to the attic to find Magnificat, but she refused to come down from the rafters. I could see her eyes glowing there. Luminous pale blue eyes.

Then one day I sharpened all the quill-pens I could find and got back to work. Still Magnificat stayed away. I got so engrossed in the story that I thought the book I was writing was the right world, the one I had to find. But it couldn't be, because Don Quixote went home to die in bed.

I delivered the manuscript to Francisco Robles and waited for the book to be published. Magnificat returned, and would curl at my feet in front of the fire, purring. Sometimes those eyes would look up at me. Luminous pale blue eyes.

I thought about her a lot.

I remembered her best the night she fled the Crown Prince, young, reckless, that glorious mane of wheaten hair dishevelled.

Who was she? Was she my sister? Was she *his*?

When I could think of her without my eyes stinging, I went to the gambling den where the Bench of If-Only used to be. It was a sentimental gesture, as close as I could come to that night in Alcalá, as close as I could come to saying goodbye to Andrea. I went straight to the backgammon table. Playing the boards for the house was a blonde wearing a little cap of gold brocade.

The man with the Aurelio Ollero lanyard asked me, 'What's yours, Don Miguel?'

I looked at his face, really looked at it for the first time. It was the face of someone skilled at what he did in a world where, under certain circumstances, losing was the way to win.

'You must be related to someone I used to know,' I said.

'It's possible. Depends on who you used to know.'

We smiled at each other.

'Feather help?' he said.

'Wrong side of the hat?' I said.

'I'm the son,' he said, and then he looked at me, really looked at me for the first time, his eyes finally fixing on what used to be my left hand.

'You're the brother,' he said, 'aren't you?'

'It's possible. Depends on who I'm supposed to be the brother of.'

Again we smiled at each other.

'Juan,' he said.

'Who?'

'Come *on*. Juan the Obscure. Juan-O.'

'You hear from him at all these days?' I asked.

'Not often. But he's up there. Main Base. Getting it all together. Well, drink's on the house. What'll it be?'

'Spirits.'

He brought the *aguardiente* and I tossed it back and sat down at a backgammon board with my five ducats, and instead of losing, as Andrea had done in Alcalá that night and as I expected to do, I won a hundred ducats. I took them to the *primera* table and before I knew it – no face cards – they grew to five hundred. I took those to the *quínolas* table and in no time they became three thousand. I shoved them all on to the *el parar* table and watched them triple to almost ten thousand gold ducats.

I told Pierre Papin's son to deliver the money to my family in Lion Street.

I went outside, and in the moonlight I saw Micaela, dressed as an English milady just like that other time, climbing into a coach. The footman stood ready to close the door and take the step away. I was going to call her name, but before I could, everything went errant. There was no Micaela, no gambling den. Not even the Bench of If-Only. What was I doing in bed, anyway? What I was doing in bed was feeling poorly, my face to the wall, so weakened by the thirsting sickness I couldn't lift a finger. Catalina was saying something, I don't know what. I felt a sudden weight on my shoulder. It was Magnificat. She wedged herself between me and the wall and looked at me with those disturbing amber eyes.

A voice spoke. Contralto voice.

It said, Demogorgon.

It said, Demogorgon dwells.

Said, Demogorgon dwells in the abyss.

Demogorgon dwells in the abyss with three fatal sisters or atop the Himalayas with elves and feys.

I wanted to say something.

Dwells, dwells, dwells.

But that wasn't it.

Say one sentence without stuttering and you'll go free.

But I could think of no sentence. Just her name.

Micaela, I said.

And as soon as I said it, everything was all right again, the right kind of errant, and I climbed into the coach.

And as soon as I climbed into the coach it began to move, and as the way was long, she asked me to tell her a story.

And I began with how my great-grandfather knew Columbus, and I didn't stop until I reached the part where Micaela and I were in the coach, racing along the old road again.

And she said, 'Tell me, Miguel – what comes next?'

A NOTE ON THE AUTHOR

Stephen Marlowe was born in New York and educated in Virginia. He served as the first writer-in-residence at the College of William and Mary. He has lived in some twenty countries and is author of the internationally acclaimed *The Memoirs of Christopher Columbus*. He was awarded the French Prix Gutenberg du Livre in 1988. *The Death and Life of Miguel de Cervantes* is his twelfth novel.